Winner

BEST FICTION &
GOLD AWARD: Best Book
1997 Sacramento Publishers Association

"A corking good story ... skillful bl
California's turbulent years." *Sierra*

"I rate the book right up there with
Sacajawea by Anna Lee Waldo." Jod. ... The Bookplace

A wonderful blending of dramatic history and insightful imagination. A delightful, rewarding read." Richard W. Etulain, Professor of History, University of New Mexico, Center for the American West

"... filled with romance, suspense, heroism, passion, and sacrifice." *Around Here Magazine*, Gerry Camp, Sundance Books

"... insightful, multicultural ... a wonderful analysis of power." Deborah Moreno, California history instructor, Cosumnes River College

"... historical characters from the Gold-Rush era jump off the pages ... a brilliant novel." William M. Holden, author of *Sacramento: Excursions Into Its History and Natural World*

Special thanks to all the readers who continue to share their thoughts. Most typical:

"Awesome research!"

"Fascinating. A side of the Donner Party story I hadn't heard before."

"I didn't want it to end, and when it did, the world looked different — the grass, the trees, everything."

"I couldn't put it down, and read too fast. So I'm reading it again."

River of Red Gold

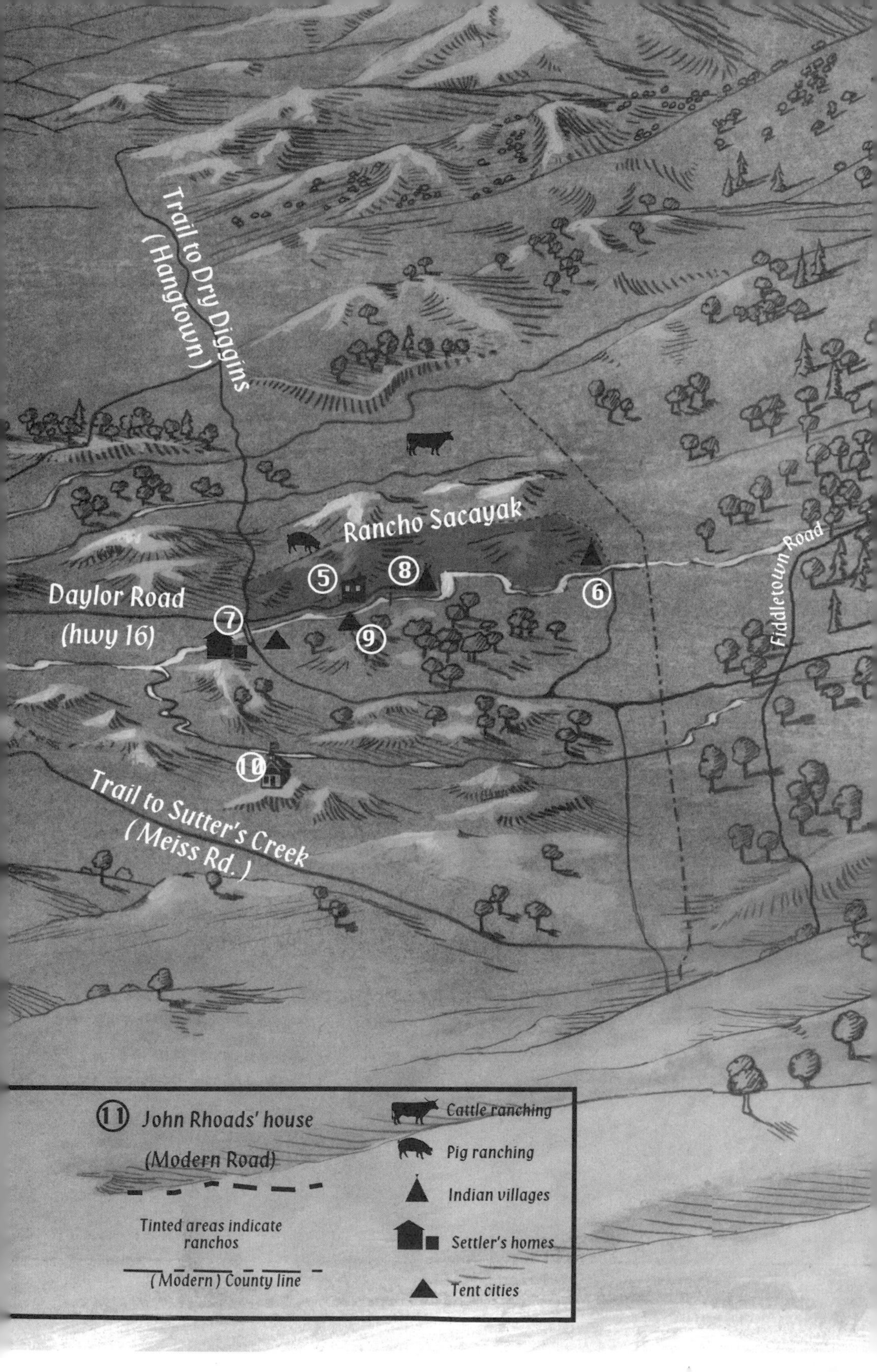

Trail to Dry Diggins
(Hangtown)
Rancho Sacayak
Daylor Road
(hwy 16)
Fiddletown Road
Trail to Sutter's Creek
(Meiss Rd.)
John Rhoads' house
(Modern Road)
Tinted areas indicate ranchos
(Modern) County line
Cattle ranching
Pig ranching
Indian villages
Settler's homes
Tent cities

I

Pedro and Maria

HOWCHIA SPEAKS:

Once I was Eagle Woman. Now I am an oak tree.

When I walked these paths, the nights came often and life in the village hurled past like the river in the time of early flowers. When I died I should have gone to the happy land. But I looked back, unable to turn away from the home place I loved. Thus, my spirit lingers. But I did not choose to inhabit a being so long-lived, or stand overlooking the dancehouse — a hollow in the earth now, overgrown with high grass — where the outpourings of our human hearts once rent the sky and the mysteries of the universe were felt so deeply. Through the dirt of a millennium my roots suckle the rotted acorn husks and bones of my people. My trunk is sculpted and broad, and even while the earth scorches in the sun, my tap root, far below, drinks from a pool of wet sand as eternal as the river.

An occasional vehicle parks here, and the new people picnic on the river beach. The laughter of children at the water pleases me, and I think how I played there as a child — and my little son and his daughter after him, and her children. But the new people leave at dark. They miss the orange moon rising over the eastern hill and layers and layers of sparkling stars. They miss the music of owls and the urgent drum of frog calls and the rustling of night animals.

In the quiet time I fathom all that happened here. But next time I die, I shall look forward and walk the pathway of ghosts. For now I yearn for the cheer and dances of the spirit world. Before an evening fire I will tell the stories, and my people will exchange sly smiles when they hear that despite the melancholy teachings and sober striving of the new people, many of them hope to live much as we did. For the spirits that live in the boulders and the river and the plants and animals are beginning to touch them too.

Rising from the heat waves over the tired grass comes Old Man Coyote. He seems to float, a dirt-brown shag on high slender legs, trotting his rounds, head cocked a little askew. He stops beneath my branches.

I greet him the old way: "Where did you come from and where are you going?"

His amber eyes are human. "Just ate a cat over in the subdivision." He licks his lips. "The pampered sack of lard didn't even have claws, heh heh. They'll blame the mountain lion. I'll rest a while, then trot over to the ranch and check on the lambs." He sits down and a familiar glimmer lights his eye. "Think I'll sneak into Stan's helicopter and wait till he's hovering over the hills trying to find me, heh heh, then bark in his ear. Woo woo woo!"

Always scheming. "The Ancients came to this river," I say, "and life was much the same for a long time. Then in a few seasons everything changed."

A yawn unfurls his lips. "You're just looking back again."

"I'll bet even you miss the Big Times."

"Those dancing clowns pretending to be me, heh heh, that was the best part. Woo! I was the only one with the power to face the magic."

"We honored the spirits, Old Man. Now, at the slightest whim the new people could bulldoze me and shoot you. We exist in their obliviousness."

He turns in a circle and plops down in my shade, tongue draped thinly over the humps of his incisors. "They can't kill me." He looks up smugly.

I chuckle. "You created us like you, Coyote, except maybe more curious. Sometimes I wonder — don't you? — how it might have been, even if the Spaniards had learned of the gold, if they had kept the North Americans from — "

"If if if," he sniffs through an amused snout.

I chuckle again, for he is right. Condor dreams the world's events, and no one can explain or change a dream. "Have you heard? People say even Condor is dead."

He jumps up like he is afraid and looks around, then lies down again. "No he's not. Ground squirrel is still chasing his wife and Heron is fishing in the mud." He smiles up into my branches. "And you still tell good stories."

I sigh. A breath of air rattles my leaves and unsettles the ghosts of the past, and I see again the man named Pedro Valdez.

1

SUTTER'S FORT, 1844

The night was warm, and within the fort's adobe wall a candle cast a moving, breathing halo on the ceiling of Pedro's small room. He lay naked on his rawhide cot, ankles crossed, restless hands moving over the ancient helmet, which he held on his chest — a pointed iron cap with a cross welded down the nose and over the eyebrows. The earthy fox-den smell of the adobe seemed particularly strong. It conjured up the disturbing memory, and the sick feeling it often brought, of the house of his childhood — the one-room adobe in San José. It had been dark then too. The wooden latch had rattled. Pedro and his brothers and sisters had bolted up in their bed. Their mother rose to her feet, the spinning-wool tumbling from her lap as the door creaked open.

Old Pepe, Father, stood in the candlelight — home at last, wearing nothing more than a vine of wilted leaves about his loins. His hair was wild and matted and as white as his beard, most of the red gone. His mouth twisted with shame and his hooded eyes avoided the stares of the family. He entered and crossed to the bed, smears of blood marking his footsteps upon the packed clay.

His voice rasped high, with the pride gone out of it. "I found *mucho* gold," he said, "but *Indios* took it again. Threw it away. Scattered it in a thorn thicket." He looked down. "The devils stole my helmet too, and my clothes, and my horse." He had walked forty leagues across the big valley.

By a miracle of the Virgin the helmet was found again in the ashes after the Indian uprisings of 1829. Pedro ran his thumb over the rough spot in the metal where a spike had broken off. He and his *hermanos* had been very young when Old Pepe first told them the helmet had been worn by an ancestor who had ridden with El Cid Campeador. The great El Cid and his heroic freedom fighters had, so many fabled centuries ago, liberated Spain from the Moors and pushed them back across the sea, saving Europe for Christ. Their manly deeds rang down the ages. Yet here lay the helmet in Pedro's hands, passed down from Valdez to Valdez in an unbroken chain of military service to the Crown of Spain. Dazzling Spain, powerful colonizer of continents.

Spain ran in Pedro's blood. Grandfather Valdez, a lieutenant, had sailed the Atlantic to serve in New Spain, Mexico now. Pepe in his turn had come north to the remote garrison on the Bay of San Francisco, to pacify *Indios* in the regions served by the northern missions. But being a bastard son, his mother an Indian, old Pepe had remained an enlisted man, the helmet his sole inheritance. Nevertheless, no prouder or more loyal servant ever served the Crown. Before gold drove him *loco. Ay Madre,* it took a proud man to go insane, one with too big a dream.

Besides, dreamers had clawed for gold in the coastal hills and valleys for sixty years and every time excitement flared, the ore proved of little value. During Pedro's lifetime men had stopped looking. All but Old Pepe. With a mad twinkle he had sworn his family to silence, declaring, "I am the only one looking far enough east." People made the *loco* sign by their temples. Children pointed to Pedro's rags and said, "See how grandly he dresses! His father mines gold." The laughter still rang in his mind.

He crossed his other ankle. Any fool could see the Indians of Upper California lived in hovels and wore beads of bone and clay. If they'd had gold like the people Cortéz conquered, some would drink from golden chalices and wear fine ornaments. A man had to be *loco* to think gold abounded where tens of thousands of Indians lived — a people acquainted with every rock and plant in their territories. Grudgingly, sadly, Pedro had agreed with the town. Old Pepe had gone soft in the head. It was the disloyalty that made him sick, he realized. It ran against the grain of Spanish pride. And those bloody footsteps held no attraction for him.

Pedro had left home as soon as possible, signing for duty when still a boy. A revolution had rocked Mexico, barely felt in this northern wilderness, yet it proved a quake with lasting tremors. In eighteen years he had served an emperor of doubtful character, more than one shadowy general, a *junta*, and "the people" of Mexico. It was hard to keep track. Now he served under Captain John Sutter, a naturalized Mexican citizen who lacked any tie whatsoever with Old Spain. Yet Sutter controlled the vast interior valley. In the five years since Pedro helped lay the first adobe brick in this uncharted land, he'd done his share of pacifying Indians — like when Maximo bolted and turned rebel.

"*Madre de Dios*," he said aloud, spreading his hands over the solid curve of the metal. In a strange way it represented his soul, his destiny, but it wasn't enough. At thirty-three *años*, a man had to think beyond barracks and mess meals, especially a man barred from rank on account of mixed blood. *Terreno* burned in his imagination — land, a sweep of it peppered with cattle, worked by his own skilled vaqueros. Land gave a man substance, a certain nobility. And soldiers were often rewarded with grants from the Mexican government. Someday when he saw the land he wanted he would apply.

Wrapping the helmet in the old sarape, he replaced it beneath the cot and puffed out the candle. As the wick-smoke scented the still air he thought about tomorrow, when he would ride up the Cosumnes River. Captain Sutter was reaching farther east for laborers and militiamen, illness having decimated the valley *Indios*. Pedro would ride to where the foothills mounted toward the great Snowy Range, *Sierra Nevada*.

He turned on his side, his sleeping position. He would practice his trick riding. *Indios* loved it. It loosened them for talk.

Maria Howchia pushed her basket into the scooped-out hole in the sandy shore where the river would leach the bitterness from the acorn meal. She heard a commotion. Barking dogs, pounding hooves, squealing children.

She straightened to listen — the tattoo of womanhood new on her chin, her black hair singed straight across her shoulders and brows — then hurried toward the excitement. The u-machas and the dancehouse were a blur as she passed, and the luck stone and amulet bounced on her budding breasts. She rounded the high berry thicket and crossed the dry streambed, then stopped in her tracks.

A completely clothed man stood upright on a galloping horse, one foot before the other. Bent knees flexing with the running gait, he flew like a bird — chest forward, arms wide, white sleeves billowing, slim black trousers buttoned down the side. He circled the field where ti-kel was played, then galloped toward her from a gilt-edged dust cloud, his reddish hair flaming in the low sun, a hat standing straight out behind. Gooseflesh rippled down her back and limbs.

The thirty-five other *umne* gaped with her as the flying rider crouched to retrieve the rein, which had been draped across the horse's neck. He stopped the horse and sprang catlike from the big saddle, arms upraised, smiling grandly at his admirers. His glance met hers. Magic shot through her.

She moved between her parents, touched the arm of her father, Grizzly Hair, who was hy-apo, headman, and asked, "Is he a black hat?" The hat the stranger returned to his head was black with a scarlet band, and it had the same stiff, broad brim Father had described as the mark of the enemy *Español* warriors, who lived near the western sea.

The polished white bones in Father's earlobes and the full black plume of his topknot glistened in the sun. Beneath the practiced calm of his broad face, she saw his agitation. Not answering, he stepped toward the man and asked in Spanish: "Where did you come from and where are you going?" The *umne* crept forward to hear, Maria Howchia among them.

The stranger threw back his shoulders, lifted his chin — the closely trimmed beard outlining his square jawline — and spoke in Spanish slow enough to understand. "I come from El Señor Capitán Don Juan Sutter, from his establishment on the *Río de los Americanos*. I would be pleased to talk with you."

She noticed that Father's name for the big northern river was used by *Españoles* too. But that wasn't on the western sea. It was only a day's walk to the west. Protectively, Etumu laid a hand on her shoulder.

Maria Howchia put her mouth to Mother's ear and whispered. "He flew like a bird." The snowy egret glided in exactly that proud manner, but the man's hair was the color of the red-tailed hawk. *Proud Hawk* she named him in her mind.

The stranger removed the wood-framed saddle, the straps from the horse's head, and the metal framework from its mouth. Watching each move, she walked with the crowd behind him and Grizzly Hair. All followed to the village center and sat in the open area before the dancehouse. Important talk would come. Father and the stranger sat opposite one another. She found a place among the people, near enough to hear.

"*Capitán* Juan," the man began, addressing Father by the name the mission long robes had given him. "*Mañana yo me voy al establicimiento del Capitán Sutter. El necessita más trabajadores . . .* " He held himself with dignity, which indicated he came from honorable people. That lent honor to Father. Not what she expected from a black hat, if that's what he was.

Most of the talk rolled over her. Covertly she examined his face — the trimmed mustache the same red-brown as his hair, the color less stunning in the shade. His gaze swept across her chest as he talked, and his eyes locked with hers. Strange eyes, the color of an evening pond, fractured as when pebbles are dropped and ripples cross from different directions. Penetrating eyes that invited her. For a moment she held her breath, not wanting him to look at other young women that way, then looked down.

His Spanish talk rose and fell, urging Father to send the people to Señor Sutter's place.

Father talked of fair trade, and she knew he was suspicious. But Crying Fox, her older brother, listened with enthusiasm, as did many others. By the end of the talk, when the supper fires were lit, she felt something new inside her.

Proud Hawk joined the family fire, his legs outstretched, one black, square-toed boot crossing over the other. As she helped Mother prepare supper, she stole glances at him and his black hat, which lay on the ground beside him. It bore a mysterious black mark on the red band. Black and red, woodpecker colors. He stirred the dust with a stick and glanced at the other supper fires. She added water to the leached acorn meal and stirred. He looked into her eyes, and a spark of magic kindled between them. He had power.

She took the blue-oak tongs and reached into the fire for the cooking stone. In his gaze her hands trembled. She dropped the red-hot stone into the nu-pah, splashing the uncooked porridge on her legs and feet. He had loosened her grip. Mother scowled. Grizzly Hair looked a question from the shadow of the u-macha. Embarrassed, she dashed down the earth-ramp into the cool and dark of the house.

Peering up from the floor of the u-macha, she heard the singing of Grandmother Dishi as she came from the river, arms before her in the way of the blind. Crying Fox sat near Proud Hawk, smiling politely between bites. Mother's moves were strained as she offered salad with ant vinegar. Proud Hawk ate that and strips of roasted ground squirrel, but refused the nu-pah. The fire brightened against the evening shadows, and she began to feel foolish.

A coyote warbled and yapped, laughing. Quietly she crept outside, embarrassed at what the curious people at the other fires would think. Grizzly Hair, Proud Hawk and Crying Fox continued to eat in silence. She sat down beside Father, who leaned against the dirt berm of the house. She ate but didn't taste.

Later Proud Hawk went to the ti-kel field to sleep near his horse. Grizzly Hair, Crying Fox and all the other men went to the sweathouse. She knew their talk would be about the *Españolo*. Tingling with strange excitement, she helped mother put away the baskets in the u-macha rafters, beneath which Grandmother Dishi already snored on her mat.

Back outside, she said to Mother, "Black hats no longer capture people for work at the missions." Father had told her that. The war at the time of her birth had achieved that victory.

Etumu's eyes widened, the light of the dying fire giving her normally peaceful face a fierce look. Her voice came a little shrill. "They can never be trusted."

Maria Howchia sighed as she scooped cold ashes over the smoldering logs. Mother never spoke of the war, but the black hats must have done something terrible. "Why does Proud Hawk want us to go to Captain Sutter's place?"

"Proud Hawk?"

Her face heated.

Etumu passed over it. "He wants men and women to collect grass seed."

"That is women's work."

"*Capitán* Sutter expects men to do it."

"Is *Capitán* Sutter a long robe?"

"Talk to your father about these things." Etumu went to her sleeping place, and Maria followed to hers, a mat of reeds beneath the u-macha shade porch, where the family slept on warm nights. She lay looking up.

The first campfires of the Immortals twinkled through the loose weave of willow branches. The river murmured, always louder at night. She inhaled the aroma of the mossy backwaters and the night moisture touching the dry grass, which clothed the hills far as the known world. Owls whooed, but she wasn't afraid of their bad luck. Things were different now. The war against the black hats was long ago. Tomorrow she would speak with Crying Fox and together they would convince their parents it was safe for them to go to Captain Sutter's place.

She lay with her eyes open, not sleepy. It wasn't long before the distant campfires filled the sky, glittering and winking in the moonless night. The mat whispered as she rose.

"Where are you going?"

She'd thought Mother was asleep. "To pass water."

"Don't go to the black hat. He will hurt you." Patient, soft-spoken Etumu never said such things. She taught by example and made no demands.

"He is our guest, Mother," she said softly, "and he is polite." Actually he shouldn't have looked into her eyes quite so long, but she knew he meant no harm.

"Black hats are cruel." The tone was flat, final.

"This man is too young to have fought in the war. Besides, the world has changed since then."

Silence.

Irritated at Mother's old ways, she left the porch, intending only to look at the man from the distance and see how he slept. She stepped quietly across the loose pebbles of Berry Creek and up to the open field, and saw the pale spot that was his shirt. A horse nickered.

She drew nearer, feet silent, listening for the sounds of his sleeping, but the drumbeat in her ears covered everything — the river, the honking frogs, even the crickets. His magic pulled her. A twig cracked beneath her heel.

"*Que va*? His voice carried like a beautiful song.

"*Yo*. Only I." It came out weak. Was he upset to be awakened? Would Etumu hear?

The pale shirt moved. She heard a scrape as he sat up. He thumped the ground beside him. "*Ven*."

Her heart galloped in her chest but she continued to step toward him, remembering the story of Mouse being pulled by the magic of O-se-mai-ti, Grizzly Bear. Never had she felt so drawn to another person. Perhaps Father had felt like this when he cut o-se-mai-ti's hair and acquired a piece of the great bear's power. She lowered herself next to Proud Hawk — the smell of leather, aromatic smoke and man-musk. Her neck and face burned hot, and it didn't feel like fear.

He ran his palm down her bare back and rested it on the curve of her waist. A fiery pathway lingered on her skin.

"*Indita mía*," he said, his sweet-smokey breath connecting them in the warm night. My little Indian girl.

She reached and felt the surprising softness of skin next to the bristly hair on his face. Part of him entered her fingertips. She wanted to go with him to his home place, but who else would be there? "Is Captain Sutter's establishment a mission?"

"No, *Indita mía, es un castillo*."

"A presidio?" The garrison of the black hats was even worse than a mission.

"Mostly it is a pueblo, where people make things and grow wheat and raise cattle. I live there." His hand retraced the glowing pathway up her back and down again. "Would you like to go there with me?"

Her heart jumped at the thought — and she wanted more. But a dog suddenly pushed its snout into her arm. Etumu's dog, who always stayed near Mother.

The man's hand remained on the swell of her hip, and he called, "*Hola*."

Someone lurked in the willows. Not a man. They were still in the sweathouse. "Go sleep, Mother," she said. "Proud Hawk and I talk. He is kind."

The Spanish rolled from his tongue like music. "Your daughter is safe. She goes to her house now." Had he understood the talk of her people?

Gently he pushed her hip away and softened his voice, but it was loud enough for Etumu to hear. "I came to make friends. Go now, *Amapolita*, Little Poppy. I have no wish to upset your family."

2

After the young *Indita* left, Pedro lay studying the stars salting the velvet black above him. He never tired of trying to link the constellations with the stories he'd been told, some from old Spain, some from his Indian grandmother. Coyotes warbled one after another, a sleepy sound in the balmy night.

It came to him like the unfolding of a beautiful dream that this was the perfect place for his rancho. Like the other villages on his ride up the Río de los Cosumnes it had plenty of *Indio* workers, but here at the start of the foothills, the land had a rugged, manly feel. Near the village the river spilled over a huge boulder face. He could build his hacienda on the hill opposite it. Then in the summer, when he sat smoking on his gracious veranda, he would watch the water and feel cool. *Indias* inside would be rolling tamales and sweeping. Red roses would crowd the veranda posts, perfuming the air, and his shy Spanish wife would sit beside him in her high comb and mantilla, glancing seductively at him. His fine clothes would be imported from Mexico, shipped from Yerba Buena, silver brads down his trousers, bleached cotton showing where they belled out. His bolero would be embroidered with colorful thread. He would be a leading citizen of Upper California, Sutter's esteemed neighbor, General Vallejo's friend, and loyal retainer of the governor in Monterey. Pedro's vaqueros would be the best in the colony, having him as teacher.

Soon he was dreaming.

When he awoke the pretty *Indita* stood at his feet, naked as Eve, watching him. Surrounding her were the potbellied children of the village, their thick black hair blunt across their brown foreheads, their black eyes sparkling. Birds chattered and whistled from thickets along the river and creek, and dawn painted everything rosy. He sprang to his feet, spread his fists wide, and inhaled the aroma of dew on the dry grass.

She said, "I go to Captain Sutter's fort with you."

He recognized the faint peachy scent of her skin, and knew Sutter would take her. The Captain liked budding young girls. "I think you should stay home," he said, realizing that in this small matter his interests and the Captain's were at odds.

"Before the sleep you said — "

"Show me where you swim."

She cocked her head and eyed him, then turned to lead, her firm little buttocks shifting, her heavy hair swinging across her tender shoulder blades. Children grabbed his hands and trotted beside him, smiling up like he was a god. *Patrón,* he corrected in his mind. The scent of peaches wafted back to him. He remembered the soft, poppy-petal feel of her. Yes, the *Capitán* would take her, and Pedro didn't want her used by Sutter, or the scoundrels he attracted. She should stay here, and soon he would be her *patrón.* At the thought he felt a sudden tightness of the prickly wool of his *pantalones.*

He followed her through the village, where naked people smiled at him and spooned their fingers into baskets of congealed acorn porridge, smacking their lips. One of the best things about clothing was that it hid this condition. What did *Indios* do when a man could see plainly that another man wanted his wife?

The *Indita* walked straight into the water with the children, and they all swam like tadpoles. *Indios* were jokingly said to be amphibians. Brown faces grinned at him from the moving water, wide where it spread out after coursing from both sides of the island. With her hair slicked back, the girl looked as beaverlike as the others, and as young. On the shore, Captain Juan stood almost hidden in the willows, gazing toward the rising sun in the way of *Indio* chiefs. Men and women came down the path and slipped silently into the water.

Pedro watched the sunrise color the dry hillsides and waited for his heaviness to recede. The water would be warm and he wanted to be a part of the morning bathing. Not the behavior of a *patrón,* but he sensed it would serve as a link today. Water was sacred to *Indios,* his *India* grandmother had said. Stripping quickly, he waded in and paddled out to where it was deep. He was relieving himself when the chief, apparently finished with his morning prayer, waded into the water with his people. The *Indita* dog-paddled to Pedro.

He asked her, "What do you call this *ranchería*?"

"Ranchería," she said.

Of course it was an Indian village. "I mean what name? *Comó se llama*?"

A crease appeared between her perfectly shaped brows, the water up to her neck. "*No se llama nada.*"

He'd heard this before. *Indios* didn't name their villages, yet they named everything else — every boulder, every flat piece of ground, every hill. "Come with me," he said, beckoning with his head.

He swam to shore and led her up the gravel bank to where they could see the face of the granite boulder. "What do you call that?"

"Sa-ca-yak."

Sacayak, he repeated. *Rancho Sacayak.* It sounded good. "What does it mean?"

A huge smile bunched her cheeks, her teeth dazzling. Then with two graceful steps, she skimmed into the water and swam away.

Later he thought of that, as he nudged his dark-brown stallion, Chocolate, up the path with seven Indians walking alongside. Sacayak clearly indicated something secret and special to these people. All the better. Rancho Sacayak.

Her parents had opposed her coming. *Está bien.* She and her brother had stayed at home. The five young *Indios* beside him walked with quivers slung over their shoulders and bows in their hands. The two young *Indias* carried their huge conical baskets in the typical manner — on their backs secured by thongs around their foreheads. The older men of the village had claimed all the horses — no doubt stolen from the missions and ranches. But the walking *Indios* wouldn't slow Pedro down. They had the amazing ability to trot all day. Besides, he was taking his time. On the way back to the fort he'd collect *Indios* from all the other villages he'd visited coming upstream. He had done well. The riding had been the key. Indians loved it.

At the top of the first hill, he turned the horse and looked down at the open area, the brown people, many big and fleshy, staring up at him. Here at the start of the foothills the natives were as unclothed and harmless as Adam. It was like an abundant Paradise before the Fall. In the Big Valley the half-clothed Horse-thief Indians — mission escapees for the most part — plagued the rancheros. Still, they rarely injured people. But on the coast, where people of all races hid beneath clothing, a man had to watch his back. Captain Sutter, when he sent Indian children to work for his creditors, specified that they not be quartered with Mission Indians, so they wouldn't learn bad attitudes.

Captain Juan was the biggest of the strapping Indians below, a man over six feet, not counting the topknot. Beside him stood the lovely little poppy. A chief's daughter often became a ranchero's mistress, but the excitement coursing through him was for the land. When he got back to the fort he would draw a map of the place and ask Captain Sutter to write a letter of recommendation to the Governor, stating that he, Pedro, was of good character. It would take time for the paperwork to creak through the Mexican government. So he must start immediately. *Rancho Sacayak.*

He memorized the layout for his map. Below on his right the Cosumnes River tumbled from the mountains, the hills mounding upward on either side. There was water in the small river, even now at the end of the long dry summer. He had examined the clay chinking on the conical huts and found it to be of fine adobe quality. The fertile soil in the ancient ox-bow where he had impressed them with his riding would nourish his corn and beans. Grapevines festooned the trees along the river and creek bed, and blackberries and herbs abounded. On the hillsides grew the best cattle fodder on earth.

Exhilarated, he galloped downhill and up the next hill, catching up with the *Indios*. A song sprang to his lips, a tune the soldiers had sung in Monterey. At the chorus he raised his voice, then at the last high note shifted into falsetto and let it fade like a wisp of fog. Pleased to be in good voice, he smiled at the *Indios* trotting by the horse, and thought again of the *Indita* — sweet and innocent in the forward way of the *nativas*. He was pleased with how he'd restrained himself. His favorite love song came from his heart, and he sang with mournful gusto:

El tormento de-amor que me-abraza
En mi pecho no-encuentro consuelo.
The torment of love that grips me
In my bosom cannot be consoled.

After Proud Hawk rode away, Maria Howchia looked at the dusty willows and the sun-baked boulders, and felt trapped in a world too small. Pounding acorns at the bedrock mortar hole, she noticed Crying Fox' crimped lips as he straightened arrows.

He too was thinking of leaving against Father's wishes. Crying Fox' best friends had gone. Her friends Blue Star and Burns Fingers had gone too. Women were the best gatherers, and Proud Hawk had wanted more of them. Hadn't he said he wanted her to come to the fort?

She remembered the faceted gray eyes, the proud bearing, the copper-tinged hair and mustache. His musty-smokey scent lingered in her mind. Her skin remembered his touch.

Later, at the family supper fire, Grizzly Hair spoke loud enough for all to hear. "Kadeema's people, who live on the river of the Americans," he gestured northward, "refuse to work for Captain Sutter now. But he sends his scout here. Why should our people do what others refuse?" It upset him that so many young people had gone.

Etumu's basket-weave cap bobbed up and down in emphatic agreement. Her black eyes flashed as she looked at Maria Howchia. "The black hats do not purify themselves," Mother said. "People who go to the place of the black hats will lose their strength."

Maria Howchia had no appetite, although the steaming basket held her favorite bulbs. She sat against the dirt collar of the house among her father's tobacco plants, feeling as wilted as they. Grizzly Hair and Etumu meant only to protect their children, yet they were wrong to keep looking at the past. Things were different now. The black hats hadn't captured people for a long time. And Captain Sutter wasn't to be feared. He only wanted seed pickers.

She said, "I heard Kadeema's people left Captain Sutter's fort because they were sick for their home place."

Crying Fox nodded enthusiastically. "I heard that too. But we would not be homesick. We would return after the harvest. Señor Sutter pays fine things for *trabajo*." That meant everybody doing whatever the headman ordered, all at the same time. Father had learned of work at the mission.

Grizzly Hair's expression remained closed.

But the stranger hadn't hurt Maria Howchia. "Proud Hawk wants to be friends with us," she said. "He would not invite us to the fort if it held danger."

Suddenly Crying Fox stood up, squared his shoulders and pointed to where Father Sun had gone to his western house. "After the sleep I go to the fort."

Maria Howchia held her breath. Would this be seen as disrespectful?

Grizzly Hair didn't move, his forearms resting on the points of his knees, a juicy turkey bone dangling in his hand. Four drips fell, then his voice came as flat as his expression. "Each man must find his own way."

Etumu jumped to her feet and looked at him with wide eyes, then turned and scowled at the distance. Disapproving.

If Crying Fox was going, Maria would too. She stood up and announced, "Each woman must find her own way too." It came out stronger than she felt.

Grizzly Hair inserted the turkey bone into the jaws of Etumu's waiting dog, stood, and turned toward the path leading west, no doubt heading for his power place. Seeing this, Etumu disappeared down the u-macha entrance. Grandmother Dishi murmured wordlessly, fumbling blindly with her food.

Maria exchanged a troubled glance with Crying Fox. They had defeated their parents, but it brought no pleasure.

Pedro squinted into the setting sun — only a few varas between him and the knoll crowned by the fort. He had collected thirty-seven *Indios* from the villages. Better than expected. They trotted along behind, grouped by village. Sutter's five-square-league New Helvetia lay in the elbow where the American River joined the wide Sacramento. It was far more than a rancho, a fledgling town really, an amazing nexus of imagination and enterprise. Someday, Pedro thought, Rancho Sacayak would be such a place, but without the scoundrels Sutter attracted. And without the squalor of San José with its four to five hundred people, not counting Indians, aging military retirees on small farms, filthy mahalas servicing the men from Mexico — an ant heap of drunkenness and broken spirits. *Señor del Cielo*, no. Pedro's brothers probably still worked the family plot, a mere square vara. Maybe they had all forgotten him.

He remembered how shame for his father had pushed him to excel at horsemanship. He'd won contests, and respect. He sank back in the saddle, resting his hands on the big Sinaloa horn, rocking with the gait. The heat, *gracias a Dios*, was leaving with the sun. He could almost feel his military life fading with it. Rancho Sacayak was the bright, happy thing.

Chocolate whinnied as they approached the fort, which was dark against the red wine of the sunset. The remaining corner of the adobe wall appeared to have been finished in the week since he'd left, the structure massive and formidable in the empty grassland. *Está bien.* He could assign the Indian adobe makers to the harvest.

Indians and Kanakas came running, calling, "*Viene el Señor Valdez!*" Sutter's bulldogs rushed at him barking. He beckoned the new *Indios* from the Cosumnes, who hung back timidly.

The gate was open as usual, and the two *Indio* guards saluted smartly with their bayonets pointed heavenward. Returning the salute, Pedro sat tall as he rode inside, the new Indians following. The grain-soup aroma of pi-no-le reminded him of his stomach. He'd have Señor Daylor put a beefsteak on the grill. Daylor, who had learned to cook on a British brig, refused to make California food — a disappointing aspect of the fort life — but the Englishman made good bread. And butter was always plentiful.

He tied Chocolate to the stair railing, heard footsteps and turned to look into Perry McCoon's sideways smile, a dimple digging a hole in one cheek. The *malcriado* of a sailor leaned on the rail and planted a shiny boot on the first stair. "Looks like the greaser's back," he drawled, the insult rhyming with teaser, "and about time it tis."

Here was the most detestable thing about the fort. McCoon and his ilk. The Captain made it clear that Pedro would lose his position if he took the bait of these English-speaking men who worked for Sutter and drank with him at night. Fortunately, not all were as bad as McCoon.

He made as if to mount the stairs. McCoon didn't move out of the way — dark hair waved to perfection over a nose so straight it could have been planed, blue eyes sparking with mean humor. The *cabrón* was vain too, a lady's man *Americanos* called his kind, and he flattered himself to think he was Pedro's equal on a horse. Pedro was imagining changing the shape of that nose, when Sutter emerged on the landing above, smoothing his mustache and arching his brows in delight at the new *Indios*. To Pedro he dipped his head in approval.

"Esteemed *Capitán*," Pedro said saluting, "these strong young *Indios* are ready to serve you."

Sutter bobbed his head and pointed at the soup troughs. "Tell dem to eat. And Lieutenant Valdez, come to my room venn you haff eaten." He turned inside and shut the door.

3

After the sleep Maria Howchia stepped from the river and brushed dry with her tassel of turkey feathers. Father stood at the edge of the sandy beach as he did each morning, facing the sun as it rose, absorbing power. It hurt that he hadn't spoken to her yet. Never had his black eyes seemed as hard as when he'd looked at her before the sleep. She forced back tears at the memory, but returned to the u-macha to pack.

Descending the ramp into the dimness, she saw the curve of Mother's small back on her mat, facing the wall. Quietly reaching into the rafters, Maria untied her large burden basket, the bottom of its cone heavy with acorns that she'd taken from the granary before the sleep. No doubt food would be at hand in the fort, but to be safe, she would carry the staple of life.

On top of the acorns she placed her folded mantle made of the pelts of bright birds. Then her cloth skirt. She must look her best for any Big Time that might be held; she would dance with Proud Hawk. She threw in her cooking basket and her polished bone awl for coiling redbud. She might need to make more baskets. She picked up her small stone mortar. It was heavy, but the fort might not have a grinding place. She lifted the mantle so as not to muss the feathers and placed the stone beneath it, then shoved her long seed beater down the length of the basket.

In the cone of light from the smoke hole lay her folded rabbit blanket. Should she take it? She hesitated. It wouldn't be needed in this warm weather. Besides, on a long journey it might be damaged. She wasn't sure what lay ahead. But if she left it here, it meant returning before cold weather. She scowled. What she really wanted was to become the wife of Proud Hawk.

She must win him soon. Crying Fox intended to return when Sutter's seeds were stored, before the time of rain. But she might need more time. And even if Proud Hawk agreed to marry her, she couldn't be sure he would return with her and live in the u-macha with her parents for the proper time while they decided if he was a good husband. She hoped he would, and she wouldn't need to carry the blanket now. But Father said other peoples didn't follow custom. Maybe Proud Hawk would ask her to stay at his house at the place of Señor Sutter. Maybe he had a good blanket, and hers wouldn't be needed. Never had she felt so unable to act, so frozen in indecision.

She gazed at the blanket, and it seemed to speak, asking not to be left behind. Dogs might come in and shred it. She saw herself making it — the care with which she had rolled the pelts, fur side out, sewed the soft tubes end to end into long hollow ropes, woven the ropes over and under, and tied the ends. The blanket spoke of suitors who had brought the rabbit pelts, and of old master hunter

Jacksnipe Song, whom Father hoped she would marry. But she had rejected them all, waiting for a special man. Only respected married women had as many pelts as she. The blanket said she was attractive to men. It spoke of all the warm glances of the hunters and the fine coupling at the two Big Time festivals since she'd become a woman. And when it had been cold and she snuggled under the rabbit fur, tucking the silkiness around her skin, she had drifted to pleasant dreams on the coldest of nights, dry even when wind drove rain down the smoke hole.

Etumu turned over and glanced at Maria. "You go?" She sounded weak, hurt.

Maria balanced the point of the basket between her knees and nodded over the big round opening. If she took the blanket, Mother would think she didn't intend to return. It was hard to explain, not a question of when she would return, but with whom. Scraping movements on the roof and the sudden dimming of the light made her look up.

"You come?" Crying Fox's broad face peered down the smoke hole. He had bathed and had been waiting with his full quiver across his chest.

Tears of frustration welled. How could a blanket do this to her? Or was leaving home the difficulty? Only older people had gone that far away, and that was during the time of the war. She had never traveled beyond the Omuchumne village — a walk a child could make before the sun was high.

"I go without you?" Crying Fox asked.

She looked up into her older brother's impatience, recalling her own bravado before the sleep. But then she remembered Proud Hawk's hand on her back, and said, "I come now."

She stuffed the blanket in the basket, leaned the full cone against the wall while she jammed on her grass skullcap and threw her charmstone necklace over her head.

She paused. Father had said the women of the *Españoles* wore skirts. Perhaps she should wear hers for the journey. No. She must protect it for the Big Times. But Sutter paid in cloth for the collection of grass seed. Soon she could make a new skirt. Hurriedly she dug under the blanket, feeling for the striped muslin, pulled it out, tied the skirt around her hips. Now she wouldn't appear old-fashioned to Proud Hawk.

The sudden return of light and the downward scuffling on the roof told her Crying Fox was leaving. She slipped the deer thong around the basket, bent her knees, rump to the basket, placed the thong across her forehead and stood with a little jerk to center the weight. At the top of the dirt ramp she turned back to Mother and said, "I will return."

Etumu said nothing. This was the way people parted, quickly so as not to bring tears. Still, she knew Mother would think of her each day, as she would think of Mother. Outside, she nearly bumped into Father, long wet hair plastered to his head and shoulders. He stood beside the house, less imposing without his bone earplugs and topknot. Their gazes locked. No anger flashed from him.

His eyes talked of pain and love. "Daughter. You are young, and the men at Sutter's place have no understanding of polite behavior."

"Soon I will have fourteen *años*," she reminded him. He had taught her to count birthdays like mission people did. But despite being adult and able to take care of herself, she felt a needle of fright, like a fledgling leaving the nest. She was moving away from the protection of this man of knowledge — not going to a neighboring village as a marrying woman should, but to an alien place outside his sphere.

The square-shouldered back of Crying Fox crossing Berry Creek without her set her into motion. She trotted after him, pulled by the magic of Proud Hawk.

The trail to Sutter's Fort was easy to follow, and each step of the way she felt stronger in her purpose, for she was following the day-old tracks of HIS horse.

So intently did she envision him, he began to seem mythical. But when she closed her eyes she could still smell him, feel his touch, hear his exotic words, his melodic voice saying, "*Indita mía.*" This was no dream. He was her man, unlike any other. She had lain awake in a fever of wanting him.

Walking ahead, Crying Fox seemed absorbed in thought. She caught up behind his big bunching calves and strong buttocks, the delicate heron bones swinging in his earlobes.

"Why didn't you bring your horse?" she asked.

"Father said it might be stolen from the fort."

"Who would steal it?"

"Raiders. Maybe Sick Rat and Gabriel. Maybe Maximo's men."

"Sick Rat wouldn't steal your horse." Gabriel's men stole horses and sold them to *Americanos* at the Lake of the Tulares — at the southern end of the Valley of the Sun. That was so far away it might as well have been on the moon. Sick Rat hadn't returned home after the war, but remained with the horse raiders.

Crying Fox walked on, feet landing perfectly on their sides, rolling to push off. "He would not know which was my horse. Raiders round them up in the night, quickly."

Would Maria be safe in such a place? She felt safe now, with Crying Fox. Surely he would protect her at the fort.

She wanted to talk about Proud Hawk. But once when they were children, Crying Fox had said to her, "Don't talk until you have thought about what you are saying four times." That had embarrassed her, and she had never forgotten it. But he was a man. He went to the sweathouse most nights and heard what was in men's minds.

She asked, "Am I pretty?"

In stride, Crying Fox turned his head halfway to reveal a half smile. Then nodded abruptly.

Relief coursed through her and she resumed thinking about Proud Hawk. More than four times she had thought about marrying him, but she couldn't bring herself to mention it to Crying Fox. He might assume an *Españolo* was an inappropriate man. In age Proud Hawk was between her and her parents — at the peak of his physical powers, so unlike old Jacksnipe Song, with his fleshy, saggy neck and worn teeth. Her man stood on the back of a running horse.

Crying Fox kept a determined pace. They passed several villages, each time politely accepting food and learning more about Captain Sutter's fort. People said Sutter possessed great power, and that he and his fighting men had killed whole villages on the southern river — with guns and a wheeled cannon. Father had told of such guns. She asked why Captain Sutter had done that.

"They stole his horses." They looked at one another knowingly. The headman spoke: "Captain Sutter cut off Rafero's head and left it on a metal spike on the gate. Birds ate it. The skull hung there several seasons." The wide eyes of the others matched the horror creeping through her.

Later, walking behind Crying Fox, she still felt queasy. But Proud Hawk's magic beckoned. The path left the river and headed west over open, flat country, which had been burned. The lowering sun felt hotter than ever. Perspiration stung the chafed places where the basket rubbed her back and shoulders.

At last Crying Fox stopped and pointed. She followed his finger to a flat dark line against the blazing sun. The fort. The great size of it frightened her and she turned, looked back up the trail, but couldn't see the comforting line of green that marked her own river. The fort was supposed to be on the *Río de los Americanos*, but from here she saw no green line of cottonwoods and willows. Crying Fox walked on. She followed.

Cattle and sheep — animals described by Father — grazed near the fort. Men in long pants sat at the edge of a field of strange, ripe grass, now and then jumping up to scare away birds or deer or cattle. They waved greetings at Maria and Crying Fox, who walked on a trail through the full-headed grass, now pinkish in the slanting light of the blood-red sun.

Barking dogs with horrible, flat faces rushed at them. She stopped in terror. Crying Fox took a threatening step at them, growling. The dogs stood at bay. They didn't attack when he continued walking purposefully. She trotted behind, the barking din following her all the way to the huge clay wall.

The wall stood amazingly perpendicular to the ground, mauve in the sunset and nearly three times her height. A structure was built into the corner where two walls met, roofed over with large overlapping scales, like a snake's skin. Beneath the roof, on either side of the corner, poked the black snouts of two big cannons.

She adjusted her basket and trotted to catch up to Crying Fox at a big wooden gate. It had metal straps and was topped with iron spikes. But no severed head, she was relieved to see. Two blue-clothed men with long-knifed guns stood stiffly beside a wheeled cannon. Would she and Crying Fox be mistaken for horse thieves? She hung back, ready to run.

A guard's sideways glance met hers. A smile twitched at his lips. He spoke a strange tongue.

In answer Crying Fox said, "We come to *trabajo*."

The man looked at Crying Fox' charmstone, the fused cluster of elongated blue crystals he wore around his neck. Long ago Father had brought it from the coastal mountains. No one had ever seen anything like it. "*Bonita*," he said nodding at it. "Mokelumne?" He asked. They had stolen horses. Maria's heart jumped to her throat and she stepped back, afraid of the long knives, which could be used to cut their heads off.

"No," Crying Fox said sharply. "From the *Río de los Cosumnes*. The people of Grizzly Hair, Captain Juan."

The man pointed them through the gate.

Weak with relief, Maria followed as a half-clothed man stepped forward to lead them across a yard. The packed earth smelled oddly of unwashed bodies. She also smelled shaved wood, leather and steaming seeds. A thump of wood against wood sounded from somewhere as she approached a tall adobe structure inside the walls.

Near the house were two halves of a tree trunk, hollowed out and filled with gruel. People kneeled along the troughs, dipping their hands into the food and quietly eating supper. But they buzzed with talk as she and Crying Fox passed before them and followed the escort up the house-hugging stairs. They climbed high and stopped on a landing. The strange man rapped his knuckles on a wooden door. The door swung back.

Proud Hawk stood there! Not an arm's length away, his smokey-musky aroma enveloping her. She could hardly draw breath past her racing heart. But his expression was strange. Was he unhappy to see her?

Crying Fox was saying, "*Venimos a trabajar.*"

A distinct furrow deepened between Proud Hawk's grey eyes. "*De la ranchería de Capitán Juan*," he said in a tone tinged with annoyance. All her earlier buoyancy dropped away, punched down by the cold fist of disappointment.

From inside came alien talk, a man's voice. Proud Hawk answered in equally strange sounds. A tremor of fear crept up her spine. Crying Fox stood impassively. Briefly, the unseen man spoke again.

Proud Hawk stepped aside and gestured them into a dim room, motioning them to follow across a floor of level boards. She stole a glance at the man who had attracted her here, bewildered at his unfriendliness. Only two sleeps ago he had asked her to come. The wall opened to an adjoining room from which wafted an unbearably rancid smell, and the aroma of cooked meat.

In the alcove sat what appeared to be a man, though he could have been a demon. He wore dark clothing with gold buttons reflecting the light of two candles, which stood on the table before him. His large eyes were sickeningly pale in an equally pale face. His hair was the color of rotten straw — short on top, growing down the length of his cheeks and disappearing under a hairless chin. The tip of his pinkish nose slightly overhung a growth of hair — darker than the hair on his head and pointing outward like sideways bobcat ears, and his nostrils were long. Flanking this staring head was a knife, which he gripped in one pale hand, and a forked implement in the other, both pointing up. A plate of food lay before him. Behind stood boxes and baskets and blankets heaped along the wall. A long gun leaned in the corner.

Proud Hawk swept his black hat toward the man and said, "El Capitán Don Juan Sutter."

The man remained seated, studying Maria Howchia and Crying Fox from the tops of his white eyes. Then he laid down his implements, picked up a cloth, dabbed at his bobcat ears as if training them to grow sideways, and glanced up and down her length, lingering on her breasts. Perhaps he noticed that she was a woman, her chin properly tattooed. He said something in a strange tongue.

Proud Hawk responded, then spoke slowly to Maria Howchia in Spanish, almost a whisper. "He wants to take you to his bed. Do you want to make *amor* with him?" His scowl pained her.

"No." If Crying Fox hadn't been there, she would have added: I want you.

Speaking in his tongue, Señor Sutter scraped his chair back and came around the table, half a head shorter than Proud Hawk. Proud Hawk spoke back. The two stared at one another, exchanging more talk. While the strange talk filled the room, Crying Fox leaned to her and whispered, "The Captain is hy-apo. Maybe you should couple with the headman of the fort."

Proud Hawk turned and said, "I told him you are the children of Captain Juan, and your father would be angry if he takes you to bed. But the Captain says your father should be honored." Stabbing his chin toward the door, he whispered a quick, "*Vaya*! *Ahorita*!"

Go, this minute was still translating in her head when Captain Sutter raised his voice, spitting terrible sounds at Proud Hawk, who breathed rapidly, in obvious agitation.

Crying Fox said, "Perhaps she will like the captain better when she knows him longer." Beneath his outward calm she saw his fear.

It jolted down to her toes. Captain Sutter could shoot them, cut their heads off and display them on pikes. Maybe he was telling Proud Hawk to do it now. She saw alarm and confusion in the *Españolo's* face, and realized he lacked power before Captain Sutter.

She turned to run, but Sutter's hand closed on her upper arm. He yelled at Proud Hawk and Crying Fox, pointing to the door with a loud, "Go." It meant nothing to her.

She hated the look on Proud Hawk's face as he followed Crying Fox to the door, backing more than walking. He wasn't proud. The door shut behind them. She squirmed to no avail.

For an instant she faced the captain, his pale eyes, one looking slightly inward, then she looked at his foot coverings. With surprising strength for a small man, he pulled her to the far end of the alcove, to a raised platform of blankets dimly lit by the candles. A second long gun stood in the corner.

She tried to breathe, to face her death, for she had seen he was angry. This violent headman had ordered whole villages killed.

He pulled down her skirt, let it drop to the floor, put his hands on her breasts and smiled into her eyes. Maybe he wouldn't kill her. He had said he wanted to take her to bed. Maybe he only wanted to couple.

A rabbit-toothed smile parted his lips, moved his sideways mustache as he pushed her back to sit on the blankets. Breathing rapidly in her fear, she reminded herself this was only a man, not an evil spirit. And yes, she saw by the swelling in his trousers that he wanted to couple. Relieved, she thought she could endure it.

The boots beside the bed, too near her nose, emitted an odor like the putrid pink slime mushroom. A sharper smell slammed into her as Sutter threw off his jacket and raised his arms to pull his shirt over his head. Smells couldn't escape here. Doors and windows were tightly covered. The house had no smoke hole. He dropped his trousers and stepped out of them — the pale fur of his legs haloed brightly in the candlelight behind, his arousal pushing out the thin cloth of his short pale pants. He lifted a leg and pulled the foot-covering from a crooked white foot, first one, then the other, and the nauseating pink stench penetrated, though she tried not to breathe. He draped the foot coverings over the boots. Did he never bathe? She stood up, suddenly needing fresh air like life itself.

"*Nein mädchen.*" He seized her upper arms and shoved her down, then stepped from his short pants, his man's part flipping free, nearly in her face. The end of it was encrusted with a pale cheesy rot and the yellow stench gagged her. She pointed at it and said, "*No quiero.*" Again she stood to leave.

"No, mine chile." He slapped her hard across the cheek and mouth. It threw her back on the bed so suddenly she hardly knew what had happened.

She sat up, felt her burning lip. Her mind spun. She had never been intentionally struck. She had heard of it only once — a mother slapping an extremely disrespectful child. Her lip pulsed with her heart, and she feared he would hit her again. She felt like a moth in the hands of a cruel child.

He smiled and grasped her shoulders, breathing hard. "Ya, dot is goot." With those intense sounds came a stink from his mouth like vegetation rotting in warm, stagnant water — a fulsome black-green smell. Even in shadow, with candles at his back, she saw the terrible white eyes, and his stinking man's part as she sat on the bed. Her stomach lurched. She tasted bile, swallowed hard. Would he kill her if she vomited?

He pushed her back and lay beside her, her head sinking on a puffy square of cloth. A stench billowed from it — light brown and rancid, as if generations of sick animals had sweated and died there; this was the underlying smell of the house. He raised up on an elbow and groped between her thighs with a harsh finger. He shoved it inside her, the nail scratching. She jerked away.

He rolled his white weight on top of her and squeezed out the last good air. His knees parted her thighs. She wrenched her head to the side but couldn't escape green rot of his mouth, or the biting stench of his underarms as he pinned her hands down with his hands. His man's part was probing, she felt the sticky path of it on her thighs.

With a wooden bang light entered, the door opening. A tendril of good air came through the foul room, followed by rapid barefoot steps. A dark silhouette loomed — a woman by her angry voice, though the hair was long. The woman picked up a boot and pounded Captain Sutter with it. He rolled away fending off the blows and speaking in soothing, reasonable tones. But the woman was quick and fierce. As they grappled, Maria scooted off the blankets.

She ran through the room, fetching her skirt and burden basket, and out the door and down the stairs.

It was nearly dark. The clean aroma of grass washed over her, but fear and confusion pursued her. What would Captain Sutter do when the struggle was over? The courtyard was dark, deserted, Crying Fox nowhere in sight. Candlelight glowed in many little squares of windows around the wall. As she stepped off the last step, a loud metallic sound rattled her bones. She held her breath. It clanged repeatedly in cadence.

A man called: "Twenty bells and all's well." She saw a dark figure moving around the wall, sharply delineated when he passed the windows. "Twenty bells and all's well," he called again. The voice and the clanging receded.

Hunting for her? Announcing the hunt to others? She had angered the headman, and people were killed for that. Maybe Captain Sutter had gone out another door. In her mind she saw her head on a gate spike. She crept from the shadowy staircase, where anyone could be hiding, her heart drumming through her ribs. She couldn't tell if the gate was closed. Could she go through it without being seen? Where would she hide?

"*Ven!*" The smell of smoke and leather surrounded her. It was Proud Hawk. He took her hand and said in Spanish, "You can sleep in the *Indio ranchería.*"

4

The next morning Pedro had assigned the *Indios* to the fields and was on his way back through the gate, thinking how clever he'd been sending Manu-iki into the Captain's room, when he saw trouble ahead. Bill Daylor, the powerful, broad-shouldered English cook, stood cornered by three Indians and Captain Sutter. Pedro hurried to Sutter's side.

"Bill Daylor iss a — a" the captain sputtered. "Trow him in jail in chains!"

"What has he done?" Pedro wanted to know. Señor Daylor had blood on his apron but that was normal. He stood hatless, legs braced, the white expanse of his forehead gleaming in the morning sun.

"He hass made sex with Manu-iki." Drawing a noseful of air the captain added, "In da cook house! Now go, bring twenty strong men."

Right there in the kitchen! Amazed, Pedro ran to the field for Indians and Kanakas. Then it came to him. Manu-iki had seduced the cook to get revenge on Sutter for all his Indian girls. Now Daylor would pay, all because of a pretty *Indita*. Ay, ay, ay. Pedro could be in big trouble.

Soon twenty *Indios* and Kanakas surrounded Daylor, and Pedro and Luis were dragging the heavy chains across the courtyard. How peaceful it would be to run cattle at Rancho Sacayak!

"Just ye try'n taik me, ye bloody bastards," Daylor snarled through his large English nose, apparently not a bit cowed by the reinforcements.

Daylor had arrived in California the hard way, walking the plank. He claimed he had spoken for the crew, who had hoped to linger in Monterey — to take on more fresh meat, he said. The brig sailed out of the harbor while Daylor argued with the captain, insisting they turn back. But English captains did not like to be contradicted. Daylor was the only one to go ashore, all but drowned. Pedro figured the señoritas had been the lure, that and the lush countryside, which had to beckon after months aboard those floating prisons. That had been only a year ago, and now Daylor was in trouble again, hunched forward, eyes darting daggers, jaw dropped like he would eat his adversaries.

A hush hung over the courtyard. Carpenters, tanners and candlemakers peered from doorways around the wall. Indian women and children watched through the open gate. Manu-iki stood by the oven with her cowrie shell necklace deep between her golden breasts. Forbidden fruit. She knew her power over men, and wild *hombres* these foreigners were.

Sutter clenched his fists and hopped. "Hit him, hit him. *Verdammt.*" Normally he behaved like a gentleman officer, Pedro reminded himself.

Two Indians and Kanaka Henry rushed forward, but the Englishman knocked them back like a bear swatting hornets. Kanaka Henry, the big golden-skinned *mayordomo* of the Islanders, avoided Sutter's accusing stare and got up to try again. The amazing part was that Manu-iki was Kanaka Henry's woman, had been since before Sutter brought the Kanakas from the Islands. Pedro knew that if he had a wife and Captain Sutter took her to his bed, Pedro would kill him. Never mind rank. But to fight another at Sutter's bidding, and for this reason — *Ay Madre!* Sometimes he couldn't fathom Kanakas. It would be comical if it wasn't so dangerous.

A hefty *Indio* dashed at Daylor. The cook's fist thunked into his face with the sound of a ripe melon. The Indian fell back cradling his head.

Daylor growled, "John Sutter, so help me, if ye don't call off yer lackeys, I'll kill ye, I will. So help me God."

Sutter's mouth opened beneath his parted mustache. Now he wouldn't sleep well, Pedro knew, as long as Daylor lived. Threats were not lightly made. He hoped he wouldn't have to hang the man, not for playing with a woman. A few feet away hung the end of the limb where condemned Indians died kicking. But this was a white man, a man of *razón*.

Sutter shook his fists. *"Donnerwetter, Gott im Himmel!* Nay nay nay, Idiots! At da zame time! Togezer! All at da zame time!"

Kanaka Henry translated it into Island talk, Pedro into Spanish for the Indians, and twenty men closed ranks on the fighting cook. "Ya ya, iss goot," Sutter encouraged as they stepped forward.

Daylor dove at Kanaka Henry. Kanaka Henry collapsed, all the *Indios* and Kanakas piling on top. Underneath and out of sight, Daylor erupted. Naked limbs and torsos thrashed and heaved atop the volcanic force. A dust plume enveloped the pile of writhing men as knees and feet scrambled for leverage and arms flailed for holds.

Manu-iki glanced at Captain Sutter with smugness on her golden features, and Pedro wondered if the pretty *Indita* would understand what she had stirred up. At last the heap of men stilled. *Indios* regained their feet, backed away. Pedro knelt beside Señor Daylor, who lay spread-eagled beneath Kanaka Henry, Indians kneeling on his legs. Daylor kicked. Kanaka Henry cinched up his arm.

Pedro, clapping the irons on Daylor's wrists and ankles, whispered in his ear, "I am sorry, señor."

"Wrap him in chains," Sutter said.

"He cannot get away now, *Capitán*. I believe we have no need for chains."

"Lieutenant Valdez, wrap dot man in chains from his neck unto his foot. He iss a dangerous fellow."

"Sí, *Capitán*." He helped Daylor to his feet and wound him in chains, turning him around and around as Luis fed out the line. Men in the shops snickered. *Indios* laughed outright. And it did look ridiculous.

"Ya ya, iss goot," said Sutter.

Luis handed Pedro the ring of keys.

"Lieutenant Valdez" — Sutter's tone deepened with his restored dignity — "lock da bastard in the calaboose." He flashed Daylor a triumphant look. "Tomorrow, send him wit a big escort to Monterey. The Governor iss to be told William Daylor is a bad disturber of the peace. He iss to be deported."

"Sí, *Capitán.*"

Sutter's pale eyes caught the morning sun as he glared at the cook. "You goat! I hope day trow you on da same ship and next time you walk da plank and go to da bottom." He started up the stairs of the *casa grande*, then turned and announced to the whole fort: "Now, go vork."

Men ducked back into the shops. Pedro made eye contact with Daylor. "If you would please be so good as to walk, señor?" He pointed with his hat across the courtyard.

"Not goin to that hellhole, I ent."

Sutter's boots thumped back down the wooden stairs and his shrill voice knifed from behind. "Goot, I kill you now." He grabbed Pedro's gun and reached for the powder flask.

Pedro said softly to Daylor, "Señor, *por favor* walk." No one would question Captain Sutter killing a cook in this wilderness. He was pouring in the powder.

Daylor, a much taller man, looked down at them both and Pedro read the pent-up violence. Sutter clicked the lock. Then, to Pedro's relief, Daylor took two tiny steps toward the gun tower, weighed down and hobbled by the clanking chains. Sutter jammed the gun into Pedro's hands and left, thumping up the stairs. Pedro inched across the hushed courtyard, following the cook.

Jared Sheldon came from the carpentry shop with an adz in his hand. He stepped before the *calabozo* door, looking like an intelligent wolf about to lunge — chiseled face, slight overbite, narrow jaw, yellowish-hazel irises. But Pedro knew Sheldon to be a level-headed man, even if his best friend was in chains.

With a glance at the *casa grande* then Daylor, Sheldon said, "I'll get you out of this. I'm going to Monterey tomorrow to get my rancho papers moving." Sheldon was a free contractor, his time his own. He leveled a look at Pedro. "I'll explain to the Governor. He'll let him go." Sheldon had helped rebuild the Customs House in Monterey and the Governor owed him.

Pedro nodded noncommittally. "Señor Daylor," he said, "*por favor*, enter."

Daylor and Sheldon, equally tall and lean, exchanged a look. Sheldon had fished Daylor from Monterey Bay, having heard his cries for help, then taught him carpentry and brought him to the fort. No doubt he would save his friend again. Sheldon turned back toward the carpentry shop and Daylor crossed the threshold. Relieved, Pedro saw that neither blamed him.

It was dark inside, even with the outer door ajar. Excavated beneath the circling stairwell that led to the cannon ports above, the *calabozo* reeked of stale urine. Pedro inserted the long, rough key into the lock of the barred inner chamber, turned the lock, and stepped back as the iron door squealed open.

Above his tunic of chains, Daylor's jaw worked and he said, "I vowed to meself I'd die before gittin locked up again."

"Go, señor, *por favor*." He kept his voice gentle.

Daylor sighed and shuffled inside the cell. Pedro exhaled. He liked the man. Some of the runaway sailors and fleabitten trappers who hung around Sutter were cheats to the bottom of their souls. Some treated Pedro like an outsider in his own country. But not Daylor and Sheldon.

He swung the heavy door closed and the clank echoed up the gun turret. In the light from the open door, Daylor looked over the chains and through the bars. Nothing was more tragic, Pedro thought, than a strong man made helpless. Anyone could sneak in and fling a knife through the bars. Sutter wouldn't, but impulsive men vied to do the Captain favors. And with the babble of tongues nourishing misunderstandings, anything was possible. The outer door had no lock.

"Do not worry señor," Pedro said, "I will sleep here tonight, and ride part way with you in the morning. You will be safe."

"Why would you care?"

"You are good man." He considered, lowered his voice. "Captain Sutter, he is a little *loco* about the women, no?" He cut his reassuring smile short. With the light at his back he'd be nothing more than a black shape under a sombrero. "If I can help in Monterey — without embarrassing Captain Sutter — I will."

Daylor's throaty, emotional tone surprised him. "Thankee mait. I understands your position." Then his jauntiness returned. "Ah but Manu-iki loves me manly body, she does. And she the fairest female to walk the earth!"

All day Maria Howchia worked in the field. Her seed beater wouldn't dislodge the strange golden seedheads, so she twisted them off with her hands. Blue Star did the same beside her. They stepped steadily, rhythmically, as their mothers had taught them, tossing the seed into their burden baskets. The barbed stalks began to hurt her hands. She wiped sweat from her eyes and looked across the plain where a line of green marked the big river. How she wished to be swimming! Or sucking in a long drink of water! She glanced at her sore palms.

"I'm going to dump my load," Blue Star said with an envious glance at the men swinging huge metal hoops at the wheat. They moved rapidly, purposefully. "You too?"

Maria looked back toward the river, thinking how she had run from Captain Sutter. The memory pricked her along with the hot sun. Proud Hawk, who was known here as Señor Valdez, had told her to go home, but Crying Fox hadn't wanted to leave, and a woman couldn't travel that far alone. Blue Star was waiting. "Yes. Let's walk back," she said. Her basket was only half full now, but she had gathered two full loads earlier, and her hands told her to quit.

Blue Star opened her own palms — red, cut, swollen. She had worked two days. This is how Maria Howchia's hands would look tomorrow.

As they started back through the field toward the high white walls, the man who scared birds jumped up and ran toward them, the tails of his red bandanna flapping as he leaped over the stubble with his long gun. Puzzled, they stopped.

"No, fill them up," he said the moment he arrived before them.

"We are tired and our hands hurt," Maria Howchia said.

He stepped back and leveled the gun at her nose.

She sucked air, the shock tingling. Blue Star covered her mouth.

With his long hair hanging on either side of the wooden stock, the man pointed the gun from Blue Star to Maria. "I shoot you if you leave. Pick seeds."

They did. Only at the signal of a gun's bark did they join the two hundred other people and dump the last of their loads on the growing seed mountain in the adobe corral. Maria could hardly wait to jump into the river. Almost faint from thirst, she hurried along the path, hands screaming with pain, throat choked with dust and wheat chaff. And her soul still hurt after being struck by Captain Sutter. Where was Proud Hawk? Her desire to see him was mixed with the fear that he would take her to the headman.

She dived into the cool water, which was already filled with people, and surfaced, cupping the water, sucking it down. Then she floated on the watery bed, undulating her hands to stay stationary in the current. Above, the giant trees tried to meet over the broad river. Her stomach growled. The morning gruel had been too thin, but the bread tasted good. Maybe she would get more tonight. She closed her eyes and remembered its taste, but strangely, it was nu-pah that came to mind — its thick, oily goodness.

She swam to shore, not having spoken to Blue Star of Captain Sutter, and searched for her friend among the swimming people. Other men and women stepped from the water, whisking themselves dry with turkey feather tassels like the one she had forgotten and left in the home place. She asked a tall woman, "Who cooks while the women gather seeds?" Supper would be ready, Blue Star had said.

Pressing water from her hair, the tall woman said, "Señor Daylo and Manu-iki. But people say he is gone now. Maybe Manu-iki and her women make food alone." She started up the path. Manu-iki was the long-haired woman who had beat Captain Sutter over the head with his boot, the woman who had given Maria an unfriendly look while putting bread in a mud dome that resembled a beehive.

Blue Star stepped up the bank, water sheeting from her. "Ah, that felt good." She flipped water as she whipped her head from side to side, and joined Maria and the others on the path through the high thicket, heading back to the fort.

When they caught up, Maria asked the tall woman if Manu-iki was Captain Sutter's wife.

"Yes, and she is Kanaka Henry's wife too."

Stunned, Maria exchanged a look with Blue Star. Sometimes a man had more than one wife, but no woman had two husbands.

The young woman glanced knowingly at her. "Captain Sutter tells all people how to live." Reaching for a clump of grapes, the vines cascading from a high tree, she popped one into her mouth. "He couples with many young women, many girls too."

Girls! It was as Father had said. Good behavior was not observed here. She plucked a cluster of grapes as she walked, and asked, "What does he do if they run away?" The grapes were sweet and ripe, slippery morsels with crunchy seeds.

"Most do not. He gives good presents. And it insults his honor if a woman resists. Once he slapped a girl in the face and said she had stolen a cooking pot from the kitchen. He had her locked in the *calabozo*. She was to be shot the next morning, but the men of her family helped her escape. Her brother was hanged by the neck for helping her get away. He died."

A shiver ran down Maria's spine despite the warm air blowing over the grasslands. "He smells bad," she said trying to stop the memory. Like a taunting demon, it had swirled in her head all day.

The woman's laughter tinkled, her eyes saying she thought Maria had coupled with the Captain. "They all smell bad, the men with pale skin. But they give nice presents and do not expect a woman to cook or gather for them in return. You'll get used to it."

Blue Star asked, "Don't they bathe?"

"Almost never."

Mother had warned about this. People were impure here. But Proud Hawk hadn't smelled bad, had he? Strong but not bad. Even so, she wasn't sure she wanted him now. He lacked power here, where the white fort dominated the grasslands. She felt like a young child blundering into a den of rattlesnakes. She wanted to go home. But a man would point a gun at her. Father had said the long robes at the mission made people work in just this way. Father had escaped, but she must not ask Crying Fox to help her get away. He could be hung.

"If I run away, would Captain Sutter hunt for me?"

The tall woman shrugged. "People bet on what the Captain will do next. We never know." She smiled, but her eyes conveyed sympathy.

Maria shut her eyes. She must regain her calm. She would not leave unless it became absolutely necessary. Besides, she'd feel foolish to appear at home so soon after defying her parents. She got herself into this quagmire and she would get herself out. But what if Captain Sutter came for her? Coupling wasn't supposed to feel bad. Why did the thought of him repel her? She had never heard of women being forced. Except — was THAT what happened to Mother during the war? What bothered her most was knowing that Proud Hawk might send her back to Captain Sutter.

A breeze cut past her wet skin. The season was turning — hot days and cooling nights. It was Acorn Time. At home people would be playing games and singing and looking forward to First Rain. Ahead loomed the fort, a malignant white growth in a friendly sea of tan grass.

5

That night after supper, and after making sure the pretty *Indita* was safely hidden in the huts of the *Indios*, Pedro closed the outer door of the jail behind him. Removing his sombrero, he sat leaning against the wall, and placed his gun over his lap. The stench was as deep and pervasive as the night was black.

They sat like that for a long time, Daylor behind the bars in the dark, Pedro outside the cage. Then Daylor talked, telling of the time he'd ridden after stolen horses and found Sutter's herd grazing at the Omuchumne village. He and Jared Sheldon had made a deal. Sheldon would petition the Governor for the land and give Daylor half in exchange for clearing brambles and building corrals.

Daylor said, "Bet me boots Jared gets his papers, 'e does. When I gits meself free, I'll set me sails fer that Omuchumne rancho."

Pedro remembered the place — a fertile stretch where the Cosumnes turned south, only about two leagues from the Rancho Sacayak of his imagination. "A good idea, señor." Something big scurried across his boot. He jerked his leg back and said, "I'd like to get some land too."

"I didn't peg you for a farmer."

Peg. Strange English words kept popping up, but Pedro understood the meaning. Farmers were rancheros, men who worked the land, and Daylor was like most men around the fort; they saw Pedro only as a soldier.

He explained, "I've been with Captain Sutter five years. It is time I have a rancho in this beautiful land." He had been a good officer. Enlisted man really. He would never rise above corporal, but one day the Captain had simply started calling him lieutenant, and who was Pedro to argue? Captain Sutter was a law unto himself. But Pedro could have lost everything over the *Indita*. Now he would walk on thorns to keep her from Sutter.

Daylor grunted. Straw rustled, chains rattled.

Silence fell between them, Pedro sitting in the dark thinking of Captain Juan's *ranchería* and hoping Sutter would write the letter of recommendation. He thought back over the years at the fort, back to when he'd first seen Captain Sutter in Monterey. The little Swiss had emerged like an emperor from the Commander's headquarters. As he strode up the revelry yard, his blue jacket bristled with brass and red trim, the fringe on his gold epaulets swayed, the white plumes flounced on his tricorn and his fancy scabbard glinted in the sun. Every soldier had been impressed by his deportment. Even now, knowing the Captain's weaknesses, Pedro admired the man, who often alluded to his distinguished military service in Switzerland and France. But something about that puzzled him.

"Why would a French captain establish himself on the California frontier? Daylor was an Englishman, he might know.

Chains clinked. "I'd say he's runnin."

"Running?" The joke was that every man at the fort was escaping something. But surely not Sutter, with his connections in European courts. What were friends for if not to help a man through his troubles?

"At's me guess," said Daylor. "Eatin me alive, the damned critters is. Have ye measured the size o' them that hop about in here?"

Pedro grunted and shifted to his other hip, recalling the speech that changed his life. The Commander had introduced Captain Sutter and said he needed volunteers to serve in his new garrison in the interior — men to pacify the Horsethief Indians. The commander went on to say that Captain Sutter was now alcalde of the entire interior region. "The Governor will pay close attention to Captain Sutter's recommendations for land grants," he continued, "Men, this is an opportunity to serve with a distinguished officer and civilize the interior."

Pedro beat five others to the line. Sutter took them all, and Pedro never regretted the move. New Helvetia had proved an exciting place. Within a year Sutter started building the fort and stocked it with a wealth of animals, tools, guns and furnishings purchased from the Russians, who were vacating their holdings on the coast. Pedro had become the Captain's right-hand man. He didn't worry much about the little tussle in the *casa grande*. Sutter didn't hold grudges. But perhaps Pedro had performed his duties too well. Had he become indispensable?

Would Sutter write the letter?

Morning. At seven bells Pedro mustered the militia, now nearly eighty *Indios*, and marched them in two straight columns under the red, white and green flag. Sutter waited on the stair landing, in his dress uniform. Among the women and girls watching from the shade of the big oak was the pretty *Indita* from Captain

Juan's village. She had looked at him strangely last evening, but he knew she had successfully evaded Captain Sutter the last two nights. Besides, Manu-iki had occupied the Captain.

"Company halt," Pedro called.

The *Indios* returned his salute. The new men learned quickly. They enjoyed the morning ritual as much as he did. He employed every flourish he'd ever seen in Presidio Monterey.

As Captain Sutter came down his stairs, Pedro stepped back. The Captain strolled down the lines, a dignified officer inspecting his men — some naked, some in shirts but no pants, others in tattered mission loin cloths. The Kanakas and the best of the *Indios* were absent, escorting Bill Daylor for the next week.

"Lieutenant Valdez."

Pedro snapped his heels, "*Sí Capitán.*"

"General Mariano Vallejo comes to us late in der day. I giff him a formal velcome. Trousers and shirts must be on the new Indians. Find some in da Russian crates."

"*Sí, Capitán.*" Pedro saluted.

Sutter turned and mounted his steps.

"At ease," Pedro said, then beckoned the women and girls forward. He explained the day's work. Each Indian was to cut three loads of wheat by twelve bells. Men and boys, who had no burden baskets, were to use cowhide bags. These were now ready in the leather shop. At eleven bells all *Indios* were to dump their grain, police the grounds and put on as many clothes as they had. "Report to the token room if you have no clothes."

The girl was looking at him. *Bonita.* He almost forgot what he was saying. She could well be the key to making his rancho a success, being the daughter of the chief. "Dismissed," he barked. As men dispersed and women secured thongs around their foreheads, balancing their big conical baskets, he went to the little *Indita*. "*Momentito,*" he said in a soft tone, laying a hand on her arm.

Her wet hair was tidy from her morning swim and her breasts tilted up toward him as if to say good morning. He felt his response tingling. But her large black eyes had developed the glazed look of her people when they didn't want to speak. She turned toward the men and women exiting the gate.

"It is good you are staying out of *Capitán*'s sight," he said. Most Indian girls thought it was an honor to go to Sutter's bed, and he hoped she wouldn't change her mind. "I tell you again, I will help you leave."

He detected a tremor in her lower lip as she glanced briefly at him. Was she upset with him? He had noticed this before. The door of the *casa grande* swung open. Captain Sutter stepped out surveying his courtyard. The girl dashed for the gate, the big basket hiding her shapely backside.

Pedro smiled to himself. She was doing her part.

6

General Mariano Guadalupe Vallejo and three men went up the stairs with Captain Sutter. Pedro dismissed the militia, which had looked remarkably respectable. Now they crowded before the door of the armory to hand in their guns. When that was done, Pedro mounted the stairs. He had been asked to attend the meeting.

"*Momento*, Señor Valdez," said a North American voice.

He turned to see John Bidwell and Pablo Gutiérrez, both dusty from the trail and hauling saddles through the gate. They worked at Sutter's north ranch, Upper Farm, Sutter called it — *Hoch* in German. Pedro waited.

"Is there a *batéa* at the fort?" Pablo asked.

Pedro shook his head. So far as he knew, there was none. In Mexico those wide wooden bowls with ridges were used for panning gold. Had these two found gold? The familiar sick feeling touched his gut as he watched the two place their saddles under the oak and head for the *casa grande.*

"I'll ask John," Bidwell said.

Pedro held up a hand. "Señores, sorry but the Captain is occupied with important matters. Help yourselves to refreshments in the kitchen."

Disappointment showed in their faces and the two men retreated, trying to talk with one another, Pablo with poor English, and Bidwell with poor Spanish.

Pedro opened the door and scanned the room — the talks not yet started — and entered. There sat General Vallejo, John Sinclair, Sutter's closest English-speaking confidant, and Vallejo's three men — all seated at the elegant Russian table. The Captain was in his alcove. Vallejo's blue uniform looked a bit shiny, but distinguished, and Pedro felt a thrill of pride to meet the grandest of his countrymen. Respectfully he took off his hat and swept it to the floor, then seated himself and waited for Captain Sutter.

General Vallejo talked pleasantly of the journey from his Sonoma rancho and the launch ride across the Sacramento River. His round white face was flanked by dark muttonchop sideburns, and he didn't seem much older than Pedro. Pedro didn't know the General's three men. They nodded in unison, a silent chorus to their superior.

On previous occasions when General Vallejo had visited New Helvetia, Pedro had wished to speak to him personally. Finally he had the chance. "I owe you a personal debt of thanks, esteemed General," he said.

Across the table Vallejo tilted his head in puzzlement. "How so?"

"You had my father's helmet returned to me."

Vallejo pursed his full lips. "I don't remember . "

"In 1829, Estanislao's rebellion, after the last batt — "

"Yes, yes. Now I remember. What a long time ago! It was remarkable finding that ancient relic in a field of ashes. Blackened, I recall. It must be precious to your family."

"Sí, General. It was worn by my ancestor in the Holy Wars."

The General raised his brows in appreciation. "Did you fight Estanislao? Or, no. I think you were too young."

"I was young, but I fought and got a shoulder wound. Nothing serious."

Vallejo smiled, "We were both young." He had led the final engagement and emerged a hero, and was soon promoted from Ensign to General.

Sutter entered bareheaded, without his too-tight jacket. He carried a writing plume, ink bottle and paper. Bowing formally to each visitor, he sat at the table head. Formalities consumed the better part of an hour, with Pedro translating when necessary.

General Vallejo was eloquent in his agreement with Sutter that Upper California must rid itself of the criminal depredations of the *cholo* soldiers brought by Governor Micheltorena from the jails of Mexico. "But Captain Sutter," he said, holding him with a pointed look, "I draw your attention to an important fact: the scoundrels are leaving."

General Vallejo paused as Pedro translated, then continued, "Twelve days ago Governor Micheltorena agreed to send them away. Still, my *Indio* runner informs me you are amassing soldiers. The alarm is finished, *Capitán*. It is over. The *cholos* are going home. No need for your big militia."

Sutter lowered his chin and his eyes floated to the tops of white seas. "Den for vhat reason is General Castro collecting troops in San José, hmm?" He didn't wait for an answer. "Iss perfectly clear da agreement iss soon broken." Sutter's look changed to pity. "Perhaps your information iss un-fresh, hmm?"

It could have been taken as an insult, but Vallejo didn't flinch. "Captain Sutter, I sorrow for my country, which, I'm sure you have no need to be reminded, is your country too. You have written certain letters, and I have seen your enlarged militia. Rumors fly quickly up and down California that you sympathized with the foreign invaders from the United States — an unauthorized and armed invasion, wasn't it?" Pedro recalled the bedraggled, starving men of Lt. John Frémont, who had been *loco* enough to traverse the Snowy Range in winter.

"General Vallejo," Captain Sutter said, "I giff dem every kindness you would. Please, for me, say to your Californio friends dot my generosity not be misunderstood. I love Mexico so much as you."

The furrow between Vallejo's brows remained. "If you fight General Castro, you do yourself harm." He looked up at the ceiling then at Sutter. "*Capitán*, I came here determined that you, how shall we say, understand. No matter what Governor Micheltorena has told you, war will endanger both our collective futures.

Please, *Capitán*, do not let old troubles between us color your understanding. I come today clean of grudges. For the sake of our country, I implore you, go back to your farming."

The talks continued. Captain Sutter insisted it was his duty to train a militia. General Vallejo surprised Pedro by hinting that Micheltorena and Castro were actually allies. Pedro glanced at both men and paused in his translation. How could he, a man of poor birth, presume to interpret the velvet subtleties for which Spanish officers were famous into English, for a man whose native language was German? A man inclined to flat-footed thinking?

Like stepping from stone to stone in a fast river, Pedro selected his words. He couldn't simply blurt out what he thought the General had implied. He might be wrong, and the reputations of distinguished Californians — Castro's and Vallejo's — were at stake.

He stuck to the literal translation. Sutter repeated his determination to support Governor Micheltorena against the rebel general, to war if necessary. Vallejo approached his request from new angles until light faded at the windows and it was hard to see the faces. Pedro hoped for an opportunity, later, to explain his hunch to Sutter. Then all could be repaired by letter. That was Captain Sutter's way.

Sutter pushed back, scraping his chair noisily on the plank floor, and bowed deeply. "Esteemed General, I would be honored if you and your men would partake of our humble supper." He rang his little cow bell three times — his signal for the servants to set places. Playing host was a great strength of his.

General Vallejo took his tricorn from the table, pressed it to his belly and returned the bow. "The honor is ours, esteemed *Capitán*."

Rising, bowing all around the table, Pedro realized he wouldn't get a chance to speak to Sutter alone until tomorrow. Meanwhile the matter of his rancho churned in his mind.

Outside, the sky was still light though the days were shorter now. The breeze came from the southwest. As he descended the stairs Pedro saw the Indians crowding before his room, waiting for the day's tokens.

He got the key from Luis in the armory, crossed the courtyard and moved through the *Indios*, who stepped back politely. Unlocking the door, he lit the two candles on the iron wheel overhead and nodded the people into the warm room. By summer's end, even adobe heated all the way through. He pulled the box of tin tokens from under his bed and began handing them out, staring intently at each face, assuring himself that the *Indio* had actually worked this day. They threaded the tokens through their neck thongs to jingle with the other tokens. On Saturday they would redeem them for the brightly striped cloth they all loved, and beads.

Half way through the line, he looked up to see the daughter of Captain Juan offering her reddened palm. Her downcast lashes lay on her soft, brown cheeks. "*Hola,*" he said, noticing that his voice had softened.

She looked away, seeming less confident, different than when they had first met.

He whispered, "Do not forget to stay out of the Captain's sight," and slipped her an extra token.

"Gracias," she murmured, and turned away.

The next morning Vallejo's party galloped away toward the Sacramento River. Pedro signaled the *Indios* flanking the road to fire their guns in the air. Once, twice, three times, as the party shrank into the dust and distance.

Dismissing the men, he headed for the *casa grande* and reviewed in his mind what he would say to Sutter. First the nuances of Spanish speech, then the matter of Rancho Sacayak. Señor Bidwell and Pablo Gutiérrez met him at the stairs.

"*Buenos días,* Pablo," said Pedro. "Did you find a *batéa?*"

"No. We are here to request two *batéas* from Mexico on the next ship."

"Have you found gold?" Pablo's land grant lay in the foothills at the *Río de los Osos,* Bear River.

"Sí."

Captain Sutter flung open the door, practically in their faces. "Oh, yust da men I look for." He nodded to Bidwell. "Good day John, I am heppy you are still here."

Bidwell removed his hat and was about to speak when Sutter suddenly hurried down the stairs and called across the yard, "Jared and Perry, in fife minutes ve meet." Jared Sheldon and Perry McCoon. He turned back to face Pedro and Pablo and John Bidwell. "Please. You attend too. All of you. Now I zend for Sinclair and da others."

Watching Sutter disappear around the corner, Pedro felt frustrated. When would he get the Captain's attention? Inside, the ink, plume and notebook remained on the Russian table from the day before. As Pedro seated himself, Perry McCoon entered and slouched into a chair. He grinned in his unfriendly way, the single dimple stabbing his cheek.

Pedro stared at a spot on the wall. In Monterey he'd often been assigned to hunt ship jumpers like McCoon, disloyal men who hid until their short-handed captains sailed without them. Strangely, Captain Sutter made no distinctions. He treated all English and German-speaking men like gentlemen, no matter how dishonorable. It grated.

Señor Sheldon entered nodding politely at Pedro. Taking a seat, he joked with McCoon. Even lightly sparring, Sheldon had a wolf's expectant expression.

He was in his mid-thirties, like McCoon and Daylor. Pedro too. All at the peak of their manhood. Pedro admired Sheldon more than any other *Norteamericano.* The story was that before he came to California he had been left for dead on the Southwestern desert, left by traders on the Santa Fe trail, but he was tough. Apaches had doctored him and he had learned their language and ridden with them. Now he spoke fluent Spanish and counted the Governor of Alta California as his friend.

Sheldon was saying to McCoon, "You're so full of shit, you wouldn't know the truth if it harpooned ya."

McCoon's dark blue eyes sparkled in his tanned face. He whisked a leather flask from inside his sheepskin vest, uncorked it and raised it. "And I suppose ye never rode with the Horse-thieves?" A teasing, one-sided grin.

The humor dropped from Sheldon. Men didn't say that to his face. Besides, there was another side to the story. The Alcalde of Los Angeles had gone after Sheldon because the man he worked for couldn't pay his debts and ran from the law. Sheldon admitted hiding with the Horse-thief Indians. But not to plunder ranchos and sell Spanish horses to the *Norteamericanos.* He seemed to measure McCoon, then rolled his eyes.

McCoon gave him the flask. "Jared, ere's to the good times. All speed." The dimple deepened. Again Pedro found himself thinking that if the captain closed his distillery, the worst scum would vacate the fort. But Sutter liked the noisy bunch.

Sheldon took a swig.

McCoon retrieved the flask, turned his smirk on Pedro and slowly, deliberately inserted the cork and pocketed the liquor. Pedro swallowed a passion to flatten him.

The door banged open and Sutter came in with Sinclair, Bidwell, a French trapper, two Germans — one a cooper — and Pablo Guţiérrez. Sutter nested his rump in the captain's chair and began. "My goot men. Our friend General Mariano Vallejo iss playing his tricks again. He says he vill not fight on behalf of our esteemed Governor Micheltorena. And more, he makes the fool of me." He tapped a stubby forefinger on the table.

The men exchanged looks.

"Mine *Indios* have told of General Castro's activities. He iss preparing three-hunnert soldiers to march on Monterey. Ve must go and support Governor Micheltorena. If not, one day Castro comes marching his troops here, and — Ya, iss better we fight now, wit da Governor, not vait, doing nothing, as General Vallejo advises. You men, I need you to collect American trappers. Day shoot goot. We march as one grand army against da rebels." His face had the look of a benighted warrior of God.

He turned to Pablo. "You and the other Schpanish men who haff landt on account of my help and so fort, you vill of course fight wit us. Not so?"

Pablo looked down and shifted on his crate. Thinking about the gold?

Pedro said, "Señor Sutter, I believe General Vallejo knows more than he is telling us about General Castro. Perhaps we should consider his counsel not to march."

A lost-boy look briefly replaced the benighted warrior, then haughty indignity. "Loyalty stems from da land, Lieutenant, and landt binds men to der country. If I vant to know who are da leaders of my country, I look who granted mine landt. The Mexican government hass giffen me New Helvetia; mine loyalty I own to Mexico. You who haff landt are just zo in mine debt. Not zo? Ya. You march wit me."

Pedro had spoken boldly and dared not push it further. For better or worse, his fate was with Captain Sutter. Even if he had been a real lieutenant, he wouldn't second-guess a captain. A hunch was only a hunch, and Captain Sutter was a distinguished European officer. Besides, Pedro needed a letter from him.

"Lieutenant Valdez is a fine officer," Sutter said, to Pedro's pleasure, "the best I haff seen. He hass prepare mine Indians goot. And now, if each man speak his mind, please, hmm?" The Captain glanced around the table twirling his mustache, his pale, expectant eyes glittering.

"The Captain's right," said John Sinclair, owner of the big rancho across the river. "We owe the government loyalty. I'll get forty Indians to march with us."

John Bidwell, a reasonable man who had been with Sutter for several years, agreed. "I'll bring fifty Indians from Hock Farm." English speakers couldn't say *hoch* with a German's rasp. Neither could Pedro.

Jared Sheldon's wolf eyes scanned the men. "Don't s'pose I can hold my hand out fer a land grant and stand by while Castro fights the Governor. Count me in." Sheldon scowled. "But if we're in a fight, I'm in it to win." His jaw was flint.

Sutter stopped twirling his mustache. "The *cholos* of da Governor fight wit us, fight like cornered dogs, so day not go back to the calabooses in Mexico." His lips turned up slightly, like the painted figure of San Joaquín in the mission church. "I giff you mine vordt, we vin. When iss finish, all get reward." His smile twisted into pained sympathy. "General Vallejo iss an unhappy chile. He dreams of ruling all Alta California. He fears he make his hands dirty in war." He snorted softly. "I listen not to him."

"Ve fight," said a German, the other nodding.

"And you, Mr. McCoon?" Sutter asked.

All eyes turned to the *malcriado* slouched in his chair. He grinned in his lopsided way. "Kiss the arses of the powers that be, I will."

Sutter slapped his palms on the table. "Iss finish. Pablo, ride fast to Monterey. Talk to the Californios. Tell dem to join us on da march. Most important: deliver a letter to Governor Micheltorena." He opened his portfolio and scratched out two lines, dipping his plume twice. He waved the paper dry, folded the letter, and presented it to Pablo. "I write dot ve ride to his defense." He looked pleased.

He pushed back his chair and stood looking intently at each man. "Perry, go nort to San Rafael, and bring trappers back. Careful. Vallejo hass spies. Jared and John," he said turning to Sheldon and Sinclair, "help me recruit settlers and trappers. We need goot marksmen." He smiled warmly around the table.

The men put on their hats and stood to leave. Pedro pressed forward to speak with the captain, but Bidwell elbowed in front of him, and Sutter had the look of a man preoccupied. He wasn't interested in *batéas* or land. He motioned for all but Pablo to leave.

As he went out the door Pedro saw Pablo remove a false sole on his boot, insert Sutter's letter, and stamp down. He'd have a long ride to Monterey before he could return to the hills and look for gold.

But what if General Vallejo had been sincere in his advice? It was too late. The die was cast, and Captain Sutter was Pedro's only chance for a land grant.

7

Maria Howchia waited with Blue Star among the milling people, and looked through the gate. Manu-iki was pulling a long wooden paddle from a dome oven, her assistants pouring buckets of pi-no-le into the troughs. At the end of Manu-iki's paddle a loaf steamed in the morning air. Maria wanted to learn how to make such bread.

Two men in loincloths stepped into the courtyard, one with a bell, the other with a drum. The drum roll purred and the bell clanged. The eating signal. She moved through the gate with the crowd, careful to remain hidden.

Blue Star said, "My fingers are so swollen I wonder if I can eat."

Maria glanced at her own sore hands, and kneeled before a trough, watching for Crying Fox among the naked men and women coming through the gate.

He came in and found a place opposite her, his crystal charmstone reflecting blue light as he looked after the bread, which was quickly disappearing as it was passed down the trough, each person tearing off a piece. Hungrily, he scooped the gruel, then licked his fingers and studied his hands. Cut. Swollen.

By now all the people were eating and she and Blue Star were wedged in tightly. Maybe a hundred and fifty people at her trough, an equal number at the other. Many didn't know how to count in hundreds, but Grizzly Hair had learned it at the mission and taught his children. She spooned her fingers and scooped up the thin soup, looking down the trough. A flurry of hands churned from gruel to mouths, the level of soup lowering as if draining through big holes.

Manu-iki approached Crying Fox from behind, with a loaf of hot bread. She looked at Maria with black eyes glazed — a large-breasted woman with no chin tattoo — then tapped Crying Fox on the shoulder. He spun around and, like a child who'd done something foolish, took the loaf she offered. Manu-iki smiled warmly at him and left. Maria watched him look at the lively motion underneath the red strips of the cloth tied about her hips. He tore off a hunk of bread, still watching, and passed the loaf across to her.

Realizing her brother liked Manu-iki, and worried for him, she sank her teeth into the delicious bread. Didn't he see what happened to Señor Daylor? She watched Manu-iki pinch off a piece of dough and hand it to her pale-skinned child. The child popped it into her mouth, then Manu-iki slapped the dough back and forth in her hands and stretched it over itself and laid it carefully in a basket. Maria craned her neck to watch her take an inflated lump from a basket and place it on the end of her paddle. What magic made the bread fatten with air? Manu-iki bent forward — shell necklaces and long hair playing about her wrists — and pushed the paddle into the dome. Crying Fox was watching too.

Suddenly Maria's neck prickled. She turned toward the big house and locked eyes with Captain Sutter, who stood on his landing. She drew back, behind Blue Star. But it was too late. "Lieutenant Valdez," she heard Sutter call.

Almost immediately Proud Hawk came around the *casa grande*, from where he and other *Españoles* ate. A sombrero darkened his face but she felt his glance.

She dared not look at Captain Sutter as Proud Hawk spoke to him, his square-toed boot poised on the first step, his knee snug in his dark trousers. Then he walked away and went back around the big house. She nibbled bread without tasting. The gruel vanished before her. The bell sounded, and she lined up with the others to hear Proud Hawk speak. She heard nothing, and when the talk was over, she rushed out the gate with the others.

A hand touched her elbow.

She whirled around, afraid it was Captain Sutter. But it was Proud Hawk, Pedro Valdez. He lifted one of her cut, swollen palms and said, "You can make yourself a good cutter from a split willow."

He spoke to Blue Star and Crying Fox, who had caught up. "Go to the river and cut willows, split them lengthwise and make hoops. Bring one for her." They left.

The gray faceted eyes searched her, looking deep. He released her hand and spoke softly, "Captain Sutter wants you to go to him after supper."

She looked down and her voice came out rough. "I didn't stay out of his sight."

"I am sorry, but he says you are the prettiest Indian girl he ever saw."

She didn't correct him for calling her a girl, and no happiness came from being called pretty. The good feelings of the morning had evaporated with the dew on the stubble fields, leaving sharp reality. All she could think to say was, "Captain Sutter's woman will not want me to couple with him."

"Manu-iki?"

She nodded.

"She fears another woman will have his children."

"I do not want his children," she said. "I want to go home today."

He studied her, his magic gone, and she sorrowed for the reckless soaring of spirit she'd once felt for him. He spoke for Captain Sutter. Beads and striped cloth couldn't hold her, if she had to couple with the white-eyed man.

"Then go," he said in a kindly tone. "Do not wait."

She couldn't ask Crying Fox to leave; he might be hung. Besides, she'd seen the way he looked at Manu-iki; he wouldn't want to leave. Father had spoken true. Each man must find his own way, and each woman. She would go alone. If she left now she might make it before dark. But she couldn't just walk away. How? When?

The sound of many horses drew near, and Pedro Valdez glanced around as if to assure himself he wouldn't be overheard. "Captain Sutter will be angry," he said. "He doesn't want *Indios* to leave during harvest."

She knew that.

He raised his voice to be heard over the approaching horses, his voice regaining the rich musical quality that had once enthralled her. "Especially you. If you are asked, *por favor*, say nothing of our talk, or of my help." The thundering of hooves grew louder.

She searched the kindness in his face, beneath the sombrero, the strands of hair curling down, glinting reddish in the sun. Did he fear for his life? She didn't want Captain Sutter to kill him either. "I will say nothing." But she was glad he had lost his magic. It would be easy to leave him.

The running horses, maybe thirrty, were being herded by *Indio* riders into the corral where she'd poured the contents of her burden basket. They made so much noise — the horses and the yipping men — that she had to yell to be heard. "When should I leave?" She would be conspicuous on this level plain.

He inhaled through his downturned nose, placed his hands on his waist sash and pushed out his chest, scowling pensively at the horses, now running around the corral. "Pick wheat this morning. Then when you move to the south field, go into the bushes to pass water. Stay below the uncut grain. I have a spy, so be careful, *por favor*." In the lines around his eyes and mouth she saw a look she had seen when she first met him.

A spark still smoldered inside her, she realized, and she knew the fire for him wasn't entirely gone, just covered by heavy ash. "Maybe you can come and visit us," she said over the whooping of the vaqueros, who were replacing the poles of the gate. They could be friends.

The horses ran up and over the hills of wheat, sliding, scrambling, snorting and wheeling toward the wall, the vaqueros trilling their tongues shrilly — heads and waving hands visible over the walls. Then the horses whirled and stampeded back the other way, skidding on the grain as the men leaped behind them.

Proud Hawk was watching too. "I will come, *Amapolita.*" Little Poppy that meant. A flower the color of the stripes on his sash, which moved about his slim dark pants as he began walking toward the corral.

"Wait," she called, and he turned. "My rabbit blanket is in the house where I slept. Will you bring it when you come?"

A smile softened his face. "The pleasure would be mine."

For a moment she didn't recognize the man who came through the fort gate and stood at the entrance to the corral looking between her and Señor Valdez. But when he pushed his sombrero back on his head, she realized with a shock that it was Captain Sutter. Never had she seen him in such a hat, and trousers with straps over his shoulders. She whirled away, heart pounding, and positioned her basket.

Dread drove her up the path through the stubble toward the uncut field where she would pretend to work, and as she walked the pandemonium in the corral grew fainter.

Pedro joined Captain Sutter at the corral gate and watched the Indian vaqueros run the horses over the wheat. In an hour a thousand bushels would be threshed. On the next windy day he'd start the winnowing, the shovelling of wheat and chaff into the air. Then they'd bag the grain.

Captain Sutter yelled over the noise, "I see dot you haff talk with da *muchacha.*"

Pedro nodded, avoiding his twinkling eyes, and looked at the horses. But as they leaned on the gate poles, he knew he must reassure the man, lie to his superior officer. It came out rough. "She will come to you."

Sutter smiled, and said "Ach ya, iss goot." His cheerful tone continued, a poor match for his words. "This year we haff wheat enough for our needs only. Pity."

None for the Russians. Each autumn the Russians sailed up the Sacramento to collect payments in grain. It was amazing how the Captain kept putting them off! Not that the harvest was small. It increased every year. But there were more and more men to be paid for cutting wood in the mountains and building corrals and starting shops, everything from coopers to shoemakers, and men of commerce supplying the fort. Besides there were more *Indios* to feed. The enormity of Sutter's debts secured by promises of produce was stunning, beyond what any ordinary man would conceive. How he kept it all straight was a mystery to Pedro. Each fall he half-expected Russia to claim New Helvetia as payment. It seemed they had the right.

Sutter yelled over the melee, "After harvest, we plant dopple so much again. Next year iss different, ya." Delight lit his features as he watched the vaqueros whip the horses into frenzies on the spreading mountain of wheat, much of the chaff already powdered into dust.

"*Capitán, por favor,* I need a word with you — " The dust made him cough.

"Yes, mine son. Come wit."

The captain turned and walked through the fort gate, Pedro followed, silently rehearsing his speech about needing to be his own man, wanting Rancho Sacayak. But as they neared the *casa grande* Perry McCoon came from the kitchen with a hand up. "John," he said, "I needs to palaver." When had he returned from San Raphael? Had he even gone? His dark hair was clasped neatly at the nape of his neck, his boots blackened and shiny. A dandy, the English called such a man. A snake.

Sutter smiled from Pedro to McCoon. "Both want talk wit me. Both come." The spring in his step as he mounted the stairs no doubt came from his thoughts of the pretty *Indita. Madre de Dios*! Pedro was in treacherous water — again. And he wouldn't speak of Rancho Sacayak in McCoon's presence. "*Capitán*, if you please I'd like a moment. Alone, *por favor*."

Sutter stopped and turned to look down at them. McCoon, above Pedro, turned too. He could have been made of syrup. A smile poured across his face and his body melted into the railing. Only his blue eyes stayed hard, challenging Pedro before he turned back and said to Sutter, "The greaser's hidin something, me thinks."

Pedro kept his expression placid.

"Perry," Sutter said, "you must not call mine officer dot name. Understand? I not have dot at mine establishment." He looked at McCoon as though he were a beloved child who had forgotten his manners.

McCoon straightened as far as the syrup would allow. Sutter glanced at the sun and motioned them both inside. "Komm!"

Pedro felt like he'd been walked on by a horse. But how could he be angry with a man he'd just lied to? He sat on the polished Russian chair opposite McCoon. He would listen to what the man had to say, then speak to Sutter later.

The captain folded his hands on the table and arranged his mouth in his judicial expression. "Ach zo, vhat brings you? Hmm?" As expected, he addressed McCoon first.

"I've been talking to Jared Sheldon about the pretty piece o' land he's wantin on the Cosumnes River. And I'd like to try my own hand at farming. There's a bonny piece some leagues east of Jared, on the north side of the river, Indians aplenty. At the start of the hills." *Rancho Sacayak?*

McCoon continued. "Like to see if farming's to me likin. Talk is, you're looking for a hog farm. Let me breed yer hogs, and I'll bring your pork to the fort." He grinned at Sutter with a dimple boring into his cheek. Pedro hid his shock.

Captain Sutter queried, "Far away, iss not? Vhat? Forty kilometers. Too far?"

"Me thinks the farther a hog farm, the better." McCoon laughed and his eyes lost their tease. "Help us both, hit would. I'm looking at that land for a rancho. And ye'll git half me crop o' pigs. Start me off with a couple of brave lookin sows and a boar from Hock Farm, and we'll both prosper." *A rancho!*

Sutter said, "Perry, you be a sailor, not a farmer."

"Have ye not seen me ride? Better'n any man on a horse, I be."

Disgusted at that, Pedro cleared his throat. But Captain Sutter raised his brows and nodded in a parody of a wise man. "Ach zo. Iss true."

"Help run yer cows too, I will, till I get me paipers," McCoon continued, sending a smug look Pedro's way, "but it's done for good, I is, with the briny deep. And what red-blooded man could turn his back on the beauteous and willing brown lasses such as grace this fine land, captain sir?"

Sutter smiled like an oriental potentate and Pedro searched his mind for the word *lasses*, but nothing came. McCoon was saying, "I wants me own pick o' the crop, if you gits me drift. An' fer that, a man figures t' get twenty-five miles outa your range, all due respect sir." He grinned a dimple.

Captain Sutter threw back his head and guffawed, but Pedro was still reeling, and puzzling over *lasses*.

Sutter bobbed his head up and down. "Ya ya, iss goot. I want mine men to settle all sides of mine establishment. We be strong together. I write today a letter to Johann Bidwell dot he giff you two zows and a boar. Tell Herr Brüheim to drive the hogs in mine oxcart to da Cosumnes. We see how farming likes you, hmm? Ya ya." Smiling, he smoothed his mustache back from its part, his eyes bright.

At the start of the hills. North side. Rancho Sacayak for sure. And, *Madre de Dios*, McCoon intended to petition for a grant! This was a joke of Coyote, as old Grandmother Maria used to say. Just when men thought they knew where they were going, things like this happened.

"And you Señor Valdez? Can I help you, hmm?"

Mind skimming over every possible rouse, he remembered the war. "*Capitán* Sutter. Our soldiers are excellent, as you see each day, but we need more men if we mean to fight a war." He could ride farther up the Cosumnes, maybe find another place. But then he realized he'd be McCoon's neighbor.

Sutter punctuated his words with sharp nods. "Ya ya. Absolutely." He scowled. "Go on the morning." He rang his cow bell, slapped the table, scraped his chair on the plank floor, and stood. "Iss not every day I make all happy, hmm?" He glanced between McCoon and Pedro, looking pleased.

Summoned, Manu-iki came through the door and stood waiting for instructions. Seeing the ripe fruit of her breasts, Pedro suddenly recalled *lass* was an English word for woman. McCoon would go after the young *Indita*. And Pedro wouldn't be there to stop it.

But then, if he found different land just as good, and if the new headman had an unmarried daughter — If, if, if.

8

The air was chill, the path dark as Maria Howchia hurried toward the home place. She tried to watch her footing, but the crescent moon gave little light. Rattlesnakes might lie in the path, absorbing the remains of the day's warmth. Mountain lions and grizzly bears roamed at night. But mostly she worried about Bohemkulla, the spirit who prowled the night paths scrambling the minds of travellers.

If she hadn't run most of the way, she wouldn't be this close to home. It had been dark since she'd left Omuch's village. She had accepted their food, but hadn't wanted to stay for the sleep. Now she wished she had. Exhausted, she bumped her sore toe on unseen root, and almost cried out.

The night was alive. Owls screamed and moaned throughout the forest. Straining to see into the shadows of the trees, she heard deer move in the dry grass. Sometimes skunks ambled before her on the narrow path. But no spirit wailed. Did Bohemkulla overtake people without their hearing? Part of her might be stolen. People said it had happened to old Grandmother Dishi. Never had she felt so alone, so small. Still, this was better than coupling with Captain Sutter, and soon she would be in the u-macha. That kept her moving.

The moon floated higher and the home path began to feel familiar. She went down the gully where the little creek joined the river, and climbed the last hill. With a sigh of relief she saw the glow of the sweathouse — the unchinked cracks — through the trees. Father would be inside.

A deep rumble moved the roots of her hair. She looked toward the boulders on her right and saw the moon's reflection in a pair of green eyes. She reached down, felt for a rock, let the burden basket slip from her back. No rock. Four-legged hunters, especially cougars, enjoyed the chase. She must not run.

She found a small stick, hurled it at the eyes. They disappeared, then reappeared a short distance away. Looking for them she saw another pair glinting behind a clump of vegetation, just as near. She whirled to look behind her. Two more eyes. Wolves travelled in packs. How long had they been following her? They knew a woman with a burden basket carried no weapon. Wolves didn't bother men.

Don't run. Her heart galloped beneath her ribs as she stepped carefully from the path, searching with her feet. She needed a big stick. A tree was overhead. Limbs fell in the wind.

Don't let them smell fear. But it was too late. Eyes moved toward her. Any animal would smell this much fear. Scrambling around for a weapon she screamed, "Father, Father." He could be within earshot.

The grass swished, coming at her. She dodged, whirled, caught the thick odor of wolf. She felt a fallen tree limb with her foot, then lifted it though it was huge and heavy. She swung wildly, moving her back against the tree for protection. *I must be fierce.*

A snarl came from the side. She whirled, every hair on her body tingling. Out of her mouth came the most hideous and inhuman noise she could make. Courage and anger coursed through her. *Bad wolves to attack a human!* She yelled for Father, swinging the weapon from side to side in great arching swoops.

From the side a heavy animal hit her, knocked her on the ground. She twisted, jammed the branch into its jaws. The animal gagged. She felt a spray of saliva, smelled bad breath as she shoved. Hind paws shifted back and forth over her groin, digging in for balance. Fore claws cut her from chest to neck as the wolf fought the branch. *How dare you jump at my throat!* Focusing all her anger, she screamed for Father.

Teeth clamped on her ankle. The second wolf yanked her. Wanted to drag her away so Father and the men wouldn't know! Anger mounted to blind fury and she kicked with her free foot, gouging her heel into the animal's eye as she struggled against the wolf on top. *I'll show you how strong people are!*

The top wolf jerked free of the branch. She rolled to the side and swung hard at the spot she had just vacated. A thunk and a yipping squeal answered. Her leg was free and she jumped to her feet.

Her return swing pounded the other wolf. Growls and snarls surrounded her and she swung the limb and hit another. Ribs boomed. How many? Swinging blindly, she was relieved to see glowing firebrands moving up the hill toward her. The growls ceased and she heard the rustle of animals skulking away.

In the torchlight Grizzly Hair and Jacksnipe Song and several others came to her. She lost her strength, dropped the branch. Although she was supposed to maintain a period of pretending not to see Father, a space to recognize the time spent apart, she put her arms around his thick middle and stood there on quivering legs.

He held her and petted her hair. Also ignoring custom. She closed her eyes and melted into his warm power.

The next morning, after Mother applied herbs to her lacerated ankle, Maria

Howchia went with Grizzly Hair to check his turkey snares. Relieved not to be badly injured, she walked easily. But her tongue felt paralyzed. She could not speak of Captain Sutter.

Father didn't ask. Bending over, big haunches taut, he wrung the neck of a flopping turkey, then straightened and sang a wisp of a song to send the spirit on its way. Many men sang only to the spirits of deer and bear, but father wasn't like other men. He was a man of knowledge.

His topknot shaded his wide cheeks as he reset the snare, then Maria Howchia walked with him as he carried the bird down the trail. The black-walnut trees had turned golden and the ground beneath them was thick with yellow leaves and black round nuts. She bent, tossed them into her burden basket. Walnut paste balls would be good with turkey stew.

Grizzly Hair sat against the tree. "You were brave, daughter," he said, startling her. It was the first he'd spoken since the sleep. His admiring tone resonated and a smile twitched the corners of his mouth. But she didn't feel brave. She felt foolish for having expected Proud Hawk to become her husband. And ashamed she had lacked power in Captain Sutter's room. The memory made her skin crawl. She frowned.

"You remind me of your mother's sister," he said. Since Oak Gall's death that name was not spoken.

"Tell me about her." Satisfied that she had enough walnuts, Maria removed her head thong, balanced the basket upright against the tree and sat beside Father, hoping for a long story to lull her.

"She was brave." His gaze grew pensive, and he appeared to watch a red-tailed hawk crying over the brown hillside. "She went to the mission with me. Running Quail's oldest son also went. Just we three. Everyone else was too afraid."

Maria Howchia wanted more about Oak Gall. She waited.

"People told me not to go. Even my mother, who was a spirit tracker. She said the danger was great. Everyone told Oak Gall not to go."

He seemed to be finished.

"But you learned many things at the mission," she prompted. People in the village respected Father for his knowledge of the *Españoles*. Wasn't it a good thing that he had gone there? He and the old woman he brought back, old Maria, had taught the people to speak Spanish.

He brought his knees up and rested his forearms across them, hands hanging between. "Yes." After a pause his voice changed to a teaching tone. "Clarity comes when fear is defeated. Fear can be in anything. Sometimes it is well founded and we must be clever. But often we fear looking foolish or struggling hard. Defeating fear brings *seeing*. That clarity is the first step on the pathway to knowledge."

"By *see* you mean more than look?"

He looked at her. "Can you *see* what was hidden before you went to the fort?"

"I know more about Captain Sutter." It came out soft.

He appeared interested.

"He makes men and women do his bidding. When he is angry, he has his enemies wrapped in iron chains. They live in a bad hole behind metal bars. Sometimes they are shot with guns or hung by their necks until they die. Or their heads are cut off."

She looked up through the fringed yellow of the leaves into the azure sky, disappointed about Captain Sutter's power over Señor Valdez. No longer Proud Hawk to her. "Captain Sutter is hy-apo, but different than you. Here each man decides for himself. Each family decides who is to be married, who is to be punished. Who is to couple —." A catch in her throat stopped her.

Tenderly he patted her knee, his face showed rare emotion. "You are so very young," he said as if to himself. Then he was teaching again. "Maybe you *saw* a different kind of power."

"Señor Sutter couples with other men's wives too, and girls." She wished her voice wouldn't shake. "He forces them."

"The long robes teach women to hate coupling. So their men force them."

Silence fell between them as she thought again about Mother during the war. Then she thought about Father's wisdom, the way everyone came to him for advice. Now his knowledge was aimed at her, and she felt honored. It gave her strength to ask, "Do you think I could become a doctor?" A woman of knowledge.

He glanced at her, then beyond. His big warm hand reached around and came to rest on her shoulder. "You are brave enough," he said.

This thrilled her. Strength flowed from his hand. It straightened her back and steadied her voice. Few in this world were capable of achieving the power brought by knowledge. The steps would be painful and frightening. But with Father's guidance, she might convince old Bear Claw, of the Yal-umne, to agree to teach her magic medicine. Grandmother Howchia had been a singing doctor. Maria Howchia would follow Eagle Woman's tracks. She realized she had indeed been brave; she had defeated her fear of leaving the home place. She had faced Captain Sutter alone. She had even defeated bad wolves. "What must I do to become a woman of knowledge?"

"What do you fear most?"

She shivered, suddenly knowing where this was leading. "Captain Sutter's power."

"That is your enemy." His face was impassive.

"I must defeat him?"

"Yes."

Was she that brave?

"You are thinking it will be difficult. But it will be easier than the next step on the pathway to knowledge. After you have defeated Captain Sutter and gained new clarity by it, you must defeat the clarity you gain. That *seeing* will be your new enemy. Each step of the way, the enemy becomes stronger, slyer, more difficult to conquer. Many strong men have failed to defeat their clarity. But you must continue to face your enemies if you are to become a woman of knowledge." He seemed to be remembering.

"I don't understand. How can clarity be my enemy?"

"Fear is straightforward. But clarity is devious. It refreshes you, lulls you, makes you think you know everything. It is a far more powerful enemy." He turned to her. "The warrior sees clearly and believes in his heart that the peace chiefs are wrong. That makes him a good fighter. The long robe sees clearly and believes in his heart that all others are wrong; that makes him a good teacher. But the warrior and the long robe can never become men of power unless they triumph over their hard-won understanding, no matter how clear. See that boulder?" He pointed at a giant stone splotched by overlapping lichens. "Does it appear strong and eternal?"

"Yes."

"Some day it will be sand. You cannot know that unless you *see* its soul. It is like removing your hands from your eyes." He cupped his hands at the sides of her head making a vision tunnel, then removed them. "You gain knowledge by defeating clarity."

"What is my next enemy, after clarity?"

"The respect bestowed by people upon one who *sees*. People come to one who can *see* like hummingbirds to nectar. Their advice is solicited. They can make others do as they wish. It is a very sly enemy. Few can defeat it. But you must, if you are to become a woman of knowledge."

This was almost too much to comprehend. "But how do I defeat my clarity about Captain Sutter's power?"

He stood, looked down at her. "Each person finds a different trail. If I tried to tell you, it would be wrong. I have different eyes." His worried expression said he would rather she lived as any other woman, pounding acorn flour, cooking, marrying, and having babies. The pathway to knowledge was treacherous.

But, as she positioned her head thong and burden basket for the way home, she felt determined. Next time she met Captain Sutter she would defeat his power.

9

It was the middle of the Big Time, the third day of Cos, Salmon, Festival. Maria Howchia's hands had recovered. At meals she filled her belly and her old energy had returned. But, in the place where dreams were born, her spirit felt different. She hadn't wished to couple after First-Salmon rites. She'd watched other pairs move toward the hillside, then went quietly to her own mat and lay thinking about Captain Sutter, his smells, his power, and the men who did his bidding. She missed nothing about the fort except Blue Star, and had all but forgotten about Pedro Valdez.

Now, running hard up the ti-kel field, she was surrounded by over fifty players, each with a pole pointed upward — a thrilling sight. The teams were well matched, and she was lost in the fun. Cousin Quail Song intercepted the scrotum, as it was jokingly called, and raced for the goalpost whirling the attached deerskin balls around his pole. She ran after him to protect him from the other team that converged from all sides with poles pointed, all trying to hook the scrotum.

A man passed her, fast enough to catch Quail Song. She grabbed his arm. He yanked it. Her feet slipped. She hung on, gritting her teeth as she skidded along the ground behind him, pole dragging. Another man hit from the side and both men fell on her. It knocked her wind out. When the air came back she tried to laugh, but lay under a pole pressing into her ribs. By the crowd's screaming roar, she knew Quail Song had made a goal.

Realizing she must have a drink or pass out, she disentangled her legs from arms and legs and got to her feet. She'd been running from one goal line to the other for half a day. She gave her staff to a man on the sideline and turned toward the river, still breathing hard.

The screams of the game receded as she passed through the village and down the path to the bathing place. Young mothers on the beach were hanging split salmon to dry on the racks. Toddlers played around them in the sand. The river was warm on her ankles and knees, cooler on her thighs. She fell forward, gratefully sinking until the roots of her hair were under water. Soon the spirits would send rain — Turtle Claw had beseeched them — and she looked forward to colder water. Even now the salmon creased the surface, faithful red-fleshed sojourners who offered themselves in rich abundance to the *umne*. This was a river of red wealth.

Underwater, stroking along the bottom, she opened her eyes to watch the slack-jawed salmon, then popped up near the island and pushed back her hair. Sun sparkled across the wrinkled skin of the blue water — this blue only in salmon time. The oaks on the hills were turning brown, but the shoreline was bright green with herbs. Treading water, she stilled herself and inhaled the purifying smell of peppermint. A deep-voiced roar came from the playing field and then it was quiet again, except for a clown bird knocking on hollow wood, resting between attacks. Her spirit floated as easily as her legs. The bright river narrowed downstream, held in by water-sculpted boulders. Alder branches shaded the family fishing hole. She was glad to be home.

The bushes thrashed. A sombrero and pale shirt pushed through the thicket. She blinked. No one at the festival wore a shirt and *pantalones*. Had Pedro Valdez come to return her things? The man came to the water's edge, which was hidden from the beach, and she knew by the sling of the hip — one boot on an outcropping, long gun in his hand — it wasn't Pedro. And too slender for Captain Sutter. The face was darkened by the hat, but she felt she had seen him before.

Looking her way, he sat down on a rock shelf, gun over his knees. She felt his eyes and her skin prickled with fright, but she watched and continued treading water. No doubt he had seen the ti-kel game, and hadn't caused trouble there. As she faced him her fear dissolved to curiosity, and she decided to go closer. She slipped into the current kicking downstream, carried by the water, stroking only a few times. The bottom came up rapidly. Rocks met her knees and she found footing.

The stranger had deep blue eyes, as if holes had been bored in his head and the sky came through. Looking calmly from those eyes as she stood up with water sheeting from her body, he smiled in a lopsided way, causing a cunning dimple to appear in his cheek. She thought she remembered him from the fort, but if he'd come to capture her, he didn't act like it. He was a handsome man with a perfectly straight nose, a man in his prime. But he smelled bad.

"Hello, pretty lass," he said.

She heard the friendliness in his voice. She stepped closer, from submerged rock to rock, a breeze prickling her wet limbs with gooseflesh.

He patted the boulder beside him, smiling in an inviting way.

She remained standing and asked in Spanish, "Where are you going?"

He opened his hands like he was sorry he couldn't understand.

"You come to our Cos fiesta?"

He shrugged again and said, "No palaver."

He didn't speak Spanish.

He placed his gun on the bank behind and tilted his teasing smile toward her. "Palaver *poco*," he said, and she understood the word for little. "*Bonita*," he said. Pretty. He brushed his gaze down her length, his long dark lashes lowering to his cheeks. Unlike other *Americanos*, he had no bush of hair on his face; the clean lines showed. His brown hair, tied neatly at the nape of his neck, made a wavy tail down his pale shirt. His smile dazzled.

"Wot's the nime o' this plaice?" he said, gesturing up river.

She marveled that people made such strange sounds.

"*Nombre*," he said, gesturing around.

That meant name, and she recalled Proud Hawk asking the name of the boulder over which the river spilled in time of rain. "Sacayak," she said.

"Sacayak?"

She smiled and nodded, but he needed a bath. In the spirit of the Cos festival, she laughed and grabbed his hand and pulled him toward the water.

He lurched to his feet. "Wait a minute," he said, throwing his sombrero on his gun. He sat down and yanked off his boots and placed his bone-white feet in the water.

She pulled him up again, but he stopped and undid the square of buttons at his front, letting his pants drop, then tugged his shirt over his head — the stench not unlike Captain Sutter's — and tossed everything over his boots and gun. She marveled at the skin below his neck — white as Coyote Man in his ash paint, with patches of dark hair under his arms and on his chest and around his man's part. Hair grew on his legs too, like on Captain Sutter, but on this man it was black against white. It looked preposterous, clownlike, and she couldn't hold back a giggle. Wrinkling her nose at the bad smells, she yanked him toward deeper water. He came haltingly, picking his way over rocks. She pulled him upstream against the current, now to his knees, and laughed to see a man walking like a baby holding its mother's hand. His attention never left his footing.

At the deep water where the bathing pool spread before them, she tugged his hand. He braced his feet on a submerged rock, upon which he had struggled to stand, and shook his head in solid refusal. But he was only just above his knees in the river, and he looked so precarious on the slippery rock and acted so serious, it struck her as hilarious.

On shore, toddlers and their mothers watched in awe between the racks of red salmon. Could he be afraid of them? But she knew how to get people into the festival mood. She dogpaddled around his rock. He turned and looked at her with questions in his blue eyes, and, she realized with a new seizure of giggles, he didn't know what she was about to do. Any of the home men would have.

She shoved him off his rock, plunged on top and held him under. He thrashed and grabbed at her, but she held on, sputtering laughter, and thought maybe he knew this game after all. He wasn't really trying to get to the surface. Sometimes men pretended to struggle in water fights, as a way of showing they liked a woman. She hooked an arm around his chin and swam strongly, towing him face down under water against the force of the flow. He thrashed ineffectively. She smiled. Soon he would be clean.

She pulled him through the braided currents to the calm place where she'd first seen him. He had assumed a limp posture, and she admired the length of time he could hold his breath; but she tensed for a surprise move, perhaps a sudden burst out of the water with both hands pushing her head down in retaliation. She knew that trick. But her smile faded as another possibility began to dawn on her.

She pulled his head up. Thin crescents of blue showed above white orbs. She stared. *Drowning.* He wasn't pretending. She turned him over and swam hard for shore holding his chin up.

Her cousin-sisters gathered around as she dragged the man to the sand. Little children pointed at his furry chest. With help, she heaved him to his stomach, head to the side, and pressed sharply between his shoulder blades, trying to force water from his lungs. "Run. Get Grizzly Hair!" she said, as she pushed rhythmically on the white man's back. She hadn't meant to hurt him.

A cousin disappeared toward the playing field as the cheers of another goal rocked the air. The wait seemed long. Beside her, a big-eyed boy child asked, "He sick?"

"Drowning," she said between pushes. "I thought we were playing."

"He no play."

At last Father came and knelt over him, heaving him to his side. The motion triggered an explosion of coughing and vomiting, and she exhaled in relief.

The man struggled to rise, but got only as far as his hands and knees. On all fours he hung his head, shaking it from side to side like a bear, coughing and coughing.

"He will live," said Father. "Who is it?"

"I don't know," she said loudly, to be heard above the coughing and the burst of cheers from the field.

The dripping white man coughed a fine mist, then grew still. He rotated his head to the side, looked at her from the holes of his sky blue eyes, and said, "You bitch." The teasing grin was gone.

She was so happy to hear him speak, she didn't care that she didn't understand his meaning. "Sky Eyes," she named him in her mind. The little boy squatted, peering at the man from underneath. With a rigid index finger the man poked the child hard in the chest, making him cry and run to his mother's arms.

Puzzled at the meanness, Maria Howchia watched the man struggle to his feet and walk slowly downstream, his white buttocks blotched with patches of dark sand.

As Maria Howchia and the other women steamed poison oak leaves and other greens for the feast, word came that Sky Eyes had been joined by another light-skinned man, this one driving a team of large animals. Food could wait. She joined about a hundred people hurrying along the hilly path.

Where the grassland sloped gently toward the river, she saw Sky Eyes and a man with a long frizzy yellowish beard. A curtain of pale hair curled about his shoulders but the scalp was barren and shiny on top. Downwind, even at this distance, she could smell him. At the fort she had seen oxen like the two that tossed their horned heads, but what were the animals dancing inside the cart?

The two white men spoke loudly to each other in a tongue that made it sound as if their mouths were full of mush. She stepped close to one of the wheels, massive slices of oak skewered by a peeled pole, and looked through the weave of the cart. Three dark, sparsely haired animals snuffled and grunted inside. All had round flat noses and short tails coiled at their rumps. Horn-like teeth jutted from the sneering lips of the largest.

When the white men stopped talking, Grizzly Hair, who stood in the crowd of festively decorated people, pointed to the animals and said, "*Puercos.*" She knew he'd seen them at the mission.

Sky Eyes approached Grizzly Hair, who greeted him courteously. "*De donde viene y a donde va?*"

Yellow Beard slowly said, "*Nosotros víven aquí.*"

They had come here to live! Maria looked at the assembled people, all smiling at one another. Many understood Spanish and she knew they were thinking, as she did, that it would be fun to have interesting neighbors.

Lockl, headman of the visiting people, stepped forward, speaking with Grizzly Hair, but one of the *puercos* squealed like a hurt child and she couldn't hear. The animals rocked the cart violently. People giggled and she crowded closer.

"They bring you *puercos.*" Lockl was saying.

"I don't know," Grizzly Hair countered.

Yellow Beard spoke in halting Spanish. "We need a *cerca.* You *Indios* make fence." He gestured around the crowd and pantomimed the piling of sticks.

Sky Eyes gestured wildly, his face twisted in anger. The other white man faced him and shouted. Sky Eyes shoved Yellow Beard. He glared. People gaped. Children looked up at their parents with questions in their eyes. Showing anger in public was a sign of weakness. Maria Howchia covered her mouth, careful not to laugh aloud, as some did, and wondered what the men were saying.

But she waited and watched the low sun cast its glow on the world — the oaks, the people, the bleached grasses, the boulders in the river canyon, the blue river snaking past. She loved salmon time. Ripe red toyon berries winked along the river bank. It was the time of fat ducks and the coming of geese. A cock quail called ki-ka-go, a sharp sound that soothed — the constant of the world. At last the white men stopped speaking and glared silently at each other.

Yellow Beard furrowed his brow as if concentrating hard and spoke to Grizzly Hair — slowly, thinking between words. "*Adobes. Indios fabrican una cerca de adobes.*" They were to make a fence of mud. He had wanted it of brush, but Sky Eyes had prevailed.

Grizzly Hair glanced at the *puercos* and at the sun, and said, "Soon the sun goes. After the sleep we make the fence." He turned to explain to those who had not understood, then said to Yellow Beard, "We have fiesta now, fandango. You come. Bring *puercos*. They watch from the *carreta*."

People smiled and moved about explaining what had occurred. Maria Howchia felt happy anticipation, and not just for the dance. The world was changing. No longer did the home place seem too small. Exotic men and *puercos* had come. Father was encouraging the changes, and Captain Sutter's power didn't extend here.

With her toes skimming the path and her amulet bouncing, she and her cousin-sisters raced ahead, lifted by exuberance. They passed the cart and Yellow Beard, who drove the oxen as he stood, buttocks braced against the jolting cart wall — a weave of branches — and she realized every bird and animal would flee from the unearthly screech of the wheels.

Sky Eyes rode past on a brown and white spotted horse. He looked at her and she could tell he thought she was pretty. He puzzled her though. He hadn't seemed amused, as many men would have been, to be nearly drowned by a playful woman. Was he really that weak? Unable to swim or laugh at himself? Unable to hide emotion? Surely not. Different people had different ways, that was all.

She hoped to see his dimpled smile again. She wanted to get to know him. Maybe he would teach her his strange tongue — the tongue spoken at Captain Sutter's place. That would help her face the captain. As she was thinking this, a horseman appeared on the hilltop, dark in the low sun. But she knew by the proud bearing as he sat in the saddle that it was Pedro Valdez.

10

Shadows on the circular wall loomed black and huge in the firelight. Maria Howchia danced as a fiber in a rope of people circling the fire in the dancehouse, feet patting the earth to the heartbeat of the log drum. Turtle Claw chanted the song of the Ancients to conjure the spirits. She awaited Molok, Condor.

Turtle Claw raised his arms and began to sing the most powerful spirit into the dancehouse. The log drum throbbed more slowly. Goose bumps pricked her scalp. She and the other dancers stopped and made their way across the pine boughs to join the spectators. She sat with her family against the circular wall, the air in the sacred house purified by the pine scent as the cleansed people quieted to watch the enactment of first things. An infant whimpered, but that was the only sound.

The spirit bird entered to the whoosh of people sucking air. Towering over Turtle Claw, he walked on long skinny legs as a bird walks — chest out — and fully extended his enormous black wings as he circled the fire, turning this way and that to show the white undersides. The shadow of Molok Impersonator darkened the entire wall and ceiling, and when it fell on Maria, a tremor shot through her. She was glad she had scrubbed and purified herself, glad all the people had. Such power could kill. But with the proper precautions, the strong could absorb a little of it.

Big brother of Raven flapped his wings, then seemed to fly around the circle, flapping as he bounded and "landed," and Turtle Claw's deep voice chanted the story of the beginning of earth. Coyote Man entered from the smoke hole — white, tailed — and hung by his knees poking fun at Condor Impersonator. Only Coyote could do that. Then, after a few jokes about Turtle Claw and Grizzly Hair, Coyote Man jumped before the fire and he and Turtle Claw enacted the creation story — Turtle bringing mud from the depths of the endless gray sea to the light above, Raven making it into land. Three women singers embellished the chants, their polished voices weaving high and low through the story.

Pedro had come, he told himself, to collect Indians for Sutter's militia, and to return the *Indita's* things. But he also came tracking Perry McCoon. And it was just as he had thought. The Englishman was here on this very *terreno.*

Now Pedro sat uncomfortably near McCoon and the German named Brüheim, the three watching the bright arch of the roundhouse door about eighty feet away. Any other place along the rise wouldn't let him see. Captain Juan's daughter was inside among the tightly packed *Indios*, more than a hundred, focused on a speaker with a tall headdress and cloaked entirely in black feathers. McCoon seemed a little less obnoxious than usual, no doubt feeling vulnerable away from the fort, but he was also clearly absorbed by the happenings inside the roundhouse. So was Pedro.

Inside the dark dug-out structure, the Indian on stilts opened the wings of his costume, and each wing looked longer than a man. The wings were intact. The costume had been made from the skin of an actual condor.

"Blow me down," McCoon said, standing up. "If that ent the damndest thing."

Pedro was fascinated. Grandmother Maria, who had come from the lower Cosumnes, had told him that the condor was sacred, and sometimes when he was riding and a condor flew overhead, he understood what she meant. He had felt the thrill of fear as the shadow swept over him — heart stopping until he realized what it was, like a mouse must feel beneath an eagle. Then as the gigantic bird would glide away across the empty grasslands, he felt gratitude that it hadn't attacked him. It did seem a miracle that anything that size could fly. No wonder *Indios* revered it.

McCoon went to the doorway and stood there blocking Pedro's view. Pedro got up to see better, Brüheim following.

Peering over McCoon's shoulder, he felt the steamy smoke on his face and saw the source of the relentless beat, an Indian stomping on a hollow log. It unified the weird singing, the guttural chant and the dance of the giant condor. Entirely covered with black feathers, the Indian was nimble on stilts and appeared even taller with the headdress. The wings opened and closed as if pulled by unseen strings as he strutted around the fire, and the eyes of the seated Indians glinted like stars around the wall, reflecting the fire that blazed in the square of oaken pillars. Lashed to these posts, the ceiling beams were decorated with streamers of colorful feathers. Another performer — in whitened skin — dashed around howling. This would be Coyote, who signified everything confusing and chaotic in life. *Indio* humor revolved around that. They laughed hardest when somebody got caught in a trap of his own making.

McCoon turned and tilted his head for Brüheim to follow him inside.

"Don't go in there," Pedro said. They ignored him and stepped in.

The Indians closest to the door looked at them as though they were invading bears and picked up pine branches and brandished them. But most were intent upon the ceremony and didn't appear to notice.

"You'll set them against us," Pedro said in a voice to be heard over the drum and the chanting. Before the dance, he'd got several Indians to agree to go to war with Captain Sutter, and he didn't want them to change their minds. He wouldn't have thought McCoon would want to antagonize his future hog herders either.

"Ent hurtin nothing." McCoon handed his gun to Brüheim as if to show the Indians he was harmless. They shoved branches in his face; he crossed his arms against them, snickering. Brüheim backed out. McCoon yelled in a parody of being hurt. "All right, all right. 'Ave it your way, you 'eathens." He ran out, giggling and jumping in an exaggerated fashion, hands crossed behind, like a child escaping his mother's whipping.

Pedro was back on the rise where they'd been sitting. McCoon sat down, took the leather flask from his vest, downed a swig, and handed it to the German. "Those niggers'll conjure up the Devil, they will." Brüheim, had the flask tipped to his mouth.

Pedro said, "They want the condor spirit to be good to them."

McCoon turned to him. "Aff-breed like you oughta know." The firelight caught his perfect teeth, his dimple.

Pedro's voice came low, measured. "Sometimes I think, Señor McCoon, that you would like to fight me." He had promised Sutter he wouldn't take the bait, but he was a hair's breadth from his limit, and twenty-five miles from the fort.

McCoon took the flask from Brüheim, swallowed twice, wiped his mouth and drawled, "Ashamed o' yer nigger blood?"

Pedro ground his nails into his fists and decided to educate the bastard. "Both my grandfathers were distinguished officers of the King of Spain. My mother's father was Don Pedro Fages, a nobleman and governor of Upper California."

It didn't matter that both grandmothers were Indian, his father illegitimate. He let his anger and pride speak, "I am Spanish. Señor." His back was straight, and he used the polite address to satisfy himself, not the English cur.

"All the same," McCoon drawled in a bored tone. "Greasers."

Pent-up rage exploded in Pedro's arm as he rammed his fist into the source of that word. Half amazed, he felt flesh slide beneath his knuckles and heard the hollow sound of McCoon's head hitting the ground.

He jumped to his feet looking down at the man, who was curling like an injured worm.

Brüheim grabbed Pedro from behind and yanked his elbows together. *Strong.*

As he struggled to throw him off, McCoon got to his knees and snarled, "You filthy, rotten maggot infested piece o' shit!"

Brüheim yelled, "Schtop! Both of you!" Pedro jerked, but the German hung on.

McCoon was on his feet, tonguing his lip out. In the orange firelight his normally handsome features were twisted and ugly and his lip bled. He pulled back his arm.

Pedro jerked free just as the fist slammed him. Something snapped. Pain seared past his right ear and up through the top of his skull. He stumbled and caught his balance. His vision doubled, then swam back to focus as he steadied himself. McCoon was braced to strike again.

Pedro was faster. His knuckles found McCoon's teeth a second time. He heard a crack and felt something give. McCoon reeled and fell.

Agony pulsed through Pedro's head. His jaw was frozen. His knuckles hurt as he stood over the writhing lump in the dirt, watched it start to get up.

This time Brüheim grabbed McCoon when he got to his knees, and pinned his elbows behind as he had done Pedro's. "Herr Lieutenant Valdez. *Bitte*, please. Enough. No more. Do not hit him again. I beg of you."

McCoon looked spent, dazed, bloody. A tooth dangled in his open mouth.

Pedro's stomach rose. From the sight of the blood or the pain in his face, he wasn't sure. Still, if the *desgraciado* hadn't been immobilized, he felt he would have silenced that tongue forever.

He stepped into the shadows. The throb of the hollow log and the wails and yells from the roundhouse mixed badly with the throb in his head. Brüheim's spitting words came through it. "He iss officer on Captain Sutter's dragoons." Admonishing McCoon.

In the dark Pedro unclenched his sore knuckles, placed the heel of his hand against his face, and pushed. With a rip of knifelike pain, his jaw popped back into alignment. Instantly he felt better, carefully opening and closing his mouth.

The German was still talking, ". . . and you are my partner, in need of Sutter's goot vill."

Pedro figured McCoon had Sutter's good will no matter what. No doubt he'd tell the captain Pedro had attacked him without provocation. In New Helvetia, he realized sadly, foreigners were treated better than native Californianos.

A large figure darkened the roundhouse doorway. Then the orange light flashed again, illuminating Condor Man with stilts in hand, and another Indian. They were leaving. The hushed footsteps receded into the moonless night. A pig squealed from the cart. A coyote, a real one, yipped and howled.

Abruptly the drumming stopped. McCoon spoke loudly as if for Pedro's ears, though he addressed Brüheim. "Show that greaser who's the best vaquero, I will!"

Pedro smiled in the shadows at the call for a showdown on horseback. Pedro had delivered two delicious blows to McCoon's one. And nobody, but nobody, was better on a horse than Pedro Valdez. The light dimmed as Indians crowded out of the dance house, speaking softly to one another.

"We ride tomorrow," Pedro said, noticing the daughter of Captain Juan in the doorway with glowing firelight behind her curvy, naked figure.

McCoon growled, "We'll ride when *I* say, not before."

"As you wish." He used his velvet tone. "Any time you say, señor."

Satisfied that McCoon wouldn't enjoy the night, Pedro approached the *Indita* from behind. In the dark and surrounded by Indians, he hurried so as not to lose her. Bright stars pricked a tapestry of holes in the black sky but gave little light. What was her name? He knew it was considered rude to ask.

She and another girl headed toward the river. "*Hola*," he called and the girls turned. He sensed more than saw the one with skin like a poppy petal, a head shorter than he.

"Señorita, may I speak to you a moment?" The fragrance of peaches floated back to him against aromas of dew-dampened absinthe, sage, and straw. She waited. He imagined her uptilted breasts. Indian girls were a delicious mixture of innocence and lust.

He felt himself stir. "I brought your blanket and mortar stone. I'll bring them to your house." His voice was rougher than expected. Sounds of joking and splashing came from the river, and crickets pierced the dark all around.

"Gracias, señor. Put them inside." She seemed anxious to leave.

He had hoped she'd be more receptive. Unlike most of the men at the fort, he wouldn't force himself on a girl, and it made him ache to realize Indians were doing it all around him. They did it in front of their families and had few qualms, especially after roundhouse ceremonies. "Are you going swimming?"

"Sí. You come and swim with us?" Her voice had a vanilla tone of maturity.

Hope swelled in him. "Yes." If that's how it started, he'd bare himself in the cool night air and swim.

"Come." She turned away with her friend and walked quickly and quietly ahead of him. He was drawn by her scent. At the river she waded and submerged as he undressed. He heard the lapping of swim strokes, too many. Where had she gone?

He'd expected the men would go to the sweathouse, but no, they were out there fooling around with the women. He heard their chuckling. It was entirely dark, the air so cool the water felt warm on his legs. He waded deeper. Indians darted past. Black heads wove chaotic patterns like shuttles loosed from their looms, a crazyquilt of ripples, a bubbling of strange talk.

The rocky bottom fell sharply as he waded to his chest. Warm on his torso, a layer of cold water swept his legs. With games being played around him, he dogpaddled into the midst of the Indians, hoping to find the girl. *Indios* glided by like fish.

He sensed the girl saw him, saw that he swam poorly, and he was helpless to find her. He treaded water, waiting. Water lapped in his eyes. In all this splashing he wouldn't know the chief's daughter from a snaggletoothed old man. He gulped water and coughed, out of his element. She wasn't helping, that was clear. He paddled back to where he could stand, and felt foolish.

Onshore, he stood shivering, holding his pants, letting his feet dry until he could brush the sand away. A breeze had picked up. *Ay Madre*, late autumn! His lusty feeling had shriveled. He saw himself in his mind's eye, a shivering stranger among people who didn't feel the cold, and didn't like what he saw.

But this could be his some day, if McCoon gave up on the pigs. Chances were he would, or maybe he'd catch valley fever and die, or drink himself to death. Or was that wishful thinking? Gathering his clothes, he left the water and headed for his horse. The girl's things were in the pack behind his saddle. Ay, ay, ay, the worst was that Captain Sutter and Perry McCoon were drinking *amigos*.

He dried with his blanket, left Chocolate hobbled on the playing field near the creek, dressed, and groped his way back to the huts. He remembered which one was Captain Juan's.

At the entrance the vanilla voice shocked him pleasantly. "*Otra vez gracias*." She took her blanket and mortar.

"*De nada*." He reached through the dark, touched, explored with his fingers until he recognized an upper arm, wet and cool. She didn't flinch. He moved his palm across to a handful of resilient breast with a nub of nipple, and almost groaned.

She stepped back. "You speak for Captain Sutter." The tone was quiet, sullen.

So that was it. He was thinking what to say when an older woman's voice came from inside — guttural sounds.

The girl responded in kind. It gave Pedro hope. He was apparently interesting enough to talk about. He wanted to tell her about the verbal abuse Sutter had heaped on him the night she left the fort, and how he had lied about knowing the whereabouts of her village, but said only, "I don't always do his bidding."

The older woman's voice rasped new sounds, drawing nearer. The mother. Small with slit eyes, he remembered. She had been about Pedro's age, and had spied on him that first night. She shifted into broken Spanish. "My daughter no talk to black hat. Go from house. Go from ranchería. Go or I bring man, make you go."

The vanilla voice said something, perhaps in protest. More wishful thinking? Soon it was quiet except for a few soft voices in the dark as people moved about the huts.

Swallowing disappointment and wishing he'd followed one of the other young women — all were occupied now — Pedro wouldn't antagonize the chief's wife. "I go, señora."

The *Indita* asked, "You go to the fort?"

"Yes. I must go tomorrow. With all the men who will ride to war with me."

"You come back?"

Aha, hope! "Yes. after the war."

"You live in house with the blue-eye men?"

Her vulnerability clutched at his gut. "Perry McCoon," he said, "is a bad man. And you, señorita, should stay away from him. I would never live with him." He bowed formally in the dark. "Señora, I go. *Buenas noches*."

The next day Maria Howchia glanced at the gray sky. Cool air moved against her skin. "This is not a good season for making adobes," she said to Sings-with-Frogs, a young man about her age. "The rain will spoil them."

He smiled like a child. "But this is fun."

She laughed, mud oozing pleasantly between her toes. All around her, people talked and sang as they stomped clay. Some hauled water from the river, others brought baskets of dry clay, still others scooped the sticky mud into the forms that Yellow Beard had laid out beside the mud pit. Adobe-making had become a game, a part of the festival.

The corral for the *puercos* was to be located here, at tai yokkel, not far from the river. The white men were setting up camp. Proud Hawk had ridden back to the fort, she supposed. He was nowhere to be seen. That was well. He belonged there.

"When the mud melts and the *puercos* escape, we'll have a feast," said Sings-with-Frogs, smiling at Maria Howchia. Last night he had tried to interest her. A cousin-sister had told her he was trying to get the nerve to offer her a marriage present. But she didn't want to marry him, or anybody. She was careful not to give Sings-with-Frogs the wrong idea. Crying Fox had told her men hated that.

While Yellow Beard talked broken Spanish with three young boys, Sky Eyes stood near the adobe pit watching Maria. He looked like he'd fallen on his face. He was badly bruised and his dimple wasn't to be seen.

"I'm going to war with Señor Valdez," said Sings-with-Frogs, stepping beside her so that his foot slid by hers beneath the mud.

Others stamped the mud around them and she pretended she hadn't noticed it was his foot. "You didn't go to the fort with him."

"My cousins and I are going after the festival. Señor Valdez said they won't leave the fort for ten sleeps." His young face conveyed pride, hair blowing across his face.

She knew the men had talked of going. Long ago nearly everyone had gone to fight the black hats, women as well as men. This time it seemed more of a game. No one mentioned danger. "Are most of the men going?"

"No. Most are going on a horse raid with Sick Rat." He pivoted as he stamped and brushed his thigh against hers. His man's part had begun to swell.

By their amused expressions, she saw her friends had seen too. A strong gust of wind swept up from the river, blowing her hair into her eyes. She caught her cap just before it sailed away.

Sings-with-Frogs bent forward, scooped clay and slathered it down along her body. She drew in her breath, glanced at her friends, pointed at him in mock anger, saw the gleam of willingness in their eyes, and pushed the young man into the mud. He sputtered and flailed.

Laughing, she sat on him and held him down. When she looked up, sky blue eyes were watching. The white man's swollen, purple lips were bent into the ghost of a smile, but no dimple dug into his cheek. A tooth was missing. What had happened?

The tussle in the mud continued without her as she smiled at Sky Eyes. He interested her, and his *puercos* interested her. Why had he brought them here? Would he teach her about Captain Sutter's power. Would he teach her his tongue? His face had clean lines, the skin almost as dark as healthy people. She was intrigued, and sorry she had nearly drowned him. She wanted him to smile his dimple at her again. But why had Pedro Valdez warned her against him?

Salmon Time ended and Maria Howchia's family went indoors as rain roared off the steeply pitched roofs of the village. Often during the long rainy nights she thought of Crying Fox, who hadn't returned from Sutter's fort. Blue Star had, telling of Crying Fox being sent to the eastern mountains with *Americanos* to take food to people in need of help. People had given Crying Fox a new name. Salvador, Savior. Perhaps he had stayed at the fort after the wheat harvest because of Manu-iki. Was that the reason he'd been sent on the dangerous journey?

At tai yokkel rain melted the adobes, as predicted. She often went to the *puerco* corral to help place brush along its sloughing walls. The two white men also needed women's help tying bundles of cattail leaves for the roof of the adobe house, to keep the rain off the melting walls. Whenever she came near him, Sky Eyes smiled at her.

Twice he followed her home, and she hid from him. But she grew more and more intrigued, and wondered why he and Yellow Beard shivered so before their outdoor supper fire. And why they argued loudly. Then Sky Eyes left his new house, leaving the *puercos* alone with Yellow Beard.

One day she was tearing herself a new ceremonial skirt from the bolt of cloth Father had brought back from a horse raid on the coast. She would tie it around her hips like Manu-iki did. Etumu entered the u-macha, sat beside her, and said in a strange tone, "Our acorns will be gone long before next acorn time."

Maria Howchia lowered the cloth. This had never happened before. The cha'ka held more than a year's supply. Oo-lah must be served at ceremonies, and nu-pah was eaten every day. It wasn't possible to live without acorns.

"You and Crying Fox were gone during the harvest. We didn't gather enough."

Shamed, Maria Howchia watched streams of rain fall from the arch of the doorway and flow down the ramp into the house, pooling near the firepit. She set the cloth aside and ducked outside, cringing as cold water struck her shoulders and ran down her back. She would see for herself.

The cylindrical cha'ka of woven vines stood like a tall sentinel beside the house. From her earliest memories it had held the promise of something to eat, a knowledge so deep and sure she'd never really thought about it. A floor of crossed wood raised the storehouse to discourage ground animals, and a roof higher than Father's head kept out the tree squirrels.

She glanced through the rain at the other silos — so ordinary she'd hardly looked at them before. Were they full? Could her family trade cloth for the acorns of others? She parted the vines at face height. No acorns flowed. She restored the hole, and made a lower opening, finding the nuts at waist height. This is where they normally were at the end of the long dry, when acorns were ripening in the trees. That was six moons away.

Grizzly Hair came through the veils of rain shouldering a soaked goose. Seeing her, his eyes registered something, and she knew he'd talked to Etumu about the acorns.

"Father, I am sorry. I should have stayed and helped gather." She had gone to the fort in the middle of the harvest. Mother always warned that squirrels and woodpeckers would have them all in five sleeps if the people didn't gather them first. It was true.

Rain washed down Grizzly Hair's cheeks, and without his topknot his hair was plastered to his broad shoulders. "The blue-eyed men take our food for the *puercos.*" He swung the goose from his shoulder, the limp head resting in the mud, and indicated she should take it.

Later, while skinning the goose, she heard Father's voice outside the u-macha and put the goose down and went up the slippery ramp. Yellow Beard stood there, bucket in hand, his heavy blue cloak soaked, his face shadowed beneath his pulled-down hat. People peered from their doorways.

"No acorns," Grizzly Hair said in a matter-of-fact tone.

Yellow Beard went to Turtle Claw's cha'ka, parted the vines and poured a bucketful. At their doorway the doctor looked at his wife. She shrugged.

As Yellow Beard waded Berry Creek and headed west, Grizzly Hair spoke quietly with Turtle Claw, then returned to the u-macha. He lay on his mat and closed his eyes.

Rain continued to fall through the smoke hole, wetting the fire pit. Maria Howchia struggled to blow the damp charcoal to life. She wished for a sunny day and worried about Crying Fox. She also wondered where Sky Eyes was, and what he and Yellow Beard would do when all the people refused to share their acorns with the *puercos.*

Grizzly Hair spoke without opening his eyes. "Soon we will celebrate First *Puerco.*"

11

JANUARY 3, 1845

Chocolate pranced nervously as snare drums rolled and the fife squeaked in the heavy air of the overcast dawn. "Steady," Pedro said patting the proud animal, the likes of which ought to be leading the march.

Meanwhile, ludicrous on a she-mule, Sutter was exiting the gate. Pedro closed his eyes and took a long breath. He was Sutter's lieutenant — almost — and he would serve honorably. He opened his eyes. But if General Castro saw his opponent on that mule, he wouldn't be able to shoot straight for laughing. The captain's military finery and plumed tricorn made it the more ridiculous. Only a woman rode a jenny!

Pedro glanced at the three waiting *Californianos* — half of the six who had come from the Presidio four years ago, the numeral three still visible on their fading hat bands. Their blue waistcoats and trousers were frayed like his, but all rode *macho* animals. This was the first real war since the battle of 1829 against Estanislao and the valley Indians, and Pedro felt the spirit of his ancestors in his veins.

The drummers wove a snappy rat-tat-ratatat beneath the whipping red, white and green and the sky threatened the storm of the decade. "Easy boy," Pedro crooned. The leather-clad riflemen were riding out behind Sutter, some spurring their horses rudely past the captain, laughing and whooping. Former sailors rode with them, including Perry McCoon — disloyal men from five or six countries. Pedro had a bet with Jared Sheldon that less than twenty riflemen would report for the march. Sheldon had more faith. Why, Pedro didn't know. Each autumn Captain Sutter begged the Russians to wait for their payment until the winter-harvest beaver came in — having supplied the trappers for the winter. But every spring they spread their hands helplessly and claimed the harvest had been unaccountably poor. If the captain didn't know they cut deals with the fur companies, he was blind and deaf. Why didn't he stop indulging them? Small wonder so many dishonorable men hung around him. Like squirrels in the granary. It grated. He counted beaver-felt hats, slouched leather hats and skull-hugging hats — fifteen, sixteen, seventeen, eighteen. Sheldon owed him three plugs of tobacco.

Seven immigrants rode out with the riflemen — men who had just, astonishingly, crossed the Sierras with wagons. The Indians Luis and Salvador had guided the last of them safely down the mountains, then rejoined the militia. The immigrants looked hungry, but carried excellent weapons. Pedro coveted the long Kentucky rifle with a maple stock, striped with growth rings of the straight tree it had been carved from. Fitted into this distinctive stock was an equally distinctive hexagonal barrel that sent balls straight and far. It made a toy of Pedro's musket.

Following the riflemen, six Kanakas fell into stride. Four wore pants and two had colorful sarongs stretched around their haunches. Besides French guns, they all clutched long spears, the fighting tool of their native islands.

"Company march," Pedro called. The hundred-seventy Indian foot soldiers queued up five abreast, stamping their bare feet in place until the forward lines moved. Pedro's drills had transformed them into a disciplined force, dressed as well as could be expected. Pieces of French uniforms that the Russians had seized from Napoleon, a pair of pants here, a shirt there, an occasional peaked hat. They held their muskets against their shoulders more smartly than any soldiers he had known. Even the naked men, the new recruits, marched flawlessly out the gate, bows swinging in their left hands. The drummers and fife player closed ranks behind the marching men, providing a fast beat.

Pedro nudged Chocolate. The big horse danced before settling down beside the other three stallions — the cavalry. Lastly came *Indio* vaqueros leading thirty loaded pack mules in lines of ten, and three brass field pieces. No presidio in Alta California had ever fielded a larger force. Pedro couldn't help but feel proud. He only wished some of the California rancheros had joined them — Rufus Chabolla, José Amador, Antonio Suñol at the least. Word must have spread that General Vallejo was sitting out.

At the thought Pedro exhaled a chest full of air. It misted, then disappeared in the wind, like his doubts about this campaign. General Vallejo might have had a hidden purpose. Things were rarely as they seemed in Spanish politics. And Pedro wasn't born to it. He knew he missed the undercurrents. Complex matters were handled in riddles of courtesy. Anyway, the die had been cast.

Two days later, with the storm still gathering, Pedro decided to talk to Captain Sutter about Perry McCoon's hog farm and find out if it was a serious enterprise. He rode past the trotting Indians and joined the Captain, who, under his bouncing feathers, looked like a pink-cheeked boy on an adventure.

"Iss goot vetter," Sutter said, eyeing a gap in the otherwise implacable clouds. His eyes sparkled as he bumped along, boots sticking out from the mule's ribs.

Pedro forced himself to nod, but looked straight ahead toward the coastal *sierra* and *Diablo* Mountain, where *Indios* said Coyote came from. He had grown up hearing tales of the feathered devil who roared down out of that mountain. The *Indios* looked skittish, and Pedro wasn't the only Californiano surreptitiously crossing himself as the peak loomed. Ahead rode the dark knot of riflemen, seemingly unconcerned.

The captain's white plume was blowing straight back. "The Governor iss heppy," he said, "dot I bring troops to help him." He expected a doubling of his land grant in exchange for this expedition. "You know I haff big debt wit the Russians." He cut his eyes over to Pedro.

"Sí, *Capitán.*" They'd probably seize New Helvetia if the fort weren't bristling with their own excellent cannons. A Coyote joke for sure.

"Soon Herr Rotcheff comes from Russia and brings wit him a gentleman who studies Indians. He pays for baskets and zo fort. But now he is looking for someting very special to take back to Russia for da Tsar's private collection."

From his higher mount Pedro looked down at him and wondered what that could be. *Indios* didn't have special things. They didn't make jewelry and precious objects of art.

"I would like dot you help me find someting. Understand? To make da

Russians go away heppy, hmm?" He smiled in a way calculated to make him look wise.

Watching a rider approach — coming back from the riflemen — Pedro said, "I will think about it."

"Gracias, Lieutenant." Sutter looked toward the approaching horse, and Pedro was disgusted to make out Perry McCoon on its back.

McCoon turned his horse alongside the Captain and said, "Me and the other blokes'll be ridin on to the mission." He looked at Pedro. Red spots still marred his mouth where the scabs had fallen off and he had a satisfying gap in his otherwise perfect set of teeth. Sutter spoke confidentially to McCoon, in a way that left Pedro out.

Only too glad to return to the rear with his *compadres,* Pedro wondered if Captain Sutter could command McCoon and his ilk. He knew he couldn't. Drops of moisture fell on his knuckles. He looked up. Fat globules of water splashed on his face. Inky clouds boiled as far as he could see. *Ay Madre*! But swimming the *caballada* across the San Joaquín River, which spread before them, would be easier now than later.

Drenched and restive in the shadow of the Devil's Peak, they camped in torrents of rain and ate cold jerky, the riflemen gone to call on Dr. Marsh, the eccentric *médico* on his *Los Meganos* rancho. The next day the rain continued and Pedro stayed near the back where the *Indios* trotted. Daylight vanished quickly and rain slashed, the company pushing past Señor Livermore's rancho.

At the end of the fifth day he followed the *Indios* into Mission San José, the riflemen already drunk and loud, sprawled over the wind-sheltered corridors, Dr. Marsh among them. Candles inside a number of rawhide cylinders gave off soft light. The Captain's tent had been erected in the corridor and a gray-robed *padre* moved silently from one door to another.

Pedro lifted up his soaked sarape and shook it out, and dumped water off his hat. He was glad to see mission *Indios* bringing food and wine. As he munched beef and tortillas and felt the warmth of the wine spreading through his limbs, he saw Jared Sheldon sauntering over, lips parted in a wolfish smile. "You win," he said, and opened a hand with three plugs of tobacco.

"Gracias, Joaquín" — his Spanish name. He took the tobacco and patted the ground beside him. "*Siéntese.*"

Sheldon arranged his long legs, leaned back against the adobe wall and bumped his floppy leather hat over his eyes. His English was quiet. "I hear you're looking to git land."

"Sí." Daylor, who was building a trading post on Sheldon's rancho, must have told him. The two were partners now.

"Perry's on a big stretch," Sheldon said, "five, six leagues along the north bank of the Cosumnes. How much you looking to get?"

"I'll try for that much." He didn't want to say that the land he wanted was occupied by McCoon, because Daylor and McCoon were friends. "If I don't get killed." He meant it as a joke, but it quieted Sheldon for a time, during which Pedro remembered this man didn't die easily. From beneath the hat came: "You planning to hang up your soldier hat any time soon?"

"Maybe when this war is over."

"Might be a good time at that. I hear Sutter's got the go-ahead to grant land direct. You hear that?" To the point, the way New Englanders talked. But what he said wasn't right.

No doubt Sheldon knew about the Governor's portfolio that had come to the fort before the march. The letter had been read to Pedro and he had helped translate for Sutter. That's why Sutter marched when he did, after he got what he thought he was waiting for. But Pedro had heard the qualifier, and Sutter seemed deaf to the part he didn't want to hear. "The authority is not absolute," Pedro said in Spanish.

Sheldon lifted the side of his hat, gave him a look, and dropped it. "In life nothing is absolute." Fluent Spanish, with good accent.

No wonder he liked this *Norteamericano*. He raised his voice to be heard over the raucous riflemen — loud despite the crashing rain. "Well, maybe grants will move a little faster for Captain Sutter's friends now. But to you, *amigo*, it makes no difference, no?"

Sheldon went back to English. "Yup. Got my final papers. But I wouldn't bet a weasel's ass on the rest of you gettin ground if Castro wins this war. I'd wager all foreigners'd be exiled. And even you Californianos on Sutter's side might have trouble. S'why I said, we're here to fight, we'd better win."

Pedro looked at the black curtain of night with drops flashing through it and silver stripes of water pouring from the valleys in the roof tiles, and thought of General Vallejo cozy in his *casa grande* — a *patrón* surrounded by loyal landholders and catered to by foreigners, many hoping for a letter of recommendation. No matter what happened on the field of battle, Vallejo wouldn't lose. But Sutter could lose everything, and so could those who followed him. *Ay Madre.*

Sheldon said, "I were you? I'd move my grant papers right along. Last letter from Vermont, my brother wrote that a man named Polk was runnin for president, hell bent to take California. Now maybe that's already happened. You'd need clear title. Even then you could run into trouble."

Pedro appreciated the advice. He also appreciated the man.

An immigrant came over and sat down beside Sheldon. "I heard the Californios around here are joinin up on Castro's side," he said, "Did that priest say anything about it?" He glanced at Pedro and handed Sheldon a bottle of wine.

"Wouldn't surprise me," Sheldon said lifting his hat and taking a swallow. He handed the bottle to Pedro.

The immigrant exhaled loudly. "That don't set too good, do it?"

"Nope." Sheldon's jaw dropped in sudden sleep — despite the rowdy riflemen — his shoulders sagging.

Amused, Pedro smiled and took a swallow of good mission wine. The immigrant nodded he should keep it, and left. Pedro was already feeling light-headed and exhausted; the complications swam together. Captain Sutter came down the corridor and sat down before his tent. He reached inside and pulled out writing paper.

Feeling the cold, Pedro drew his sarape around his shoulders and watched Sutter alternately tip a flask to his lips, then pen a few words. Soon he sipped more often than he wrote. Seeing Pedro's glance, he said, "I have angst about da fort venn I be away."

"You left a good man in charge, *Capitán*. Señor Reading keeps everything *bien*."

Sutter arched his brows in an expression of gravity, and his accent was thick with liquor. "But can I trust dot he keep da men from Manu-iki? I write Herr Reading to lock her safe in her room, ya, till we come again. Melons, Lieutenant. Dot iss big problem."

Melons? Pedro felt his jaw drop, and snapped it shut. The mind of his superior officer was far from war, but *melons!* Forbidden fruit. It seemed uncaptainlike the night before their probable first engagement with Castro, whose rancho was on the way to Monterey.

"Manu-iki vant dem be planted, zo she go outside and plant da seeds, and all men see her bent down." Hic. He shook his head, and Pedro caught up with his meaning and envisioned lush Manu-iki bending over. "I write my order now, dot she have a sure place in the garden, for her melons. Ya, *ganz sicher*, and she be locked in da room till venn I come again. She plant later and not have anger." He scratched on the paper, then looked confidentially from the tops of his eyes. "She grows big melons, ya. And sweet. Biggest in da vorld." Hic.

Pedro closed his eyes, recalling a few melons he had known. A man never knew another man's mind, especially one born in a foreign land. Maybe Sutter was more subtle than he'd thought. For all he knew the Captain was planning his war strategy, beyond the melons. Sleep was unravelling Pedro's thoughts, pulling the loose threads apart. Paper rattled.

"Ve show ya strengt," Sutter said, jerking Pedro awake. "Men join strengt. Soon we haff independent empire, you vatch." He finished folding the letter and put it in the tent.

Independent empire! The Captain had hinted that before, but Pedro thought of it, not exactly as a joke, but certainly not serious. Yet empire was precisely what

General Vallejo worried Sutter was developing. Many top *Californianos* did. And now Pedro wondered if Sutter had something else in mind besides aiding Governor Micheltorena.

"I haff word, very hush *por favor*, very hush," he was saying. "Ten tousand Nort Americans next year be coming." A tipsy smile parted his mustache. "Loyal to me."

Pedro looked at him. Ten thousand was beyond comprehension. No more than five hundred people lived in the entire crowded pueblo of San José, and about that number in Yerba Buena. Maybe a hundred farmed around Sutter's fort, the same around Sonoma. But ten thousand? That was more than all the civilized people in Upper California. He felt like he was dreaming. Sutter was supposed to keep North Americans out. "Why?" he asked, "Why are so many coming here?"

"Mormons. Hic. Farmers, goot craftsmen. Families mit children. Mormons be hard vorkers, goot people. Iss vhat I need. Iss vhat I pray for. I write letters. I giff dem landt. Now ve see empire, a-yah." He pointed down the corridor at the trappers and sailors. "Bad men. Silence please." He tried to put his finger across his lips, but missed. "*Por favor*, silence about letters."

Everything would change. The thought of such a throng pledged to Captain Sutter banished sleep like owls startled in a belfry. Whether or not he had the authority, Sutter had the power to give land, Pedro realized. He had built an impregnable fort and armed it well — that was power, and Pedro knew he'd better understand this better. "What are Mormons?"

Sutter upended the flask, swallowed. "People of a religion dot vant no interference from government." He wiped his sleeve across his mustache. "Mormon men haff two, tree wifes, see. I have write dem dot California haff no care how many wifes."

The padres cared. Vallejo cared. But Sutter ruled the Big Valley. Marriage didn't exist for him and his trapper friends. A man simply took a woman — as many as he wanted. Indians didn't care. The noise intensified in the riflemen's corridor, McCoon's voice jumping out, "You bastard! Heard of cuttin a bloke a bit o' slack ave ye?"

Pedro realized that the ten thousand would claim the riverbanks for themselves. Furthermore, Sutter was easily influenced by *Norteamericanos*, whom he liked better than Californianos. He would listen to the Mormons. And what if the United States attacked? Would he and his Mormons fight? Against Mexico? Would Pedro? Ay, ay, ay, it was too much for his wine-befuddled head.

Some of the candles had gone out. The one nearest the tent flickered wildly. Sutter listed like a ship in high wind — eyes closed, mouth gaping. Pedro nodded to Kanaka Henry, who watched from where he lay in the corridor with the other Kanakas, and the two of them dragged the Captain inside his tent.

All night rain cascaded from the roof and the riflemen drank themselves unconscious. Pedro sat against the wall in his sarape drifting in and out of sleep. Golden melons careened at him and ten thousand North Americans fornicated across the land.

12

Black paled to gray behind the cataracts from the roof. The roar of it almost overwhelmed the see-saw of mismatched snores echoing up the corridor. On their haunches and ready to march, the silent *Indios* lined the walls. Good men. Pedro was shaking out his sarape when Captain Sutter crawled from his tent and handed him a sealed letter, and said, "To Herr Reading."

Pedro handed it to his best runner and watched him speed through the rain. Important news from the front. Melons. Mission Indians offered platters of refried beans and tortillas. They tasted good to Pedro, but Captain Sutter covered his mouth and lurched into the rain.

Pedro finished his breakfast, then tented his hat with his sarape and went a polite distance from where Sutter stood in the rain looking down at his vomit. *This is no Emperor*, he thought, waiting to discuss the day's military strategy. More than likely the wine had done the talking last night, and Sutter was innocently supporting Governor Micheltorena against the rebel general. Strange that some men drank themselves sick every night.

Sutter wiped his chin, picked his tricorn off the ground, shook it and turned.

"Capitán Sutter, *por favor*, I would like your assessment of our position."

"Ve march now to Monterey." He jammed on the hat with the sad wet feathers and headed for the corridor.

Assuming he had been embarrassed to be observed, Pedro followed and said, "Sorry *Capitán*, I was only meaning to say in private we must march around Castro's — "

"You tell me mine command, Lieutenant, hmm?" He had stopped short of the corridor and was glaring from the tops of his eyes. "Governor Micheltorena meets us, coming da udder way." His accent was thick with agitation.

Pedro hadn't heard that. "Before we get to Castro's rancho?"

Color replaced the pallor in Sutter's cheeks and his large blue eyes sparkled. "You vill make as ordered, Lieutenant, and no questions. Iss clear?" He turned and walked, carefully, back to his tent.

"Sí, *Capitán*." But he burned with the rebuke. He bore more responsibility than a real lieutenant, yet was being treated like a common soldier. He returned to his fellow Californians, nibbled breakfast and tasted nothing but resentment.

Two hours later the riflemen still couldn't be roused, except for Jared Sheldon and the immigrants. Sutter paced up and down the corridor before the snoring men, alternately holding his forehead like he had a headache and fingering the pearl hilt of his sword scabbard as if he might skewer them. Pedro remained with his countrymen.

"Stand up, if you please," he heard Sutter say. "Ve march now." Pedro knew they wouldn't be able to shoot straight for hours.

"*Donnerwetter noch ein mal, AUFSTEHEN!* Sutter yelled. Still the riflemen didn't move. He stood with his hand on sword hilt, then turned and approached Pedro. "Lieutenant Valdez, ride to the pueblo . . . "

And gather support where Castro controls the countryside?

" . . . and tell every cantina proprietor not to giff my men liquor of any kind. Iss clear? No matter how much day vant to pay. No liquor."

Stunned, but hiding his disapproval, Pedro saluted. Within minutes Chocolate's sleek muscles were expanding and contracting beneath him, Pedro's consternation boiling so hot he didn't feel the rain. Bad enough that he was heading into the cesspool of his hometown — he'd keep his hat low and hope they wouldn't recognize him after all these years — but Virgin save us, he might as well shout in the plaza that Captain Sutter couldn't control his foreigners! That would chase even more men into Castro's camp. From what the padre said this morning — Don Antonio Suñol's runner having informed him — *Californianos* on the coast were flocking to Castro to fight what they feared was a massive army of barbarians and armed Indians sweeping across the countryside. Some thought they'd be eaten alive. This was the opposite of what Sutter had expected. His strength repelled them.

The *Indio* Coyote came to mind. But Pedro didn't laugh.

Later that afternoon the last of the riflemen rode out of San José and the townspeople who dared peep around corners crossed themselves like they'd seen *el Diablo* himself. Pedro sighed, vowing again never to return to this place. He had been recognized and seen as a traitor — he saw it in their eyes. Sutter had requisitioned horses for all the *Indios*, and though that unpleasant action buttressed the widespread view that Sutter was nothing more than a robber chief, Pedro was glad they were mounted. People had run in every direction when the riflemen stormed into the cantinas, stealing liquor if they couldn't buy it. Pedro realized his family would hear that he served a thief, a ludicrous one on a jenny at that!

Not far out of town he saw that something was wrong. He spurred Chocolate past the *Indios* toward where the riflemen were stopped. A long shape dangled from an oak. Reining closer, he saw to his horror it was Pablo Gutiérrez. His head was tilted unnaturally above his stretched neck and the death smell was bad. Pablo's shredded tongue lolled on his black lip. His eyes had been pecked out. Pedro looked away and moaned to himself. Pablo, disgraced in death. Images flashed — Pablo strumming his guitar, Pablo happily brandishing his title to his Bear River rancho, Pablo wanting a *batéa* for panning gold. Nausea churned in his gut.

"Cut him down," The Captain ordered. Indians dismounted.

Pedro placed his own bandanna over Pablo's face, accidentally touching, jerking back from the clammy skin. When the *Indios* had the body buried, he rode on, still imprinted with the putrid sensation. But gradually it was transformed into blood lust, and he tightened his grip on the rein. Vengeance tasted metallic in his mouth. He patted his musket, secure in his saddle holster at his left knee. Pablo had done nothing. He was only a messenger with a note in his shoe. Pedro was glad to be riding to war against the *desgraciados* who had hanged him. General Castro deserved to die in disgrace.

They were camped on a wide green field on the bank of the rushing Río Salinas when Governor Micheltorena high-stepped in on a magnificent white stallion. He had fine features and dark shoulder-length hair and sat straight and still in the saddle — the picture of Spanish aristocracy, a leader of unshakable military poise. Pedro was glad Sutter and his mule were parted for the meeting. He felt an overpowering sense of relief to see this ally for the first time, and his desire for vengeance flowed beneath the surface of a new and powerful purpose. Micheltorena rode like El Cid. Not only did he inspire complete confidence, but he commanded a large cavalry of foreign riflemen and a hundred and fifty hungry-looking Mexican soldiers — all dismounting outside the camp. These combined forces would surely prevail over Castro. General Vallejo had erred in refusing to defend the Mexican government.

The Captain and the Governor met formally, stiffly bussing one another's cheeks. Proud of his Spanish heritage, Pedro shared a glance with Sheldon. Then Sheldon stepped forward with his hand out and shook the Governor's hand. "Joaquín Sheldon," he said, "It is a pleasure, your excellency. Your signature is on my land grant."

"The pleasure is mine."

The meeting was short. Micheltorena said a huge force had joined General Castro and gone south on El Camino Real, heading for the big ranches on the plains of Río de los Angeles. They would pick up strength as they marched and leave ambush parties along the road. Therefore Sutter and Micheltorena should go down the Big South route along the coast and meet Castro's forces in the southland. But, said the Governor, "I must wait here a few days for reinforcements. So you go on ahead. You are slower, with the field pieces. I will catch up with you."

The *Indios* pitched tents, unpacked mules and cooked supper. Afterwards — Governor Micheltorena back in his own camp — Captain Sutter walked around, head high, chest out, using his pearl sword scabbard as a cane, saying, "Ve vin, ya sure."

The next morning Pedro got up and found that Perry McCoon and several other riflemen had skulked away in the night. Deserted.

"They will steal my horses at da fort and go to Oregon," Sutter grumbled.

If only McCoon would! "I think Perry will go back to the hog farm," Pedro said. Where he could take advantage of the pretty *Indita.* But at least now the Captain wouldn't vouch for the scoundrel's character. Surely he wouldn't.

Several days later torrents of water pummeled Pedro's felt hat as he looked ahead at the sinuous line of mounted men and pack mules. Veiled in bluish rain, they seemed to shrink to insignificance along the narrow ledge cut into the black cliffs. Bringing up the rear, Chocolate picked his way along a shelf two hundred feet above the roaring ocean. The wiry branches of a stunted shrub — exposed roots clutching the vertical rock — plucked Pedro's sarape from his right shoulder, the sheer wall towering overhead. The line of men and animals disappeared around a bend, then reappeared, hugging the distant wall of the cliffs.

Quick movement caught his attention. Toylike across the chasm, two pack mules toppled over the edge. They turned slowly as they fell, feet up, and disappeared into the booming turbulence below. A tendril of fear tickled down his spine. He reined Chocolate to a stop. All men stared down at the frothing violence that had devoured the mules. Long white arms of spray reached upward as if for more sacrifices.

Pedro looked down at the footing under Chocolate's hooves. Slick, inclined toward the ocean. Across the chasm the line crawled forward, toy *Indios* carrying toy field pieces on their shoulders. Toy mules. He patted the horse, "*buen caballo*," and nudged him onward.

High overhead, a hawk screamed. Birds had to hunt even in the rain, but the sound brought an ache of loneliness. Human life was nothing against these brooding cliffs. The military campaign seemed insignificant alongside the restless, uncaring ocean stretching beyond a hundred horizons, dwarfing the cliffs, devouring them like a child's pile of sand across aeons as old as God.

Who would miss Pedro if he fell? John Sutter? A few friends at the fort? Not really. Indian girls he'd enjoyed? No. He didn't even know if any of their babies were his. His family? He hadn't kept in touch. What mark had he made on the world? Did training *Indios* count? Maybe he'd made a scratch for having helped settle the frontier — running, in his way, like so many others. A silly *Norteamericano* trapper poem said it:

Oh what was your name in the States?
Was it Simpson or Johnson or Bates?
Did you kill with a knife and flee for your life?
Oh what was your name in the States?

He had never committed a crime, but felt just as footloose. At thirty-three he should have a wife and children and his own rancho. Something more *simpatico* to put his roots into than these rocks, to which the plants clung so fiercely.

He came to where the mules had fallen, and saw the paler rock where the ledge was chipped away, the path narrower than ever. Head down, Chocolate never slowed, though his withers brushed the rock face. "*Buen caballo.*" Pedro said, patting his rain-slick neck and glancing ahead at the fluted cliffs. His horse truly was his best friend.

The pale spot over the sea where the sun had been trying to brighten the clouds faded into the gloomy horizon.

For several days they traveled along the cliffs, camping in the *barrancas* and wild cañons, and Pedro wondered why Governor Micheltorena didn't catch up. Before light one morning a grizzly bear attacked a mule and it had to be shot. Even the mountain lions, watching from the trees, seemed bolder than anywhere else. Because it rained so much of the time, Pedro often shivered standing up at night, instead of sitting or lying down in the torrents that rushed toward the cliff. But where was Governor Micheltorena?

Then one morning the riflemen refused to mount their horses, though Sutter ordered them to march. The Captain backed down. Pedro was glad for the rest; even the mules looked tired. Besides, this would give the Governor a chance to catch up.

At day's end the rain had lessened to a heavy mist. Out of it trotted a wet *Indio*. The slick brown man rounded the bend on foot and handed a portfolio to Captain Sutter. Sheldon translated to all who gathered around:

"Esteemed Captain Sutter, please be so good as to pardon my most recent delay. I remain near the Salinas River waiting for a suitable carreta to carry me over the Big Sur mountains. My Indians have gone to Monterey to search for a wagon. Strong axles and wheels are needed and a bed for me to lie down. The conveyance must be narrow enough to be carried by the Indians on their shoulders. Regrettably I have a bad outbreak of hemorrhoids and cannot mount my horse. Please be patient. I will overtake you.

Together we will defeat General Castro. Your governor and servant, M."

El Cid with hemorrhoids.

Sutter scowled and said, "He waits ya for a carriage."

Sheldon clicked his tongue and looked into the distance, his jaw working.

"Ve send a message back." Sutter said suddenly. He went to his tent, sat down in the entrance and scratched out a letter. Handing it to the courier, he said. "Ve march ahead and attack Castro's flank."

Pedro kept quiet; Sutter looked determined.

After two more long days on the cliff trail, the nights almost as miserable, another Indian arrived with a message:

"Captain Sutter, please continue into the San Luis Obispo valley, but do not attack. Wait for me. A united front is necessary. M."

Sutter grumbled but, to Pedro's relief, announced he would wait.

Several days later, when the trail left the cliffs and the countryside spread out, a messenger delivered another letter. A suitable carreta had been located; however, it would be some time before it could be brought to the Governor's camp on the Salinas River. General Vallejo's warning rang in Pedro's mind, and he began to feel he was in a poor *comedia.*

An ancient vaquero reported from the opposite direction that General Castro was gathering strength like a tarball rolling through feathers — the settled rancheros of the Santa Barbara coast and their numerous *Indio* vaqueros and a hundred foreign riflemen.

"The Governor may not intend to fight," Pedro said to Sutter, "and I doubt we could defeat Castro's forces alone."

"Iss *kvatch*!" Sutter waved him away and struggled onto his mule.

Pedro hoped he was right that it was nonsense. But he kept trying to imagine Governor Micheltorena lying on his back, looking at the sky while being carried along the cliff trail. That was *kvatch* too.

The grasslands were dotted with cattle. Haciendas nestled among the rolling green hills and the air was warm, but the women and old men who could be glimpsed near the buildings ran inside at the approach of Sutter's militia. Up close they trembled with fear. But one wrinkled old woman in a black kerchief stood her ground at her door.

"Ve not hurt you," Sutter said. Pedro translated, adding they'd like a side of beef if it could be spared.

She met his glance. "Tell Captain Sutter I do not fear his armed savages. I am too old to care when I die. *Mátame!*" Kill me. She held up her chin as if waiting to be shot, then added, "But you should know guns are trained on you."

The bravery in her eyes sapped Pedro's spirit. Castro had taken all the men of fighting age. If any had been present, a man would have come to the door. He removed his hat and made a sweeping gesture of respect. "You are in no danger, gracious Doña. We are retainers of Governor Micheltorena, come to fight Castro's rebels, not to plunder."

She stood like stone. General Castro had sown his lies well. Pedro turned to the sound of a horse. An Indian in fine Spanish clothing pulled to a halt and spoke in good Spanish. "*Capitán* Sutter," he said doffing his sombrero, "Don Cristóbal would be honored to host you and your officers at his table this evening."

The *casa grande* stood like a vision in the center of formal gardens, which were flowering in winter. Verandas wrapped around the house on both upper and lower stories and the roof was a civilized tile. Don Cristóbal and his mantilla-draped lady showed Captain Sutter, Pedro and Joaquín Sheldon along a tiled corridor, past carved oak furniture, to a room with several men waiting to be seated at a long table. On one wall a fireplace radiated cheery warmth, and quiet Indians brought platters of steaming food of the kind Pedro had been dreaming about.

Toasts were exchanged, and Pedro felt proud of Sutter, who always comported himself well at formal occasions. Several wine refills later, Don Cristóbal gazed across the table and said, "Capitán Sutter, General Castro is Governor Micheltorena's godson." He paused for the translation, then added with a riveting look in his dark eye, "They are *familia*. I doubt they would make war on one another."

The faces on the other side of the table betrayed the ghosts of smiles. General Vallejo had tried to warn them. Sheldon's wolf eyes cut from Cristóbal to Sutter, then to Pedro.

But Sutter was undaunted. "Esteemed Don Cristóbal, perhaps you haff been misinformed, hmm?" He told them about Pablo Gutiérrez, but their expressions didn't change.

They arrived at the wide flat plain through which the Río de los Angeles meandered, and spent two long weeks chasing Castro — following the directions of old men with hooded eyes. More convinced every day that he was engaged in something other than war, Pedro continued to express his reservations to Captain Sutter, but Sutter dismissed them as poppycock, a word he'd learned from the immigrants. But why was Castro evading them? And where was Governor Micheltorena? Neither ally nor foe reported for battle.

Then suddenly the Governor appeared, offering a formal apology. He and his men camped on the river, and, like magic, General Castro materialized on the opposite shore with several hundred fighting men and a number of field pieces. In the evening messengers crossed the river from Castro's tent to Micheltorena's bivouac downstream. Twice.

The campfires were banked. Pedro lay under the stars, head on his saddle, wondering if Sutter's march all over the southland had forced Castro into a fight his honor wouldn't let him avoid. Approaching footsteps made him sit up. A voice from the past said, "I've come from General Castro's camp to talk with you, Pedro." It was Jesús, from Monterey Presidio.

Obligatory questions about family were asked and answered, then Jesús said, "Do not shoot to kill. Governor Micheltorena only needs to make a good impression before he returns to Mexico."

Good impression! "But he is the Governor of Alta California."

"He dislikes the office."

"So, why this form of leavetaking?"

"Honor. He must be defeated. Your side must lose. Then he can say the right things in Mexico City. It's been worked out. Pio Pico will become governor down here, and Castro will act as governor in the north. We'll shoot over your heads. You shoot over ours."

Honor. Pedro stared at the clouds moving across the quarter moon and considered the word. What of Captain Sutter's honor? And Pedro's?

Jesús' tone was confidential. "We'll capture Captain Sutter. Don't worry, he'll be quartered in a fine house and questioned like a gentleman. He will be released, that is if he's innocent of inciting foreigners and Indians to rebellion."

"You were the rebels, remember?"

Jesús chuckled low in his throat. "I'm not so sure about that."

But when Pedro went to Sutter's tent and explained, he threw down his pen and yelled, "Iss treachery vhat you say. My riflemen day go to the udder side. Running dogs! And now I need every gun shooting straight. Ve shoot to kill. No poppycock stories!" Many riflemen had indeed gone to Castro's side, not out of liking for him, but to join their *Norteamericano* trapper friends, who, Pedro surmised, had enticed them with liquor. Besides, Dr. Marsh had urged their sedition.

Pedro returned to his saddle and blanket. Did honor demand that he protect Sutter's interests even against Sutter's wishes? Was there a larger honor than strict obedience to his superior officer?

Joaquín Sheldon came and squatted at his side saying, "An old *amigo* of mine just came across the river and gave me a good chew of tobacco. They're told to fire clean over our heads. Says we're to do the same."

"Do you trust him?"

"Sí."

"Will the riflemen follow orders if you tell them to shoot high?"

"Sí." Considering that wild bunch, that was a large promise. But this was

Joaquín Sheldon.

Pedro said, "Shoot high. I will take full responsibility."

"I s'pose," Sheldon said in English, "it wouldn't do John a hell of a lot of good to rile both sides in this friendly war." He snorted. "Even one side."

Pedro thanked him and left on his rounds, thinking. When he looked into the world of the Mexican military elite, he saw only darkly and from a great distance, but it seemed that the leaders of Alta California had manoeuvered a delicate balance by which the rancheros in the northern and southern halves could govern themselves without interference — men like Vallejo. And in Mexico City, where central authority over the colony was desired, it might be accepted that a split in Alta California had been forced by this rebellion, which had also forced Governor Micheltorena's resignation. In this fragile balance, Captain Sutter was more than irrelevant; he was a clumsy threat. Pedro's countrymen were asking for an equally delicate action from him, one that put his future in jeopardy.

13

The sun fired the tops of the encircling mountains and spread across the plain. The tules along the river shimmered in the dewy light, but Pedro's head ached from lack of sleep. He had decided to speak to Sutter one last time. As he walked along the lines toward the captain's tent, the *Indios* greeted him with their flicker of a glance and continued piling cannon balls.

An *Indio* was buttoning the brass buttons down Sutter's royal blue jacket. They stood outside the tent, the captain's chin high, the square sideburns and mustache neatly trimmed. Pedro forced himself to repeat, "Captain, I am convinced we should shoot high."

The chin came down and he sputtered harshly in German, his face flushing red as his upright collar. The *Indio* bowed away.

Pedro kept his expression level. "I believe the Governor delayed so long not because of hemorrhoids, but to give Castro and Pico time to negotiate the treaty."

"Lieutenant Valdez," Sutter spat, gripping his sword hilt, "of all der men in der world, I expect loyalty from you. Vhat you tink Napoleon do wit such an officer hmm? Run you through for treason?" He whirled away and marched up the lines, excitedly ordering the men to shoot straight. "Kill the dogs! Show you are men!" Perhaps that was the problem: he saw himself as Napoleon.

The Indians, who spoke no English, looked toward Pedro and he signaled them to fire high. Sheldon nodded and sent the same signal to the riflemen —

those who hadn't already ridden for home or waded to Castro's camp.

When the first rifles and cannon boomed, Pedro knew he'd made the right decision. Castro's crack riflemen fired high. Sutter screamed at the Indians and shook his fists over his head. But they looked to Pedro, who had always been their actual commander. Cannons exploded with regularity on both sides, the balls landing harmlessly until mid-morning, when one of the Governor's pack mules dashed into the line of fire just as a rebel fieldpiece was torched. The cannonball struck its neck and, in a fountain of spurting blood, its head toppled off. Briefly the animal stood headless, a sight Pedro knew he would remember whenever he thought of this war.

At about noon the shooting sputtered to a stop — one month and twenty days after the march from Sutter's Fort. Casualty: one mule. Three if you counted the mishap in Big Sur. And Pablo, maybe. Unless he had been killed for some other reason.

Fortunately Micheltorena and Castro were *familia*. The treaty would be amicable. Land grantees beholden to Micheltorena would be unharmed and therefore unlikely to foment a real civil war. Where that left Captain Sutter, Pedro didn't know. But even if his powers were snipped, it was better than losing his skin to no purpose. Pedro felt no regrets. But he knew his military days were over.

Looking over the river he saw Captain Sutter being captured. He seemed a boy in grand trappings as about thirty riders surrounded him and herded him toward the Pico-Castro camp. The last act of the farce.

Whooping came from the hundred or so riflemen, who had splashed to the center of the river from both sides, raising flasks. Pedro realized that if they ever fought on the same side and really cared about their cause, they would be hard to beat. And if they were joined by ten thousand Mormons — ay, ay. He looked beyond, to Sutter's escort on the green plain and hoped Castro and Pico would satisfy themselves very soon that the Captain had never intended to turn the foreigners against Mexico or incite the *Indios* to riot. Maybe the Captain would realize Pedro had done the right thing in countermanding his order — a hanging offense. But he didn't fear punishment. If there was one lesson in this long campaign, it was that Sutter was all bark and no bite. He had grumbled to Pedro when the riflemen defied his direct orders and killed the rancheros' cattle. He had threatened to have them flogged and they had all but attacked him. He had backed down and actually tried to pacify them with hints of land as a reward for following orders! Amazing that a man so lacking in military leadership had become a captain in the French army. No, he didn't fear Sutter.

He turned to catch Chocolate. As he walked across the hill, the pretty *Indita* came to mind, the vanilla sound of her voice. The thought of Perry McCoon with her twisted his gut, though he didn't know why he should care. No, McCoon wouldn't flee to Oregon, as Sutter flattered himself to think. More than likely the two would soon be friends again.

He led Chocolate back to where the gear was stowed and looked over the river from his higher vantage point. About fifty riders from the Castro-Pico camp had surrounded the *Indios.* About twenty more were galloping for the horses. Booty! That hadn't been mentioned as part of the *comedia.*

He spurred Chocolate past his fellow Californians, who were running for their horses, and went down to the river where the *Indios* were being herded across.

"Corporal," he said to the man apparently in charge, "*por favor*, these *Indios* are under my charge. I request their release into my hands."

"Sorry," he said, "they belong to us now. Payment. We had considerable cost as you can imagine." The man's gap-toothed smile flashed beneath his presidio hat, number 2 on the band — San Gabriel. His uniform looked as threadbare as Pedro's — as all Alta California soldiers'. The half-naked *Indios* carried the three cannons on their shoulders. More booty. In contrast, Pico's Los Angelinos were nicely dressed in embroidered black boleros with white linen showing below their trouser knees.

Pedro calculated. With the riflemen celebrating with the supposed enemy, maybe four or five could be induced to ride for the Indians, against at least two hundred. It would be useless. And most of Sutter's *remuda* of horses was being herded across.

Three *Californianos* rode up, turning their mounts to watch with him — the mass of men and horses heading across the grassland.

"Nothing we can do now," Pedro said swallowing a lump. Then he knew he couldn't just ride away and allow these men to be slaves to the southerners. "But I will not leave here until I get them back. No matter how long it takes." His jaw worked along with his mind. There would be supper talks and diplomatically dangerous strolls in gardens. Maybe he could dictate a letter to Vallejo, and get help from that quarter. The lack of casualties made everything easier.

He saw that his friends were examining what must have been fire in his eyes. Like chanting acolytes they echoed his feelings about the Indians.

"They never complained."

"They were completely loyal."

"They kept the powder dry."

Pedro's voice cracked. "They can do anything with their hands. They understand . . . It's their . . . " He struggled for the right word. *Nobleza*? Yet in the descending scale of comprehension that defined this ridiculous war, they had toiled at the bottom. Pedro felt as if he loved these men as much as he'd ever loved anybody. Complex, warring feelings flooded him about his *Indio* blood.

He rode over to where Joaquín Sheldon sat with his spare horses watching the departing men and animals. "You return to the fort," Pedro said, "I'm staying until I get the Indians back."

"Glad to hear it. Castro and Pico oughta listen to you, after you played their game." His wolf-like gaze turned back to the prairie. "I might even have a friend or two left in Pueblo de los Angeles."

Pedro glanced at the celebrating riflemen and his words came out strong. "Could you and Señor Daylor use a good vaquero at your rancho?"

Sheldon cocked an interested eyebrow. "Of yer caliber, any day. But *dinero's* scarce. I'd have t'pay in calves."

It made no difference. He could build up a herd while waiting to see if Mexico City made Castro governor of Northern California, and if McCoon left Rancho Sacayak. "After I finish here, I'm working for you."

Sheldon extended a hand. "My *mayordomo*."

The hand was hard and dry. Smiling into Sheldon's solidity, he felt some of the weight lift. "Maybe I'll petition for the land across the river from you."

"William Hartnell has title to that ground."

"Then I'll wait, maybe find another piece."

"Might be a spell before they figure out where to go from here. In the meantime the You Ess of A is about to declare war for Texas and California. I heard that last night from a man who should know."

"Would you fight for Mexico?"

"Nope. I'm through with war." Not a moment's hesitation.

"Me too. And I am your *mayordomo*." It felt exactly right.

14

Maria Howchia felt paralyzed as she stood before the door of Sky Eyes' adobe house. That was odd because she had just danced the O-se-mai-ti. The Grizzly Bear had left her with the light, easy feeling of a joyous animal. Walking up the dark path with the blue-eyed man, she had felt O-se-mai-ti's power. But now that she was here, what kept her from entering?

The cold wind brought the promise of more rain. Shivering momentarily she felt Sky Eyes' hand on her arm. He pulled, but she jerked back. She had been glad to see his dimple in the light of the ceremonial fire, and had felt drawn to him. But she didn't want to go into his house.

With Yellow Beard gone to the fort, Sky Eyes had come alone to the ceremony and danced, removing his shirt in the smokey dancehouse. The thick hair on his chest made her think of a bear. It was intriguing to think of coupling with such a man.

Jacksnipe Song had watched her leave with Sky Eyes, but it was her right to choose. She didn't feel sorry for him any more. She had been telling people she wouldn't accept a marriage present from any man. She was pursuing knowledge.

Sky Eyes turned, hooked the cowhide drape aside and stepped through the door. She heard a little pop, saw a sputter of light, then a blaze as a candle flared. His shadowy form turned toward her. I could run, she thought. Then she remembered she should face her fear of the house and learn from it. It would bring clarity.

"Me thinks its cold ye be, lass." His voice sounded intimate, seductive in the quiet night. What did the talk mean?

She forced aside her uneasiness and stepped to the threshold. He was experienced in ways she wanted to learn. He might even help her understand Captain Sutter's power. Proud Hawk had told her to avoid Sky Eyes, but why should she listen to a man who spoke for Captain Sutter?

Sky Eyes drew near. She smelled him beside her. The rain had washed his clothes many times over, and he was less pungent than in Salmon Time. She welcomed his odor now.

"Come," he said reaching around her, pulling her buttock toward him. "I needs ye." Almost a whisper, hoarse, intense.

His other hand dragged a slow finger between her legs. She sucked in air as pleasant lightning shocked her. It wasn't newborn. This lightning had been hiding, waiting during the dance and the walk up the path. She wanted him.

He took something from his shirt, uncorked it, put it to his lips, swallowed, corked it, then closed the space between them. She didn't pull away when his lips touched hers. With his odor came a nose-flaring smell and the taste of fiery liquid. She ran her tongue around his lips, tongued his tongue.

It numbed her lips and tasted like — what? She was curious, wanted more.

He handed her the flask.

She swallowed a mouthful, then coughed without knowing she would, her throat on fire. He chuckled, intimate, friendly.

"Here, I'll feed it to you." He took a drink and put his mouth on hers. The cold wind stole her basket-weave cap, but standing against him, she didn't care. She sipped through his lips, rolled the liquid in her mouth, swallowed. She wanted more — the magic, the spark of his blue eyes, the dimple, the sharp odor, the fur on his chest.

He knew it. His hand was on her again. This time it lingered lazily, and she felt herself grow wet. Setting fear aside, she entered his shadowy house. A gust of wind swirled around her, the flickering candle nearly expiring. A spirit warning?

Sky Eyes pulled the hide across the doorway, slowing the wind, and lifted the blazing candle to her face. She saw his dimple, his approval of her, his wanting, and was glad.

He set the candle-dish on the floor beside the bed, gentled her down on the blankets beside him and taught her to drink the fiery liquid. "*Aguardiente*," he called it.

"*Aguardiente*," she repeated, learning to sip tiny amounts. Warmth hit the bottom of her belly and mixed with the other warmth. It ran to the muscles of her arms and legs, weakening them. It settled in her woman's parts and made them voracious. Her breasts grew heavy from wanting him. Her heart thudded for him, and with each sip she forgot her foreboding.

"Perry McCoon," he said pointing to his chest.

"Perrimacoo," she repeated, pointing at him.

He pointed to her chest with a quizzical expression. Pale people had no qualms about speaking their names, and she had already thrown her scruples to the winds. Pulsing with longing, she spoke her name aloud for the first time. "Maria Howchia."

Moments passed and nothing bad happened. That made her feel strong and she drank in the pungent aroma of his skin along with the fire of *aguardiente*.

"Maria," he said. A thrill passed through her to hear it on his lips. "Mary," he repeated, cupping her breast, kneeling before her and licking it like a dog. "Mary." They lay slowly back, together. "Mary."

As his clothing came off he rubbed his face in her breasts and belly, between her legs, moaning like a lost spirit.

On fire, she rolled on him, moving against him, unable to get enough. The friction of his white body against hers fueled her hunger. She fed him her breast, her earth body, her femaleness, craving his bigger finger, the one weeping, criss-crossing her with wanting. She needed his milk. When at last she clutched his hips and sucked him in, lightning electrified her. The shadowy corners of the room revolved, spinning in a sickly way. She whirled and thumped down a steep vortex to a place where her soul was lost in bad dreams. There she wandered, crying out where no one could hear, no one could console her.

In the upper world the man groaned and flopped on his back.

When she opened her eyes, harsh light crept inside on the packed dirt beneath the hide drape. Light from the window hole hurt her head. Her tongue stuck to the roof of her mouth. Scratching new itches, she lay in a filthy blanket beside the snoring man. Lice lived in his bedding.

She lifted the covering, stepped over him, and carefully replaced the blanket. Swallowing to keep her stomach down, she went to the door, lifted the hide and glanced back at the light-washed square of the room. Perrimacoo slept. In the corner, behind the table lay a big heap of something soft and dark. Feathers? The urge to vomit gripped her. Everything about the place was bad.

Outside the door Father Sun struck her face. The spirits had warned her not to go inside the adobe house, yet she had done it. She had spoken her own name. An owl blinked at her from a naked oak limb. Bad luck. Bad luck.

Walking up the path through hillsides green with First Grass she smelled the man all over her. Because of it, deep within and against her will, her body prepared to receive him again, even as she walked away from him.

The people were assembled before the dancehouse for the final oration of the O-se-mai-ti festival. Father's talk had begun. He was admonishing the young men to avoid arguments and exhibit patience. When he finished with that, he stood quietly on the roof of the dancehouse, the focus of every eye.

In formal tones he continued, "My son Crying Fox and all the young men who went to the white man's war are prisoners in a southern place called the Town of the Angels . . ."

Shocked into stonelike stillness, Maria Howchia listened as Grizzly Hair explained that they worked like men in the mission — lines of them carrying loads to large boats. They were now *esclavos*, a word not understood in the people's tongue. She couldn't imagine Crying Fox forced to carry such loads. Wouldn't he leave in the night? What power kept them there?

". . . Captain Sutter is a prisoner inside a big house." Grizzly Hair paused. "Headman Micheltorena left for the far southern place."

Grizzly Hair stood quietly, as if focused on some distant point, but she knew his focus was inward. What he said next puzzled her.

"Our condor robe is gone."

People stared at him. She glanced at Turtle Claw — impassive, eyes glazed. This was not new to him. Grizzly Hair continued, "Someone stole Molok's vestments." His head fell to his chest. His hair glistened, wet from his morning swim. Maria Howchia's breathing came rapidly. People looked at one another in horror. Molok's robe had been stolen.

Bad luck would fall on the people, terrible luck, and death. No one would know when, or upon whom, or for how many generations. They hadn't protected their most sacred possession.

As from an almost forgotten dream she recalled the dark, ominous pile in Perrimacoo's house. It couldn't have been the robe. Anyone who touched Molok's vestment without purification would have been struck dead immediately, and the unleashed powers of the universe would have killed her too, if not immediately then as she slept in its presence. Yet the robe was missing and bad luck already stalked the land.

The acorn supply was low. Crying Fox and others were enslaved. Even Captain Sutter was imprisoned. Tragedy would spread everywhere, touch everyone. Scrambled power rained like daggers. And what of her? Maria shivered.

15

SECOND GRASS FESTIVAL, the home place, 1846

The suns lengthened and the fluffy clouds had sailed away. Maria wished she didn't feel distant from the joy of Second Grass and the jubilant mood permeating the village. The short grass of the colder rainy season had burst into luxurious second growth, waving tall across the hillsides, shouldering high against the cha'kas and u-machas. Its gladness reflected all around her. She felt the gentle southwestern breezes and Father Sun's growing strength. Excitement trilled in the songs of nesting birds and mating frogs, but didn't flow into her, even when she danced and sang the spirits into the dancehouse.

It is the way with people, to forget troubles, she realized. They had buried thoughts of the lost condor robe beneath feasts, games, laughter and coupling. But she felt the evil spirits — a soreness in her breasts and a quickness to tears. Mother said she was pregnant and Father said she should marry the man who put a baby in her blood. She hadn't been to the woman's house for four moons.

All her relatives said she should marry. But she didn't feel like being a wife. She didn't want Perrimacoo or any man to move into her parent's house for the trial period, and she didn't want to go inside his house ever again, though she sometimes lay with him under the trees. Her cousin-sisters and -brothers were friendly enough, but somehow the feeling of being a bad daughter separated her from family and friends.

Besides that, she couldn't make her legs run as fast as usual. Club in hand, she trotted across the hillside on the trampled grass, playing the Yokuts game Father had taught people many years ago, the game he had learned on his way back from the Mission. The Omuchumne team wasn't far behind, and that kept her going. But her mind wasn't on the ball. She recalled that before the sleep Turtle Claw had looked at her abdomen in a disapproving way, and she had left the dance line to sit against the dancehouse wall. Why did a woman need to be married? Grandmother Howchia hadn't remarried after the black hats killed her husband, and Great-Grandmother Dishi had never married.

Ahead, Grizzly Hair smacked the little burl ball hard. As it flew high and long, Maria Howchia raced forward. But she was well behind her four teammates, and couldn't outrun Blue Star even in the best of times. Blue Star, who had started running while Father was still hitting, had a head start on everyone.

Blue Star got to the ball, set her feet and swung her club, all in one graceful move. The ball sailed well, but Maria Howchia wasn't even up to the place where it had been struck. By the time it landed, Grizzly Hair had covered half the distance, two other teammates on his heels.

He was bracing himself for the next shot when something cracked Maria hard on the back of the head. She reeled, dizzy with bright pain. She grabbed her head and realized she had been hit by the Omuchumne team's ball.

She glanced back to see them tramping around in the long grass, parting it with their clubs, searching for what had bounced off her head. Bad luck.

She didn't even try to run toward the last hole. As the five Omuchumne people raced after their ball, a young woman on that team glanced back at her and wrinkled her brow in sympathy. Pain still pulsing, Maria saw Grizzly Hair retrieve the burl from the last hole and hold it triumphantly overhead. Her team had won.

He saw her coming and his smile faded. Tossing the ball to Turtle Claw's son, he strode back to her. "Are you well, Daughter?" Perspiration ran down the creases of his wide cheeks.

"A burl hit me."

Still breathing hard, he felt in her hair, probed the bump and pursed his lips. "Come." He guided her with a hand between her shoulders. "Or do you need to sit down?"

"No, I can walk."

In the u-macha she shoved her polished club up into the rafters beside his — making them had been a shared pleasure.

"Come with me to the sweathouse," he said.

Something was afoot. She waited outside. Quickly he emerged with his bow. She kept quiet as he slung the otterskin quiver over his shoulder, four feet and tail dangling. It was filled with arrows.

Midday was not a time for so many men and women to be walking the path to tai-yokkel — with weapons. They moved determinedly, all the men clutching bows and watching Grizzly Hair from the corners of their eyes. Why was she, a woman, being brought on a hunt? Why were so many women coming?

When she and Grizzly Hair arrived at the adobe corral of the *puercos*, men began ramming the butts of logs into the weakest adobes. Grizzly Hair turned to Maria Howchia and said, "Tonight is First *Puerco* feast."

Stunned at that, she looked at Perrimacoo's house. He stuck out his head, hair mussed from sleep, the whites of his eyes looking red. He would be furious.

"What the bleedin fuck's going on?" he yelled.

The battered adobes collapsed and men scraped away the debris to let the *puercos* go. A sow stuck her head out, grunted and glanced at the countryside with small glittering eyes.

Barefoot, Perrimacoo half hopped over the rocks and sticks until he came to where he saw the hole. "Ye bloody savages broke me fence!" he screamed. "I'll blast ye I will!" He picked his way tender-footed back to his house.

Grizzly Hair signaled, and about forty men stepped from the surrounding trees and boulders, bows drawn. Maria Howchia sucked in her breath. Would they kill him?

Perrimacoo reappeared on the flat rock before his door, ramming powder down his gunbarrel. He jerked the stock to his chin, looked down the barrel, then, eyes sweeping around at all the arrows pointed at him from all directions, lowered the gun.

The sow, swollen with young again, rushed to freedom trailing a string of half-grown *puercos*. The boar ran the opposite direction. Grizzly Hair's arrow entered the mother pig's eye. She fell immediately, without sound. Maria Howchia was shocked. How could he do that? She had loved watching the ten piglets nurse in two neat rows on their mother's belly. Sometimes she and Perrimacoo stood smiling and pointing over the fence at them. She scowled at Father, saw his calm dignity as he approached the fallen pig, and knew she could trust him.

The young *puercos* ambled around, unafraid as Grizzly Hair lifted their mother's snout and yanked out the arrow. He accepted a basket of water from Jacksnipe Song, then knelt on one knee and tenderly poured water into the animal's open mouth, and sang. His song floated over the loud talk of Perrimacoo, who stepped forward, but the encircling men drew their bowstrings tighter.

Father sang the animal's spirit to the pathway of ghosts. The song apologized for the need to kill one who had been penned, fed and taught to trust. Goose bumps pricked on the backs of her arms to think of that. Then she grew fearful as she looked at Perrimacoo's angry face and recalled his delight that the sows were about to give birth a second time in six moons.

The last singing note faded and Grizzly Hair signaled. A group of older boys picked up the sow and carried her up the path toward the village.

"Ye filthy, bleedin 'eathens." Perrimacoo raised his gun again.

Arrows whispered through the air and quivered in the ground in a half-circle around his bare feet. He stared at them.

Maria Howchia's heart hammered, glad they hadn't killed him. Paralyzed with conflicting feelings — knowing Father had the people's interests at heart, but also knowing her man had expected to exchange the new piglets for goods at the fort — she locked glances with Perrimacoo. She felt sorry for him. But he stabbed her with such a hateful expression that she looked down. Did he assume she had known of this?

Grizzly Hair's bow hung in his hand and his voice came low and strong. "Daughter, invite him to the First Puerco feast."

Her words quavered. "My father invites you to the feast. We celebrate Second Grass, and," she hesitated, then blurted out, "First Pig."

"First Pig!" he shrieked. "Damnation ye nigger bitch!" His eyes were round.

She trembled. What would he do to her?

Grizzly Hair was calm. "Tell him his presence at the feast will honor the *puerca.*"

When she conveyed this, Perrimacoo screamed, "Just ye tell this to the honorable pig!" Without lifting the gun or aiming, he fired.

One of the men in the circle clutched his foot, fell and grimaced. Blood seeped through his fingers.

Before Perrimacoo could reload, several men grabbed him and jerked the gun from his hands. He yelled about hell and demons and kicked their shins, but without his boots, the kicks had little effect and seemed to hurt him more.

"Daughter," Grizzly Hair said, "tell him he owes us four half-grown *puercos* in payment for the injury to this man. He held up four fingers and pointed to the animals now leaving the corral with the other sow.

Arrows hummed. Four half-grown *puercos* fell as their frantic mother rushed about nosing her young ones, one after the other. They lay kicking in the grass. Feeling as if her voice belonged to someone else, Maria explained why the animals were shot.

His face twisted with ugly anger and he glared at her.

"I not know of this," she said as the men lifted the snouts of the dead pigs, giving them a drink for their spirit journey.

He jerked, but couldn't escape the grasp of the men. "Like hell." he yelled. She didn't know what that meant.

Patiently Father said, "Tell him we will take him to the feast." He signaled the people to round up the escaped pigs and lock them inside.

At least a hundred and fifty people crowded around watching the skewered animals cook over three different fires. Father had invited all the related villages, and this was the most people Maria Howchia had seen at a Big Time. But the person she watched most closely was Perrimacoo.

He had been forced to walk up the path by the men who had taken his gun. Now he sat on the ground and stared into the flames, which were all but invisible in the bright day. Every once in a while she glanced at him and saw fury in the sky eyes. The skins of the *puercos* burst and crackled before him, the popping sound of cooking fat. Everyone else gleefully watched, anticipating the feast, murmuring with their heads together and pointing at the roasting animals. However, Father sat against the big oak as if in thought. The strange sweet aroma pervaded the village and all Maria's senses.

Cloying, too sweet, too rich. Feeling sudden nausea, she swallowed hard and went to the river for salad makings. She inhaled the soothing fragrances of her plant friends and took her time, upwind of the cooking smell. Again, she felt the painful separation between her and the *umne*. Like a bird making its home among fish. Yet she belonged nowhere else.

When Father Sun had gone to his western house, strips of meat were distributed, but she wanted none of it and tried not to watch people on every side smacking their lips and exclaiming over its taste. She stared into the distance to keep her stomach calm. Grizzly Hair ate the heart of the sow, then chewed several ribs. Perrimacoo refused food. Father laid down a rib and looked around at the many people, signalling with his eyes that he intended to speak. Everyone quieted to listen, and he addressed Maria.

"Daughter, tell Perrimacoo he is welcome in our village."

She told him in English. He rolled his blue eyes and looked away.

"Tell him he does not know polite behavior."

She told him and he snorted rudely.

"Tell him I will teach him polite behavior."

His jaw dropped and his sky eyes widened.

"Tell him that when a woman is pregnant by a man's blood, he should bring her family a gift so they can decide whether she should marry him."

Unnerved at this unexpected turn of talk, and queasy in her stomach, she repeated it brokenly.

Perrimacoo's lips twitched. "Wot kind o'gift."

She asked Father the question.

"Tell him we think the *puercos* taste good, and we would accept the other sow, or all her remaining young that were not killed today."

"But Father, I do not want to marry him."

He scowled and raised his voice in a way that shamed her. "Then send the gift back. I am only telling him how to behave." The twilight was darkening, but she could see well enough to know he wasn't angry, just serious in his purpose. She told Sky Eyes to offer the sow and her young.

He tried to jump to his feet, but the surrounding men were quick. He gritted his teeth and twisted back and forth in their hands. "Why don't ye bloody 'eathens just shoot the lot of em and get it over with! "

"Doesn't he want to learn good behavior?" Father asked.

Moisture suddenly blurred her vision, though she didn't feel sad. It often happened. All she could do was listen to the frogs bellowing in the dwindling light and wonder what spirit made her weep.

Grizzly Hair didn't demand an answer. He collected his long legs, stood like an oak — the people clearly enjoying the entertainment — and spoke in a commanding tone. "Tell Perrimacoo we are honored to have him as our neighbor, and we appreciate his *puercos*. They taste very good." He rubbed his stomach and waited for her talk.

"Tell him we will be honored if he brings you a marriage present."

Without looking at Sky Eyes, she murmured that in the few words she knew.

"Tell him if he becomes my son-in-law and the father of my grandchild, his wants would be my wants, his rancho, my rancho." She struggled to say it all and Perrimacoo listened quietly.

"Tell him we enjoy helping him take care of the *puercos*. However, the females have too many babies and are pregnant too soon afterwards. These oaks," he extended his arms and looked up at them, "provide enough for my people and a few *puercos*. Each year we will have a feast such as this."

Perrimacoo's outbursts seemed to be over.

Grizzly Hair studied him in the last light of day, reached down, picked up the gun. "Tell him I do not want his gun. It is his, as long as we are polite neighbors."

She repeated this as best she could.

Grizzly Hair placed the gun over his wrists and walked toward him.

Perrimacoo reached up, took the gun, checked its working parts, placed it on his knees and shifted his glance from side to side as if looking for an escape route.

"I am finished," Grizzly Hair said, returning to his place beneath the oak. He sat looking at nothing.

Maria Howchia knew all the men were watching Sky Eyes, though they appeared not to. She felt calmer now, seeing that he was in a thoughtful mood. She also felt proud of Father, and a little less separated from the world.

Perrimacoo nodded at her and said, "I will bring a marriage present."

Earlier she had thought she would return any such gift. But seeing his respectful demeanor now, it occurred to her that the way to knowledge was to marry him. Then her child would have a father and her relatives would look at her approvingly, and Perrimacoo would be part of the *umne*.

16

TIME OF GATHERING ACORNS

It felt good to be replenishing the family cha'ka, the vine-woven storage silo, but the baby's constant howling grated because Maria Howchia couldn't do anything about it. He couldn't be hungry already. She straightened her back and looked at him across the shade of the oak where she was gathering. He stood upright, laced to the neck in his bikoos, which leaned against the tree trunk. He wept bitterly. Beside him two other laced-up infants stood in perfect peace. Their faces were tan. His was red. Dogs shared the shade, lying with their muzzles draped sleepily over their paws, eyes checking.

"He is not well," said Mother's second-cousin-sister. Her big haunches and fat breasts and stomach rippled as she gathered acorns under the samc oak.

"Have you seen illness of this kind before?"

The big woman reached behind her head and dropped acorns into her full basket, the thong cutting visibly into the woven cap on her forehead. Her black eyes reflected the wisdom of one who was older. "Grasshopper Wing's grandchild cries like this."

Grasshopper Wing had left her husband's house and gone to another man. Perhaps that brought bad luck. Maria Howchia took a long stick and reached high into the oak, sharply prodding a branch. Acorns showered onto her cap and rolled off her shoulders and breasts. "Can it be cured?" she asked.

The woman shrugged her basket between her shoulders, bent under its weight, said, "The bad luck is in the child's spirit," and waddled away under the load.

Maria Howchia winced. It wasn't the first time she'd heard that. Picking up nuts she mentally ticked off what she'd done right while she was pregnant, never looking out a door or backing out for fear of breech birth, never looking at Great-Grandmother Dishi for fear of blindness, never looking at a sick person or animal. All the bothersome precautions she had taken. But no help came from this recital.

The baby howled, his puffy face streaked with tears. It was the same whether she held him or not. The baby's father must have brought this, she thought. Perrimacoo had little power. Such a person brought bad luck, like a hole dug in a dry riverbottom filling with water. He rarely purified himself. He also took too many acorns for the *puercos*. Twenty-three lived in the corral, now that the remaining sow had twice more given birth. Twice he had struck Maria. Once he had chased her with a burning stick. No other man except Captain Sutter acted like that, and she would never mention it to anyone. It was shameful. His bad behavior brought bad luck.

She sighed and bent forward, sweeping up acorns with fluid motions. She too had behaved badly. No other woman refused to enter her husband's house. With so much wrong, no wonder the baby cried. Etumu's dog got up, stretched, and barked repeatedly into Billy's face, turning toward Maria as if telling her to make him quiet. But the barking made him cry louder.

She shut her eyes. It was Molok, the power of the universe going bad. With Crying Fox's recent return from the south land, she had hoped it wasn't so, but she had been fooling herself. She felt she must sit or fall. Hurrying to Billy's side, she sat and bounced the bikoos on her knees.

She had never been inside the bad house since that one night, and whenever she asked Perrimacoo about the robe, he became angry and raised his fist. Now she never mentioned it. She moaned aloud — the sound lost in Billy's howling — feeling almost as sick as she'd been that morning long ago in the man's bad luck house.

Crying Fox stepped around the blackberry vines and squinted into the sunlight at her. She could tell by his mussed hair that he had been napping. "The men in the sweathouse are trying to sleep," he said. "they want you to take the baby away from the village."

Shame! The baby had disturbed the men. Rushing away with her angry bundle, she watched her brother duck back into the sweathouse, the muscles of his buttocks and calves sharply defined now that he was thinner. As she passed the entrance, several male faces frowned from the shadows. The thump of a woman pounding acorns beat time with her rapid footsteps up the east hill.

She couldn't ask the doctor to cure Billy. He'd want to be paid more goods than she had, but that wasn't all. Turtle Claw might die confronting the power of Molok, and she was honor-bound to warn him. But then she would owe him much more in goods. Instead she would endure the crying and the horror. She couldn't tell anyone she thought her man had stolen the robe. The doctor would kill him with magic and that stopped her cold. A child needed a father.

At the top of the hill she adjusted her head thong, breathing rapidly. Billy had apparently fallen asleep. She heard the rushing river and smelled the blue-lavender brush flowers blooming at the end of the long dry. She leaned down, picked a sprig and brought it to her nose. These were tough plants, the harsh vinegary scent almost too much up close.

Shifting the cradleboard to the other arm, she headed downhill toward an oak that may not have been picked. The flower was a sign. Maria Howchia was strong too, and the only protection against unloosed power was one's own power.

At sunset she cooked rabbit strips over the fire while Mother busied herself with greens. Perrimacoo arrived and settled himself against the family u-macha.

He put his leather hat on the ground and ran his fingers through his dark wavy hair. "Mary, tell yer daddy I needs to palaver."

Grizzly Hair turned to face his son-in-law.

"Mr. Brüheim's gone fer good," Perrimacoo said, "And I'm sittin in yon house like a ship becalmed, I is. I wants yer daughter t'cook me food over there like a regular wife. In me own 'ouse." His voice raised. "Or 'as ye forgot, it's me bleedin wife she is." His blue eyes drilled into Father, then into her as she talked for him.

Father sighed. "Daughter, he gave me the present of a fine leather hat and the piglets to roast. You accepted that, and so did I. And the other gifts he brought later. A wife lives in her husband's house after a decent time." He stared toward the river. It was hard to deny Father's wishes after he'd made a bargain, but he didn't know of the robe.

She extended him a basket of fresh nu-pah, watched him scoop it with his curved fingers, and knew how much he'd missed it during the past three moons. But the caring lines on Father's broad face remained in place. He was waiting. She said in her own tongue that staying out of that house may have saved her life, and little Billy's. She looked down.

Perrimacoo stared rudely at her. The baby cried in his cradleboard. Without her permission he unlaced him, and by the time she presented him roasted rabbit on cress and two boiled quail eggs, the baby was naked and laughing on his father's knee, clutching the pale sleeve of his shirt.

"He's fat," Sky Eyes said with pleasure, standing the baby on his feet, tiny toes clenched in the powdery dirt. Then his expression darkened. "I wants me answer."

The baby grinned up at Maria Howchia, big dimples creasing both cheeks, chubby knees pressed together. When he smiled like this it seemed the entire world consisted of his sweet, pale face framed by his light brown curls. She couldn't do anything to endanger him — any more than he was endangered already. "My husband's house is not safe," she told Father.

He sat thinking, then said, "A woman does not marry a man whose house is unsafe."

For a moment she couldn't respond, and when she did, it felt too private. But she forced herself to say, "Sometimes a woman is sorry she married a man." It came out very quiet.

Father sighed. "Tell him his house is unsafe, then think about your death." This was Father's way of reminding people to live each day with joy.

Hearing again that his house was unsafe, Perrimacoo grabbed his forehead and gnashed his teeth at the ground. "Mary, ent a bleedin thing wrong with me bleedin 'ouse." He exhaled noisily as if forcing his anger out. "Listen," he said in a calmer tone, "I needs ye to come with me to New Helvetia, so I can show off me babe."

He had said this before, and the thought of Captain Sutter made her stall again. "Should I tell my family what you say?"

"What the hell difference does it make? Just say you'll go."

She didn't want to face Sutter yet. She had no more power than the last time she saw him. On the other hand Perrimacoo was her husband. He would protect her from guns. And she was curious about the fort, now that so many *Americanos* were there. People said they had brought women and children over the eastern mountains in big wagons. It would be fun to see *Americanas*. Crying Fox and other men planned to help Perrimacoo herd the *puercos* to the fort, and she would enjoy travelling with the crowd. It might keep her man's mind off coupling too. Besides, the cha'ka was full of acorns. Her parents didn't need her. She nodded she would go.

He grinned, handed her the baby, bit into a rabbit leg and talked with his mouth full. "Stop and see Jared Sheldon and Bill Daylor, we will."

And she could see Blue Star! Her friend had married Quapata and gone to live in his village. Maybe Blue Star would show her the wonderful seed-grinding machine Señor Sheldon had made. Everyone was talking about it.

RANCHO OMUCHUMNE, Late September, 1846

Pedro sat on his horse resting his forearms on the big round pommel horn of his saddle. From the high ground north of Daylor's trading post he saw the whole sweep of the countryside — golden hills sloping down to the green bottomland of the Río Cosumnes. Wonderful pasture where it wasn't choked with berry vines. Midway between him and Daylor's adobe, Quapata leaned into his horse's mane, bare heels tight, and cut a cow from the herd. Pedro had to smile. These *Indios* were natural vaqueros, and Quapata was the best of the boys now becoming men.

About a mile farther downriver he could barely see Sheldon's millhouse, where he bunked. You had to know the shape of the peaked roof between the cottonwoods. He liked the privacy of that upstairs room, and its size — larger than any place he'd lived — even if he did share it with flour bags and a family of mice.

Madre de Dios, Quapata looked good. The *Indio* turned his head back over his shoulder to see if Pedro was looking. He waved encouragingly.

Sheldon and Daylor were men of their word. Life was good on Rancho Omuchumne, with no troops to drill, no sessions with Sutter on everything from soup to buttons, no prickly translation, but Pedro's enjoyment came more from what he did than what he didn't do. As surely as Quapata was whirling *la reata*, the *patrones* needed Pedro on this huge rancho. He was a good *mayordomo*, and he got more enjoyment from training vaqueros than he'd thought. Working on horseback every day gave him a feeling of — what? The beauty of life? Maybe the sense of fitting well into the scheme of things. He felt born to this life.

Oh, no question about it, a man his age should have his own place, but Mexico City hadn't recognized Castro as governor, Pico having taken over, and Señor Sheldon said it would take a while before it was clear how to petition for land. Petitions had stagnated. The United States hadn't started a war, yet, and the *malcriado* Perry McCoon was still raising hogs on Rancho Sacayak. So there was nothing to do but enjoy life. And the *Indias*. Tomaka was as comfortable as a feather mattress. Heavy of flesh, slow moving, happy disposition, she accepted the temporary arrangement and gave him his privacy. Besides, Big Times gave him other opportunities. *Indios* held their fiestas at least once a month, and had themselves several days of guiltless, rollicking fun. *Españolas* were too religious for that. *Indio* fandangos pumped euphoria into Pedro until he took his shirt off and sang at the moon. Even the sourest puss could laugh at himself at those celebrations. All without liquor, which Señor Daylor refused to provide, though the Indians would have liked it. Of course Pedro didn't let the *patrones* see him doing that.

That *muchacho* could ride! Quapata handled the horse like his brown body was a part of it. He was moving in tandem with a really crazy cow, zig-zagging across the hill. Quapata whirled a nice big lasso. Wild, these long horns. Vicious.

The cow turned suddenly, thundered uphill toward Pedro. Quapata closed the gap. Pedro heard the bellowing herd shy behind him, felt the ground tremble. Quapata's powerful thighs spread over the mustang's ribs as he threw the *reata*, catching only one horn. The cow twisted wickedly and changed course. The *reata* whipped free of Quapata's hand and streamed behind in the dirt.

Pedro tightened the hat bead under his nose and nudged Chocolate toward the cow. Just as Quapata let his body slip to the side, legs clamped, and reached down for the dragging rope, the cow turned, and the *Indio* missed the dragging lariat. But he was doing well. Nothing was harder than this. With Chocolate loping smoothly alongside, Pedro yelled, "*Míra*, watch!"

He touched the horse with his spurs and overtook the cow. The trick was to keep her on a straight course, but she swerved. Again Pedro overtook her, looking back to see Quapata galloping behind, watching.

This time the cow held course long enough for Pedro to rotate down with his leg under the horse's belly. "Steady, *está bueno*." He kept up a patter of encouragement to calm the stallion, help him tolerate the lopsided weight. No question, this was dangerous work, every time.

Face near the pounding hooves, sombrero skidding, he gritted his teeth against flying dirt and kept his narrowed eyes on the cow's hooves. The horse was slowing a little because of the dropped reins, and she was gaining. Pedro made a kissing sound. Chocolate accelerated. He stretched his right hand after the trailing *reata*. Debris stung his wrist and he felt the tip of the leather licking up and down off the bunch grass and dirt.

"Hah!" he yelled, "Hah!" The horse surged ahead and Pedro gripped the leather. This was the worst part, inching back into the saddle with a thousand pounds of craziness attached to your arm, but Chocolate was the best. He kept pace with the cow, and she didn't twist away and jerk him.

In the saddle again he spat a mouthful of dust and tried to blink away the grit. Would this *vaca* ever wear out? Glancing up, he saw with horror that he was heading straight for Sheldon's wheat field. The harvesting Indians seemed frozen in place as the crazed longhorn bore down on them.

He spurred. The big horse lunged ahead, cut off the cow and turned her up the path toward Daylor's adobe. At last she slowed to a trot.

Pedro breathed easier, pleased he hadn't lost his touch. He looked back to see Quapata not far behind, face cracked in a wide, admiring grin. Looking ahead, Pedro was astonished to see a herd of pigs and *Indio* herders. At the sight of the cow the pigs squealed and tried to run, but the herders raised sticks and threatened them back. Perry McCoon had to be nearby.

"Hold, boy." Pedro hopped off Chocolate and made his way along the taut *reata* toward the heaving, blowing cow. By the look in her eyes, she expected to get her throat cut. He was talking to her when suddenly a boar broke free and careened toward the cow. She panicked, twisted her head, and the *reata* slipped off her horn. Galloping in a crazy circle, she lowered her head to charge the boar.

It turned and ran toward Daylor's yard, preceded by its knife-like tusks. Pedro jumped on Chocolate and coiled the rope. The cow veered away, but the boar kept going. *Indios* and Perry McCoon scattered, the boar charging at a young *India* with a baby in her arms.

Pedro gauged the speed and let fly. The animal ran neatly into the noose and he yanked the horse to a stop. The boar flopped to its side with its hind legs kicking and its tongue out.

The *India* stared at the animal, which was only an arm's length from her, then looked up at Pedro, her big black eyes wide. It was Captain Juan's daughter! The pretty little poppy McCoon had taken to bed. Pedro hadn't seen her since that night before the farcical Micheltorena war. Her face was so beautiful now that he hardly heard the baby screaming in her arms, or noticed the foul smell of pig excrement all over the place.

Her expression had changed from shock to admiration — for Pedro. With a red skirt tied about her rounded hips, bone and clay beads tight between her full bare breasts, she was a woman now, yet young enough that her stomach was flat and her waist nipped in between the curves. His insides went soft at the sight, and it felt good. He had missed feeling that way. This was the tenderest looking girl-woman he had ever seen. The Heavenly Señor must have enjoyed making her.

"Next time, lasso both horns," McCoon said in a syrupy tone.

Pedro leveled him a look, then signaled the herders to take his *reata* and tie the boar. He spurred Chocolate toward the fighting cow, which Quapata had lassoed over both horns this time and was struggling to hold onto. Pedro aimed his spare lasso at a back hoof, tripped the cow, jumped down and whipped his riata around her kicking legs. In a few moments the animal was immobilized. Pedro noted she was pregnant and healthy, the right ear notched out round, the left cloven. Daylor's cow.

Quapata said, "Maybe I will be good like you someday." He untied *la reata*, jumped on his horse and herded the cow up the hill, expertly cutting back and forth.

Pedro smiled after him and led Chocolate the few rods back to Daylor's yard, where the herders had the boar hog-tied. "*Buenos días*, Señora McCoon," he said sweeping his sombrero before the beautiful *India*, ignoring McCoon. He spoke loud enough to be heard over the baby's crying. If it angered McCoon to see her treated like a lady, that felt good.

The flies rising from the pig dung belonged to the Englishman, who was hunkered down against Daylor's big cottonwood with his rifle over his knees, grinning as if enjoying the sight, as if he were a king entertained by a buffoon, as if he hadn't dodged the fight between them. "Appreciate it, I would," he drawled, "if ye'd keep the cows away from me 'ogs." His grin was closed enough to hide the missing tooth.

"I am waiting for our riding competition, señor." Pedro tilted his head at him, "Or maybe you are afraid?" It had been well over a year. The man had no *cojones* and Pedro was ready to flatten his handsome nose.

McCoon pointed his rifle at Quapata, who was receding toward the hill. Looking down the sights, he muttered, "I told you, greaser, I name the time."

Pedro snorted derisively, mildly relieved that Quapata had gone out of range though it was plain the coward was only trying to unsettle him. He glanced at the *Indita*, who was looking at him, and was pleasantly startled to see that she held him in high esteem. A sudden sorrow gripped him — so profound and unexpected that he couldn't keep it from his face. McCoon had her and the land too. The baby made her doubly the man's wife, the way *Indios* thought. Pedro found it difficult to look at the weeping child — living evidence of McCoon's foul touch.

He hardened his jaw and met McCoon's insolence. "Any time señor, any time." He brushed away the flies rising from the pig dung. A MAN raised cattle.

Señor Daylor pounded up on his gray, his long face shaded by a big sugar-loaf sombrero. "Well blow me down if it ain't me old mait," he said sliding his lanky frame off the horse and looping the rein over the rail.

McCoon got up and went to him and clapped him on the back. "A wee visit on the way to the fort with me 'ogs. Why, a bloke'd mistake ye for a Mexican in that git-up." A head shorter than Daylor, McCoon was less of a man in every way.

Pedro reined Chocolate away.

"Pedro," Daylor called. Pedro turned. "Take that adz back to Jared." He nodded toward a carpentry tool by the hitching rail.

"Sí señor." Without slowing he swept the tool from the ground and cantered toward Mill Ranch, already planning a visit to the fort. Señor Sheldon was waiting for a package from Yerba Buena, and Pedro could fetch it for him. He also wanted to see how McCoon treated his wife at the fort. He'd leave in the morning, after arranging it with Señor Sheldon.

Besides, it was time to talk to Captain Sutter about land. A growing herd of cattle bore Pedro's earmark and he was restless to give them a permanent home. Sutter had no doubt forgotten any bad feelings from the Micheltorena war. Even William Johnson — that scum of a sailor who hadn't reported for the war and caused the Captain to complain so loudly — now held title to Pablo Gutiérrez' old rancho. Pedro shook his head. He had wanted it, the only land Sutter had the legal authority to give — land properly granted by the governor but to an owner who had died. Instead, Sutter had held an auction for it and accepted a hundred and fifty pesos from Johnson. Pedro's partial herd hadn't measured up. *No importa*, he had enjoyed life at Rancho Omuchumne, and McCoon might still leave. But now, seeing the girl made him feel an urgency he didn't entirely understand.

17

On the trail to Sutter's Fort, Maria Howchia promised herself she'd see Sheldon's mill on the way back, no matter what Perrimacoo said. It was disappointing to have missed both Blue Star and the fabulous seed-grinding machine. She realized she was more interested in coming back through Rancho Omuchumne than going to the fort. Most of all she wanted to see Proud Hawk again.

The same magic she'd felt the first time she saw him had sizzled through her, and she disliked the distance lengthening between them as she walked behind the pigs and her cousin-brothers. Proud Hawk no longer did the bidding of Captain Sutter, but rode for the *Americano* hy-apos of Rancho Omuchumne. She couldn't wait to see him again.

The sun was low when the fort came into view and she was surprised how different it looked. A new adobe structure now shared a wall with the corral, and yet another new adobe house — a long one — was half built. A town of wagons had sprung up near the gate, many with pale cloth stretched over big hoops. Beyond that she saw strange hornless cattle with sleepy white faces, and beyond them reed houses that hadn't been there before, with horses and *Indio* people moving about. A separate town of tents had been erected by the wagons and she saw many long-skirted, completely clothed women, some stirring pots over fires.

Children with yellow hair turned and looked at her. They followed the pigs and men and ran alongside. "They're nekked," a child shouted. "That buck's got a necklace!" said another. More children joined them, with hair of different colors. Some wore shirts and trousers, others long flowing dresses. The girls stared at little Billy in his cradleboard.

"Hello," she said to them. They smiled at her wonderingly.

Two blue suits with long guns stood at the gate. Perrimacoo signaled the herders to wait outside with the pigs and beckoned her to follow him into the courtyard. Walking behind him, she stumbled on a rut, so intent was she on the changes. Fully clothed *Americanos* were everywhere. Overhead, the red, white and green banner was gone, replaced by a pale cloth bearing something that looked like a brown pig, or bear. In addition to men in fringed buckskin, she saw many others in trousers and shirts like Perrimacoo's. One had a face as dark as the black lizard, the braids tailing from his hat as fat as her wrist. Everyone talked in loud voices and stood before tables heaped with hides and other objects.

Some of the women wore hats with big wings that tunneled their vision and all but hid their faces. But when she got a glimpse, she saw skin of all hues — some normal, some pink with small brown spots, some white as demons. Their hair ranged from black to orange to yellow. Some were tall, some short, but even those who looked older were lacking in flesh. One had a straight, narrow nose like Perrimacoo. One had a nose that looked cut-off — too much nostril showing, and still another the beak of a fierce eagle. That one scowled at Maria's breasts and sucked her tongue with an audible snap.

Then she was suddenly at the foot of Captain Sutter's stairs, Perrimacoo tugging her hand. She pulled it back and shrugged out of the bikoos and handed Billy to his father. "You take him," she said. He wanted Billy's name marked on the captain's paper-that-talks. Billy woke up and began to fuss.

Perrimacoo looked at her with disgust, took the baby and went up the stairs.

She dashed around the house, out of view of the Captain's window, and nearly stumbled into a group of blue suits sitting in the shade of the building. They stared impolitely. A slow smile spread across the features of one and he got to his knees and reached for her. She darted among strangers and ducked inside the iron-making house, which was attached to the fort wall.

Luis, a young *Indio* she had met before, smiled in a friendly way. Dressed in a leather loincloth, he sweated as he pumped the big bellows on glowing coals. He spoke in Spanish. "Is Salvador here?" Crying Fox's fort name.

"Outside with Perrimacoo's *puercos*," she said.

She peered out the window and saw Manu-iki, her long black hair tied in a tail at her back like a man's. "Are *Americana* women friendly?" she asked Luis, who began pounding a piece of glowing iron.

The hammer clanged. "Not to me." He glanced up with a humorous twist in his smile.

She smiled back. Then, through the window, she caught a glimpse of Perrimacoo on the landing of the *casa grande* — looking over the busy courtyard, for her. The baby was crying. She stepped out the door.

"Come to our fandango tonight, you and Salvador," Luis said.

She smiled back. She would like that.

She was part way across the courtyard when a crowd came through the gate. Through the jostling people she saw men helping two men walk. Living skeletons in torn *Americano* clothing. This amazed her. Why would anyone starve at acorn time? In the midst of plenty?

Perrimacoo appeared at her side, handing her the crying baby. The blue-suited men poured around the corner of the *casa grande* and stood in the path of the bony men. So many people had pressed together that she was in little danger of being seen by Captain Sutter, who stood at the back of the crowd, and she had to hunt to find a crack to see through.

The stick-like arms of two thin men were draped over the shoulders of those who helped them walk. The tops of their skull faces hung with long brown hair that joined the huge, bristling dark beards on their chests. She could feel bad power crackling around them, and remembered Molok's robe.

A thin man talked. "Please. I must speak with Mr. Sutter."

"I'm in charge here now," said a blue suit.

"This is Mr. Sutter's fort isn't it?" The thin man asked. "I have a letter for him from George Donner. We had hoped our families could benefit from Mr. Sutter's famous generosity. People are in dire need. They need his help."

"Who are you?" The blue suit showed not a trace of embarrassment in speaking for the actual headman of the fort.

"I am James Reed," the thin man said. "This is Mr. Herron. There are nearly ninety people in Donner's party back on the trail." He rolled his eyes as if searching for strength in the sky. "My wife and children were almost out of food when we left. They won't make it without supplies. You or Mr. Sutter or whoever is in charge must immediately send a pack train of food over the mountains to meet them."

The blue suit yanked at the belt of his trousers and said, "Two men come in about a week ago, to get help for that same Donner Party. Stanton and McCutchen, they was. Said you'd be dead, if you be Reed. Mr. Sutter's gettin relief together now, is my understanding." He eyed the thin man. "You men musta had a bad crossing."

"Some of us had to leave our wagons in the desert and walk. We couldn't carry food. Our oxen died. We almost didn't make it. I'd like to give this letter to Mr. Sutter. Is he here?"

The blue suit looked suspicious. "The men that come in said you was involved in foul play and was exiled from the Party without provisions."

The skeletal man's voice rose loud and clear, and Maria Howchia heard the pride. "Defending myself and my wife, sir. And Corporal, that's no crime. I'd think a man in uniform would hold his opinion until both sides were told."

A big straw-haired man with a bushy reddish beard boomed, "Way I recollect, you warn't about t' listen to no reason. You was too high falutin." The nodding *Americanos* murmured agreement.

James Reed took his thin arms from the shoulders of those who were helping him and looked at the crowd. Fire smoldered in his sunken eyes. "Mister," he said, "if you're speaking of the cutoff, we followed Lansford Hastings' guidebook. Maybe our mistake was being able to read, unlike most of you." *Americanos* exchanged surprised glances. "If there's a criminal in this sorry mess, it's Hastings." His bones seemed to melt and men grabbed for him.

The blue suit cleared his throat. "Now let's keep our shirts on."

The thin man raised his head. "How far did Stanton say the wagon train got?"

Captain Sutter pushed his way through the crowd. Beside the others he looked short, and he had gained flesh since she had seen him. "I am Colonel Sutter," he said extending a hand toward James Reed. "Herr Stanton hass say he tinks the Donner people be in da high mountains now."

Unhooking an arm, James Reed reached and grasped the captain's hand. "I am so relieved to see you, Mr. Sutter. These men said you aren't in charge here. I don't understand."

Sutter looked down in an embarrassed way, then brought up his knob of a bare chin. "Iss mine landt." He gestured broadly. "Mine establishment. Haff you a letter for me?"

"From Mr. George Donner, a good friend of mine." He pulled it from his pocket. "It says he will pay you for supplies, if you could have them sent back up the trail. Immediately, if you can, sir."

"To you, Mr. Reed, my storehouses are open. Please be so goot as to come to mine rooms, and ve talk about beds and so fort. Alzo I show you provisions ve pack for your Party." He glared at the blue suits, who raised their eyebrows to each other as they departed for the other side of the *casa grande*.

Maria Howchia watched Señor Reed and his companion being half carried up Sutter's stairs. As the crowd dispersed into chattering groups, Perrimacoo headed for the gate. She trotted behind, saying, "Is the blue suit the captain? I don't understand." The English had been difficult.

"Campin 'ere, they are, till the Americans figger out wot they're trying to do." He reached the gate and shaded his eyes against the late sun, surveying the wagons, the tents and reed huts.

"Is Captain Sutter the headman?" she asked.

He waved at the men from the home place, who held the pigs in check, and strode toward them.

Hurrying behind, she called, "Who is headman now?"

He whirled to her with flat eyes. "See yon flag a'flyin?" He pointed back toward the courtyard. "Things ent the same, at's all. Now shut yer trap, or I'll pop ye good." He raised a hand.

Molok swooped through her mind, his huge shadow darkening the world. Yes, things were different now.

After supper Maria Howchia scrubbed every bit of her skin in river sand and swam into the current of the giant Río de los Americanos. She plucked cleansing herbs and tucked them into the bikoos. Walking back on the trail to the fort, she promised herself she would behave correctly in all things in preparation for the spirit dance. She would connect with power. Only power stopped bad luck.

Later, she laid the sleeping baby against an oak near the big ceremonial fire and joined Luis and many strangers in the dance lines, women stepping one direction, men the other. The different languages of the dancers didn't matter as the fire licked high against the dark plain. She sang her own chants, ignoring those who sang them wrong. She ignored the *Americanos* on the outside edge of the firelight, people who hadn't purified themselves. White children hopped and laughed alongside her. They had no idea how to speak with spirits, and that was bad. But she did her part properly, opening herself to power, hoping to seize a little of it.

A crisp breeze carried the smell of pigs smoking over a fire. Perrimacoo had sold them to *Americanos*. Now he sprawled in the shadows between the fires, drinking with his old friends. It occurred to her that *aguardiente* would help her forget the world and ignore the hopping *Americano* children. She left the dance line and went to her husband and signed that she wanted a swallow from his flask.

He handed to it her, his friends eyeing her.

The second time she left the dance line and went into the shadows and was drinking the fiery liquid, she heard a big graybeard say, "McCoon, that thar's one sweet lookin *bolsa*." She knew the word that reduced her to her woman's part.

"At she is." Perrimacoo reached, she thought for the flask, but grabbed her skirt and pulled it off, yanking her down.

"No." She yelled, rolling away in dirt powdered by animals and wagons. "The baby still drinks milk." She fought him, dust in her nose. Molok's powers were abroad. Things must be done right. Nursing women were not supposed to couple.

He giggled. She could almost see his tongue between his teeth when he sounded like that. "Help!" he said in a mocking tone to his friends, as he struggled to hold her. One grabbed her leg as she twisted to get away.

"I go dance!" she said.

"A spitfire!" Perrimacoo giggled, fighting to pin her hands down. "Johnson, ye auld fucker, give ye a poke, I will, fer a peso. Warm the bitch up." Laughter exploded from all the men. "I'll warm her good," said another leather shirt. "Me too," said another.

The big graybeard fell on her with his stinking beard thick in her nose and mouth. Gasping for air, she tried to heave him aside, but couldn't. Rough hands spread her thighs and held her shoulders down. Knees crushed her hands into the dirt. Horror squeezed her heart as the man opened his trousers. The man's part rammed her, making her breath suck inward in an inverted scream. She saw the slavering men waiting their turn, and bit her lip. The spirits hovered and Coyote laughed. She tried to focus her powers and make the men leave her alone. But she was too weak.

She choked back sound. A grown woman didn't cry.

All the next day she hid in a secluded corner outside the fort, a place where adobes were stacked, beyond the eyes of the leather shirts. She hurt, inside and out. All her husband's friends had coupled with her. The spirits could kill her. Strong power was loose, and she couldn't stop it.

A woman with a basket of nu-pah hesitated as she rounded the corner. Smiling in a kindly way, offering it, surprised to see her among the blocks of clay? Having refused to eat with Perrimacoo in the morning, Maria felt hunger squeezing her insides, and tried to smile in thanks. The woman sat beside her and they ate in silence, but the mush didn't fill the emptiness or quell the pain. Tears threatened, and she was grateful when the woman left with her basket. Maria Howchia felt no joy in the change of seasons, even with the coming of the time of rain.

Through a gap in the blocks she watched seven mules being loaded, tied with bulging leather bags. Then Luis came through the gate with Crying Fox and Captain Sutter. Still hidden by the blocks she crept nearer to hear the men, the baby asleep in the bikoos.

"You hang if mine mules die," Captain Sutter's voice said. "Iss clear? Even one." Fear gripped her. Her brother was in danger.

Crying Fox said, "No mule die." He was dressed in trousers, moccasins and a long-sleeved shirt, open at the chest revealing his pendant of blue crystals.

Luis added, "Big snow no come for a moon."

They were going to the eastern mountains again!

A small *Americano* in a big floppy hat and worn clothing approached on a horse, pulling two other horses tied together. Crying Fox mounted one and Maria Howchia forgot about being seen, forgot to be afraid of Sutter. She walked into the open.

In their own tongue Crying Fox said, "My sister, you look like you saw Bohemkulla." Even with that name on his tongue, he looked almost jovial as he sat on the fine horse.

She closed her eyes and moaned. "Molok."

Some of the joke faded from his eyes.

"Big bad luck comes. You must stay." Somehow she knew.

He dismounted and put an arm around her. "If bad power flies free, Sister, I am no safer here. Molok flies where he wishes."

"Don't go," she said, surprising herself with the urgent tone.

"Salvador," said the *Americano*, "let's git on up the trail."

Crying Fox patted her shoulder and mounted his horse.

She couldn't stop him.

Luis said "*Adios*." He and the small *Americano* eyed her a moment, then reined their horses around and trotted up the path that forded the American River. Crying Fox followed, and the three men headed toward the mountains.

She watched her brother disappear around a bend, then the string of mules, until nothing remained. Clouds were gathering, night coming. No one began a journey at night. No one went to the eastern mountains in time of rain. Last time he had gone it had been earlier in the season.

"Hello, *Liebchen*," said a voice. She turned. Captain Sutter was reaching for her.

18

It was overcast, nearly dark and somewhat chilly by the time Pedro arrived at the *terreno* around the fort, littered by canvas-topped wagons and campfires. He'd worn his sombrero from habit, not necessity. He wished he'd brought his sarape. Campfires winked beside the wagons under a darkening sky. He smelled coffee, ham and beans, and cattle dung and the oniony scent of human beings. Quick motion caught his eye. An Indian woman ran through the *Indio* huts pursued by a short man that looked like Captain Sutter. Could he be reduced to that?

Curious, Pedro nudged Chocolate through the immigrant camps, more than fifty wagons he guessed. These had to be the first of Sutter's Mormons, who were supposed to make him emperor in his own nation. But what were North American soldiers doing at the gate? He'd heard that Captain Frémont had come again, but not that there had been a takeover.

Passing wagons, he glanced at the immigrants, maybe ten or twelve to a campfire, all staring at him. More than one woman for each man? Yes. And swarms of children. Polygamists? More wagons arrived each day, he'd heard, and Sutter was letting them use his land. But not ten thousand. Nowhere near that number.

A child with a loose trouser strap ran toward him pointing and screaming, "Look, look, a Spaniard!"

Chocolate started to rear. As Pedro worked to control him, he was amused at the comical freckled face with brown hair slicked on either side of a center part, the boy gazing at him in admiration.

A woman with a determined gait approached, more children following. "Jonathan Rhoads, you know better'n point. Now git back to yer supper. All a you! Hear?" She pointed.

They slunk away, never taking their eyes off Pedro. He smiled to himself. The boy's tone implied the immigrants held Spaniards in esteem.

The woman said, "I'm sorry my kids got no better manners than that."

"It is nothing, señora."

An older man approached with a Kentucky ring maple rifle. He had a stocky build and thick, white hair. His pressed-together lips turned down like a horseshoe. "Thomas Rhoads is my name." He extended his hand.

Pedro reached down and squeezed leather and iron. "Honored to make your acquaintance, señor. I am Lieutenant Pedro Valdez." He nodded around at the wagons, "Are you Mormons?"

"All of us here." He gestured at a circle of ten to twelve wagons. "I am an Elder."

"Elder?" It was the term Indians used.

"A church leader."

Pedro jumped from the horse and swept his sombrero before the man. "Glad to make your acquaintance, esteemed Elder. Captain Sutter told me he was expecting ten thousand Mormons." He glanced momentarily toward the Indian huts and saw the Captain trotting like a child seeking a lost playmate.

"Ten thousand?" he asked incredulously. His deep brown eyes crinkled and his horseshoe mouth straightened in what must have been a smile. "Well, that'd be fine and dandy, but only a couple hundred came with me. You might say we're scouting. If it looks good, we might could get several thousand at that."

All looking for land. Time was running short. "With your permission," Pedro said, excusing himself.

He nudged Chocolate toward Sutter, cutting him off between wagons. "*Buenas noches, Colonel Sutter.*" Governor Pico and Sutter had made a series of agreements, one of which was Sutter's higher rank. Still most people called him Captain.

"Ach zo, Lieutenant Valdez. Vhat brings you here?" He glanced around for the girl.

"I came for Señor Sheldon's mail and to speak to you about land, Colonel." To his surprise he saw the pretty *Indita* peering around a hut behind Sutter's back, covering the baby's mouth, and he realized with a shock it was she Sutter was after. But she was revealing herself to Pedro, and he felt a rush of warmth that she trusted him to help.

Sutter was saying, "I am occupied now, Pedro." A man-to-man tone.

Pedro used the direct approach. "I noticed it was Perry McCoon's young wife you were after." Peeking from the hut, her large black eyes pleaded. He took care not to betray her location with his eyes.

Sutter raised his brows. "Iss zo? Perry McCoon hass taken my pretty little *liebchen?*" Then he laughed. "Now I know why he iss vanting der hog farm. Ha ha. And only yesterday I write in my journal dot Perry hass a son, and da mama iss Mary." He pressed his lips in a closed, confidential grin that spread his mustache. "Perry giffs me a half hour wit her, ya ya." He nodded toward a group of wagons near the west wall. McCoon was perched on a wagon tongue surrounded by *Norteamericanos*, mostly women, his *pinto* tied to the wagon.

The girl ducked out of sight, the gathering darkness helping, the clouds hastening the fall of night. "Colonel Sutter," he said, "I have an urgent matter I must discuss with you."

"Find yourself a *muchacha*, lieutenant. Ve talk on the morning." He whirled, searching.

McCoon was on his horse galloping around the wagons. The fires lit his antics and the faces of his enthralled audience. As the horse reached a measured stride, McCoon slowly rose to a crouch, almost standing, arms precariously at his sides. Then he fell back into the saddle.

A cheer exploded. The Englishman had been practicing. Now he rode through the parting crowd, leaned down from the saddle and picked up a coffee pot. He righted himself, brandishing the pot aloft. A loud, collective sigh of approval rose. McCoon's smile flashed across the distance, his face clean-shaven. His perfectly waved dark hair was clasped behind. A lady's man showing off for the ladies.

Pedro turned Chocolate back toward the fort gate, against the flow of North Americans hurrying toward the cheering. As he dismounted at the rail, the Rhoads family approached, two attractive girls, one short, one tall, following the older couple, numerous children bouncing around. *How many wives?* "*Hola,* señoras and señor," Pedro swept his sombrero to the ground.

The boy with the hair parted in the middle said, "We're gonna see that buck-arrow do tricks. Look Dad!"

"Vaquero," Pedro corrected. But it wasn't the fractured Spanish that bothered him. It was hearing the term applied to that scum of a runaway sailor.

The Rhoads family left and a full-throated shout exploded over by McCoon. As it trailed off, a small voice said, "*Gracias* for helping me Señor."

He whirled to the vanilla voice. "*Indita*, is that you?"

"Sí, Mary."

The tenderness of the tone took him by surprise and he went to where she stood, indistinct in the shadows behind the gate. The baby seemed asleep in its cradleboard on her back. Her skin smelled faintly of peaches. He touched a velvety shoulder, her thick hair brushing his hand. She seemed to welcome his touch. Unable to form words around his surging emotions, he put his arms around her and gentled her to him, his chin on her hair. Soft breasts yielded to his chest. He stifled a moan. "*María, María, María.*" What was happening? Where was this leading?

"Señor Sutter might come," she whispered, taking his hand, pulling him along the wall. Her warm little palm shot pleasant lightning into his depths, and he never wanted to let go. In the dark overcast no moon or stars illumined the plain; he saw her curvaceous figure by the faint light of the campfires. She rounded the corner and headed up the north trail past the adobe pit, toward the river.

She crouched and pulled him beneath the canopy of a large oak, a curtain of low branches catching his sombrero, which he removed and ducked down. Only one distant campfire glowed through a rounded canvas top and almost no light filtered inside the hanging branches. The dry grass and fallen leaves whispered beneath their feet and his heart labored in his breast.

He half saw, half heard María remove the cradleboard, set it in the leaves, and reach for him. He trembled inwardly as he kneeled beside her, so powerful his desire, so soft the breeze moving his hair as it came through the branches.

She pulled back and said, "I must not couple. It is bad now, when the baby still sucks milk. I want only to embrace you."

"Have no fear. I will hold you, *sólamente*." He touched her cheek and was surprised to feel tears. He traced them from her eyes to her trembling chin, then stroked her fragrant hair.

She put her arms around him and laid her cheek in the hollow of his throat. She felt small, soft, precious. If he couldn't lie with her, he would fill his mind with her. She seemed little more than a child, yet had a child of her own.

"How many years do you have, *Amapolita*?"

"Fifteen."

A poppy just opening. An owl hooted softly. Coyotes warbled. A screaming cheer said McCoon was still performing. Except for these bursts the night was quiet. "It honors me to hold you," he murmured into her hair. "I would hold you for a thousand years and not couple if you did not want it."

"*Muchas gracias, señor.*"

"For nothing." He felt a shudder in her. "I think you are unhappy. Maybe you dislike your husband looking for the attentions of the *Norteamericanas*?"

"I hope he couples with them all night." Not peevish.

"But he is the father of your child."

Without removing her cheek from his throat: "I am sorry I married him."

His pulse quickened. Regardless of what lay ahead, he felt he loved this girl. At first he had thought of her in connection with securing rancho labor. Now the land didn't enter in. He knew his love for her would heighten his conflict with McCoon, but the feel of her in his arms, the velvety skin of her back, the narrowness of her waist and roundness of her hips made him dizzy with *amor*. And now she didn't want McCoon. It was more than he had hoped. "Let's lie together in each other's arms."

She lay back, her hand warm through his shirtsleeve, pulling him down in the rustling leaves. He gathered her length to him, sorrowing that he had left her with Captain Sutter more than a year ago, and that McCoon had started his pig farm on her people's land.

She mumbled into the crook of his shoulder, "I trust you, Señor Valdez."

It opened his heart. "I am honored." He stroked her petal-like skin, cupped her full breasts and ran his thumbs over the toughened nipples. "If it does not worry you, I would like to remove my shirt. Only my shirt and bolero."

"My brother says not to lie with a man, except to couple."

"What do you think, señora?"

"I want your skin next to mine."

He pushed to his knees, tossed the vest aside and drew the shirt over his head.

She was saying, "Salvador said do not talk unless the thought is there four times." She paused. "I have not thought about this at all."

"Neither have I, señora." A roar of approval came from McCoon's side of the fort.

When it subsided, she said, "Please do not name me that."

He laid out the shirt and indicated she should lie on it. "I meant it only for respect. What should I call you?" He was naked to the waist and leaning down to meet her, the soft firmness firing his loins to exquisite pain.

"Name me anything but Señora McCoon."

Luxuriating, nearly dying of *sentimiento*, his voice came gravelly, "María." Her warm hand explored his back, banished the cool air, heated every part of him. He moaned, "María." It was a prayer, and though his lips hadn't uttered a Hail Mary for a long time, he thrilled to the name that meant the most blessed of women. He rubbed her cheek with his nose and felt hot tears. "You cry because of me?" *Señor en el Cielo, no.*

"Yes."

He held his breath. "If you do not want me, I will leave."

"No!" Then she was quietly sobbing, her whole body jerking. He hugged her tightly, trembling to contain his wild passion. "I do not want to make you cry."

She was trying to stop. "I — Talk later. Now love."

Ay Madre, the erupting desire he felt for this girl!

The roar from beyond the fort sounded to Maria Howchia like the growl of a menacing animal. She held this man in her arms and rejoiced to hear the thudding of his heart. It spoke of closeness, and she felt almost as a fearful young child feels in her father's safe arms, and that made the tears leak out. She felt cherished, and knew she would crave it always. That was the crux of the pain. Debasement and humiliation had crept up on her unawares, even before her husband's friends had coupled with her. She hadn't realized until now that her power had been so depleted. Her Spanish was too clumsy to put it into words.

"Does McCoon hurt you?" A quiet tone.

She was strong. McCoon's slaps didn't injure her, and when he picked up sticks and threatened, her body wasn't hurt. She felt embarrassed to be treated that way, and never admitted that it happened. But suspecting her husband stole her people's most sacred possession left her weak beyond consolation. Made her feel she had wronged the world. Made her feel like a bad thing that ought to be slapped, and she could only stagger away with eyes unfocused, trying not to care. Made her feel she deserved the husband she had selected, a man who gave her to his friends for their amusement and made her feel like a thing instead of a person, and she would welcome her death except for the baby. The magic of the man in her arms revealed all this to her. No tongue could convey half of it.

"No need to talk if you do not want to," he said in a deeper voice. "But if McCoon hurts even a hair on your head, *Amapolita*, my little poppy, I will kill him."

This frightened her. Men didn't make idle threats. Killing brought more killing, and retribution. She must not tell Proud Hawk that McCoon hit her. But perhaps he could do one thing. "When you talk with Captain Sutter, *por favor*, ask him if anyone at the fort has heard of the condor robe. Someone stole it from my people."

19

All night he lay with María in his arms. She slept toward morning, and at dawn, certain of her *sentimiento* for him, he kissed her cheek. She didn't wake up. The baby moaned in his sleep. Quietly Pedro took his sombrero and ducked through the curtain of hanging limbs. Making water outside the canopy, he smelled coffee and bacon. North American women bustled around their campfires with shawls over their shoulders, and as far as he could see, clabbering clouds dulled the sunrise. It looked like an early winter, a good time for setting his life in order.

He buttoned his flap and strode around the high wall toward the gate. First he would speak with Sutter, but it was early. The Captain was no doubt asleep. And what about McCoon? Brushing leaves from his *pantalones* and bolero, he walked beyond the gate toward where the *malcriado* had held his little show. Curiosity, and perhaps a little manly pride, drove him.

Only a few women and children moved around the wagons. A lanky woman straightened from a fire and stood, back of the hand on her forehead as she squinted at him. Beside her, a young boy stared openmouthed.

"Pardon me, señora, but I wish to find the man who rode his horse here last night. I would be grateful if you could tell me where he is."

She raised a leg and slapped her thigh. "My land! I wouldn't a believed if I hadn't a seed it!" She pressed her lips and lowered her voice to a conspiratorial tone. "Don't rightly know whar he went. Last I seen, that young widow Lewis was a hangin on im fer dear life. And her man only three weeks gone!" She rolled her eyes.

"I seen 'em!" screeched the boy. "In yonder trees." He pointed at a bunch of willows west of where Pedro and María had spent the night.

The woman raised her cloth to swat the boy.

"Geeman-ee Ma, he wanted to know!" The boy danced around the fire, easily escaping the swats, and flashed a grin at Pedro like he did this every day.

"Gracias," Pedro said, walking toward the willows. He saw McCoon's pinto tied in the thicket, and it was all he needed.

"Ach zo," Sutter said scratching his side, his bare toes wiggling as he stood at the door. "You be early on da morning. Come." He gestured Pedro inside and to the table. "Zit down. I dress now."

Pedro sat and placed his sombrero on the varnished pepperwood, hearing Sutter in his sleeping alcove — where he had handled María. How far had he gone? A chair scraped on wood. A boot dropped. The loathsome sweetish odor of unwashed bedclothing permeated the room.

Sutter called, "You interrupt a most unfortunate moment last evening." He emerged with a flask, his hair wet-combed, his mustache waxed. Sitting opposite Pedro, he handed him a letter postmarked USA for Jared Sheldon, rang his bell three times, and smiled. "Vhat bring you to mine establishment after zo long a time, hmm?" He offered the flask.

"No, gracias." He looked into the pale, watery eyes. What did Sutter think now about the mutiny in Los Angeles? Pedro wouldn't remind him. "I have two things. First, I have wanted land on the Río Cosumnes for a long time, the very piece, I am sorry to say, where Perry McCoon has the *puerco rancho*. *Por favor*, tell me if you think he will be granted title."

"I giff him already title." Sutter's expression lay between irritation and challenge. He tipped the flask to his lips.

Pedro's mind shot back to the letter of authority he had helped translate before the farcical war, the qualifying words — if the land has been properly granted, if the owner has died. Sutter couldn't grant the land at María's village. Unless — "Did Governor Pico extend your powers after the war?" Pico was to be the acknowledged governor until the territory was officially split.

Sutter's cheeks turned pink and he glared at Pedro. Then Manu-iki opened the door and came to the table, her golden fruit as lush as ever. Sutter ordered breakfast and gazed at her with somewhat less attention than before. He looked at the door shutting behind her and turned to Pedro. "My powers haff been sufficient before my unfortunate arrest."

Translation: no land-granting authority. Pedro set aside vagaries. He had waited too long to let courtesy stand in the way of understanding. "I recall that Governor Micheltorena gave you authority only to re-issue land which — "

Sutter jumped to his feet and slapped the table with both hands, chair tipping behind his legs. "Enough. Ve finish."

Pedro stood, half a head taller. "Please forgive my rudeness, Colonel Sutter.

Accept my humble apology." But he was glad he knew the true situation.

The large sapphire eyes glared and the waxed points of his mustache quivered above his parted teeth. Pedro picked up his sombrero and turned to go.

Again, Manu-iki pushed open the door with her shapely, tightly covered backside. She carried a full tray to the table — steaming cups, fried pork, fragrant rolls, a cask of butter and tin pitcher of milk.

The flush drained from Sutter's face and he sat down and flapped his hand. "Sit, Lieutenant. Eat." He sucked on the *aguardiente* and offered it to Pedro. "Trink!"

"No, gracias." He wanted to get back to María, but he remembered that playing host brought out the best in Sutter, and he needed the man's goodwill. Sometimes what people believed was more important than writing on paper. If Sutter thought he was handing out land titles, why shouldn't Pedro get one?

He placed his hat on the table, smiled at departing Manu-iki, sat, poured milk and spoke in a courteous tone. "Muchas Gracias, Esteemed Colonel. Forgive me please. I have been badly out of touch at Rancho Omuchumne. Perhaps you would be so good as to grant me another piece of land."

Sutter poured the liquor into his coffee. "If you haff ask before summer, maybe. Now tings change. Captain John Frémont says he hass authority of the fort, and mine trappers and immigrants say they haff seize Upper California for an independent nation. They arrest General Vallejo, so iss unclear."

Buttering bread as that sank in — General Vallejo arrested! — Pedro saw Sutter's confusion as he continued. "But Captain Frémont leafs again. As before. Den I haff mine establishment back. Den I grant land, ya." He was about to pour *aguardiente* into Pedro's coffee.

He flattened his hand over the cup. "No, no, *por favor* no. But Colonel, where is General Vallejo now?"

"In the calaboose." Sutter flicked his wrist over his shoulder.

Horrified, Pedro jumped up. "General Vallejo! In the *calabozo*? Here? Now?" It was barbaric to throw a noble officer in that lice-infested place like a common soldier! How could Sutter sit there calmly eating?

He patted the air over Pedro's side of the table. "Zo unfortunate. Zit. In da beginning I entertain General Vallejo here in mine rooms." His eyes had a sorry dog look. "I sent a barrel of brandy and other delicacies from Yerba Buena, and showed the General mine hospitality." He raised his brows. "Zit please."

Pedro sat and Sutter continued. "Captain Frémont iss no goot officer. He scream at me dot I know not how prisoners be treated. I say to him, ya I know." He nodded like a wise man. "I haff myself been a prisoner."

Pedro listened to a story of how Frémont had declared Sutter incompetent to manage the prisoners. He had left a young Lieutenant, an Army artist named Ned Kern in charge of the fort. General Vallejo's lodging in the *calabozo* was Kern's doing. Sutter selected a slab of fried pork and stuffed his mouth, talking and chewing. "Before he leaf, Captain Frémont says to me I am to be arrested! In mine own establishment! If I even walk wit General Vallejo by the river." He leaned forward. "Frémont iss *schlecht!*" With that wet word a particle of moist food flew to Pedro's cheek, and stuck. "He says if Vallejo escapes, I be hanged!" He tipped the flask to his lips.

Pedro surreptitiously wiped his cheek with two fingers. "Where is Captain Frémont now?"

Sutter shrugged. "Chasing after General Castro. Ach zo many troubles I haff now! Men haff been shot. Iss war now wit the United States." An expression of helplessness spread over him. "But I vait. Frémont leaf some day."

So, it starts. Pedro recalled the *Norteamericanos* drinking in the middle of the Los Angeles River. Now they would fight on the same side. The United States controlled the fort, perhaps claimed the interior. And Sutter, the ranking Mexican officer, hadn't resisted. What would happen to New Helvetia? Sheldon's rancho? Pedro looked across the table at a pathetic figure whose powers, whatever they once were, were crumbling, and knew he was talking to the wrong man about land.

Unless the Mormons ... He swallowed his coffee without tasting. "I met Señor Elder Thomas Rhoads outside. Maybe his Mormons will help you fight Frémont and help you get the fort back."

Savagely Sutter ripped a roll and plunged it in his liquored coffee. "No. They come far, running from bad fights in Illinois." He popped dripping bread into his mouth, chewed and shrugged. "One cannot ask dot men fight the United States Army in da moment der vagons schtop." He scowled. "*Gott im himmel*, some of dem ride wit Captain Frémont! The son of Elder Rhoads also!" The lost-boy expression Pedro had seen on the Los Angeles plain flickered across his features — a man who couldn't even ride properly.

Suddenly Pedro knew as surely as he breathed that this was no European gentleman officer. Somehow he had acquired a uniform and fooled the authorities with his grand manner. No doubt he selected the California wilderness because it was far from those who knew him. "Colonel," Pedro said, "I can't rest while General Vallejo is in the *calabozo*." He selected his words so as not to offend. "Has Lieutenant Kern given you reason to, ah, fear the United States Army?"

"No. Kern iss weak, hass a bloody cough." He described the pitiful condition of Frémont's men when they arrived, and how Sutter had brought them back to health with food and liquor, the second time. Sutter's voice lifted and Pedro almost saw his mind coming to a conclusion. "I try wit General Vallejo again. Ya ya." Smiling with his old confidence, he reached across the table and put his hand on Pedro's sleeve.

"*Está bien.*" Pedro disengaged the touch by reaching for a rind of pork. He wished he could as easily shake the thought of Sutter with María. "The second matter I come to speak of."

"Ya ya?" He straightened in his chair and assumed the look of the justice of the peace of the Big Valley.

"I have learned that a condor robe was taken from the village on the Río de los Cosumnes where Perry McCoon has his pig farm." He recalled McCoon's fascination with it the night they watched the *Indios* dance, and how good the pain had felt when his knuckles smashed into those perfect teeth. "Do you know anything about it?"

"It makes da Russians heppy. I giff to dem."

"Where did you get it?"

"I best not say." He looked at Pedro as if assessing whether there would be a recurrence of doubt about his authority.

Only a man like McCoon would do this, Pedro knew. "Where is the robe now?"

"In Russia by now."

José y María! He had hoped to get it back. After a moment, in which he wondered how María would take this news, he said, "*Por favor*, I would like to visit General Vallejo."

In the courtyard dogs were fighting over scraps from the kitchen. *Norteamericano* carpenters planed boards between sawhorses and children of immigrants darted about. Walking with Sutter, Pedro thought he felt María's eyes on him, and it felt good. A plan was forming in his mind, but first he must see if there was anything he could do for the General.

Halfway across the yard they met Lieutenant Kern and three soldiers. Sutter was obsequious. "Your Worship," he said to Kern, "mine friend Pedro Valdez here tells me Californios be sad dot der esteemed General Vallejo is by us treat as a common soldier while he is zo unfortunately detained by you."

The birdlike young man — probably ten years younger than Pedro, but a real lieutenant with a red stripe on his sleeve — said, "The opinions of this greaser, or, fer that matter, the one over there, don't make no never mind to me." He jabbed his thumb at the gun tower.

Pedro felt possibilities evaporate. A lieutenant in the United States Army would be unlikely to speak rudely to a native Californian unless it were condoned by his commanding officer.

Atop the pools of white, Sutter's eyes were focused on Kern. "I am sorry to report to you, esteemed Lieutenant Kern, dot our supplies be down. From now on, all men be served gruel for breakfast, corn cakes for dinner, and perhaps a little jerked beef for supper. The brandy iss unfortunately, entirely gone." He signaled Manu-iki, who watched from the kitchen house.

The young officer looked at her, then back. "Why didn't you say nuthin yesterday?"

"I haff heard it today. Zo many guests! Ach zo much eating! And food for the starving Donners!" He threw out his hands helplessly. "Now, if you excuse us, I must say this bad news to our honored prisoners."

Kern's bird eyes snapped. "My men will examine the storage rooms."

Sutter's pupils leveled like gray gunboats. "You not trust me, hmm? Haff I not feed you like a king? And my cooks criticize? And now ve all eat poor, hmm?"

Kern asked to speak to Sutter alone. Pedro headed for the gun tower, three North American soldiers trailing. He opened the door and held his breath against the stench. The light from the door revealed several figures sitting and lying in straw, one scratching under his shirt, the other clawing his beard. Vallejo's men were also jailed. "General Vallejo?"

"Sí." A short stocky shape came to the bars.

Mindful of the soldiers at his back, Pedro whispered. "I am Pedro Valdez. Perhaps you remember — with the helmet? It humiliates me more than I can say to see Your Honor in this place. Somehow I will get you out, and take you to Joaquín Sheldon's rancho. You will be safe there."

A warm chuckle and a conversational tone surprised him. "Of course I remember you. And the helmet. But Lieutenant, we have considered the situation and we believe our interests are well served by Upper California coming under the control of the United States." He sighed. "We must stay prisoners for a while."

What was this? It was as if sand shifted beneath his feet. He whispered, "Because they listen?" He thumbed over his shoulder.

"They speak no Spanish and I wouldn't care if they did." General Vallejo sounded like a man spreading glad tidings: "The Mexican revolution has been a grave disappointment. Each time we Californians try to govern ourselves, centrists take over in Mexico City and the government ignores us. Not one square league of land around Sonoma has been granted in over a year, though I have sent numerous petitions. Meanwhile, the United States has just granted vast lands in Oregon to its settlers. In the United States people of geographic areas rule themselves. That's what we need in Upper California. In the United States trade is wide open. We would prosper. We would receive help in fighting the Horse-thief *Indios*. Señor Valdez, I have been in touch with *Norteamericanos* about this. For years."

More sand shifted. Small wonder Vallejo hadn't fought General Castro. He had other things on his mind. "But it is an outrage for you to be in this hole."

Vallejo chuckled. "The lice in New Helvetia are huge, it is true, and I may have little blood left, but I must wait here until Frémont and his rowdies finish terrorizing the countryside. You see, Mexico will lose without question. It is sad, but when the laws of the United States replace the tyranny of Frémont, I want no man charging me with subversion or resistance. I came peacefully. I stay peacefully. I endure the lice with fortitude. That must be understood."

Mexico will lose without question. Pedro let out his air. All ties with Old Spain would vanish. But if he couldn't rescue the General, he might as well learn from him. "What is the meaning of the Bear Flag?" Flying in the courtyard.

Vallejo snorted. "An excuse to plunder my rancho. Frémont is encouraging those men who came to Sonoma and declared their so-called Bear Flag Republic. My guess is he's humoring them so they'll ride with him to fight Mexico — did you know there is great resistance in the south? Then watch, as soon as he doesn't need their rifles, he'll hoist the U.S. stars and stripes. The bear flag will be forgotten. Would you do me a favor?"

"Sí, General. Anything."

"Tell Joaquín Sheldon, Rufus Chabolla — all our countrymen — not to resist Frémont. We native Californianos must be seen as friends."

"I will tell them." Sheldon wasn't about to fight anyway, and Pedro's mind was on land. "The Captain told me he issued a land grant after his release in Los Angeles."

"Impossible! He hasn't the authority."

"That was my belief. I would like to petition for that same piece."

The General whickered like a horse. "To whom? Wait *amigo*. We are working with the United States to assure that those who have land will keep it. Next comes the treaty with the United States. After that we'll learn what agency to petition for new grants."

As Pedro tried to imagine petitioning the United States, Lieutenant Kern's voice came from behind, speaking to the soldiers.

"Escort Mr. Vallejo to Mr. Sutter's rooms," he said.

Pedro smiled in the dark. Sutter had won. It was amazing what men did for food and liquor. And gratifying to know he, Pedro, hadn't served six years under a fool. As they herded the prisoners out of the cell he was also amused to recall Sutter's testiness about General Vallejo. Now they were on the same side. Pedro watched the portly little General being escorted across the yard toward the portly little Captain who might have become an emperor. *If* ten thousand Mormons had come. *If* he'd been that breed of natural leader known as a European Military Officer. If if if. He could almost hear his Indian grandmother say, "Coyote is smiling." She had a point too, about the schemes of men. But General Vallejo had revived Pedro's hope about Rancho Sacayak. No land had been granted. And, unlike Sutter, the U.S. government cared nothing about Perry McCoon. As soon as the war was over, Pedro would petition the United States. Maybe Señor Sheldon would help.

But now it was time to take María. Never had he felt so sure about anything. She made him appreciate the Indian in him, and the Spaniard in him wouldn't let any other man possess her, not after last night.

20

Billy slept and Maria Howchia sat quietly inside the cattail u-macha, where several *Indios* called Maidu lay napping. Little work was being done at the fort now. She had an unobstructed view of the gate, and hoped to see Pedro soon. He had come back to her, where she had waited beneath the tree, and, with something new and wonderful in his eyes, told her to hide in an *Indio* house until he came for her. He had kissed her with passion and power. She would wait for him no matter how long it took. He had men to see, he'd said, including the bootmaker. His boots opened like little mouths.

A horse pounded up to the gate, frothing with sweat. A blue suit jumped off, unlaced a saddle pack, and handed a package to the blue suit who stood beside the wheeled cannon. The latter glanced at the package and the two trotted across the courtyard and up Sutter's stairs. Soon afterward Sutter came to his door ringing a handbell. *Indios* climbed the stairs, then ran down and sped away. Runners. Later Captain Sutter came down, and the drummer appeared ratatat-tatting like a frantic woodpecker, the signal for people to gather. Something important had happened.

The napping people yawned and looked out the entrance. Wagon people and *Indios* were streaming through the gate. The Maidus wasted no time in answering the call of the drum — a break in routine was always exciting — but she stayed. Proud Hawk had said wait.

The Walla Wallas, a wealthy people who for many sleeps had been camping beyond the wagons, were now arriving at the gate. The Maidus had said Yellow Snake, the Walla Walla headman, was here with his people negotiating reparations for the killing of his kinsman by one of the Captain's friends. The Walla Wallas had been trying to talk to Sutter for more than a moon, and if he didn't satisfy them, they would make war on the fort. Now they moved through the gate like tall Immortals in their supple deerskin suits, the men gripping fine bows. But the most amazing was Yellow Snake's daughter. The morning clouds had blown away and the sun shone full on her shimmering form. She moved like a column of sparkling water. Coils upon coils of bright reflecting beads hung about her neck, descending in opulent ropes to her waist. Sprays of the little mirrors dangled from her ears to her shoulders and looped between her braids and over her forehead. Rows of them blazed from her long skirt and moccasins. To look at her was to be struck in the eyes. Her beauty blinded. Captain Sutter would negotiate with caution in the face of such wealth.

Beyond the shining form Maria suddenly saw Pedro — beckoning.

She picked up sleeping Billy, shrugged into the straps of the bikoos and hurried toward the man who made her a woman again. Dirty leathershirts were arriving on horses, dismounting and greeting their friends. Rancheros and their women were rattling up in wagons, excited children jumping out. She walked with the crowd into the courtyard, where the Walla Wallas stood patiently waiting alongside men and women of every hue of skin and form of dress. Several blue suits stood facing each other at the high pole from which the bear banner hung limply.

Pedro stepped to her side in new brown boots, the star-shaped wheels on his heels jingling. His grey eyes invited her into him, and she stood beside him, thrilled, caring little that Perrimacoo would see them.

He took her hand, and a current of power fused them. This too was fated, Molok dreaming, not for her to question. "Did Captain Sutter speak of the robe?"

"Later," he said with a squeeze of her hand, holding it between their thighs.

Captain Sutter came down his staircase with something under his arm. A broad-shouldered, *Americano* almost blocked her view, and more people were squeezing in. She caught a glimpse of Sutter pulling the rope attached to the bear banner. It squeaked and jerked down the pole. Then, after much moving about by the blue suits, a new banner jerked up the pole. Thrilled by the magic in Pedro's hand, she watched the flag arrive at the top, all the faces in the courtyard upturned, and as a breeze luffed it, she saw red and white stripes and white stars sprinkled against a square of blue.

A BOOM compressed her heart. The earth jumped. She felt it up her bones. Instinctively she grabbed Pedro's arm. The baby wailed on her back; other babies screamed. Dogs howled and barked. Pedro's lips formed a word, but another boom sounded. "Cannons," he repeated with a smile. She covered her ears. The booms continued. Window glass shattered and tinkled around the courtyard. *Americanos* laughed and pointed. At last the cannon thunder stopped and she stood rubbing her ears. All the babies were crying along with Billy. Young *Americano* children wept into their mothers' long skirts and their mothers patted their backs.

Captain Sutter was about to speak when a blue suit stepped forward and began to orate. She was trying to see Sutter's reaction when the big *Americano* blocked her view by leaning over and quietly speaking to his woman.

"Ladies and gentlemen . . . " the blue suit began, but with Billy crying at her back she heard little.

The people in front moved, which left Maria open to Captain Sutter. He was scowling and blinking at the orating blue suit, who spoke loudly to be heard above Billy, most of the other babies having stopped. Then both Sutter and the blue suit turned and looked at her. She stepped behind a man with a brown beard down to his waist. He was bobbing his head and saying, "Ach ya." The woman beside him wore a high comb and mantilla over smoothed black hair and a full black dress gathered at the sleeves. The high comb blocked Sutter's eyes, but Billy continued attracting attention by his howling.

" . . . as President Polk . . . Manifest Destiny . . . California into the fold."

People cheered but turned to stare at her and Billy. Proud Hawk smiled down at her, the crow's feet at the corners of his gray eyes speaking his happiness that she stood beside him, telling her not to worry. He looked back at the blue suit, and she glanced around at the assortment of peoples, many looking between her and the speaker — the Mokelumne, Wapumne, Ochehamne, Nisenan and Maidu, Walla Wallas, wagon people, women with tunnel hats and chalky skin, blue suits with shiny buttons, *Españolo* ranchers in boleros and sombreros, leathershirts with huge bushy beards — including the one with black skin and strips of red cloth woven into his fat braids. She was embarrassed to recognize some of the leathershirts who had coupled with her, but glad the gray beard named Johnson was not there. Suddenly she saw Perrimacoo on the other side of the flag pole, standing between *Americanas*, one in a yellow dress. As if feeling her eyes, he turned and looked at Maria, and at her hand in Pedro's, then at Pedro. He might kill them both, if he knew about last night. Men had the right.

She started to unclasp her hand, but Pedro squeezed it firmly, and looked at Perrimacoo.

" . . . common tongue to be the English language." She moved behind the comb and mantilla. The tightening of her stomach told her to leave this place immediately. Perrimacoo had stepped to the side to see her better and Captain Sutter was looking at Pedro. *Americanas* were staring too, with angry faces. Billy continued to scream — the only baby still crying.

"My man is looking," she said trying to take her hand away. She had to leave.

"Not a problem," Proud Hawk said, firmly holding her hand and looking over his high nose at the speaker. "He is a coward."

The blue suit leveled terrible eyes at her, but continued, " . . . soon a star for California . . . flag represents that destiny. Commodore Sloat needs . . . We shall respond." She couldn't understand any of it.

Unable to bear more, she said, "I go," and wrenched her hand loose and slipped back through the gawking people, wedging between them, nudging them aside, and never looked back. She ran out the gate and around the corner of the wall to the big oak where she and Pedro had spent the night. Fearful Perrimacoo would follow, she crawled in behind the wide trunk and peered out from it. Perhaps Pedro would follow too, thinking Perrimacoo would kill her. He said he would kill him if he touched her in anger. They could all die. But perhaps — she hoped —*Españoles* didn't follow women and crying babies.

Heart pounding with fear and confusion, she shrugged out of the bikoos and hugged Billy to her breast, his lashes and red face wet with tears. She must quiet him or go hide by the river. With one eye on the corner of the wall, she crooned him a sleeping song, and gradually the hiccoughing sobs grew further apart. Up the trail by the fort wall, dogs sniffed around the wagons. She listened for the speaker, but heard only bursts of cheering — as she had before the sleep. With Pedro's arms around her, she had felt warmth and peace. Some of the dread had lifted from her spirit after she confided to him about the missing robe. But now, perhaps he would never want to see her again. Did it matter? She was Perrimacoo's woman. She could only hope she hadn't brought them all to their deaths.

No one came around the high adobe wall, and Billy slept. Through the branches she caught glimpses of the red, white and blue banner above the high wall. The clouds were thickening over the eastern mountains. She felt moisture in the air and smelled leaves beginning to molder on the earth. The season was changing. Beyond the fort the golden grasslands stretched peacefully, expectantly, as far as she could see.

A thunderous roar continued for a longer time. Then the first people appeared — *Americanas* and their children. They climbed into wagons left standing with harnessed horses. But no Perrimacoo. Maybe he didn't care about her. And Proud Hawk? Would he be angry with her for leaving as she did?

Suddenly a dark horse was galloping wildly around the wagons. She slipped the bikoos on her back and crawled to the tree's drip line to see better. The rider wore a sombrero. It was Pedro! What was he doing? People jumped out of the way as he came through the wagons. He slowed, sitting the horse sideways to her, then lunged directly toward her. She stood up in the path not knowing where this dream was going.

He didn't slow and she assumed he wanted a passing glimpse of her before leaving the fort. But the horse was upon her and hands squeezed the breath out of her as she was whisked off the ground and up into the saddle with the high round knob — Proud Hawk leaning into her from behind, the baby between. They tilted to the side as the horse circled around, pounding back toward the wagons and staring people.

She couldn't help but grin into the wind, thrilled at the way he had picked her up, strangely fearless about Perrimacoo. People were pouring from the gate, returning to huts, wagons and camps. They backed out of the way, watching the horse cut expertly through, the harnessed horses stepping fitfully about. Pedro seemed to be looking for somebody, the big straw hat turning this way and that as he guided the animal. Then they were racing full tilt outside the large encampment, all eyes upon them as the horse stretched beneath them. They passed by Captain Sutter at the gate, hands on his hips, staring at them. The horse slowed to a fast walk and Pedro guided it toward the gate. She felt like she was in a story she'd never heard before, and didn't know the end. But one thing was certain, Pedro Valdez had his own power; he no longer did Captain Sutter's bidding.

He veered left, then stopped abruptly, hugging her so she didn't lurch forward.

There stood Perrimacoo before them! He had his arm around the waist of an

Americana in a yellow striped dress, one who had been beside him at the oration. She was a little older than Maria, her pale face looking perplexed inside a yellow tunnel hat. Perrimacoo looked beyond Maria as if she were a stranger. She watched his hands, afraid he would pull his gun on Pedro. But his arm stayed around the *Americana* and his shoulders were slack, his weight slung to one hip.

"I take her to my house," Pedro said.

The *Americana* turned the tunnel toward Perrimacoo. He glanced around as if trying to figure out who Pedro was talking about, gave the woman his best sideways smile. Then said to Pedro, "Hit's about time, greaser."

The woman frowned at Maria's breasts and said, "I don't understand."

Perrimacoo guided her quickly away, murmuring to her as she looked back over her shoulder.

Confusion swirled around Maria — relief that her man hadn't pulled his gun, joy to be with the man she wanted, and puzzlement and anger that her husband had denied her. He was Billy's father. She felt a slight tremor in Proud Hawk, then with a tinkle of spurs the horse lunged into a rocking gallop, flying east up the trail. When she caught her breath and felt secure gripping the knob, she turned partway back in the saddle and yelled to be heard over the pounding hooves, "He looked like he didn't know me." All she saw was the wide curve of the sombrero.

"He has another woman."

"Is that how *Americanos* leave their women?"

"Maybe."

Hope lifted her spirit with each lunge of the big animal. The long black mane flew back toward her and Pedro squeezed her between his arms as he pulled on the rein, slowing the horse to a walk. They were already well beyond the fort, a speck in the midst of an endless sea of grass and she loved him behind her, his warm breath on her ear.

"Can a woman of your people leave her husband?" he was asking.

"Yes."

"How?"

"Throw his things out of the house."

He was quiet a while, then said, "*Españolas* cannot do that."

"What stops them?"

"My people are married by God. In His eyes they are married for all time."

The Great Spirit in the sky. What power it must have! To marry people for all time. "Are you married?" It came out weak, for she feared his response.

"No."

A wondrous word. She let out her breath and almost laughed at a flock of quail racing comically up the trail before the walking horse, beating their wings into roaring flight at the very last moment before they got stepped on. But he had said nothing about marrying her. And nothing about the condor robe. She knew he wouldn't have it in the saddle bags; she had warned him not to touch it, even look at it. He understood that he must arrange its handling with Turtle Claw.

For a long time she rocked with him in silence, savoring the warmth of him through his shirt and trousers, and trying not to think how the world was fracturing into a scramble of unaligned power. But at last she asked about the robe.

He sighed. "Captain Sutter says it is in Russia."

"Can you get it back?"

"No, *Amapolita mía.*" My precious little poppy. He nuzzled her neck. "Please do not be unhappy with me. I would do anything else for you, but I cannot go to Russia."

Of course he couldn't. She hadn't thought about that four times. Russia was across the western sea. Father had told her that. Now the robe couldn't be retrieved, except by very powerful magic. She shivered to think of the feather vestment in faraway places, gazed upon without scruple, touched by unpurified people. Terrible luck would plague the Russians, and Captain Sutter and — "Did Perrimacoo take it?"

"Captain Sutter would not tell me."

It didn't matter. Doom would fall on the *umne* who had allowed it be stolen, and upon her. But for the moment, cradled in Pedro's arms, she felt like she could fend off whatever was coming. She felt lucky. "Where is my brother?"

"With Luis and an *Americano* named Charlie Stanton. They are taking food to the Donner Party, in the mountains."

She remembered the spirit warning. But nothing could be done about that, or the robe. Welded like this to Proud Hawk and swaying with him as tight as the babe in her bikoos, it seemed they were all one person, and it felt so good that she dared start talk that was a man's prerogative.

"How do your people become married?" Many more than four times she had wondered about that.

Almost afraid to breathe, she watched a herd of antelope flow like water over the high grass, rising and falling like salmon swimming upstream, legs tucked beneath their bellies. Then one of his hands gave the other the braided rein and the free hand cupped her breast and pressed it. His hand felt calloused and strong but gentle and his voice was husky in her ear.

"*Amapolita*, touching you like this has married us. *Comprendes*? In God's eyes we are married. Later a *padre* can say the matrimonial mass." He slid his hand down over her waist and hip and caressed her thigh as he murmured, "Now you must throw Perry McCoon's things out of his house."

Happy tears blinded her as she twisted around in the saddle and kissed the slightly down-curved tip of his nose, then his mouth, pulling back to say, "I never lived in his house. I am your woman and we are married." Strong emotion overpowered her.

"María, my sweet *Indita. Te quiero.*" He reined the horse to a stop and pulled her to him and kissed her hungrily. A spot of power near the tip of his tongue electrified her, a metallic taste and she lost herself in the world of softness between the bristles of his mustache and trimmed beard. She wanted to kiss him forever but after a long time her back felt sore.

She turned and gazed happily down the hill. They had stopped overlooking the valley of the Cosumnes, the ancient bluffs and gently rolling hills that channeled the river southward, the line of white mountains far in the distance, more white on them than she'd ever seen in this season. She pushed away the thought of Crying Fox up there. Here, longhorns grazed peacefully in the lowlands and smoke curled above the yellowing cottonwoods. Pedro's home was beautiful. She was eager to live here in her new man's house and cook and gather for him. Blue Star lived here too, with her man Quapata. Life would be good in the bottomland.

He hopped off the horse and reached for her. She leaned into his arms and slid down his length and stood in his arm, the baby cheerfully cooing at her back — a sign that this was right. And as they gazed at the quiet scene, a rush of strength coursed through her, enlarging her in every way, and with it came the aching hope that the Great Spirit with the power to marry people for all time would help realign the loose power careening through the world. She would do her part by observing the rules of living and not couple while nursing.

She felt lucky — for now.

II

Elitha

21

SIERRA NEVADA MOUNTAINS, December 1846

Snowmelt from the heat of the fire leaked through the rotting hides laid over the canvas tent. Plink plink plink reverberated in the enclosed space. Fourteen-year-old Elitha Donner wondered just how deep under the snow the tent was now, with the storm so bad up above.

Icy water dripped on Pa, who lay quietly against the oozing tent wall. It dripped on Tamsen, who Elitha called Ma, lying next to Pa where she could feed the small fire. It dripped on the quilts over Frances, Georgia, and tiny Ellie, who were huddled together for warmth, silent now after talking about mashed potatoes with milk gravy. Plink — into the muddy pool between the beds. Plink.

It dripped on Mrs. Wolfinger who lay by the living pine on the other side of Leanna. Leanna was Elitha's only one-hundred percent sister, and not much of a talker. Thankfully she rarely complained of hunger, and Elitha was glad for her warmth coming through both sets of stockings, petticoats and cloaks. Sometimes she and Leanna changed places and for a time Elitha warmed up in the middle. But she was two years older and had a stronger constitution, so most of the time she lay on the outside.

Wiping off a drop with the edge of the quilt, she recalled the time when she and Leanna had a different mother. Then Mary Blue had died, and not long afterward Pa married the school teacher, Tamsen. Some said a women in her forties was too old to be having babies one after the other, and it was true the three little girls had made a lot of work. But Elitha had been eight and Leanna six when it started, so they helped a lot. And Tamsen had a way of making work seem fun. She also taught them to paint with pigments and told them of the ingenious ways that plants spread their seeds. The young people of California were lucky to be getting a school run by Tamsen Donner, with stacks of books and glass vials for plant specimens. That is, if it didn't all spoil in the wagon. Winter was only half over. Elitha sighed. At least they knew where the wagon was, unlike the poor frozen cattle.

"I wanna go up and see the sun." Ellie's baby voice.

"The sun's not out," Tamsen said.

"Is it night?"

"I don't think so."

Elitha listened for the fap fap of the tent door and knew it was still storming up above. To save their strength the family stayed in bed. Ma insisted.

It was quiet again, except for the fap fap and the plink plink. Elitha spent most of her time reflecting on how life had been up to now. They all did. She knew Pa felt terrible that they hadn't got through to California before the snow fell. People blamed him and Mr. Reed for taking the cutoff. Stupid, they said, to chop a road through a forest when a fine broad trail lay to the north. But they were wrong about it being Pa's fault. Every one of them agreed to leave the main trail and go the way Mr. Hastings' book showed. And they'd still have gotten through if it hadn't snowed so early. Even Mr. Sutter's Indians had said it never snowed much in November. So maybe it was God's fault. But He wouldn't do that on purpose, would He? At this point her thinking always came to a dead end.

In the firelight the tent had a fleshy tint flickering with dark shadows, day and night the same. And day and night the smell of mildewed hides simmering on the fire kept her on the verge of nausea. There was nothing else to eat. Added to that was the stench of the honey pot, and people adding to it.

When would this storm end? So the honey pot could be carried up the ice stairs and dumped. Up on top the snow would glisten in the dazzling sunlight and she would fill her lungs with fresh, cold air. She could sit on the firewood, drying her cloak. Sometimes when it was clear like that, Ma brought up the pigments, which she'd thought to take from the wagon, and paint the white mountains on canvas. Elitha loved to watch.

But now wind whistled down the tunnel of ice stairs and Elitha tugged the quilt around her shoulder. At least they had fire now. During that first bad storm the wind had snuffed it out and the family lay in blackness for eight days. Pa counted. How he knew day from night mystified her. She had shivered so hard it made her back sore, and, staring into the teeth-chattering blackness, she'd had the terrifying thought that she was already dead and this was the real hell, and everybody had been mistaken about hell being hot. But then she'd stopped such foolish thinking and hugged Leanna.

Jean Baptiste had put boards outside the tent door to stop the wind. Only small drafts teased the flames now, made them flicker and jump. She worried about Jean Baptiste on account of the hired men's wigwam being so poorly made. That first night when the wind blasted and Pa decided to make camp and wait out the storm, she had wondered how the men got their lean-to up at all after struggling so long with the family tent. She had seen the desperation in their faces when the wind stole the canvas from their stiff fingers.

She sighed. All the hired men were dead now, except Jean Baptiste. Pa had gone to their tent when the first one slipped away into happy delirium. He thought he was a boy again, warm and eating at his mother's table. Ma said the next one died like a tired child going to sleep. The third confessed that back on the plains he'd helped kill Mr. Wolfinger. That's what Ma said, that last time they sat above sketching the mountains.

Elitha had felt a thrill of fright. "Why did they kill him?" She put down her paintbrush.

"Greed," Ma said. "Mr. Wolfinger carried a bundle of money. Must of had more in his wagon." Tamsen cocked her head at her artwork, adding, "That's why people call gold the root of all evil." Her sharp-boned face was hidden in the shadows of her hood, but Elitha could tell she wasn't really looking at the painting. It was often so, as if she stared at an unseen presence. The silence of the mountains was almost painful, the tall pines whispering so faintly up in their snowy tips you had to strain to hear it.

Now a blast of wind rattled the boards at the door, and Elitha turned over in bed, remembering the fun of helping Ma sew ten thousand dollars of gold coins inside the apple-green quilt. They had also stashed money in a cunning little money cache built into a false side of the wagon, and there was more in Pa's fat money belt.

Killed Mr. Wolfinger. The murderers might sneak back and try to steal the Donner's money too. Mightn't they? And kill everybody? The other people of the party were stranded miles and miles up the trail. She knew this because Mr. Reed's teamsters had come back to see if the Donners were all right. At first Pa had figured the rest of the wagon train had made it over the pass. But they hadn't. And if Reed's men could come back, so could the murderers. It was something to worry about, because last summer on the prairie she'd caught a fragment of conversation as she passed the Rhoads' family fire, big John Rhoads saying, "The Donners are wealthy people." At the time she'd felt proud. But now money seemed a danger, and all the gold in the world couldn't get them through to California. Only God could melt the snow choking the pass.

Each day she prayed more. "Please God, make the storm stop. Please God, help the Murphys and the others in the forward camp, and protect us from the bad men, and please God save Jean Baptiste." Only a little older than Elitha, he was the only one left to cut the firewood now that Pa had weakened so, and if the fire went out, they'd have to eat the spoiled leather uncooked. It was bad enough in a gluey mass. And even if he was a halfbreed — people said they were unreliable — she hated to think of him alone in the men's wigwam. But Pa wouldn't hear of him staying in the family tent, and besides it WOULD be immodest, so she could only pray.

Five-year-old Georgia's whimpers were bracketed by plink plink. She had never been a healthy child. Little Ellie, who was a year younger, had taught her to walk.

"I'm hungry." Georgia wailed and Elitha gritted her teeth.

Ma's voice was low and patient, "Georgia baby, we'll all have supper soon. It's almost ready." The mess of moldy gel.

Elitha thought of the apple tree back on the farm in Springfield to divert her mind from the stench. She had sat in a high crotch inhaling the perfume of the crisp white blossoms with pink ruffled edges and felt like a fairy princess. Overhead a mother robin kept landing and stuffing worms down the throats of hatchlings. The summery sound of bees visiting the fairy blossoms surrounded her. Splotches of sunshine kissed her shoulders and hands. She had thrown her sweater and bonnet to the foot of the tree and run her fingers through her braids, letting her hair fall in a silky dark-brown mass around her shoulders. Would she ever be that warm? Ever see green grass again?

Tears of wonder had filled her eyes then, on account of the beauty of the world. Why didn't everyone sit in apple trees? Maybe they didn't smell springtime the way she did. It was like she had a secret engine inside her that started up at snowmelt. *God gave me that memory just so's I would have it now*, she suddenly realized. And worms would be juicy and good. She had been like a baby bird then, with her mouth open, expecting food to be brought. Meals were constantly being prepared in the sunny farm kitchen with two hired girls helping. She had known, without even thinking, that meat and potatoes would soon be steaming on the dinner table and hot biscuits would be snuggled under a cloth, and butter standing full in its tub, scraped across the top with a knife. Oh, how her empty belly ached and twisted!

"Ma, I'm hungry." Little Ellie's piercing whine.

Something made a scratching sound. Elitha listened through the plinking. Perhaps a mouse. The scratching came again. She raised up on an elbow and squinted across the dimness. "Don't move. Everyone quiet." She' had done this before.

"Catch a mousey! Catch a mousey!" squealed little Ellie.

"Hush now." Lifting the quilt, she eased herself down on her hands and knees in the cold puddle. Ice water drummed on the back of her cloak, but she didn't move. All her life she'd watched cats do this. Whiskers twitched. She narrowed her eyes toward a tiny triangular face peering from an aperture in the pine boughs beneath Ma. The mouse stepped forward, sniffing in all directions, green-eyed in the firelight. Larger than the grey mice at home. Browner, with a fluffier coat. She hoped her sisters would keep quiet while the animal lost its fear. Minutes passed.

It scurried toward the hide. Her arm struck lightning quick. "I got it!" The mouse bit her little finger. She cracked its neck.

"Hurrah, hurrah," filled the tent.

She raised it by the tail for all to see. Ellie, tiny inside her bulky cloak, scrambled out of bed wanting to hold it. The limp warm thing was passed around. Pa declined, so did Mrs. Wolfinger, but Tamsen took it and passed it on, then took the empty cooking pot from the fire and lifted the flap, pushing the boards back, stepping up a few ice steps for snow.

She backed in, the wind flattening the flames. Though she was no bigger than many twelve-year-olds, Tamsen's shadow was huge on the canvas. She put the pot of snow on the fire. Moving out of Ma's way, Elitha jammed a switch down the rodent's throat, then held it over the hottest part of the fire. The smell of burning hair momentarily covered the bad odors, and four sets of tiny toes clenched.

"Cook the parts separate," Ma advised.

The fresh mouse would need little boiling. She cut and placed the parts on the melting snow, counting the innards as two of the eight portions. The back would make a portion, and the head, boiled a little longer to soften the skull. "Pa, you want the liver and the lights?"

"You womenfolk take what you want, give me the rest." Even with fresh meat coming his voice sounded tired and high. Would he ever sound cheery and bluff again? His haw haw haw used to make her think of the way St. Nicholas was supposed to sound.

A sniffle came from Mrs. Wolfinger as Elitha struggled to cut through the animal's shoulder. It was horrible about Mr. Wolfinger being murdered, and she a lady as elegant as any Elitha had ever known, whimpering at odd times like a child with a toothache. Even the little ones knew better than ask what the matter was, though in normal times that might be polite.

As Elitha arranged the meat on the slush, she pictured Mrs. Wolfinger as she'd looked last summer strolling on the meadow with her pale hand resting on the dark cloth of her husband's elbow. Her ivory brooch was admired by every female in the wagon train. Herr Wolfinger touched his bowler and smiled in a distinguished fashion and Pa said people shouldn't expect him to cut down trees like a common laborer. Now Mrs. Wolfinger had nothing but the soggy clothes she lay in, and it was more than a pity to see a grand lady thrown utterly on the hospitality of others. It wouldn't do to remind her, but Elitha decided to give her the haunch, which she did so crave for herself, and worried Mrs. Wolfinger would feel the charity.

The water in the pot melted. "Let's sing," Elitha suggested.

"That's a splendid idea," Tamsen said. "But first, you girls turn your heads." She rustled in her things, fetching her secret stash of flour, Elitha knew.

"You can look now!" Sure enough, Ma sprinkled two teaspoons into the pot to thicken the broth. Her alto voice began, "Rock of Ages, cleft for — "

"Sing bout gravy," piped Ellie.

"Whatever song is that?" Ma asked.

"You know," Ellie intoned.

"Not unless you sing it."

The little girl's faltering voice tried to hook itself to a tune. Then she gave up and said peevishly, "Bout roses!"

Elitha, watching bubbles form, couldn't remember such a song.

Georgia suddenly burst out with, "I know! Let's sing that!" It had been the longest time since she'd said anything except *I'm hungry.*

Ma was patient as always. "Sing the first part, dear, then we'll know it."

It came from Georgia like a bright trumpet skipping upward. "Up from the grave he arose!" Her voice sagged as she came to the end of her words.

Elitha recognized the hymn. "Yes let's sing that." It had a triumphant feel.

Pa started the verse in a low, scratchy voice, and everyone hushed to hear the part that sounded like a funeral.

"Lo, in the grave he lay, Jesus, my Sav-ior
Waiting the coming day, Jesus, my Lord."

Elitha and Ma and the girls chimed in at the chorus, bouncing up the stairs of the happy notes:

"Up from the grave he arose!
With a MIGHty triumph o'er his foes
He arose the victor of the dark domain
And he lives forever with the saints to reign."

They all but shouted the end:

"He aROSE! He aROSE!
Hallelujah! Christ arose!"

"Sing it again!" Ellie said. And they did. This time Elitha sang the somber part along with Pa, lying in wait for the explosion of the chorus. At the end, fishing with a spoon for mouse parts, she felt enlivened. Tamsen handed her the series of plates and she ladled the thickened broth over each portion.

"Why did Jesus wait so long? To come out a the gravy?" Georgia said, taking her plate.

Elitha was trying to figure out why she'd say that, when Frances corrected in her grown-up voice, "See Georgia, he was low down in there, and it was a big s'prise when he jumped up, cause he was p'tending to be a rose!"

Tamsen laid her arm across Elitha's shoulders, shaking. Elitha had to look at her to understand that Ma was laughing. They were on their knees beside the fire and she was no heavier than an empty feed sack shaking in the wind. In her mind Elitha imagined Jesus as Georgia did, and though it was a sacrilege, it struck her so funny she caught Tamsen's hysterics. They hugged each other, tears streaming. Pa's guffaw boomed like in old times, and the little girls tried to laugh too, though it was plain they hadn't the first idea what was funny. Just when it seemed everybody would stop, somebody would erupt again, and it was a long time before the pervading hush settled.

Ma took her lightness from Elitha's shoulders and in the sudden quiet she felt a swooping feeling that raised goose bumps. Like something spooky had entered on a wisp of wind. It disturbed the fire and sent a shadow through her mind. Would the family rise from this hole?

Shoving that firmly from her mind, she picked a tiny morsel from the outside edge of the heap of gray entrails and placed it on her tongue. This was the way she made food last longer and it didn't hurt so bad when it got to her stomach. But mostly she didn't want to be finished while others were still eating. Her sisters imitated her, each trying to finish last.

Georgia muttered, "Ebbrybody laughed at me."

"Because we love you," Ma said.

Leanna said, "No, silly! Because Jesus was in the GRAVE."

Not about to let that linger, Elitha shot back, "I just know we'll get through to California."

"Of course we will, dear," Ma said in her teacher voice. "Why, Milt and Noah said people are getting ready to go out on snowshoes, up in the forward camp. They'll bring help. Mr. Reed will see to it they come for us. He can be counted on."

"They have snowshoes?" Elitha said. The Donners didn't, and she figured they'd packed just about everything that had ever been thought of to take on the overland journey.

"One of the men is slicing oxbows, and making strips of the harness leather," Tamsen said, "to weave over the wooden frames."

"Help will come soon then," Elitha said, suddenly believing it. There was a whole hide left to eat till then, and Pa's arm would get better any day now. In California they would buy a nice farm from the Spaniards, and Ma would start her school. The Murphys would visit and spring would come. And surely they had apple trees in California.

22

WEDNESDAY, DECEMBER 16, 1846

Coyote turns three times and lies on the snow, enjoying the sight of fourteen people testing their awkward snowshoes. "They expect to escape from the mountains," he observes wryly.

The death bird does not blink. "It is a hundred miles, and the snow already fifteen feet deep."

Fifty malnourished people observe from dark oversized cloaks. *Maybe I should be going too* plays on every mind. Solemn children are surprised to see men and women tumbling in the snow, to hear their laughter shattering the frozen air. They sense the mounting heart of the snowshoers, who hope to bring help. Laughter sounds so strange in these frozen heights, where life is suspended, drawn within itself.

Uncle Frank, nearly sixty years old, lifts an oxbow high before he plunges it forward. Snow dusts him to the armpits.

"He looks like my baby sister tryin to walk in Ma's shoes!" somebody says.

"Quitcher cacklin and see how it's done!" says Uncle Frank high-stepping on the brow of the pristine snow. It was his idea to make the awkward footgear.

He catches one snowshoe on the other, teeters, and yells a waterfall of sound as he pitches forward. It echoes from the granite wall towering between the camp and California. It flies over the frozen lake and loses itself in the quiet pines. He flops like a fish in a powder box, trying to regain his feet.

They will fail, the spectators think, recalling how it snowed for five days and nights while the fourteen worked in their noisome dens, cutting hides to ribbons, tying knots. Their hands had something to do besides feed fires. *The fires here will die,* they know — when the people grow too weak. Laughter sounds so strange.

Amanda McCutchen will leave her pitiful baby and walk through the snow for help. She falls. The spectators don't smile as she giggles and flops, trying to get her knees under her.

Salvador and Luis, the Indians from Sutter's Fort, master the technique of walking in snowshoes. They have seen the trail once, without snow, and would be amazed to know the *Americanos* call them guides. Captain Sutter will hang them if they return without the mules, which were eaten long ago, so they plan to go quietly to their home places when they see the Valley of the Sun.

Coyote smiles. "Last time a blizzard whipped them back to their dens."

"They think it is different now, with snowshoes," the bird says.

"I doubt they'll go half the way."

"They won't come back." The beak snaps shut.

Among the people, all the excitement of the huge wagon train as it first rumbled out into the prairie is cut back to this one fine stream, like water funneled into a nozzle. They call themselves The Forlorn Hope. THEIR life breath won't ebb away in stinking holes, they think. They will fetch help or die with wind in their teeth. Those who will stay in the dens think, *Maybe I should be going.*

During the night the death bird lights in camp, and Baylis Williams is stiff by morning. Everybody recognizes the omen but no one speaks of it. And when the fourteen snowshoers and three who will go without footgear squint toward the high mountain wall, no laughter rings over the white valley of the Truckee.

"Hit don't stick," Uncle Frank observes, lifting one foot from the snow. "Hit's a good sign."

They remember the real omen.

"Time to go," Charlie Stanton says with false cheer, posing as a man of inexhaustible vigor. He signals Salvador and Luis.

Those who will remain stare with sunken, smoke-reddened eyes at those who have blankets slung over their backs. Departing mothers hug their children and kiss their bony faces. "Mrs. Murphy will take care of you, precious. Be good, and remember, no matter what happens, you are my children."

Wives cling one last time to husbands.

"We'll bring help," Bill Eddy promises his Eleanor, knowing her lot is harder here with little Jimmy and the baby. He ties on his blanket with six days' lean rations rolled inside.

Charlie Stanton leads across the trackless powder, followed by Salvador and Luis. All sink past their ankles despite the footgear, which they lift straight up, thrust forward, and place before them. The death bird hops behind the seventeen as they move single file through the dazzling brilliance.

The five women, not one over twenty-five, step resolutely into the big tracks. After half an hour their shriveled muscles ache. Their husbands lead, keeping their weakness a secret, as do the Irishman, the Mexican teamster, Uncle Frank, Charlie Stanton and Bill Eddy. Dutch Charley and the two Murphy boys trail at the rear, lacking snowshoes, stepping into the holes. Much of the time they break through to their thighs. The dark line crawls away from them, lengthening up the slope toward the pass.

Thirteen-year-old Lem Murphy stops to catch his breath and sees only the figure of the last snowshoer far ahead. The sun has slipped behind the cold mountain wall, erasing the surface features. Night will come and he will be far behind. The death bird cranes his scrawny neck and pecks him on the shoulder. He throws himself into the trail. The bird hops back to Dutch Charley and William Murphy, who are trembling with the weakness of malnutrition and, looking back, realizing the folly of coming without snowshoes. The mountain's blue shadow sweeps all the way back to the smoke rising from the snow. The bird cocks his head, asking.

They think how good the pine-boughs would feel. The poking twigs won't bother them after all, or the stench. They'd rather die in bed. Dutch Charley cups his mouth toward the moving figure up ahead, "Lem. Lem! We're goin back."

Lem Murphy turns to see their small shapes, arms beckoning.

"Come back with us!"

"I'm goin on to Californy!" The snow gives way and he sinks to his waist, but flounders onward, not from any strength in his emaciated limbs or thumping heart, but his zeal to live, his vision of food ahead, and his promise. "Ma, I'll be back with help in a few days." She and all those children are waiting. Besides, it feels good to just get up and go.

Soon the stars glitter through the white-shrouded trees, the only witnesses to his wild struggle. His legs are dead below the calves, his arms below the elbows. The wind is picking up, dusting snow in his eyes, but the trail is easy to feel. Others will be resting ahead. He just needs more time to cross the same distance, that's all.

At last he sees muted light ahead and crawls toward it. The fire is behind the blankets on a cross of green logs, poles connecting the angles. The people sit around the fire holding blankets over their heads. He squeezes in with the men, unties his pack and adds his blanket to the overhead canopy, fumbling to put the spilling meat and sugar lumps on his lap. People reach over, pat him, glad to see the youngest made it. He tells them the others went back.

"Wouldja look at that," Lem says, picking up his dead feet and placing them near the fire. "My arms and legs are still a goin!" They jerk and tremble.

People chortle about their cramps and shakes. "Look at mine!" says Uncle Frank, who is striking his calves, careful not to disturb the blankets.

Charlie Stanton says, "We already et." He means Lem should do the same.

Lem pops a sugar lump in his mouth and breaks off a meat string as long as a finger. The rations have been calculated for the estimated distance to Bear Valley.

Here's some coffee," says Charlie Stanton, handing him a tin cup. He admires the boy's bravery but says only, "It's a might nippy out."

"Yup. An' we didn't git fur, neither." Not even up to the pass. Cold bites through the wool blanket and coat.

"Not more'n four miles."

All know they must make far more than that each day to get to Bear Valley, or their six days of rations will give out. At least that's how Stanton estimates the distance, and he thinks the snow won't be so deep down there and Reed and McCutchen will be bringing up supplies.

The death bird squats a little ways back and folds his wings, knowing McCutchen's big frame lies in bed at Sutter's Fort, malnourished beyond a quick recovery, and Reed got up too soon and tried to lead a rescue party, but the eight-day storm turned him back. The Forlorn Hope are the only people in these mountains. And even Salvador and Luis can't find roots and berries under snow this deep. The silence is loud to the Indians. Bears and marmots sleep in their dens. Deer and birds are far away grazing in green valleys. Only people, who imagine themselves clever, struggle in the frozen heights.

"What do you think?" Coyote asks. "Will they reach Bear Valley and see their hopes dashed?" His lips pull back in a grin.

"Charlie Stanton can't make it and he's the only one who knows the way."

"He looks strong to me, in the prime of life."

"That's why he rode for help. But look what he's been through. Wait and see." The bird doesn't blink.

"Lem," Charlie Stanton says, "when I was a comin up the mountain the other way, I hung a pack saddle up in a tree."

"What fer?"

"Hold yer horses. I'm sayin mebbe I can make you some kind of snowshoes."

The next day fifteen people scale the wind-swept snow to the summit and make another platform fire, weak in the thin air. Stanton heads into the knifing gale and finds the Spanish saddle. Later, when Lem drags in, Luis and Salvador are tying leather strips around the frame, and soon an odd pair of snowshoes is ready. Lem almost weeps with joy. "Aw gee, thanks."

Wind cuts through wool like it isn't there, and nobody sleeps. They roast their backs, then turn toward the fire until their backs shrink with cold. Men take turns with the axe, bringing wood. Blankets are retrieved from the wind and rearranged. Several times the smell of burning wool or shoe leather brings the cry, "Som'ns burnin!"

At dawn the gaunt people stare eastward one last time. In the mountainous cleavage beyond the frozen lake the pink sky pushes a streak of pale color across the white valley. It looks like a scene on a canvas. They stamp their feet to be sure they're living.

"Hey look!" Sarah points at wisps of gray just visible in the stillness.

"Hit's their smoke alright!" This ghost of a link with their families holds the Forlorn Hope spellbound.

Salvador nod-blinks at Charlie Stanton that they need to make tracks. Stanton is waiting for his morning surge of strength, which he relies on like his eyes and ears, but it doesn't come. "Well, we'd better git goin," he says.

The fifteen trudge down the incline toward a frozen unknown, Lem bringing up the rear on his new snowshoes. Legs are stiff, feet already numb. Their rations will last four more days.

Later in the day, Charlie Stanton stops and waves the line forward with his hat, lets them pass. Bill Eddy and Salvador and Luis can break trail. His vast cauldron of strength is drained. It fueled a thousand-mile walk across the plains, a lightning ride from the desert two hundred miles over the mountains to Sutter's Fort, then back with the Indians into Humboldt Meadows and up the steep face of the mountains again, helping the wagons cross the Truckee River twenty-seven times. In camp it kept him going for thirty days almost without food. Now his snowshoes are too heavy for his quivering thighs. He is like a very old man, though he is twenty-eight years old. Breaking trail is too hard. The sun glancing off the snow stabs his eyeballs. For hours he has imagined his teeth mashing into hunks of cured pork and his tongue pressing the sweet, salty pulp against the roof of his mouth. He wonders if he's losing his mind.

When Lem passes, Stanton feels the boy's courage like a snake feels warmth. "I'll bring up the rear," he tells the boy. "Tomorrow you walk behind the Indians."

"You all right?" Lem peers into his red eyes, the man no taller than the boy.

"Oh, sure. Just fixing to watch from the back."

The death bird hops along behind.

Late that night Stanton drags into camp. For him the following day is dark, though others say the sun glistens on the snow like fields of diamonds. Squinting hard, he follows the tracks, proud of getting a good group together, a bunch with grit. He waves the bird off, saying, "I'm takin my time, is all." A luxury now that others lead.

Stanton wonders why he of all men volunteered to go for help, he with no family to save. Only three months ago he was in the Sacramento Valley eating pork and corn grits. But he hadn't taken the time to flesh up. People needed him, and hell, he always had so much stamina, small as he is.

Coyote shows himself, under the trees, standing with his bushy tail low. "Thought you'd be the hero of the Donner Party, didn't you?"

Stanton scowls. "Well, if I hadn't brought those seven mule-loads of flour and beef, half of them would have been dead by now. Bill Eddy, for instance." He points to the distant line where Bill Eddy is leading. "Why that man and his little family were about famished down there at Truckee Meadows. People weren't sharing their food."

Coyote barks a laugh. "You gave everyone the same amount when some of them still had cattle to eat."

Stanton isn't about to argue with an animal. He lifts a shaky leg and sets it forward. God knows, with all the bickering and concealing of food, nobody could have figured it any better. He doled to each family according to the number of persons, big or small. But why think of that now? What's done is done.

The amber eyes follow his progress. "It's your fault they didn't make it over the summit. You should have made them leave sooner."

"Well hell!" he shouts, bristling at the familiar accusation, "those oxen needed to graze on the grass that was there."

"And where are they now?" Frozen solid beneath the snow.

Trudging far ahead, the Mexican teamster turns and looks back at Stanton with a strange expression. Sound carries in the thin air. Stanton lowers his voice. "Sure I advised them to rest a week. It was a gamble, that's all. A gamble, and I lost by one day. We would have made it if the snow had held back just one more day." *Sweet Jesus, I need to lie down.*

"Would-be heros always think, just one more day, just one good shot, just one less mile," Coyote says, clouds puffing from his mouth. Then he trots out of sight.

Stanton toils along the lumpy trail with his smarting eyes closed. Snow sticks to the webbing, heavy as anvils. He knocks it off once in a while and sits down, heart banging behind his ribs. He is not going to make it, he knows, and more than likely neither is anybody else. But they had to get out of camp or crazed men would take food from babies.

Long after dark he crawls to the fire and sits next to Bill Eddy so he can tell the new leader which way to go. "The Indians don't know the way," he confides. They exchange a look. Stanton touches Bill Eddy's shoulder, "They've only seen the trail once, when there was no snow."

The next day the sky is clear, but Stanton drags farther behind. He crawls into camp in the middle of the night. In the morning as the people pound their muscles and tie their blanket-packs on, Stanton pulls out his pipe and fixes a smoke. "Lem, would you mind?" His voice sounds muffled, like a creek under the snow.

Lem finds a stick with a live coal and holds it to the pipe. Stanton sucks, puffs. "Thanks, son." He wishes he could see the boy's face as more than a blur. Wishes he had a son to live after him, any child at all. "You're a real brave kid."

"Aw shucks."

"No foolin. You got what it takes." He smiles, noticing the calming effect on his heart. He senses people standing around and flicks his hand at them. "Git going! I'll catch up. Go on, git! See you at the next camp."

As the blurs fade, Charlie Stanton smiles at the bird. "Just a little longer now." He puffs his tobacco, a man's last joy.

Then he is surprised to hear squeaking, crunching snow. Somebody is coming back. "Who's there?"

Salvador squats, places a hand on his shoulder. "Señor Cholie, come." He knows a few words of English.

"Gracias, Salvador, but I want to sleep now." He holds his hands together, miming a pillow under his head. "Understand?"

Salvador touches Stanton's inflamed eyelids with the tips of his fingers. "You, I help walk." They have journeyed far together. The other *Americanos* were not generous and Charlie Stanton never ate until he gave equal portions to the Indians. Salvador doesn't want this friend to freeze on the trail.

Stanton shakes his head. "No. I sleep now."

After a pause, strong hands grip his shoulders and give him a friendly shake. Stanton can't hold back the tears, and can't see the moisture in Salvador's eyes. The Indian releases him.

Waiting for the sound of receding snowshoes, Stanton is startled to hear the sustained tones of a mournful song. In the silence of the mountains the song carries across canyons and vast spaces. It seems to come from all around him, from the very sky. It is not of the world.

"Now, spirit go happy," Salvador says when he is finished.

"Thank you, friend. Gracias. Go now. Take the people to Sutter's Fort."

The seventh morning is clear and cold, and no rations remain. The fourteen shiver as they eat snow and wonder how much farther it is to Bear Valley.

Uncle Frank says, "At least we can walk without the cuss-ed snow stickin."

Coyote smiles and says, "They are hopeful." But a storm is coming.

The death bird does not blink.

Later, carrying their heavy footgear, the Forlorn Hope scale a ridge. Twelve pairs of worn shoes dig into the crusty snow, following the bloody tracks of Salvador and Luis, whose feet inside their torn moccasins have frozen, thawed and split open many times.

"Ifn we can jes git up there and see, we might figger a better way to go," Harriet says.

"I sure never thought as how I could climb another thing!" Sarah starts to get to her knees, then almost falls as black vertigo grips her in a liquid swirl. She grabs Harriet.

It happens all the time. "Bill Eddy must see something," Harriet says.

Sarah's vision slowly returns and she makes out Bill Eddy with the two Indians, thin as sticks, gazing west. Maybe seeing the promised land, as some call it. Maybe she'll see green grass and smoke from Sutter's Fort. But before she gets to the lookout, the men's faces betray bitter disappointment. Then she gazes across a world of quiet mountains, high ridge after high ridge, white and peaceful beneath woolly clouds. Anger nips her in all her hungry places. She studies the Indian guides. Their eyes seem to look inward and their wide cheeks cut sharply to big teeth, overstretched with thin lips. Only the Mexican teamster can speak Spanish, and she hasn't heard the Indians say a word on the entire march.

Sarah puts her hands on her bony hips and demands of them, "Which way from here?" Seeing no response, she turns to the Mexican.

He translates. Salvador and Luis point northwest.

"No!" Sarah's voice breaks with frustration. She points at the faint salmon glow over the farthest ridge. "We're s'posed to go west. "That's WEST, can't you redskins see that! Don't you even know which way the sun sets?" She feels like crying, though she has nothing left to cry with. "No wonder we're still out here a killing ourselves! We're headed the wrong way!" Her face contorts and she plops down, refusing to look at anybody.

Coyote enjoys this. The winter sun sets in the southwest, and he knows the northern route through Bear Valley is much easier, though a little farther as birds fly. A grin lays bare the tips of his fangs and he says, "They'll get lost."

The death bird's beak is shut.

Bill Eddy pats Sarah's shoulder. "You're just tired. Let's make camp."

They obey this man who carries the gun, though the mountains seem devoid of game. The two husbands take the hatchet and look for firewood. Everyone else examines the stitching of their blankets for crumbs, picking over them like monkeys.

It is bitter cold and late when Uncle Frank pokes the blankets. Sarah and Mary lift the cover and he crawls in by the fire. Mary touches his face. "We was afeared for you."

"I said I'd catch up." His voice is a high rasp.

"How far to Sutter's Fort?"

Bill Eddy says, after a silence, "Mebbe seventy miles."

No one speaks in the presence of this terrible knowledge. In a week they've gone a third of the way. Each knows they must have food immediately, yet nothing is to be had. Arms trembling, Bill Eddy, who poses as the strong man, struggles to cut wood. Others take turns with the hatchet.

The next morning the wool is thicker in the clouds. Salvador and Luis point toward Bear Valley in the northwest. Sarah shakes her head. She is adamant. Uncle Billy and the two husbands agree just as adamantly, pointing southwest. Bill Eddy recalls Stanton saying the Indians do not know the way. "It can't hurt to go due west," he says. He straps on his snowshoes and starts down the mountain.

Crying Fox-Salvador says to Luis, "Maybe they know a better way than Señor Stanton's trail." He scans the deep gorge into which Bill Eddy is headed. The other steep side must be scaled.

Luis shrugs and inhales the smell of the coming snow. "Yes, maybe they know a better trail." He follows Bill Eddy.

The first flakes fall as fleeting and innocent as an afterthought. Then for two days the fourteen wander in swirling whiteness, confused as the wind. At the bottom of each canyon they crawl up the next steep ridge. The distances widen between them, and all human purpose is reduced to keeping the dark figure ahead in view, for if the chain breaks they'll be lost.

They camp on a windy ridge. Bill Eddy is spent and can't get wood. Sarah's husband raves about bacon frying on a phantom fire. The Irishman prays the same mumbling thing over and over. They eat snow.

The next morning they dig out and realize the falling snow is too thick to see in any direction. No one can walk. Lem searches for a crumb and eats what turns out to be a nub of wool. He recalls his foolish promise to be back in a few days with help. He is exhausted and suspects they are lost, but says nothing.

Bill Eddy knows they are lost, but pretends to lead. Blindly they struggle onward.

In camp Crying Fox-Salvador squats under his blanket next to Luis while Bill Eddy tries to start a fire. He tries to cup his frozen hand and blows on the green needles, using match after match.

Luis says, in his own tongue, "They didn't know a better trail."

His friend nod-blinks in agreement.

"Let's go back to the lake camp," Mary's husband says.

Bill Eddy scowls. "That's crazy. We've come so far."

Silently agreeing with that, Lem notices Harriet's husband glowering at him with a strange and wild expression. Bill Eddy looks at the men and women around him. "I'm spent," he admits. "Somebody else get firewood."

"I'll go," says Lem to show he is a man.

The death bird pecks at his guts. It hurts so bad he can't remember any sensation but hunger. At least now, he thinks, there's no food to hit his belly like a fist. And if they keep walking west, they can't miss California. He swings at a branch, closing his eyes to the white avalanche from the tree. Each branch seems tougher than the last. He dumps his green boughs beside the fire, and extends the hatchet to the group. Harriet takes it and leaves to cut another branch.

"Blessed are they that hunger," the Irishman chants, "for they shall be filled." In the silence of the late afternoon snow, his voice is squeaky and high. "I think we should kill somebody for food. Maybe draw lots."

"He's outa his head."

"No. He's right."

Bill Eddy mutters, "By thunder, I ain't no sacrifice lamb. If it comes to that, two men should fight it out with knives. Draw lots to see which two. The loser gits et. That's fairer."

Lem isn't sure he is awake. Would he be considered a man? He is glad the women refuse this plan. The Mexican explains to the Indians what has been said; their eyes widen in horror.

Coyote chuckles, but the death bird sits unblinking.

The next morning the storm whirls from every direction, obscuring the Indian leaders. The line stumbles forward, almost dozing, not realizing they are going north.

"They're tougher than I thought," Coyote remarks.

"They don't know what they're doing," the bird says, giving the Mexican's flesh a good peck. The teamster is crawling behind the others, moving by force of habit through the mounting storm. Hours later he collapses beside a poorly made fire. His breath rattles and his hand flops into the whipping flames.

Lem lurches for it.

Bill Eddy stays his arm. "He's a goner."

The hand shrivels into a black fist and the aroma of cooking meat blows with the smoke. Stomachs knot in blind anticipation, but hunger must wait. Another enemy is upon them — wind screams in their ears, pounds snow in their eyes and steals their breath. They drag the Mexican from the circle, then hunker down and wait. A little peace settles over the Forlorn Hope. Food is again in camp.

Without the cross of green wood to support it, the fire melts down inside a widening snow cup. People sink with it, and are somewhat sheltered from the wind. They take turns with the hatchet, their most precious possession. Each climbs out, shoulders into the blizzard, chops a branch, slides down, and places it on the fire, which is suspended precariously above a pool of water.

In her turn, Sarah throws back the hatchet and it flies from her numb fingers. In the howling snowstorm she crawls around patting the snow, feeling for where it sank. Tears of frustration freeze on her cheeks. She gives up, flops on her back for a peaceful moment, and knows how easy it would be never to rise. The death bird hops near.

Her eyes fly open. "Lordy, my babies!" She crawls back to the fire, sinks down the slushy bank and tells them about the hatchet. In the glowing snow cup, all stare at her. Bill Eddy rises to fetch a branch with nothing but the knife in his belt. When he returns, Crying Fox-Salvador manages to shove the upended limbs under the sputtering wood, and the miraculous fire burns brighter over the pool of water. Luis arrives with two limbs, stumbles down the bank, knocking a sidewall loose. A small avalanche snuffs out the snapping fire and the world is black — the only sound the roar of the wind and the crack of trees bending too far.

No fire can be rekindled, and their feet will freeze solid in the slushy water. Crying Fox-Salvador rouses Bill Eddy, who sits in a stupor, and pulls Sarah's sleeve. Soon all are struggling from the sheltered pit, dragging Lem, the Irishman and Uncle Frank, who are unconscious. Out in the wind they kneel and dig like foxes in the flying snow, then huddle with their backs to the outside of the excavated circle, heads on knees, the unconscious propped between them. Every few minutes the wind steals a tail of a blanket, and they fight to get it back. The hollow clacking of teeth seems loud even in the wind. The thirteen quake with cold, consuming strength they didn't know they had.

"If I live, I'm never complainin of heat, ever again."

"Pat stopped shiverin."

Mary feels his face and pronounces him gone.

The twelve roll him out and reposition the blankets.

Uncle Frank rasps. Sarah hears it over the wind, "Mary, listen, he's talkin."

They put their ears to his mouth.

"Eat of my flesh....and ye shall be saved." His lifts his head and speaks so all can hear. "Eat of my flesh....so's ya can git help....fer them babes." His head flops down.

They roll him into the storm.

Suddenly conscious, Lem Murphy shrieks, "I'm goin' to Californy." He tries to run. His legs thrash. Men and women lunge to hold him. Blankets fly away. "Gitcher hands off me," he yells. "Lemme out. Leggo! Oohwheet!" His kicks are violent and painful, his screams incoherent. Harriet and Sarah kneel on his legs, the Indians his torso, Bill Eddy grasps his hands while the husbands of Sarah and Mary lurch after the blankets.

At last Lem lies still. Mary cradles his head and says, "He was the best of us." In turns they kneel over him and hug his light bones, thinking, *We will lose heart.*

"He was brave," somebody says. They roll him out.

In the morning the snow falls steadily. Seven stick people in hooded cloaks bend with their knives over the remains, ripping cloth and frozen flesh. Bill Eddy builds the cross and kindles a fire on it. A distance away, sitting at their own fire for the first time, the Indians sing mournfully, backs to the abomination. They sing to help the ghosts find their way from this place, and, they hope to stop the bad luck.

Weeping, the five women saw along a thigh bone and lay out pink portions. Sarah's husband, his hand deep in Lem's chest, looks up as Eddy approaches. "It's Christmas Eve," he says excising the liver, cutting off a frozen slice, offering it to Eddy on the tip of his knife. His eyes glitter with challenge.

Bill Eddy staggers past the singing Indians and falls in the snow, sobbing for the first time since he was a child. He is debased by the knowledge that he would eat with the others if he hadn't found the bear meat his Eleanor had put in his possibles pouch. He notices the silence, the singing stopped. The pines stand uncomplaining.

Crying Fox sees Condor slicing across the white mountain, and recalls his sister's warning. It is for Molok and his brothers, big and small, to tear at the dead without misfortune. But now Molok's robe lies in unclean hands and Crying Fox sits unprotected in this dangerous place where people eat of the human dead. Sometimes, he knows, Condor kills to eat. Power careens out of control with the snowflakes. He hears Coyote laugh and, knowing he chose this fate, almost laughs with him. He calls in song to the spirits that make the living cling to life beyond all expectation, then touches Luis and feels him surface from his trance-like state. "Do you see your death?"

"For two sleeps, when I turn my head a certain way, I have been seeing the bird jump away."

"I too, but first let us see the green grass again."

On the stem of a neck, a skeletal face turns to him and lips slide across inflamed gums. It is a smile, and a bargain.

23

JANUARY, 1847

I must go to the home place, Maria Howchia thought as she stood looking out the rain-streaked window of the room she shared with Pedro. The room was above Señor Sheldon's millhouse on the riverbank. Pedro sat on the bed playing sad music on his guitar, lulling the baby to sleep. A runner from the fort had said Crying Fox hadn't returned from the mountains, and she knew her parents would be very worried, and lonely.

A tree hurtled down the brown river, swift as a galloping horse. The rain never stopped. Even the old ones in Omuch's home place could not remember so much rain. Power was unleashed, and water, which was so necessary to life, could kill. Snow would be falling in the mountains, piling deep. She wanted to go home and speak to Father about learning magic from Bear Claw.

Pedro's singing stopped, the drumming rain the only sound. Then Pedro's voice came, almost a whisper. "María, are you sorry you left Perry McCoon?"

She turned to see his fingers stilled over the strings, bare feet crossed on the bed, auburn hair framing his face. His gray eyes were filled with puzzlement and sorrow. She shook her head emphatically, her bluntly singed hair brushing her shoulders, and turned to watch another tree sail past, the roots standing like branches. "For three moons I have enjoyed living with you," she said. "Now I want to go visit my people and learn from a doctor. But I am your wife."

His fingers strummed a haunted chord that lingered and faded in the wooden room. "Are you worried about your parents?" His voice was kind.

"They are not at peace."

A board creaked, Pedro approaching. His hands massaged her shoulders. "I thought maybe, since McCoon's new wife died, you wanted to go back to him. You seem unhappy."

Perrimacoo's *Americana* had sickened and died. He had taken her to the fort for burial. Her death confirmed that there was evil in the adobe house. "He is no longer my man," she said. "You are." She turned, looked into his gray eyes and hoped he understood the strength of that.

His hands continued to work. "He will probably return to his house soon."

She wished he never would, but she could no longer live in this suspended state. She adored Pedro with the tenderness of a mother loving her child. She wanted to couple with him, and it was a constant source of hurt between them. He honored her wish to abstain while the baby nursed, but he often crept quietly from the room in the night. She knew he went to Tomaka's hut, for the kindly woman told her, always with a report of Pedro's love for her. This made her love him more, because he respected her need to wait. Some days she laughed to see how earnestly he encouraged little Billy to eat mashed food. Maybe Bear Claw would tell her how to protect against the bad luck, and she could be a full wife.

Boots pounded up the wooden stairs. Pedro's hands left her shoulders. He opened the door and admitted a blast of wind-driven rain that hurled the sombrero from its peg on the wall. Señor Sheldon stood at the door in a flapping, wet cape, trying to be heard above the storm. "Come with me to Daylor's. Quapata says bring a shovel. The levee's breaking."

"Come in, *Patrón*. I'll put on my boots."

As Pedro shouldered the door shut, Joaquín Sheldon removed his dripping hat and nodded a greeting to Maria Howchia. She picked up the awakened baby, sorry Pedro would leave so soon again. Only yesterday he had added dirt to the embankment behind Daylor's house. It was odd, she thought, that *Americanos* chose to live where a river overflowed in time of rain. She feared this was only the beginning. Soon the snow would melt and add to the torrent.

As Pedro stamped into his new boots and pulled his red and white sarape over his head, she suddenly knew she wouldn't wait for him all day again, as she had yesterday. She shrugged into the cradleboard without bothering to change the baby's rabbit skin, and wrapped herself in her blanket.

"Where are you going?" Pedro asked.

"To visit my parents." She would accompany him to Daylor's house, then continue to the home place.

Sheldon swung his wolf-like eyes between the two, and Pedro said, "It's Satan's brew outside."

Not wanting to talk with Señor Sheldon present, she touched Pedro's shoulder and gazed at him to impress on him the permanence of her love.

He compressed his lips and scowled a nod. Leading the way, he descended the stairs, Sheldon following. The wind stole Maria's breath as she closed the door on the square room that smelled of her man.

Pedro clutched the shovel under an arm. Beside him a grim-faced Joaquín Sheldon pointed the top of his leather hat into the storm. They walked the half-mile because the horses shied from the mud. María followed, and he could tell her mind was made up. He ached for her already; why couldn't he ever say no to her?

Freezing rain drove through his *pantalones* and trickled down inside his boots. Overhead, branches whacked together and dark clouds roiled. On his right the roar of the river drowned out talk. Pedro stepped off the trail and walked between the trees where a mulch of willow, walnut, and oak leaves buffered the mud. The wheat field on his left was a choppy sea.

In normal winters rain came in bursts, a day or two, followed by sun. Now it had rained for seven days and nights, and Señor Sheldon's cattle stood on the hills marking the ancient bluffs of the Cosumnes, the boundary of the Rancho. But as Pedro had lain awake last night he'd had more than the high water on his mind.

It seemed that ever since he'd brought María to his room, he'd been waiting for a stretch of contentment. But McCoon's baby lay between them. Maybe McCoon himself. He sighed. *Dios mio*, if she wanted the Englishman, there was nothing he could do about it, though it would break his heart. If only he could love her as a real husband!

The cursed condor robe, which surely McCoon had stolen, interfered too. It was why she wanted to become a medicine woman, to fend off bad luck. *Aye Madre. Indios* didn't let go of things once they got it in their heads. Pedro had tried to make her forget the superstitions. On stormy mornings he told her she didn't need to bathe in the raging river. But she insisted. She even dunked the poor baby in it. She refused to eat meat unless the Omuchumne medicine man had sung to it, and she didn't want Pedro to eat it either. Sometimes he had the impression she prayed to every tree and bush. Even he had begun to think of the damned condor costume as a curse.

Pedro rounded the last bend. Daylor's adobe and the Rhoads' covered wagon came into view in a watery yard. A bulky man was coming through the rain, apparently on his way to the trading room, where the Rhoads family was staying. Behind the house naked *Indios* shoveled mud on the bank. In a flapping oilcloth coat, Elder Thomas Rhoads worked with them. Bill Daylor shoveled in his shirtsleeves — hatless, pants rolled to his knees. As he looked up at them, water streamed from his long face and thin hair, his shirt wet as second skin. With his broad shoulders sagging, he called instructions to Quapata, then pointed to his adobe, indicating they should go inside.

Approaching, Daylor said, "I thanks ye both fer coming," and followed Sheldon, Pedro and Maria inside.

The cold room smelled dank and clammy. Daylor's *India* gestured toward the dripping fireplace in explanation for the lack of heat. Ceiling leaks added to the puddles on the mud floor. "I have no cooked food for you," she said in Spanish.

Pedro glanced at María, who stood against the wall holding the baby in his cradleboard, her eyes soft black pools. She was as brave as any man. It was only that she felt some big supernatural thing coming at her.

Señor Daylor sat, touched two willow chairs indicating the men should sit. "Jared, methinks it's hopeless. Even if the bloody rine stopped this minute, too much water is washin down the hills." He stabbed a hand east. "It's get out, or build us an ark, it is."

Señor Sheldon turned his wolf stare on Daylor. "What about the wheat?" Señor Rhoads had helped plant it in exchange for a chunk of Sheldon's land.

"I'd bet me last shilling ever kernel is washed away."

Sheldon wiped a drop from his face, glanced at the ceiling, then nodded at Pedro. "We two can move a lot of dirt." He glanced at the shovels they had left at the door.

"Jared, we're holding back an ocean, and not fer long. I say we go to McCoon's for a time. Hit's high and dry there, and 'e might bring a demijohn o' brandy from the fort. The Rhoadses should go back to the fort." He gave the smile of a strong man who'd done what he could.

Sheldon swung his eyes over to Pedro, "I can trust Señor Valdez with the stock."

Pedro considered the Horse-thief Indians, always looking for an unprotected herd, but the bonds forged with the local *Indios* over the last two years were strong.

"Sí, *Patrón*, I will stay with the herd." He wasn't free to go with María while his employers needed him.

Three bangs sounded at the door. Daylor's *India* threw it open. Wind and rain pressed her skirt between her legs as she stepped back to allow señoritas Sarah and Catherine Rhoads to enter, shaking out their kerchiefs. Following them were Señora Rhoads and the huge, drenched man he'd seen riding up. Mormon Elder Rhoads came in last, rolling his pantlegs down over powerful, muddy calves. Pedro stood up, as did señores Sheldon and Daylor.

Bowing toward Señora Rhoads, Pedro said, "I would be honored if you take my seat." Smiling thanks, she sat and Pedro joined María at the wall. Willowy seventeen-year-old Sarah Rhoads cast a secret look at Señor Daylor as she seated herself in the chair he'd vacated, and Catherine grinned at Señor Sheldon. A quiet smile tugged his lips. The *patrones* liked the daughters of the Mormon elder.

Señora Rhoads said, "This is my son, John Rhoads." She touched the stranger's thick arm. "Go ahead, son, tell them."

The man, probably in his mid-twenties, ran a massive hand though his dark hair, wet peaks of which touched the ceiling. His beard was dark and full. "I just come from Johnson's Ranch, been workin there," he said in a strange tone. "Saw a terrible sight." In the pause Pedro recalled Johnson, the *desgraciado* of a sailor who had bought Pablo Gutiérrez' 22,000 acres on the Río de los Osos for a hundred and fifty pesos.

Señorita Catherine bounced impatiently on her chair. "Tell how you tied logs with belts and floated down the rivers." She flashed a warm smile at Señor Sheldon.

John Rhoads glanced kindly at her. "My little sister is right. This here valley's a slough from one end t'other. The only way I could get from Johnson's was on the water. There's no footing fer horses anywhere near the rivers. But I had to talk to you good men of California."

His manly features twisted with emotion as he shook his big head. "The most pitiful, most famished people you ever saw come down the mountain. Skeletons is all they are. Couldn't even walk. Injuns come in half a carryin a man named Bill Eddy. Six more was back up at an Indian village. We had to go carry em in."

María's hand tightened on Pedro's arm, and he realized these famished people were probably the same ones her brother had gone to help rescue.

The big man continued, "They come from the summit, where the rest are camped, and got through only by eatin them that died." He let that hang, then pointed eastward. "Eighty more Americans, includin women and children a starvin up there right this minute, bad off as them that got through. I'm rounding up help, and was hopin you men would come with us. Mr. Sutter is headin up the relief. He says to tell you he needs any flour you got left, and horses and mules. But mostly we need strong men."

Señor Sheldon scowled and cocked his head. "Who are those people at the summit? Friends of yours?"

Elder Rhoads stepped forward, his dark eyes intense under flyaway white brows. "They're the James Reed and George Donner Party, part of the wagon train we come across with. They're good men, but took some kinda fool cutoff. Got caught in the early snow." His lips pressed down into an inverted U.

Pedro glanced at María and saw her inward-looking expression, her eyes not tracking. He knew she was thinking of her brother, and the damned condor curse.

Across the room Señor Daylor seemed to be measuring the giant of a man, and Pedro read the expression: No sane man would venture into the high Sierra in this weather. Sheldon looked skeptical too. "You say John Sutter's headin up the relief?" He swung his eyes east. "He going up there with you?"

John Rhoads shook his dark shaggy head. "No. He's dryin beef and gittin supplies together. Sendin word to Yerba Buena. Part of the United States Navy's anchored there. Askin em to send volunteers, that kinda thing. Maybe you know that Englishman named McCoon he has workin for him? He's sailin supplies up to Johnson's place." Pleased at that, Pedro looked down at María, but saw no emotion. "They're puttin a relay team together to take packs on up to Bear Valley."

"'Ave ye men to hike up with ye?" Daylor asked.

"Not yet. That's why I'm here. To ask you."

"You're new to California," Daylor said, "and wouldn't know what kind of winter blows up in yon mountains."

John Rhoads looked at him with his deep brown eyes. "We got winter back in Illinois."

Señor Sheldon, standing before the cold fireplace, narrowed an eye. "I don't know what kinda winter they got in Illinois. I'm from Vermont. But I'm tellin you," he looked east, "it's not atall the same up there. My advice is, take a good gander at John Sutter. He's not going up. Hell no. Heada relief or whatever you call him, he's staying in the valley. Cause he knows no horse or mule can git through the snow and men can't pack enough on their backs to feed that many people. Why they'd be lucky to feed themselves, goin to the summit. It wouldn't accomplish a thing." He stabbed a hand toward the window. "More'n likely you so-called rescuers'll starve too. It sounds hard, but you gotta hear. I don't think Sutter's leveled. This is a real bad winter, and I'd hate to see a man as brave as you lay down his life fer folks foolish enough to git stuck up there."

That was a long speech for Señor Sheldon, and Pedro sensed it was as much for the ears of Señorita Catherine as her brother. These people might not know that Sheldon had survived by stamina and cunning, living with the Apaches when he was young. A brave and wise man, he disliked foolishness.

Daylor said, "We got goods and cattle what needs lookin after." He glanced at his partner. "Jared, you got any flour left?"

Sheldon raised one finger. Pedro saw that the decision was made. The partners would donate food and stock to the relief effort, but not sacrifice their lives.

The door flew open. Quapata stepped in with water coursing down his body, cutting trails through the mud on his shins. "River come now. We no stop it." Beneath the practiced calm, a hint of horror showed in his brown face.

Pedro pulled María out the door. A churning arm of mud was pushing around the corner of the house. The Rhoads family bustled out to their covered wagon. Sheldon and Daylor went for the oxen and horses.

Pedro and María splashed up the trail, faces into the storm. Pedro stopped at a point where he knew the higher bank would safely hold, and looked into her big black eyes. "I'm going back to the millhouse. I must stay with the cattle now, but I'll come to your ranchería when I can."

She stood tenting her head and bare shoulders with the rabbit blanket.

"Will you be at McCoon's house?" He swallowed a lump.

She shouted over the lashing rain, "Never! But no go back to the millhouse. The water is coming. The house will float away."

He smiled at the "never" and said, "I must fetch my things."

"Things are not important," she yelled.

"My horse is important, and my helmet, and my guitar. Now go. I must hurry. And María, you were right to leave today." Grateful for the understanding in her eyes, he kissed her mouth, tightened the bead under his chin and pointed his black hat toward Daylor's.

The swollen mud arm had advanced beneath surging brown water. Pedro broke into a run. The Rhoads oxen strained at their yokes under a cracking whip, Elder Rhoads on the buckboard yelling, "Haw, haw!" Outside the wagon, John Rhoads prodded their rumps with a pole, his thick legs in water to his knees. The wagon wheels moved. The Rhoads family would make it out.

It was a poor time, Pedro reflected as he splashed through the water, for the men of Rancho Omuchumne to be asked to rescue people in the mountains. The partners had their own duel with nature, to save all they had worked for.

24

Sleet cut into Maria Howchia's face and legs as she struggled homeward, hoping to make it before nightfall. A mental image slammed into her. She pictured water rushing faster than a man could run, a galloping tree knocking Pedro unconscious, sweeping him downriver. Her feet stopped. *Pedro and Crying Fox could die in the same storm.* The rabbit blanket flapped at her knees.

What if it never stopped raining? Condor could dream that. All living things would drown. Muffled under the blanket, the baby wailed and she turned from the wind to catch her breath.

She reached inside for calm then turned to the wind. By the time the trail headed up the first of the home hills, she had faced her fear of Pedro's death. With that came clarity. If he lived, she would savor each moment. She would encourage the baby to live on food other than milk. In every way she would love her man. She would do everything to help him get the land paper he wanted, the one that allowed him in the eyes of black hats, blue suits, long robes, *Americanos*, leather shirts and Captain Sutter to live at the home place as Perrimacoo had.

Morning dawned overcast, but not raining. It was a sign. Visiting the home place was right. Outside the u-macha the earth smelled washed, and first grass bent under heavy beads of water. Her breath made clouds and her feet sank in wet loam as she took the baby down the trail to the bathing place.

The raging brown torrent had torn away the earth nearer to the village center than she had ever seen it. Stepping up to her calves, she felt the goodness of the icy stream and hugged the naked baby to her breast. Since the time of the ancients her people had lived here. Every hump in the ground was familiar to her, and it warmed her to see blind Grandmother Dishi walking with confidence down to the water, singing to the river-baby spirit. Maria Howchia watched her bent figure step into the river to bathe.

"Daughter, it is good to have you home."

She turned in the water and smiled at Father. His large size was only part of his impressive presence. His eyes crinkled in a loving smile, his face framed by his long, full black hair. She splashed to him and hugged his solidness with her free arm while he hugged both her and the baby. She felt some of his power enter her, and it was good. To honor the time spent apart, neither she nor her parents had let slip even a hint of recognition the previous evening. She had crept into the house and lain on her old mat, knowing how a young bird feels when it returns to the nest. Now, however, a show of emotion was permitted.

Grizzly Hair patted her head and dove into the torrent, stroking to the center where the two writhing currents met around the island. His black head disappeared, then he swam back through the hurtling water, thick arms pulling to keep from being washed downstream. With an invigorated grin, he waded ashore and stood with strength as he gazed toward Father Sun rising from his eastern house — a red glow behind the clouds. Steam rose from his torso and floated upward with his prayer.

Today she must tell him her belief that Perrimacoo stole the robe, and that she had slept in its presence. Secrets stole power. But now he was meditating, so she waded deeper and submerged, holding the baby out of the water. The cold water stung her chest and back, quickening her mind. She thanked the river spirit for purifying her of cloudy, cowardly thought, then dunked the sputtering baby. He howled and she laughed at him, holding him by one arm as she washed his lower parts. Despite this, he had been much calmer of late, ever since she had left Perrimacoo.

Father was still gazing at the dawn. She returned to the house, where Mother was emerging. They hugged, Etumu half a head shorter, smaller than Maria Howchia remembered, the skin of her back and upper arms looser than she remembered. The distinctive smell of her brought memories of when she had seemed large and had leaned near to show the proper way to weave a basket. It was good to be home, even with bad news. As Etumu left to bathe, Maria Howchia noticed the strong oak growing from the refuse mound at the back of the dancehouse. She had always liked it, growing straight and branching in perfect symmetry, different from those on the hills, which though older were gnarled and smaller. The corky smell of the wet bark drew her to the trunk and when she touched it, a peaceful, life-giving calm entered her hand. It travelled up her arm and suffused her entire body. Her breathing slowed. She leaned on the trunk and closed her eyes.

The tree said, *Granddaughter, you are strong. You can walk the path of a medicine woman, as I did.* It was Howchia, Father's Mother! People had called her Eagle Woman, for the black and white eagle that wintered here. No other person had been named for that powerful spirit, but Grandmother had been the singing doctor. She knew magic. It was a great honor that she had spoken to Maria Howchia, her namesake, and part of her spirit was coming through the pungent bark. Everyone thought Eagle Woman had gone to the happy land, but here she had been, all this time! A powerful ally. Maria would cherish Grandmother's secret.

Later in the day, ready to speak of the condor robe, Maria Howchia took a rat to the mortar holes, along with a basket of leached acorn meal. As she expected, both Father and Mother joined her for talk, and she could see they had missed her. While she skinned the rat, Grizzly Hair rolled fibers on his thigh for a new fish net and Etumu, with a lap full of loose black feathers, bent notched quill tips over netting twine and snapped them into place, making a new ceremonial robe for Father. She asked Maria about Señor Sheldon's *molino*.

She was glad to talk first of something easy. "It has flat stones that turn and rub together," she said. "You could grind an entire basket of acorns this fast." She put down the obsidian knife and clapped her hands. After a short time she clapped again and picked up the knife. "It grinds seeds to dust."

Grizzly Hair glanced up appreciatively from his fibers.

Mother paused with her feathers. "Who turns the stones?" Beneath the hair across her forehead, her infolded eyelids gave her a crisp, distinctive look.

Maria considered. It would be difficult to explain *el molino*. "Remember the place of the Omuchumne, when we went to a Big Time there?"

Etumu's cap bobbed up and down.

"Remember the long tongues of yellow sandstone at the river's edge?"

"Yes of course. The Omuchumne use it for mortars and their nu-pah is salted with sand." She put her teeth on edge and made a gritty smile, glancing at Grizzly Hair with a look that said their home place was best.

He smiled in an agreeing way, the love between them visible. It had always been there but now that Maria loved Pedro, she saw it more clearly. In no hurry to mention the condor robe, she continued.

"Omuch's men dug deep channels in the sandstone, one to bring the river to a paddled wheel, the other to take the water back to the river. A wooden gate keeps the water out until it is needed. When the gate is lifted, water rushes in and turns the wheel, which twirls an oak pole jammed into the wheel's center. The top of the pole is fitted with wooden teeth."

Her parents paid close attention as she demonstrated with stiff fingers how the teeth interlocked with more wooden teeth embedded in a log, and how that log spindle made another one turn, and yet another, each faster than the last. "This happens beneath the millhouse, and the fastest log pokes up through the floor of the mill and spins the flat stone. A matching stone is raised and lowered to it. Señor Sheldon's stones are very hard. His people have no sand in their meal."

Etumu exhaled audibly. "We need a *molino*." She looked at Grizzly Hair. "Would you make one for us?"

"First I must see Señor Sheldon's." He added a handful of fiber to the twine on his leg and, with a flat palm, spun it up and down his thigh.

Maria Howchia said in all candor, "A *molino* is hard to make. The cutting of channels through our greenstone would be impossible, I think. And the spinning logs are braced with many pieces of crossing wood; it looks like a giant spider's web under the millhouse. Señor Sheldon is very clever."

"Many newcomers are clever," Grizzly Hair said. "When the next runner comes from Omuch, I'll let him know we would attend their Second Grass Big Time if we were invited." He acknowledged Etumu's grateful smile, and watched her flying fingers.

Then he glanced at Maria Howchia and said, "What else have you learned?"

Now it comes. She tossed the rat into the meal and pressed with the pestle to split the gut. But first there was something else. "The men of Sutter's Fort honor paper — fiber pounded thin as a leaf. Marks on these papers talk for the headmen, even when they are far away. The papers say who should live at places and who owns the earth." Under her pestle the mash turned dark with rat innards and bristled with bones. She added more meal.

Grizzly Hair nodded. "When I was in the mission I saw paper with black and red marks. The *glav-nyi* of the Russian fort also had paper that talked." Thoughtfully he asked, "What is the meaning of this, owning the earth?"

With a crunch she crushed the rat's skull. "It is like owning fishhooks and baskets. The men of Sutter's Fort look to the paper to tell them which man possesses everything on that piece of earth — plants and trees and river and fish and all the animals. The paper tells that man to build a house. That is why Perrimacoo came here."

"And what of the people who have called it their home place since ancient times?"

"They cannot ask the man to leave, even if he is bad, if he holds such a paper."

His eyes flashed with humor and his lips twitched in a little smile. "When the men of a home place wish a stranger to leave, he will leave."

Father had made Perrimacoo stop raising *puercos*, but that didn't stop the power of the land paper. Pedro had explained it. She repeated his words. "A man with such a paper has the right to kill anybody who bothers him. Captain Sutter and his men would kill people who did not honor the paper." Cannons on wheels and racks of knife-tipped guns came to her mind.

Father was unfazed. "We are many, and our relatives in the surrounding villages are many. Paper holds no magic for me. Any man who comes here must learn to be our friend."

Maria Howchia squeezed the pink mash. Feeling the prick of a bone sliver, she resumed pounding. "I want Pedro Valdez to live with us. I want him to have the land paper. He is my new man." Ignoring Etumu's look, she explained that Perrimacoo only pretended to have such a land paper.

Etumu attached feathers so rapidly her fingers were a blur. "Pedro Valdez is a black hat," she said.

"Not now. He is Señor Sheldon's vaquero." Maria Howchia pounded with extra vigor although she thought all the bones were crushed and blended with the acorn mash. "He is my man. I want to have his children."

Grizzly Hair raised his brows at her. "Have you told Perrimacoo he is no longer your man?"

"Not yet."

He regarded her closely and said, "He had a pale wife."

"Yes. She died." She stole a glance at Father, indicating she had more to say.

He waited.

"Remember I said Perrimacoo's house was unsafe?"

"I remember."

She laid down the pestle, wishing the sound of the rushing river, which filled her ears, could wash her clean of what she must say next. "I believe he stole the condor robe." Her parents seemed to turn to stone. "I slept in his house when the robe was there. I think I saw it in the corner."

Etumu jumped up and ran away, the pile of feathers scattering, the half-made cape flying. Saddened, Maria watched her pass the u-macha — her own mother terrified by her presence. Grizzly Hair, who had stood up, stared down at her, something rarely done. His broad cheeks seemed paler, his eyes wide with horror. But she also detected sorrow in the tents of his lids.

There was more. Quietly she scooped rat paste into the cooking basket and wiped her fingers on the rim, and said, "Crying Fox has not returned to the fort from the eastern mountains."

He turned toward the mountains and spoke in a low voice. "The snow came early." She could tell it had been reported.

"Starving *Americanos* came from a camp in the mountains," she said, "and were carried by *Indios*. We must learn if Crying Fox was among them."

They glanced at one another, both thinking, she knew, of Condor, the power of the universe gone wrong. Seeing his pained expression, she added, "I have not died." It was a good sign. Perhaps Grizzly Hair would not fear her. Her voice caught in her throat as she finished her bad message. "Molok's robe is in Russia."

He squatted and put his head in his hands. Unmoving as stone.

She waited with eyes unfocused, swallowing sorrow. "Father, I would like to learn from Bear Claw, but I have few things to pay him." Once Grizzly Hair had said she had the gift to become a woman of knowledge. A doctor was one step beyond; many people died opening themselves to the spirits, but Grandmother Howchia said she could succeed. She would try to straighten the scrambled power around her, for it was partly her fault. She could live for periods of time in Bear Claw's village and relieve her parents of her dangerous presence. Grizzly Hair had good tools and his men had given him several bear robes. Maybe he would pay for her training.

Never had he looked this discouraged. At last he looked up and spoke. "You are alive. Therefore you did not sleep in the presence of Molok's ceremonial cape. Someone else stole it."

Feeling certain that was not true, she didn't respond.

"Other strangers saw it," Father said.

She tried to think back, but he remembered for her. "Yellow Beard and Pedro Valdez were here at the Big Time. And the unruly young men of Sek's village."

She looked at him in dismay. "Pedro would not steal it."

His face said he didn't trust Pedro. Such trust, she realized, would take much time. Sighing, she asked, "And what of Bear Claw?"

"I would be proud to have a medicine woman for a daughter." He laid his hand on her shoulder, displaying his lack of fear. "Go to Bear Claw. He will say what presents to bring." He turned and walked away under the ashen sky.

She watched him speak to Etumu, who had stopped on the hill where the dancehouse of the Ancients had once stood. Was he saying their daughter was not to be feared because the thief might have been Pedro? A Coyote joke. Or was he saying that since she'd been in their house so many times, they were in no more danger now than before? Or that he, Grizzly Hair, had the power to protect them?

Gladness and sorrow wrestled within her like the river currents around the island. At last things were straight between them, and tomorrow she would go to Bear Claw's village and begin her dangerous learning, if he would let her. It was a terrifying honor that Father and Grandmother Howchia trusted her to do this. She rose to take the rat mash to the u-macha, then realized she couldn't enter until Etumu felt less fearful. She would start the fire and heat the cooking stones.

The air around her moved, as if something invisible swooped past. Goose-flesh prickled the back of her arms. She looked up and saw that the clouds had parted over the mountains and in that distant wash of afternoon sun, the mountains showed like huge white fangs. Not only the pointed tips were white but the slopes all the way down. It was a treacherous smile, and she had never seen the snow that low. Dread turned her soft. As a mouse knows its size against an eagle, she knew her smallness against Condor.

25

FEBRUARY 19, 1847

"Men are coming!"

In the fine weather Elitha Donner was sitting with her three youngest sisters on the felled firewood tree above the family tent, now twenty feet below the surface. It took a moment for her to understand what Jean Baptiste had said, less on account of his accent than the abruptness of the shout in the quiet afternoon. She shaded her eyes against the glare of sun and snow, and saw the half-breed high in a pine, excitedly pointing through the trees.

Three-year-old Ellie cocked her head at Elitha, "What did he say?"

She stood, let black vertigo pass, and squinted in the direction of Jean Baptiste's finger. "I'll go see." She felt hope surge in her heart as she lifted her skirts and plunged into the powdery snow.

He yelled again, "Three men come, with big packs!"

She struggled forward until she saw dark figures coming single file across the little white meadow, as real as anything. Two were enormous. Not the skinny men from the forward camp. Breathless with excitement, she reversed directions and fought her way back. Ellie and Georgia and Frances were still sitting on the downed tree, staring from huge eyes in sharp little faces.

"Those men are gonna take us to California," she told them, backing down the ice tunnel.

Halfway down she slipped and bumped to the bottom. Rubbing her smarting hip bone, she laughed and yelled, "Ma, Pa, relief is coming! The snowshoers must have got through."

Ma turned from where she kneeled, washing the fat, discolored sausage that was Pa's arm. "We are saved then," she said, weeping and laughing and hurriedly tying on a new bandage. "Help me clean." She began straightening things.

The place did look a terrible mess and smelled worse. Elitha stuffed dirty clothing under the blankets. Ma laid a blanket over the chamber pot.

Mrs. Wolfinger got up from the bed and ran long bony fingers through her hair. Catching her heavy skirts, which slipped from her hips, she tied the ends in an hasty knot and carefully mounted the icy steps using her hands. Leanna sat up in bed blinking.

Elitha kneeled beside Pa. "Did you hear? Help is coming."

He moaned.

"Pa! We're saved! Men are coming. Big men. One as tall as Abraham Lincoln and twice as broad!"

"Bout time that odd duck got hitched. Set his sights fer governor I hear."

"Oh Pa, Pa!" It nearly made her cry. His young friend from militia days had been married for years, as Pa knew perfectly well — he had personally welcomed Mr. Lincoln to the farm to talk to a crowd of neighbors, and Congress was what he said he was running for, not governor. It worried her terribly to see him confused like this. And this wasn't the first time. He was having such spells more and more often. Could a bad arm cloud the mind? She gentled her tone. "Pa, I said men are coming to rescue us."

He opened his eyes to slits. "Oh. I'm glad." He added, "For you."

She caught her breath. "Don't talk like that!" She threw her arms about him, loving him more than anything in life.

Wincing, he shrank back.

"Oh, Pa, now I hurt you, and you smartin so terrible! I'm so sorry." Feeling like a clumsy ox, she turned toward the stairs, tears welling.

"Elitha lamb."

The old tone. How long since he had called her that? She turned to see his good arm reaching, his brown eyes melting her with a love she felt for him in equal measure. She knelt and clasped his big hand.

"I just wanna say, Elitha, you got the Donner blood. Good stock. Nothing can stop you. Just remember, when there's trouble, just keep going on down the trail."

She swallowed hard, Donner blood coursing through their clasped hands. She couldn't bear the sound of his giving up. Not the Pa she knew. He had settled the Kentucky wilderness with Daniel Boone, then carved a farm out of the rank growth of South Carolina, and done miracles with his homestead in Illinois, buying up the neighbors' ground when they failed, until he had the biggest piece around. Mr. Lincoln's father had made the same moves, but ended up with nothing. Pa was a tower of strength. He kept moving to virgin land whenever the human race got too thick, packing for California at the age of sixty-two, ready to start over. People had tried to talk him out of it, but he had an iron constitution. Donner blood.

"Now gitcher self on up there and see who's come." He gave her a friendly shove.

Darkening the tunnel, Leanna continued to crawl up the ice stairs, moving like she was ninety years old. It tried Elitha's patience. By the time she followed Leanna into the sunlight, three strangers in floppy leather hats and heavy beards stood at the entrance gazing at her. Jean Baptiste, scrawny beside them, touched the biggest one as though assuring himself they were real. Mrs. Wolfinger watched, sedate as a lodgepole pine. Struggling across the snow from Uncle Jacob's tent came cousins Mary and George Donner, Aunt Betsy and her son Will Hook.

Elitha asked the biggest rescuer, "Are you from Fort Sutter?" His thighs were like tree trunks.

He turned his deep-set brown eyes on her and Elitha recognized him from back on the prairie. "I'm John Rhoads. This here's ole Dan Tucker." He pointed at a large man with a bushy red beard, opened in what was apparently a smile. "That there is Mr. Moultry."

"You were on the wagon train," she said to Rhoads. He had made the remark about the Donners' money. *Come to murder them?* The thought fled before his whiskery smile. She felt the goodness in this bear of a man, and could almost see herself in his eyes, a sorry sight despite washing her face in snow each morning. Her frock and cloak were stained and badly creased from being slept in.

Ma emerged from the hole yanking her skirts straight. Her face was wrinkled beyond her forty-five years and, standing erect, she was shorter than anyone else except the little girls. She had a smile in her voice. "I'm Tamsen Donner. Are you men from heaven?"

The man with the red beard chuckled and doffed his hat. "Reasin P. Tucker, ma'am. And I haven't seen heaven yet."

Timidly, Georgia asked, "Are you the Dan Tucker in the song?"

The man laughed and said, "It's not my real name."

"Well, land sakes!" Ma said, "Never have visitors been more welcome." A wide smile compacted the lines on her face like an accordion. "We'd be pleased if you'd come in and rest. You must be tired."

John Rhoads swung the pack off his back. Unlacing it, he reached inside, brought out a biscuit and placed it in Elitha's hand.

Amazed, she curled her fingers around its floury bigness, felt its hard substance and ran her thumb along the browned edge where it had touched grease. Tears sprang to her eyes. Saliva shot under her tongue and her stomach knotted. She was about to break the biscuit into parts for everyone when she realized the men were handing one to each person.

All stared at the biscuits, except Jean Baptiste, who had stuffed the whole thing into his mouth and was chewing hugely. Mrs. Wolfinger sniffed hers. With the flat of her hand, little Ellie pressed hers against her cheek lovingly. "Can we eat it?" She cocked her head at the man.

"Little girl, if you don't eat that blamed biscuit that I carried all this way, I think *I* will cry. Now you wouldn't want to see a grown man do that, wouldja?"

"No SIR!" Ellie broke a nub from the bottom edge, tongued it like a frog, and grinned close-mouthed at Elitha.

Elitha put the browned edge of her biscuit between her teeth and sucked in the feathery aroma of flour and bit off a little, savoring the hint of lard, baking soda, and salt, which she hadn't tasted since back on the prairie. It stung the raw, swollen roof of her mouth.

"Well, eat the goddam things!" Mr. Moultry demanded, then lifted his hat at Ma and Aunt Betsy. "Begging you pardon, ladies. Been a while since I seen white women."

26

"I am the daughter of George Donner," Elitha marched to that rhythm as she placed cold-deadened feet into the furrowed snow. Wool stockings, shoe leather and pieces of a blanket tied around her shoes separated her from the snow. She and Leanna followed the rescuers, walking single file — Mrs. Wolfinger and three other women ahead. Seventeen children, six men, and a rescuer brought up the rear.

Three days out, and Elitha couldn't for the life of her imagine Fort Sutter, where she and Leanna were supposed to wait for the family. Nicer than the forts on the prairie, people said. Sort of Spanish. John Rhoads had said another rescue party, now on its way, would take the rest of the Donners through to the fort. Any time now they would meet those second rescuers on the trail. For three days she had kept a vigilant eye out, but the dark things she saw in the distant snow always turned out to be trees.

"Smile often and be friendly," Ma had instructed. "Nobody likes a sourpuss. And tell people you are the daughter of George Donner." Tamsen was rightly proud of the Donner name and the nice house and well-kept place in Illinois. In California Elitha planned to behave in the manner that spoke well of her upstanding people.

But now the snowy mountains seemed endless. Behind her Mary Murphy whined like a hurt puppy. Leanna limped behind among the children, including their seven-year-old cousin George Donner, named for Pa. Elitha turned, but they were all so far behind snaking through the trees, she could scarcely see them.

I am the daughter of George Donner. She felt tired, her head light, and she longed to lie in the snow. But they must get to the food cache first. Today they were supposed to find it, and a good thing too. Shivering around a fire all last night, she had eagerly joined the crowd for rations. The rescuers handed out the usual cube of jerky the size of a thumbtip, which they served each morning, and one teaspoon of flour, which they spooned out twice a day. But that had been the last of the supplies. Dan Tucker scraped the last flour from his pack, with the little ones crying, "me, me, me."

John Rhoads had said, "Don't worry, we'll reach food today." Like St. Nicholas with his pack, he'd slung his blanket, containing little Naomi Pike, over his shoulder and plunged up the trail. Elitha noticed he hadn't eaten even in the morning.

Stomach pains turned her inside out, the more so for walking all day. Ma had been right; lying in bed saved your strength. And with each step it seemed little knives stabbed up into her legs. The hazy sun had moved across the sky. Never had she longed for anything as much as rounding a bend to see John Rhoads removing a big leather bag from a tree limb.

Behind her Mary, a year older than Elitha, was saying, "I'll bet Lem's down at Mr. Sutter's just asuckin up pot roast with potatoes and gravy." Mary was Lem's sister.

Gravy again. Shutting her mind to food, she said, "He was brave to go out with the snowshoers."

"What?"

She turned around. "I said, Lem's brave." It felt good to look away from the glare off the snow. She turned back and saw John Rhoads giving her a strange look.

Mary called, "They said Lem got frostbite pretty bad."

Well, who wasn't frostbit? Elitha hadn't the strength to talk. She looked at John Rhoads' broad back, a silhouette in the blinding haze, and watched the brightness drop behind a mountaintop. The snow turned bluish. In only a few minutes it crunched differently beneath her wrapped shoes and the sound told her the cold would be bad again tonight. She could smell it sitting down on the frosty pines. But if Lem Murphy could get through, she reminded herself, she could too.

Ahead, John Rhoads swung the child off his back. Joy moved her legs more quickly. She turned to Mary and called, "They found it!" The rescuers stood beneath a tree looking up.

Catching up to them, she saw dark shreds on the snow at their feet.

Dan Rhoads was saying, ". . . maybe bear or wolves."

John Rhoads squatted, fingered a scrap as if weighing it, and scowled at the distance. "Some'm big."

Mr. Tucker added bitterly, "Ate every bit."

She understood.

Mary caught up and linked her arm in Elitha's, staring. A growing pack of children arrived. From John Rhoads' green blanket Naomi Pike wiggled out like an inchworm, blinking.

"Where's the me-eat?" Mary half-whispered. John Rhoads looked at the solemn children peering at him from dark cloaks and Elitha read his despair. What would they do? They had to eat.

Mrs. Wolfinger pressed her palms together like a tall sad nun. Elitha followed her glance to the smear of coral clouds above the mountain, the only color in the landscape. The pines stood quiet in their white upholstery.

There was no food. A hard shiver passed through her and she recalled Pa saying, "Just go down the trail." He must have known the crossing would be worse than she'd figured. Foolishly she had thought the presence of rescuers meant an end to trouble.

Big John straightened up and announced, "Gimme the hatchet, Ned. We'd better make camp."

Her knees gave way and she sank to the snow, her stomach a grinding monster. She closed her eyes and silently prayed. "Please, God, if you let me get through, I will always be good." Never had she felt so small and weak as out here on the mountainside. *How long did people live without food?*

Mary lay sobbing. Mrs. Keseberg cried aloud, hugging Mrs. Wolfinger, who comforted her in German. Surrounding them, a dozen children whimpered. "I wanna biscuit. I'm HUNgry!" Elitha jammed her mittens over her ears.

Virginia Reed arrived with Leanna, and Elitha watched the pain in their twelve-year-old faces as comprehension hit.

Elitha threw her arms around her hundred-percent sister, hardly able to feel her light bones inside the layers of wool. "We'll get through. You'll see." She rocked Leanna. "No. No, Don't cry. Remember what Pa says. You can always go more than you think."

Leanna's sobs eased and they watched John Rhoads make the cross for the fire while the other rescuers whispered in a huddle. Later, when Elitha, Mary and

Leanna and all the whimpering children sat near the fire trying to warm their feet, John Rhoads stood and spoke in a voice that sounded like God:

"Children, everyone, listen. In the morning four men will go ahead to the next cache. They can go a sight faster'n you. They'll be back with food in a day or so. But you gotta keep walking, so they won't have so far to come. Understand? The farther you walk, the sooner you eat."

"Will you stay with us?" Elitha asked.

To her relief, he nodded his big bear's head.

"I'm HUNgry!" a child whined, and others chorused.

Mrs. Wolfinger said, "Giffs a schtorm coming?"

Everyone looked where the coral had left the sky. Gray clouds pressed down over it. Mr. Tucker wrinkled his nose in several directions and said, "I hope it holds off a while." He didn't sound hopeful.

Elitha buried her face in the hammock of her cloak-covered knees, tucked her cold fingers beneath them and felt spent, exhausted. She ached beyond sleepiness. *Please God, no storm.*

"What the god-damned hell!"

Elitha's eyes flew open to gray light. She saw the pine, a limb dangling with snowshoes, a rescuer brandishing an empty frame. "You low down, shitty vermin!" he said, glaring at Elitha and the other people by the frozen, sooty pond where the fire had been. She felt guilty though she'd done nothing.

"Which a you bastards et my snowshoes!" His eyes were terrible in his hairy face.

John Rhoads placed a hand on his arm. "Hush, man. You might can walk on top. The crust froze pretty hard last night."

He threw off the hand. "I'd like as hell t' see YOU walk on top!"

"Here, use mine." Rhoads handed him his snowshoes.

He snatched them and said, "We gotta punish the thief."

John Rhoads' voice was low and patient. "You complain of feeling poorly after two weeks of low vittels. Man, these people been starvin for three months." His look said end it.

No more was said. The angry man and three others headed down the trail for the next cache. Rhoads and the two strongest rescuers remained to prod the children into line. Elitha scooped a handful of snow and noticed the clouds had thickened. A wind was picking up. She took her place beside Leanna, the ice granules hurting her inflamed mouth, then numbing it. Would the weather hold? This was the longest break since that first storm had stopped the wagon train. *Please God, no storm.*

She helped Leanna walk over the humps between the packed-down steps.

Then they discovered the surface beside the trail held their weight, and it was much easier walking. Seeing her, all the children walked on the crust and Mrs. Wolfinger and Mrs. Keseberg. Even they didn't fall through, until afternoon.

But John Rhoads did. Bringing up the rear, he floundered to his thighs as he coaxed the children. "Keep going," he'd say, "That's a good boy." Once Elitha heard him say, "I'll give you a lump of sugar when we get there if you walk up to that rise."

Every so often Mrs. Keseberg's little girl lay down, limp beyond crying. Elitha dropped Leanna's arm and helped the child. "Get yourself up now. Go on," she'd say, imitating John Rhoads. "That's right, keep going." She knew the girl's mother had no more strength than it took to keep herself upright and couldn't carry the child. Elitha, too, moved by force of mind, and felt she couldn't have carried a fly.

Ahead, the line bunched as if snagged. Momentarily she thought the forward rescuers had returned with food, but they'd only lit out this morning. She wasn't thinking straight. When she caught up to the crowd, she saw a man curled in the snow like a baby in bed. John Rhoads stepped forward with his bundle over his shoulder. "Mr. Denton, get up!" He yanked the frail man's arm, but only dragged him in the snow.

Mr. Denton's dull eyes pleaded from his withered face and his voice scratched, "No. I'm too tuckered. Leave me be."

The other rescuers exchanged looks with Rhoads, and the red-bearded one said, "We already tried, John. It's no use. Leave him be."

Mrs. Keseberg's little girl curled up beside Mr. Denton. Several more children lay beside him. Leanna plopped down, explaining to Elitha, "I can't go on either. I'll just rest a little with Mr. Denton, and come along later."

John Rhoads used his God's voice and Elitha jumped in her skin. "You children git up this minute, hear? Or I'll TAN YOUR HIDES!" He looked ferocious scowling that way, with his thick legs braced and his deep eyes flashing.

Leanna slowly pushed to her feet. The children staggered up and crossed their hands over their bottoms, whining, "Don't whup me Mr. Rhoads." All except the little Keseberg girl, who lay motionless.

"Then git yerselves on up that trail," John pointed over their heads. "What would yer folks say? To think you got no more gumption than this here old man!"

Elitha knew Mr. Denton was a lot younger than Pa. The children struggled onward, but Mrs. Keseberg's daughter did not rise. Mr. Rhoads swung down his green blanket, spread it, and placed the little girl next to three-year-old Naomi Pike, Mary Murphy's niece. Two inchworms, Elitha thought, as he slung them on his back.

Mrs. Keseberg's lips stretched back in a toothy wail. "Oh, *dahnke, dahnke.*" Elitha couldn't help but remember Mr. Tucker scowling and saying, before they'd left the lake camp, "No child who has to be carried can come." The rescuers needed their strength or all would founder. John Rhoads had nodded at Naomi Pike and said, "Cept that one. I'll carry her. I never saw a woman as pitiful as her ma down at Johnson's ranch, a crying for that girl."

Mr. Moultry had tried to change his mind. "Man, yer gun weighs twelve pounds!"

Rhoads had looked from under his bushy dark brows, and no more was said. He had a soft heart, Elitha realized, and it was a blessing he was also the strongest. Now she admired his ability to do what was best for the children. Sometimes people needed a scolding. She never looked back to where Mr. Denton lay, though a fearful shiver passed through her to think he would freeze.

Leanna muttered, "He's mean." She threw her arm over Elitha's shoulders, using her as a crutch.

"Mr. Rhoads is keeping us all alive. Why, Mr. Denton couldn't even make a fire. All of you would have froze back there. Don't you know you never could have caught up?"

The snow was softer now, and John Rhoads sank deep with each step and sweat glistened on his dark brow. The monster gnawed her insides. Snow stuck to her feet and had to be constantly knocked off. Every several steps she sank too. Nevertheless she supported Leanna and took charge of tired children who wanted to lie down. Helping them along kept her mind off her stomach and smarting feet.

The rescuers called an early camp. Mr. Moultry offered his snowshoes to be cooked and Elitha gratefully accepted half a leather string.

27

"I'm afeared we ain't gonna make it," Mary Murphy said at dawn the next morning. Sitting beside Elitha, she looked like an old woman with her kerchief tied beneath her chin, her blue eyes terribly exposed to the cold on account of their bulging. She'd hardly said a thing yesterday.

"Course we will." Elitha rolled on her hands and knees, and stood erect, skirts crackling, backside stinging with the cold.

"The men who went ahead? I was thinkin they mayn't come back atall! What if they done et everything, and gone on?" Her face wrinkled up to cry.

Elitha saw Virginia Reed listening, and knew she couldn't let Mary's supposing spread. "They'll be back. You'll see." Two days had passed since the men had gone ahead.

Mary arranged her bluish lips in a pout.

Glancing at John Rhoads, who was rolling the two little girls in his blanket, Elitha realized he'd heard. The pain in his eyes reminded her of Pa. Was he sorry he had come to rescue them? He swung the blanket and its contents over his shoulder.

Well, she'd let him know he'd done good. "You just watch," she said to Mary and Leanna in a voice meant for him, "Those men'll show up before you can say Jack Spratt. Come on, the faster we go, the sooner we meet them." She stuffed a handful of snow in her mouth and waited for it to numb the sores.

As she helped children walk, she recalled a time last summer when the sun had been hot. It was back then, in the Rocky Mountains, where she and Mary had become friends. They had stretched out their legs on a flat-topped boulder and looked over the scuffed toes of their shoes to the stalled wagon train below. Men hacked at trees and women sat mending clothing. How sweet the summer air had smelled! With the scent of shooting stars and lupine all abloom!

"Most of us in this here wagon train 're Mormons," Mary offered, flouncing her skirts. "Now you keep that under yer hat, or Ma'll whup me go-o-od." Mary had a way of making a syllable last three beats.

Elitha crossed her heart. "Are you Mormon?" She glanced at Mary's head, but saw no horns poking through the curly dark hair.

"Alla us Murphys."

Shocked, but recognizing opportunity, she started with, "You got on holy underwear?"

Mary grinned sidelong at her, the neat stub of her flat nose near her full lips — a mouth fascinatingly near the bottom of her face — then hiked her skirt above her buttoned shoes. Saggy longjohns covered her legs.

"Is that it?" Never had she imagined anything so plain being called holy.

"Yup."

"Don't you ever take them off?"

"Not never, less I got a leg in my clean pair." Mary flounced her skirt over her shoes and looked at the working men below. The bridge of her nose was so low both blue eyes could be seen at once bulging over it. That too was fascinating.

"How do you bathe?"

"One leg at a ti-ime." Her lips turned up.

"You allowed to get them wet?"

"Not sposed to."

Glancing across the summer meadow where the Wolfingers were strolling, she tried to imagine washing like that, standing with one leg in the tub. A light breeze billowed the sleeves of Mrs. Wolfinger's creamy silk blouse. They might have been king and queen, she wearing her ivory brooch. The thudding of axes paused, and the murmur of the little stream running through the meadow carried far up the boulders in the thin air. She lowered her voice and got to the worst thing. "People say Mormons are cannibals."

Mary pressed her lips like it made her mad to hear such whoppers. "Folks prattle that way t' make people hate us."

"Mormons don't ever eat human flesh?"

Mary scowled ahead. "Course not!"

"People say Mormons have hundreds of wives."

"I never heard of one with tha-a-at many!"

She was on to something. "Would you marry a man if he already had a wife?" Ma said polygamy was barbaric, and she thought so too.

Mary flung her dark wavy hair from side to side, but something in the shake gave away a glimmer of a maybe.

"Isn't that what Mormon men do?"

"If they've a mi-nd, but ain't nobody can make a lady marry a man ifn she don't wa-a-ant."

"What if he married you first, then got himself another wife, ten more? What could you do about it?"

She blinked and watched the Wolfingers. "Nu-u-thin I guess." Her turned-out lip said Elitha had gone far enough.

"I got a secret," Elitha gave, ignoring the horror of Mary's answer.

Her bulging blue eyes lit up. "Cross my heart I won't te-e-ell." She slashed the air over her chest.

"Hope to die?"

"Burn in Hades." A smile stretched the bottom of her face.

"I think Lem's a looker." Maybe it wasn't enough to balance Mary's secrets, but it was all she had.

"Le-e-emuel?"

Elitha glanced back to be sure her little sisters hadn't followed. "Shhh. Yes, Lem."

"Well he's just a ki-i-d!"

That hurt. She tucked a flyaway strand of hair behind her ear and said, "Well, you're his sister. Maybe you don't see him the way I do." Lem seemed a lot older than fourteen. Or was it thirteen? It didn't matter.

Mary scooted closer and put her arm around her. "I didn't mean nuthin, honest. Lem's a good boy. Ma says he's worked like a man ever since Pa died."

"I'll say! Just look at him down there." Laboriously the men were axing through the trees, Lem swinging in steady rhythm, and if he was only thirteen he sure didn't look it.

"I guess Lem's a looker," Mary allowed.

Now it was winter and they plodded through the snow, angling down yet another steep mountainside, a skitter of clouds over the sun. She turned to see big

John Rhoads toiling behind. There was a real man.

Later he swung his green bundle to the snow and called up the line, "Make camp!" It was early, but even he had to be exhausted. No one had eaten a crumb for days and a big man needed a lot of food.

Mr. Tucker waved his snowshoes and called, "Come and get it!"

John Rhoads unrolled his blanket and little Naomi Pike sat up. Mrs. Keseberg was staring down. John squatted to look, and they both reached down, touching. A scream came from Mrs. Keseberg and echoed across the mountain. John picked up and carried a stiff child behind the trees, Mrs. Keseberg wailing and stumbling behind. When they reappeared later, his arms were empty. Mrs. Keseberg shrieked at the sky, "*Du lieber Gott, nehm mir auch!*"

Elitha felt small and helpless as she sat where the fire was being built and sawed at the leather with her teeth, working shreds away from the whole. She had made that little girl walk. Now it seemed cruel. She didn't know how near to dying the child had been. Poor Mrs. Keseberg!

No one spoke. Across the fire, John Rhoads hunched over his knees like he couldn't face anybody. But despite the death and Mrs. Keseberg's bone-rattling howls, Elitha fell into a stupor-like sleep.

The next day was cold, but thankfully clear. It seemed a miracle, that and the way her feet kept moving across the frozen crust. Now Mr. Moultry and Mr. Tucker each carried a child who couldn't walk, and again camp was made in the early afternoon. When Mr. Tucker's blanket was unrolled, another child was dead. Again they buried the body in the snow. Elitha sat with Leanna, shutting out the cries of hungry children. *Please God, bring the men back with food.* Three days and two nights now with nothing but snow in their bellies. Who would die next? It could well be Leanna, who looked very poorly.

Then, just before dark two burdened men staggered through the trees and fell on their huge packs, moaning in pleasure to be lying down.

"I told ya they'd come!" Elitha said to Mary and Leanna.

"Yer brother and Glover got too famished to come back," Mr. Coffeemeyer said to John Rhoads. "They headed fer Sutter's. Said they'd send supplies back to the springs."

"How far didja have to go?" Mr. Tucker asked, patting him like a good dog.

"All the way down to Bear Valley." The men sat up and shrugged out of their leather packs.

"What about the cache at the head of the Yuba?" John Rhoads said as he untied one of the packs.

"Eaten clean by varmints. My guess is squirrels gnaw the straps, then varmints git to it on the ground. But John, there's no relief at Bear Valley!" He waited in the silence, then added, "We gotta take these people all the way down to the springs. That adds two days at the least!" He gasped for breath. "What do you spose happened to the Second Relief?"

Straddling a bag, working the ropes, John said, "You done good gittin all this way in only three days." He hefted the bag and raised his bushy brows. "With the likes of this." He patted the bag, pulled out a handful of smoked beef strips and raised his voice, though it was unnecessary, so intent was the watching crowd. "Each person gets a piece as big as my thumb."

"Good thing it's hi-is thumb," Mary whispered, watching Mr. Coffeemeyer. Like a doctor in an infirmary, he was distributing teaspoons of flour to lined-up children.

Will Hook, Aunt Betsy's son by a former marriage, sneaked a hand into the pack behind John Rhoads, but Rhoads whirled and cuffed his arm. "Haven't you never heard of people dyin by gorgin? Bloatin their stomachs till they pop? You gotta be careful after starvin."

Will glowered at the huge man, and Elitha felt ashamed of his bad manners, even if he wasn't a genuine Donner. Uncle Jacob had his hands full with that one.

Mr. Coffeemeyer glanced at the boy, then back at John Rhoads. "It was a hard trek, but I wouldn'ta traded places with you three, left with the likes of them." He cocked an eye at the children around the fire.

Elitha caught a shade of brightness or finality in his tone that somehow announced the end of trouble. It shot strength into her veins along with the biscuit and jerky. Sitting at the fire, ignoring her pounding head, she hugged Mary in one arm and Leanna in the other and grinned. "We're gonna get through!"

Then for the first time on the trek, she let her mind drift unchecked. She saw a dinner plate with schnitzel swimming in gravy the way Grandma Donner used to make it. Sharing the gravy were heaps of mashed potatoes with butter pooled in the craters and overflowing down the sides, and a pile of creamed snapbeans with big hunks of pork that fell apart in the mouth and a crust of buttered crumbs folded through. She saw herself forking through everything with abandon, then digging into a deep pan of apple-pan-dowdy awash in sweet clotted cream.

The snow had thinned and was edged with a dripping lace of ice. With the sparse but regular infusion of food Elitha's spirits soared, when she wasn't thinking about poor Will Hook, and she looked forward to riding on a mule. That would feel like heaven after walking on painful feet — it had been five days since Coffeemeyer's return, and two days beyond Bear Valley. The rescuers said they'd reach the springs today, where Mr. Sutter was sending mules to carry them to Johnson's ranch. She hoped they weren't mistaken.

But her relief at the warmer climate was tempered by sadness. It started when they met Mr. Reed and several men coming up the trail. Mrs. Reed had fainted at the sight, and Virginia clung to her pa like she'd never let go. Mr. Reed handed out sugar cakes, which he and the men had made at Bear Valley. Oh, how wonderfully sweet they were, though they stung Elitha's raw mouth. The rescuers figured Mr. Reed's party had missed Mr. Coffeemeyer's group by only a day or two. One final hug for Virginia and Mr. Reed and his men hurried up the tamped trail toward the lake camp, where his youngest children, Patty and Tommy, were still stranded. Thank goodness Pa's best friend was on his way, thin but determined. He would not forget the Donners.

That same day Elitha's group arrived in Bear Valley, where men were baking bread and more sugar cakes. The camp was full of it. But before two hours had passed Will Hook was rolling in pain, having gorged despite the warnings. The men forced him to drink tobacco juice that they'd chewed and spat into a cup, and he had vomited. But when they saw him gorged again the next morning, they couldn't save him, even with tobacco juice. They'd found bread jammed in his pockets even as they buried him in the snow, and took out tight wads of it. Poor Will! Poor Aunt Betsy. Elitha figured she'd be the one to tell her.

Now, a scattering of oaks spread horizontal branches among the monotonously vertical pines. In a sunny place she spied a dark patch in the snow, went to it, and realized it was bare ground — the first she'd seen since October. Wet dirt, a remembered friend, with a tatting of melting ice. In the center, a fur of infant grass spears was already up. She kneeled and laid her cheek against the cold ground and thought she heard the whir of life.

People gathered. Children stared. Adults smiled, and John Rhoads grinned.

Elitha and Mary and Leanna hooked arms and the three limped along on throbbing, cracked feet, sometimes yelling in pain and laughing about the yelling. They passed larger and larger brown spots in the white, until the snow appeared as bedraggled and tired as they all felt.

The cries of the little ones had changed from I'm hungry to, My FEET hurt. But soon it would be over. She felt a smile on her face. They had broken out of the quiet fastness of the mountains. They had survived the deepest snow and worst winter the rescuers said anyone could remember. Not even a storm could spoil it now. God had answered her prayers.

Later in the day she unbuttoned her cloak and felt fresh air creep through her sweater, linsey-woolsey dress and cotton petticoat, all the way to her skin. Air was no longer the enemy. Once again she felt allied with nature, part of the spring ready to burst forth. Every hour the grass was a little taller, where the sun shone, and she could hardly wait to see the first farm at the foot of the mountains — Johnson's ranch, the guide book called it. Farms were called ranches or ranchos in California. She pictured painted white fences, neat barns, a large house, and fashionable buggies.

"Look!" Mary pointed ahead to where mules and horses nibbled grass as if it were the most natural thing in the world. Elitha recalled poor Belle and Pal and all the other gaunt animals that had frozen under the snow, and how Jean Baptiste couldn't find them even with his metal-tipped probe. Those poor animals would have loved this. New life was beginning.

Tents came into view, and men tending fire. She caught a noseful of sour dough and knew it came from the dutch ovens on tripods. She let out a squeal and hugged Leanna and Mary. More men came into view, young and old, standing, staring awkwardly as if not knowing what to do with their hands.

Soon she was sitting on bare ground with Leanna and Mary, and laughing right through the embarrassment of being gawked at by the men. A man in buckskins staggered over to John Rhoads with a cup, but he refused it. More spirits were flowing from an oaken barrel. Some of the men collected around Mrs. Wolfinger and Mrs. Keseberg, who had stopped crying. *Little Ada buried in snow, and cousin Will Hook.* Wolves and bears would get the bodies.

"Will you marry me," asked a pug-nosed young man in apparent seriousness.

Elitha looked around. "Me?"

"You is the be-oootifulest sight I ever seed!" His face was a comical pout.

She stifled a laugh. She hadn't even combed her hair for two weeks. "You don't know me."

"What's yer name?"

"Elitha Donner, daughter of George Donner."

"Will ya marry me, Eliza?"

"I said Eli-THA."

"Oh, sorry ma'am, I thought you was a lisper."

She turned to giggle with Mary, but Mary was busy with her own admirer, a drunken older man. Still another man was sweet-talking twelve-year-old Virginia Reed, though she lay in an exhausted heap. Propped up on an elbow, John Rhoads watched from his deep eyes. Elitha looked earnestly at the freckled face and said, "No. I won't marry you." All the other men were looking at her too.

To pass water in private she had to speak to John Rhoads, and he made sure the men — most looked like trappers and mountain men — didn't follow her. During the evening a cold wind swept down the mountain and she hunched toward the fire, flanked by Mary and Leanna. Three times she awoke to push men's hands away and say, "Please stop waking me up."

In the morning the freckled boy removed his hat apologetically. "We don't hardly have no white girls in Californy," he said. "A looker like you won't last."

"What do you mean won't last?"

"You'll git married."

Glad when it was time to mount her mule, she was relieved to see all these men would stay and keep camp for the Second Relief, as people called Mr. Reed's party.

"We don't have enough gear," John Rhoads announced. "Half of you git saddles, the other half git bridles. The critters'll foller each other." He had the bearing of a leader.

Elitha whispered to Mary Murphy. "I wouldn't mind marrying HIM."

She rolled her blue eyes. "Well, he-e-e-'s already married."

Even though it was a joke and she had no intention of marrying any man until she was at least fifteen, she felt a twinge of disappointment. Then it dawned on her. "Is he Mormon?"

Mary pushed out a long, uphill "Uh-huuh."

"You never know then, do you."

Mary gave back a conspiratorial grin.

When all were mounted, John Rhoads waved them into a bunch and backed his horse so he was looking at the whole skinny, ragged crowd of riders. He swallowed and said, "You're a brave bunch. Alla you. You kids done more'n I woulda thought."

He looked at his saddle horn and all were quiet, even the horses. When he brought up his head, she saw his eyes were wet. "I'm tellin' yer folks what good kids you were." He kicked his horse to the front of the line, and led out of camp.

Mary looked over at her from her mule, lips pressed in a knowing smile at the bottom of her face. "Last I heard, you was likin Le-e-m."

She nodded at John Rhoads. "Oh, I'm just joshing about him." She was just happy to be, at last, entering the fabled land called California.

28

Rested after a night in a covered wagon, the first night in three weeks under a roof, Elitha shrugged out of her cloak in the morning sun. She and Virginia Reed were watching John Rhoads stuff dried beef into cowhide bags and tie them, and she had the oddest feeling that if she didn't restrain her hand, it would reach over of its own accord and touch him.

Virginia said, "Ain't you coming on in to the fort with us, Mr. Rhoads?" They had arrived at Johnson's ranch last evening.

"No, I'm hightailin it up yonder." Rhoads nodded up the trail. He was forming another relief party with some of the mountain men, who had congregated here at Johnson's. "No way yer pa and his men can bring down all those people by theirselves, Virginia."

Elitha was relieved this tireless giant was going back. Mr. Reed might not be able to rescue so many Donners — Aunt Betsy and little Simon and Ma, and

Elitha's three half-sisters, and Pa so sick. Pa might need to be carried on a litter.

She glanced beyond the big man to the green hills splotched with dark oaks — leafless yet — wishing by some magic her family could see what she was seeing. Grazing on the lush grass were crowds of beasts they called cattle in California — brown and white spots, slim hips, horns long enough to skewer a horse. Swatches of yellow and white flowers streaked the low places. Flowers! And only a few days back it was the heart of winter. California was more beautiful than she'd dared hope.

The land bordering the trail from the mountains had funneled down through the hills into this cottonwood draw beside the Bear River, and here on the first flat land was Johnson's ranch, not much more than two sad little houses of mud brick, called adobe. No fences, no barn, no garden, no orchard, no buggy. Only an outdoor firepit and drying racks furry with pelts. But a world of birds piped and whistled, and cottontail rabbits scampered all around.

John Rhoads straddled a leather bag and looped a rope under it, his back muscles shifting visibly beneath his red flannel shirt as he pulled and tied the rope. The smell of coffee floated across the yard, and she heard the faint sound of women's voices coming from the adobe. She turned to look. The scene wasn't pretty. Tumbled boxes and broken barrels littered the pocked and rutted mud of the yard. Naked Indian men strolled around as calm as you please, as did bare-breasted squaws with babies in cradleboards. A gang of naked brown children, a few suspiciously white-looking, darted between the covered wagons. She counted eight. The leather-clad mountain men who leaned against the cabin smoked, drank, and told loud jokes she tried to ignore. They didn't lower their voices even though Elitha and Virginia were a stone's throw away. This farm, or rancho, sure wasn't anything like Pa's place.

But it was spring, and she was in California, only two or three days from Fort Sutter. She almost felt ashamed to feel this good while her parents and sisters struggled down the mountains. Energy entered her pores with the sun and her scalp tingled, it felt so clean. She had borrowed soap and a comb from Elizabeth Keyser, a sister of John Rhoads who lived here, and washed her hair in the cold river. She felt good underneath too, because a woman at Sutter's Fort had sent fresh underwear for all the rescued girls and women. She had buried her old drawers.

"Top 'o the mornin, John." A hand came down on her shoulder, and she turned to see the same Englishman who had brought supplies from Sutter's on a small sailing vessel. She'd seen him asking the trappers for help unloading the barrels and boxes, and heard him joke with them. His accent fascinated her, and he was the first clean-shaven man she'd seen since Illinois. The hand remained while Rhoads offered a howdy and the two agreed the weather was nice. She smelled liquor. The man was handsome, his straight nose right out of the pages of Tamsen's art book, the part on Greek sculpture, the slashes of his brows matching his dark wavy hair. He wore no hat, and his bright blue eyes were surrounded by the longest black lashes she'd ever seen on a man. They nearly lay on his tanned cheeks when he grinned down at her — fringed eyes.

He handed her an apple with a blush of orange streaks. "It's from Sutter's farm." The tips of his teeth showed white from perfect lips, but one tooth was missing. His smile poked a dimple into one cheek — a teasing smile.

The apple felt good in her hands and she couldn't help but smile back into his fringed eyes. Saliva shot under her tongue at the smell of the apple even though she knew it would punish the sores in her mouth. Yes, they had apple trees in California, and very few white women. What was he seeing? A tall, young brunette in a dirty dress — some people said she was comely. At least she'd scrubbed her face and hands with good lye soap.

"Well, eat the bleedin thing!" His eyes crinkled irresistibly. He handed another apple to Virginia Reed and beamed at Elitha. "Me nime's Perry McCoon."

She curtsied. "I'm Elitha Donner, daughter of George Donner. I'll eat this later if you don't mind."

He grinned, the dark tapered brows straight as sticks over those amazingly blue eyes. "Expected ye'd be starved enough to eat me, I vow." The mountain men had joked about man-eating women. She looked at them and saw they had listened and were laughing and slapping their thighs. She didn't understand, but felt embarrassed anyway.

"Elitha! Elitha!" A scream.

She turned to see Mary Murphy coming at her from the door of the main adobe, her expression distressed, her arms out. She hit Elitha running.

She steadied herself and hugged back. "Mary, whatever's the matter?"

A keening wail.

She patted her back, mystified. Mary was crying. Crowding around were John Rhoads, the naked Indians, Perry McCoon and all the children, white and Indian. Elitha said into Mary's ear, "Let's get off by ourselves."

She guided her with an arm about her waist and Mary laid the soft pad of her swept-up hair against her cheek and cried like her heart would break. They found a secluded place near the rushing river, beneath budding trees.

"Oh, Elitha, Elitha," she wailed. "Lemuel's dead!" Her shoulders rocked with weeping.

Somebody had said such a thing? It galled her. "No, Mary. John Rhoads said all the snowshoers got through, and he's straight-arrow."

"They said they a-a-te him!"

Her skin crawled from head to toe. "That's crazy. Who said such a horrid thing?"

Mary had her long fingers in her hair and was rocking up and back and crying, "Oh Lemue-e-l."

"Who said that?"

She sobbed out, "Harriet."

Mrs. Pike. Mary's sister — two older Murphy girls had been in the snowshoe party. John Rhoads had carried Harriet's little Naomi all the way down the mountains and laid her in her mother's arms. But from what Elitha had seen of Harriet this morning, she was strange. "Maybe she's outa her head," she said, patting Mary's back. But why say such a crazy thing? The mountainous desolation came back to her — the emptiness of seeing the food cache gone, the hard edge life cut when it needed to survive. But Lem Murphy! Her own breathing came shallow.

Mary rocked frantically. "Well ifn she's crazy, where IS Lem, and Uncle Frank? And my — " The rest dissolved in tears as she collapsed face down, convulsing over her arms. The noisy river rushed by. Mary lifted her head, "Sides, them others didn't even stop her from sa-a-yin it." She went back to sobbing.

Ate him. Elitha felt like she couldn't catch her breath. Small faces peeped through the willows, curious children — orphans until their mothers were brought from the mountains. To weeping Mary she said, "I'll find out the truth. Lem and the others musta gone on to Sutter's, or Yerba Buena."

Leaving Mary, she grabbed the hand of the nearest child and ordered the others to follow. They walked obediently with her as they had done on the long march. "Sit here," she said pointing to a grassy spot where Leanna lay. "Now you all leave Mary in peace. Hear?"

She pushed passed the pungent cowhide into a small, low-ceilinged room that smelled of must, damp dirt and strong coffee. The two small windows were deeply recessed in the adobe. As her eyes adjusted to the dim light, she saw Mrs. Wolfinger, Mrs. Keseberg, Mrs. Reed, Elizabeth Keyser and Harriet Pike, the last holding her bony three-year-old on her lap — all looking at her. Trembling deep inside, she felt like a child in a room full of women, the air thick with secrets. A blackened pot and dented tin cups were scattered on the crude table, which all but filled the room. The only other furniture was a humpback chest beneath one tiny window and a stack of crates below the other. "I've come to learn the truth about Lem Murphy," she said.

They all looked down or away. Elizabeth Keyser, John Rhoads' sister, who couldn't have been too much older than Elitha, stood up and said. "Take my chair. You got no flesh. I don't see's how you can even stand up." She pulled up a crate for herself. Married to a partner of Mr. Johnson, Elizabeth was hostess.

Elitha sat in the crude willow chair and teetered on uneven legs. Sudden light washed into the room and she looked up to see Perry McCoon lifting the leather, but she ignored him and said to the women, "Lem and them wasn't my kin so you don't have to save my feelings. I just want to know if they made it through." Nerves made her squeeze the apple in her lap.

Elizabeth Keyser poured coffee and shoved a dented cup at her. Harriet Pike closed her eyes and let out a ghost of a moan as she rocked the child on the uneven floor, or uneven chair legs. Her bony hand, cracked and red, looked huge on the little girl's yellow sweater. The others were looking at Harriet, leaving it to her to speak.

Elitha prodded, "Mr. Rhoads said all you people on snowshoes got through."

Harriet spoke in a detached tone. "Bill Eddy made it t'here. Brother John fetched the rest of us from an Indian camp a ways back."

So they did make it. "Lem?"

Suddenly a male voice boomed through the doorway, "Well tar my scuppers if it ain't Perry McCoon! Caughtcha in the henhouse!" Coarse laughter snarled. A big gray-bearded man wearing dirty leather clothing was slapping Mr. McCoon on the back.

The Englishman looked pleased. "Where ye been hiding all mornin?"

Elizabeth Keyser said, "Please, Mr. Johnson, we women was atalkin."

Johnson dashed in like a wild animal and grabbed her off the crate, and as cups slid and spilled from the disrupted table, yanked her to him. "Kiss kiss fer yer man's pardner." His red lips jutted from his matted beard and she wrenched her head away just in time for his lips to press her cheek instead of her mouth. Elitha caught the sour eggs whiff of him.

Suddenly locking eyes with her, or rather one eye, the wild man set Elizabeth down and slowly put words together. "My my. Wouldja look at what's come down the mountain!" His unruly gray brows elevated and one eye looked at the wall. He turned his good one to Mr. McCoon, who observed the scene with a teasing dimpled grin, and said, "No wonder yore at my door!"

Elizabeth was rearranging the cups, tears shining in her eyes.

Mrs. Wolfinger, regal despite her wrinkled blouse and wasted appearance, straightened her back and said, "Herr Johnson? *Nicht so*?"

"Last time I heared." One eye kept staring at Elitha and she felt undressed by it. She'd envisioned Mr. Johnson, the first American they'd meet, as a prosperous gentleman farmer whose hired girls would serve food and nurse them back to health. But this was about the worst-looking man she'd ever seen.

In a trembling voice Elizabeth said, "Oh, excuse me, I didn't introduce you. Mr. Johnson, this here's Mrs. Wolfinger, Mrs. Keseberg, Mrs. Reed, and Elitha Donner. They come in last night. You know Harriet."

The German women bobbed their heads and said "*freude*," which Elitha remembered, from Grandma and Grandpa Donner, meant glad.

Johnson hawed and snored by turns in what passed for a laugh. "My pardner allus said the Germans'd take over this here country." Looking around the table he roared, "Why looky here. Ifn he coulda kept his trousers buttoned, he mighta snatched hisself a genu-ine German female. Haw haw haw."

Elizabeth Rhoads Keyser, who apparently had been snatched instead, quietly repeated, "Mr. Johnson, we was atalking." Her tears were gone.

How can she stand it? She had to love Mr. Keyser a great deal to live with him here on land they apparently shared with this horrible Mr. Johnson.

Perry McCoon winked at Elitha and steered Johnson from the room, telling him he'd heard some good stories. Quiet settled over the room and dust danced along the sunbeam angling over the chest from the window, but something still quivered inside her.

Mrs. Wolfinger said, "Elitha Donner iss a strong maiden, strong like iron. You can, ya, say all to her."

She braced herself.

Elizabeth Keyser took in a breath with her eyes closed, then looked at her. "Seven come through. The poorest bags of bones you ever did see. Bill Eddy got here first, poor man. Come to the door and I shut it right in his face afore I knew what I was about. It was like lookin at something not even human."

Seven. "How many went out on snowshoes?"

"Fifteen, wasn't it Harriet? Not counting the Indians?"

Harriet nodded and said, "Here dumplin, take s'more milk." Her big red hand held a cup to the frightfully thin child. *Half had died.*

"Elita, vhat dey not schpeak," said Mrs. Wolfinger, "iss dot the dead, the living haff eaten. Dot has needed been. Understand?" She sucked back her chin in an aristocratic manner as if trying to belie the terrible reality showing in her eyes.

"Lem?" It came out thin. Not one woman at the table met her eyes. Mrs. Pike rocked little Naomi, and the thought of this hard, rangy woman eating Lem's flesh made her insides feel like jiggling jelly. Yet by the faces around her, she knew she'd heard the truth, though it would take time to fully understand. "And Sarah?" Mary's other sister.

Elizabeth Keyser answered. "All five women survived. Sarah went to Yerba Buena. Said she never wanted to hear about the troubles of getting to California ever again."

Light washed over the table, Perry McCoon entering. He touched Elitha's elbow. "Too much doom 'n gloom in here," he said, "Come and I'll show you me bonny schooner."

She stood, pain knifing up from her feet, her knees as weak as her stomach. She felt unreal, like a girl in an improbable story, and knew this moment would turn in her mind the rest of her life. Then she remembered the apple. She asked Elizabeth, "Would you happen to have a knife?"

She looked thunderstruck. "Whatever for?"

"To cut this apple."

Mr. McCoon pulled a horn-hafted dagger from his belt and handed it to her.

Thanking him, she laid the apple on the table and cut it in eighths, a white juicy sunburst erupting with apple fragrance. Pocketing the seeds — someday she would plant them — she handed back the knife, told him she had somebody to talk to, reassembled the apple and hurried across the yard. Men had caught the horses and mules and were saddling them. John Rhoads was still packing. "You didn't tell us the truth, Mr. Rhoads," she said.

He looked up, then back at the leather bag he was filling. "Now if I'd atold it all, who woulda left the camp? More'n likely you all woulda thought the same thing'd happen to you. As it is, all but four made it, outa twenty-three. Way I figger, that's pretty derned good. Saved what little food there was for the others." He looked up the trail. "Old California hands said it couldn't be done atall."

Still, she felt belittled. "You coulda told me."

He straightened to his full height and his beard lay like a dark brown blanket on his chest. His brows drew together in a frown. Men didn't like females telling them their business.

"We sure did get through, didn't we," she said. "I guess you knew what was best." He nodded, cut a length of rope from a coil, and whipped it around the mouth of a bag.

"Will you tell my parents the truth?"

"About you and Leanna being fine, yes. No more."

That made her feel better. He wasn't treating her like a child. "Why did the snowshoers die, Mr. Rhoads?"

Tying off the bag, he put his thumbs in his belt and blew air through his nose. "They got lost. And storms got 'em." He squinted toward the mountains.

"You think they did wrong to eat the dead?" Cannibalism was a fearful sin, maybe the worst.

"Not fer me to say."

She thought about that. Nobody knew what those people had suffered. They didn't have food bags hanging in the trees, or bread and sugar cakes being baked in Bear Valley. Would her parents and little sisters get caught in storms? Would they eat the dead? Jean Baptiste had suggested it long ago. "If Mr. Reed doesn't bring my family down, will you?"

He glanced at the sky the way she'd seen him do a thousand times. Clouds shrouded the mountains. "Yer ma and the little girls. He turned his deep brown eyes on her and she felt the shock of their connected glances. "Elitha, your pa's far gone with the gangrene. You know that, don't you?"

Gangrene. That word hadn't been used. Gangrene killed if the limb wasn't removed. "Maybe he could be carried down to a doctor."

He shook his shaggy head and looked endlessly sorrowful. "He's a big man, even starved."

John Rhoads had a soft heart and amazing strength. Yet even he couldn't do it. Tears tickled her face as she realized her father, a generous man with many friends, a father who approved of her more than she deserved, would die alone in the quiet mountains. But she managed, "Well I guess he'll have to stay up there then." She wanted to run and hide from Perry McCoon, who was eavesdropping, and the leather-clad men who never stopped gawking at her. But she held on to herself and said what she'd been thinking throughout the march. "You're a good man, Mr. Rhoads."

Suddenly he was hugging her, her head on the cushion of his beard, and she heard the steady thud of his heart. This heart would risk another trip to get Ma and the girls, and she couldn't ask more. He put his hand on her head and it felt like a warm cap. "Elitha Donner, you're the bravest girl I ever met."

Perry McCoon interrupted. "Settin sail fer Sutter's, I is." Pronounced Suiter's. He hiked a brow at her. "Happy to take ye aboard."

Gently Mr. Rhoads pushed her away and said, "That's a good offer. You'd be there in a day, stead a two. A lot easier than on muleback."

She caught sight of Mary hobbling around the adobe, steered by Mr. Johnson, and felt sorry she hadn't got back to her sooner. "How many can you take?" Leanna sat playing cat's cradle with some younger girls.

He smiled his dazzling smile at her. "Two or three."

"Just a minute." She turned to Mary, her face wet and vacant, like she was cried out, and handed her half the apple slices. "I guess Harriet was right." Afraid to get her started again, she put a protective arm around her shoulder and added, "Let's go to Sutter's Fort on Mr. McCoon's boat."

On the other side, Mr. Johnson snaked an arm around Mary's waist and pulled her firmly to him. "She's a stayin right here."

"Mary, you sure?" The wall-eyed man smelled to high heaven.

Her glistening eyes turned to the hills. "I guess I'll wait here fer my ma. That way I'll see her sooner."

Inside the tangle of matted beard, Johnson's lips parted in a tobacco-stained, snaggletoothed smile. "Doncha worry, I'll take care a her."

Mr. McCoon tilted his head at Leanna. "I'll taik you and her in me skiff."

Suddenly she needed to be gone from Johnson's ranch that very instant. Mary had made up her mind to stay, and well, that was her wish. Elitha had been bouncing on a mule for three days on her sharp sitting bones and she couldn't wait for the long journey to be over. She ached to forget the hunger and the filth and the snow and children saying My FEET hurt, and mostly she wanted to be far from Mr. Johnson and Harriet Pike and all these ogling trappers — she knew now, she thought, what their jokes meant. With Mr. McCoon she and Leanna could float effortlessly to the rainbow's end and wait there in comfort for the rest of the family. People said Mr. Sutter was a fine host who set a generous table for immigrants.

Besides Mr. McCoon seemed like such a gentleman.

29

Despite the sad news about Pa, Elitha loved watching the busy birds swoop over the river. The leaves of the high trees were only in bud, so the glorious sun streamed through the tracery of branches, which formed a canopy over the water. With the mast cleverly folded down, Mr. McCoon threaded his way through the trees, using a low back sail and a tiller. The Bear River flowed into the Feather River, then the wide Sacramento. "Sail now, she will," he said, braced in the manner of a sailor, which he said he had been. He steered with two fingers on the tiller. Elitha and Leanna sat clinging to the rail.

The narrow boat skimmed the roiling brown current so fast they passed uprooted trees at a good clip. Elitha's hair streamed behind, and it seemed to her they were flying to Sutter's Fort. New Helvetia, Mr. McCoon called it.

"When did you sail on the ocean?" she asked. Leanna looked eager to hear.

"Nine years old I was, when I hopped on that first brig. Came here with Cap'n Sutter nigh onto eight years ago. Sailed ever minute between, cept when we hove into port."

"You were just a boy," Leanna said. "Didn't your folks try an stop you?"

"From sailin?" Seeing her nod, he threw back his head an hawed once. "Not hardly."

"Did the captain make you work hard, when you were a boy?" Elitha asked.

His smile faded momentarily, then the twinkle came back in his eye, "What think ye?"

She tried to imagine life aboard a sailing vessel, but all that came to mind were horrifying tales of becalmed seas and men dying of thirst and being flogged. "I think they made you fetch things?" He nodded. "And clean up after everyone?" He nodded. "Did you like it, I mean when you were a boy?"

He chuckled through his nose, like it was a private joke, then shrugged. "Put food in me mouth and give me a bunk to sleep in."

"Didn't you miss your family?"

He hawed again. "Me daddy was quick t'blow, and he blew hot 'e did, when he was drinkin."

"He beat you?"

"Oft enough."

"Did your mother try an stop him?"

"Dead me mum was, at an early age."

"Did you sail all the seven seas?" Leanna put in..

"Ay lass. And then some." He seemed to enjoy talking into the wind, his tan, sculpted face finely lined.

"Do you remember your mother," Elitha asked, thinking of her own real mother.

"A wee lad I was, but now and then when I close me eyes, I see her face comin." He paused. "A beauty, me daddy says to me she was."

Looking at him, Elitha believed it was true. "You must have lived in a seaport."

"When me mum was alivin?"

"When you signed up to be a sailor."

"Aye, then, if ye calls London a seaport. Me daddy and me went to London after she died. No 'ealthy plaice for man ner boy, that town." He shook his head in amused recollection. "Like to perish, we did, movin from one room to another, then livin on the streets." His voice took on a faraway quality as he stared into the wind. "Niver got over her dyin, me daddy. S'why he took to gin so hard, I guess." Suddenly he was cheerful. "Hail from Illinois do ye?"

"How did you know?"

"Them wot come down before ye, them poor ragged wretches? Said most of the emigration come from Illinois, so I figgered ye might. And wot might yer daddy be doin there in Illinois?"

"He's a farmer. Cleared every place he owned."

"A bonny big farm did ye leave then?"

"Oh yes. Wasn't it, Leanna?" She nodded enthusiastically. Neither of them had been anxious to leave it for the wilds of California.

"What kind of farm? Hogs? Chickens . . . ?"

"Oh yes. And cows. And corn and oats. We had big storage barns and silos, and an orchard. Pa sold boxed fruit to all the neighbors, and took it in to Springfield." People said George Donner had a magic touch when it came to making good on the land.

"A nice 'ouse?"

"Real nice." She thought of the room she and Leanna shared, upstairs, with the climbing yellow Rose of Ophir at the window making the summer nights smell so fine.

"Yer daddy keep the farm, did he?"

"Oh no, sold half interest to my brother before we left."

"Your brother?"

"Well, fifty-percent brother, grown now, with a family. From Pa's first family." People joked that Pa had three lives. Three wives.

"Taik ever penny, did it, to provision the journey?"

"Oh no. We had plenty left over."

"To get started in California?"

"For a nice place, and for Tamsen to build a school. That's my ma, my stepmother actually."

He smiled warmly and she felt a stirring inside her. She'd never seen such deep-blue eyes set in such a tanned faced, or features so perfectly proportioned. He was a man at ease on the water, and talking to girls. He seemed to enjoy the splashing of the water against the prow and the multitude of birds playing overhead.

The passing green vistas patched with yellow and purple flowers reminded her of Tamsen's book of German fairy tales, in which the goddess of spring, Easter, floated in a gauzy robe, as spirits do, over the greening land. She wore a crown of flowers and everything she touched with her magic wand bloomed and hatched and sang — eggs in a thousand nests, spotted and blue, rabbits and deer unafraid with their young, and oaks with wispy halos of pastel green. Exactly as spring looked today. This was the paradise Pa had uprooted them to find. She could see now that he was right to do it. In the midst of so much springtime, hope pushed up in her. The rescuers might yet find a way to carry him down the mountain.

From the helm Mr. McCoon announced, "Making fifteen knots, I'd wager." He looked at Elitha. "Fancy me schooner, do ye?"

"Is that what this boat is called?" Leanna asked. He explained it had been a ship's long boat, meant to be paddled by up to twelve men. For river use it had been decked over so the interior could be used as a hold. The rails and masts had been added.

Elitha admired the way he manipulated the sails and used the wind. He made a series of changes and the boat rounded a right angle corner, tacking back and forth across the inflowing American River. "Westerly'll help, it will," he said. "But sometimes the devil himself can't sail up this river."

Huge trees jutting from the banks limited the boat's range, so he changed the booms every few minutes. Leanna curled up out of his way and napped.

Exhaustion was pressing on Elitha too. She sat against the rail looking at the passing branches, the sky changing from blue to gold, and a powerful longing to get to the fort seized her. Fine accommodations would be waiting, according to Hastings' guidebook. Perhaps she would sleep in a real featherbed for the first time in nine, maybe ten months. She'd lost track. She was almost asleep when the boat bumped wood.

"All ashore for New Helvetia!" Mr. McCoon said, stepping to the prow. Light was fading above the enormous trees — a shadowy, unearthly forest.

Leanna sat up and rubbed her eyes. "Where's the fort?"

He chuckled as he tied the boat. "In good time ye'll see."

Elitha's legs felt rubbery after the long ride. Walking up a trail through the thicket, she stumbled on a root and it hurt her sore foot terribly — both feet still very tender. Mr. McCoon caught her and pulled her to him. A little longer than necessary? Then quite suddenly they stepped out onto a flat grassy plain that reached to the horizons. The mammoth oaks spaced across it looked black in the twilight. Ahead stood the massive fort. Even with so little light she could see it was more substantial than the wooden forts on the prairie — larger, the walls solid.

Approaching the structure she stopped, puzzled. The top of a flag showed above the wall — the stars and stripes. "The book said California was in Mexican territory."

Mr. McCoon scratched his head and replaced his hat. "Maybe it tis."

"But that's the United States flag."

"Any fool's guess, it tis, what country we're standin in." He put his hand on her back and they resumed walking up the trail beside the high wall. "Why, not so long ago I heard the British fleet was taikin California. Might have by now for all a bloke'd know, and that'd make me a naytive now, wouldn't it?" He snickered. "that flag don't mean a thing. Always tryin to cast lots with the winner is John Sutter." Suiter.

Elizabeth Keyser had said a war was going on in some distant California place, and most of the emigrant men had gone to fight, the Rhoads men being exceptions.

"Ever day some bloke rides into the fort," Mr. McCoon was saying, "all in a dither about the bloody war." He turned to her. "A curious lass, ye be."

They rounded a corner and she saw a gate topped with spikes and flanked by cannons. Around it lay covered wagons with the tongues down, like huge toys left by disorderly children. Beyond the wagons was a row of square tents and beyond, Indian wigwams made of bulrushes. Across it all came a breeze with the fragrance of dry grass and coffee.

Women and children came from the wagons and followed them through the gate, but no one spoke. She thought she recognized some of them, but it had been so long since her part of the wagon train had split off from the main migration, she couldn't recall any names. A soldier asked, "You comin in from Johnson's?"

Mr. McCoon lifted his hat, smoothed his hair and announced — his voice heavy with significance — "Donner girls these be, from the stranded wagon train."

A mutter bumped through the crowd and a high-pitched "oooo" scratched into Elitha like chalk on a slateboard. Three children ran a distance away then crept back looking at her and Leanna like they were a side show in a circus. Wondering what on earth was wrong, she exchanged a puzzled look with Leanna and squeezed her hand.

The people followed them across the courtyard and watched them mount a flight of stairs, and she felt their eyes like a physical force. Inside Mr. Sutter's rooms, which weren't anywhere near as grand as she had expected, Perry McCoon introduced them to a man in a military uniform, Lieutenant Kern, and John Sutter wearing ordinary brown trousers and a muslin shirt. A third man with muttonchop sideburns sat in a chair reading a book by candlelight. Mr. Sutter nodded in his direction and said, "General Vallejo." The Spaniard stood, bowed formally, and said, *Mucho gusto*, and returned to his book. The first genuine

Californian they had seen.

Remembering what Ma had said about sad faces making no friends, Elitha smiled at everyone and answered all Mr. Sutter's questions. "No," she said smiling, "we couldn't carry anything." They had no sundries, not even a penny. She looked at Leanna standing on the sides of her shoes to keep the pressure off her toes, her frock hanging from her scarecrow's frame and dark circles under her eyes, and realized she didn't look any better. Like something the cat dragged in, Tamsen would have said. *Where were the beds?* Mr. Sutter, a man about her height wearing an Austrian mustache, made his face into the picture of pity. "Haff you girls hunger now, hmm?"

Perry McCoon answered, "They ate on the skiff."

Elitha smiled and nodded. *Where was the guest room?* She didn't feel up to talking. Exhaustion weighed her down.

Mr. Sutter's pale eyes seemed to swim as he looked at her. Then he turned and went into an alcove, lit a candle and returned with paper, ink bottle, and plume. He scratched a short note, waved the paper dry. "Giff to Mr. Mellus in der store," he said, handing it to her. "He giff supplies. Lieutenant, show dem to mine traveller quarters."

Relieved, she followed Lieutenant Kern to the door and Mr. Sutter laid his hand on her waist. "You are yoong to suffer zo hart." His breath smelled of liquor.

"Thank you very much for helping us," she curtsied, then remembered. "What is the date today, if you please?"

"Martz two."

"March the second?" He nodded and she repeated in her mind, March second, eighteen forty-seven." She would remember this day, her first in California proper, and she would count the days until the rest of the family arrived. With a smile she said, "Spring comes early here," and curtsied good-bye.

Lieutenant Kern led the way out the gate, the people from the wagons following —she couldn't fathom why — to a dark building that looked about a hundred feet long and twenty feet wide. Rounding the butt end of the structure, she saw it was divided into small rooms, none of which had a shutting door, even a curtain. Pointing through a doorway, the lieutenant said, "There you go."

"No plaice for fine young laidies such as these," Mr. McCoon said.

"It's all we have." The small young Lieutenant sounded tired too.

"I know better," Mr. McCoon shot back, and she felt embarrassed to be causing trouble.

The lieutenant snapped, "Mr. McCoon, the rooms inside the fort are occupied by officers of the United States Military."

"This is fine," she interrupted, walking inside the musty cubicle — completely dark. Leanna and Mr. McCoon followed. She stumbled on a loose pile of dirt, perhaps a gopher mound. "Really it is," she added for McCoon. *Why are those people gawking?*

"Firepit's in the middle of the floor," Kern said. "Firewood's catch as catch can." The room had no window, no furniture. She forced a smile and curtsied to Kern. "Thank you ever so much, sir. We are much obliged." Hardly a featherbed, but it was good enough if everyone would just leave. She felt she could put her head on the gopher mound and sleep for a week. At least it was a roof over their heads.

"Are they man-eaters?" asked a child from the doorway. Her scalp crawled.

A large woman grabbed the boy by the ear, twisted it until he was on his toes, and ordered, "Now you say something NICE to these poor girls who are starved and frozen, and all alone in this wicked world."

He screeched, "Sorry Ma, I'm sorry! Stop!" His desperate eyes shifted to Elitha and he said in a nicer tone, "I'm sorry ma'am." His mother liberated his ear.

All alone in the wicked world. They must have thought they'd come down with the snowshoers and their parents were dead. Apparently everyone had heard about that and were mixed up. Quietly but firmly she said, "My sister and I came through with the relief party. Our parents will get here in a week or two." People looked at her. She took a breath and added, "We ate no human flesh."

"Ooo-ooh" squealed a child with a face that might have sucked a lemon. Others circled in playful horror as children do, apparently not caring to know the truth. She looked at Leanna in the dark, her head down, shoulders sloped, and took her hand.

Lieutenant Kern was leaving at last. "Now remember, sign for food at the store."

"Thank you sir," she curtsied and forced another smile, although her face could hardly do it. "Thank you both for your kindness." She and Leanna would be here for a while, so she'd straighten these people out. But tomorrow would be soon enough, in the light, when she could see them. It would help, she thought, to be a little older.

Everyone else left, but Perry McCoon lingered. Much as she liked him, she had hoped he would be tired too. Leanna stretched out on the floor despite his presence. They had both done it on the boat, but in the small room such an action seemed disturbingly intimate.

"Liked sailin with ye, I did. Hits not ever day I gits company, and comely company at that."

"Thank you ever so much Mr. McCoon." She couldn't see him in the dark.

"Call me Perry."

She became aware of her muffled heartbeat, and wondered if he was married.

Leanna pulled her cloak to her chin, turned over, and began a soft even snore.

Perry said, "Check on ye tomorrow at noon siesta, I will. That's what they calls it 'here. Siesta." She could feel his grin. "I'll be workin with the cows till the

Captain puts up another load to taik to Johnson's."

She was glad he'd come tomorrow. She'd make herself more presentable.

The next day dawned overcast, and by noon rain threatened. Mr. McCoon, freshly shaven, came as promised, and Elitha walked with him around the fort wall, leaving Leanna. When her feet hurt she sat on a stack of adobe blocks, Perry beside her. He surprised her by saying he owned a big spread of land. "In California high birth means nothing," he added with a happy crinkle in his eyes. "Me land is as big as any squire's in England."

"Oh, I thought you were working for Mr. Sutter." Suiter, she pronounced it.

"Being naighborly, I is. Sail 'is sloop to Johnson's and back, an 'elp with 'is cattle. Ranchers lend a 'elpin 'and in this country."

"Who's tending to your farm while you're gone?"

"Gots me fifty niggers, big strong bucks, workin the plaice." She couldn't decipher his strange expression.

"Niggers?"

"Indians."

She'd heard that before, slang for dark skin. Is it like this? Your farm?" She opened her arms at the fields and grasslands, upon which hundreds of animals grazed — cows, horses, mules, sheep and goats. Mr. Sutter was said to own the land as far as the eye could see and to employ many Indian riders to do the herding, called a Spanish term that sounded like buck-arrows.

"Ay, but I got no fort or stores, and Sutter's land is a sight bigger, a bleedin barony, it tis."

She was feeling the first drops of rain and trying to imagine this sailor working a farm with fifty Indians when he turned his face, his blue eyes, to her, and said, "Would ye like to be the mistress of such a rancho?"

Heat flushed up her neck and ears, and, having no idea if he was proposing marriage or passing the time, said, "Well I don't know. I'm going to help Tamsen, that's my mother, set up her school and I guess I'll teach in it for a while."

Sounds of talking came from the trail that led to the river. They both turned toward it and saw Mrs. Wolfinger and Mrs. Keseberg. Behind them came two men and several children, all walking toward the fort. The relief party arriving.

"I'll get back to the cows," said Perry McCoon. "See ye laiter."

He left and the sky opened up. Elitha ran to the room to get Leanna and a broken half-barrel they'd found. They stood in the fort yard holding the barrel above their heads, watching as Mr. Sutter and Lieutenant Kern greeted the immigrants in the rain. Mrs. Wolfinger and Mrs. Keseberg chattered in German with Mr. Sutter. How dignified they looked bowing their heads to each other!

When Mr. Sutter was talking to the men, Leanna tugged the barrel toward

Mrs. Wolfinger, who had smiled them a hello, and said, "Where's Virginia and Mrs. Reed?"

"Day schtay wit da Sinclairs, udder side da river." That was the lady who had made all the new underwear.

Leanna looked crestfallen. She and Virginia Reed had been good friends on the trek down the mountains; she wanted to see her.

"Frau Reed haff bad pain in der head," Mrs. Wolfinger explained, joining them under the barrel. "Goot vooman. Care for dem till der man come wit Patty and Tommy."

"Come and see our room," Leanna said.

They hurried, all holding the barrel over their heads, like three girls in a funny Fourth of July race — Mrs. Wolfinger about twenty years old — and when they stood looking at the room, Mrs. Wolfinger had a far-away expression, the way she'd often looked in the tent. In the light from the open doorway, the pot they'd got from the store for frying and boiling looked untidy in the ashes.

"Well," Leanna said, I guess it's better'n being under the snow."

"Ya. Iss better." Her expression hadn't changed. Thinking about Mr. Wolfinger? And his stolen fortune? The hired-man who'd confessed that he helped kill her husband and blamed it on Indians?

"You can sleep with us," said Leanna, pointing at the wood shavings that they'd collected from the carpentry shop.

"No, Herr Suiter say Frau Kaysabergher and I schtay in number tree." She pointed toward the other rooms.

On the second drenching day, Perry McCoon brought oranges and sat beside her on the sawdust bed, now hemmed in with poles. "Wish the bloody rine'd quit, I does." He whacked his hat on his knee and moisture sprayed in her face.

"Spring rain brings the flowers," she said cheerfully, intensely aware of the side of his hand touching the side of hers in the wood shavings.

"Ent a pretty sight up there."

"Where?"

"Yon mountains." He turned his eyes eastward. "Snowing like the devil, it tis."

"Snow?"

"Hard rine means blizzard up there. Never fails."

It hadn't occurred to her that anything in this green valley of springtime could be connected with the nightmare in the mountains. But now she realized this storm was hurling snow on the Second Relief. Leanna looked like she'd seen a ghost. The family could die in the storm.

Perry was kissing Elitha's hand. She forced a smile, retrieved her hand and said as courteously as she could, "I spose me and my sister want to be alone now."

30

She couldn't remember rain like this in Illinois. It was as if a demonic sky giant hurled slashing torrents at the huddled humans below. Streams from the roof eroded the corner of the building and pale rivulets of mud sloughed down into the room. It was cold inside and out. Freezing water pelted her face when she went to look at the trail to the river, and the pond by the wall was an overflowing lake hopping with miniature eruptions. She asked herself questions that had only one answer. Could the rescuers keep enfeebled people walking through a blizzard? Could they find the food caches and keep to the trail? Tamsen and the little girls and Aunt Betsy and the Donner cousins and Jean Baptiste and Mrs. Murphy and everybody else could be dying this very minute. Could already be dead. She hugged herself trying to stop the shakes.

She wished Mary Murphy were at the fort, so the three of them could help each other endure the wait. And it would have been nice if the Sinclairs had invited Elitha and Leanna to stay with them, where they'd have the company of Virginia. Mrs. Wolfinger and Mrs. Keseberg spoke German together, and spent a lot of time in Mr. Sutter's quarters. She and Leanna were seen as children, who were less interesting to talk to, yet too old to need help. The children Elitha had helped on the long walk, including cousin Georgie Donner, had been distributed to farms being established nearby. She and Leanna were alone among strangers, except for Mr. McCoon, who, she had learned, was unmarried.

It rained four continuous days and nights and when it stopped, the goddess of spring had gone into hiding. Snuggled close to Leanna under their cloaks, Elitha awoke to a clear sky framed in the doorway and felt the cold burning her toes all the way up through her insteps.

She sat up, removed her stockings and stared through breath clouds. Her feet were alabaster white, except for her toes, which had been an unnatural shade of red and were now turning dark as charcoal. Red cracks showed at the joints. She hobbled painfully to the door. Under a cloudless sky the green grass sparkled with frost and the naked oaks were traced in white. How cold it must be in the mountains! She shuddered.

Leanna whined, "My feet hurt." The dreaded words.

Glimpsing Mr. Mellus heading through the gate, Elitha said, "I'll get some flour and make us some flapjacks." She already had saleratus to make them light.

She pushed her feet into her shoes, biting her lip, and hobbled up the path, glad the store wasn't too far inside the gate. Mr. Mellus was unlocking the door — one of many along the fort's inner wall. From the hood of her cloak, she smiled her friendliest smile and followed him in. No return smile.

She pushed her hood back and surveyed the goods while he shuffled things on boards laid across barrels. It smelled rich inside with so many bags of flour, jars of pickles, and crates of oranges — a luxury of California. Leather bags and furs were stacked beneath the window. He didn't look like he'd finish anytime soon, so she curtsied and said, "If you please, I'd like five eggs and four cups of flour."

He pursed his lips over toward one nostril and ridges appeared on the wide expanse of his forehead. "How long's this sposed to go on?" he said.

"Pardon?"

"Me supplying you."

Horrified, she sucked in air and said, "I didn't know we were a burden," then hurried out. Donners were taught to carry their end of a load and never to expect handouts. All she'd done was follow Mr. Sutter's instructions. Tears pricked her eyes as she hobbled back to the room.

She was telling Leanna when Mr. Mellus darkened the doorway. Without invitation he entered and stared down at the two of them on the wood shavings.

Unable to meet his eyes, Elitha said, "Go ahead and take the salt and the saleratus back." She nodded at the little Mexican cloth bags against the wall. "And the pot." At least they hadn't eaten that.

"Oh fer — I'm no ogre. Jes gittin blamed tired a John Sutter givin away my goods so generous like. Now THERE'S a fella who never pays up, on time or otherwise!"

"Ma'll pay what we owe when she gits here." It came out squeaky.

"Look. I know you girls gotta eat and I guess John Sutter's emptied his stores to Captain Frémont and his men and the relief effort and just about everybody else in the whole blasted territory. I jes come to say I could use some cleanin up, clothes washin, wood gatherin, that sorta thing. In exchange."

Relieved to see a way out, Elitha eagerly agreed. "We're good at tidying up and washing clothes, aren't we Leanna." She gave her the elbow.

"Yes, we do real good."

"Good. Start by going down to the river for wood. Stack it in the store by the stove. Danged if this here fort ain't picked clean. You'll git yer eggs and flour when I git my wood." He was gone.

She felt relieved, but spent — and glad for Leanna's hug. Next time she'd figure things out on her own and pay no attention to Mr. Sutter's promises. "Come on," she said, "we got wood to fetch."

That afternoon her feet sent swords up her legs. She was hungry, as usual, and thinking about supper when Perry McCoon came in. He lifted his hat, smoothed his wavy hair and said, "Nobody's got through at Johnson's yet. Jes delivered goods, I did."

"Maybe they all stayed at the lake camp till that storm died down." *Please God.* But she knew that too much time had passed before the storm; they would have started.

"Maybe." His steel-blue eyes moved over her. "Lass, you oughta make yerself a new gown. Got fetching stuff at the store, Mellus has."

She shook her head. She felt ashamed of her frock, which had once been her best, but she wasn't about to buy things she didn't really need even though it was bad that she couldn't wash her dress, having nothing to wear while it dried on the rocks. "We just gotta wait till Ma gets through, that's all. And when the snow melts, they'll bring the wagon down. I've got a pile of gowns in there." *How wonderful if they could bring Pa in the wagon!* She forced a smile.

He reached in his pocket and pulled out a sparkling handful of blue crystals on a leather string. He dangled it and she saw that the crystals were stuck together in a sort of haphazard star, perhaps a dozen dazzling points jutting in all directions. It was a beautiful bauble that almost looked man-made. He stepped in front of where she sat and placed it around her neck.

Holding the lovely thing away from her face to admire it, she felt unsure of the propriety of accepting such a present. But his intimate and admiring look prevailed. "Why thank you, Perry," she said, "It's beautiful." She stood up. "Where did you get it?"

"Johnson's ranch." He flashed his dimpled smile. "Glad ye likes it."

He stepped closer, his eyes narrowed to dark fringes, and before she knew what was happening, pulled her to him and pressed his lips on hers. She felt the prickles where he'd shaved and smelled tobacco smoke and the tang of liquor, but his lips made her forget all else. It was her first kiss. A rush of heat took her breath away, and she didn't know what to do except hold her lips to his.

He pulled back and looked at her. "Would ye marry me, Elitha?" His eyes danced. Teasing? Happy? She couldn't tell which.

"You mean it?"

He chuckled and glanced at the eroded wall. He looked at Leanna on the sawdust bed, then back at her, the whole time keeping his dimpled grin. "Serious as I ever gits."

"I — I don't know. I'm waitin on the folks. I, we're going to . . ." She needed her parents' approval.

"Want ye on me rancho, Elitha. You and me together can civilize that wild plaice and build us a fine barony. Our babes'll 'ave land to call their own." He took her by the shoulders. "Think on it, lass." Then he was gone.

Leanna sat in the sawdust hugging her knees, the light from the doorway whitening her thin face and making her brown eyes translucent, but her smile goaded. "He's the best looker in Californy." She stood and lifted the blue crystals from Elitha's chest, admiring them, and her smile was gone. "I wish I was pretty like you."

"Well, you're only twelve." But Elitha knew Leanna didn't have the big brown eyes and swan neck and high forehead that Perry praised. The heat lingered at her throat and she could still taste his lips. She felt like a leaf in a twister. What would Tamsen say? And Pa, assuming they got him down the mountains.

In mid-March Elitha and Leanna gathered with Mrs. Keseberg and a few other anxious people before Lieutenant Kern, who was to read a list of names. Word had come that the Second Relief would soon arrive at Johnson's ranch, to which Perry had sailed with supplies. Lieutenant Kern started by saying that severe storms had overtaken the Second Relief, Mr. Reed's party. Then he looked at the paper and enunciated each survivor's name, waiting each time until the joyful shouts subsided. Elitha and Leanna cheered to hear the names of their cousins — Mary Donner and Solomon Hook, brother of Will Hook who died of gorging. But the lieutenant looked up and his lips were pressed together. That was all. It had been a mere handful.

The absent Donner names left a howling hole, and Elitha felt like she was sinking in when Lieutenant Kern announced, "Now the names of them that perished on the way."

She squeezed Leanna's hand and stopped breathing each time he arranged his mouth to speak. Cries followed each name and her stomach tightened a notch. "Isaac Donner," he read, and they looked at each other. Aunt Betsy's five-year-old. Kern looked up from the paper and said, "That's all."

Leanna gave a crippled little happy hop, but Elitha looked into her brown eyes and said, "We don't know why they didn't come." She watched that sink in.

Lieutenant Kern turned the paper to the other side and cleared his throat and announced: "This here's a list of them that was left alive at the summit."

First on the list were George and Tamsen Donner and three daughters. Then came Elizabeth Donner — Aunt Betsy — and two young cousins. Uncle Jacob had died.

Nevertheless, even with the terrible news about Uncle Jacob, Elitha grabbed Leanna's other hand and they jumped around in a hobbling circle of joy. God had heard. Pa was alive and the family hadn't come with the Second Relief. A miracle had happened.

MARCH 23, 1847

Perry had suppered with Elitha and Leanna in the room, and had left. It was evening after a warm day and still light. Elitha was surprised — her shoulders bare in her petticoat — when he stuck his head in and said they should come with him to Mr. Sutter's quarters. Some Donners had been brought in. Elitha and Leanna threw their frocks back on, quickly buttoned them, gathered up their skirts and hurried out where Perry was waiting.

Jean Baptiste Trudeau, to Elitha's joy, was sitting on the bottom step, even more emaciated than when she'd last seen him. He was resting his sparse black beard in his hands and his elbows on his knees, his long unkempt hair falling about his face. At first she thought he was unwell, but as his black eyes registered recognition, a smile spread over his bony face. He stood up with an expression one sees in artwork when mortals witness heavenly beings.

"Jean Baptiste," Leanna said touching his shoulder, "you got through!" No names from the Third Relief had been announced, but it was said that they had overtaken the Second Relief, which had been slow on account of so much suffering.

Elitha felt a strong sisterly love for him — not much more than a boy really, yet he had cut all the firewood, chopped the ice stairs and done a thousand things for the family. Sometimes after he had cut the wood, he had laid out his sarape, rolled the little girls in it, and swung them until they screamed with pleasure. Now, after what they'd been through together, he seemed more than a hired man. And where Jean Baptiste was, the family couldn't be far behind.

"You looking good, healthy," Jean Baptiste said, smiling from one to the other. "Many times when I come back from hunting with no animal in my hand I feel very bad, and when I no find the cows under the snow I feel very bad, and when I eat your family food I feel bad, and now I see they give you plenty food here and I am happy."

"But where's everybody else?" Elitha asked.

"Your cousin Mary and Sol up there," he tossed a look up the stairs at Mr. Sutter's door. "Your three little sisters are healthy and they sleep this night at the rancho up the river. Sinclair." He looked in that direction and looked down, his long black hair falling over his face.

"Ma and Pa?"

He didn't look up. Had Pa died in camp?

"Dead?" Leanna squeaked.

Not looking up he shook his head. "No. When I go they are live."

Both alive! "But where are they? Johnson's ranch?" Maybe one of the higher camps, recuperating for a few days. Maybe Bear Valley. But why was he so glum?

Still not looking up, he said, "In the wigwam."

It came like a slap, the family word for the tent — Jean Baptiste having directed its construction that first blizzarding night. Ever-faithful Jean Baptiste had left his employers. But then she realized they had entrusted him with the little girls. "You brought our sisters through," she said.

He never looked at them, but walked away, across the fort yard and out the gate, his feet obviously hurting. Elitha watched him go.

"'Aff-breed is he?"

She'd almost forgotten Perry was there, and didn't like acknowledging that's what Jean Baptiste was. Leanna looked as perplexed and disturbed as Elitha felt. The girls had been brought down, but not Tamsen, and Jean Baptiste had acted as guilty as a boy caught scooping pie with his fingers. With a last look after his limping figure, Elitha nodded at Perry, and they all went up the stairs and knocked on Mr. Sutter's door.

The room seemed crowded. Mr. Sutter introduced Elitha and Leanna to three bearded men with their boots off. Perry knew them all. Elitha recognized the powerful man sitting on a crate with his legs wide apart. Hirum Miller had signed on as a driver for Pa in Illinois, then left the family in the middle of the prairie to join a faster-moving company. She also recognized Lt. Woodworth, having met him in Bear Valley. Cousin Mary Donner, looking more like a rag doll than a seven-year-old girl, lay on a bed of four chairs — the backs of two serving as side rails — one of her feet heavily wrapped in colored cloth, the skin of the other blacker than Elitha's had ever been. The angry red cracks in the dead skin wept much more. Mary's little face was as white as the bones underneath, which so unpleasantly shaped its contours, and she was clearly in pain, her eyes squeezed shut. Sol Hook looked about as famished, but he was half-sitting against the wall, a fuzz of new beard brown against the white of his face. "Howdy," he said, voice cracking in the way of fourteen-year-old boys.

"Howdy," Elitha said, wondering if he knew that Will, his hundred-percent brother, had died of gorging, and that their father was dead.

Perry pulled up the last chair and joined the four men. They drank from cups and watched over the rims as Elitha and Leanna squatted beside Sol.

"We heard you came through with Mr. Reed in the Second Relief, and the blizzards gotcha."

"Yup." Both his feet were wrapped in cloth.

She didn't mention little Isaac Donner, who had been among the casualties. "We saw Jean Baptiste outside and he told us Tamsen and my pa are still up there in camp, and our little sisters are at the Sinclairs."

"Yup."

Mary moaned from her makeshift bed.

Elitha wanted to ask why Jean Baptiste had behaved so strangely, but was shy about mentioning it in front of the men. Instead she said, "Mary going to be all right?"

Sol looked at the men.

Lt. Woodworth, who, she had just learned, was stationed in Yerba Buena with the United States Navy — though garbed like a mountain man — cleared his throat and said, "I'm taking these two to Yerba Buena to see the ship surgeon. Fraid Mary there won't make it unless her foot's amputated. She burned it bad in a fire. It was so numb she couldn't feel it. Now Sol here," he raised his brows at him, "maybe. He did a fool thing. Took off his shoes, then had to walk barefoot 'cause he couldn't get em back on."

With the horror of amputation ringing in her mind, Elitha said, "My sisters all right?"

"Looked in fair shape to me. These two was in the worst condition."

She looked at Sol. "What about Aunt Betsy, yer ma?" Sister of Elitha's real mother.

Sol closed his eyes and wagged his head — high up on the ribbed neck. He nested it against the wall as if he needed sleep. Elitha stood and asked, "You men all with the Third Relief?" They would have seen the Donner camp.

Lt. Woodworth seemed to be the spokesman. "These two here went up," he blinked at the other rescuers. "I coordinated provisions and transportation."

She looked at Mr. Miller, realizing she'd never particularly liked him, and Pa certainly had been disappointed in him for taking up with what he considered a better company. But it was good of the man to risk his life for others. "How were my parents?"

Mr. Miller and Mr. Oakley exchanged a look, which made her fear Jean Baptiste hadn't told the truth. She was trying to harden herself for what would come, when Mr. Miller said, "We heard yer Pa was hangin on t'life. But Tamsen was in good condition. We saw her at the lake camp."

"She sent the girls — "

"She wouldn't come with us. Them other men was bound and determined to git on the trail afore the next storm hit, wadn't they Howie? And she was just as determined not to leave without seein if yer pa was still livin. Wanted us to wait and see."

"So you left without her?"

"Oh, she knew we would. Asked us to take the little girls."

"And Jean Baptiste was there to help."

All the men, including Mr. Sutter, looked at each other. *What was it?*

Hi Miller said, "That low-down mongrel, cut out on his duty to yer ma. Insisted on coming with us."

"She asked him to go back to the camp with her?"

He rolled his eyes. "Think she fancied cuttin firewood herself?"

"I don't understand. Why was she there at the lake in the first place? And our sisters, if they didn't mean to — "

Lt. Woodworth cut in. "Loithy — what was the name?" Perry corrected him and he continued, "Elitha, what happened up in those mountains was very complicated and it would take too much time to explain it all just now. The main thing is, your mother was in the best shape of anybody, and she'll surely be coming with the party I sent up. John Rhoads is among them, and he's a veteran. Your little sisters should get here sometime in the morning — they stayed at the Sinclairs' tonight. Your mother should come in maybe, ah, let's see, two, three weeks. Now, we're all feeling tuckered and need to get an early start."

She and Leanna left, but Perry stayed.

The next morning when they went to the pond to wash, Mrs. Wolfinger told them Lt. Woodworth's party had carried Mary and Sol to the landing at first light; Jean Baptiste had helped. Hoping to talk to him, Elitha left Leanna to buy something to eat and ran down to the landing to see if he was still there. But the towering trees entwined with vines were her only companions, Mr. Sutter's boat gone, Perry gone. She looked upstream. The early sun was blinding, and she saw nothing but sparkling ripples on fast-moving water.

She sat on tender vegetation near the water's edge, thinking if Jean Baptiste was hiding, he might eventually come from the trees. But he didn't appear. Leanna came down the trail with biscuits and oranges, and they sat peeling oranges and listening to courting birds — a cacophony of shrieking and chattering as the water lapped on the dark earth near their shoes. The crusts of black skin had peeled off their toes, and to Elitha's great relief, new baby skin had grown underneath. Today they were supposed to clean fort rooms, air out blankets, sprinkle and sweep dirt floors, wash laundry and gather firewood. But they had the time, even with the girls coming; the days were longer.

They gathered fallen branches and twigs and made a pile, careful not to snag their new frocks, which they had sewn by the firelight. Elitha's was noticeably skewed at the shoulder seams. She'd never been good at sewing, hired girls having done it.

"Look!" Leanna shouted, pointing.

An Indian boat of the type Californians called a balsey appeared at the bend in the river, the point of its tule-bundle prow turned up so high she saw only a dark man with a pole standing at the back. She grabbed Leanna's hand, not sure it was the right boat, until it came closer and three small heads showed above the side.

"Big sisters!" the little girls yelled as the buoyant craft was poled to the landing. Frances, Georgia and Ellie. Eyes too large, even from the distance.

Laughing and crying at the same time, she got her shoes wet catching them —birdlike beneath their dirty frocks, their hair matted — as they scrambled up the side of the strange craft and all but flew into her arms. Their dirty frocks were rumpled, though made of expensive material — brocade and velvet — too large, oddly cut and hastily sewn. These were the fine frocks Tamsen had made that winter in Illinois, thinking of the future. She had obviously cut them down for the trek down the mountains, wanting the girls to look as presentable as possible.

Six-year-old Frances said, "Ma said you was to care fer us till she comes through."

"Yes. I know she stayed up there."

"Takin care a Pa," Georgia explained.

"He's ailin bad," Frances added, her hard little face serious beyond her years.

On the wooded path they walked slowly, because the little girls were hobbling like crippled old women.

31

That evening after Elitha and Leanna were finished with chores, they trapped Frances and Georgia and Ellie between their knees — their pelvic bones so light beneath their petticoats — and combed as gently and best they could through yards of hair. The girls smelled of good lye soap, and though it wasn't dark yet, their eyelids were droopy with sleep, even while their hair was being combed.

Smoothing the silky dark hair over the subterranean bumps, Elitha smiled into Ellie's sleepy brown eyes and said, "How old are you?"

A coy smile curved her lips. "Four?"

"That's right. You had a birthday on the way down the mountains, didn't you? And I didn't get to say, HAPPY BIRTHDAY!" With that she jumped on her and squeezed her little bones and gave her a smack on the cheek.

Frances said, "Now give her a spanking."

Elitha moved her arm in a slow-motion parody of four spanks. Ellie looked worried at first then pleased in a self-conscious way to be the center of attention. Then Elitha laid the three girls side by side in the wood shavings and covered them to their chins with their cloaks. Tomorrow she'd borrow some scissors and cut out the hair mats, and see about their stained frocks.

Georgia wanted a song, so Elitha and Leanna sang about Tom Pierce's old gray mare, as many verses as they could think of, and all the verses of the one about the three gypsies. By then it was almost dark and all the eyes were shut. Quietly she and Leanna moved the warped boards they had used to hem in a bed for Ma and Pa, and pushed all the springy wood curls together so there was just one big bed, and lay down on either side of the girls. The sharp smell of fresh wood came up around them and mosquitos winged through the open doorway with the cool night air.

Leanna wasn't a talker, but she was awake and maybe thinking the same way as Elitha. Elitha lay staring into the dark, seeing the endless white mountains and the cold and the children left buried in the snow. It must have been hard for

Tamsen to send these girls on such a terrible journey. She must have believed they'd starve to death in the tent. And it *was* a miracle no blizzard had overtaken them.

Much later a high-pitched scream jerked her awake. Then Ellie frantically saying, "He's gonna get me!"

Elitha struggled to her knees in the shavings and hugged the tiny little girl, who was standing in the dark. She was shaking and her head was wet with perspiration, though the night was very cool.

"He's coming!" she wailed into Elitha's shoulder.

"There now, you had a bad dream is all."

Frances sounded thick with sleep in the dark. "She's feared of the scary man at Mrs. Murphy's."

Murphy's? "Now Ellie, you just lie down and I'll sing some more. Poor little thing, you had a nightmare is all."

"No!" Pitched to break glass. "He's gonna kill me!" Even her bawling was shaking.

"It's not real, Ellie. There now, there's no such man. Why you three weren't even AT the Murphys' cabin."

"We was TOO," said Georgia.

Elitha stopped to think. Of course, they had stayed there with Tamsen, when the Third Relief arrived. "But your ma was with you. She and Mrs. Murphy wouldn't let anyone hurt you.

"NO! She wasn't there. And we was there a long long time."

"A VERY long time."

"And we was so hungry."

"And SOOO cold. They didn't have no fire."

"Frances," Elitha said to the eldest, a six-year-old not given to fanciful stories, "how did you come to stay at the Murphy cabin without your ma?"

Frances said Tamsen had paid two men to take them all the way to Sutter's Fort, but when they got to the lake camp the men went on alone, leaving them at Mrs. Murphy's. Greed and chicanery had saved them. "But Mr. Reed would have taken you. He was in charge of the Second Relief."

Frances said, "Mr. Reed took Patty and Tommy on ahead."

"We was sleepin in their bed," Georgia added.

Recalling the night she'd stayed in the cabin occupied by the Murphys and Reeds — a log hut built by a party stranded at the lake the previous winter — Elitha figured out that the two men had secretly stolen back to the Donner camp without Mr. Reed. But why hadn't Mr. Reed taken the Donners?

"Frances," Elitha asked, "do you know how much Ma paid those two men?"

"I think five hundred."

Greed had indeed saved the girls.

"It smelled ROTten," Georgia said.

Elitha lost the thread. "Rotten?"

"Mrs. Murphy's house."

"They didn't never empty the bucket and there was dead people on the floor with big holes in em."

"And we was SOOO cold."

Sobs and hard sniffles.

"Cause the man what eats people don't fetch wood."

Elitha's scalp prickled. She heard the thud of her own heart and felt the slight rocking of it as she stood on her knees holding Ellie. "Now, now — "

"And the old lady can't see to go out for wood."

"And can't walk good neither."

Just as Mary Murphy had described her mother. Starvation had done that, and people said the rescuers had found mutilated dead in the cabins. So that much was true, and it must have frightened the girls out of their wits to see that. But no man was left in Mrs. Murphy's cabin after her sons-in-law and Lem went out with the snowshoe party. *Oh Lem!*

Gently she pushed Ellie down to sitting and said, "Now let's all forget about that and go back to sleep. Bad things happened but you're all safe now." She tried to push her back in the shavings.

"No!" she screamed, fighting to her feet. "That man's gonna kill me!"

Leanna spoke for the first time. "He say that to you?"

"He said it to ebbrybody. If they cried."

"And he WOULD OF too," Frances said.

"So we didn't cry none." It was Georgia's grown-up tone, but then long sobs started choking out of her like they'd been building up for years.

"You put your hand on my mouf an it HURT!" Ellie accused through her sniffles.

Elitha felt as if she was in her own nightmare. How cheerful Ma and Pa had tried to appear! To make them think being snowbound was a perfectly normal part of getting through to California. Elitha and Leanna had played their part too. These were hardly more than babies. Surely no man would threaten them.

But Georgia was crying like she'd never stop. Elitha knee-walked over to hug her too, one girl in each arm.

Ellie sobbed, "he's coming."

Still lying in the sawdust, Frances said, "He's way up in the mountains, Ellie." Sticking to the story. But what man?

Leanna's voice was soft in the dark. "DID he kill somebody?"

"No," Elitha said firmly, the black of night being a poor time to prolong this, "Now you all just go back to sleep."

But Leanna had them talking, one over the other, a waterfall not to be stopped.

The story emerged. A little boy died in the bed of the bad man who had a very long beard and very long hair. He had stood over Mrs. Murphy's bed and complained of the cold and insisted he needed the boy in his bed to keep him warm, so Mrs. Murphy gave him the boy. In the morning the man said the boy had died in his sleep, and he hung the lifeless body on a nail in the wall. From time to time he got up from his bed to cut off pieces. He told the girls it was the best he'd tasted. Mrs. Murphy screamed, "You killed him. You murderer." After that she stayed in bed except when she'd slip the girls crumbs.

"She didn't want him to see we was eatin."

"We chewed under the bedclothes."

"YOU cried," Ellie accused.

"I stuffed covers in my mouth!"

Frances said, "Mrs. Murphy said to take turns sleeping, but we was scared anyhow."

Elitha quivered like her bones and everything else inside her had melted into a sickening gel. She gathered Frances up too so all three girls were in her arms, foreheads together. Leanna hugged them from the other side and after a while they all lay down in one big hugging mass. Then sometime in the night, still in each other's arms, the sisters fell asleep. Elitha was the last awake, thinking Lord in Heaven, these girls had been protected from everything harsh in life, and now this! And who was that man? One of those who killed Mr. Wolfinger? And why had Tamsen gone to the lake camp if she thought her daughters had gone on ahead?

Every night nightmares interrupted sleep. All three had them. Elitha tried to soothe their fears, telling them the bad man would die in the mountains and not come to Sutter's Fort. And most likely that was true. Those left at the lake camp were too weak to walk. John Rhoads had said that over a month ago. Poor Mrs. Murphy.

"Will Ma and Pa die too?" Frances asked.

"Of course not! The rescuers say she's in the best condition of anybody."

"Don't leave us," the girls would plead when the flapjacks were eaten and she and Leanna were leaving for work. The weather was very warm now, and Mr. Mellus didn't need firewood. They'd caught him up on his washing too, so now they worked for other people, often away from the fort at the new farms being settled by immigrant women, most of their men gone fighting the Mexicans. The money went for cloth, sundries and food. Food, food and more food. They were hungry all the time.

"Don't you worry," Elitha said, "We'll be back at the end of the day. And you know I'll never leave you." They weren't alone in the wicked world. "And don't pay any mind to what children say. Remember, sticks and stones can break my bones but words can never hurt me. And if people look at you funny, you look straight ahead and just walk away." Since the arrival of the Third Relief things had changed at the fort. Some of the rescuers had told gruesome stories of cannibalism — though few as bad as the one the little girls had told. Women and older children sat talking in low voices around the wagon tongues, repeating the stories, exaggerating them. The children appeared to be mesmerized; women turned to each other with open mouths. Whenever Elitha or Leanna or the three girls drew near, they quieted. Sometimes it seemed like the unfriendliest place in the world.

Each evening Elitha would ask, "What did you do today?" Frances would recite, "We held hands wherever we went, just like you said. And Indian ladies gave us some of their mush."

"And we made the papooses laugh."

"And watched a man make a chair."

"And the Indians marched with their guns."

"And a man made a hat. And pounded an iron hoop."

Ellie contributed, "And the mule go round and round." Turning the grist stone. Elitha imagined they watched that often, for it was a wonder the poor animal kept going with so little prodding.

"Now you girls wear those bonnets we made you," she would say. "Or when Ma comes she'll say you look dark as Indians and I'll be in dutch." She kissed their serious little faces and smiled the joke away. Tamsen wasn't like that. She treated even the youngest as supremely sensible, and never raised a hand. She would know what to do about the nightmares, and Elitha waited for her like all the Christmases she'd ever known rolled up into one.

One day when she was coming back from the persnickety French woman's place — Perry gone to Yerba Buena for four weeks — thinking how she hated being a hired girl, a hot wind stole her flyaway skirts and dust devils danced across the trail. Perhaps Pa had died, she thought, knuckling grit from her eyes. *No.* That was pure superstition. She'd been tired all day after not sleeping most of the night on account of drunken men talking in the doorway, scaring her half to death. And the French woman had been cross all day because Elitha had cracked her crock lid in the morning. She had walked two miles under a dawn sky and was returning before sunset. Every day seemed longer — actually was. Leanna worked at another farm, and Elitha felt lonely as she milked cows, churned butter, built fires, heated water, washed clothing, stacked brush for fences and shoveled out deep-rooted grass for new gardens. She felt lonely even though she worked alongside the women and their children. During the long days she never forgot that in Illinois she read books while hired men and girls from less prosperous families toiled at the heavy chores. Everything in California was primitive. They didn't have pipes, so she hauled water from the river with splashing buckets banging her knees.

But soon it would be over. Tamsen would come and care for the girls, and Elitha and Leanna wouldn't hire out any more, and with the ten thousand dollars from the quilt they could pay men to build a house and school. She hoped the books in the wagon weren't ruined. And Tamsen would advise her about Perry. After all, a girl's whole life depended on getting a good man.

Was he a good man? Once she'd seen him mercilessly whipping a snubbed horse. "Beatin sense into 'im," he said with a smile, and it was true, most men believed in that. Another time she'd been surprised to find out he'd never heard of the Golden Rule. "Do unto others as you'd have them do unto you," she'd explained. "It's from the Bible." He had narrowed his eyes as if looking over the sea and said he remembered one of his shipmates saying that. Then he had smiled sidelong — a teasing look — and said, "Do unto others afore they do unto you, I'd say." A harsh rule, one that Jesus had tried to change.

She knuckled more grit from her eye. To make matters worse she had her courses, which luckily Tamsen had explained back on the Platte River last summer. It was a sticky mess, and she'd been embarrassed to borrow a rag from the French woman. She couldn't imagine putting up with it the rest of her life and hiding it from a husband. God's curse on Eve.

Ahead the blazing sun whitened the walls of the fort. The long adobe outside the gate looked white too, and she saw a few people gathered at the butt end of it where their room was. Excitement pumped into her and she gathered her skirts and broke into a halting run with the rag shifting and the devil wind blowing hair across her face.

Smoke came from the doorway and the smell of cooking meat. Ma had to be here! Cooking supper. She pushed past several children and three women standing at the door. But only Georgia, Frances and Ellie were inside, squatting around the firepit in dirty frocks. Georgia and Frances were toasting slices of liver. Ellie had a big quivering piece in her hands and was chewing it. Blood was smeared all over her hands and arms and cheeks. She grinned up at Elitha and said, "Big Sister!" Red teeth. That's what everybody was looking at.

Elitha turned to the spectators. "What are you doing here anyhow?" They looked at her with round eyes. "Go away until you're invited!" she said.

"Cannibals!" a boy sang out, pointing at the girls.

"Go on! Git!" She reached for the blackened frying pan and made like she would throw it at him. "And don't let me see you here again!" With disapproving looks, mothers tugged their children away. Never before had she spoken crossly to grown people and she almost couldn't believe she'd done it.

When at last they were out of earshot, she turned to the girls, her voice unnaturally sharp. "What in heaven are you doing!"

Frances looked up, about to break into crying, the liver trembling at the end of her stick. "Eatin," she squeaked. Flies were all over her face, all their faces.

"Well I can see that. But where'd you get that liver?" She pointed at the meat. Leanna wasn't here, so the only money was in her pocket.

"The man what sells meat, in the fort." Her chin quivered. "We was watching him cut it and he," she sniffed, "give us some."

"Cause we was HUNgry." Georgia's meat was nearly on fire.

Frances tried to sound adult. "I didn't let Georgia or Ellie play with the matches, honest Injun."

Elitha grabbed the liver from Ellie's bloody hand, jammed it on the end of the blackened switch and thrust it over the flames. "There." She wiggled it down over Ellie's head to get her to take it. "Now you cook it till it's good and done, you hear? Good and black!"

Ellie assumed control of the stick and her voice shook. "Yes Big Sister." Pink tears ran through the blood and down her neck into the staining collar of her frock.

Elitha lay back on the shavings and forced a softer tone. "Ellie, you were eating it raw." Then, like the powerful blasts of the wind she'd battled all day, something exploded in her and demolished every bit of self control she'd tried to hold on to. "YOU WERE EATING IT RAW!"

She knew, yes and everyone else in the whole blessed fort knew. People said these girls had helped eat Uncle Jacob and the hired men. She turned away and wept into her arms. Tamsen wouldn't have let them know, but still the thought turned her stomach. She was no better than the ghouls around the fort. It seemed that God had forgotten the Donners.

"Big Sister," Georgia whimpered, "What's a cannibo?"

"Hush about that!"

But then she realized that at fourteen she must set the example, and it was up to her to keep their spirits up. It was just that too much had landed on her and she didn't want to keep leaving them alone all day with strangers. She couldn't stand this hovel either. Tamsen would buy chairs and gas lamps for the new house and wouldn't have to sew at night by an open fire, getting ashes and dirt all over the goods. Low in her abdomen something seized up and she gritted her teeth until it passed.

Flies hummed in lazy circles and lighted on her face, and rose when she swatted at them, only to come back. "Ellie," she said. All three turned to look, "I'm sorry I felt out of sorts. None of you did anything bad. Nothing bad at all."

Several days later, the Donner sisters stood at dawn watching the last Relief ride out — John Rhoads, five men and a string of mules trailing. Sadly, the men's previous attempt had been aborted because of snowmelt, and the impossibility of getting the mules through. Elitha recognized two other men from the First Relief.

In addition there was Sebastian Keyser, Elizabeth's husband from Johnson's ranch, and a man in buckskins the size of John Rhoads — Fallon le Gros people called him. He was one of the trappers who liked Mr. Sutter's distillery, a complex arrangement of barrels and pots and pipes.

The mules carried only a bit more food than the men needed. No caches would be hung in the trees, Lt. Kern had said, because it wasn't necessary. Only Tamsen Donner would be left living. Nevertheless, long-faced Philippine Keseberg also stood watching the men and mules depart. Her husband hadn't come down yet, and her little Ada had died, never having recovered her strength.

"I heard this is a salvage party," Leanna said.

"They don't want Indians getting into the wagons when the snow melts," Elitha said. The packsaddles were meant to be filled with precious goods, so it was a blessing Ma was there to keep a sharp eye on the apple green quilt, and Pa's money belt. Most of these men looked as wild as the Second Relief. But on the other hand, she thought as the last mule went around the bend, it seemed fair for the rescuers to be paid from what they found in the wagons. Tamsen would know how much was fair.

"Well, they're off," Leanna said with a sigh. There were fine lines around her eyes as if she were older.

Frances looked up. "How many days till Ma and Pa git here?"

That would be asked many times, Elitha knew, and she hadn't told them how bad off Pa was. "Don't know," she answered truthfully. People said so much snow had melted that the men would reach the summit in far less time than the first reliefs. The mules might even make it the whole way up, and Pa could ride. She sent a silent prayer to God. Four faces were turned to her.

"About a fortnight, I guess."

Elitha said good-bye and walked up the east trail on her way to work. On either side of her the wheat was already golden and headed out. The plain was flat as an ocean and she scanned the horizon, seeing a distant line of white. Cloudlike, but she knew it was the mountains. A long time ago she'd heard that thoughts could be sent through space. She closed her eyes to concentrate and tried to make her thought fly across the distance.

Pa and Tamsen, the girls got here safely. I'm taking care of them till you get here, so don't worry. Leanna and I have to work, so we can't be with them all the time but they'll be alright. A man here wants to marry me, but I told him I need your permission. And Tamsen, I've seen California and you were right. They need a school real bad. So don't you worry about anything. Just live, and eat what you have to. John Rhoads is coming for you, and he's a real good man.

It was a difficult fortnight, in many ways worse than the wait beneath the snow. The family had pulled together then. But now ever more gruesome rumors about the Donner Party crackled like wildfire through the fort. The details of bodies "broken into" worsened all the time. The most awful stories were about the "starved camp" where Mary Donner and Sol Hook had suffered so badly. A baby whimpered, people said, as it clung to its mother even as her chest was ripped open and her heart and liver removed and eaten.

One day Elitha went to the outhouse and found a copy of the *California Star* folded on the seat. She read with horrified fascination. The date was April 10 — a week ago — the paper published in Yerba Buena. An article entitled "A MOST SHOCKING SCENE" told of little Mary Donner matter-of-factly suggesting to the families left stranded in the snow cup that they eat the dead people — her younger brother being one of the first to die. The report quoted her as saying it was done all the time at the Donner tents. Then, to Elitha's horror, a terrible falsehood was printed, one that apparently referred to all the stranded immigrants:

> Calculations were coldly made as they sat gloomily around their gloomy campfires for the next and succeeding meals . . . various expedients were devised to prevent the dreadful crime of murder, but they finally resolved to kill those who had the least claim to human existence . . . so changed had the immigrants become that when the party sent out arrived with food, some of them cast it aside and seemed to prefer the putrid human flesh that still remained.

Now the worst horrors known to the human race — cannibalism and murder — were linked with the Donner Party — the Donner name. At Elitha's approach women arranged their faces in exaggerated pity, but she saw something else — a sense that females who had eaten such terrible fare had lost all claim to daintiness and feminity, all the gentle qualities that elevated them above the naturally coarser males. Mothers had apparently grown weary of telling their children to stop gawking and pointing. The little girls didn't understand it, and Elitha couldn't explain why they were not accepted into the little tribes of children that ran through the fort waiting for their fathers. And when a boy milked a cow and gave Ellie a cup of fresh milk, she was overjoyed just to be treated kindly.

Elitha no longer tried to contradict people. It was clear they wanted sensation and perversion, not the truth. People also blamed "Captain Donner" for taking the cutoff and not foraging for food in the mountains. He was called a failure as a leader, a man who had no business coming west. The trappers called him a greenhorn, though he wasn't by a long stretch. They didn't take any account of the fact that while he was in the mountains he lay badly injured, miles and miles from the people in the forward camp, who in any case had never paid attention to his advice. The wagon train had been a loose aggregate of families travelling together — as most of these women knew quite well — and yet rescuers returning from the mountains, some recruited by Lieutenant Woodworth, seemed to think Pa had commanded a disciplined army. They said openly that he bore the responsibility for all the suffering. Most painful of all, Elitha wondered in her heart if she could ever again proudly tell strangers that she was the daughter of George Donner.

Most of the survivors of the Party had now dispersed across the countryside — Mary Murphy still at Johnson's ranch, cousin Georgie Donner still at a nearby farm — so they didn't have to endure this. The Reeds never stayed at the fort, so they were spared. The Breen and Graves families from the Second Relief rested at the fort only a few days, then went quickly to other places. So the only other person left waiting was Philippine Keseberg, whose husband remained at the summit — alive and a little crazy, people said, feasting on what lay about.

Perry McCoon said with a mocking look, "Ye tender 'earts 'ave to learn to smile at the tales. And 'ave ye thought, praps there's truth in them?" He was hard to talk to.

One Sunday they were walking with him to see the Indian vaqueros race their horses, when four boys came careening around a corner and skidded to a halt. One pointed at the little girls and said, "Ooooh!" The boys dug into a giggling run, pretending to be terrified.

Perry trotted after them and quickly caught one. He took him down kicking, removed his shoes and trousers, cackling the whole time as he dodged the kicks, and, still laughing, ran away with his clothes. The boy ran close behind, covering himself and yelling, "Mister, them's my new shoes. Please. Ma'll switch me, please mister." At the pen where Mr. Sutter's bulls were resting in close confinement, Perry threw the shoes and trousers among them, startling a particularly mean-looking animal to its feet. It glowered at the boy when he got there — the horns as long and pointed as hay rakes and five times as thick. All the bulls were up now, moving around and trampling the boy's belongings into the reeking muck. The other boys left their playmate, who was about to burst into tears, standing outside the bullpen.

Still chuckling, Perry led the way to the horse races. The little girls looked up at him in timid admiration, but it struck Elitha as just a tad bit severe — shoes being so very dear at Mr. Sutter's bootery. But people had different standards.

32

On April 27, seventeen days after the scavenger party headed for the mountains, the Donner sisters were eating boiled potatoes with meat gravy when a man's cough startled them and something big eclipsed the twilight. Elitha looked up to see the dark shape of a man at the doorway. John Rhoads! She felt a sting of joy. But where was Ma?

When he stopped coughing he said in a tone lowered by a chest cold, "Elitha, I need to talk to you, in private." *Pa.* But where was Ma?

With a fist rising in her throat she got up — the other four watching — and went out the door and followed him around to the dark side of the adobe. Tamsen had to be ill and they'd taken her to Mr. Sutter's quarters. Only bad illness would keep her away while John Rhoads came with the news. She tried to get ready.

He dropped his hat on the ground and clamped his hands on her shoulders and said, "We brought in one survivor."

"My m — "

"Not yer mother. Lewis Keseberg." He turned his head, coughing, but kept holding her.

"You said you'd bring her!" She could almost hear, *Yer ma's a strong little lady. She'll live.* Everybody said she was the strongest one.

"Keseberg claims she died."

Her kneecaps melted. "Pa?"

He shook his bushy head and his brown beard from side to side. That much she had known.

"Did you see her, the — " A powerful force came up and grabbed back the word.

"We didn't see her body."

Hope rekindled. She was lost, that was all. Lost, wandering someplace. They'd missed her between the camps. "Please go back up. You've gotta find her!" Why would he believe a man like Mr. Keseberg? Somebody said he was out of his head.

"Elitha." His shaggy head tilted back as if appealing to heaven. "My God, how can I say it?"

Her heart was in her ears.

"Keseberg knows she's dead. No, let me finish." He coughed and his fingers dug into her shoulders. "He killed her." It blackened the twilight and smothered newborn hope.

Out of the void, "He say that?"

"No."

The flame roared again, red hot with anger. "Then how do you know? You didn't even see her." He didn't know that woman. She would walk down the mountains alone if she had to, but she would come to her children. But she had to be nice. "Oh Mr. Rhoads, please go back and look for her. I just know she's alive." She was losing ground to an avalanche of wild weeping and he was coughing and they should have stayed up there and looked until they found her.

"Elitha, oh Lord," he said when he found the breath, "I wouldn't say this, except you'll hear it all. Tongues'll flap a good long spell. Now you gotta be strong and keep this from yer little sisters. But you see," it came through his teeth, "we wanted to strangle that cowardly son of a bi. . . that low-down excuse for a man when we figgered out what he'd done. But we all agreed, this here is to be a civilized country and we gotta stick by some kinda law. So we charged him with murder. Mr. Sutter says there'll be a trial."

"But you don't even know if she's — "

"Keseberg admitted — he ate her." He grabbed and hugged her like he could squeeze out the horror. "We saw evidence."

A high-pitched sound floated up around them and she didn't know at first it came from her. *Ate her*. All else fell away into a monstrous hole that opened in the universe and time and space vanished down the hole along with her past and future. She stood unbreathing. Then her mind snagged on the nightmares.

"Was he in Mrs. Murphy's cabin?"

"Yup."

She pulled back, and, though the anger had gone down the hole and she was like an empty frock on a clothesline, blurted out more hope. "Then it couldn't of been Tamsen. She was miles away." *Please God.*

Leanna's timid voice pricked the twilight. "That you Mr. Rhoads?"

"She'll be a minute," he said, and when she had gone, growled out, "We found his tracks going down to your folks' tent."

MAY 5, 1847

"Corpses don't bleed," Mr. Coffeemeyer declared, his eyes finding Elitha across a courtyard full of people.

It was warm for May. She stood in the crowd that had gathered, as far back from the man on trial as she could get and still hear. She felt like a sleepwalker, drawn by horror, not volition. Looking at him now, she recalled the intense gratitude she'd felt for Mr. Coffeemeyer when he'd come back with the food cache. He'd seemed an angel in buckskins. He pulled his eyes away and pointed a finger at Lewis Keseberg.

"You killed Tamsen Donner," he accused. "Cut her up and drained her blood and stewed her in her own pot!" A hiss went through the crowd. Women covered their mouths and exchanged horrified glances. Lewis Keseberg, a hairy skullface, sat halfway up Sutter's stairs, his sunken eyes pale in the bright day, his blond beard a pendulum moving back and forth across his dark shirt, ticking denial.

She was glad she'd insisted on Leanna staying with the girls and keeping them beyond the gate. What all had Coffeemeyer said? She felt dull, like a sleep-starved child trying to learn higher division. Soon the man would hang and the nightmare would be over.

John Rhoads joined Coffeemeyer, a head taller, his voice heavy with chest ague. "Ed's right. Seven men surprised this sorry excuse for a man before he got his lies untangled. The motive was fresh meat. We all saw the blood in the buckets. We asked why he didn't eat the mules and cattle that was coming up in the snow-melt. He said it was too dry." Several male voices called assent. Talk buzzed all around Elitha.

She closed her eyes, suddenly thinking of what Perry had told her about his being lonely out at sea when he was a boy, with his mother dead and his father so deep in drink he might as well have been. She felt a connection with Perry, and wished he were here. She fought the hollowness that was coming up to get her and knew she must sit down immediately. But then she'd see only the backs of skirts and trouser legs, and no decent girl would do that. She looked back toward the gate and thought she could sit there without drawing too much attention.

She excused her way through the crowd, a man orating about proof and evidence, and sat down leaning on a gate-post. Captain Sutter was climbing the stairs to be seen above the crowd. People with pitying expressions turned to look at her. The Captain was talking, but at this distance she understood only a few words.

". . . iss not a bad man . . . no different dan udders. . . . All haff eat flesh of . . . "

". . . character assassin — " another man charged.

Fallon le Gros didn't need to climb the stairs, and his voice carried farther.

". . . killed her for the Donner riches," he said. "When we tightened the rope around his filthy neck, he admitted where he'd buried two hundred dollars. Claimed he didn't know where the rest was. I woulda hung him on the spot, cept the others wanted a trial."

Hirum Miller stood nearly as tall as Fallon le Gros. He told the assembled people, to Elitha's amazement, that he knew for a fact that George Donner had received ten thousand dollars from the sale of his land in Springfield, Illinois. Heads bobbed and people turned to talk to each other, as if they had known this all long.

Suddenly the hollowness sucked everything black. She put her head between her knees until she thought she could walk, then pushed to her feet and kept her head low, hurrying out the gate, gripping her stomach to hold it down. It seemed a hundred miles to the adobe room, but she got there and gratefully flopped on the sawdust, glad the girls were gone. She pulled her cloak over her head to shut out the world. The moist warmth of her breathing mingled with the image of Keseberg's pale eyes and pendulum beard, and the pot of Tamsen's blood and . . . *Oh dear God.*

Even if he was hanged it wouldn't erase the pot.

But, she realized with a sudden lessening of tension in her shoulders, she could marry Perry McCoon and become the mistress of a big cattle ranch. She could take her sisters away from here and try not to think of any of this ever again.

I pause in my spirit-tracking and look at Old Man Coyote, who appears to be asleep at the foot of my trunk. "That poor young woman," I say, "walked a strange trail without strong allies."

Coyote jerks his head up. "For crying out loud, she had all the help she needed, and talked to the God-spirit all the time."

"He was so far away he didn't even have a shape. And she knew nothing of catching spirit help in dreams."

"She dreamed of apple trees."

"You know very well what I mean."

Coyote smacks his muzzle to loosen a morsel of cat wedged between his teeth. "Well, I wouldn't need any magic," he says laying his chin on his paw. "if I had men breaking trail and making fires and handing out food. The only thing I wonder is why John Rhoads didn't hump her. And Perry McCoon — what's he waiting for?"

"Patience, you promiscuous old man. Anyway, I feel sorry for her."

"You're just being sentimental. Remember, the new people judge everything by their own comfort." He chuckles like he can't stop, chuckles through: "I like the way they wander around in their messes and can't figure a way out. It's hilarious."

"You, of all animals call people hilarious! What about that time you insisted on bringing fire to the world? Wanted to be a hero, so you whined and schemed and wore the other animals down until they let you carry it, against their better judgement. But you burned your fingers off short and set the whole world on fire. Why, if you hadn't found that hollow oak, you would have fried."

That wipes the smile off him, and I see him glance covertly at his paws. But Coyote never quits. The corners of his lips curl up again. "Get Perry McCoon back in the story. I like him."

"You would."

33

JUNE 1, 1847

Dawn. Planks of the deck grew distinct. Sycamores and cottonwoods changed from dark to summer green. Elitha could now see the dark stubble on Perry's face, which was slack with contentment as he braced his back with his hands and stood looking up at the thick canopy over the river.

She was far from content as she rose from the blanket on the deck, smoothing her linsey-woolsey frock. She had sinned — the very night he returned from Yerba Buena — though God had let her live. She'd broken her solemn promise to be good. Earlier, while Perry had dozed and darkness blanketed what they'd done, she'd realized she had probably committed the Unforgivable Sin. Aunt Susanna had spoken about that, shooing Elitha away when she'd been maybe six years old. In all the years that followed, nobody had given her a straight answer about exactly what the Unforgivable Sin was. It seemed to her now that the thing she'd let Perry do, being unspeakable, was undoubtedly it. She fastened buttons from waist to chin, realizing she could burn in hell for all eternity. Life was full of pitfalls and she shouldn't have surrendered, shouldn't have disappointed Pa. *Elitha is an obedient girl,* he used to say. Apparently not, but now all she could do was go forward and try to make it up to God and Pa, if he watched from heaven.

Her voice came quiet and smooth. "Let's go up to Sinclair's and get married now." She pushed the last button through its loop. Sinclair was the justice of the peace — *alcalde* in California.

He raised his straight brows at her. "Now?" At her deliberate nod he chuckled, checked his trouser buttons, slipped the rope and yanked the main sail aloft. The canvas barely luffed, and he grinned as he coaxed the small craft upriver. "Now is a fine time, lass. Indeed it tis."

His contentment with boom and sail made her wonder why he'd left the sea. Would he be sorry one day? With a mild shock she realized such matters were now central to her life, not mere curiosities. But she liked his dream of becoming a wealthy squire, and liked what he'd said about her greater "learning" being what he needed to make his dream come true. It felt strange and wonderful to be needed by a thirty-six-year-old man. The skiff inched upstream and she stood beside him at the tiller sailing swiftly into her new life, needing the assurance of his touch. She felt like a young animal entering a strange forest.

He craned his neck to watch the curl of green water at the prow. "Neptune's Bones, never seen it so deep in June." He pointed at the river and looked at her. "This be the ford, lass, for horses, wagons, right here. Would ye believe? We'd be shoaled up here good most years." He changed the rigging and they tacked across on the diagonal. "That's why they call Sinclair's plaice *Rancho del Paso. Paso* means crossing."

Upriver the V of sky was a glorious orange-pink in advance of the sun. A doe jerked her head from the water while a fawn sipped at her side. Elitha inhaled the fragrance of morning and vowed she wouldn't permit, on this day, the ugly visions that had bothered her since Keseberg walked free. That was nearly a month ago. It was time to go down her trail. When the crying was over, that's what people did, no matter the setback — Pa had lost two wives. No matter the deaths, or ruined crops, or burned barns, whatever, people showed their grit by going forward. Heaven or hell would just have to wait. Her children would grow with the new land, from the union of a British sailor and the daughter of George Donner.

The skiff parted a forest of green cattails where hundreds of red-winged blackbirds squeaked like rusty gate hinges. Piloting through, Perry stepped over the rail, crouched, watched, and when they bumped land, grabbed a rope and pulled the boat to a tree. She jumped across to mud and it occurred to her that the Reed family might still be at Sinclair's. She'd be pleased to see Virginia again, and have them all witness her wedding.

A beaten trail led through lush growth to a ridge. On it perched an adobe house ringed with tall blue flowers — a sort of multiplied lily she had often admired. An outbuilding, a lean-to and a milch cow stood to one side. Several half-clothed Indians glanced up from a little fire, their wigwams of dry rushes standing beyond.

An Indian got up and spoke Spanish, a language Perry didn't know very well. "Fetch Señor Sinclair. I wants to palaver," he said.

In a short time Mr. Sinclair, who with Mr. Sutter had officiated the trial, teetered before them jamming on a boot, his dark hair mussed and his shirttail out. "You old tar," he said, casting an approving eye at Elitha, "what brings you out this early?"

"Getting married, we is. If you've a mind to 'blige us."

Mr. Sinclair, who was about Perry's age, nodded from one to the other, then waved them inside. "Make yerselves to home while I gits respectable."

Elitha glanced around the homey room, but saw no sign of the Reeds. Patterned carpet covered the floor and blue chintz hung from glass windows, sparkling clean. A tidy fireplace was plastered into the adobe corner. The place had a woman's touch.

"Mornin." A female voice.

She turned to see a smiling woman in a neat red-striped frock and dark hair hanging lose to her waist. "Good morning." She curtsied and, almost without thinking, removed Perry's hat, handing it to him. Seeing his raised eyebrows, she smiled in hopes of conveying that she hadn't meant to criticize, but men were to remove their hats indoors. She asked the woman, "Are the Reeds gone?"

"Left a week ago. Visiting the Younts over in the Napa Valley. Till they get their health back. Then I 'spose they'll go to that ground of his in San José." She made a sorrowful face. "Those poor little tykes. Never saw living children so poorly as when Patty and Tommy come down!" She brightened. "Nothing good cream won't cure."

"I'm so glad the whole Reed family lived."

Mrs. Sinclair rearranged her face to pity. "A blessing, ain't it? You poor, poor dear."

Perry shot a sparkling grin at the woman. "Here to get hitched, we is."

Her voice jumped up an octave. "So the Mister says." She pointed at the chairs and excused herself.

Elitha sank in upholstered floral print and watched Mrs. Sinclair's neat pin-striped figure move through the bedroom, into an adjoining room and disappear around a corner. Perry sat squirming like he felt uncomfortable. On a small table between them was a glass of the same pretty blue flowers that were blooming outside. She hoped to make Perry's place this cozy — hoped they could leave today and get started. Mrs. Sinclair came toward them with a tray of silver and teacups.

They drank coffee and spoke of the fine weather. Over her cup Elitha looked at the man about to become her husband — boots apart, teacup balanced on a thigh, combing his hair with his fingers. He was an enigma, a man who'd sailed the high seas then become as fine a horseman as any Spaniard. She felt the mystery of him, and pride at his wide experience.

Mr. Sinclair entered with trimmed beard and clean shirt, wielding two leather-bound volumes. "My marryin books," he said with a wink.

Mrs. Sinclair pushed the table out of the way, arranged bride and groom before the fireplace, and took the flowers from the glass, shaking water from their stems, and pushed them into Elitha's hands. Mr. Sinclair gave his wife a book — *The Bible* it said in large print on the cover — and read phrases Elitha had heard before, but paid little attention to.

She put her hand on the Bible and said in her turn, ". . . to love and cherish, to honor and obey, in sickness and in health, till death do us part." *Death.*

Mr. Sinclair snapped the book closed and said, "Yer hitched and that thar's my first weddin." He looked like a boy with a shiny new top.

"Neptune's bones!" Perry said, "I'm the first?"

Mr. Sinclair twisted his mouth in thought. "That time Sutter wedded'ya? What, a year ago?" He grabbed his beard and pursed his lips, "At's right. A year ago. That was his last marrying."

Stunned, she turned to Perry, "You been married before?"

"She died."

Mr. Sinclair said, "Waitin fer Christmas, man? Kiss the bride!"

Perry drew her into his arms and she closed her eyes. Stubble stabbed her mouth, slightly sore from last night, and brought the memory of a much younger Elitha sitting on Pa's lap, giggling, squirming for freedom as he playfully whiskered her. Then, in the darkness behind her treacherous eyelids, she saw the scene the rescuers had described —Pa's breast cleaved open, his heart and liver gone, his empty skull sawed wide open, but somehow his eyes, beneath the chasm, were kindly, looking at her. She pushed Perry away and turned to the fireplace.

A hand came down on her shoulder. "My dear," Mrs. Sinclair's voice said, "I hope you're not poorly on your wedding day."

"Just something in my throat." She feigned a cough and turned around.

"It's the flowers, dear. Sometimes the dust of them chokes me too."

Mr. Sinclair suggested they stay for another cup of coffee. While his wife made another trip to the kitchen, he explained that Mr. Sutter was feeling "low" about Captain Frémont leaving Lieutenant Kern in charge of the fort, and appointing him, Sinclair, alcalde. "Why don't you let him shine a little and host you a wedding feast? It'd smooth his ruffled feathers I'll wager."

"A fine idear that is," Perry said.

Since the trial, Elitha had been avoiding Mr. Sutter, who had acted as advocate for Lewis Keseberg — Mr. Sinclair having pronounced the verdict that Mr. Coffeemeyer was to pay Keseberg a dollar for defamation of character — but she kept quiet. This was Perry's wedding too. Besides, she didn't entirely understand all her feelings.

Mr. Sinclair added, "Hell, the war ain't over yet. Fer all we know, the Mexican flag'll fly over the fort again and I'll be happy to hand this duty back to John."

Perry had a way of smiling directly into a person's eyes that could be construed as a challenge. "Me thought Captain Sutter was a damned fine constable at that," he said.

But Mr. Sinclair only chuckled. "An odd Mexican Frémont musta thought he was!"

"See eye to eye with him pretty much, does ye?" Perry asked.

"John Sutter?" He smiled. "Oh shore. We're pardners, kind of." He went to the door, signalled an Indian, and must have dispatched a runner.

The Indian runner, or boater, must have been quick, because by the time she and Perry docked at Sutter's and hiked to the fort, people were congratulating them and women were bustling around the clay ovens that resembled giant beehives. The little girls were not in the courtyard that she could see. Had they been afraid last night?

Feeling mounting remorse at leaving them, she nearly collided with Mrs. Wolfinger at the foot of Sutter's stairs — Dorothy Wolfinger, who at the trial had called Lewis Keseberg a fine gentleman who "never tink to kill a vooman." Elitha backed up and murmured, "Sorry," then said to Perry, "I'm going to look for my sisters."

Mrs. Wolfinger drew in her chin and tilted her head and said with a kindly smile, "Elitha, not to vorry. Frau Brunner make dem clean. You be da bride. Go up and zit!" She pointed the way and Perry, in obvious agreement, took her elbow and led her up the stairs. Mrs. Wolfinger followed with an Indian basket of bread rounds, and Perry went into Mr. Sutter's adjoining room.

Uneasy feelings struggled within Elitha as she sat at the big table, along which

Mrs. Wolfinger cheerfully distributed the bread. The worst was she feared Keseberg would come through the door; since the trial she'd noticed he was tight with Mr. Sutter. The Man Eater, as people called him, walked around the fort appearing to bask in the notoriety, while she and her sisters watched their step and pressed into the shadows trying to avoid him. She doubted she could abide being in the same room with the repulsive man. Maybe Perry would make him leave.

She heard Perry talking and joking with Mr. Sutter, the thick odor of unwashed bedclothes wafting from the alcove. Sunlight dazzled and dimmed the room as immigrant women entered, set things on the table and left. Food aromas competed with the other smells, some of which came from the stacks of woolen blankets and crates along the wall. Bearded trappers with slicked-down hair came in, waltz-stepping comically around the women. They smiled at Elitha and drank from skins. She had no idea their names, but smiled back. In a way she was the hostess. But as she sat with her hands folded in her lap, she felt reality fading into a cloudiness, as if her feelings bore no relation to what was happening. Part of her wanted to run away. A light ache in her privates reminded her of the night — she'd loved the feeling of being rocked on the boat, loved the way he'd said she was beautiful. His hands made her forget everything. His insistent kisses lulled her right up to the moment of shock and pain. She'd almost pushed him away, but couldn't because she needed his arms around her.

People filled the chairs and pulled up crates — no Keseberg yet. She remained in her cloudy realm, a step back from the happy bride she'd always imagined she would be, and smiled at the Sinclairs as they entered. A finger chucked her chin.

She whirled to see Captain Sutter beaming down at her. "Perry iss a lucky fellow, hmm?" He wore his military finery, a blue jacket with gold epaulets and red trim. His chubby thighs strained the white fabric of his tights, which disappeared into blackened knee-high boots. He nodded a welcome to the Sinclairs and others, and made a signal to an Indian girl. A few minutes later the girl staggered in with a demijohn and put it at the head of the table, where Captain Sutter had seated himself like a king, one chair from Elitha.

Perry sat between them, his teasing smile and brandy breath pouring over her. In a blaze of sunlight a group of small people entered. When the door shut she saw an older woman in a brown frock with Leanna, Georgia, Frances and Ellie — stricken little faces above clean dresses. Ellie's chin quivered and her high voice penetrated the buzz of talk in the room. "You're not our sister anymore!" Tears were running from her eyes. Georgia and Frances wore pouts too.

"Of course I am!" she said, hurrying to them. "Whatever gave you such an idea?"

The small woman with her hair pulled severely into a bun said confidentially, "I haff say you be der sister no more."

Their sister no more! She searched the frightened eyes, two brown pairs, one blue, aware of the listeners in the room. "I shall ALWAYS be your big sister. It's just that I am Mrs. McCoon now too." She squatted and hugged them, their legs thin beneath the cloth.

Ellie murmured into her cheek. "But you're not my fambly now."

"Nonsense!" she wiped Ellie's tears on the corner of her dress, then steered the girls to chairs on her side of the table.

Mrs. Brunner muttered, "I vork hard *mit dieser mädele zauber zu machen.*"

Zauber meant clean. "Thank you very much for taking care of them, Mrs. Brunner." Irritated at the woman but knowing she must be polite and grateful, she curtsied and took her seat between Perry and Leanna, the sense of unreality mounting. Soon so many were squeezed in at the table that she could scarcely move her arms. People who didn't fit sat on crates against the wall.

Captain Sutter stood at the head clearing his throat for attention. He raised a full glass. "*Prozit* to Mr. and Mrs. Perry McCoon."

With a loud scraping of chairs, all except Elitha stood and raised glasses. *Prozit* rumbled from more than thirty throats, and she tugged at Perry's trousers to make him sit, but it was useless and no one seemed to notice him toasting himself. Then Sutter spoke in heavy accents about Perry, his "long friend and associate." She held a half-smile until her face hurt, and didn't understand the winking aside about rustled calves, which made old California hands laugh, and felt embarrassed to be sitting while everyone else was standing. Captain extended his glass toward her and finished, ". . . such a great beauty zee iss, and a kind spirit alzo." Everyone looked at her as they drank their liquor, and her face burned like a hot poker.

Mr. Sutter leaned forward to fork the first piece from a sliced ham.

Perry patted her hot cheek and said, "She's shy, this one." Polite laugher.

The pink meat trembled on Sutter's fork. "And now, all eat," Sutter commanded, sitting. They all sat.

People smiled and a blizzard of arms and forks and spoons shot out to the dishes. She stared at the meat as it plopped off Sutter's fork and rippled on his plate. Like an unbraked wagon down a mountain, images careened at her. The pot of blood. Mr. Coffeemeyer saying, *Corpses don't bleed.* She looked down and kept her gaze from the pots on the table. Tamsen's small form materialized before her, quailing before Lewis Keseberg — skeletal combatants. She couldn't look at people eating with fragments of food on their teeth, couldn't stand the peck peck of talk and forks. People said Lewis Keseberg fed them information about how best to saw a skull, how long to simmer human brains, how much tastier human liver is than any other kind. But at last she felt again the cushioning fog of unreality, and spooned succotash and bread pudding on her plate. Handing the dishes to Leanna and the eager girls, she remembered that not long ago they had dreamed of a meal like this. Across the table the talk was German, Mrs. Wolfinger and Mr. Zins and Mr. Kyburz inclining their heads toward Mr. Sutter. Mrs. Brunner craned her neck over a man and joined the conversation. "Kaysaberger" came through the babble. She exchanged a glance with Leanna and found and squeezed her hand beneath the table.

Mrs. Kelsey called: "This here's a weddin. Stop talkin about the de-parted."

Heads bobbed approval. Mr. Sinclair stood up ringing his fork on his glass. "A toast to the bride," he announced. "The pluckiest girl I ever seen and so like her sainted mother, whose name will be remembered for all time." The *California Star* had praised Tamsen as a model for all women because she had stayed with her dying husband instead of saving herself. The writer never mentioned her duty to her children.

But then, Elitha realized, Tamsen had planned on caring for Pa and the girls, with Elitha's help. She didn't expect to be murdered. And here sat Mr. Sutter and Mr. Sinclair, the old and new lawmakers calmly eating. But at least Lewis Keseberg didn't appear. People cheered and drank liquor, even the women.

Mr. Zins pinged on his cup with a fork. "I haff announcement." A short man, he stood patting the top of Mrs. Wolfinger's head while the talking stopped. "Dorotaya and I be married Saturday June twenty at tswelf noon," he said, "All invited." Shouts erupted. The tip of his large red nose hung down over his lips, which curved in the smile of a concave quarter moon. Not handsome like Mr. Wolfinger.

Mr. Sutter shouted over the hurrahs, "Ya and we haff feast here. All invite." He slapped the table so hard the plates jumped.

As Elitha clapped along with the crowd, it dawned on her that no inquest had been held in the matter of Mr. Wolfinger's death, despite the deathbed confession, and no one gossiped about the whereabouts of his money. With new sympathy she looked at the young lady beneath Mr. Zins' hand — the color and flesh back in her cheeks, the ivory brooch at her throat. How wronged she must have felt! And lonely, even surrounded by the Donner family. No doubt she had vouched for Lewis Keseberg because of her friendship with Philippine Keseberg. A person needed friends. And now Doris, as people called her, was going down the trail. It showed in her face.

"Till death does ya all part," said a trapper. Wine sloshed as glasses were raised.

People cheered and Perry lifted Elitha's hand like a prize.

34

She had hoped to leave immediately after the wedding breakfast, but by the time it was over, Perry had drunk too much *aguardiente* and fallen asleep on Sutter's floor. Later, looking a tender shade of green around the eyes, he explained he needed money to buy a wagon and team. She and Leanna handed over the coins they'd saved. Pocketing that, he said, "I need more," and went to Captain Sutter for "Donner money."

Elitha was unclear on the details, but people said that after the rescuers were paid from the wagon booty, an account had been set aside for the Donner orphans, with Mr. Sutter in charge. She didn't know how much was in the account — did it include the $10,000 from the quilt? At the trial the rescuers had acted like they'd found very little —but she knew she couldn't talk to Mr. Sutter without getting blubbery and appearing awfully young, though she'd actually be angry with him. The other thing she didn't know was whether the money was to be shared with her cousins despite the fact that Mr. Reed — a man of means — had taken them in, and despite her belief that her father had left Illinois with a great deal more money than her Uncle Jacob. She knew that Mr. Reed and Mr. Sutter had become good friends, and she wasn't about to contradict Mr. Reed.

In any case, Perry had returned looking satisfied. "I'm glad you're taking care of the money," Elitha had told him. It was good to have a husband to see to these complex matters — good that money was the province of men.

Now it was the next morning. Leanna scanned the room and pronounced it clean. Elitha agreed. The woodshavings were neatly hemmed in and the switches laid straight by the firepit, the ashes removed. They had all pitched in, bouncing around, cheerful for the first time in a month. Their hair was braided and the carpetbag filled with their extra clothing, which had been so laboriously sewn. In the bottom were Elitha's apple seeds.

Georgia dandled Tamsen's black silk stocking with the fancy gold TD embroidered at the top. Elitha knew she would be devastated to lose this one keepsake from her mother, which she had brought down the mountains in the pocket of her cloak. Ellie held the other stocking.

"Stuff 'er in." Elitha said, pushing the carpetbag at Georgia.

She shook her head and laid the silk against her cheek, looking mournful.

"You can't hold it the whole way. We'll be six hours in the wagon."

Georgia shoved the stocking down the neck of her dress, and looked pleased.

Remembering her own sorrow, and Leanna's, when their real mother died long ago, Elitha sympathized. "Sure it won't fall out? Here Sugar," She untied and tightened the sash of the frock. "There. That'll hold it in."

Ellie, having watched this, stuffed Tamsen's other stocking down the front of her dress, then turned her back and waited for Elitha to retie her sash as well.

That done, Elitha twirled her around and squeezed her, so sweet she was with her large brown eyes and cheeks grown plumper. Tiny for her age, like Tamsen, with a mind as keen as a tack. Suddenly aware that Frances had not a stitch to remember her mother by, she hugged her too and tried to revive the cheerful mood. "We're going to have such fun on Perry's farm! You'll see. There's a nice stream near the house, and you can watch him with his cattle. He's a wonderful baquéro." Sometimes she thought that word started with v.

"Is a buck-arrow a man what gits bucked off? And Indians shoot at him?"

Elitha smiled. "Ask Mr. McCoon what it means, Ellie." He would be a full-time rancher now, and, she hoped, a little happier than he'd been of late. Recalling how he'd acted last evening, she felt her smile fade.

She had gone with him to the skiff, the *Sacramento*, and he had petted the rail as if it were a living thing. "A land lover I is, from now on."

He had laid out the blanket. Knowing what he wanted, she stepped back, uneasy about the girls. "I need to go back to the room and tell my sisters where I am," she said. "They'll fret." Like they had the night before.

He gave her a steady look. "You're married now."

"It won't take long," she said. It was a half-mile, but she'd hurry.

He took her by the shoulders and his eyes glistened strangely.

"I'm sorry, I just — "

His mouth came down on hers, then he drew back enough so his lips grazed hers as he whispered hoarsely, "Hit won't take long." Mocking what she'd just said? He was unbuttoning her frock.

"Somebody might see us." The days were long now and drops of golden light filtered through the trees, playing on the restless green water around the rocking boat. Anybody could happen upon them here at Sutter's landing.

His fingers worked the buttons. "So what if they does?"

She had lain on the blanket feeling conspicuous with her skirt up and her bodice apart. Moaning, he moved over her, trouser flap down, and fondled her breasts. Then he pulled back and looked at her privates. Embarrassed, she squirmed, wishing he'd get it over with so she could go to her sisters.

"Ent never seen nothin to match the whiteness." He ran his hand up and down between her thighs. "Like heaven's milk they is, here in the light of day."

No doubt he'd seen the legs of every kind of dark-skinned woman from Africa to the Sandwich Islands. She felt excruciatingly uncomfortable being examined like this. "Please just — "

"Big Sist — " A small voice was smothered out. Leaves thrashed on the bank.

Shocked that the girls had followed, she pushed Perry away with strength that surprised her, threw down her dress and scrutinized the shore. All she saw were leaves. "Where are you girls?"

Perry was on his knees with his extended self visible. The four stepped shyly into view. "I told 'em we shouldn't acome," Leanna said looking down.

"I should of told you I'd be a while," Elitha said.

"Well, you got an eyeful," Perry barked, "now get the hell out of here!" They shrank back, a step at a time, Frances stumbling.

Elitha softened it. "Go on back to the room. I'll be there in a while."

When they were gone, Perry proceeded. He seemed distant, and she worried somebody else would come, and worried that she'd handled the situation badly. She didn't know much about being a wife.

Now, clasping the handles of the carpetbag and smiling at the girls, she tried to put that scene behind her. Things would be better at Rancho Sacayak. "I can't wait to get on the trail," she said.

"Me neither," they repeated one after the other. She tied their bonnets.

"Let's go to the gate," Georgia sang out.

"Yeah!"

"I'll beat you."

"No you won't."

The string of laughing girls ran out the door, their feet mostly recovered, and Elitha's steps felt light as she followed them to where Perry would come with the wagon. As the bouncy sisters darted around the young soldier at the gate, Elitha felt the sun through her frock — surprisingly hot despite the wind. It tugged at her bonnet and blew the girls' hair from their braids and bonnets and across their faces — the strands she'd cut to get the mats out.

"Don't touch the cannon," the soldier grumped.

They hunched in a circle covering their guilty grins. Elitha looked up the west path, but saw no wagon, only a dust devil. *Someone died.* That was past.

"You gonna teach me to read?" Ellie grinned.

Elitha chased after her, caught her up in her arms and growled into her neck. "Didn't I promise?" Ellie giggled a perfect arpeggio and kicked her legs in the air.

"We're going to have our own school." Georgia told the soldier, who, having made a leaning post of his gun, wiped perspiration from under his hat — crossed guns on the band.

"She's gonna be our teacher!" Pointing at Elitha.

"At Mr. McCoon's farm."

"And my big sisters won't go away to work no more!"

He gave them a tired look.

Glancing inside the gate, Elitha saw Lewis Keseberg coming down the stairs with Captain Sutter; they vanished into a shop. Impatience tore at her. When would Perry come? The air smelled like tinder. Then came a sound she had never heard before — like a high note singing down around them, a prickly hum within the wind. Maybe fire searing through the dry grass. She looked all around but saw no smoke. The girls stopped playing. "What IS that noise?" Frances asked.

Elitha looked to the soldier, who restored the gun to his shoulder and frowned uneasily at the plains. He didn't know. Sam Kyburz, who a couple of weeks ago had tried to interest her in marrying him, drove a team of oxen past the fort, pulling a load of bulging leather bags. He smiled and lifted his hat, apparently unconcerned about the sound. She didn't ask. Riders came and went, seemingly oblivious. Then a team of horses materialized in the dust of the west path. The girls saw it and jumped in place, holding hands. "He's coming, he's coming!"

But the wagon's driver turned out to be a dark-skinned Indian woman wearing white woman's clothes. She pulled the team to a stop near them and hopped down to secure the team, one thick black braid swinging.

Elitha said, "Pardon me, but do you know what that noise is?"

The woman looked at her and said, "Grass opens."

The eavesdropping soldier looked as perplexed as Elitha felt. The woman reached down beside the cannon wheel and plucked a stalk of dry grass, pointed to the papery seed pods, then gestured around the horizons. "Open when dry."

Elitha understood. A single pop was too faint to be heard, but millions cracking and popping at the same time made this noise — surprisingly loud to be heard over the wind. She explained it to the girls, and Ellie's eyes lit like candles. They bent forward, ears to the blowing pods, hands on knees, listening.

With the mystery solved, Elitha's impatience heightened. Intent on looking for a wagon, she didn't pay attention to a horse with big brown and white spots galloping toward her. Then she saw his face, pinched and hard beneath his leather hat, the dust blowing rapidly away.

"Get aboard," he said with an expression like last evening.

"Where's the wagon?" she asked. The girls circled her like chicks.

"Can't get one now. Next time."

"We can't all fit on the horse." Her stomach felt hollow.

"Mrs. Brunner'll see after the girls, she will. I tended to it. Now get on." He gave her a look so steely she almost couldn't speak.

"But you said — "

"I said get on."

She felt the girls clutching her dress, heard them start to whimper.

In a vexed tone Perry yelled at a man who was strolling toward the outhouse. "Taik these girls, will ye Ned? Give 'em to the Brunner laidy when ye sees her." A man in buckskins turned, stroked his beard, ran his eyes over Leanna and said something Elitha couldn't hear over the whoosh of wind and whine of the grass.

Looking at Perry's narrowed eyes, she wondered with a shock if he'd planned this. The thought made her feel like a scrap of paper blowing in the wind. Her fourteen years were nothing against his thirty-six. She felt weak and trembly. He could have bought a wagon; they were cheap with so many having come over the mountains. The man with cruel Spanish spurs seemed a total stranger. But only yesterday she had promised before God and witnesses to obey him till death did them part. She couldn't balk at the first obstacle, no matter how much she hated leaving her sisters.

She squatted before the girls and looked into their tear-streaked faces, so recently dry and happy. But no words came. She inclined her head and they all touched foreheads.

"Oh fer Chrissake git on the bleedin 'orse." She looked up to see his fingers close on the braided coil of leather hanging from his saddle. His face looked ugly. Women and children who were walking by stared, pity on some faces, amusement on others.

She felt bafflement as alien as the singing grass, and stammered, "How long before we come back for them?" She saw the flicker in Leanna's eyes, knew she'd heard the resignation.

He dropped the lariat, left it hanging in its coil. "A few daiys."

Murmuring that they'd have to be brave and stay with Mrs. Brunner for a while, she hugged the little girls one by one. Georgia collapsed crying in her arms. Ellie's brown eyes were frenzied as she flung herself at her neck, nearly knocking her down. She hung on fiercely while Elitha tried to hug Frances. "But Grandma Brunner isn't here," Frances bawled. A desperate, last-resort argument.

It made her feel better to know they had a name for the woman, one that suggested familiarity and friendship. She pushed the carpetbag into Leanna's hand. Then like magic Mrs. Brunner appeared, disentangling Ellie's fingers and peeling her from Elitha's neck. The German woman corralled the weeping girls while Elitha stood stranded in their heartbroken gazes. *All alone in the wicked world.* She was leaving them, as Ma had. But it was only for a few days. People travelled back and forth to the fort all the time, she told herself.

Suddenly Perry was on the ground shoving her at the horse. She put her shoe in the leather stirrup-housing and mounted. He landed heavily behind her. Then they were galloping away. She turned back. Mrs. Brunner flapped her hand goodbye. Sad-faced Leanna stood behind the weeping girls, the devil wind whipping their skirts before them.

35

"Damned norther!"

It was the first thing Perry had said since leaving New Helvetia. It had been hours. Afraid if she spoke, she'd accuse him of deceiving her, she watched waves moving across the ocean of golden grass and listened to its unearthly wail. *Ma said you was to care fer us till she comes through,* Frances had said when they came down from the mountains. That meant forever now. Tamsen's trust in her felt like a sacred bargain. It made tears come and they blurred the landscape mile after mile, the wind drying them on her face. But she never stopped countering with, *We'll fetch them in a few days.*

"Brings the bleedin 'eat, hit does."

The last time it blew like this, when she'd found her sisters roasting liver, the grass had turned brown and the fort had sweltered for a week.

Something large and dark was suddenly sweeping toward them across the grass, faster than any earthly thing. She shrank back, heart clamped in her throat. It was nearly upon them before she realized it was a shadow and looked up to see a giant black and white bird — a condor. She'd never seen one so close. The center of the bird looked like a black man with white arms outstretched, body tapering down to nothing at the tail. Surrounding the white arms were huge black extensions of its shoulders and arms, tremendously long black feathers at the tips open as if grasping the wind. The bird glided closer in the cloudless blue, correcting, looking down at them with the ugliest head she'd ever seen — naked, blotched, pinkish — the neck swollen and loose-skinned like an old man with a goiter. Her scalp prickled and fear jangled in her limbs as she met the bird's fierce scowl, its unblinking red eye, the bony curve of its beak.

Perry shouted, "Vamoose!" He grabbed his sidearm and fired. But the bird had already surged forward and, with two wing flaps, shrank before them until it was nothing but a black spot in the sky. He stuffed the gun in his belt, grumping, "Take calves from their mum's teats, the bleedin bastards does."

It seemed that the biggest of everything was to be found in California — mountains, bears, trees and birds. Ahead was a herd of about thirty antelope, peach-colored with white markings, pronghorns erect. Like the others they'd seen, these bounded away as fluid as fish in water. She saw many deer nesting in the shade of the whipping, thrashing oaks. Sometimes the horse passed so near, she could see their fur riffle in the wind. But no matter what she saw, the faces of her sisters haunted her. Had they stopped crying? The worry that Perry had planned this came at her as relentlessly as the wind, as prickly as the howling grass.

Suddenly the horse lurched off the trail at a run and she grabbed the horn to keep from bouncing off. Ahead Perry's hat tumbled over the grass at a high speed. He spurred the horse and overtook it, maintaining a gallop beside the hat. She felt him slip and feared he'd fallen. But he swept up the hat and pulled himself up, yelling, "Hang on, lassie." Back in the saddle he jammed the hat on his head and turned the horse toward the trail. A man at home in the wind, as skilled on a horse as a boat.

A strange wind too, she thought as the horse slowed to a walk. Every north wind she'd heard of brought cold air. This one blasted like a blow furnace. Her lips were cracked and dry, her back wet and tight against the man she'd married — a man as alien as the wind.

They topped a rise and she was surprised to look down into a valley with a swath of green running through it. She hadn't known they'd been climbing. Far in the distance stretched the mountains — from horizon to horizon — capped in white. It felt eery to see, with all the haze blown away, those broken, angular surfaces, and to know that she'd walked across them and her parents would remain forever in those heights.

"There be Rancho Omuchumne," he was saying. "Sheldon and Daylor's grant."

She looked at the green bottomland. "Rancho Omu — "

"Named it for the niggers, Jared did."

The horse swayed as they descended into the valley, whinnying to another horse on the slope where a dark-skinned rider sat with the cattle. The bottomland was a tangle of trees and vines, except for the trail, on which they galloped until they came to a tiny wooden cabin. A saddled horse stood outside.

"Ahoy!" Perry called, reining in. In her ear he said confidentially, "A naighbor."

The door opened and out stepped a short girl about Elitha's age, maybe younger, a pink frock stretched across her plump bodice. She wasn't pretty, her nose being a little on the fleshy side, but she had a generous smile and a likeable, impish grin. The wind stole locks of her brown hair from the bun on top of her head.

"Well blow me down!" Perry said from behind, "Me eyes was set to see that man o' yours."

"He's here abouts." The girl placed her hand on her forehead, holding back the hair. She seemed pleased with what she saw.

"This 'ere's me new bride, Elitha." He clapped her on the shoulder. "That be Catherine Sheldon."

"Catey," the girl corrected, grinning impishly.

A man stepped from mounds of berry canes as high as the house, a muddy shovel in hand. A hat shaded the hard wedge of his face but didn't diminish the power of his level gaze. "Howdy," he said. A man who is never surprised, Elitha guessed. Probably in his mid-thirties, same as Perry.

Catherine disentangled a sweating pottery gourd from a noose hanging on the shady side of the porch and held it out for them. Her hazel eyes twinkled as she ordered, "Well neighbors, gitcher selves on down fer a drink."

The surprisingly cool water eased Elitha's throat. She couldn't get enough. It felt wonderful spilling down her bodice too, while the hot wind flapped the wet linsey woolsey on her back, the fit still loose after these three months. Handing the gourd to Perry, she saw the teasing love Catherine was sending Mr. Sheldon, and the intimate look he returned.

Catherine said, "Shame on you for not telling we was to git neighbors." She winked at Elitha. "Come on in outa the wind."

But Perry glanced at the sun and said, "Thank 'e, no. We'd visit a spell but we're late enough. Stopping at Daylor's too, we is." He turned to Sheldon. "Expected you'd be at yer new house up yonder." He nodded his hat at a trail cut through the thicket.

Catherine answered, "We're helpin Bill and Sally clear the slough." Sheldon seemed easy with his wife doing the talking. The same wouldn't be said of Perry, Elitha knew, though she didn't know how she knew.

Perry tilted back on his heels, "Now a man with two houses could get muddled about where his boots lie, couldn't 'e?" Catherine was taking in his dimple and the long dark lashes over his cheeks, the kind women wished they had.

Mr. Sheldon swung his gaze from Perry to Catherine and back again, lining up his lips in a hint of a smile. "No sense in tearing down this old bachelor cabin." He nodded at it. "We call it Slough House, to keep ourselves straight."

"Slough House!" Perry hawed.

Elitha wasn't sure what was funny. *Slew?*

Perry said, "A bloke'd think it were a fine inn. But slough!" He shook off another chuckle. A thing was either fine or a slough, but not both.

Catherine said, "Just never try'n spell it!" She grinned and Elitha liked her.

Then they were on their way, waving at neighbors she looked forward to seeing again. A mile or so beyond Slough House they came to Daylor's Trading Post, a two-room adobe backed up to a river bank and surrounded by cottonwoods. The bare earth yard was littered with green leaves, which had been torn from the trees. If it hadn't been June and hot, she would have thought autumn had come. The gale tired her.

Stepping out to greet them was a tall, broad-shouldered man with a prominent nose, lopsided smile and receding hairline — also about the same age as Perry. His greeting came in Perry's accent. But he looked wiry and powerful, especially beside the willowy girl who followed him to the porch. Maybe eighteen years old, blonde hair parted in the middle and tied up in a neat bun. Elitha didn't feel the rush of liking she'd felt for Catherine, perhaps because of Mrs. Daylor's greater age and beauty.

Inside, Perry bought flour and beans and talked to the man. Elitha told Sarah Daylor, "I met Catherine Sheldon back up the trail."

Sarah smiled, her eyes pale blue. "That's my little sister."

"Sister? Why, how nice you're so nigh one another."

"Yes, and Mother and Father Rhoads aren't far either."

"Rhoads? That's the name of the man who rescued me and my sisters." Their bawling faces came at her.

"Would you be talkin about my brothers John and Dan? They went up to rescue the Donner Party."

"Both. I'm a Donner. Came through with the First Relief." Dan Rhoads had gone ahead to the fort when Mr. Coffeemeyer brought back the cache. "John's a good man."

"That he is. Took in a passel of youngins when my sister-in-law died. Brought them across to Californy just like they was his own. Matilda's a dear too." Perry was counting coins into Bill Daylor's hand.

"I met your sister Elizabeth at Johnson's ranch. Is John's place nearby?" She knew he was farming on the Cosumnes, or Cosumney, as some called the river.

Sarah flapped her hand south. "Less than a mile. My folks' place is down that way too, a little farther."

"How grand, to have family close by."

Perry and Bill Daylor hauled small bags of flour, beans and sugar to the horse and strapped them with salt pork behind the saddle. Then, too soon, Perry was spurring, and they were riding east, following the same double track — much fainter now.

"Sutter's trail this is," Perry said. "His woodcutters, goin up to Piney Woods."

"How much farther to your place?" Hills stretched before her.

"Bout seven miles."

She settled back, watching the sway of the awkward shadow — horse, riders and bundles, low sun at their backs — and worried about her sisters. The devil wind blew ceaselessly over the feral hum of the grass. At last Perry pointed past her bonnet and said, "Thar she be."

She followed his finger. On the brow of a hill beneath two oaks she made out a small adobe cabin, pink in the setting sun and dwarfed by the hills behind. The place seemed sad and remote, with the nearest neighbor seven miles away. Dark windows flanked the door, windows that would have reflected the sun, had they been glazed. The cabin stared blindly down a slope that led to the green trees that had to be the river. Strewn on the hillsides were shed-sized boulders. It came to her that someday the house would melt into the earth without a trace, but the boulders would remain.

"Me 'ome sweet 'ome," he crooned as they drew near. "Where a sailor finds his rest. And a good barrel of *aguardiente*." He threw back his head and hawed. "Me 'aunted 'ouse, it tis."

Haunted house? Headachy after the long day, she didn't feel like talking, and stored that away in her mind.

The horse stopped before a cracked hide beating at the cabin doorway. She dismounted and pushed the drape aside, peering at the interior. It was dim, noticeably cooler and rank with the smell of rodent scat. In a corner she made out a tangle of dusty blankets. In the middle of the room stood a crude table piled with candlewax and littered with white bird guano. A round of a tree stump, a dusty barrel and a bucket completed the furnishings — all connected by spider webs, webs that choked the twin window holes. Big tits of dried mud clung to the walls and ceiling, enough nests to harbor every wasp in Illinois.

She pulled her head out and, as Perry unstrapped the bags, glanced around at the rolling landscape — the ever-present oaks, boulders frosted with gray lichens. Then it hit her. The devil wind had stopped and the high hum of grass had weakened, as if the retiring sun had sapped all energy. A bird whistled, the first she'd heard all day. She caught a whiff of something familiar. Damp moss? A muddy creek bottom of a summer evening? A wayward memory of the stream at Donner farm, where she and Leanna had spent so many hours? It was the smell of the river.

The aroma soothed, and the absence of wind. Here, far from whispers, far from Lewis Keseberg, she would find relief. In a few days she'd go back for her sisters, never mind how terribly far it had turned out to be. She set aside her doubts about Perry and told herself this was her home. "I don't see any cows," she remarked in a light tone.

"Be fetching em, I will," he said, hanging tack on a peg by the door.

"But where are they now?"

The point of his jaw moved and a crust of a salt outlined his lips. "Better learn this now, lass. Me own affair, it tis, 'ow I run me rancho." His eyes punched hard as steel.

She felt slapped and hadn't recovered when he said, "I gots me an idear." Clamping a hand on the back of her neck, he steered her inside toward the filthy blankets.

36

The next morning as he was leaving, Perry took a pocketful of glass beads. "For tamin me niggers," he said. With that teasing grin of his, she could never tell if he was joking. "Now don't get near 'em," he added, "Wild as banshees, they is."

"They haven't hurt you, have they?" *Or your last wife?* The worst she knew was that they had eaten his pigs.

She followed him through the leather drape and watched him whistle for his horse. In Illinois most men had signed up for the Black Hawk War, and across the plains the cry "Indians" had brought a terrified clamor for guns. But the California redskins she'd seen were completely docile.

"Just stay nigh the 'ouse." With a teasing snicker he added, "Ent about to touch ye in there."

"But Perry, I was going to wash the blankets." That meant going to the river.

He turned to her and the lines of his face were soft, amused — not like he was worried. Then he turned and walked up the hill to meet his horse. Puzzling over how he could frighten her yet appear amused, she realized the Indian village was only a half mile away. If they wanted to do mischief, they could have by now. But in the end she decided that this was only his strange way of showing that he cared for her. She went inside for the knife and a length of leather strapping she'd found on the floor, then went to the river to cut willows and tie them in a broom.

No Indians were visible. She gathered a good bunch of switches and, back in the house, swept animal droppings and flattened gopher mounds. She broomed down masses of crinkly spider webs and, using the bucket, scooped out a grainy, six-inch deep nest of ant eggs she found when she picked up the bucket, the ants scurrying all over her. Then she went back to the river and took off her frock and washed the ants out, submerging long enough to drown the ants in her underclothes and hair. She dressed and carried water from the river and poured it over the floor to make the clay smooth and hard underfoot, as people did in New Helvetia, then flooded the heaps of bird guano and scraped it from the table with a rock.

As she worked, Pa's stories came back to her, stories of his youth fifty-five years ago. Even the eastern Indians had been peaceful then, and he admired the brave pioneer women giving birth, settling problems with Indians and handling bloody accidents that befell their children while the men were away. With a lift of his chin he had finished his stories with, *You gotta be tough*. Wary, but not fearful.

It was stifling outside, her clothing already dry, but she remembered her vow never to complain of the heat again. She carried Perry's moth-eaten bedclothes to the river and rolled up her sleeves and scrubbed them. *What did Indians do for soap?* The splashing refreshed her. Steam rose when she stretched the blankets over the boulders, which were hot to the touch. She left them all day — to fry any nits — and folded the sweet-smelling blankets at dusk, feeling pleased with her progress. The only setback was that a wasp had stung her hand when she'd bumped a nest with the broom.

Perry returned, tight-lipped about the Indians. After supper he removed his trousers and — as he called it — poked her. Despite the fact that her sisters were on her mind and he was dirty from the long day and they both perspired terribly, she was glad he wanted her and she liked the feel of him against her. Afterwards she ventured, "Perry?"

"Mmm." He was nearly asleep.

She decided to start with something besides the girls. "I got stung by a wasp."

She held up the back of her puffy hand. "See?"

He didn't look.

"Well, I was wondering . . . "

"What?"

"How do people in California clean out wasps?"

"Leave the sons-o-bitches be." He flopped toward the wall.

In the presence of ladies or children, Pa had always shifted to son-of-a-gun.

"But they're flying in and out all day and I have to watch my step."

"Leave a body alone at night, they does."

Before she could say more, he was snoring.

As the dark intensified an emptiness opened in her, in the place where Leanna used to be. She realized this was the first time they had ever been apart. In Pa's world, with children from three wives, Leanna and Elitha had been "the girls," quiet and useful, four-handed, bracketed in the middle. Drifting toward sleep at last, she saw the circle of sisters in her mind's eye, heard them crying with the wind, and knew Leanna would do her best to care for them until she got there, in a day or two.

Three days later she said to Perry as he was leaving, "When we go to the fort for the girls, we should buy window glass. I saw some in Mr. Mellus' store."

He held the leather drape over his shoulder in a way that made the early sun strike his eyes, the pupils pinpoints. Outside, not a leaf stirred. "Warm weather we's 'avin now," he said. "No need fer window glass till fall." He dropped the hide and whistled for his horse.

"We gotta get the girls anyway," she said, following him out and feeling ever more uncomfortable with the way he put her off.

He gave her a strange look and went to Paint, his horse.

She knew her sisters were looking for her. It cut at her like a knife.

Twilight came but no Perry. She sat under the big oak near the door and ate a lonely supper of salt pork and beans, leaving his portion in the pot. Afterwards she hauled it high into the tree in the rope pulley he'd made. He had warned her never to keep food in the house, or grizzly bears would come. *Grizzly bears*. The most ferocious creatures in the world. At the fort she'd heard how they could be shot ten times and still tear a man from limb to limb.

The sun's last red smudge vanished on the hill, but the air remained very warm. In her camisole and underdrawers, she crawled on top of the prickly wool blankets, feeling her way, then lay listening for Paint.

The dark thickened before her eyes. Aware of her heart thudding inside its own dark room, she felt small and fragile at the bottom of the moonless dome of night, the drape at the door no comfort. Sounds were louder in the dark. Coyotes warbled and yipped, some nearby. Mosquitos came through the windows and sang in her ear. She batted at them and wondered, was Perry injured? Lying alone somewhere?

She listened, but no horse came. Only the ghostly owls landing in the branches overhead. Oo-ooo-oo. Several owls. Some in higher or lower pitches, dissonant at times. It added to her jitters. Was he dead? Something screeched above the roof. She bolted upright, heart hammering. A bird? An Indian signalling? Tentatively she lay back on the blankets. Maybe a screech owl.

A half-moon rose and traveled across the sky, invading the window through the tracery of limbs on the wall. A wolf howled nearby and she bolted up again, gooseflesh rising. Other wolves answered, hollow tones sliding upward in unearthly falsettos. She reached down, checked the tree limb she'd laid beside the bed, glad to feel its rough surface. The keen edge of the knife met her probing fingers beneath the folded blanket she used for a pillow. Did grizzlies make warning sounds? *You gotta be tough.* Women mustn't expect to be coddled. Sometimes a man went hunting and got on a trail he had to follow. After all, Perry didn't have cattle yet, so he wasn't like a settled farmer who could be counted on to come in at sundown.

To quiet her mind, she mimicked the owls and hoped predators would think no human was inside. Sometimes she did so well she silenced the real owls, and imagined them sitting perplexed on their branches. Then she began to think Perry had something else under his hat, that he'd gone to fetch the girls. It seemed the best explanation, the only one in fact. He would surprise her. And what a surprise it would be! With this thought, she sank in and out of sleep, and toward morning felt cool enough to pull a light blanket over herself.

The orange sun fired the eastern hillside when she awoke. Relieved to be in one piece, she straightened the fresh-smelling blankets, looked around the tidy room and didn't know what else to do. She had no fabric to sew — not having wanted to beg Perry to buy a bolt of calico she'd seen at Daylor's, not knowing then how much she'd need for curtains. She pulled on her petticoat, frock and bonnet, tied the thong with the blue crystals around her neck, and went out. She ate Perry's supper from last night, thinking that if he'd gone to the fort, he wouldn't arrive before sundown today, at the earliest, or the next day if he had other business. She hardened herself to the thought of a second night alone.

Already the sun burned the backs of her hands and perspiration trickled between her breasts. She moved to the shade and watched birds busying themselves before the worst heat set in. She'd seen that yesterday. They hopped up and down vertical trunks, stabbing for insects or playing tag in the branches with no sad thoughts of the past, no fears for the future. *His eye is on the sparrow,* Tamsen used to say. About thirty quail pecked their way toward her, fat gray creatures with a bauble quivering comically before their beaks. Then in a great startled roar, they winged away.

She looked up to see what frightened them, and met cat's eyes. A gray-striped cat the size of a coyote rose from a crouch and strolled away on long striped legs, dark spots on its belly and a tail no longer than her finger. When the cat was gone, a cottontail rabbit dashed across the open space and disappeared into a tunnel of grass. She'd seen them everywhere, scampering around despite the hawks crying overhead and the cats and wolves prowling the grass. She felt herself settling into a peaceful frame of mind, not waiting, but joining the buzz of life in which all creatures, hunters and hunted, enjoyed the day for its own sake. She went down to the river to explore.

Deer clattered over the rocks at her approach. The river, not much wider than a creek by Illinois standards, was slow-moving, and on its banks she entered a lush, green world. Swallows dived and swooped over the sparkling surface, playing.

She removed her frock and stepped into the warm mud, moss tendrils tickling up between her toes. She clutched her petticoat around her hips and waded deeper. But it was silly to keep her skirt dry, so she dropped it and it billowed. Curious fish studied her. One stood on its nose examining her enlarged, water-distorted foot. The fish didn't leave, even when she wiggled her toes. The sun pierced the water, illuminating a forest of wavy underwater plants, flashing through the blue crystals at her neck. No breeze moved the loose hair enveloping her shoulders. The bonnet protected her head from the sun, but intense heat reflected from the water's bright surface to her face.

Not knowing how to swim, she stepped cautiously on the slippery submerged boulders, watching her feet. Scattered in the silt were golden scales that threw the sun's glint back at her. Too light for gold, Perry had said. Her feet stirred up tadpoles, fat heads propelled by tails darting into the muck. With heat pressing into her bonnet, the chilly water felt good inching up her waist and torso and breasts.

She was up to her armpits, feet braced against the lazy current, when a much bigger yellow gleam caught her eye. Careful not to stir the silt, she moved toward what looked like a twist of metal, like slag she seen in the ashes of Pa's forge, except for the color. She touched it with her toe. It was firmly lodged in a crack between rocks. Gold? In a story Tamsen once read aloud, a boy found a pirate's treasure trove. *His heart leapt*, Tamsen had enunciated significantly. A silly thing to remember now. Even if this were gold, it was no trove. She felt curious more than anything. Why would gold be in a river? Didn't it come from mines under the earth?

Trying to move it with her toe — she'd get it out and see if it was heavy — she heard rocks clatter on shore and looked up to see a naked squaw. Off-balance, she jabbed a foot downstream, afraid she'd step in over her head. But, thankfully her foot lodged on another rock. She braced herself and saw that the Indian, who looked about her age, had a young child. She glanced around, but no other Indians were to be seen. The young squaw sat down in the shade of the willows as if to observe her. Like all Indian women in California, she wore a woven skullcap, a leather string of objects between her bare breasts and a tattoo of dotted lines running down her chin, which from a distance resembled a hideous beard. Otherwise she was very pretty, in a soft brown way, and her expression was as calm as the morning.

She unlaced the cradleboard and sat the baby in the sand beside her. The paleness of his skin against his mother's struck Elitha. He looked like one of the half-breed babies at Johnson's ranch. But Perry was the only white man around, wasn't he? No, she recalled. A German had once helped him raise hogs.

The Indian girl beckoned. The yellow lump could wait. Elitha moved toward the shore. The baby squeezed sand in his fat fists and grinned at her. She stopped cold. That grin. Those dimples. Perry was the only man in California with that smile. She filled in blanks, why he'd asked her to stay away from Indians. Was this his wife? *Dear Lord no.*

Suddenly coming at her was the talk she'd had with Mary Murphy about plural wives, and she had seen that the rough men in California had as many Indian wives as they pleased — maybe that's why the Mormons wanted to come here. Then it hit her that Perry might be spending time with this girl while she was alone. Might have been with her last night. Feeling like a wind-up doll, she stepped out of the water onto the hot sand.

"*Hola*," the girl said.

"Hello." She felt her petticoat plastered on her legs, water streaming down her body, cooling the sand as she stepped across it.

"You be Perrimacoo's wife?"

Be. Just as Perry would use it. Lowering herself on a flat stone, she summoned her courage. "Yes. Are you his wife too?"

"No. My man is Señor Valdez." She looked not into her eyes, but at the blue crystals around her neck.

Wringing water from her undergarment, Elitha examined the baby, who was patting the sand, and realized Spaniards might well have dimples. "What is your name?" she asked the baby's mother.

She gazed at the river, her eyes large black pools in which the pupils could not be distinguished. "*Americanos* lose power through tongues," she said.

What did that mean? She noticed the girl's posture, somehow dignified despite the exposure of her privates, and repeated, "What is your name?"

Her bluntly cut hair grazed her shoulders as she briefly turned full face to Elitha, then back to the river. Her expression remained calm, her hands quiet beside her raised knees, but she said nothing.

"My name is Elitha McCoon."

Nothing came back. The baby got up and toddled to Elitha, his brown eyes much paler than his mother's, the pupils visible. His hair was light brown. He grabbed the crystals.

In one fluid motion the girl disengaged his hand, whisked him to her lap and rubbed his fingers and palms with a bundle of leaves hanging from her neck. She intoned mournful sounds, then rushed him to the water, waded to her waist and dunked him repeatedly over his head, each time turning him a different direction. He sputtered but didn't howl, as any baby Elitha knew would have. Then the girl returned, laced him in the cradleboard and jammed it upright into the sand where he could see, but presumably not touch, Elitha.

Feeling insulted, not only by that, but the fact that she wouldn't tell her name, Elitha looked at the child beneath the built-in sunshade. Water from his hair streamed over his face, which was stretching into a slow grin and narrowing his eyes in a way that laid his long lashes on his chubby cheeks. This was Perry's baby! Had Perry been with this girl last night? Had she come here to flaunt the child, calm as you please? No wonder Perry had tried to scare her away from the Indians. He didn't want her to find out!

"I am daughter of Captain Juan," the naked brown girl said, with pride in her expression.

Indian chieftains in California, Elitha knew, called themselves captains in imitation of Captain Sutter, and Juan was the chief of the local tribe, the one Perry said he was trying to tame. Apparently he'd tamed the daughter. Well, Elitha wasn't about to sit here and have her think she was anybody just because her father was called a captain.

"I am the daughter of Captain George Donner," she responded with a lift of her chin. Nevertheless, she felt terribly uncomfortable talking to this savage bedpartner of her husband, but couldn't get up and leave. There was more she needed to learn.

The girl seemed to be looking at a distant point. "Luck charm of my brother," she said, then lifted a hand to point briefly at the crystals.

Had Perry got them here instead of Johnson's, as he had claimed? A discrepancy wouldn't surprise her — she no longer expected the truth from him. She held the bauble away from her neck. "You sure?"

Her black eyes moved over it. "My brother luck charm. Where from?"

If it was her brother's, she'd know where. "My husband gave it to me."

"Where?"

Had Perry stolen it? If one thing was impressed on emigrants, it was never to take Indians' belongings unless they were given. Gruesome retaliation could follow. Surely Perry knew that. "He said he got it from Johnson's ranch."

The girl gazed silently at the distance while Perry's baby looked from one to the other. Then the mother said, "Where Johnson Ranch?"

"North of here a long piece." She pointed.

More silence. Elitha took off the necklace. "Here, you can have it back."

She shied at the crystals like a horse at a snake. "Rock have power. Kill," she said, shrugging the cradleboard on her back. "Your man house bad luck." She turned and started walking away.

That didn't fit with a girl flaunting a man's attentions. But it did fit with Perry saying the Indians thought his house was haunted — a barrel of *aguardiente* had stood there for months without being touched. The firm brown buttocks were resolutely shifting away. "Please don't go," Elitha said. It came out before she could think

The girl turned halfway, the small likeness of Perry peering around her brown shoulder.

"I'd like us to be friends." She didn't know what made her say it.

A full, genuine smile came back at her.

37

An hour or so later Elitha headed out to where she'd seen the yellow rock in the river. She laughed aloud. The girls would love it here and they were surely on their way, because the Indian girl had said Perry had gone to New Helvetia for his cattle. Surely he intended to surprise her. She had misjudged him, and could hardly wait to see her sisters.

As she searched for the nugget, she thought about the strange visit with a girl from the stone age. She seemed totally without guile. Elitha believed her when she'd said Perry was no longer seeing her — she admitted the baby was his. What she didn't want to say, she didn't say at all, like her name. Talk would grow easier in time, she thought, spying the sparkle beneath the moving water. And it pleased her — she still didn't understand why — to have an Indian friend, even if Perry had once known her carnally.

She nudged the lump up the crack between rocks, quickly grasped it in her toes, trying not to lose it in the murky bottom, and walked it toward the shore. The twisted yellow metal lay heavy across her palm, as long as her hand was wide. Clearly fashioned by nature. Rubbing her thumb over its slick smoothness, she stepped through the muck — miniature frogs leaping out of the way — up to damp sand, wondering if it was gold, and if so, how it came to be in the river.

Part of her didn't want to show it to Perry just yet. He might laugh at her for being childish, and say this was a common rock that lay all over California. Mr. Daylor, a trader, would recognize gold. But he'd tell Perry and she didn't want to be in dutch for showing it to him first. Walking up the hill to the adobe, she decided to hide it. Then after Perry arrived with the girls and the cattle and things had settled down, she'd bring it to him and ask ever so off-handed, "You think this is gold?" If he said yes, they'd have a merry time deciding what to do with it — maybe have jewelry made at Sheldon's forge. This was easily enough for a locket for each of her sisters.

The place she'd named "split rock" was the perfect hiding place. It was near the house — two head-high boulders as far apart as her outstretched elbows. Lichens covered the outer surfaces like tough ruffled doilies, but the inside walls were clean and nearly vertical. Indentations on one side matched the protrusions on the other — some awesome force having wedged them apart long ago. Tamsen would have known what caused that, she thought as she buried the nugget in the dirt between the walls. Now all that knowledge, forty-five years of studying the natural world, was lost.

The remainder of the day she explored along the river, where Captain Juan's daughter said no harm would come to her. She found a piece of oak with a hollowed-out gnarl and put some rich damp soil in it so her apple seeds would get a good start. Then she cut armloads of cattail leaves to make mats for the girls, the way the Indians made beds. Once in a while she saw Indians near the river, but as the hours went by, all her apprehensions disappeared.

The June day was long. She was beginning to think she might spend another night alone, when she felt as much as heard a rumble of hooves. Excitement rippled through her. They were coming! She ran down the swale and up the hill opposite the house.

A phalanx of bawling cattle appeared along the ridge, then poured over the top and down the hill in a flowing brown and white mass. Hundreds of upturned horns bobbed in the late sun, all angled the same way. It made a stunning pattern. The herd passed her at maybe fifty rods away, and she stood on one foot then the other, knowing Perry was behind. She could almost feel Frances, frail Georgia and Ellie in her arms. And Leanna!

But when Paint topped the ridge, one rider was on his back. She shaded her eyes inside her bonnet and squinted into the fiery sun to be sure. Perry rode alone in the saddle. She looked toward the other two riders, waited for vision to return. They were Indians. Each alone. No sign of anyone else.

Suddenly feeling the full intensity of the heat, she closed her eyes and shut out the dust of the bawling animals, all moving down the swale then trampling up the hill past the little adobe. With disappointment hurting so bad, she was relieved Perry didn't stop when he passed by. She couldn't even raise a hand.

Later, as she prepared beans and salt pork, he rode back from the hills behind the house. Anger seared through her disappointment, and she hardly glanced up from the firepit. "You didn't bring my sisters." *And didn't tell me you were going to New Helvetia.*

He yanked the cinch and removed it. "Expect a bloke to tend fifty long-horns and three baby girls at the same time, do ye?" He turned and the crust of dried salt around his mouth gave him a clownish look, but his steely eyes were hard, the radiating lines around them darkened with dirt, aging him. He turned back to hobble the sweat-soaked horse.

"They could have ridden a mule tied to your saddle." He'd had money for cattle — what Sutter owed him for his work was only about half what he herded here. A mule would have cost little more. Besides, he had the Donner money, didn't he?

He gave her a look like they were opponents and he was winning. "What makes ye so sure I went to Sutter's?"

She felt limp from being so upset. He looked tired. Maybe when he'd eaten and rested, they could talk. She went to the pot hanging over the fire and stirred the thickening beans.

Later, after he'd eaten and poked her, though she hadn't wanted to, she lay silent, waiting for him to speak. When it didn't seem likely he would, she brought it up again. "We'd better go after the girls tomorrow." Tomorrow would be six days.

The first owl hooted near the cabin. "When I gits meself settled."

"Settled?"

He exhaled in a vexed way. "Now, the very minute I gits me cattle, think ye I'm about to turn meself around and go back?" He snorted and turned over. "Daft!"

Panic for the little girls mounted. Every minute they would be watching for her. She recalled that last morning at the fort, and realized she shouldn't have got on his horse. She should have insisted on his getting a wagon, made him whip her if that's what it took. He might have backed down, or someone might have taken pity and helped. She hadn't persisted. Hadn't tried hard enough to keep her word to her sisters. She had been duped.

As if sensing her thought, he softened his tone. "Aw now lass, doin me best, I is. I'll git the niggers to give me one of their colts. We'll train it. Then one day soon enough we'll both ride back to the fort and fetch the little lasses." He patted her rump. "Now you just nod off. There's a good girl."

"Colt? How old is it?" It took more than a year before a colt could be ridden.

"Not foaled yet."

She couldn't stop a thin sound that came out like a wounded animal. "That's too late. We can get a wagon and — "

"Ent none out here."

Of course, but he could send an Indian to New Helvetia to fetch one. The Indian girl said their young men would do almost anything for trinkets or tools. Anger flamed through her, stoked by the urgency to pass water, which she had just done, passing only a few painful drops. It was a maddening condition she'd noticed since about noon. She rose to her knees, staring down at the twilight curve of his pale skin against the dark blankets. "I promised Ma," she said. Louder, "I promised my sisters I'd come for them in a few days! They're orphans, Perry." He of all people should understand that.

He leapt to his feet and grabbed her upper arms and shook her, shouting, "I'll go to the bleedin fort when I'm damned good and ready, and not a minute before! Ye hear? Now leave me sleep or I'll tan ye good, I will." His fingers dug painfully into her flesh and his eyes were big and terrible. Fear crept into her anger.

He dropped her arms and flopped on the bed, hissing through his teeth. "Damned if I'll abide a scold fer a wife. Now lay yerself down and shut up."

Long minutes passed, her mind racing over being called a scold. *Elitha's an obedient girl.* She went outside to pass water. Again, only a few drops answered the urgency. The poking had worsened it. When the pain subsided, she went back in and lay carefully beside him, not touching. Was this condition a punishment from God? For her sin with Perry before they were married? But her thoughts returned to the way Tamsen had been happy to mother her and Leanna — women did that all the time. But maybe sisters were seen as different from the bride's own children, and a man didn't want that responsibility. Still, he should have told her. He had led her to believe he'd accept her sisters, then made her betray them. Rage resurfaced as a hot hook in her breast. She barbed him with, "I met an Indian girl today."

His breathing stopped.

"She said her baby is yours."

He exhaled loudly. "Mary."

Mary. An English name. The girl had said she didn't like Perry any more, and Elitha believed her.

"Stay away from her," he said, "Or those bucks'll see you talking all friendly like, and they'll stick ye, they will, just like they do their own. Anytime of the day or night."

She weighed that, coming from a man who had deceived her.

The days fell into a pattern. At dawn Perry slipped from bed, grabbed a hank of jerky and rode away to teach the Indians to use the braided ropes called lariats and tend the cattle. He returned for *siesta* during the hottest part of the day, then left when the heat lessened. They ate before dark. During the day Elitha learned useful things from Indian Mary, like where to dig the soaproot plant, which sudsed and cleaned her hair and clothing. But she rarely saw the herd of cattle anywhere near the house.

Then Indian Mary disappeared. Two weeks later Elitha saw her again and learned that she often went to another Indian village — *ranchería* Californians called it, where she was becoming what sounded like a witch doctor's apprentice. All this time Elitha suffered more each day whenever she passed water, and in her mind it became the pain of knowing her sisters were watching for her, and she was not on her way.

One morning she woke up and decided to make a door so she wouldn't worry about animals coming in at night. With no tools or knowledge of carpentry — not even a plan — she walked past the *ranchería* to the hills overlooking the river where tall gray pines leaned like drunken sailors. Pine was easier to work than oak, that much she knew, and she suspected it was the material from which the Indians made their cone-shaped huts. She hoped to find some leftover boards. The grass was tamped around the pines, and she found evidence of people having taken away much of an old fallen giant. Half of it was still there. She put her foot on the loose, rotted part and pulled and yanked at it, but all she got was a piece about three feet long. She was standing there thinking, when she heard a noise. She turned to see two naked Indians with bones in their ears coming at her, one with a club in his hand. They were practically upon her.

Panic buzzed to her extremities, Perry's warning in her mind. *Wild as banshees.* She'd grown up hearing of Indian atrocities. But instead of braining her, they straddled the downed pine, rammed the odd-shaped "club" into a crack and pounded on it with large rocks that lay conveniently alongside. As her heart slowed, she realized that she was in their woods, watching them doing the very thing she wanted to do — wedge out slabs of wood. Then she saw more Indian women and children back in the trees.

Indian Mary came to her, smiling. "How many?" She pointed at the steadily working men.

"Two." She'd been teaching her English, and thought she would have known that.

Mary said something guttural to the men. They straightened, smiling broadly at Elitha, and presented her with two flakes of pine, each about six feet long.

"Oh, boards, you mean." They had seen her, and come to help! She pointed and repeated, "Boards." Quickly she calculated and said, "I want six."

Mary talked to the men, and they went back to work. When six boards had been wedged out, the two men carried them for her, walking at either end, Mary, with Perry's baby, walking beside Elitha. But when the adobe came into view, the men put the boards down. Mary asked, "Where build house?"

"No. I'm just making a door," she said.

Clearly disappointed, Mary spoke to the men and they left. Then she repeated what she'd said before about Perry's house being bad luck, and turned to leave. But Elitha asked her how to fasten the boards together. Soon they were down at the river at a wide sandy place where the willows stood back from the river, Mary showing her how to tease out the long, thin roots that sought moisture. When they had a large pile of them, Mary dug out a backwater and coiled the roots in it to soak all night.

The next day Mary showed her how to weave the tough, pliable roots over and under the boards and tie them securely. The result was a little like a giant accordion, and it stood higher than the roof and very uneven, but it would do. For hinges she would cut strips of the old cowhide, maybe tripled for strength, and nail them — when she went to Daylor's for nails — to the doorframe. Figuring a way to fasten the door shut would be easy. For now, feeling very pleased with herself, she stood the door against the side of the adobe.

By the time she had the biscuits and beans ready for Perry's evening meal, she'd been thinking about going up to the mountains to see if any bolts of cloth were left in the Donner wagons. She could make bedclothes, lace curtains, a gingham tablecloth, and velvet frocks for the girls. Now she realized she should have gone to Mr. Sutter to find out how much had been salvaged.

In high spirits Perry rode up and jumped off Paint. He hobbled the horse then bowed to her like a country squire and accepted his filled plate. "Thankee kindly, milaidy." He sat beside her on the log by the firepit, his fringed eyes sparkling and his clean-shaven face as handsome as ever.

She said, "Let's ride up the mountains and see what's left in the wagons." She felt strong enough to view the camp now, and wanted to have him share her private thoughts. Maybe it would bring back the tenderness he'd shown when he'd first learned the terrible news about Tamsen.

He threw back his head and hawed and eyed her like she was weak-minded. "Think them blokes what went up didn't sniff out every ha'penny? Wye, they splintered the wagons with axes, they did!" Found every cranny." He tossed the remainder of the biscuit into his mouth and chewed hugely — no longer the country squire.

"I helped Tamsen sew ten thousand dollars into one of the quilts."

He choked and coughed, and a doughy projectile flew by, creasing her nose. He struggled to find his voice. "Why . . . . didn't you say nothin?" His face was red, his eyes wet. "Keepin it from me was ye?"

"No. I mean I didn't mean to. I just, well, figured it would be a pleasant surprise if it was given back to me, a surprise for you. But I didn't know, maybe they'd already found it and paid the rescuers out of it," *and given it to you*, "and sometimes I thought Mr. Sutter would ask me to come to his rooms and talk about it. But then I suppose I was bothered by the trial and all . . ." She'd assumed a heavy quilt jangling with gold coins would have been the first to be salvaged, but why nobody mentioned it was a mystery. However, the bolts of cloth might well still be up there, some of it unspoiled.

Slack-jawed, he stared at her. "They was right about the money then."

Hoping to revive his happy mood, she said, "Yes. And we could make the house nicer." *For the girls.*

"Aye, that we could, lass." He stared past her.

"Will you take me then?"

He looked at her, then brought his plate to his chin and wolfed down the rest of his beans and swallowed. "Like I said," he wiped his sleeve across his mouth, "I've only just come 'ome with me cows." He reached down and patted her knee — oddly, like there was something was on his mind.

But she knew better than to probe. She sat a few minutes thinking about his reaction, then, every step provoking false urgency, took the soiled tins down to the river in the last light of day. It came to her that the affliction in her privates could kill her eventually. Women died from mysterious conditions all the time, Perry's first white wife included. Looked at that way, goods didn't matter. Her life — who knew how much time anyone had? — was here at Rancho Sacayak. She had to get it in her head that everything from the old life was gone, and a grueling ride on horseback to see the camp of starvation and death wouldn't bring it back. Perry was right.

"Lass," he said when they were in bed, "we're going to Daylor's. It's a cookout they're 'avin."

"That's grand! We can see Sarah and Catherine, and buy nails."

"Nails?"

"I made a door."

38

They dismounted before Mr. Sheldon's two-story millhouse — three stories if you counted the understructure down the riverbank. The new house across the yard had the same look. With wooden peaks and vertical lines, the buildings could have come from Ma's picture-book of New England. Before the millhouse stood a pair of sleepy oxen hitched to a wagon filled with big leather bags. Trying not to jiggle with urgency — she'd made Perry stop three time on the trail and used the Daylors' outhouse when they'd stopped for nails — she looked around for Catherine.

Sam Kyburz came from the millhouse, accompanied by an Indian in a loincloth. Mr. Kyburz tipped his hat and Elitha half-curtsied. He and the Indian swung bags from the wagon to their shoulders and headed for the millhouse. Then suddenly she recalled that the morning she'd left the fort, Mr. Kyburz had gone out with a full load of wheat —to be milled here, she now realized. Her sisters could ride with the next load!

Jiggling absentmindedly and excited about the prospect, she wished Perry hadn't followed Mr. Kyburz into the mill. She wanted to talk to Mr. Kyburz alone. But Catherine bounded around the corner of the house, skirts hoisted, a bauble bouncing on her breast. Full of vinegar, Tamsen would have said. They hugged, the top of Catherine's bonnet fresh-smelling under Elitha's nose, then held each other at arm's length, grinning. It was exactly as Pa had said. People on the frontier became instant friends.

Catherine, who seemed younger but wasn't, stood half a head shorter. She yanked Elitha's hand. "Come, gotta secret."

Wondering about that, and thinking she could just as well talk to Mr. Sheldon, she followed Catherine behind the house and tiptoed across rows of young green beans and vigorous squash. An outhouse came into view — peaked like the other buildings — and it seemed the height of civilization. Did she really need to pass water again? She felt that way all the time now, and when she did, the pain was so intense she put it off as long as possible. God was mortifying her with a condition she couldn't mention to a living soul.

Catherine sat down in the shade of a giant tree, its limbs dense with dark fringed leaves. Tamsen would have known what kind it was. Elitha settled beside her on soft, silty ground, birds chattering overhead. Catherine bunched her shoulders up around her elfish grin and said, "I'm in a family way."

She opened her mouth and searched the twinkling hazel eyes. "Why, that's grand! And Mr. Sheldon seems like such a nice man."

"Oh, he is, he IS. I love him SO much!" She extended the gold watch hanging around her neck. "He gave this to me, for a wedding present." It had a tiny winding key. She popped it open for Elitha to admire.

She praised its ornate interior and, barely able to endure the pressure, asked if she could use the outhouse.

"Silly goose, go on!" Catherine gave her a friendly shove.

Dropping the wooden latch in its slot, she sat on the well-sanded seat. Long ago she'd heard of a disease prevalent among "women of the night," females so wicked they were mentioned only in whispers. She felt sure she had their affliction. The water started. Pain knifed upward from her privates to her chin, pulsing with terrible sharpness and intensifying as the stream stopped. In the luxury of complete privacy she allowed herself to voice a moan, clenching her teeth at the ceiling while the sting throbbed on and eventually subsided. How wonderful an outhouse was! She hardly noticed the acrid smell in the pit or the buzzing flies. *Forgive me, Lord. Lift this punishment if you see fit.*

When she settled on the dirt beside Catherine, the urge to pass water was already agitating her again. "Good thing yer Ma is so close by," she offered, looking at Catherine's plump middle, her pink-cheeked happiness matching the pink of her frock and bonnet.

"Yup. She's real good at birthin all right."

Elitha didn't know the first thing about it. When Tamsen's daughters were born, she and Leanna had been shooed outside.

Catherine said, "I hope my folks stay in California."

"Why wouldn't they?"

"Well, Pa got a letter from Brigham Young — a friend of his — wrote on the trail. You see, just about all the Mormons have left for the West, and well, they decided to stay near the Great Salt Lake."

The trek across the salt flats came to mind and she couldn't imagine anyone settling there, especially if three of their daughters were married to California men. But to Catherine she said, "Well I sure hope they won't leave before your baby comes."

"Oh they wouldn't." She wore the comfortable smile of a child who knew love and support came from all directions. "Besides, Ma hasn't got her strength back after the crossing."

It occurred to Elitha that she probably couldn't have a baby, her condition being located where it was. More than likely she would die first. Just then, two large mushroom-shaped objects rose jerkily from the riverbank — wide straw hats of the type Spaniards called *sombreros* — men pushing them up as they climbed. Under one hat she recognized Mr. Sheldon. The other man wore a short black vest over a muslin shirt and a red and white striped sash around the waist of his dark trousers, which split open over his boots. He looked at Elitha with interested gray eyes, his nose turned slightly down.

Mr. Sheldon touched his straw brim. "Howdy ladies, Where's Perry?" He glanced at Catherine with a look of love.

"At the millhouse with Mr. Kyburz," Elitha said.

"Wheat here already?"

"Yup," Catherine said. Mr. Sheldon started to walk on.

"Mr. Sheldon," Elitha blurted out, "I was meaning to ask — "

He turned, his eyes penetrating and yellowish.

"Next time Mr. Kyburz comes, maybe he could bring my little sisters. They could ride right on top of the wheat. Then we'll figure out how to get them out to our place."

He bobbed his sombrero and said, "I'll see to it."

"Oh, I'd be SO obliged!" She felt giddy with relief. It had been so simple!

At sundown the air looked like a gilded veil, so filled it was with particles of dust and pollen, and then the daytime heat faded into a balmy night pulsing with crickets and frogs. Over everything floated the magical music of the Spaniard —

the one she'd seen that afternoon.

"I love that," Elitha said to the Rhoads women, ignoring her urgency. "What is that instrument?" Its haunting sounds suggested exotic places and stories like Ali Baba and the forty thieves.

"Guitar," Sarah Daylor said, reaching over to pat Elitha's shoulder. "I'm so glad you're here. You should come visit regular."

"I'd like that."

The elder Rhoadses were here too, and John with his pregnant Matilda, and a wagon load of children. Elitha felt like royalty — sitting on a log and visiting with the women while Indians served peppermint tea and tended the fire. They cooked the beans, turned half a bullock on a spit, prepared greens and watched the children, Indian and white alike, as they romped and toddled. Elitha's hands were free. She couldn't remember a time in all her fourteen years when she hadn't helped with supper.

She knew Mr. Sheldon had talked to Sam Kyburz but had been busy with company ever since. She was anxious to hear that the arrangements were confirmed. Except for her affliction, she felt happier than she had in a long time.

The men kept to themselves, visiting on the other side of the fire. Wisps of talk about ranches and cattle came through the music and the bellow of frogs and treep of crickets. Perry passed his leather flask and Elitha knew by his stance that he was already slurring his words. At the end of a musical line a single treble guitar note trilled, and then the Spaniard began to sing — a rich baritone.

"Who is that?" she asked, enthralled with the Spanish words.

"Pedro Valdez, our *mayordomo* — our top vaquero," Catherine said.

Wasn't that the name of Mary's husband? With heightened interest, she listened to his words of *amor*.

Sarah Daylor said, "I heard your sisters are a big help to the Brunners."

News! "When did you hear?"

"About a week ago. Mr. Chabolla told me when he came to mill his wheat. I mentioned you was our new neighbor."

Elitha searched Sarah's perfect face. "How are they?" She kept her voice low.

Catherine and Mrs. Rhoads looked intrigued. Sarah said, "All I heard is Mrs. Brunner's feelin her age and with the work on the farm and all, your sisters are a big help."

Mrs. Rhoads tilted her gray head toward Perry across the fire and said, "Don't he want them with you?"

She felt disloyal to be whispering about him. "Oh, we've just been too busy to fetch them," she said cheerfully. "Maybe they'll come on the next wheat wagon." She flounced her skirt and smiled at the women. "My but it's a pretty night."

"It is at that," said Mrs. Rhoads, staring at nothing. She turned to Sarah and said, "Ever mornin I wake up more tuckered." Elitha thought that was to be expected of the mother of nineteen living children.

Beyond the firelight children shot tiny arrows at make-believe animals. In the dark it was hard to tell which were Rhoadses and which were Indian. She asked the women, "Did you know the Murphys?" She figured they did, because they had all been in the wagon train hiding their Mormon identities, many escaping the Nauvoo massacre.

"Yes," Mrs. Rhoads said. "She hired out on the crossing, got her supplies that way. Poor thing." She shook her head. An Indian woman cut a sliver from the sizzling haunch and tasted its doneness.

"I'd sure like to know how Mary's doing," Elitha said.

"She married Mr. Johnson," Catherine said.

"That awful man?"

"That awful man," Sarah repeated, rolling her eyes. "Like to lost her mind when she learned of her ma passing on and all. Then she just up and married him."

"Abused her with his farmhands," said Mrs. Rhoads in a tone that warned away further inquiry. She pursed her wrinkled lips and stared at the fire, looking very old.

Abused. Elitha feared she knew the meaning of that. But farmhands? The only white men she'd seen around Johnson's looked wilder than the Indians. Poor, poor Mary!

Catherine said, "Elizabeth writes us regular. Says Mary wants to leave Mr. Johnson. She's thinking of leaving Mr. Keyser too. Both got pickaninnies all over the place callin 'em pa. More'n one squaw too."

Mrs. Rhoads scowled at Catherine. "Now, now, dear. Mr. Keyser has every right to expect Elizabeth to try her best." She turned her tired face to Elitha. "I'm hopin they'll move here near us, and git away from those squaws." She looked ahead like she had a bad taste in her mouth.

But Elitha was thinking no girl could just walk away from a husband. She wished she and Mary weren't separated by fifty miles. But this was a party, and she steered her thoughts to the joyful side of life — visiting instead of listening to owls and coyotes and watching Perry get drunk. "It's fine here," she said suppressing the urge to jiggle. "You got each other, and your Indians are such a help."

At that moment she heard Perry say, "'Ear ye be finding gold hereabouts."

He hadn't mentioned it to her, but then he often kept secrets. She had one of her own, in the split rock.

Pedro fingered a series of crisp, rippling chords and watched the people around the fire react to McCoon's mention of gold. From the tree where he played his guitar, he could hear everything and see the women's faces. Indians turning the spit made no acknowledgement. *Americanas* taking their ease listened. Señora

McCoon — a serious girl about Maria's age with dark hair coiled around her ears and a *bonita* face except for her thinness and enormously sad eyes — brightened at the mention of gold.

Apparently Perry McCoon was just learning of it, and, comically, trying to sound *casual.* Señora Catherine said, "Isn't it grand! Ma keeps finding it down at their place, doncha Ma?" Before Señora Rhoads could open her mouth Catherine added, "Pertanear ever time she washes the clothes, she sees gold pokin right outa the bank!"

"Not every time, dear."

The elder Señor Rhoads wiggled a thick finger toward the dark. "Mother, we're among friends. Go get the little pouch. Give our sons-in-law a gander."

Pedro rippled a chord in a different key. So, they were finding it down there too. He lifted his hand and let the strings vibrate. A huge orange moon was silently rising behind the dark trees, while nearby, life crackled and hummed. The spit and snap of the roasting meat, the murmur of the *Indias*, the rustle of the river and bawl of distant cattle wove a tapestry of sound in the warm night. Wishing María were here, he watched McCoon.

The *malcriado's* eyes glittered with a *loco* expression Pedro knew all too well. "'Ow much be ye findin then?" Not even beginning to hide his drunken excitement, he widened his stance to keep from falling.

Señor Sheldon said, "A tad bit around here." The *patrones* had made Pedro promise not to mention gold to anybody outside the rancho, and now they were telling Perry McCoon! But then, he supposed, he would have heard it sooner or later.

Señora Rhoads emerged from the dark, coming from the wagon. Firelight accentuated the creases in her face as she handed a leather pouch to her husband.

McCoon hovered like a fly as the elder Señor Rhoads loosened the string and poured the contents into his palm. He stepped to the fire and lowered his hand down where the women could see, McCoon shadowing. Even at this distance Pedro saw the shine of the yellow gravel. It was *mucho* indeed.

McCoon asked in a cracking voice, "Where'd you git this?"

Señor Daylor answered, "Like she said, down at Dry Creek." He winked at Señora Sarah, a look of *amor.*

It occurred to Pedro that Old Pepe might have been to Dry Creek thirty years ago. He ran his fingers over the guitar, quickening the mood as the pouch — restored of its contents — was passed from hand to hand. Señora McCoon reached in and pinched the gold, her full lips parted. Maybe McCoon would abandon his ranch and search for gold at Dry Creek — encouraged by his wife.

Fingering a sad melody fragment and underscoring it with a trill, he reflected that gold wrapped men in the arms of hope, then strangled them with discouragement. Even in the presence of so much, he felt no excitement. His fortune would come from land. Like Don Cristóbal in Santa Barbara, he would be a *gran ranchero* with a rose-perfumed patio. Ay, *Californianos* knew how to live. Señor Sheldon was from New England. He worked too hard. A distant, hollow beat began to interfere with Pedro's rhythm. He lifted his hand. The *Indio* Big Time was starting.

Señora Sarah sighed, handed the pouch back to her father and said, "There they go again." The Indians, who had finished cooking, turned up the dark path toward the drum — children trotting behind — and Pedro knew they'd dance and sing for the next four or five days. They didn't need gold to make them happy. Maybe they had taught the *Californianos* to fandango for days at a time. It was a good tradition.

"Cap'n Sutter know about the gold?" McCoon asked.

The elder Señor Rhoads said, "Sure. I told him. Figgered I owed the man fer the use of the land." His mouth turned down like a horseshoe.

McCoon pressed, "That 'IS land? That far south?" *Not until the Devil dances in heaven*, Pedro knew.

Señor Rhoads turned his backside to the fire and wiggled his interlocked fingers at it. "Them Mexican survey papers is the derndest I ever seen. Looked at Sutter's map myself. Couldn't make out if he owns the land he lets me farm."

McCoon's questions were coming fast. "Sutter claimin the gold, is he? Seein it comes from land 'e says is 'is?"

The horseshoe mouth locked down. "Takes his share."

"'Ow much?" McCoon was hooked like a fish and Pedro smiled in the dark.

Sheldon held up a hand. "That's the business of Father Rhoads." The elder Rhoads scowled at him. "S'all right, Jared. This here's a neighbor." To McCoon he said, "Takes his piece."

"Piece o' wot? Sutter wouldn't know 'ow much gold you take from the brook now would 'e?" He swayed and narrowed his eyes at the dour old man.

Señora Sarah straightened her back. "My pa's fair," she said. She held herself like a *reina*, queen.

The Indian drum throbbed in the distance and the full moon had risen up over the trees. The *Norteamericanos* were filling their plates. With his elbows akimbo, McCoon looked from face to face. "'Ow're we to keep this secret?" he demanded, "with Sutter's drunken tongue awaggin?" He sucked from his flask and wiped his sleeve across his mouth.

Pedro enjoyed the silence of the *patrones*.

McCoon jerked on the line, "Wye, ever bloke on the continent'll be out here minin for gold, I vow, with that man writin 'is infernal letters!"

Pedro ran his thumb down a mournful chord and let it fade. Señor Daylor's melancholy tone seemed to reflect it, or perhaps he realized his friend was flopping in the wrong waters. "Look mait," he said, "hits up to all of us to keep our tongues tied. Sutter's doin' his part, he is. He's the one telling us to go all the way to Yerba Buena to cover our tracks when we change the gold. Don't worry. He won't leak it. Nor his friend who weighs the gold. Keeps quiet, that one does."

Reflecting on that and strumming an engaging pair of chords, Pedro realized more of this gold changing had been going on than he'd thought. And now, for the first time, he could see a reason why McCoon might leave the land he'd squatted on and squat in a different place — gold. Pedro would tear McCoon's house down to make his *Amapolita* happy. She would have his children and forget the nonsense about magic. Ay, it was a lovely vision. As the others began eating, he played *El Tormento de Amor,* singing quietly the words that always evoked his feelings for María. The bliss of their embrace had been well worth the waiting. It was more beautiful than he had dreamed. His *tormento* was wanting her all the time. He visited her village at every opportunity, but he had much work to do here. The *patrones*' cattle were multiplying rapidly, every tenth calf earmarked for Pedro. He had a good start on a herd already, but his work separated him from her every bit as much as her witch doctoring kept her from him. Ah, his bosom could not be consoled! The words precisely expressed his *sentimiento.*

But his stomach was growling. He leaned the guitar against the tree, took his knife from his sash and approached the spitted beef. As he leaned over it, considering which part to cut, McCoon said, "Maits, surprised I am ye let that greaser eat with ye."

Pedro froze.

McCoon continued, "Blab about the gold to every Spaniard on the coast, 'e will! Them niggers'll stampede all over yer rancho."

Pedro flayed a curl of meat. This was the supper feast of the *patrones*, and he wouldn't add violence to McCoon's repulsiveness, not in front of the señoras. But that didn't stop him from imagining how cleanly his blade would slice through McCoon's windpipe.

Señor Sheldon's clipped words came over the crickets and distantly singing *Indios*. "Señor Valdez is my *mayordomo,* and my *amigo.*"

The *desgraciado* persisted. "But Jared, ye can't trust his kind. I 'ear they ent even abidin by the treaty. Fightin again in Pueblo Los Angeles. I vow, this'uns no better." He swayed.

A muscle twitched in Pedro's knife arm, but he blinked a nod at Señor Sheldon meaning: Don't worry. I will not disturb the peace of the señoras. But he wouldn't let McCoon off entirely. He spoke as if to the beans he was ladling onto his plate. "A sailor who deserted his captain speaks of trust." He turned to McCoon — a man of words, not deeds — and said softly, "A deserter with no *cojones* speaks of honor." Casually he wiped his knife on his thigh, turned his back and walked beyond the firelight.

Señor Daylor broke the tension. "Methinks it's time we took Mother Rhoads to 'ome." He stretched and winked at Señora Sarah, who, in the bright globe of the moon, looked like a goddess. Pedro envied him for having his woman near at hand. No longer wanting to share any part of the evening with McCoon — a total coward who for more than a year had failed to name the day of their competition — he put his guitar under his arm, took his full plate and was about to head for his room.

Señor Sheldon got up and came toward him. In deference Pedro waited, but he would not apologize to McCoon. He had taken enough insults.

Instead Sheldon stopped at the log where Señora McCoon sat and spoke to her. "Sam Kyburz says Sutter's done with milling for the year. Today was his last load. Sorry."

Her face was white in the moonlight, her eyes huge and dark. Her voice seemed too small. "No more wagon loads will be brought out to here?"

He wagged his head at her. "Not this year." He never even looked at Pedro.

On his way to his room he reflected that all together it was not a bad night. Perry McCoon had gold fever, and the gold he was crazy for lay three or four leagues from Rancho Sacayak.

39

Maria looked into the tunnel hat at the pale *Americana* and said, "Power make you *fuerte*, strong." They were sitting in the sand in the shade of the willows.

"What exactly do you mean by that?"

The *Americana* had no more knowledge than a nestling bird. But her sad eyes were intelligent, and Maria liked her. She had illness in her bladder. That was plain even from a distance. It was difficult to heal people with so little knowledge, but *oam'shu*, angelica root, had honored Maria by coming in a dream and telling her to make the *Americana* well. Maria would do as her ally directed.

"Live right," she said. "Go in water each morning." She pointed at the water but realized it might not cooperate. "Sing to river spirit, she cry like baby. Sing. Make her happy, make her friend."

She saw confusion in the sad brown eyes and felt the enormity of her task. All her life she had known about health. She knew that daily bathing and medicine tea, isolated from all else, were inadequate. Yet she must begin somewhere.

"Come. We go to Grandmother. She make river happy." Hoisting Billy to her hip, she led the way, glad to see the *Americana* following.

The riverbottom was wider in her family's special place, paved with flat rocks and tufted with redbud and giant lupine. The air was thick with the aroma of the yellow-crazy, which was blooming on the hills now. She found Great-Grandmother Dishi camouflaged in the low limbs of her oak, her hands resting from her drill, wrinkles blending with the shade tracery of the branches. Maria stepped on the warm, smooth rocks she loved so well and beckoned the *Americana.*

Clattering to attract the old one's attention, Maria explained, "Grandmother not see." She massaged her shoulders, her special greeting, which Dishi loved. The skin felt loose and the white top of her head smelled clean. Since the old one never carried a burden basket any more, she wore no cap, the talisman at her neck being her only adornment.

Grandmother began to sing, staring ahead with clouded eyes. Maria took Elitha's hand and held it to the old one's cheek. "She sing to river-baby spirit. Come to Grandmother, learn how to sing."

"Is she here all the time?"

Maria smiled. "In house at night."

Leaving Grandmother, she climbed the boulders that led up the bank, careful to watch for rattlesnakes.

Following, the *Americana* said, "You didn't talk to her. She didn't talk to you."

"She no talk."

"But she sings."

"Sí. She sings."

No more questions came.

In the shade of the sumac people, now adorned with red berries, she said, "I make medicine tea." She was about to sing when the *Americana* said:

"I don't think it will help. God is punishing me."

That surprised her. The powerful spirit of the mission, the *Dios* Pedro mentioned so often, had not seemed an evil prankster. She tried to explain. "When you weak, evil find hole. Get in." She pointed between the woman's legs. "God there? Play tricks?"

Elitha ran into the sun and covered her face inside the hat, her fine hair veiling her cloth-bound shoulders. Her defeated posture suggested sorcery had been aimed at her. If so, the cure would call for more than bladder tea. Only Bear Claw could suck out such evil, if his magic were stronger than the other sorcerer's. But first the simple remedy must be tried.

Glancing back to be sure Billy was toddling toward her, she said to Elitha, "You have enemy? Someone want God to hurt you?"

Elitha dropped her hands and looked at her through wet lashes. "No. God did this for a reason. And he is not evil. You must NOT say that!" Said with strength.

Good. She had some power. Then she recalled that Pedro had another word for power when it injured people. Bad power. "*El Diablo,*" she corrected, pointing again. "The Devil go in. I no talk good." She took Elitha's wrist, gently tugging.

"Come. We talk to Sumac."

Maria sang, telling Sumac of Elitha's need. The *Americana* seemed to listen with interest. Next they went to a stand of nettle. Maria pointed to a handsome specimen and said, "He help you." It was necessary to speak to this woman as one would a young child, explaining what was normally understood.

"Ooh," said Elitha making a face, "that's stinging nettle."

Quickly Maria shoved her out of the plant's hearing. "He is proud," she whispered. "Flatter him." Seeing astonishment replace repugnance, she returned to the nettles and said in her own tongue:

"We are poor women in need of your beauty and strength. No one else will do. Won't you please give your top leaves to this young woman? Her bladder hurts." Maria waited until Nettle said it was all right, that he wasn't offended. She pinched off three spear tops and sang her thanks.

Elitha asked, "Doesn't it sting your hand?"

"Talk right to him and he will not hurt you. But you touch him with cloth." She pointed to Elitha's skirt.

Then she showed her how to pull a strip from willow and cut a plug of oak bark. Each time she sang her songs of thanks — first in her own tongue, then in English, so Elitha could learn, for later she must do her own gathering.

In the village Elitha glanced curiously at the people who remained here at this time of day — mostly old ones and children. They looked at her politely from the sides of their eyes. Maria selected a medium-sized cooking basket from the rafters of the u-macha, handed Billy to Etumu, then took the basket down the path to the river, Elitha following.

She laid the herbs comfortably in the shade, pleased at the *Americana's* attentiveness, and sang to the basket to calm its fears about holding strong herbs. She took it to the river, wading into the current and opened the basket's mouth to the water. Ashore again, she sang to the water, for although it was a special ally of hers, she knew she'd need to cajole it into giving itself over to the herbs for a stranger.

Elitha murmured, "I won't remember the songs."

"You forget sing?"

"I will forget the melody, the words."

This puzzled her. Then she remembered Pedro teaching her *Ave María, Madre de Dios*. He had insisted the chant be spoken precisely the same each time or the magic would be spoiled. Maybe Elitha thought plant people insisted on that too.

"Your power different," she explained. "Plant knows. You speak from dreams, quiet talk with plants. Listen. They talk. You, me have different helpers, some plants, some animals. Good helper is good friend and maybe no need sing to friend. But you sing. You listen. Long time to learn. Understand? Billy too young." She fingered her talisman, which contained pieces of all her plant allies. "Helper no want same song from you and me."

Elitha looked skeptical. Maria was amazed that a person who resisted knowledge hadn't been killed by the house, or Crying Fox' crystals. Warning her not to touch the herbs or basket, she went to the family firepit, dug live coals, piled on tinder and spoke to the fire. When it was hot, she selected a cooking stone, placed it in the fire, then returned to Elitha. "Sit here, in shade. We wait."

Etumu came to the water with Billy and went to the far end of the beach with the other women and children. Perhaps they all had noticed the blue crystals and feared them. Fortunately, Bear Claw's wisdom had given Maria considerable protection around strong power.

When the rock was hot she fetched it on her blue-oak tongs and lowered the stone into the sizzling water. When it boiled she added chunks of oak bark and the nettle leaves, letting them roll with the boil. Then, removing the rock after the right interval, she picked up the other herbs, one at a time, and broke them into the water.

"Break with honor," she explained, giving the plants words of encouragement as they landed on the steaming brown water.

"Willow bark cures pain," Elitha said.

"Yes." Maria said, glad the *Americana* knew at least one thing about plants.

"Your mint is different than ours back home."

"Mint? Which is that?" She liked to learn English talk.

Elitha approached the stand of mint at the water's edge. When it seemed she might pluck it, Maria stayed her hand. "Sing first, but why pick?"

"To show you."

"I look now," she said gently. "*Españoles* call that *yerba buena*."

"Yerba Buena is the name of a town."

"Yes. By ocean."

"Why is the town named Mint?"

"*Españoles* like." She smiled. "Make stomach quiet after *mucho aguardiente*."

When the tea cooled, Maria showed her how to cup her purified hand to the surface and scoop it, not upending the basket the way Pedro did. "Drink five basket every sun. Full basket."

Her eyes widened. She showed her palm and stiff fingers. "That much?"

"*No mucho*." She gestured toward the river. "*Mucho* there. River run clean, *puro*."

"I don't understand."

"Come." Maria led her to a backwater on the river, where the water was green and murky. "Water bad," she said.

"What has this to do with me?"

She pointed to Elitha's bladder. "Water slow, bad. People and *salmón* same. You know *salmón?* Fish?" Seeing her nod, she pointed first to Elitha's mouth, then down her body and between her legs. "Fast water give power. Medicine run fast and make strong. *Fuerte.*" Comprehension flickered in the young woman's eyes, followed by a blush on her pale cheeks. Ashamed to learn? Surely not.

"May I take the basket of medicine home?" Elitha asked.

"Perrimacoo house?" Seeing that was exactly what she had in mind, she found it difficult to remain calm, so horrifying was the thought. "Insult for medicine. Basket sad. Take and keep outside. Bad medicine come if Perrimacoo touch. Medicine hurt you too. Understand?"

Horse hooves sounded. Maria went up the bank far enough to glimpse Grizzly Hair riding with Perrimacoo. She went to the *Americana* and told her who it was.

"I don't want my husband to see me here," Elitha said, as she had before.

Maria pointed down the river. "Go in river. Pass Grandmother. Your bath place be two river turns. No spill medicine, or bad luck comes."

Elitha smiled with strong friendship, not in a defeated way. Then she disappeared below the willows. Perhaps the medicine songs were working already. Maria hoped so. Grizzly Hair topped the bank, a man of power. His tone rang with it: "Perrimacoo needs you to talk for him."

"Pay ye damned 'eathens I will then!"

Maria repeated it in the tongue of her people, who gathered before him, men having come from their tool-making, their snares, and the cattle.

"How much?" the son of Fat Beaver wanted to know. He was a strapping young man who hoped to marry the daughter of the headman from the Walnut Grove village. A marriage present would be on his mind.

"One blue bead each day," Perrimacoo said.

Maria repeated that and people sat impassively.

Grizzly Hair stood. "When we take a beaver skin to Señor Daylo's, he gives us three blue beads."

The sky eyes flashed around the crowd. "All right then, two bleedin beads every bleedin day. But that's all!"

Grizzly Hair walked to the back of the dancehouse and up the dirt ramp to the roof. Over the doorway he stood like an eagle on a high perch looking at the people below. His tone told Maria not to translate.

"He wants us to leave home and live in a strange place," Father said to the people "He does not say how long. He wants us to wash gravel in a stream. When we are finished we will return home with beads."

He paused, then continued, "If you stay here and trap beaver for Señor Daylo, you will earn more beads." The *umne* loved the home place and never wanted to leave.

Running Quail's son said, "My family will stay."

Other men repeated that. Grizzly Hair nodded at each one and instructed

Maria to tell Perrimacoo the people would not go to Dry Creek to collect golden gravel.

Perrimacoo elevated his pitch. "Ent I been the soul of justice? Give ye 'eathens all them beads? Don't I mark every tenth calf yours? Alright then, five beads apiece and that's final!"

Grizzly Hair walked away. One by one the families left the dancehouse, some returning to their u-machas, some to the mortar rocks, others heading up the eastern hill.

Perrimacoo's face reddened. He yelled at Maria, "Ye bleedin bitch! Said it wrong, ye did!" He touched his gun.

Grizzly Hair turned. All the men froze.

Perrimacoo's weakness showed in his sagging shoulders. Then, clutching his gun, he jumped on his horse and disappeared up the path toward his house — where, Maria knew, Elitha would be by now.

"Well, if they won't work for you," Elitha said, "try the Indians between here and Daylor's ranch."

"Daft."

"Why not?" Before they were married he had said fifty Indians worked for him. How different the reality was! They did what they pleased.

"I can't, that's all." He leaned over the barrel, yanked the cork from the bung hole, and held his trembling cup beneath it. An amber drop pinged into the tin. He stepped back and kicked the barrel with such violence that it gouged out the wall, and bounced back and crashed into the table legs. "Hit's their damned bloody jabber!" Flakes of adobe skittered down the wall.

Nothing she could say would help. Besides, the irritating urgency was upon her as always. She pushed open the door — which served very well — thinking she'd pass water then drink the rest of the tea, which she'd left in the split rock.

His fingers dug into her shoulders and from behind she felt the wet words on her earlobe. "Where ye be going?"

Her heart raced at the tone — soft and threatening. Facing the tranquil outdoors, she murmured, "To pass water."

The fingers didn't let up. "Every other minute ye be pissin." The P spit in her ear. "Gone long enough to meet a buck, too. Think I'm daft, does ye?"

She recoiled. "I'd die first." She meant it. Donner women didn't cheat on their husbands, much less with Indians.

"Oh fer Chrissake, git!"

She didn't expect the shove. The toe of her shoe caught on the new threshold stone Perry had laid in an excavated hole, not quite deep enough. She fell on her hand, trying to brace the fall, and her thumb, taking most of her weight, was forced back. Pain bloomed in her hand, and her cheek and knees stung as she lay in the dirt. A little urine leaked out, burned. Picking herself up, she limped toward the bigger of the two oaks, ashamed of being so clumsy — he hadn't pushed hard. She brushed embedded sand particles from her cheek as she went behind the tree and was gathering her skirt.

He was there glaring at her.

She dropped the skirt, her voice quiet and polite. "Please, I'd like to be alone." *Oh for an outhouse with a latch!*

"Makin sure ye be alone, I is." He grinned a deep dimple, steely eyes boring through her. "Go on, do it then." He placed his knuckles on his hips, elbows out.

"Please, I need privacy." She didn't want him to see her pain.

His eyes were glassy. "Stayin right 'ere, I is. Ye can bloody well do it now." He swayed with too much drink.

"I can't. With you there."

He threw his head back hawing. "Show ye, I will." He unbuttoned his trousers and flipped out his member, which, with the cloth hanging between his thighs, was framed by a square of black hair. He released a shimmering golden arc not far from where she stood, then, holding his enlarging self with the blind eye staring at her, his tone softened. "Then again, I gots me another idear."

Pain drummed in her hand and she felt about to scream with false urgency. Yet her aunt in Illinois had said marriages were good when a wife let a man have his way. If only it didn't hurt so! Most of the pain came with the first thrusts. More would come later, she knew — the longer it went on, the worse it would be.

Indian Mary's advice came back to her. *You need power.* She seemed to believe weakness caused everything bad, but the amazing thing was her assumption that Elitha had a curable illness, not a killing plague visited upon her by God. As Perry pumped, she kept her injured hand out of the way and thought how casual Mary's attitude had been, even pointing to it. Her manner suggested that all Indian woman knew about this — they even had a remedy! Tamsen had admired Indian medicine and Elitha's real mother, Mary Blue, was mostly Indian — a secret she didn't often share. She resolved to give the tea every opportunity to heal her.

But as she watched the strained cords in Perry's neck, inches from her nose, she wondered again what on earth Indians meant by *power.*

40

Several weeks later as Perry pulled on his boots, Elitha stood scratching another neat line on the adobe wall beside the bed and called over her shoulder,

"It's October 16."

"So?"

"My birthday." And she had a pounding headache, but her thumb was wrapped in a heavy Indian splint — she'd told Perry she made it herself.

He came to her. "Fifteen is it now?" His hands closed around her waist, his blue eyes sparkling.

She nodded, fearing what she thought was coming, but instead he put her over his knees, pulled up her dress, pulled down her knickers, and spanked her hard, counting. By the fifth smack her backside hurt bad, but she wouldn't cry. It stung her pride, and he was snickering. At fifteen, he pulled up her knickers and turned her to her feet.

"Birthday spankings are to be light," she said, hating the break in her voice.

"Won't do no good, ifn it's light." He headed out the door chuckling.

Later, her headache was so bad she decided to go out and find Indian Mary and see if she had a remedy. The tea had entirely cured her of the pain in her privates.

Mary led her to an elderberry tree, more like a large bush, and crawled beneath it — multiple trunks and branches fanning upward and outward into a thick canopy of soft green leaves. They lay there looking up, and she detected a subtle fragrance coming from the greenery, and really tried to listen, and thought she felt the particular nature of the tree. Inhaling and appreciating it, she felt her headache begin to lift.

"How do you make glue from soaproot?" she asked.

"Shh. Now talk quiet to Elderberry. Maybe helper for you." Then she glanced up, grabbed Billy and vanished through the foliage.

Perplexed, Elitha sat up and was about to call to her when Perry's bootfalls sounded on the trail. Mary, respecting Elitha's wish to keep their friendship secret, had heard it much sooner. The acuity of Indian hearing was amazing. Elitha went to him.

Perry smiled in a jaunty, teasing way. "So there ye be lass. Come tidy yourself. Goin on a journey, we is."

"To New Helvetia?" *To fetch the girls!* A birthday surprise.

"To Yerba Buena."

Still, New Helvetia was on the way! And a town full of whites and Spaniards would be a wonderful sight. But she'd about gone wild out here. When had she last seen her hairpins? She worried her face had become browned, so often she forgot to wear her bonnet. But now she felt it stretch with a smile. "We can get my little sisters."

"We can't take them to — "

"I mean on the way back."

"We'll see, we'll see."

Yes! She wanted to jump up and down.

"Now lass, try'n guess our good fortune?" A merry dimple cratered his cheek and his blue eyes sparkled.

"What?" She couldn't imagine.

"Tell ye on the way, I will. We got to hightail it."

She trotted to keep pace with him. "Tell me now!"

"Well, seems the good citizens of Yerba Buena is feelin sorry about the plight of the Donner orphans."

"So?"

"A gift, they's givin ye."

"A gift! What?" She could hardly believe strangers were thinking of her. "Tell me what! Right now!"

"Ground."

"Ground? You mean land?"

"That I does."

"They're giving us land?"

"Neptune's bones they is! Drawing up streets to make a proper town and givin a whole two blocks of it to you Donner waifs. You being the eldest, I sent word you'd be there to collect the papers."

"But what can we do with land in town?" She was a farm girl and he already had a rancho. Topping the hill she saw Paint saddled before the adobe and glanced from the horse to Perry, realizing he meant to leave immediately.

"Hit's but dirt now, but mark my word, smart money is on Yerba Buena, it is. The deedin ceremony is eleven days from now, at noon. It'll take all that time to get there. So git yer things, lass."

That evening they camped in an adobe room two doors from where she and her sisters had waited so long. Mr. Sutter said the girls were nowhere near the fort. "Zey be heppy wissout you," he said.

She swallowed the pain of that, doubting the girls had forgotten her. Sutter said the Brunners farmed on the other side of the river, above the Sinclairs.

"Oh please," she said to Perry, "borrow the boat. Let's go see them!"

He looked at the sunset and shook his head. "Late, it tis, lass."

She felt her face fall. He was right. They'd be caught in the dark.

"I promise ye lass, we'll stop on the way back." He strode away with Sutter, to drink spirits, she knew. Mr. Sutter's boat, the *Sacramento*, would leave for Yerba Buena first thing in the morning. Outside the familiar gate she saw only a couple of broken wagons in the twilight — most of the men back from the war, the reunited families working farms — and realized these "prairie schooners" were already relics. Life went forward.

She hunkered down in sawdust and picked out the sounds of rowdy men inside the fort walls. Distant coyotes yipped mournfully, bringing back the nights she'd spent with her sisters, and the weary waiting, and the nightmares. Did they still wake up screaming? The coyotes brought better memories too, of a time back on the prairie when she'd been secure in her family.

Pulling her cloak to her chin, she wondered if bad luck really came from the feather robe that Mary said Perry had stolen and stored in his house. *Leave house or maybe die*, Mary had said more than once. Elitha had been relieved to learn his other white wife had not died in the house. Still, the woman had lived there. Bad luck was supposed to touch everybody even remotely involved with the feathers — Perry, Captain Sutter, the Indians, the Russians who took the robe, and all who looked at it. However, her own bad luck had happened long before she got to Perry's house, so it wasn't connected.

And besides, she and her sisters had survived. Her burning pain was gone, and the citizens of Yerba Buena were giving the Donners land. This spelled good luck, perhaps the beginning of the prosperity Pa had envisioned. If there was a curse, it wasn't on her, or, as Indian Mary would say, she had enough "power" to stop it. She would take her sisters to Rancho Sacayak and care for them, and Pa would smile down from heaven.

She didn't hear Perry stagger in and fall beside her.

He left the adobe early the next morning to turn Paint into Sutter's herd where he would graze until their return. She rolled her hair around her ears and pinned it, put on her bonnet and rearranged Perry's straight razor with her extra underwear and nightshirt in the carpetbag. Then she went to Mr. Sutter's upper room, where she and Perry and several others were eating breakfast.

Over his cup of cinnamon chocolate, heavily spiked with *aguardiente*, Mr. Sutter said a man named Sam Brannan had brought two hundred fifty Mormons around the Horn, and they were all establishing businesses in Yerba Buena. "They be vonderful skilled peoples." She couldn't wait to see that town on the ocean bay.

After breakfast she and Perry joined the other passengers on the trail to the river. Three men walked ahead with Perry, gripping rifles. Mrs. Kelsey held a newborn babe in her ropy arms. As Elitha helped her keep her three others corralled, she reflected that this young woman had known trouble too. Five years before the Donners and Reeds formed their party, Nancy Kelsey had left Kentucky pregnant and with a baby in her arms, insisting on staying with her husband, who would have gone to California with the small Bidwell Party without her. The oxen gave out in the desert and all wagons were abandoned. Nancy's shoes gave out too. By the time they got to the Sierras, which they knew nothing about, not even having a guide, she was barefoot, big with child and winter was coming on. They scaled the trackless mountains and ate their mules, but at least the snow was scarce that year. Nancy looked older than her twenty-one years.

"I heard you were the one that sewed the grizzly bear flag," Elitha said.

"Yup." Her plain frock hung straight from board-like shoulders and her small blue eyes drilled out from a face like pitted granite.

"Didn't last long, did it? California being independent."

"Nope, Martha Ann, git back here!"

Cascades of blood-red grapevines draped from yellow and brown trees, the stunning colors reflected in the river. The *Sacramento* bumped gently against the sycamore, which was dropping leaves the size of dinner plates all over the deck — a deck Elitha well remembered. But now the morning air had a damp chill in it.

Sutter's Indians held the rope through a ring while men and Nancy boarded. The skiff lurched and banged. Feeling limber and happy, Elitha jumped on, anxious to see Yerba Buena then come back and collect her sisters. Sutter's Indians smiled and waved from the shore. She waved back. With a sailor's rolling gait, Perry left her and went aft to the pilot, who was swinging the small boom around, reversing directions across a wide spot in the river. When the lurching subsided and the vessel headed downstream, Elitha, in a mood to match the sunshine on the blue water, went to join Perry.

The captain turned to her — familiar pale eyes. She stopped breathing. The wild hair and pendulum beard had been trimmed, flesh added to bone, but it was Lewis Keseberg. Loathing and nausea hit her. She looked at Perry, who stood at Keseberg's side as if they were friends.

"You should have been hanged," came out of her mouth. People stared.

Around the aperture in the long pale beard, the man's mouth twisted into an obscene smile, and that instant of time stretched long in Elitha's mind. She recalled a rescuer saying at the inquest that he knew for a fact Tamsen had gone to the lake camp because someone had warned her that Keseberg was planning to kill her daughters. Elitha realized she should have testified about what the little girls had told her. The man was guilty — hadn't men seen the pot of blood? Hadn't he admitted he ate her, and buried some of the gold? Oh why hadn't they finished what they'd started and hung him then! Instead of taking him to the fort where justice was a joke. And here he stood an arm's length away, looking saucy after getting away with cold-blooded murder.

She lunged at him, to punish him for Tamsen's sake. She felt skin give way beneath her nails, but hands grabbed her from behind and pulled her away. Keseberg was covering his wounds and looking surprised.

She battled the hands — it was Perry and another man — and felt her heels rattling over the deck planks as they pulled her away. They pushed her down at the prow rail, where a pile of goods obstructed her view of the killer. Her face felt hot and she breathed like a bellows.

Perry glowered down at her. "What the devil! Eat loco weed, did ye?"

That made her shake so hard she couldn't speak. In her mind she saw Keseberg eating Tamsen's brains. The Kelsey children crowded around Perry as if for protection from her. She said, "If I'd been a man, I'd have killed him and no one would blame me." It would be expected of a man, who would simply move on to some other locale and Alcalde Sinclair would forget all about it. People would say the cur had it coming.

Perry looked at the gawking passengers, put his hands on his waist and spoke to her through his teeth, "The man was declared innocent, or has ye forgot? Now you behave proper like, hear?" He raised a stiff hand as if to strike, then let it drop. "Thought I had me a laidy, I did." His mouth made a thin line, his eyes a mean thicket of lashes.

She sank against the rail feeling her breakfast in her throat. She wrenched herself up and tried to lean over the water. Not in time. It hit her frock and shoes. Perry looked disgusted.

A man said, "Haven't even started yet, little girl. You'll get your sea legs." He cast a secret glance to the spectators. *Ghoul.*

Perry went back to Keseberg, put his arm around his shoulder, and spoke into his ear. Rage almost asphyxiated her. Had she been able to swim, she would have jumped over the side rather than spend another minute with either one of them. Instead she avoided all eyes, thinking maybe there was a curse of the condor robe.

The voyage down the American River seemed to take forever, though it was probably only a half hour until the boat eased into the wide brown Sacramento, heading south. People continued to stare at her like she was crazy. Her mind seethed. Never in her life had she done anything like that, yet what the man had gotten away with would hurt her little sisters as long as they lived. But attacking him! It was as if an uncontrollable monster lurked inside her. And the sight of Perry's arm around that man hurt so much she never wanted to touch him again, even if he was her husband.

"There's Sutter's Embarcadero," said a man. Logs tied together at the water's edge, backed by a slough of bulrushes and cattails. She glimpsed the trail threading east, where they might have to walk on the return trip, if sailing against the current on the American River was impossible. In her heart she was sailing against the current of her marriage.

"Ole Sutter oughta sell that land here fer a town," a man said, cradling his gun across his bent knees.

"Naw," said another. "Don't you got no horse sense? This here's swamped GOOD come spring."

They were losing interest in her, she was relieved to see. The boat had the benefit of sluggish current, but little breeze. Perry and Lewis Keseberg swung the boom back and forth, though Keseberg didn't need any help. With anger bubbling beneath her forced calm, she sat gazing at the red and green grape vines meeting their images in the water. For months she had tried to forget the past, yet how could she, on a boat piloted by Keseberg?

By afternoon the passengers, seated on the deck, had quieted and Mrs. Kelsey's youngsters slept, one in her arms, two with their heads on her lap. The men sat in a circle, including Perry, and were passing liquor.

A man in buckskin gazed up the river and said, "At this rate hit'll take a month of Sundays to git there."

"It dad-blamed better not!" said another, turning a slippery eye her way. "The cap'n might git hungry." Hard laughter erupted all around, including from Perry and Nancy.

She couldn't meet Perry's eyes. How could she live with him?

After sundown the boat pulled to shore and everyone waded through the mud. Elitha helped Nancy Kelsey with supper preparations. After eating, the men took their blankets to a thicket and Elitha went on deck to try to sleep with Nancy and the children. Perry jumped on board and pulled her aside. She jerked away from his touch, and didn't look at him.

His whisper was strained, "Think ye I don't know what I'm about?"

"You knew he'd be piloting the boat."

"Now lass. Think. Ye wouldn't a come, now would ye? If I'd atold of it?"

Of course not. She looked down.

"Likely as not they'd give the ground away to someone else." The boat lurched as a man jumped on, apparently searching for something. Perry steered her aft, his mouth near her ear. "'Ave me reasons fer cozyin up to the likes o' him, I 'as." He tapped his temple and winked.

Stunned, she stared at him.

"Methinks to catch more flies with honey than vinegar."

She felt exhausted and hated talking to him.

"Some starry night on this 'ere trip, ole Keseberg'll get drunk and tell me where he's hid the quilt." He looked at her like she should be pleased to have such a clever husband.

"I don't care about the quilt any more."

That stopped him for a moment. "And the little lasses, spose they don't care?"

That stopped her, but only for a moment. "You're daft if you think that man will tell you a thing. It took a noose around his neck to get him to admit to two hundred dollars."

"Like I said, honey's the better way."

For seven days the boat tacked through the widening waterway, Perry acting as comrade and sailing tutor to Keseberg. Each night he drank with the German while Elitha and Nancy Kelsey and the children slept on deck. Elitha felt like a sleepwalker, trying to pretend Keseberg didn't exist. But she learned the other passengers were not ghouls. They pitied her and made it plain that they thought Perry shouldn't be associating with Keseberg in her presence. Nancy Kelsey said she would have "hauled off an give him a lick."

During the day birds filled the air — ducks, geese, cranes and herons, sometimes blotting out the sun's light. In places they blackened the water for what looked like miles and it seemed the boat floated through a river of feathers.

"Lansford Hastings' place," a man said pointing across the water. "Calls it Montezuma."

Elitha saw a white house, the second structure of any kind she'd seen. Tiny across the broad water, it sat at the foot of rolling brown hills with a toylike boat at its embarcadero. The other passengers gazed with admiration, but she wondered how Hastings could live with himself, knowing that half the Donner Party had died because of his so-called guidebook. Her throat tightened. Again she was being pulled into the past.

The next day the shore receded to hazy rims as the boat skimmed into the widening bay. Sea birds replaced the geese and ducks. The wind that filled the sails carried a salty odor. Large brown birds with hamper-like bills flew in squadrons, diving for fish — pelicans, the men called them. She looked beyond a white island to a far shore at the foot of high peaks, clear but distant — Yerba Buena.

"High-tide it tis," Perry announced to the passengers. His blue eyes looked bright, less steely, as if absorbing the color of azure sky. "That means we'll take 'er to the mole at Montgomery Street."

"A mole!" shrieked one of Mrs. Kelsey's towheads. All three jumped up and down at the prospect of the voyage's end. Adults were on their feet smiling, gripping the hand rail.

Perry helped stow the sails and pole the craft into a pile of rocks and bricks. Elitha — never looking at Keseberg — tightened the strings of her bonnet and grabbed her carpetbag. Beyond a two-story building and up a brown hill was another, steeper hill. White clouds sailed rapidly over the peak, dragging shadows across its flank, on which long-horned cattle grazed — ant-like in the distance. Here and there among the cattle stood a shack and a stick fence containing hogs. Groves of oaks resembled old apple trees. She stepped over the rail onto the "mole" — a pile of rocks.

Water lapped the soles of her shoes. Wind whipped her skirt and tugged her bonnet, nearly turning it inside out. She read the placard on the brick building,

MELLUS & HOWARD. Mellus, same as at the fort. It was the only brick building among the town's adobe and wood houses, many under construction.

The travellers said their good-byes. Elitha was relieved to see that Keseberg stayed on board occupied by hiring Indians, one of whom jumped into the hold and was visible from the waist up, handing up one bag after another. She breathed easier, the first time in more than a week.

The little town looked like a picture in a book, so intense was the quality of the light. Tamsen would have painted it. Whitewashed adobes gleamed in the fresh air. Ox carts and horse-drawn wagons creaked along intersecting trails. Most spectacular was the vast bay with many vessels bobbing on it — masts like matchsticks, flags of all colors whipping, but mainly the red, white and blue. The stars and stripes also showed above an adobe hall.

"That's a three-master," Perry said, pointing at a ship. "Learned on one like that, I did." His mood remained high, as if he didn't realize she was cold toward him. He pointed again, "There's a four-masted windjammer from the Norseland." She began to wonder if he'd got something out of Keseberg, but she wouldn't broach the subject.

By the back of the neck he guided her up a dusty road, telling her how much he liked this little town. Passing a tent saloon that was nothing more than planks balanced on barrels, he tossed a jaunty "Ahoy!" at the proprietor, who raised a hand and shouted, "Perry!"

He pointed to the far end of the long curve of beach. "See yon shanty?" She made out a structure. "Will Clark's place. Buildin a wharf. Plannin to get rich, that one." He lifted his hat and scratched his head. "Last time I was here he had Kanakas divin down there plantin beams. Swim like fish, they does." He replaced his hat. "Landed there, we woulda, at low tide."

He steered her to the porch of an unpainted wooden structure with JOHANSON HOUS painted under the peak of the roof. He knocked. Chickens clucked under the stoop. Opening the door was a Nordic giantess. Looking fondly at Perry, she smoothed her apron and said in a Swedish sing-song, "Wouldja look at what the sea's vashed in!" Turning to Elitha she asked, "And whose pretty ting iss dot?"

"Me own wife, it tis!" Perry looked Elitha over then grinned at the giantess. "You got a room? And vittels?"

"Venn you haff da money, ha ha."

"Taik me for a rascal, do ye?" His grin was angelic.

The woman rolled her eyes, turned, and beckoned them with a hook of her arm, her broad back and yellow braids leading down a short, narrow hallway. She opened a door and stepped back.

The room was so small a narrow bed nearly filled it, but it had a door with a latch, and Elitha had seen an outhouse in back. After sailing for eight days, it looked luxurious. Civilization felt good. Almost as good as the peace in her privates. She exhaled and felt her anger at Perry blow out with her breath. He was only being Perry, just trying to nose whatever he could out of life when he saw the chance. She wouldn't fight him. Besides that, the people of Yerba Buena were giving her and her sisters and cousins a nice block of land. She unpacked her blue calico dress and smoothed out the wrinkles.

41

Salt wind whipped Elitha's blue calico skirt and tugged her matching bonnet as she stepped across the deeply rutted road. She felt the pins tight in her hair, which she'd rolled around her ears. Walking beside her, Perry was clean-shaven and dapper in his polished boots, and cheerful since their lovemaking — the first in a long time she hadn't minded. The sun was bright, though it was late October — a year and two weeks since the first snowflakes had fallen on the Donners.

He steered her by the neck toward the plaza on Montgomery Street, where the stars and stripes whipped above a low adobe with a tile roof. Men stood smoking in the packed-earth yard — not one Spaniard, though she knew they made up most of the town's population. A man in bell-bottomed trousers slapped Perry on the back. "Wall, ifn it ent me mait from the King's naivy! This be yer little Donner girl then?"

Heads turned. Feeling reserved in the presence of so many strange men, she continued across the yard where a sign proclaimed "Clay Street." Wooden forms crusted with white dirt were piled beside a large mud pit. She looked up the road at the adobe houses and realized they had been built from this clay. The street was aptly named.

A bell clanged, the kind a schoolmarm would ring. A man at the hall entrance. Perry came for her and steered her through the crowded doorway — people coming from every direction — and up a center aisle between benches, upon which about twenty women sat as if in church. The buzz of talk lowered as she and Perry passed by. *They assume I'm a cannibal*, she knew as she sat demurely, folding her hands, hearing the room fill behind her.

A hulk of a man dressed like a banker banged on a table with a wooden mallet. The room quieted. He introduced himself as Sam Brannan, then spoke in an Irish accent about the "misfortunes" and "tragedy" of the Donner Party. He praised the heroism of the rescuers and talked of the "glorious end of the Mexican War" and the "manifest destiny of the United States linking the continent from the Atlantic to the Pacific shores."

His hair was shiny black, his topcoat tweed, and he had an Irishman's gift of gab. "Mark my words," he intoned, "California will prosper under the red, white and blue. And now, in recognition of our new station as a territory of the United States, we, the Citizens' Committee, are giving this town a new name, one that will no longer be the devil to spell and a tongue twister to boot. Henceforth this fair city will bear the name of Saint Francis, to whom the old Spanish mission was dedicated in 1776. And a more fitting name couldn't be found, for Saint Francis it tis who blesses the weary traveller." He looked down, fondling the mallet, then lifted his head.

"And that we all are, ladies and gentlemen, are we not? Weary travellers at the end of our journey? But in recognition of the contribution of the Spanish friars to this peninsula, St. Francis' name will be in Spanish. So, unless I hear serious disagreement to the contrary," he struck the table so sharply she jumped, "this town is henceforth to be known as San Francisco."

Applause erupted, men stamped, and Brannan banged along with the noise, using the table like a drum. With his black eyes snapping, he reminded Elitha of a snake oil salesman at a Chicago fair.

When it was quiet again, he resumed but she found it hard to listen to the names of all the citizens on the committee and the flowery language describing the thinking they had done to draw up a plat grid for the "south of Market" side of town. But at last he wound down and introduced a smaller man of military bearing — Mr. Bryant, Alcalde of San Francisco.

Mr. Bryant, who held a scroll of paper tied with a red ribbon, beckoned Elitha. The room hushed as Perry helped her to her feet and placed her hand, tender without the splint, on his elbow. Intensely aware of being stared at, she remembered the Wolfingers strolling in just this way across a mountain meadow.

They faced Mr. Bryant and she saw the crowd — sixty or seventy people beneath a low-beamed ceiling, light angling through windows like short hallways. And as Mr. Bryant was speaking about the starvation and suffering of the Donner Party, saying the two lots were a token of the pity of the citizens, she suddenly remembered seeing him before — back on the prairie. This was the leader of the faster-moving party for which Mr. Miller, the driver, had deserted the Donners. Had he stayed to fulfill his obligation, perhaps he would have died with the other hired men and not been available to rescue the three little girls later. And Mr. Bryant, who had so vexed Pa, was now smiling and handing Elitha the scroll with the red ribbon.

Applause was roaring all around. People stood, shouted, whistled, stamped and clapped their hands. Smiling as though he were the object of the crowd's approval, Perry steered her down the aisle and outside, and she couldn't help but think how quickly things changed. One day a man was a scoundrel, the next a hero. And what was Mr. Miller today? Perry had told her he had been appointed guardian of the Donner money. Pa would surely be turning in his grave — and he was in a grave. At the fort she'd heard that General Kearny and others had buried him properly on their way over the mountains and, though he'd been opened up, he was still in the sheet Tamsen had wound him in.

In the yard men smiled and took turns congratulating her. "Proud to do it," said swarthy, woolly headed Mr. Leidesdorff, one of the leading citizens mentioned by Mr. Brannan.

She curtsied, "We are ever so grateful, sir."

Perry jabbed a thumb at him. "Would ye believe? Once upon a time this 'ere fancy nigger mastered a ship. Now 'e owns a big rancho up on the American River."

Mr. Leidesdorff raised an eyebrow over a penetrating black eye, but no doubt heard Perry's underlying admiration. "I prefer to reside on the seashore," he said, "unless I want to go mad as a hatter. How in thunder do you tolerate that wilderness out there on the Cosumney?" His British accent sounded entirely different from Perry's.

"Workin on it, ent we lass?" Perry looked at her.

She twisted the scroll and smiled.

She met Mr. Clark, who was building the wharf, and Mr. Mellus' partner, Mr. Howard, after whom a street near her property was named. Two young lieutenants in the United States Army came to meet her — William Tecumseh Sherman and Edward Ord, both stationed in Monterey — and Mr. Oakley, a rescuer who had been at the fort the night Jean Baptiste had come through. She met many others she couldn't keep straight. Former sailors gathered around Perry, urging him to slake his thirst with them.

"Blow me down if that don't sound good at that!"

Two women talked quietly, looking at her, and she heard "Pretty thing."

After Perry "stowed" a few drinks, Elitha stood with him at a sturdy post with a paper nailed to it. Second Street, the sign said on one side, Folsom on the other.

Wind riffled the brown grass in every direction — from the gentle curve of the beach, across the mud flats and up the hills. She saw the canvas stores of Market Street about a quarter of a mile away and several untidy houses between. An intervening post marked Frémont Street, after Captain John Frémont, who figured prominently in the war. Running perpendicular and starting at the water, posts marked First Street, Second, Third, Fourth and so on, marching in a disciplined line up the hill. Lonely heralds announcing streets in a wasteland of ground squirrels and jackrabbits.

Above, seabirds cried as she untied the ribbon and stretched out the scroll, turning her back to the wind to keep it from flying away. Below the fancy lettering was a grid. South of Howard, Mission Road connected the town with the old Spanish mission. She looked up and saw a "carreta," a peculiar California cart that Spaniards hitched to the saddle of a rider, hurtling toward the mission as if flying over the grass.

Over her shoulder Perry pointed at the inked square at Second and Folsom. "Hit's about three times as long as tis wide," he said.

"My but it's big for two town lots!" She squinted west toward the Third Street post. "Enough for a small farm." She couldn't imagine roads would ever appear where the ruled lines were drawn.

"Ah, but it will have stores on it."

"But Perry, it's not anywhere near the town."

"Some day, lass, some day." Always hoping and scheming.

At about noon the following day they stepped from the porch of the boardinghouse into a bracing fog. Feeling better after a hearty bowl of mush and Swedish coffee, the grind of which had been soaked in egg yolk, she still felt a dearth of sleep. Her neck and shoulders ached from sitting on a chair while Perry gambled long into the night. Unaccustomed to sleeping late, she'd visited with the proprietress, helping with the chores while he slept.

"Ever time I see this place, it's sprung more houses," Perry said.

He persuaded a teamster to let them ride in his delivery wagon to the old Spanish Presidio. Amid bags and bundles they bounced along the waterfront road. Passing Clark's Point, Perry said, "They call that Broadway."

Glancing up the narrow road of that name, she saw a few scattered huts, and couldn't help but smile. But she'd learned that the town was filled with optimistic men. The sun was clearing away the fog, and they were circling a peninsula, the restless bay ever on their right.

"Mrs. Johanson said people here send their wash to China," she said, exhilarated by the wind. "Do you believe that?"

Comfortable against his leather bag, Perry sucked his Mexican *cigarrito* and winked in the smoke, "Ent enough females to do the wash. Brannan and the boys get their shirts back neat and folded in a month or two."

"They do it then, really, send it to China?"

He nodded.

"I'd think they'd lose things on such a long voyage, or get the linen mixed up."

"Nothin gets lost on a ship, lass. All stowed neat and tidy like."

In an hour they'd passed only a few houses, then they came to a cluster of dilapidated adobe buildings. Leaving the wagon, they hiked up through aromatic evergreens to a point overlooking the Spanish buildings, and gazed across the isthmus where the ocean entered the enormous bay. The tan hills on the opposite shore looked soft and round. Battalions of pelicans circled the rocky island that reared up in the center of the bay, white with guano.

"Alcatraz the Spaniards call that bird," Perry said.

She hugged herself, amazed how little warmth the sun gave, and listened as he told of arriving at this strait with John Sutter on the ship he'd acquired in the Sandwich Islands. Señor Valdez had said Perry deserted his captain. When had that happened? Maybe in those distant islands.

He feigned the creaky voice of an old-timer. "That were in eighteen and thirty-nine." He counted on his fingers. "Eight years. My, my things has changed. I'll wager nigh five hundred souls dwells in Yerb — San Francisco now, countin the greasers, if they got souls." He laughed, then added wistfully, "Send our wash to China, we will lass. When I strike it rich. A man can git rich in this country, if he knows what 'e's about."

42

Three nights later she sat on the same chair in the same room where Perry had gambled every night. Only the men at the table differed. Sometimes she wondered if he was waiting for Keseberg and the *Sacramento*. Sick at the thought and anxious to get to her sisters — the voyage could take eleven days upstream — she twisted on the chair. Perry had said, "Win me loot back tonight, I will."

She rotated the scroll in her hands, the ribbon worn and wrinkled — he'd asked her to bring it so he could show it off. She had touched him on the shoulder with it and hinted they leave, to no avail. She had counted twelve planks down one wall and fourteen on another, eleven at her back, and was intimate with every knothole and adz gouge. The room was cramped, her chair inches from Perry.

Opposite him sat the cabin owner, Greasy Jim, who had once been Perry's partner on the ranch. Behind the table the floor sloped down to a stove, from which rancid odors wafted up with too much heat. The smoke of the *cigarritos* gagged her. It was midnight or later and she'd been awake since early morning. She turned on one hip and rested her cheekbone on the chairback, watching the gamblers and praying for signs of quitting.

Greasy Jim raked in five piles of coins. Perry upended his flask, gulped three times, let out an ahhh, and wiped his sleeve across his mouth. Cards were slapped on the table. Perry shoved coins before him. Eventually others would collect them, as they had all night. She hoped he'd lose every cent, and quickly, so they could leave. But he won that hand. He turned to her and winked, then turned back and shuffled the deck.

She leaned forward and whispered in his ear, "I'll find the way to the boardinghouse by myself. I'm plumb tuckered." She stood up.

He twisted around, scowling, and pointed at the chair. "Sit down and wait till I'm done. Ent no time o' night for a white girl to wander alone. The greasers'll git ye." He flashed a pathetic grin around the table as if telling the men what a burden a wife was, and added, "We'll go when I gits me money back." He chuckled. They looked at him over their cards, not caring about her.

She looked down at the chair that had tortured her so long and knew she wouldn't spend one more minute on it. The Spaniards she had seen were gentlemen compared to these men. She shouldered the door open a crack. Cool air beckoned her into a fresh, misty darkness. The leather hinges creaked as she slipped outside. He hadn't even looked up. But he had seen.

The bite in the air stung her awake and her heart pounded. Gripping the scroll, she ducked behind a corner of the adjacent shack, where she could watch the cabin door, and try to think. Why had she done that? *Elitha is an obedient girl.* What would he do? Maybe she shouldn't go to the boardinghouse. He'd been drinking a lot, and might hurt her. But where could she go at this time of night? *Away.*

She trotted up the road, amazed the door hadn't opened, a feeling of terror and outrage jamming her esophagus like a whole melon. Maybe, she told herself, he'd pretend her actions didn't count for anything and he'd keep playing cards. But then he'd make an excuse about being tired, and come for her.

Her legs felt free and limber, as if a mysterious force pulled her away from Perry. The road rose steeply beneath her and the fog blurred the crescent of a moon. The empty fields between the cabins grew wider. A candle flickered in a window. A horse whinnied. Her breathing grew labored as she climbed. Girls didn't do this. She sat down to rest near the iron gate of an adobe, realizing she had no plan and no reason to run from the man she had promised to obey. Gasping for breath, she shivered in the cold and damp.

"*Qué pasa*?" A male voice.

She jumped in her skin. She couldn't ask a Spaniard to hide her; he'd think she was a woman of the night. She pressed her back against a tree trunk and stifled her rasping breath, hoping the man would think he'd been mistaken. Moisture penetrated her frock from the grass. Her thumb throbbed. She would keep quiet, then go back to the boardinghouse — before Perry left the card game. Maybe he was glad she'd stopped pestering him. She caught a whiff of mint. Dogs barked in the distance. A drop of condensation fell on her face from an overhead limb. An owl hooted, and her breath slowed.

"Git yer arse the bloody hell over here afore I knock ye to kingdom come!"

Her heart stopped; he was across the road.

"Who goes there?" The Spaniard.

"A law-abiding man lookin fer 'is bleedin wife!" Perry hove from the darkness, coming at her.

She stood up stammering, "I'm sorry. I, I — "

His palm cracked against the side of her head and she fell to the ground before she knew what happened. Instinctively she covered her ear to stop the ringing pain.

A soft chuckle. "Señor, please take your *mujer* away from my *casa*."

"Don't trouble yer greasy head over it!" Perry yanked her injured hand and pulled her to her knees.

She yowled involuntarily — the pain racing up her arm.

He dropped her hand. "Oh, fer Chrissake, git up!" A hard object hit her back, knocking her on all fours before she could stumble to her feet. He had kicked her. In the misty moonlight she saw him retrieve the scroll where she'd dropped it.

The whole way down the hill he never released her wrist, and never said a word. She couldn't explain to herself, much less to him, why she'd run away, so she was quiet. Closing the door of their room, he turned to her and said, "Let this be a lesson to ye, lass." In the faint light from the candle in the next house, she saw his balled fist coming. It rammed her solar plexus. She hit the wall and curled over onto the floor, unable to make a sound. Like a broken bellows, her lungs wouldn't work.

He fell back on the bed with his lower legs and boots hanging over the side, by her head. Her air seeped back, but she suppressed the urge to gasp and breathed in the aromas of the new cedar floor and rodent scat. Hugging her aching stomach, still feeling the pain in her back, the ringing in her ear and the ache in her hand, she realized the only women she'd heard of who were hit by their husbands were women of bad character, from bad families. Had she fallen that low? She felt more like a trapped animal.

Maybe she was losing her mind. Attacking Keseberg, right in front of people, then running away from Perry. She had to get it into her head that she was a married woman — for better or for worse — not an undisciplined child. She had always imagined she would become a gracious farm wife. Her place was beside this man, the squire of Rancho Sacayak. Nonetheless, she stayed motionless on the floor, breathing imperceptibly, hoping he'd think he had hurt her bad. Then maybe he'd apologize.

The candle next door blinked out. The dark was profound. A cold draft blew under the door. She clenched her teeth so they wouldn't chatter. A long time went by, but no snoring came from the bed. He never moved. She'd meant to outlast him, but couldn't bear the hard floor any more. Quite sure he was awake, she got up and carefully lay down, crosswise on the bed, as far from him as she could get.

The next two days Perry was noticeably nicer, though he never mentioned what had happened. He took the property deed "to show the blokes," and allowed her to go her own way. It felt good to look around the town alone. At mealtimes they met at the boardinghouse, and he was almost like when he'd courted her. Prowling the stores, she began to think maybe he saw her a little differently now — less like a horse or trained dog. Maybe she'd done right not to apologize any more than she had. A wife was to be obedient, but maybe there was a limit.

She admired lacquered boxes from Japan, silks and bracelets from China, checkered wool from Flanders, scissors, needles and knives from England. Mellus & Howard was truly a fine store. Leaving, she found a folded newspaper on a bench outside the door. She opened *The California Star*, Sam Brannan, Publisher, and read: "YERBA BUENA NOW SAN FRANCISCO." The front page told of the winning of the Mexican War in the town of the Angels, *Pueblo de los Angeles*. On page two, scattered among advertisements, articles told of the opening of new businesses by Mormon proprietors, and a few sentences about how Lansford Hastings was available to help people win title to their land. Then an editorial by Brannan gave reasons why the San Francisco Mormons should convince Brigham Young to bring the "saints" to San Francisco. She recalled that Mr. Rhoads had failed to get them to settle the Cosumnes area, but Brannan was more persuasive. Maybe he would prevail.

On the back page she didn't read the article about President Polk and General Zachary Taylor. Instead she wondered if Abraham Lincoln had won his seat in Congress. Nobody cared about that in California.

She returned the paper to the bench and walked up Market Street, passing a saloon partitioned from a shop by a length of red calico. BARBER AND HORSE DOCTOR, the placard stated. Beneath that, a smaller sign proclaimed: "New Battery Device Cures Ague." The proprietor, who had tightly bound a man into a chair, placed his boot against the patient's chest, told him to open wide, and clamped a pair of pliers on a back tooth. She hurried on.

The next store had wooden walls and a canvas roof. The sign said: "Mr. Green, Proprietor." Inside a man pried the lid from a wooden box. Sugarcane, the same as she'd seen at Daylor's trading post, was packed inside. With a smile Mr. Green handed her a joint. "From the Sandwich Islands," he told her.

"Thank you kindly. I'm just looking at the wares, if that's all right."

"Go right ahead, miss." He went back to his boxes.

Gnawing the cane and admiring the goods, her eye was taken by a familiar-looking young woman who was entering the store. She wore a smart black jacket with matching skirt and checkered shirtwaist. Her black bonnet hid her face, and she glanced away, as if a crate of oranges had suddenly seized her attention.

Moving to a better angle, Elitha realized it was Sarah Murphy Foster, one of the seven snowshoers who got through — Mary's older sister. Elitha removed the spent cane from her mouth, dropped it on the dirt floor, and approached.

Under the soft light through the canvas, the young woman's cheeks could have been made of white porcelain, and her jet black hair hung beneath her bonnet in springy corkscrews. *Black Irish*, Tamsen would have said. When she saw Elitha, a shadow passed across her luminous blue eyes — so like Mary's — and her voice was rough. "You're a Donner, ain't you?" She hadn't been at the ceremony.

"Yes, Elitha Donner. Aren't you Mary Murphy's sister?"

"Yup." She looked prosperous. Mr. Foster had done well here.

When nothing more came, Elitha said, "Mary and I were friends on the crossing. I'd sure like to see her again, and would be obliged if you got word to her. I'm married to Perry McCoon now, living at his place out on the Cosumnes River, past Sheldon and Daylor's." Most people in California knew them.

Sarah didn't let on if she did. "I don't never see my sister now." Her voice was husky, her eyes veiled by her lashes. She seemed eager to leave.

Awkward in a silence screaming of the grim connection between them, Elitha ventured, "So sorry about Lem. He was a good boy."

Sarah turned away and dabbed at her eyes with a handkerchief, which she pulled from her jacket pocket.

Suddenly Elitha remembered somebody at Johnson's ranch saying Sarah never wanted to be reminded of the crossing ever again. Wishing she could reel back her words, she said, "I'm awfully sorry. I should have known not to speak of it." Seeing no change, she put her hand on the dark fabric of Sarah's arm and added, "You did no wrong. People shouldn't judge us."

She turned, bright ribbons of moisture streaking the porcelain. "They judge you too?"

Elitha nodded, not caring about the misunderstanding. What did it matter? A high-combed, mantilla-draped Spanish woman was approaching the oranges. Elitha whispered, "Let's go outside." She led her up a dusty trail toward the boardinghouse and stopped at a stack of adobe bricks that would soon be part of a building. They sat on the bricks. Three men rode by on horses, but most of the people must have been behind walls eating their noon dinners. The streets were quiet and ships bobbed on the choppy water.

"Thank you for talking to me," Elitha said.

Sarah, looking intently at the blue crystals at Elitha's throat, said, "People can be downright mean." Her cheeks were drying in the wind.

"My husband gave this to me," Elitha said touching the pendant.

"I know. I got it off an Injun. Gave it to Mr. McCoon."

So, she'd met Perry at Johnson's! "Did the Indian give it to you?"

"No. He was dead."

Dead. On the prairie they had passed dead Indians left on scaffolds for the vultures. Taking objects from such corpses had been strictly forbidden because the

Indians believed it would cause dangerous spirits to be visited upon Indian and white alike. Nevertheless, Lewis Keseberg had taken a buffalo robe from such a scaffold, and Mr. Reed had nearly banished him from the wagon train. All across the continent the bad blood between them had never abated. "Where did you find the Indian?" Elitha asked.

"The guides. Don't you remember?" Sarah stood up and glared down at Elitha, and it seemed the fragile bond of friendship was broken. "Mr. Stanton brought them from Mr. Sutter's fort. Or maybe you Donners was too far behind to notice."

"I didn't mean anything by it." She got up, for it was clear Sarah would leave.

Sarah looked at her with terrible thoroughness and said, "Well, if you must know, my husband shot them. Now I never want to hear no more about it. They was about to die anyhow, and we was starvin!" She wiped an eye with her handkerchief.

"I didn't mean to pry." Deflated and more than a little horrified at this turn of events, she spotted Perry's swagger far in the distance, coming toward the boardinghouse, and absently touched the crystals at her throat. They were supposed to be charmed. For good or ill she didn't know, but they had come from a dead Indian, a murdered Indian. *Killed for meat, like Tamsen.*

Anger dropped from Sarah's face as quickly as it had appeared, and a monologue spilled from her about blizzards and being lost and men freezing to death. As Perry drew near, her pace accelerated. They had kept track of the meat, she said, so nobody would eat their kin. "The Indians was grubbing for roots and acorns. I didn't want him to shoot. Harriet tried to stop him too, but he didn't pay no mind." She turned her face away as Perry arrived at the boardinghouse thirty yards away. He put his boot on the step and looked Elitha a question.

She ignored it. "Do you know where those Indians were from?"

"Well, Sutter sent them. But they was no guides atall. Didn't even speak English. Lewis and Salvador their names was. Salvador means Savior in Spanish, ain't that funny?" She looked at Elitha with a blend of apology and timidity. "I'm jumpy lately. Didn't mean to be rude." She touched her arm. "You know, if it hadn't a been for that Injun meat, we'd of starved for sure. Then nobody woulda got through, would they?"

Sarah was right; Elitha too had been saved by the flesh of an Indian named Savior. Indian Mary's brother? She got a prickly feeling, realizing that there might indeed have been a connection between her and Rancho Sacayak before she married Perry. The blue crystals at her neck felt warm and heavy. Good luck, or bad? Indians seemed to believe in magic that could go either way, depending on a person's "strength" or "power." She recalled Mary's reaction when the baby had touched the crystals, and thought of Lewis Keseberg taking the buffalo robe off a dead Indian. He certainly hadn't purified himself. It felt like a bottomless well of confusion, no explanations fathomable. Salvador saving the Donner Party, Indian Mary healing her, all tangled up with condor feathers and magic crystals.

Sarah was saying, "It tasted better than white meat." A confidential tone.

It came so unexpected that Elitha couldn't hide her feeling of shock and revulsion.

Sarah stiffened. "Well, what difference does it make? It's alright if it tastes bad? Sinful if it tastes better? We done no wrong, Elitha Donner. Jes wanted to live."

Watching the Nordic proprietress come out the door to join Perry on the stoop, Elitha wasn't sure about anything any more. "Tell your sister I wish she'd come visit."

Sarah was already whisking her expensive skirts up the lane.

Shaken, Elitha went to Perry, who was humbling himself before Mrs. Johanson —the backs of her hands on her waist, her color high.

He flashed her a glorious smile. "Next time I'll pay ye, I vow."

She dropped her hands to her sides. "Next time den? Shore?"

"Me solemn oath." The look on his face was a kiss, dark lashes jutting toward her. Then he turned to Elitha and clucked as one would at a horse, "Hurry girl, or we'll miss the boat."

Relieved to be going at last, she dashed inside, fetched her bag and followed him at a half-trot. Then it came to her. The scroll didn't project from any of his pockets. "Where's the deed?" she asked.

His silence answered.

She stopped walking. "You lost it gambling." She felt an odd sense of fate, as if she'd known all along that this would happen.

He turned to her, his face ugly. "Git to the boat, or I vow — " He stepped toward her with a raised hand.

She hurried on, humiliation and disappointment mounting with each step. She tried to sound adult, to keep what she was asking from cracking apart. "I don't see what good the paper is to those men. Their names aren't on it." *To the children of George and Jacob Donner*. It was like a sacred trust, another one.

Tight-lipped, he strode beside her. "I signed it over."

"But they gave it to me, for all of us, and I didn't sign it over." She didn't know much about property papers.

"Forget, did ye? Ye be my wife."

"I didn't know you could sign it over is all." She felt the melon hurting her esophagus again — he was treating her like a disobedient child. Glancing at the windswept hills of San Francisco, she told herself the land wasn't worth much anyway; it was the principle that hurt. A gawking row of frightfully unkempt men looked up at her as she passed the tent saloon.

She looked beyond, to the *DICE MI NANA* nosed to the mole. A man other than Keseberg was directing the loading of goods. She felt a little better.

"Win the ground back next time, I will," Perry tossed back at her as he stepped toward the captain.

She sighed, doubting that. The scroll with the red ribbon had vanished like a dream, and maybe because of a curse. But that, she realized with a shake of her head to clear the cobwebs, was whole-hog Indian superstition. This was the nineteenth century! Tamsen had taught her the scientific way and syllogisms of logic like: all wheat is grain, but all grain isn't wheat. Logic was the way of the white man, of progress. If she let herself drown in superstition, she'd be lost. The Donner Party got trapped in the snow because Mr. Reed and Pa followed Lansford Hastings' untested route. Period. Half of them survived because they ate what they had to, and because of the bravery of men like John Rhoads. Period. She had married a man whose ways were different than she'd hoped, but that happened to girls all the time and had nothing to do with feathers and crystals. It had everything to do with making the best of things. Soon she would be caring for her sisters under her roof. And if Perry stopped her? Well, that wouldn't be bad luck, but something else entirely. She'd figure out then what to do about it.

43

Twelve days later they disembarked at Sutter's Embarcadero, the water being too low to navigate the American upstream. Keseberg, Elitha knew, was not at the fort — they had passed the *Sacramento* going the other way three days out. She and Perry and Joe House, the only other passenger, waved good-bye to the skipper of the *Dice mi Nana* and walked the trail through brown cattails that looked as exhausted and untidy as she felt. Soon the trail stretched east like a plumb line across the flat plain. It was three miles to Sutter's Fort, past the farm of the French woman — the man apparently back from the war; the couple and their children both waved from the field.

It being late in the day, all three were hungry and glad it was Mr. Sutter's habit to host anyone who came through the fort. But as they rounded the gate and approached the stairs, she stopped to read a paper nailed to the railing.

> NOTICE: My wife Mary Johnson, having left my bed and board, I would inform the public that I will not be accountable for any debts of her contracting after this date. William Johnson, Bear Creek. Nov. 20, 1847.

Mary Murphy had actually left Mr. Johnson! Where was she now? And who on earth had written this? Surely not that horrible, ignorant man. In confusion she glanced at Perry, who had looked at the notice only a few seconds and was now half the way up the stairs. Mr. Johnson was a friend of his, yet Perry had seemed uninterested. Mr. House chuckled beside her, then clumped up the stairs ahead of her.

Inside, she wasn't surprised to see Mr. Johnson and a colorful assortment of men already eating, Mr. Sutter at the head of the table. They all smelled bad, but Johnson was the worst. His gray beard was as long and matted as she remembered, and his bad eye still wandered. She watched in fascinated loathing as he got up and clapped Perry on the back, and Perry said nothing about Mary leaving.

In his turn, Mr. House said, "Looks like white women ain't 'ny easier to keep than Injuns." Men snickered and looked with open speculation at Elitha, who was seating herself. Perry seemed like a boy left out of a joke.

"The whimperin bitch," Johnson replied. "Ifn she wants the slimy Frenchy, she can have him."

She left him for another man. Perry sat down looking at Mr. Johnson as if the Oracle of Delphi were carved on his forehead.

Mr. House said, "You lookin to git another white woman?"

Mr. Johnson's red lips opened and a pink tongue flapped through the hole in his beard. "Headin to the Sandwich Islands, cause them Kanaka wahinees is acallin this old tar."

"What about your ranch?"

Mr. Sutter said Sebastian Keyser was buying out the rest of the grant, but Elitha was looking at Perry, absolutely sure he didn't know how to read. He had lied to her about it. A bald-faced lie.

Two Indian women brought more food, and the men talked endlessly about the war, the Pathfinder's latest actions, and something about General Kearny, but she was tired and barely remembered that the Pathfinder's real name was John Frémont. They speculated with liquor-loosened tongues about California becoming a slave state.

"We could get the black niggers to work on our ranches."

"Hell, they cost a fortune. Sides, our niggers are free."

"And the woolly heads don't work near as hard as Injuns."

"Yeah, but you gotta figger, Injuns eat like horses and die like flies."

Sutter gulped liquor and reminded them a lady was present.

Casting her the briefest glance, a man named Zeke Merritt growled, "We shoulda had the *cojones* to keep our skins free under the Bear Flag."

Perry leaned forward on his elbows. "But I'll wager the cap'n gits to be gov'nor under the stars and stripes."

Sutter blushed like a girl at the compliment, but Mr. Merritt pounded his fist on the table. "Well damnation man, he coulda been KING if we'd kept Frémont the hell outa here!"

Mr. Johnson rammed a hunk of meat into his mouth and chewed hugely, his cockeyed glance dragging over Elitha. She thought, *Good for Mary.*

"That's right," a man said, "Now Frémont's claiming to be governor."

"Not if he's court-martialed," came the rejoinder.

She couldn't stand a minute more. Excusing herself, she went alone to the adobe room and lay on the flattened wood shavings. A team of wild horses couldn't stop her from getting to her sisters in the morning, even if she had to walk there alone. With that thought, she fell asleep.

Up and up she circled, higher and higher on a mountain peak. When the wagon arrived she saw a log cabin and felt uneasy, because it appeared to be a house with no windows. The driver said he'd wait. Cautiously she opened the cabin door. But the room was glowing with soft gaslight and filled with people holding crystal goblets of red wine, as if a friendly party were underway. She saw Pa and Tamsen looking happy and healthy, visiting and smiling. Pa looked up and came toward her through the crowd, and in the link of their gazes she felt cherished. Tamsen came over and introduced Elitha all around. The people spoke to her in the manner of beloved aunts and uncles, though she'd never seen them before. Accepting a glass of wine, she said, "A pity you have no windows. It wastes a view from the mountaintop."

The murmur of talk quieted. People stepped back from a draped wall, and two women began to draw the curtains. Pa cupped her elbow in a steadying way, and she watched as a floor-to-ceiling grid of window panes was revealed, but instead of sky and trees, she saw a solid wall of dirt. Brown earth, with tiny air spaces, as if a battalion of men had recently shoveled it up against the windows. The realization hit. *The cabin was buried.* The people, including Pa and Tamsen, showed no sadness for themselves, but looked at her with enormous kindness and commiseration.

The women drew the drapes over the windows again, and the friendly buzz of conversation resumed. Pa turned to her, his voice deep and steady. "Elitha lamb, my only sorrow is not being able to talk to you."

She opened her eyes, Perry snoring beside her. The first gray light of dawn made a hard rectangle at the doorway, but she felt oddly peaceful. She had seen the other side. Life after death was different than what she'd been taught. The dead couldn't see out, but were surrounded by souls of compassion and love, and were having a good time! She couldn't wait to tell Leanna.

Like a pastel wash over an inked scene, the peaceful feeling stayed with her through breakfast in Sutter's quarters, and afterwards. It lingered when she and Perry forded the river on Paint, heading up the trail toward Rancho del Paso, leading a borrowed horse. She could hardly believe he was calmly riding to the

Brunner's place without excuse, without a word of protest.

Not wanting to spoil it with anything he might misconstrue, she said only, "Thank you very much, Perry."

He was so quiet she wondered if he'd heard. Then he said — his breath warm on her neck — "Elitha, I did bad to hit ye, there in Yerb — San Francisco." He cleared his throat like he had a wad of cloth stuck in it. "I shouldn'ta done it and I hopes ye don't get notions bout leavin me."

Mary Murphy had made an impression! The last thing Elitha had expected was an apology, yet it somehow seemed perfectly natural in the peaceful aura of the dream, and the fact that she was drawing near to her sisters — five months since she'd seen them. It seemed that everything was connected, but in a good way — and not by logic either. Maybe this feeling was a little bit what Indian Mary meant by power.

"I'm not leaving you, Perry," she said, but something made her add, "Not with you saying you shouldn't have done it."

"I couldn't help meself. Hit was like a dark shade acomin over me and tellin me a man gots to beat a woman to make her . . . I needs ye, Elitha. You be the one wot can change this mean ole tar into a right gentleman."

She knew a hidden part of him had opened, and wouldn't stay open for long. And who was she to cast blame? Hadn't she felt an uncontrollable monster rear up in her and try to kill Lewis Keseberg? Some things weren't to be explained by logic. "Perry, your saying that makes me feel like we did right to get married."

"We did at that, lass," he said patting her thigh. And about losin the papers, I'll make it up to ye, I will. A bad run o' luck I was 'avin, is all. Never saw it so bad in all me livin days."

"Perry, I need to tell you I'm sorry I jumped on Keseberg like I did. It must have shamed you." They were approaching a man guiding a handplow behind a mule, and she wanted to get this out. "I've been meanin to ask if he said anything about the quilt?"

"Nay, sorry lass. But 'e said Fallon le Gros went back up. Turned around right after they brought Keseberg down. So 'e thinks that big bastard 'elped himself. Then, not a fortnight after, General Kearny and Sam Brannan and a bunch of military men marched back through, turnin everything over. Neptune's bones, ent a chance in Hades a farthing's left anywhere there abouts, an' those men ent daft enough to breathe a word of it either, or write it in their reports."

It looked like Dan Rhoads ahead, but she had one more thing to say. "I'll teach you to read if you like." A necessary skill for a gentleman.

She felt him release his breath — exasperated? She hoped she hadn't closed him up again. But after a moment he said, "Ent about to learn letters, Elitha. Tried before."

"But — "

"Bill Daylor can't read, and he runs his store shipshape. Now if a man can run a store without letters, 'e can run cattle." He sounded determined, and she saw that it really was Dan Rhoads they were approaching — John Rhoads' brother.

"How about signing your name? Can you do that?"

"Now I might can learn that, with a little 'elp."

"Good. We'll start there."

"Howdy," said Dan Rhoads, whoaing the mule.

"Tearin up God's green earth be ye?" Perry grinned.

Dan Rhoads smiled. "Best I can. Plantin winter wheat for Mr. Sinclair." He wiped a streak of dirt across his brow — she remembering how weakened by hunger he had been when he'd gone on to the valley early. Now he was working to put aside money to buy land of his own, Catherine had said.

He gave directions, and in two more miles they were approaching the Brunner farm. She saw a neat frame house — maybe four rooms — and fences, and realized with a pang that she would be taking the girls into worse circumstances. Then she saw them running toward the horse.

"Big Sister, Big Sister!" they called, holding up their skirts — Georgia and Frances ahead, little Ellie trailing with a barking dog. Where was Leanna?

She slid off the moving horse and hit the ground laughing. The dog barked in her ear and she sat hugging all three girls. The dog was so noisy she couldn't ask about Leanna. Perry rode ahead to the house. She got up and enjoyed being pulled along by the bubbling, laughing girls, all neat and clean in new frocks. *Well cared for.* She couldn't answer all the questions flying at her. "Yes, silly, we have a house at the ranch. No, no children, except Indians."

When she got to the house, Perry was leaning on the doorframe. She passed by him as she entered, curtseying to Mrs. Brunner, but intensely aware of the indoor fireplace and adjoining rooms with wooden doors. *Much better house.* Now that the girls were standing still, she saw the healthy roses in their cheeks. "Why, you three put on flesh!" she said, "Especially you Georgia. Where's Leanna?"

The answer came from Mrs. Brunner — smaller and older than she remembered, her hair drawn into a severe white-streaked bun.

"She vorks on a farm, far away." She flapped her wrist toward a framed daguerrotype on the whitewashed wall.

"Where? We'll have to get her." Leanna would be thirteen now and Elitha was anxious to introduce her to Indian Mary.

A balding man with a drooping handlebar mustache and a full gray beard stepped through the door, giving Perry what looked like a meaningful glance. "Not possible," he said. "Too far avay. Frau Rotweiler needs her."

The room seemed cramped with so many people, although it was larger than Perry's entire adobe. Panic pricked her. If she didn't take them now, they'd all be working in far-flung places and excuses would be given as to why she couldn't have them. She used her motherly voice. "Now get your things and we'll all ride to the ranch." Searching each pair of eyes, two pair brown, one blue, she detected resistance.

Turning to Mrs. Brunner, she said, "I'll help them pack."

Mrs. Brunner said, "Day not vant go."

Dumbfounded at that, Elitha saw Mr. Brunner give Perry a look. Perry said, "Step smart lass, there's weather brewin." To Mr. Brunner he said, "I'll leave the mare with ye. Be pleased if ye'd taik er back to the cap'n."

The row of small faces before her wore troubled adult expressions, and no denials came from them. "Please, Mr. and Mrs. Brunner," she said, "I promised Ma I'd care for them. We Donners need to be together."

The girls looked up at the woman. Fearfully? Asking permission?

With a helpless shrug Mrs. Brunner opened her palms. "I not schtop dem." Peering down at the girls: "Iss so, *klein mädele*? Grandma schtop you?"

Georgia, Frances and Ellie exchanged glances, then slowly shook their braids, saying in practiced unison, "*Nein* Grandma."

Mrs. Brunner tilted her bun toward Elitha, all the while holding them with a fierce eye, "You vant go with diss one?"

"No Grandma," came the unison monotone.

Baffled, wishing to talk to each one alone, Elitha knelt, took Ellie's hand and said, "I've been missing you." She petted back the fine dark hair around her face. The elf hadn't grown taller, but was padded now. "Won't you come keep me company? I am SO lonely on the ranch, with Perry out with the Indians all day." She glanced at him, his arms folded, boots crossed as he leaned on the doorframe. No help there.

Mrs. Brunner nodded at Ellie. "Dot one go maybe."

Ellie nuzzled her velvet cheek against Elitha's. "I'll come, Big Sister."

"Oh, thank you Baby." She swallowed and blinked back tears as she hugged Ellie, then pushed her away. "Now run get your things." She saw Georgia and Frances locked in Mrs. Brunner's gaze. Afraid?

Recalling Sarah Daylor saying how much the girls helped the Brunners, she gripped Georgia's thin hand and turned to Mrs. Brunner. "Surely you can find a hired girl?" But hired girls were paid and her sisters worked for nothing. And besides, Mr. Miller was giving the Brunners Donner money as long as they lived in the house, or was supposed to be. Elitha didn't trust him. And she knew she shouldn't be thinking it, but she wondered whether Perry was somehow involved in a scheme with Mr. Miller.

As she turned to him, his hand clamped on her upper arm. "We'd best be on the trail," he said. Trial. "Bring the young one." To the Brunners he added, "We thanks ye kindly," and pulled Elitha out the door, Ellie and the others following.

She kissed Georgia and Frances, mounted the horse, then leaned down from the big Spanish saddle and lifted Ellie by her tiny hands, one of which gripped Tamsen's silk stocking, and put the child in her lap. Frances and Georgia called good-bye as the horse plodded away from the farm. A warm tear crawled down her cheek — so many tears in the last six months! It was a wonder she had any left. She twisted around to wave, and saw Mr. and Mrs. Brunner like shadows in the window. Chickens clucked and a young pig sniffed in the dirt.

"Good-bye," Ellie sang out. Elitha hoped she'd done the right thing to separate her from the others, to take her to a house with no indoor cooking, and winter coming.

What would Pa and Tamsen say? *Do your best.* She had. Hugging Ellie, who gripped the silk stocking as if her life depended on it, she swallowed the disappointment about Leanna and vowed she'd do well by Ellie. After all, most things didn't work out the way people expected. Pa didn't expect to die before getting to California. Tamsen didn't expect to be murdered, and the Citizens Committee didn't expect Perry to lose the deed.

They hadn't gone far before the sky clabbered up and wind whipped the ocean of grass. The days were short now, the air chill. Ellie whined, "My FEET hurt."

The dreaded words. Elitha's toes hurt too, more than they should have, a legacy of the frostbite — perhaps a lifelong reminder whenever it got cold. She squeezed Ellie and said, "You'll be fine. Old man winter's in the air, that's all. But don't worry, it never snows in California, except in the high mountains."

III

Golden Dreams

44

Coyote rises, stretches his forelegs before him, pleasantly cracking his back, then trots through the trees. He hears the voices of María and Elitha, and stops to listen. Elitha brings something from the pocket of her blue dress, holds it on her palm and asks, "Do you know what this is?" Coyote sees the glint of gold in the late November sun.

María takes the twisted shape, bites it, and hands it back. "*Españoles* call it *oro.*" The *Americano* word hides in her mind.

"Does that mean gold?"

"Yes."

"Where did it come from?" Elitha thinks someone may have dropped it in the river.

María smiles, thinking this is a joke. "I not find. You find." Her expression is playful. Coyote thinks this might prove amusing.

"Does Mr. Daylor take gold in exchange for goods?" Elitha is not playful.

"Señor Daylo take skins, not rocks." She is trying not to smile.

"Rocks?" Her little sister is pretending to mother Billy, who is running free of his bikoos. "Wouldn't Mr. Daylor accept gold? It is very valuable, if that's what this is."

"Come," María says, "We talk to Father. He will know." She walks toward the village.

Elitha hesitates, but Mary is well up the trail with the nugget, so she follows, as do Ellie and Billy. Coyote trots along behind, pleased to have nosed out something fun.

Naked Indian women sit in the sun beside their mud-plastered huts. Some are working with feathers in their laps, others powdering herbs in the mortar holes. Children play around the cha'kas. María asks for Grizzly Hair and a boy is dispatched.

Elitha stands in awe of the village, the people, the houses and cha'kas packed with acorns, the dancehouse dug into a hill. Ellie grins conspiratorially, enjoying fooling Perry McCoon, who has told them both to stay away from this place. Grizzly Hair emerges from the sweathouse and Elitha stares wonderingly at his naked height and fleshiness, at the bones piercing his topknot and the string of bear claws around his neck, each claw as long as a man's finger. "Palaver," he says gesturing to the ridge overlooking the river, more patient than Coyote would be if his nap were interrupted.

The two young women sit for talking. Billy and Ellie are happily feinting and dodging with the browner children. Coyote, smiling in his luxuriant winter fur, finds a little shade beneath my branches, which spread over half the village. He sits in the fallen leaves, able to see and hear the humans, though they no longer see him as they did when the world was new. "Now they'll go crazy," he says to himself.

"Do not forget," I say, "my son is a cautious man."

Startled to all fours, Coyote jerks his head around, then, remembering that I am here, snorts indignantly and circles three times. He wishes the spirits would stop scaring him with their infernal commentary from random bushes, rocks, baskets — you never know what. Embarrassed beneath his gruff exterior, he plops down again, huffing, "Your son is no different than the others."

I sigh, for it is true. He wants wealth for trade like everyone else. From my lofty vantage I see my lovely granddaughter hand him the gold nugget. People are seating themselves where they can hear, and small brown hands are touching the silky hair falling from Elitha's bonnet. "It is long like a man's," murmurs a child. Ellie dashes happily through poison oak.

Elitha feels enlarged by this pow-wow with the Indian chief who refused to find gold for her husband. She recalls Tamsen's tale of Delaware, a majestic chief who helped white men wage war. Captain Juan appears to be a similarly grand savage, though he is naked and that, to her, is a disturbing condition. But she forgets about it, seeing the fond expression in his face as he looks at his daughter, and she is sad to know her own father will never again look at her that way, and never again see the perfection of a sunny autumn day and a long wedge of geese gabbling overhead.

"What does she want with this gold," Grizzly Hair asks, looking at the nugget. But before she can answer, the sound of Pedro's horse approaches and all heads turn.

Dismounting, Pedro looks lovingly at María and feels a slight pique that Elitha McCoon is present. María runs and hugs him, petting his reddish sideburns and mustache. Powerful surges of human emotion pump through him as he holds her to him.

Elitha sees this is the same Spaniard who traded insults with her man, the one Perry said would tell all the Spaniards on the coast. She wants to get the gold back from the chief and leave, but even so it is too late. Perry might learn that she showed the nugget to Indians and a Spaniard before mentioning it to him. She struggles in her mind to fashion a falsehood to explain it.

Pedro pulls himself reluctantly from his beloved and sweeps his hat before Elitha. "Señora McCoon," he says, "the pleasure is mine to see you again." But he is not pleased. He hopes to complete his marriage to María, hopes her parents will accept his gift and will warm to him one gift at a time, as winter changes to summer one day at a time. He is sorry the McCoons didn't stay in Yerba Buena for good or move to Dry Creek. Maintaining an expression of proud politeness, he steps to his horse and retrieves a Nipponese lacquered box from his saddle bag. The villagers say ohhh as he extends it to Grizzly Hair.

Grizzly Hair thinks a man who stole the condor robe would be unlikely to bring so many presents, and maybe Pedro Valdez is innocent after all. But Etumu's expression says no and a wife's opinion is important. Grizzly Hair sets the box on the ground, deciding to finish the other matter first, for Elitha is looking at him with impatience. He opens his hand, revealing the elongated lump of gold and asks why it is of interest.

María invites Pedro to sit beside her and talks Spanish for her father's sake. "Señora McCoon wants to know if Señor Daylo accepts such gold in exchange for goods."

"Why would he do that?" The corners of Grizzly Hair's mouth twitch into a tiny smile, and though Pedro is hurt that his present merited no comment, he is amazed at the size of the twisted nugget and confused by the response and the bemused smile.

"Elitha says gold is valuable," María explains.

The smile fades. Grizzly Hair masks his shock, and his mind races. That would explain some odd behavior, he thinks, like Perrimacoo begging the *umne* to leave home and gather gold for him. And long ago the funny old black hat he and others had captured didn't run, though they slapped his bare buttocks and he was clearly afraid. Instead he looked longingly after the hatful of gold they threw in a berry patch. And later the excitable Russian ally, whose gun was supposed to kill the cannoneers in the war against the black hats, kidnapped Etumu instead and deserted on the eve of last battle. The quiver full of golden musket balls was what he wanted, Grizzly Hair realizes now. The Russian wanted it more than winning the war; maybe he wanted her to guide him to the source of the gold. Yes, Grizzly Hair realizes, gold is valuable to the new people. It explains much. "Ask Señor Valdez," he says, handing the nugget to him. "He knows the value of gold to the *Americanos*."

It is heavy in Pedro's palm but it drops even more heavily into the quiet pool of his mind, rippling outward to the shores of the known world. He realizes Old Pepe was right. Gold lies in many places in these foothills, and the Indians knew about it all along. They simply didn't value it. The ripples move a generation back, to his grandfather Don Pedro Fages exploring for gold around *Indios*' necks and in their huts. He never imagined they would leave it lying where God put it. Pedro has difficulty breathing, because he realizes Spain lost Alta California for want of knowing what Old Pepe knew. His voice is rough with emotion. "The Spanish king would have sailed a large armada into Yerba Buena and Monterey if he had known. Nothing would have been spared."

Coyote lets out a joyful yippity-yip.

"Hush," I say, "I can't hear."

"What is he saying?" asks Elitha, tired of the Spanish, which she cannot understand.

María sees moisture brightening her beloved Pedro's eyes, and waits politely for him to finish. In an entranced monotone he says, "No wonder my father went crazy." A tear runs down his proud face, but he does not wipe it, preferring his sad betrayal of his father to be fully expressed.

Grizzly Hair is quick to see Pedro's emotion. "I do not understand. Gold reminds you of your father?"

Pedro snaps out of his trance. "Yes. Please excuse me. He was a fine man once." Seeing no reason to keep the secret from the girl he loves, or her father, or her people, he offers his words like jewels. "Gold is the most valuable metal. All trade is measured against it. The King of Spain would never have forfeited this land if he had known of the gold."

María turns matter-of-factly to Elitha. "Señor Valdez says gold is very valuable." Then, glancing at her father — the words clearly striking him hard — it hits her too. Gold lies all along the river. Grandmother Howchia once collected a basket full of pleasing shapes, which Father took to the war against the black hats for melting into balls.

But Elitha is irritated. "Of course it is valuable. What I asked was, is this really gold? And what would Mr. Daylor give me for it? She is tired of the foreign talk, every utterance followed by long pauses and staring into space. She is sorry she showed the gold to Indian Mary, and the Spaniard makes her anxious. Coyote smiles.

María translates for Grizzly Hair, who nods at the nugget in Pedro's hand. "This is gold. Its soul is very dense. Señor Valdez will say what it can be traded for. I do not know. But I do know the Russians would have fought the *Españoles* for so much gold."

"Maybe. But Spain would have defeated Russia," Pedro says.

Grizzly Hair doubts that. "When I was young I went to the Russian town on the western sea. I saw their many big guns and a room full of guns with long knives. I was told they had many more across the western sea, and their big boats travel fast. You black hats had not so many guns."

Elitha's frustration peaks. To Indian Mary she says, "I asked a question!"

María says to Pedro, "She wants to know the value of this gold."

In English Pedro says to Elitha, "It is a pretty piece. If it is pure, maybe you could buy six excellent horses. Maybe more."

As María translates, Grizzly Hair's thoughts tumble back to the war, the hundreds who died from the Spanish cannon that chewed through the stockades, all because the Russian was not there to shoot them with the golden balls. Coyote would enjoy that, he thinks.

"You bet," says Coyote, circling into a cozier nest.

But then Grizzly Hair realizes his united *Indios* succeeded in stopping the *Españoles* from coming up the rivers to capture people, and that prevented them from finding gold. Just as Grizzly Hair stopped the funny old man, and the bear stopped the Russian from returning to his people with the gold, all was done for another purpose. And the gold remained hidden in the fastness of *Indio* indifference.

Heh heh heh heh, Coyote pants.

Elitha is thinking she could buy a team and a wagon, but who would she buy them from in this wilderness? And besides, what would Perry do? She decides to put the nugget back in its hiding place for now, because he is a gambler. She hopes neither the Spaniard nor the Indians will mention it to him, but has an unpleasant feeling they will.

Pedro asks, "Where did this gold come from?"

"She found it." Grizzly Hair inclines his plume toward Elitha. Mentally he is shaping his next oration, in which he will ask his people to collect gold, to amass huge amounts so they will be trade rich.

In English Pedro asks, "Where did you find it?" He is quite sure it came from the riverbed, and fears McCoon will never leave if he thinks he owns a gold mine.

Elitha looks at the yellow lump in his palm and says, "I'd rather not say." She hopes he will think it came from Dry Creek.

Incensed, Pedro stands, head lifted. "It is all the same to me, Señora McCoon. Gold is of no interest to me." In Spanish, to keep it from Elitha's ears, he asks Grizzly Hair, "Have you seen gold in the river around here?"

His eyes skim over Pedro as if in passing. *Much gold,* he recalls, *enough that my wife nearly lost her life over it.* Despite his daughter's love for this man, he thinks he should be careful. Señor McCoon might bring Captain Sutter with his wheeled guns and armed men. Above all a headman must protect his people. Instead of letting the silence speak, he answers vaguely, "Some." Then, curious about this man who courts his daughter, he asks, "You say gold is valuable, yet you do not seek it?" He presents the glassy expression of a well-bred leader, I am proud to see.

Pedro glances at the big Indian he hopes to make his father-in-law and fears McCoon's ear notches will forever mark Sacayak cattle. Lost opportunities weigh on him, and he sits unhappily, one boot over the other, unconsciously rubbing the smooth gold between his fingers, wondering how to explain why gold-seeking is distasteful to him. Seeing Señora McCoon's impatience, he lets his Spanish flow in a languid stream:

"Captain Juan, I adore your daughter. More than anything in this life. I want my cattle grazing on these hills and my hacienda over there with my woman in it." He reaches for María's hand and uses the chief's Indian name, "Yu-seh-o-se-maiti, I want my children to be your grandchildren. You and I working together can produce thousands of cowhides — Spanish dollars they are called in the outer world — to be shipped through Yerba Buena. We will make a fortune from the lust of bulls. Cattle will be our gold. Your people will have much more than Perry McCoon gives them. Gold drives men crazy."

Grizzly Hair nods, recalling the crazy Russian and the crazy old black hat. He knows Pedro Valdez speaks true.

With a glance at Elitha's impatient face, Pedro continues, "My father scratched for gold in the hot sun. He cooked his brains, lost his eyesight, and when he claimed to have found a helmet full of it, he came home empty-handed as always. People called him *loco*. Gold does not excite me." He is glad to see Elitha rising.

María sees something in Grizzly Hair's eyes, and she alone notices the quickened pace of his tongue when he says, "I do not know this word, helmet."

"A metal hat to protect men in war," Pedro says, caressing María's hand.

"You are the old one's son then." Grizzly Hair reaches across and fingers a lock curling from beneath Pedro's hat brim. "Your father had hair of this color when he was young, and a missing ear." The helmet taken from the old man had saved Grizzly Hair's life in the second battle against the black hats. "The helmet has strong magic, but I lost it in the last battle."

A chain of connections snaps together in Pedro's mind. He is stunned. This *Indio* knew of his father's missing ear, his hair color, and the helmet. He had to be one of the demons who smashed Old Pepe's pride and stole his prized possession. An ocean swell lifts Pedro from *terra firma*. To hold footing and keep his voice from breaking, he looks steadily into Captain Juan's eyes and says, "You knew my father." *The father of my beloved María is the very Indian I once dreamed of dismembering.*

"Yes." Grizzly Hair says, and knows Pedro's honor demands retribution.

María is thrilled by the friendship between families. No longer will Proud Hawk be viewed as an enemy black hat. Her face shines like a spring day. "You knew his father!"

Grizzly Hair stares into space as he says, "I took his helmet."

Springtime flies from her face. The families are enemies, she thinks. No woman marries a man from an enemy family. Molok's black form swoops through her mind.

Anxious to relieve her, Grizzly Hair pats her woven cap and says, "Coyote played a trick on me is all."

Coyote lifts his smug muzzle.

Pedro looks at the Indian who sent Old Pepe to an earthly hell, but melts with love to see María's pained face, and wonders if there is indeed a curse.

Tired of the Spanish babble, Elitha swallows noisily to get Indian Mary's attention and rustles her skirts. "I don't think they are talking about the gold now, and I would like to have it back." Calling, "Come Ellie, we're leaving," she points to the gold.

So crushed is María, she hardly sees Elitha take the gold. Grizzly Hair watches the long mane of her fine brown hair sway out of sight against the back of her blue dress, the child trotting behind. Then he turns to the pair of crestfallen faces.

"Señor Valdez, the old woman María, who came here and taught my people the Spanish tongue and gave us knowledge of the *Españoles,* was your grandmother." He detects a hint of Old María in Pedro's brow. "I went to her house in San José to warn her when the war was to start, and saw that same old man sitting in her yard."

Pedro swallows in mute astonishment. It is not possible, he thinks. Grandmother María was captured as a child and lived only in Spanish settlements — on the coast.

Grizzly Hair places a hand on his daughter's shoulder, feeling her bewilderment. His voice is husky with remembering. "Old María saved my life with her good medicine after I escaped from the mission. Little One, you are named for her. She came with me to our home place and was a second mother to me after your grandmother died. All our people loved her. I wish you had known her."

If a spirit could weep I would now, recalling my joy when my son returned from the mission. Old María had indeed been a very good friend.

A storm of confusion swirls in María Howchia's mind. She cannot reconcile what has been said. "My name? After his grandmother? But you said you stole his father's helmet."

A dim memory rises from the ashes of Pedro's past, when he was a new recruit at the Presidio trying to distance himself from his family, not caring about the comings and goings of the independent old *India* Grandmother. His mother said she travelled to the interior, and he hadn't honored her enough to care. Yet, looking at Captain Juan's honest smile, he rides a wave of renewed hope despite the confusion. But why did Captain Juan treat old Pepe so badly if he honored Grandmother María?

Seeing Pedro's confusion, Grizzly Hair selects a morsel from his memory that only a good friend would know. "Your grandmother was once the woman of the Spanish hy-apo, *Comandante* Fages."

A concubine, Pedro corrects in his mind, but she considered herself his woman. "Sí. Don Pedro Fages, the first explorer of Alta California." Bewildered hope is rising in him. Captain Juan must be, he realizes, the war chief Grandmother María spoke highly about. He remembers that the *Indios* were valiant warriors, and he feels a strange pride that Captain Juan, father of his little poppy, was one of their principal leaders.

"*That* is the María you named me for!" María is saying, "The wise woman — his grandmother?" At a nod of Grizzly Hair's plume, joy flashes through her, fills all the tight, fearful places. Her life is unlocked. The families are indeed friends. If this had been known when Proud Hawk first astonished the village with his horsemanship, she never would have gone to Captain Sutter's bed or married Perrimacoo. She puts her arms around Pedro and kisses his rough side whiskers. Tears dampen both of their faces as she inhales his manly aroma, secure in the knowledge that her family, at last, will welcome him as a son-in-law.

Pedro strokes her and listens as Grizzly Hair says, "When we humiliated your father, I didn't know him. I owe you retribution. Name the goods that will return honor to your family." He adds, "My friends wanted to kill him. I asked them to release him."

Pedro looks into Grizzly Hair's eyes and hopes the older man understands the strong sentiment in his words, "*Muchas gracias, Capitán Juan.*" Turning to María's happy face, he can hardly remember the meaning of retribution, much less demand it. He could happily drown in her tears. Then he remembers. "*Por favor*, I want to marry your daughter. Please accept my marriage present. And perhaps you could make Señor McCoon leave this land."

Grizzly Hair inclines his head, considering. Of course he will accept Pedro as a son-in-law — he hands the lacquered box to Etumu, and she smiles. But retribution is paid in baskets and tools. To make Perrimacoo leave would be difficult because the *umne* enjoy eating the calves — one for every ten born in exchange for help raising them. And a hy-apo guides by consensus, not demands. Besides, Perrimacoo is the father of his only grandchild. A strong tie. But he says, "I will think how to accomplish this." He reaches across and claps Pedro's shoulder. "I will find a peaceful way."

Coyote rises and yawns with a disappointed whine, preferring stories that are filled with conflict and chaos. "Do not worry, Trickster," I say, "the gold will bring plenty of strife."

"Good." He cracks his back and trots away, and I am left to look upon my unsuspecting son and wish the lovers could forever gaze into each other's eyes as they do now, and the village were as eternal as the river.

45

So many redbud roots were gathered that scarcely enough were left on the nearby bushes. The days were chill now. Women threw deerskin capes over their shoulders, talking while the bone awls flew in their fingers, excited about all the goods they would get in trade for the gold they would wash in these baskets. Skillfully they curled the wiry roots around the guiding stays, making a new kind of vessel — broad, flat and nearly watertight.

On the final day of the Salmon Dance, Grizzly Hair had orated about Mission San José, telling the people how much can be achieved by doing the same thing at the same time. But this was not a mission. "You should stop when Father Sun is highest, so you can save plenty of light for hunting, sleeping, playing and storytelling. And no *padre* will take the product of your labor. We will put it all in the same basket. We will be trade rich."

Maria was proud of the way he guided the search for gold. Lines of young girls and boys squatted beside their mothers at the river's edge, swirling sand and water in big flat baskets until their feet grew numb. Some dug like foxes in places where grandfathers and grandmothers said gold was likely to lodge after bumping down the river from the time of the Ancients. They dug it from behind outcroppings all along the riverbank, and under the sand on rocky bottoms.

But despite Grizzly Hair's words, most of the family heads preferred to ride, rope and care for the cattle. Washing sand, they said, resembled the leaching of acorn meal and was therefore women's work.

In the sweathouse Falls-off-House pointed out, "The golden gravel has not been taken to Señor Daylo's yet and I doubt if it has any value."

"I agree with my brother," said Scorpion Trail. "We have tasted the calves. We know their value."

Running Quail said, "My wife wants me to continue herding Perrimacoo's cattle." A murmur of agreement sounded through the sweathouse. "But she will wash gold."

With his men speaking this way, it wouldn't be easy to drive out Perrimacoo, Grizzly Hair realized. Where was the assurance, the men asked, that Señor Valdez would give them as many calves as Señor McCoon? Where was the assurance, Grizzly Hair thought, that Pedro Valdez would get the land paper, even if Perrimacoo left. He didn't want violence. Grizzly Hair would wait until something occurred to him.

Each day when Father Sun was high, the women and children came with their gold to the family's u-macha and Etumu sat before the doorway holding out her large boiling basket for it. Later Grizzly Hair would inspect the level of gold in the basket and put it beside the central post. When it was full, he would take it to Señor Daylor's and return with iron tools, cloth, beads, horses, maybe even guns. Each evening talk of these goods crackled with the supper fires.

Then rain filled the sky and water rushed down from the mountains, widening the river, flooding the places where gold was found. The search stopped. "We will wait until the Second Grass Festival," Grizzly Hair told the people.

Maria had lain awake with her idea, listening to Etumu's steady breathing. It was entirely dark when she heard Grizzly Hair feel his way into the u-macha. He slept with the men in the sweathouse except when he wanted to couple with Mother. Sedge leaves rustled. "Father?" She whispered so as not to awaken Billy.

Grizzly Hair's voice came very deep. "You awake?"

"I think Perrimacoo might accept gold in trade for leaving."

"I have thought of that."

Intrigued, she waited. Etumu moaned. "We talk tomorrow," said Grizzly Hair in the same deep voice.

Good, Maria thought. The following day she would leave for Pedro's house, where she planned to remain for the O-se-mai-ti Big Time.

With the help of Indian Mary's skin washes, Ellie had recovered from a bad rash of poison oak. Now the little girl whined about her cold feet. Elitha's feet hurt too, although it wasn't nearly as cold as an ordinary Illinois winter. This morning frost had whitened the hills, and a skin of ice capped the bucket of water. Her toes and Ellie's were white as marbles.

"Frostbite weakened us last winter," she explained when they were all wrapped in their blankets. "Stay in bed tomorrow. Is your blanket warm enough?" She glanced from Ellie to Perry, who sat next to Elitha, hoping he wouldn't lose patience with the child. In the remnant of daylight from the two small windows, Elitha saw Ellie's face. About to cry.

Rising, patting her sister's hand, then limping to peer through the new glass, Elitha saw the blackening sky, which meant another rainstorm. It was late afternoon, but dark. She lit a candle. Bare branches clicked in the wind. Gusts of air came through the cracks in the door and underneath. The candle flickered and went out. Elitha had meant to go outside and lower supplies from the tree, but the sky opened again, throwing down veils of rain so thick she couldn't see the firepit.

"Well, I guess we won't have hot food." She felt for the metal box in the corner, pried it open and handed out crackers.

"Perry, tell us a story," Ellie begged. He'd told frightening tales of his childhood in London, and of intrigue and murder in exotic ports teeming with wild and vicious men.

"About the big green sea monster?" He sounded weary.

"Oo-ooh yes!" Ellie said.

"Nay. That's folly. Go to sleep." He gulped liquor, then sighed. Elitha could almost see him wipe his sleeve across his mouth.

Lying beside him with the blanket pulled to her chin, she gnawed a cracker and said, "You're not spending much time with the Indians lately." The rain drummed on the adobe, beating on the stone at the doorway.

"Ent no need now. The niggers know where the good grass is better'n I does, and wouldn't ye know. They're piling rocks along the steep banks to keep the stupid cattle from plunging to their deaths." A note of admiration rang in his slurred words.

"Well," she said to keep the conversation going, "I guess every cow that lives is one more to give birth, and they're looking for their one in ten."

"Aye lass, that they is." He gulped and expelled air.

"This must be paradise for cows," Elitha said. "They've got warm coats and green grass at Christmas." Despite night frosts, the grass grew a foot high in places. Sometimes in midday, when she went to the river for water, it felt like April.

He was quiet.

"You know," Elitha said, "yesterday I saw the strangest thing."

"Wha-at?" Ellie's tell-me-a-story tone.

"Down at the river. I heard voices, about noon I guess. I looked and there was a whole line of Indian women squatting along the shore rolling baskets in the water. Round and round." Indian Mary hadn't been among them. Where was she anyway?

"Washin their acorn mush," Perry said. "Ent ye never seen it, lass?"

"Not in such wide, flat baskets."

"Do it different ways, they does." His hand groped over her in the dark.

"Ellie's awake," she whispered.

"She don't know HOW to sleep," he growled, but left her alone.

In the morning Ellie's face was pinched and tears ran down her cheeks. "My head hurts," she whimpered. Every time she got to missing Georgia and Frances, her head ached.

"Well you just stay in bed today. And I'll get the brown paper." She kept the paper in which Mr. Mellus had wrapped the window glass. After soaking it in the bucket, wishing she had vinegar, she laid it over Ellie's face and patted it on her forehead. "There now, in a while it will feel better."

"I want to go back to Grandma Brunner's house," she murmured under the paper, still as an Egyptian mummy.

It was bound to happen. Sadly Elitha sat beside her and took her little hand, rubbing its back, wishing things had been different.

"Taik her back tomorrow, I will," Perry said brightly.

Why did that sting so?

Ellie lifted the damp paper from her eyes and smiled at him. Then patted Elitha's hand. "Don't be sad, Big Sister. I'll be warm at Grandma's. She has a fireplace."

The next morning Perry lifted Ellie into the saddle, her fist tight around Tamsen's silk stocking. Elitha waved through the drizzle as Paint headed across the green hill; the black silk dangled like an extra tail. She knew Ellie wouldn't lose it any more than a preacher would lose his Bible.

She'd done her best. To insist on her staying would be selfish. Shivering, she hobbled inside, trying to avoid the pressure on her toes. She felt her breakfast loose inside her. Was the damp air making her stomach sick? Yesterday morning she'd felt nauseated too.

Every day Perry was gone she expected him momentarily. But days became a week, then two, and more. Sometimes she felt her essence drifting into the silent foggy wilderness. She missed Ellie, missed Leanna, missed Indian Mary, missed Perry. Missed anybody to talk to. And longed for the safety of Perry's gun at night. The nausea came each morning, sometimes lingering all day. At night she pulled the covers to her chin and slept with her club and knife.

One morning as she opened the door, she saw a tawny cat the size of a huge dog looking up at her food sling. It turned and stared at her with luminous yellow eyes. Her heart banged so wildly it hurt, but she never moved, knowing cats liked to chase their prey. Then it turned its hind end to the tree and squirted the trunk, long erect tail quivering, and ambled away with its tail just skimming the ground. She released her breath.

She knew she lived within the overlapping territories of many birds and animals, such as the red-tailed hawk, who hunted the surrounding hills by day, and a pair of owls, one white and one brown, who stationed themselves in the oaks at night. It made her feel less lonely, and she got so she could identify the individuals among the animal varieties by slight differences in color and ranginess, and the notched ear of a mother cottontail. She laughed at long lines of baby quail, fuzzy walnuts on legs, toddling after their mothers, and lost her fear of the sneaky coyote who ate her leftovers behind her back.

At times her mind wandered to Illinois — to sausage-making, quilting, cooking, sleighrides behind Pal and Dotty ajingle with bells, and Fourth of July cookouts at half-brother William's place. Here the only human contact was Indian Mary's mother, who brought the morning milk. Billy toddled behind, but Indian Mary never appeared.

"Nime Billy," the child said one day with Perry's dimpled grin. *We are a strange family*, she thought.

Once she went to the Indian village and tried to ask for Mary. No one spoke English. The Indians eyed her as if waiting for her to leave so they could return to their chores, even Billy's grandmother. Feeling out of place, she walked up the faint pathway through high grass and unfolding fiddlenecks, and returned to the silent adobe.

Then she heard a horse, and before she could get outside, Perry burst through the door with a sunny smile. "Hello me pretty lass," he sang out.

She smiled, her uncombed hair hanging to her waist.

He grabbed and held her at arm's length. "Mormons is minin gold up on the American River, they is."

"That where you've been?"

"Neptune's bones, they're hauling it in by the sack! Every red-blooded man in the country's headed up there." He took her by the waist and lifted her in a playful circle, then set her down, staring at her middle. "Putting on flesh? Or is it a babe in the oven?"

"Oven?"

"By the gods, girl, I vow you're a simpleton. 'Avin courses, be ye?"

Her face and neck heated. The way she'd been brought up, you didn't speak of it with a man. And she'd had only three, one on the prairie and two last summer. "Not for a while," she murmured.

"Didn't I tell ye." He stared at her middle. "Lass, me luck's a changin, hit is! A new babe! And riches to boot!"

"Riches?"

"Daylor and Sheldon and yours truly be drivin cattle up north. To a ranchería they call Culuma. Wye, those miners be eatin like niggers! And nothing but wild game, and gold in their pockets. Just you watch, they'll pay dear for me beef. Send our wash to China, we will at that!"

It didn't seem real, coming at her so fast. "When are you going?"

"Noon tomorry. That Bill Daylor's a canny old tar."

She'd be alone again, but — "Going with Mr. Sheldon and Mr. Daylor?"

"Full in the hold and deaf to boot?"

"I want to stay with Sally or Catey while you're gone."

He narrowed his dense lashes at her, steel-blue piercing through. "Gone to her in-laws, Catey is, and Sally's minding the store. And how'd ye think ye'd get there?" A teasing smile cracked the side of his face.

"Ride with one of the vaqueros, or walk."

"Git on a horse with a nigger, would ye?"

She nodded.

"I'll not 'ave me wife prancin round with niggers and that's the last of it!"

Softly she said, "Then you take me," and waited for his rage. The certainty that she wouldn't stay alone gave her strength. She recalled that he'd become nicer after she ran away in San Francisco, and in any case doubted he'd injure her badly. It seemed little to pay for company.

His voice came as flat as the line of his lips: "Wilderness making ye cross, is it?"

"I've been alone."

"That's prattle enough. Give me something to eat, then I'll poke ye like a respectable husband. That's all's wrong with ye, hit is."

The next day she rode behind Perry as he trotted Paint after the herd, thirty pairs of ivory horns as orderly as pickets leading the way, Indians riding at the side. A third of the herd. At the junction partway to Daylor's, where the path forked north, Perry signaled. The Indians stopped the cows. They would wait here for the Rancho Omuchumne herd.

She felt willful, having insisted on coming, but not sorry. He'd explained, patiently for him, that a man had to stay on his land, in the house he built. "When I needs to be gone," he had said, "me wife stays. Then no man can say I abandoned me rancho." He had remained in high spirits at the thought of gold, and she took the opportunity to press him.

"Don't you have papers? To prove it's yours?" Pa prized such papers.

"A letter from John Sutter, I has. Says it's mine ifn I build a 'ouse and don't abandon the land."

"I'm your placemarker then?" *Human bookmark.*

"And a pretty one at that." No meanness there.

"But the place is so desolate, I don't see who's going to claim it the few days you expect to be gone." Nobody lived anywhere near; it wasn't like animals vying for hunting grounds.

Somehow she had won, and without blows.

Now, cattle and horses had their noses to the grass, and in the distance she heard the lowing of the Omuchumne cattle. Perry spurred Paint to a gallop and she hung on from behind, bouncing hard against the ridge of the wood-frame saddle. Soon they skirted Sheldon and Daylor's herd, twice the size of Perry's, and reined to a stop beside Bill Daylor's rangy gray.

Mr. Daylor doffed a sweat-stained hat. "Ma'am." His lips went to the side of his long face — clean-shaven like Perry — and his brows shot up, questioning.

"Mulish, she is," Perry jerked a thumb at her. "Bound and determined to stay with your Sarah. Now, mait, if that's a bother, I'll take her home and catch up with ye later."

Mr. Daylor said, "Sally might could use the company."

A hard-riding ten minutes later she slid thankfully from the horse before the adobe trading post. Perry left like a Spaniard, wheeling the horse on its hind legs, mouth open to the bit, then thundered away at a full gallop. She hoped the cattle brought as high a price as he expected.

46

"Your ma helping Catey with the baby?" Elitha asked the next morning.

Sarah laid her fork down. Her voice cracked. "She passed on." She turned away.

Mrs. Rhoads' sallow complexion at the cookout last summer came to Elitha's mind. A woman plumb tuckered. "I'm so sorry. She was a fine lady." Mother of nineteen.

Sarah's neat blonde upsweep was turned toward Elitha, and she dabbed at her eyes with the hem of her apron.

"Who helped with the baby?" Who would help her?

"Me." Sarah shook her head and sniffed. "It was bad. I don't know the first thing about birthing. Matty came over." *John's wife.* "She's given birth three times, but never attended one. So we did what we could." She blinked. "It's a miracle they both lived. Brother John drove Catey and the baby down to Brother Dan's at Mr. Sinclair's place."

"Well, I'm glad she's all right."

Slowly Sarah stirred the beans on her plate. "Ma's grave is lost." It was clear she wanted to talk about it.

"What do you mean, lost?"

She sighed as if commencing a long voyage. "Well, they don't have a doctor at New Helvetia, so when Ma got bad, we thought to send her to San Francisco. I made her a bed in a wagon so she wouldn't jostle around too much, and Pa and the boys drove her to Sutter's." She sighed again. "They was loadin wheat, so they made her a bed right down in the wheat under the — " she sniffed, "the deck of the boat." She closed her eyes and shook her head." Guess they got almost as far as the Hastings house, Montezuma they call it, when Ma . . . she . . . " She covered her face and shook, silently.

Elitha went to her side of the table and put a hand on the warm cloth of her shoulder. "It hurts to lose your ma." She'd lost two.

"Don't rightly know why I can't git over it." She wiped her eyes on her hem. "They buried her on the shore 'cause it was a bad warm spell — last September it was. Pa and the boys made her a marker and," she sobbed and wiped her eyes, "they had to go on with the wheat. They went back later, but the river had rose, and the — " She sniffed and her voice trailed almost to nothing. "The marker was plumb gone."

Elitha recalled the river as it widened into the bay, and the cry of the geese — a lonely place. Like the mountains. Mrs. Rhoads and Mrs. Donner and Pa were all in unmarked graves. Feeling the bond, she patted Sarah's hair. "I guess pioneers can't always visit their folks' graves." *You gotta be tough.* She steered toward the happy thing. "But I'm mighty glad Catey and the baby are doing good." She longed to see Catherine's short sassy figure as it had been, and her impish smile.

Sarah looked up. "Oh my sister's a rugged little tyke. Always was. I vow, that woulda killed me." She drew in a breath. "I'm prayin her next one comes easier."

"You in a family way yet?" Elitha hadn't told Sarah she was. In truth she wasn't sure.

Sarah shook her head and got up from the table, tall and dignified like her old self. "Nope. Been married as long as Catey too — did you know our weddins was one week apart?" She took the bread pan from its nail and put it on the table. "Mr. Daylor's afraid he can't have younguns."

As Elitha considered the evidence for that — years in California, Indian women — Sarah put the plates in the bread pan with a cake of lye soap, took a kettle from the stove and poured steaming water over the soap and dishes, then added a little cool water from the bucket. Ordinary actions, when you had an indoor stove. "Now you just sit and let me do that," Elitha said.

Each morning an Indian woman brought milk for curding, and Elitha made herself useful, minding it on the back of the stove and making soft cheese the way Grandma Donner taught her. Stirring, she admired the iron curlicues on the stanchions that held the warming shelf over the stove — where the bread rose. A chimney pipe ran through the ceiling.

Following her glance Sarah said, "That stove come from Boston. Around the Horn."

"I'd sure like to have one just like it."

The next morning her stomach rode up and down as she pounded coffee beans in the stone mortar. She dashed outside with her hand over her mouth. When she came back in, she saw worry on Sarah's face. Her hand was poised over the tin into which she was cracking speckled quail eggs.

"I think I'm in a family way," Elitha said, trying to smile, though the smoke rising from the frying pan told her the lard had been used far too many times.

"Poor thing. Lie down. You're white as a ghost." Sarah moved the pan to the cool side of the stove.

The bed was comfortable — a mattress of horsehair on crossed leather straps suspended from a whittled, decorative frame. She climbed in where she'd slept so well beside Sarah the past two nights.

"Want some eggs? Indians brought em in yesterdy. Fresh."

"No thanks."

The door began to open, quiet on its leather hinges. Elitha stared, fascinated, thinking the men had returned and were playing a trick, sneaking up on the house. Then a broad brown face thrust itself in, surrounded by thick black hair, then came the large body of a naked Indian with a huge bundle of furs on his back, he and the furs more than filling the doorway. He grinned at Elitha.

Her heart did a flip-flop and she jumped from the cot, backing into the adjoining room, stumbling over baskets. She crouched behind bags of goods piled against the opposite wall, then realized Sarah didn't seem afraid.

The Indian stood next to the stove with his head grazing the ceiling.

"You'll have to git used to that," Sarah called. "These Indians don't never knock." Motioning the Indian into the trading room where Elitha was, Sarah continued, "Mr. Daylor told 'em to just come on in." She smiled. "He won't hurt you."

Elitha backed into the room where she'd started. Restoring the fallen quilt to the bed, she watched the Indian and Sarah speaking with gestures and facial expressions. She heard "savvy" and "numero," and saw them counting. The man was no more modest about his privates than Captain Juan and his men, and she thought she'd never get used to seeing that, dangling out in the air without a hint of embarrassment.

Sarah added the furs to the pile in the corner, counted out glass beads and handed them to him along with two striped blankets. When the Indian left, Elitha asked, "Why don't you make them knock?"

She slid the pan to the hot part of the stove and whipped the eggs with a fork. "They don't think it's mannerly to pound on a body's door. They'd stare through the window. Gave me the creeps." She poured the thick yellow liquid into the smoking grease. "See. These California Indians aren't like the regular kind. Did you know they didn't even know how to fight a war till the white men came? Mr. Daylor says every buck among them would rather have a good meal than kill an enemy. Can you imagine?" She shook her head.

"I like them better than the other kind," Elitha said.

By the time Perry's few days had stretched into three weeks, Elitha felt at home at Rancho Omuchumne, enjoying the close contact with the Indians. Every evening pot-bellied children came for sugarcane and she loved their soft faces.

Sarah broke and handed out pieces to them, explaining to Elitha, "Mr. Daylor has a soft spot in his heart for these kids. He gives em all the cane." They waited their turns, calmly accepting what was offered. A far-away look of sadness came into Sarah's face as she handed a stick to the last child. "It's the only reason he buys it."

Elitha wished Sarah were pregnant, instead of her.

One afternoon as Sarah bartered with four naked Indians who had come from Rancho Seco, twenty miles southeast, Elitha went out to collect wild greens. The aroma of peppermint hung in the late spring air, and suddenly Indian Mary was smiling at her.

"Where are you going?" Mary's unvarying first words.

Delighted to see her, Elitha smiled at Billy, fat and playing peek-a-boo from his mother's knee. "I'm visiting Sarah Daylor while Mr. McCoon is away. What are you doing here?"

"My man lives here."

"Oh, yes, Señor Valdez. But sometimes you don't live here."

Indian Mary spoke to a stand of round-leafed lettuce, then gracefully pinched off some leaves and tossed them into her basket. "Live in husband house," she said. "Sometime live at home place, sometime place of doctor."

Elitha had expected she'd be a full medicine woman by now. "When will you stop learning?"

Mary had the Indian way of going about her work while preparing her answer, then it would come, calm and quiet, as if the listener had endless patience. "Learn of spirits forever."

Thinking about that, Elitha picked round leaves too, one of her favorite salad greens.

"I want talk with you. Later," Mary said.

Making an appointment to talk intrigued Elitha. With anyone else she would have said, Oh, come on, tell me now. Instead she asked, "Is it about my hand?" Her thumb had mended a bit crooked, as anyone could see. She should have left the splint on.

"No. Perrimacoo."

Was she seeing him again? She searched Mary's face for a clue, but saw only the placid expression. Then she realized nothing she could do would stop him from seeing any Indian girl he wanted. But she didn't want to hear about it. "We talk later," she said, happy to put it off. "Is that good?" She pointed at what Mary was picking.

Mary shot her a sly glance. "Put yerba buena on it."

That made her laugh. At Rancho Sacayak when she'd complained about the taste of this or that plant, which Mary had said was edible, she always advised, "Put yerba buena on it." The mint covered a world of poor taste.

Laughing too, Mary adjusted the thong across her straw cap — a protection from chafing — and straightened to leave. She surprised Elitha with, "Tomorrow we gather. You come?" She cocked her head, friendship showing in her black eyes.

She felt honored. She had seen the closeness of Indian women as they went on gathering parties, but never imagined being invited to join them. Tamsen would be proud of her. And her real mother, surely she would be pleased.

And Perry? That could wait.

In the morning Mary arrived at the door with Billy. Not far back stood the entire population of Rancho Omuchumne Indian girls and women, many with babies in bikooses, all equipped with their oversized gathering baskets, all watching her. Elitha fell into step with Mary, hoping she wouldn't talk about Perry for a while.

The late spring air soothed like balm. Birds trilled, piped, whistled and twittered in the thick green canopy and it smelled like a fragrant Garden of Eden. Ahead on the path walked the Indian women with their children hurrying alongside. The points of their conical baskets reached to their knees and the wide tops yawned behind their caps, their thick black hair swinging at their shoulders. By now she was fully accustomed to naked breasts with amulets hanging between, and the colors were arresting. The women's skin was like the red-brown clay that was so prevalent at Rancho Sacayak, and the shine of the black hair contrasted with the pale straw of the baskets and caps. Flashes of red and blue drill wrapping some of the women's hips winked through the lush green foliage as the line snaked ahead. She found herself wishing for Tamsen's pigments and a canvas.

Turning to see Billy falling behind, she squatted and held her arms to him. The two-year-old grinned and ran to her. He felt warm and strong and smelled clean in her arms, her arm under his bare bottom, and a motherly feeling came over her. Perhaps, she thought, Mormon women felt this way. Walking beside her, Indian Mary looked contented — not ready to talk, Elitha was glad to see.

The path grew muddy. She put him down, removed her shoes, tied the strings and hung them around her neck and walked on with Billy beside her. She had a busy time unsnagging her skirts from the blackberry thorns and he tried to help. The short skirts of the Indian women caught less, and those who were naked walked entirely unhampered. She felt very overdressed.

Soon the path vanished into a marshy pond. She identified cattails and arrowroot, but the women were clearly after something else. Leaning the bikooses against the willows on higher ground, babies within sight, they began stepping purposefully in the water, pulling up the roots of a purplish grass in their toes. They swished the clumps in the water to wash off the mud, tossed the roots in their baskets and continued, talking and laughing.

Mary put Billy near the babies, where he squatted to poke holes in the mud, apparently accustomed to being left. Indian Mary beckoned from shallow water choked with water plants. Elitha pulled off her frock and petticoat and waded into the muck in her camisole and underdrawers, sloshing, feeling with her feet for the roots of the purplish grass. It didn't grow in masses, but was distributed widely. It was the tiny bulbs on the roots that they were after. As she got more efficient in bringing them up, her underdrawers became muddy, but with all the laughter and sisterly talk, which she recognized through the barrier of language, she was surprised how much she enjoyed herself. Mary gave no sign of wanting to talk, perhaps because others were present.

After what seemed a long time, the tiny bulbs only a hand deep in the point of Mary's basket, the mood of the women changed. One after another they left the water, laid their baskets beside the babies, and ran happily into the thicket.

She looked inquiringly at Mary.

"They saw a, a . . . What do you call this?" She made a noise like a mosquito and made her hand into a semblance of a winged thing.

"Fly? Bee?"

Mary inclined her head and pursed her full lips. "Maybe." Brightening, she beckoned. "Come. You see. You help. First make fire."

Mary went to where two other women were fanning cattail fluff on small wooden platforms, which they'd taken from their baskets. On each scorched platform, wooden drills were positioned, points down. They operated the drills by pulling twine, the same way tops twirled to the pump of a string. Wisps of smoke rose. They pushed fluff into the smoking drill points and blew on it. "You, fetch little wood," Mary said.

Turning to find kindling, Elitha heard giggles and squeals in the brush beyond and wondered what was happening. Soon they had a fire snapping hotly, to the obvious delight of the babies, who stood laced to their chins in their propped-up boards. Billy slapped pond mud and watched. Many women were now thrusting cattail heads into the flames. Giggling, they rushed away with their smokey torches. Not to be left behind, Elitha broke off a cattail spike and held it in the flames. Indian Mary touched her arm.

"We smoke them out," she said. "You bring sharp willow stick."

"Smoke what out?"

Mary shrugged and headed for the trees. Wanting to see, Elitha followed through the jungle-like vegetation, toward the happy squeals. She saw a woman on her tip-toes push her torch into the hollow of an oak. A cloud of insects blossomed from it, and the woman shrieked and ran. Others swished their smoking torches through the buzzing cloud as another woman stuck her torch in the hole. Were they after honey? The torches drove most of the insects away, but yells, laughter and loud claps of hands on bare skin told of stings.

Then several rangy golden-brown insects came at Elitha, long legs dangling. Her hair moved at the roots. HORNETS. She stumbled back, turned and ran for the water, her toes digging into the damp ground.

At the fire she glanced back and saw she'd outrun the hornets. Billy was laughing at her. A few moments later Indian women and girls came from the thicket of trees, hands cupped together. Kneeling, they opened their hands, and Elitha saw heaps of writhing white maggots. They skewered them on switches as happily as Elitha and her sisters had once threaded popcorn for the Christmas tree. Briefly singeing the wiggly grubs over the flames, they popped them in their mouths, talking rapidly, smacking their lips, the pale flesh of the grubs visible in their teeth when they grinned.

Elitha's stomach pushed up against her throat and she lurched toward Daylors'.

Indian Mary trotted to her side, offering grubs. "Good," she said smacking her lips. The black-eyed maggots squirmed.

She whirled away and disgorged a horrible brown mass, grainy and lumpy with pieces of pork. Breakfast.

Indian Mary watched and when she was empty and reeling, placed her hand on Elitha's abdomen and put slight pressure on the cloth. "Baby in there?" A motherly look.

"Maybe."

Mary smiled. "Friends help." She nodded toward the Indian women and gave her own stomach a pat. "I have one too."

She wasn't sure she wanted Indians at her childbed. "Señor Valdez must be happy," she managed, feeling faint, but trying to be polite.

"Sí," Mary said, placing a raw grub on her tongue, "His blood is in me."

The world went dark. She twisted away, heaving, and caught herself on a tree, which blocked the sight of Mary chewing. The women at the fire began to sing.

Mary asked, "Talk now?"

"Later," she croaked and staggered to where she'd left her frock, then turned up the path as fast as she could go, glad Mary went back to the fire.

In a few minutes she felt better walking under the leafy canopy, the blooming elderberries scenting the air with delicate sweetness, *healing her*. Behind, the singing grew fainter and she assumed the women and girls of Rancho Omuchumne had settled in for a long feast. Then to her dismay she heard their voices coming behind her. She turned, thinking, please no more ugly grubs.

Indian Mary trotted to catch up and said, "People coming." Her hands were empty.

Probably the grubs were in the basket, Elitha thought, walking faster. Mary held her head at a listening angle, but Elitha heard nothing except the birds and the footfalls and chatter of women and children coming behind.

Then she heard a distant noise like a strange cricket. The sound intensified as they approached the main trail to Daylor's. Indians had amazing hearing. In a minute or two she heard horse hooves and the unmistakable sound of a snare drum. She couldn't imagine what was happening. Was Perry coming? With a drum? How angry would he be to see her with the Indians?

Stepping from the foliage, she shaded her eyes to see up the trail from New Helvetia. Dust rose around three horsemen, one in a big white hat. Over the hill came a long line of walking people, three and four abreast. When they drew near, she recognized Mr. Sutter in a planter's hat, on a mule. Ahead of him an Indian with a red bandanna around his hair was drumming as proudly as any parade master.

Indian Mary ducked back into the thicket.

47

Captain Sutter craned his neck to peer into the bushes after Indian Mary, then said, "Good day Mrs. McCoon." He smiled and removed his planter's hat.

Beside him two hugely bearded riders touched their hats and rode on. So astonished was she to see this procession, she didn't think to ask where they were heading. Nobody used this road except Sheldon and Daylor, Indians, Perry, and Señor Pico, from whose rancho the big Indian had brought the furs.

The Indian women and children, except for Mary, stood staring at the Indians, maybe a hundred, walking past. The Indian men wore tattered, ill-fitting pantaloons. Smiling at them, the watching women made appreciative, sexual gestures — which embarrassed Elitha — and looked enviously at the squaws in the cast-off rags of immigrants. The naked children of the local Indians ran with the strange children. Herded by the Indians, sheep and cattle trotted in fits and starts, dogs yipping at their heels. Dust rose in a wide band into the pale blue sky.

Behind the Indians came half again as many men and women of a different sort — the women without chin tattoos, probably Kanakas. But so many! Not nearly this many had been at the fort. They looked drawn and exhausted. The men leaned on wooden spears, the women shuffling beside them with tired black eyes, some holding babies. About half the women wore shirts, and both men and women wore hip wraps of colored cloth. The staring was mutual, the strange people giving back as much as Elitha and the Omuchumne Indian women gave. The last man, an Indian, led a long string of mules swaying beneath huge bundles. All manner of buckets, shovels, pans and axes were tied to the bindings. The scene brought to mind the biblical story of Abraham moving his tents.

Elitha ran up the line to Captain Sutter and asked, "Are you moving?"

He looked down from his mule. "Moving?"

"It looks like you're leaving the fort."

He laughed heartily. "Ve go to Jared Sheldon's, my dear. He keep us da night. Den ve go to der suddern mines. Ve find goldt." He looked very pleased, though also a little tired.

"Nobody's at the mill ranch, except Mister Valdez. Mister Sheldon's gone. Why don't you rest at the Daylors'? Sarah and I'll get water for you, or coffee if you'd like." She'd never heard of southern mines.

"Not to vorry. Señor Valdez and I be friends. I camp at Mill Rancho."

"Where are the southern mines?"

As if smiling at a joke, he said, "Nort iss Río Americano, not so?"

"Yes."

"Bad men mining dere. BAD men. They attack mine Indians. And so, enough! We go where nobody find us."

"On the Cosumnes?" Would her own quiet river become crowded with strange Indians and Kanakas?

"No mine chile, first ve look on da rancho of my old friend Andrés Pico. You hear of Rancho Seco, hmm?"

She nodded.

"Den we go to Piny Voods."

The trail east from Rancho Sacayak led there, as did the trail from Mill Ranch. "I didn't know they were finding gold around there. Perry said it was all to the north." She walked beside the mule, recalling that Mr. Sutter had kept the Rhoads' and Sheldons' gold a secret. Perhaps he was keeping secrets for others as well.

He smiled wisely. "I tink it gives gold there too."

Gold is everywhere, she thought. That's why she'd found it on Perry's property. "Are those Kanakas?" She pointed behind.

He nodded. "Not long off the shiff from der Islands. Goot happy vorkers."

"How long will you be camping?"

He looked down in an avuncular manner. "Mine chile, now we make holiday. Who knows?"

Sarah came around the adobe house with a basket of wash, glancing first at the drummer wiping his brow in the shade of the big cottonwood, then at the multitudes behind Sutter. Curtseying with the wash, she seemed at a loss for words.

Elitha explained what he had told her.

"I'd be obliged if you'd rest here, Captain Sutter," said Sarah, displaying the composure which Elitha so much admired. She set down the laundry.

He scowled. "We go to Sheldon's. Iss not far." He waved the drummer on, and the procession continued.

Thinking that a bit rude, Elitha watched the pack mules disappear up the leafy trail, then turned to Sarah. "I asked him to stay too, but I guess he didn't want to. Those poor Kanakas sure look tired."

"He and Mr. Daylor had a fight a long time ago. I guess there's still bad blood between em. My guess is he don't want to be beholden to us."

Perry had told a story about Mr. Daylor fighting off Indians and Kanakas, and Mr. Sutter having him taken in chains to Monterey. It had been over a Kanaka woman. Sarah lifted her queenly chin and turned to the garden.

Keeping out of sight, Maria hadn't lit the candle in Pedro's room. Her toe tapped in the dark as she watched the last night of the festival from the window. *Indios* joined in as the Kanakas faced each other, dancing and singing, and clacking long sticks together on the accented words.

I HEARD, I HEARD the boss man say,
JOHN Ka-naka naka, tu-lai-ay.
To-DAY, to-DAY is a hol-i-day,
JOHN Ka-naka naka, tu-lai-ay.
We're BOUND, we're BOUND for Frisco Bay.
JOHN Ka-naka naka tu-lai-ay.

On John they stamped one foot then the other, on naka, naka knocked their knees. The beat made her voracious for Pedro. He sat below with Captain Sutter in the restless shadows of the flames. She couldn't remember wanting him so much. This festival did that to women.

At last the dance ended. People joked, many passing flasks. Apparently Captain Sutter's Indians acquired *aguardiente* freely. Some staggered. Many laughed, pulling the husbands of others away from the firelight, pretending it was by accident. Hand-in-hand couples walked to the shadows. *Indios* and Kanakas.

Pedro stood up, casting a long shadow. He turned from Sutter and started toward the house. She burned for him as his boots thudded up the stairs. Then the door opened and in a wash of soft night air she was wrapped in his strong arms and breathing his manly aroma.

She kissed his hungry mouth and pressed into him.

He murmured, "Captain Sutter is drunker than his Indians." He found her breast. "He asked about you."

She froze. Had he glimpsed her on the trail this morning? Would she be hauled away? She still wasn't ready to face him.

He chuckled. "I told him you are mine." He kissed her in a tonguing way, then pulled back. "He said he would pay me a thousand dollars for one night with you." His eyes glistened in the firelight coming through the window.

She gasped in surprise. Her people were adding pinches of gold to a large basket for Pedro, to buy Perrimacoo's land. It would take many pinches to equal a thousand dollars. "That much would tempt any man," she breathed.

"Money does not tempt me." It sounded gruff but it was pride. He was Proud Hawk. He gentled her cheek back to his pulsing throat. "You must know that, *Amapolita*." In the V of his open shirt his heart spoke to her while his breath moved the top of her hair.

Absorbing the honor of his words, her legs went weak. Love for him ran as endless as the river. She had not meant to question his love for her. "*Gracias,*" she whispered, adding "*Capitán* Sutter must carry many pesos."

He petted her hair, his clean breath washing over her. "He said he would write a note of promise for it. He expects to get a hundred times that much in gold where he's going."

"There are many women in the world. Why does he want me?" She'd hoped he would forget.

The corners of his mouth twitched in a half-smile. "You ran away from him, Little Poppy. Some men crave what they do not have. Besides," he kissed her forehead, "You have the face of an angel." His kisses circled her face, "And, *Indita mía*, a body *el Diablo* would die for." His hands slid down to her buttocks and he took them in his hands.

"I am glad you want what is yours." She loosed his sash and freed the buttons.

"*Por favor*, my thousand dollar poppy," he murmured, "do not make me wait any longer." He lifted her to him.

48

Elitha wasn't sure, when she first heard the horses, who was coming. She went to the porch. The sun was high. By now Sutter would have forded the river and left for Pico's. The horses were coming from the north. "Looks like the men coming," she yelled at Sarah.

The three ranchers galloped toward her and she felt sorry her visit was over. Maybe Perry would stay for supper. He reined Paint to a stop and dismounted in one fluid motion. Beneath his two-week stubble he looked tired, but he grinned a deep dimple at her, then untied the saddle bundles. That and the way he moved indicated he'd sold the cattle for a good price. But what had detained them so long?

Mr. Sheldon saluted from his horse and reined up the leafy path toward Mill Ranch.

"Wait," Elitha called, gathering her skirts and running toward him. He stopped and looked down at her.

"Captain Sutter came with about a hundred and fifty Indians and Kanakas. They all camped at your place last night. Probably gone by now."

Mr. Sheldon's eyebrows drew together in thought.

Elitha heard Perry whip the girth through the loop and say, "Out mining gold now, is Sutter?" Suiter.

She turned to him. "How'd you know?" Sarah was in Mr. Daylor's arms.

"I told ye, every man not halt nor blind is out minin," Perry said. "Where'd he go?"

"He said Rancho Seco, then up to Piny Woods."

Mr. Sheldon's horse disappeared up the narrow tree-lined trail. Mr. Daylor, who was carrying his saddle to the porch rail, exchanged a look with Perry, then smiled at Elitha. "You and Sally be lucky lasses." He pushed back the hat on his high white forehead.

Elitha cocked her head at him. "Why lucky?" Sarah echoed, "Yes, why?"

Perry fished down the front of his shirt and brought out his possibles pouch. With the thong still around his neck, he extended the bag toward her and said, "Go on. Take a gander."

Smelling leather, old perspiration and liquor, she stepped to him, prying the pouch open with her fingertips.

Held as if on a leash, he quipped at Daylor, "These lovelies don't know they be married to gold barons."

Elitha moved her fingers through the grainy material and brought out a nugget similar to but smaller than the one she'd buried.

"Maybe now they'll put on some flesh," Mr. Daylor said running an eye over them. "We'll hire all the work done, and they can sit like queens eatin bread and honey."

Sarah made a teasing face. "Gold barons, my eye. That there ain't near as much as my folks found."

At the bottom of his long face Daylor pressed his lips together in what passed for a smile. "Madam, what you're looking at is only the start."

Elitha gave pouch and Perry to Sarah.

Perry went willingly, grinning comically from his leash while Sarah looked into the pouch. "We've got a pot full of it wrapped in the blankets, we has. Wye a body can pluck gold from the ground like eggs in a henhouse!" he said, blue eyes crinkled at her. She released him.

Excitement sparked through Elitha and her mind flew. She would send to San Francisco for a buggy and nice clothing and to Boston for a cookstove like Sarah's. They must have the house rebuilt, with a fireplace and a good door and windows that opened — a wooden house like the Sheldon's so water wouldn't seep through. And a two-seater outhouse. She would find carpenters — Mr. Sheldon and Mr. Daylor being too busy on their rancho. Most men did their own building, except Perry, who didn't know how.

Mr. Daylor had his hands around the red-striped fabric of Sarah's small waist, his cheek against her blonde bun. "Mrs. Daylor me love," he said, "we picked up that much in no time atall." He exuded strength, his height making her small, though she was as tall as Elitha. A handsome couple, Elitha thought, and rich?

"Well, lass?" Perry said, brandishing the pouch at Elitha. "Curious where this treasure trove is to be found?"

She had to keep reminding herself this was really happening, and not to let herself ride too high. "You said you were going to the American — "

"Went there, we did. Sold the cattle to Lienhard's young man for a pretty penny. But on the way back, lass, on the way back! About ten miles coming to home we stopped and tried our luck in a gravelbed by a dry creek, the worst patch of nothing you ever saw. And would ye believe! These old tars hit it rich, they did!"

He was like the boy in the fairy tale who went out to find his fortune. But the boy in the story had encountered difficult tests along the road. This seemed too easy.

"Just layin on the ground?" Sarah was asking.

"Like hens' eggs," Perry said, "Learned a trick or two, we did! Throw a shovelful of sand and gravel on a blanket, hold the corners and toss it careful- like. The breeze blows the light stuff away. Gold sticks in the weave."

"And the place!" Mr. Daylor put in with more earnest fervor than Elitha had ever seen in him, "Not a soul knows of it. That's the beauty. The miners are busy around Culuma, miles and miles away." And Sutter mining in a different direction, Elitha thought.

Perry chimed in, "Deserted as a church on Monday."

Mr. Daylor headed for the outhouse, calling over his shoulder, "We're sending the Indians back for more. Ten thousand dollars a week is my guess, what they'll get out of there."

Elitha sucked in her breath. Ten thousand dollars was the savings of Pa's lifetime, and he was a wealthy man. That much every week was more than her mind could hold. Their wealth would rival the eastern bankers. With intensifying excitement she thought what they would do with the money. She would write her half brother, William Donner, and tell him to send carpenters from Illinois. She could stake the crossing of the whole crew, and when the house was built, she'd reunite the family. The girls could help with the baby when it came. Perry's drinking might lessen a bit too, and his gambling, when he had as much money as he needed. Money helped make a gentlemen, she'd been told. *Oh Pa, you were right about California. If only you had lived to see this!*

With Billy on her lap, Maria listened to Señor Sheldon's fluent Spanish. Her friend Blue Star sat on one side, big fleshy Tomaka on the other. Omuch's *umne* circled around. Señor Sheldon was using a few of the people's words. Impressed, Maria exchanged glances with Blue Star and Tomaka. It was clear the Omuchumne admired Joaquín Sheldon. His flinty expression held firm as he spoke, and the faces of the Omuchumne — twice as numerous as Maria's people — looked toward him like flowers to the sun. He had become co-headman, and Omuch didn't seem to mind.

"Except for those who stay with Señor Valdez, every man, woman and child will come with us," Señor Sheldon was saying. "It is a three-day journey on foot. Thirty miles. Women are to bring carrying baskets, blankets, mortars, knives and basket-making tools, anything you need to live a long time. We will take more cattle with us, and leave the rest with Señor Valdez. He will select four vaqueros to stay here and help him." Pleased that Pedro would stay, Maria was disappointed her friends would leave. It would be lonely.

Blue Star whispered, "Now we will wash gold like your people."

Señor Sheldon continued, "I will pay each person fifty cents for every day you work."

A murmur traveled around the seated people. "A family with children will make *mucho dinero*," Tomaka said. Omuch nodded and Maria saw him exchange a glance with Señor Sheldon. They were like brothers.

Now the people would leave home to seek gold. Such a thing had never happened before. What was the tickle of foreboding she felt?

The next morning Maria stood beside Pedro, his warm cloth-covered arm around her shoulders, Billy at her knee. Sadly she watched Blue Star and Tomaka walk up the trail with the Omuchumne, more than fifty — old people and little children among them. Billy would have no one left to play with. No Big Time would be celebrated until the people returned.

She glanced at Elitha and Señora Daylor on the porch. They put down the roots they were peeling in their laps and their eyes followed the people walking away with sure, steady steps. At the front, a plume of white dust marked Señor Daylor's horse. Again she felt the tickle of loose power.

Señor Sheldon waited on his nervous animal, to help the vaqueros herd more longhorns to the mines — meat for the miners. Glad her friends had taken plenty of supplies in their carrying baskets, she was about to mention her unease to Pedro when Perrimacoo stepped between them.

"I needs to palaver, Mary. Alone."

Pedro said evenly, "What you say to her you can say to me." He lifted his chin and his bolero vest rode back on his shoulders. *Proud Hawk.*

Perrimacoo's blue eyes narrowed to a thicket of mean lashes. "And what if I wants to talk to her about me boy?" He jutted his jaw at Billy, who squeezed her finger a little more firmly.

In measured calm Pedro said, "Say what you like, but say it here, señor."

"You tellin Perry McCoon what to do, nigger?" *Aguardiente* fumes spilled over them.

Pedro didn't change his stance but she sensed his readiness and fear niggled into her. Was a fight what she had felt?

Perrimacoo rolled his eyes skyward. "Oh, for Chrisssake, for God-damned Christalmighty's sake!" His eyes came around to her.

"Not understand," she said.

"Every other rancher in the whole bleedin countryside tells 'is niggers what to do, and I've a mind to —" Snorting fumes, he steel-eyed Pedro, then her. "God's very bones! I wants to palaver with your daddy and needs ye to come, is all."

He was trying to force her to do him a favor, like a boy wanting his mother to cook a special treat. He, who had handed her to a crowd of stinking men when she needed to honor the spirits, was asking for her help. It was ridiculous but she didn't smile.

Pedro said, "I'm still waiting for our riding contest."

The blue eyes flashed. "In good time, greaser. In good time. When we have plenty of witnesses so you can't cheat. 'Ave a big purse riding on it too, I will." He turned to Maria. "I needs ye to palaver today, ye hear? Today!"

She looked impolitely into the sky eyes and said, "You want my father's people to find gold for you, but they will not." Pedro didn't know her people were collecting gold for him. She'd meant to surprise him when the big basket was full.

"Oh, so now you're the judge of that too. Well, no mahala tells William Perry McCoon whot 'e be thinkin!"

No longer amused, she turned to leave.

His fingers clamped into her upper arm, "Just a minute . . . "

She saw a blur, felt the blow of Pedro sidehanding Perrimacoo's wrist, felt the grip loosen, and wrenched free of him.

"And your mother's a whore too," he said to Pedro, blue eyes sparking fire. His right hand hovered over his gun.

She held her breath. Pedro's gun was on his saddle, too far away, but quick as lightening he pulled the knife from his sash.

Señor Sheldon stepped between them, facing Perrimacoo, hat brim to hat brim, glaring at him.

"Out of my road, Jared." Perrimacoo's gun pointed at Señor Sheldon's belt buckle.

The muscles of Sheldon's jaw worked but no other part of his body moved. Then he said, "I've seen enough and I've heard enough, and I'm about fed up with your drunken antics. This here's my *mayordomo*. Understand? Worth ten of you. Twenty!" Indian vaqueros circled around, knives pulled from their calf thongs. In a gnat's wingbeat they would fight for Joaquín Sheldon.

Perrimacoo's gun wilted in his hand and pointed like a crook-necked flower at his boot.

Releasing her breath, Maria listened in relieved puzzlement as Señor Sheldon added, "Don't think I don't know where you rustled half your herd. And while we're at it, let's git this straight. Every one of these *Indios* is honest and hardworking. Something you never even heard of. And if I hear of you touching a hair of Señor Valdez or that girl — " Raising an arm, he pointed at a large cottonwood tree without looking at it, his wolf eyes holding Perrimacoo. "I'll see you hang."

Perrimacoo looked down.

Maria glanced at the porch where Elitha watched like a sad-eyed doe. How unfortunate that Perrimacoo was her man! A woman wanted a man of power.

Perrimacoo holstered his gun, then spoke to Maria quietly. "I'll give you an

Americano dress if you'll talk for me."

Offering payment! She stood motionless as he strode to his horse and pulled out a garment, dangling it by the narrow straps — a once-white frock, like the one Elitha wore under her colored frock. He looked at neither Pedro nor Señor Sheldon, who mounted his horse and sat watching.

She shook her head. She was a medicine woman. She must stay pure. She wanted no gift from Perrimacoo.

"What about your mum? She might like it."

Etumu would love it. No woman in the village owned an *Americano* garment, and women everywhere were talking about them. As wife of the headman, Maria thought, Mother should be wearing the best.

Etumu came from the u-macha wearing the flowing garment. She looked proud with her neck and shoulders bare and her breasts flattened inside the cloth. The frayed hem swayed at her feet as she walked with little Billy, his chubby hand grasping Grandmother's finger. Blue glass beads and shell money swayed with her amulet from her neck. Envy showed in the eyes of the other women, and Maria was glad she had done this.

Perrimacoo, with whom Maria had ridden, came up the path from the river where he had watered his horse. "Where's yer daddy?"

Before she could answer, Billy said, "Daddy."

Smiling, he squatted and chucked the boy's fat cheek and petted his light brown hair. "Good boy. Never forget I'm your daddy."

She kept her face a mask as she said, "My father is with his traps."

"Send for him. I'm in a hurry." His blue eyes were on his son.

She interrupted the boys in their target practice. Eyes lighting with excitement at being given an important chore, they raced away with their small bows.

Perrimacoo took Billy into his arms and said, "What's yer nime little man?"

"Nime Billy."

He laughed. "Good boy. Good boy."

Billy yanked the brim of his father's hat down over his nose.

Grinning a dimple, he pushed his hat up and said, "A bonny tyke at that." He placed the boy into his grandmother's care and looked hard at Maria. "Maike him learn decent English, ye hear? I wants him to say: Me nime is Billy McCoon."

Was he not happy with what the boy said already? And what right did a man have to talk to his child's mother like that? She was relieved to see Grizzly Hair's large figure coming down the path from the east hill, the polished bones in his ears gleaming. Two other men came with him, the happy boys trotting behind.

Grizzly Hair seated himself on the shady side of the family u-macha. Maria and Perrimacoo joined him. Father's cheeks looked wide and full next to Perimacoo's pale, narrow face, and his lively black eyes sparkled with the fire of intelligence. The gathering people talked quietly among themselves, sitting in a circle close enough to hear, Billy jabbering in Etumu's arms.

Perrimacoo spoke first. "Tell your people I'll pay them fifty cents a day, each, to mine gold for me. They will go and mine with their friends from Sheldon and Daylor's plaice." Sweat trickled past his ear, disappearing in the dark stubble of his jawline.

Grizzly Hair gave him an even look and didn't reply until he had quietly gazed across the river. "Ask him if he wants us to herd his cattle or find gold?"

Perrimacoo raised his voice, "Half of the men stay here with the cattle. The other half go with the women and children to the diggings." He wiped sweat from his eyes and pushed back his hat. "I'll pay fifty cents, every day, to the adults."

She was beginning to worry, though her words flowed evenly. The small golden flakes were deep in the black sand. Finding them went slowly. Would they accept Perrimacoo's money and stop washing gold for Pedro?

Grizzly Hair gazed at the seated people and spoke their own language. "You want to leave home and work for fifty *centavos* a day?"

No, she pleaded in her heart, knowing the welfare of his people was Father's foremost obligation. They lived as they wished, voluntarily gathering gold for Pedro out of respect for their headman. He and the people were taking their time.

Perrimacoo looked back and forth between him and his men, then snorted in exasperation. "God's bones! Sit there all day like a bleedin idiot, is it?"

She flinched inwardly, knowing that wasn't meant to be translated. But a bright spot of anger flared within her. How dare he speak of Father that way! Would he never learn respect? She looked at his narrow face and with sudden clarity wanted her people to see this man as she saw him. She would not gloss over his rudeness. She would risk being seen as disrespectful for repeating his bad talk, hoping if she used the right inflection, they would hear her contempt. She spoke slowly, searching for words that meant "bleedin" and "idiot."

People stirred and looked at one another in wonderment. Scorpion Trail frowned. People whispered parts of the insult, glanced at her father, then at her, assuring themselves all was well between the two. She also saw the flicker of amusement in Father's eyes.

Perrimacoo saw it too. "Now just 'old yer 'orses. What did ye say to 'im?"

Grizzly Hair spoke over the man's words as if he didn't exist. "I say we should save gold and not work for a man who has no manners. Señor Daylo will make me a good trade for our gold. I am his trusted trading partner."

She breathed easier as he continued: "We should also continue saving gold for Señor Valdez. Then Perrimacoo will leave our home place. My daughter's man will bring his cattle and you vaqueros will earn calves. Then you will be helping the honored grandson of the old woman instead of this rude outsider." He paused, she knew, in a moment of respect for the old times, when her namesake Maria had walked in the village.

"Mary, what's he sayin?"

Grizzly Hair continued, "Harmony and wealth will increase if Perrimacoo leaves us. I say this although I am grandfather to his son." People nodded in sorrow that their headman was forced to deprive his grandson of a father, but Maria saw that the people trusted his judgment, and accepted as a gift to them his willingness to bring disharmony on his own family.

Scorpion Trail signalled. At Father's nod he announced, "The hy-apo speaks well. I agree."

"Wot's e sayin?"

She showed him her palm to stop his sputtering while others took turns agreeing with Scorpion Trail. When all the speakers were finished she said. "He asked the people what they want to do."

"Think I'm blind, do ye? It's the ANSWER I be wantin."

"They say they no work for you no matter how much *centavos*."

He jumped to his feet and glared at her. "Ye treacherous bitch!" He shoved her shoulder with two stiff fingers.

An arrow whirred into his hat and pinned it to the cha'ka.

He whirled toward the quivering feathered shaft, then turned back and fear was in his eyes and his hand was near his gun.

Grizzly Hair's hand was up. "Tell him if he touches you again the next arrow will fly lower."

She said that, and Perrimacoo's eyes remained on Grizzly Hair. Then Father's voice came calm and deep, in the manner of a hy-apo. "Tell him the men will continue to herd his cattle, but from now on, we will take two calves from every ten births." Smiles wreathed the surrounding faces.

"Two calves, is it. Me 'orse's arse!" He turned on his heel, yanked the arrow from his hat, and tramped to his animal. Jamming the hat on his head he vaulted into the saddle.

Watching him gallop away, she felt proud of her people. "Thank you," she said to them. "You will not regret helping Señor Valdez."

49

Alone in their room over the mill, Maria told Pedro of the big basket of gold her people were saving for him. His mouth dropped open.

"It is soon full," she said, feeling his joy. "Soon you can offer it in trade for Perrimacoo's land paper."

He reached out and pulled her into his arms.

Two days away from him had seemed an eternity. She nuzzled her nose into the reddish-brown hair curling on his shirt collar and grazed his neck with her lips. "Señora McCoon and I are friends. I think she can convince Perrimacoo to make the trade. She is like a young oak, frail-looking on top, but wiry and deep rooted."

"*Amapolita,* you make me happy. Your people make me happy. I am a fortunate man to have such a woman. My words cannot express how much I love you." His gray eyes, moist now, looked deep into hers, their many facets an endless source of wonder.

Pedro had selected Quapata, Roberto and two other good vaqueros to help with the herd while the rest of the *Indios* worked with the *patrones* at the diggings. Keeping the grizzlies at bay with only five vaqueros was a chore, even with only two thousand head of cattle left.

But it was springtime and he felt good in his belly as he moved with Chocolate. His blood coursed deeper, fuller, in tune with the avian melodies around him. He breathed in the sweet air and watched the golden haze of sundown over the western ridge. Making love filled him, yet emptied him, made him need more of María. What a lucky man to have such a poppy! Her petals were damp and firm with youth. *Ah, que mujer!* He had what Captain Sutter wanted. And her people were buying McCoon's land for him too! Was he not the luckiest man alive? *Don Pedro Valdez, gran ranchero*. Soon. Olé!

But he must learn the rules of land ownership, now that things had settled down after the war. He'd been meaning to ask Sheldon's help in understanding McCoon's claim to Rancho Sacayak. Possession apparently meant something. If anyone could understand it, it would be Joaquín Sheldon. He was a literate man and a *Norteamericano* before he became Mexican. Long ago General Vallejo had offered to help, but he was a grand man who shouldn't be bothered with the likes of Pedro. Besides, a native Californian would be at a disadvantage. Señor Sheldon was the key.

Worth ten of you. Chuckling, he patted Chocolate's neck. If McCoon was faking his claim to the ranch, Pedro could play along and pretend to buy it, maybe get possession for less than he'd figured. How much? Maybe two hundred dollars? Two mere handfuls? Then Sheldon could help with the papers to get title through the United States government. Of course if McCoon owned actual title and would sell it, so much the better. Maybe Señor Sheldon could pose as the buyer. How gratifying to know your employer thinks you are valuable, honest and hard-working!

Somewhere a calf bleated, the sound of pain. He touched Chocolate with his spurs and cut through the herd to a calf with a noseful of quills. Damn porcupines! They teased a baby to put its curious nose on the quills then the poor thing starved to death beside its mother's swollen udders. What a tormented way to die! *Pobrecito.*

Releasing his lasso from the saddle loop, he brought the baby animal to a halt, longhorns parting around him. He jumped down and trotted to the struggling, bawling animal, straddling it, Chocolate holding the rope taut. The mother watched in the morose way of cows while he yanked out the painful quills and the baby cried. With the last came a thought.

The gold from Captain Juan could be taken to Yerba Buena and changed to *pesos*. He could claim his family had left him an inheritance. That way McCoon wouldn't catch on to the fact that he was abandoning a gold mine. The bawling calf bounded after its mother and he mounted and called after it, "Suck a bellyful."

Don't think I don't know where you rustled your cattle, Sheldon had said. Interesting. Not from Rancho Omuchumne. He kept a good count on all three earmarks, Daylor's, Sheldon's and Pedro's. Where from? Did he have the *calzones* to steal from New Helvetia?

Worth ten of you. He let out a whoop. The startled horse lurched, turned a big eye on him, then resumed his dignified gait. Sometimes you had to laugh at a horse.

McCoon was paying double for Indian labor. Eighteen Omuchumne Indians working for a dollar a day would add up. Fifty cents of every dollar to Sheldon. Clever, but fair. A *ranchero* should be paid for the use of his laborers. Must be a *bueno* gold strike, he knew, for McCoon to agree to those terms and trot off for the diggings that fast. *Dios mío,* if he'd only stay there!

His full empty feeling buoyed him, made him feel all things were possible. The grass grew faster than the cattle could eat. No need to push the herd around. He stopped Chocolate, hooked a leg over the horn and took in the beauty of spring — purple, white and yellow flowers woven through the green. "Ay, ay!" he called to the beautiful world, and reached for his guitar in its saddle sling.

Rolling the chords of *La Primavera* in three-quarter time, he looked toward the millhouse, where María would be grinding corn. Even her terror of the condor robe seemed to be over. She hadn't talked of it for a long time.

He sucked a lungful of delicious air and poured his soul over the countryside. "*Ya vi-e-ne la PRI-ma-vera,*" Here comes the springtime, his voice strong as the leaping river. Seeing Quapata skirting the herd, he raised an arm that all was well. *"Sem-brando flor-es, ay, ay!/ De MIL color-es/ de MIL color-es."* Flowers in a thousand colors." Quapata's arm was up. *Está bien.* Strum, pick, pick. He embellished the lilt, his gaze sweeping the expanse of bovine backs, noses to the green — María's satin curves in his mind. *"Cantan las aves/ can-tan las aves/ repítan sus trinos suav-es.*" Si-ing the birds, repeating their soft trills. *Suave.* Soft. The cattle looked up approvingly. He wished he could hold her all night. But until the return of the *patrones*, he had to get up in the dark and ride herd to spell the Indians. Three vaqueros at all times. Ah, but the colors of dawn were like love in springtime!

I should buy a pistol, he thought, suddenly recalling McCoon's sidearm. Strangers were streaming inland, many dishonorable men. And with rumors of gold far and wide, north and south along the foothills, such men would soon be everywhere.

Funny. Just when things cleared up on one side of life, the other side clouded.

50

Maria noticed the *Americana* was wearing Crying Fox' blue crystals. She strengthened herself against them and felt the warm sun through her cap as she led the way up the stairs to Pedro's room. She had asked Elitha to talk, but wasn't sure how to broach the subject of Perrimacoo leaving Rancho Sacayak.

Billy fussed the instant he spied food. She set him on the floor and reached for her basket of dried grasshoppers hanging from the rafters, telling Elitha, "This is Pedro's house. He comes to eat when the sun is high."

Elitha glanced around the room. Did she notice the neatness of the baskets and salmon strips in the rafters, the soaproot brushes of different sizes arranged on the table? Her eyes lingered on Pedro's helmet in the corner, and slid past his black hat hanging on its peg, to his guitar on the bed.

Maria gestured toward the bed, remembering that *Americanos* do not sit on the floor. Elitha sat on the bed, pressing her high-buttoned shoes together on the floor as Maria stirred a handful of grasshoppers into the nu-pah and gave the basket to Billy.

Elitha asked, "Do you have family here at Rancho Omuchumne?"

"Yes. Cousin-sisters of my mother." Proud of her improving *Americano* talk, she licked her hand and folded her legs beneath her at the foot of the bed, rearranging her wraparound skirt.

"Cousin-sisters is a nice way of saying it." Elitha was saying, looking into Maria's eyes.

"Where is your family?"

The sad brown eyes looked even sadder. "Dead, except for my four sisters."

All dead? A family was a large and diverse body of people. Maria could have named more than two hundred relatives, and couldn't imagine them all dead.

"Why die?"

"They starved in the mountains, trying to get to California."

Crying Fox had gone there, but she must not think of him. "Have you no more aunts and uncles and cousins?"

She shook her head. "My father and mother, my aunt and uncle, and most of my cousins died up there." She lifted her eyes eastward, then looked sadly at Billy, who was eating.

She had meant to suggest Elitha go live with her family. "Where are other family?"

Elitha sighed a long dejected sigh, still watching Billy. "In Illinois. My half brother's married, with children, and my favorite aunt is there. Susanna."

"Home place is Illinois?" Seeing Elitha's nod, an idea struck. She didn't want to hurt Elitha by helping Pedro buy the land, but maybe Elitha could return to Illinois and take Perrimacoo. "How many sleeps to Illinois?"

"Oh my!" She sighed. "Let's see, it took six months to get from the farm to the California mountains, and another three weeks crossing over."

More than six moons! She had always imagined the eastern sea was only a few sleeps from the other side of the mountains. One didn't walk for six moons without good reason. Why did *Americanos* come so far? Queen bees, not people, scouted for new homes. Seeing Billy dump the contents of his basket on the floor, she scooped the food back in. "Did you know of my father's *ranchería* before you left your home?" Perhaps its beauty was known far and wide.

Elitha looked at her. "No. I live there because it is my husband's land, just like you live here with your husband."

She let that settle, and said, "I saw you happy gathering marsh nuts. But I think you are sad, no women, no family to talk your tongue."

"Catey Sheldon and Sally Daylor are my friends. But sometimes I am lonely. When Perry is away and I'm by myself in the adobe." Her voice lowered to barely a whisper.

"You are Perrimacoo's wife. Say to him with strength you want go to Illinois. Maybe he go with you." She would be happier where *Americanas* were more numerous.

"I don't understand." Elitha made such a bad face that Maria's thoughts stumbled to a stop. But when she followed Elitha's glance, there was Billy, plastered from head to toe with grasshopper nu-pah.

Grabbing him, Maria said, "Come to the river; I wash him. We talk more."

Elitha followed her to the sandy spot beneath the big black walnut tree, and Maria unfastened her skirt and stepped out of it. The *Americana* removed her shoes and stockings, bunched her long skirts above her white knees, and waded into the river on slim long-toed feet. Sunlight and shadow splotched her blue dress and tunnel hat, and her brown hair hung to her waist as the water lapped around her calves.

"I think Perrimacoo sell his land paper for gold," Maria said.

Elitha looked pretty, looking up, except for her paleness. "I guess you are probably right."

Yes! Politely Maria kept the joy from her face. "How much gold for land paper?" Pedro would want to know this. She crouched into the water, waiting as the *Americana* pursed her lips in thought. The cool, friendly water tickled up her scalp and her hair floated around her face. She held Billy at arms length, and he splashed like a fat muskrat. When he began to float she let him swim on his own, noticing from the corner of her eye that Elitha was still thinking.

Standing in the backwater beneath the overhanging black walnut tree, Elitha cocked her tunnel hat. "Why do you ask?"

"Señor Valdez wants Perrimacoo land paper."

"Oh." The sad brown eyes searched hers. "You want us to leave?" She climbed to a patch of dry sand and sat down hugging her knees, face down.

"Sí," She stood upright, water pouring from her nipples, afraid she might have seemed rude. She pulled Billy from the water and joined Elitha on the bank, rocking him gently. He snuggled his wet face against her neck, ready to sleep, and she explained, "Your man and my man cannot live in same home place. Señor Valdez wants Rancho Sacayak." With the charmstone blazing at her, she struggled to keep calm and strong.

As if seeing her feelings, Elitha opened the top buttons of her dress and fanned the crystals, which lay against her damp skin. "But Mr. Valdez has a good job here at Sheldon's rancho. Why would he want to leave?"

"He wants to be ranchero like Señor Sheldon. At my home *ranchería.*"

Absently, Elitha touched the pendant. "I see." She looked down, "I don't know how much Perry would sell the land for. But if you want, I'll ask, and tell him Señor Valdez wants to buy it."

Maria smiled at her, pleased. The important thing had been said. She hoped she had an ally in Elitha. Rocking Billy she enjoyed the faint breath of air coming across the river, drying her limbs. Wood ducks, male and female, paddled into view from around an overhanging berry clump, tipping tails up in the backwater. In the pleasant silence she wondered about the young woman sitting beside her. How had she avoided death in the adobe? "Maybe this give you power," she said, pointing at the charmstone.

Silence, long toes peeping from her full skirts. Then she said, "I thought you said it brought bad luck."

So like something Pedro would say! As if power were either good or bad. "Maybe bring good luck to you, bad to me, maybe bad to you and good to me." She shrugged and looked away. It was hard to look at the crystals.

"I found out who Perry got it from."

She tensed. *Crying Fox.* She must not even think his name.

"A girl. One of the immigrants. She took it off a dead Indian."

The *dead* penetrated. Billy jerked in her arms and whimpered, feeling the tremor in her. She had harbored a slim hope, had ridden magically on the wings of the eagle, flown into the mountains, but hadn't located her brother. He had seemed more than lost. Her voice came ragged. "Where? The . . . dead *Indio?*"

"There were two."

Crying Fox had gone with Luis.

Looking ever paler and sadder, Elitha said, "One of the women told me they were all starving and her husband must have gone out of his mind. He killed the Indians." Moisture pooled in her brown eyes.

Killed? She put Billy beside her on the bank, not sure she understood.

Elitha continued in a grainy voice. "You see, they were all starved, and the Indians were about to die anyway. Eating that flesh of the Indians saved their lives, so they got through and sent for help." She closed her eyes as if in pain.

Devoured. Condor flapped his wings in the maelstrom of Maria's mind. Nothing was safe. Frozen by the horror and needing to be sure, she forced herself to ask, "Names of two *Indios* killed by *Americanos?*"

"Only one man shot them." Elitha put her face in her hands and sobbed as if she understood the world's power was scrambled. Then she dabbed at her eyes with her skirt, and said, "One of their names meant Savior, I forget the Spanish for it. They were guides sent by Captain Sutter."

Salvador. She looked at a point in the southwest and unfocused her eyes, humming a melody to rub out the name, to keep from seeing her brother's proud bearing, his muscled calves — to keep from remembering Father's hope that his son would become hy-apo after him. She struggled to make herself numb to the loss devouring a wide channel through her, to ignore the roaring in her head and the flood of lifelong memory threatening to wash her away. Eaten. He would never find the happy land and his spirit would haunt the world.

She moved outside of herself, outside the pain, and felt the strangeness that the *Americana* seemed to feel everything just the same as she did — the abomination, the flaunting of the world's order, the flying loose of power. Maria had hoped her new-found power would help straighten the world. All these seasons she had struggled hard to learn Bear Claw's magic, but now —

She turned away. The swirling evil ones flew up her throat and sickened her tongue and poured out her mouth. When her stomach was empty she staggered into the river, cringing under Molok like a quail in the jaws of a mountain lion. She had so little power! No matter how hard she'd tried.

Elitha followed her to the water and touched her shoulder. "It wasn't your brother, was it? Both those Indians worked for Mr. Sutter."

"Sí, my brother."

Elitha, struggling visibly to control her emotions, said, "I'm so sorry. I shouldn't have said anything. But I know how you feel. My mother was killed too, and eaten. My father and aunt and uncle and cousins were all eaten after they starved."

Not looking at her, Maria let the horror of that soak in. *Americanos* ate their own kind.

Elitha looked at her with wet eyes and said, "The Indians never ate human flesh. They were the only ones who didn't." *They were stronger, Maria knew.* "The man tracked them to where they were digging for roots and acorns," Elitha continued, "they must have made it most of the way down. If it had been my brother, I would have wanted to know."

Salvador and Luis were taken into the bellies of the weak, to save the weak. It was backwards, power upside down. She floated away, looking down from above upon two young women, and from her higher perspective saw that Elitha was her double, their lives intertwined, bewitched, twisted in a funnel cloud of magic. All she could say was, "Power flies loose."

"Whatever do you mean by that?"

"Old times, people hear talk of plants and animals. They know the souls of rocks. They walk with the spirits. Now most people no hear. Only doctors hear. But *Americanos* have no doctors." Her voice sounded as distant as she felt. "You are my other side."

"You talk in riddles. I don't understand."

"People no tie down power like when they walked with spirits. The Ancients were in the world tight. They held power down. Now power flies free, loose, can kill you any time. No one safe. And you and your people come, and you are so far outside the world and strange to the spirits, you ask, what is power? In old time people say you crazy." She realized the signs were there; the earth could rise up angrily at any time and kill everyone. "Loose power mean end time comes." She'd always accepted that. Why did she resist it so?

"Power means something different to my people," Elitha said.

"Different?"

"Yes. Men give other men power. Captain Sutter got his from the Mexicans."

"Man no give power. People find power, alone." She let her gaze linger on Elitha's wet eyes and realized someone must bring her brother's bones to be buried in the home place. And Luis' people must be notified. "Where my brother's bones?"

"Nobody knows. They were wandering, lost."

We all wander lost. "*Americanos* sing my brother spirit away?"

"What do you mean?"

They didn't even sing. A grown woman asking such questions! Faced with ignorance this profound, she stared into the distance. For all she knew, her brother's soul lurked in the crystals, deadlier than a rattlesnake. But it was too late. Her bones began to shake and her vision dimmed so she couldn't see the umbels of blue brodiea beyond the green shore, couldn't hear any birds except the cawing of Molok's little brothers, mocking her weakness. She reached out to steady herself by grasping Elitha's waist, powerless to stop the weakness, afraid she was being struck dead. The trembling shadows of the fringed leaves fell over them and entered Maria's quivering. She didn't understand the meaning of it and knew only that she and this *Americana* had somehow become stuck together in the chaotic swirl of power, and like a young bird blown out of its nest, she must hold on to her, for they were magic doubles. Their fates were linked. Both had been Perrimacoo's woman, one with his child asleep on the bank, the other with his child in her body. Salvador linked them too, as did the condor robe. And Captain Sutter, who had sent Perrimacoo to live at Rancho Sacayak.

Maria realized her hard-won clarity had defeated her, and now her *seeing* was her new enemy. Ignorance yawned before her and she hadn't even faced Captain Sutter. She had put it off. But now she must learn to see differently. She would make preparations to face him.

Picking up Billy, she and Elitha walked back to the millhouse, where Father Sun blazed fiercely. Elitha turned and opened her hand, the blue crystals exploding into flashes of red-gold fire. "Here," she said, "this rightly belongs to you. Something to remember your brother by."

For a moment she shrank from the thing that should have been burned with his body, but then she closed her fist over the hard facets of the pendant, numb to the possibility of being struck dead — this was the same courage she needed to face Captain Sutter. She would take the charmstone home and lay it aside for the Cry. Burning the crystals could help, like a drop in a bucket of water.

A horse with two riders pounded toward them.

Pedro reined to a halt and helped Quapata from the saddle. Quapata's face was pinched with pain, blood streaming down his arms and dripping from his elbows as he clasped his bloody hands together.

"Help him, María," Pedro said in a tight voice, "He's lost a finger."

Teeth clenched, Quapata sank against the wall of the building.

Gently she parted the hands and looked into a surging red fountain. "Quick. Tie a cord tight around the stub. I bring medicine."

She trotted upstream where she'd seen yarrow and a stand of bonemend, a flesh-healer. Quietly she explained to the plants this was the injury Pedro warned the vaqueros against — a finger left too long when the rope was wound around the saddle horn, squeezed off when the cow or bull jerked. Then she plucked the allies. To staunch blood was a small thing. The river of power flashing chaotically through the world could not be stopped.

51

Billy picked at Pedro's sleeve and fussed.

The curse of the condor never ends, he thought, looking down at the small reminder of McCoon. Half the night María had paced the room, murmuring of magic and bad luck. Devil, she called it in Spanish. Raving like a madwoman.

Now she suddenly sat up and said, "Mother will feed you."

Leaning through the shaft of sun angling through the window, he kissed her sleep-warm lips, stroked back her hair and whispered, "I am sorry."

Billy wiggled between them.

"Sorry? You do nothing wrong."

"I am a failure as your husband because I cannot make your unhappiness and your troubles go away."

"They are not gnats to be swatted."

He lifted her brown hands, skilled hands that healed, hands that made him feel like a king, hands that collected gold so he could buy Rancho Sacayak. He turned them over, kissed each palm. "*Hasta luego, Indita mía.* Until siesta."

Saddling Chocolate, he shook his head sadly. He'd had to dig it out of her that Elitha thought Perry McCoon would sell the land. He'd whooped for joy, but she hardly noticed. Instead she started in about the condor robe. He was near the end of his patience when she hung her head and told how her brother had died. *Madre de Dios!* Killed like a deer. For meat. Pedro recalled Salvador, a bright young Indian standing straight for morning reveille, and shivered.

He mounted Chocolate, crossed himself and thanked God he'd held his tongue. As the proud, virile animal loped up the trail, Pedro thought, poor little María. Sweet soul. Trying to be a wise woman. Ay, what terrible luck, that this would happen to her of all people!

Sweating in the June heat, he rode to Daylor's to replace Roberto's broken cinch ring. Señor Daylor kept a stock of supplies and Pedro took what he needed for the ranch. The morning was still fresh and his shadow flickered through the trees. Already he smelled the straw of his sombrero, wet with perspiration. It would be blistering today!

He half expected to see Daylor's big gray at the adobe, the rancheros being overdue from the diggings. But no horse was there. Only an Indian sat in the packed-earth yard. *Está bien.* Señora Daylor would give him the cinch ring and record it in her book.

Drawing closer, he recognized the proud posture and hair plume of Captain Juan, his father-in-law, seated cross-legged before the porch. If he had come to trade, where were his pelts? What was he waiting for? Then Pedro saw the large, full basket shining with what appeared to be gold.

Realization shocked him down to his spurs. Chocolate lunged forward. *Ay Madre,* not the gold! Señora Daylor would have seen it.

He reined to a stop before Captain Juan, majestically serene in his nakedness. The morning sun glanced brilliantly off the gold, piercing Pedro's heart. The price of the land would be out of his reach. Dismounting, he stood looking down at the Indian, his necklace of oversized bear claws.

"Where are you going?" asked Captain Juan, the polished bones of his top-knot and ear plugs dazzling white against his black hair.

Choking out the customary answer, Pedro looped his reins over the porch rail and folded his legs beneath him where Juan patted the ground. Niceties came first. Indians were even worse about that than Spaniards. Pedro asked about Etumu and all his other relations.

When all greetings had been exchanged, Pedro took a deep breath. "Has the Señora seen the basket of gold?" He nodded at the house.

"Sí."

Of course. Pedro swallowed, looked down, blinked away stinging perspiration. The runner had garbled the message. *Diablo!* He should have ridden personally to speak with Captain Juan. Now things were complicated, damnedably so. He expelled a long breath. The basket of gold twinkled.

His father-in-law cast him a quick look. "Runner come talk. Say Perrimacoo not know we give gold to you. I say good. Perrimacoo not know."

Pedro struggled to keep his face quiet. "But you showed this to the wife of his friend!" The crack in his voice betrayed him. *Madre de Dios!* McCoon would do handsprings.

Captain Juan absorbed the unspoken alarm. "No," he said carefully. "I listen to runner. Gold we collect for you stay in my house. You see it first, when basket is full." He patted the side of the full round vessel. "This gold different. My people gather it for trade. I trade now. Get guns, blankets, *Americano* food." Briefly he searched Pedro's face and added, "My men want these things now."

Completely garbled. Pedro feared the strain showed on his face, matched the gravel in his voice. "Now Señor McCoon will know the gold came from his land, and will ask more in trade for it." *Much more. Probably won't sell at all.* Why, oh why hadn't Pedro ridden himself?

Captain Juan remained placid. "Gold not come from land."

Hope sat up in Pedro. "Where did you get this then?" *Five leagues away*, he prayed, touching the gold, hot in the sun.

"In river."

"Where in the river?"

The Indian looked at him oddly. "At my people's *ranchería.*"

Pedro groaned, "On McCoon's land."

"River not land."

Dios mío! So many chances for misunderstanding! "The river is part of the land," he said, aching to wrench time back a week.

"Land no is water." The tone was flat, final, conveying what Pedro knew quite well. Indians didn't like to repeat themselves. The morning sun behind Captain Juan outlined him in a brilliant halo and shadowed his already dark face.

Pedro leaned forward on his crossed legs, the tips of his fingers on his forehead, then sat straight, squinting at him. "Now Señor McCoon won't want to sell. He'll search for gold in your *ranchería*, so it means the same thing." He remembered he hadn't been free to go, not for a long time. He couldn't leave Sheldon's rancho for half a day with so many vaqueros gone. Anything could happen, and he was responsible when both *patrones* were absent. "Did you tell Señora Daylor where you found this?"

"Señora no ask."

Pedro pondered the possibility of a white lie about the gold's source.

Captain Juan added, "She no trade for *oro*. She say, wait for Señor Daylo. He come this day. He make trade. I wait." His dusky face remained calm, eyes unfocused.

Seeing the profound Indian dignity, Pedro knew he'd never be able to make him lie. Grandmother María said Indians thought untruth disturbed the natural harmony of life. It was best, she said, to follow the example of straightforward animals. Coyote's treachery got him into predicaments. Anyway, McCoon wasn't likely to be fooled.

Trying to be patient, Pedro explained that more gold would be needed now to buy Rancho Sacayak. Much more.

Not a muscle twitched in the Indian's face. The river barely whispered beyond the brambles, and the Daylors' dog panted noisily beneath the ripening berries. Pedro could feel the perspiration tickling down through his sideburns.

Captain Juan's voice came low. Regretful? "My people gather three baskets of gold for you. No talk of it to Perrimacoo. No talk of it to Señora Daylo."

Pedro felt limp. "Can you get that much?"

The Indian nodded. "*Mucho oro* in river." He touched the basket before him. "This *oro*, my people need trade now. Work hard."

Pedro understood. Most of the gold was in small flakes, very tedious to separate, and, as ranch foreman he knew well that it was necessary for laboring people to see rewards. His gold must come second. He was lucky to get it at all. Laying a hand on Captain Juan's thick shoulder, he said with sincerity, "*Muchas gracias, Capitán Juan.*" For trying.

Would three baskets be enough? Five? Ten? The more gold McCoon saw coming from his rancho, the less likely he would sell at any price. Damn the bad luck! It seemed like there really was a curse.

52

Gold at Rancho Sacayak! All day Sarah and Elitha talked of little else, and every few minutes they peered out the window to see the Indian seated beneath the cottonwood. Beside him the gold sparkled yellow in a basket big enough to cook a good-sized pot of beans. Sarah hadn't known what to trade for so much. Waiting for the men, Elitha felt about to burst with excitement. Her hidden nugget hadn't been lost by some passing trapper after all. A mine had to be nearby, probably on Perry's land!

When at last the three trail-grimy ranchers dismounted before the adobe, Perry glanced at the big Indian, then, as if yanked by a rope his head jerked back, and he stared at the gold. She felt something in the air, like an approaching storm.

The Indian got up with the gold, and they all came inside and Sarah told them what had happened.

"At's me gold," Perry growled, "sure as shootin it tis!" The Indian stood quietly by, the gold weighing him down.

"Think fer a bloody minute, mait!" Daylor said, chopping his hand toward the Indian, "I been trading with him for eight years now. Hits me livelihood. He's captain of the neighbor tribe. I canna of a sudden say I won't trade! Merrily take his gold and hand it to you?" Locked in each other's stare, the two glowered in equal measure, Daylor's high-boned nose inches from Perry's forehead, the grime in their crow's feet intensifying their fierceness.

"Hits me own bleedin land the bloody savage got it from!"

Elitha cringed. No matter the bad blood between Mr. Sheldon and Perry, she had hoped the friendship between him and Mr. Daylor was unshakable on account of both having been English sailors. Now she worried. On the frontier neighbors had to be friends. But who was right? If Indians found gold on Mr. Daylor's ranch, would they be expected to hand it over to him? This was complicated. Maybe if Indians were paid to mine, they should give up the gold, like workers anywhere. But Perry hadn't paid Captain Juan, so maybe Mr. Daylor was right. She wondered what Pa would say, if he were here.

Mr. Sheldon stayed out of the quarrel, nodding Sarah and Elitha aside, telling them they'd brought home "more gold than we expected." He sucked on his *cigarrito*, and blew smoke toward the tan hills, listening to the row inside. She suspected Captain Juan's gold bothered him too, though he gave no hint of an opinion. No one mentioned supper.

At last it was quiet and Elitha went back into the kitchen. Mr. Daylor had taken Captain Juan into the trading room, where he was examining the goods. Perry stood leaning on the doorjamb, half his hat, half his shirtback visible, the crusty fingers of his right hand gripping the sweat-stained shirt beneath his elbow, right boot crossed over and resting accusingly on the toe. She knew that stance. Cross.

Feeling excitement and tension, she lifted the cloth from the pan, amazed how fast the bread had risen, and floured her hands. Watching the trade room — the Indian picking up goods — she began punching down the dough. Sarah came in with the green beans and sat down to string them where she could see. Elitha rolled dough balls, stretched the tops smooth, pinched the bottoms, wiped them through the melting butter and snuggled the greasy orbs into the larded pan. The Indian picked out a stack of blankets. The crossed boot didn't move.

Captain Juan moved around the room selecting tools, knives, a sack of beans, a bucket of beads, she couldn't see what all. Mr. Daylor nodded assent each time the Indian raised an item. Patting the pate of the last greasy dough ball, Elitha placed the rolls on the shelf above the stove, covered it with the cloth, and glanced at Sarah. Snapping beans by the feel, her gaze never left the trading room.

Elitha ventured, "Looks like it's getting nigh onto suppertime. Mr. Sheldon staying?" She hadn't heard his horse go and she wanted to stay too. The later it got, the more likely she and Perry would get caught in the dark. But Sarah didn't catch the hint. It was as if the gold had cast a spell over the ranch.

Elitha ventured again, "Well, I'd best get the stove started." Wiping her hands on the sackcloth about her waist, she pushed the heavy oak door open and went outside. The hot air hit her in the face. It was hard to breathe. The sky looked white hot, the mounded briars appeared white, the leaves curled to their pale undersides. A mule with a packsaddle stood dozing at the porch rail, swishing at flies. Mr. Daylor must have had an Indian bring it. *Poor thing, in the sun.* The heat always intensified before sundown.

On the shady side of the adobe, where she went for wood, she saw Mr. Sheldon sitting pensively on an uncut log. She smiled, shy of him after the bawling-out he'd given Perry three weeks ago. Back on the porch, the door swung open against her armload of wood. She stepped aside.

Out came Captain Juan with a pile of blankets, two full buckets banging from each huge forearm. Daylor followed, piled with bags and boxes. They packed the mule, Sheldon coming around the corner to watch.

By the time Elitha had the fire going, and was again outside, the mule was swaying up the trail under its load, led by Captain Juan. Perry squinted after him, stubble darkening his jaw, a gleam in his eye. Sarah and Mr. Daylor stood hip to hip, arms about each other.

Mr. Sheldon put a boot on the step and leaned on his knee, the *cigarrito* between his fingers. "Folks," he said, startling Elitha — it had been so long since anyone had talked — "We got a problem." He turned to Daylor. "I've sent for the Rhoads. We'll talk over supper."

Sarah smiled at Elitha. "You'll get to see Catey's baby."

That added to the excitement — they should be here any time — but Mr. Sheldon was right. The gold had stirred up strong feelings, and Elitha couldn't wait to hear what Mr. Sheldon would propose to do about it.

The sun sank behind the trees and mounded berry canes, but the excitement remained. Elitha could feel it when she hugged Catherine Sheldon and heard her whispered account of the baby's birth, and when she smiled and chatted briefly with John Rhoads, still a bear of a man. It was there when she renewed her acquaintance with Matilda Rhoads, the luckiest woman alive, to have John.

Catherine's baby, named William after Mr. Daylor, lay diapered on a blanket, a shock of dark hair standing straight up on his tiny head. He had a sweet face with eyes shut, creases pink on pink like buds. Closed to the world. What would those eyes see when he grew up? Would the frontier look the same? Would Elitha live to see her own baby? You never knew. A girl had to make each day important, and she was determined not to waste a single mnute mooning about things she didn't have. Now she would have gold.

Blessed shade now stretched across the entire yard. She helped the women move barrels and boards to make an outdoor table, catching the excitement of the men's talk — Mr. Sheldon and Mr. Daylor telling John Rhoads and his father about the diggings. Perry was oddly quiet, though he'd drunk several cups of *aguardiente*.

"Now you just sit and rest, little sister," Sarah ordered Catherine, who stepped off the porch with napkins, butter, salt and pepper. The birth had taken some of the bounce out of her, but she rolled her eyes at her sister in a way that made Elitha smile. *Still an imp.*

Feeling the unreality of the day, Elitha went in — the house an oven — to check the biscuits. She lowered the stove door and the heat blew her hair back and dried her perspiring brow. Eyes narrowed against it, she bunched her skirts to protect her hands, and carried the browned biscuits to the outdoor table. A breath of air from the river felt good; it riffled the blackberry leaves where the Rhoads' children were lined up, reaching through the thorns for the ripe berries.

"You kids git over here and wash now," said Matilda Rhoads, dipping water from the bucket into tin cups. One glance at their purple faces and stained teeth and she raised her voice, "My land! You look like a bunch of Indians!"

Elitha sat opposite Perry on a wooden crate next to Catherine, who was gazing into her baby's sleeping face. Perry had washed and shaved, and seemed entranced, like he didn't know where he was. All the men were hatless and looked young with their tender foreheads showing. Or was it the excitement that made them seem youthful despite their nearly two-score years? From the outdoor fire an

Indian brought a basket of roasted beef and set it on the table.

John Rhoads said to his wife, "I've about made up my mind, Matty. I can't stay and farm while every other man is getting rich in the mines." He turned to his father. "Pa, let's you and me ride to the American River. Send for Brother Dan." He glanced at Mr. Sheldon. "What was that Indian *ranchería* called? Where Marshall built the sawmill?"

"Culuma."

"What's Culuma?" A boy piped from among the children circling the table, waiting for the adults to finish eating.

Matilda scowled. "Children are to be seen, not heard. Now you all step back three big steps."

"S'maa'm." They stepped back.

John Rhoads said, "Yes, Culuma. Now I figure if the gold's awashin down to all them rich claims on that island where the Mormons are, it's bound to lie aplenty in between. I say we stake a claim between. How big's a claim anyhow?" He looked between Sheldon and Daylor.

Holding a rib, Mr. Daylor talked through his chewing. "Ent much size to it. The boys is drawin lines in the sand with their boots. They agree on the lines." He chuckled. "Why, with all the territory up there, ever man could git a claim and there'd be plenty gold left over for the King's naivy."

Perry still gazed at the trees along the river, scheming something in his head. Mr. Sheldon swung his eyes to the Rhoads men, father and son. "Why don't you join us at Dry Diggins?"

John answered. "Naw. You got the Indians to do your work. We'll do better on the American, by ourselves." He turned to the elder Mr. Rhoads. "What do you say, Pa?"

As the white-haired man nodded, Elitha chimed in. "Captain Sutter's having good luck up at Piny Woods too."

Mr. Daylor raised his brows. "No foolin?"

"At's right," John Rhoads said. "We hear from the teamsters haulin supplies. Pertaneer every day more miners head that way, most crossing at your place."

Sheldon clipped: "Men, we need a plan."

People suspended their rib gnawing and corn munching and turned their attention to him. By her moony expression Catherine could have been looking at a god, the watch moving up and down on the tight fabric of her bosom.

Mr. Sheldon spoke deliberately. "Way I see it, we're ranchers first and foremost. Sure I mill wheat and Bill, you got yer trading. But it's land and cattle — hides, tallow, beef — gives us our way of life. And a good one it is. Here's my thinking." He laid down his fork and looked intently at each of the three men. "We can't run stock without Indians. Not atall. Same at the mines. Without Indians not one of us would have a ratskin of gold. Follow?"

His mouth hung thoughtfully slack before he continued. "Now Perry's Indians is diggin their own gold. Don't get me wrong, Bill, you done right to give Captain Juan that mule and all that gear. It don't pay to rile the Indians, cause they're all connected by marriage. But danged if I don't see trouble with a capital T galloping our way."

Matilda all but whispered, "What do you mean, Jared?"

Catherine turned modestly sideways, unbuttoned her frock, and put the baby to her breast. Elitha chewed quietly so she could hear, the warm breeze lifting her damp hair, bringing the first fragrance of night moss from the river. Mr. Sheldon's high cheekbones and narrowed eyes gave him an intense, wise look. "Way I see it, we gotta control our labor force. They been happy gittin every tenth calf, and now fifty *centavos* worth of goods for mining. But what'll they do when they hear about Captain Juan takin home that mountain of gear?" He didn't wait for a response, but turned to Mr. Daylor.

"Bill, I don't mean to tell you yer business. It just seems to me we gotta set trade standards. Git the word to Sutter and Mellus and Brannan, right down to San Francisco — all the store proprietors. Or see our workers minin' fer theirselves. Follow? We couldn't even raise cattle."

Mr. Daylor scowled. "You mean make it so mining's not worth their time?" Elitha didn't quite understand.

Sheldon gnawed a bone, spoke to it. "Unless they mine for us, maybe at increased wages." He lifted his head. "You see any other way fer us to git by out here?" His light hazel eyes held pained determination. She knew he owed a great deal of money to shippers after building his new house and furnishing it with fine things shipped around the Horn.

The table was silent, the day's fierce light softening at last.

Perry spoke for the first time since the argument with Mr. Daylor. "So what's hard to figure? Weight the scales. Hit's done all the time, at ever port in the world. Methinks Sutter'll see the gist o' that, or he'll be beggared by the 'eathens." He glanced at Mr. Sheldon, then Mr. Daylor, a little obsequiously, Elitha thought. Mr. Sheldon's wolf eyes lingered a moment on Perry before going back to the food before him.

Mr. Daylor's long stretch of pale forehead was ridged in thought, but he said, "Ye might could be right, Perry."

John Rhoads sounded tentative. "Well, you ranchers do see to it the Indians have clothes and all — horses, the works. They're better off here than any redskins back home, thanks to you. So mebbe that seems right." The elder Rhoads gave him a serious nod.

Mr. Daylor kept his scowl. "I could say I gave Captain Juan a bonus fer coming here, stead of Mellus or Brannan. A one-time thing."

Mr. Sheldon swung him a thoughtful glance, nodding.

Elitha wondered, was that cheating the Indians? As the table grew animated again, shadows deepened across the yard, and frogs and crickets competed with the men's excited talk about gold all through the California foothills. Something told her Captain Juan wouldn't take kindly to being treated differently at the scales. He was no ordinary redskin. Yet for all his savage dignity, white men could control his earnings. It seemed sad. But then, everybody knew Indians shouldn't have too much money, or they'd go wild with liquor. She supposed that made sense, but it still bothered her, even if they didn't figure out the scales had been weighted. On the other hand, Perry had to keep his ranch workers. Cattle gave him a steady income — when he didn't gamble it away. And if Mr. Sheldon's Indians stopped working for Perry at the diggings, there would be no hope of rebuilding the house — paying for the carpenters she'd sent for. But no matter how she twisted it in her mind, weighting the scales seemed like cheating. She wished Pa were here. He would know what to do.

Rising with the women to clear dishes, she suddenly thought of Indian Mary and Señor Valdez wanting to buy the ranch. Elitha had said Perry would sell, but things were different now. With gold on the ranch he wouldn't need to leave home to make his fortune.

She set out plates for the children, who were scrambling for places. "Ain't 'nough biscuits left," whined a boy.

Matilda cuffed his ear. "Watch your manners!"

"S'maa'm."

Perry smoked quietly in the shadows of the porch. What was he thinking?

53

Maria saw the glint of amusement when her cousin-sisters gathered their toddlers and hurried to the village center.

Old women giggled, taking their accustomed places. "Perrimacoo is here," they said. "Perrimacoo comes to talk." Hearing the commotion, even Great-Grandmother Dishi tottered down the path, feeling her way with outstretched arms. She always enjoyed the laughter of the *umne*. Excited children came in packs and seated themselves under the trees, close enough to hear the hy-apo. They grinned at one another, hands clasped between crossed legs, shoulders hunched to their ears like turtles. Even the panting dogs looked expectant. Grizzly Hair's sparring with Perrimacoo had become a favorite entertainment. And part of the fun was in knowing some of the men remained hidden.

Suddenly the scene struck Maria as hilarious and she turned her back to Perrimacoo, spitting silent laughter. He expected his bad manners to be forgotten, expected to be treated as an esteemed trader when not long ago he'd been sent home with a hole in his hat. When she was sure of her straight face, she turned back to him.

Grizzly Hair was seated before the house, seemingly devoid of the humor tickling through the crowd.

Perrimacoo led with, "I wants ye to mine gold for me. But this time ye'll stay to 'ome. Sit right here on your arses, doing what ye been doing behind me back is all I'm askin, and I'll pay fifty cents a day a head." As Maria translated, he looked over the happy faces.

She was fairly sure Perrimacoo's new offer wouldn't sway Father or the family heads. People whispered back and forth, smiles gone from the faces, children alert. Grizzly Hair sat in quiet serenity, not a hair of his plume moving in the noon heat while, below, the river-baby spirit bubbled and cooed.

"Set out a simple bargain, I did. Mary, tell him you people are to keep mining gold as ye've been doing, and give it all to me. Good as my word, I is. Fifty cents every day, that is if I gets nice baskets full like the one yer daddy took up to Daylor's." His voice deepened to a growl. "And no more sneaking it there behind my back. Cause Daylor'll let me know real quick. We ranchers are stickin together on this, we is!"

What did that mean?

With a straight face and a lively gleam in his eye Grizzly Hair asked, "Rancheros put on pine tar and stick together?"

Raucous laughter came from every side and Maria shrieked too, and when she finally gained control, she wiped tears and explained it to stormy-looking Perrimacoo.

Looking at the rocking, side-holding audience, he pushed up to his feet, hands on hips, and skewered her with eyes hardened to points. "The white men has talked," he said. "From now on you niggers don't git hardly nothin for gold you bring in. Anywhere. Daylor's, Sutter's, San Francisco, hits all the same at the trading posts of the white men." A slow grin spread over his face.

She translated and the laughter dwindled. Grizzly Hair sat impassively, then said, "Tell him to sit."

His blue eyes darted around, and he sat gingerly, as if on thistles. Worried about arrows? People smiled.

Grizzly Hair said, "Tell him we will make him a gold-washing basket and he can find his own gold. If he gives it all to me, I pay him fifty cents each day. But if he keeps the gold he finds, I pay nothing." People hooted with laughter, and the tiniest flicker of amusement crossed his lips. He paused for Maria's translation.

The words rolled easily from her happy tongue. Father hadn't consulted with the family heads, but from the smiles on their faces, she knew they had come to prior agreement. She needn't have worried. Grizzly Hair was a wise hy-apo.

Perrimacoo's face reddened and he sputtered incomprehensibly. Father talked over it, "No disturbing Perrimacoo," he told the *umne,* "if you see him washing sand at the river." Heads nodded sagely, eyes sparkling with sly humor as she translated.

Perrimacoo jumped up and yelled, "Work for monkeys! Not in a lifetime of Sundays, ye big — " He stared into space, hands on hips, jaw working. Surprisingly, he exhaled and dropped his head, showing only the top of his soiled leather hat. Then he lifted his head and said, "I'm finished here. Tell him, Mary."

She did. People looked crestfallen. No arrows had pinned Perrimacoo's hat.

"Walk with me to me 'orse, Mary," he said. "I gots me an idear." He looked up and down her body, but his tone was polite.

She did as asked, but only as far as could be seen by the men. He narrowed an eye and said, "I 'appens to know Captain Sutter want's to see ye."

A needle of fear pricked her, though she'd been thinking how to go to him.

"Come with me for two days to Sutter's, and I'll give ye a hundred dollars."

She recalled what Pedro had said about a thousand dollars. "No," she said, turning toward the u-macha. She had something else in mind for her visit to Captain Sutter.

"Change yer mind, ye will," he called. She turned to see him viciously yank the horse's head around. Drawing blood with the spurs, he galloped up the trail.

As she stared after him, her good feelings drained away. Vultures played overhead, the late sun catching the white of their wing feathers. Brothers of Molok.

54

Elitha penned a letter to her half brother:

July 13, l848

Dear Will,

We are expecting a bundle from the stork in about 4 months, so by the time you get this I'll be a mother. I have made good friends — two sisters about my age married to men who own a big farm. Did I tell you they call farms "ranchos" in California? I have a horse now, so I can get back and forth on my own.

Something stank. She glanced at Perry, home from another week of mining, bare feet in a V over the bottom of the bed. Flies droned over him. His forehead was white in the gloomy corner of the room, his hat on the floor beside his limp hand, his boots piled where he'd left them. His belly looked concave. He was losing flesh. It seemed he was killing himself in the search for gold, but she knew he gambled away most of what he found.

> *If the carpenters haven't left yet, tell them not to worry about the money for the passage. We'll pay the minute they get to the ranch.*

In her first letter she hadn't stressed how quickly they would be paid.

> *God is rewarding John Rhoads for rescuing the immigrants. Rhoads Diggings is proving the richest in the territory.*

Perry muttered, "Damn 'eathens." He hated paying them a dollar a day.

> *Perry is at the diggings most of the time now. Seenyor . . .*

She wanted to use Sheldon's Spanish name — it seemed so exotic, so Californian — but didn't know how to spell it. And then she'd have to mention that the recipients of Mexican land grants were given Spanish names, and Will would wonder why Perry didn't have one. She scowled. Why indeed? Oh well, Will was unlikely to think of that, or know how to spell in Spanish.

> *. . . Wakeen Sheldon and Mr. Daylor are still getting a lot of gold, mined by their Indians. Indians are real useful in California., and I've never heard of an uprising.*

Dipping the quill she paused over the paper. There was more she couldn't write. Sacayak Indians refusing to mine for Perry. Perry drinking more than ever, and thinking she didn't know he buried fat little bags of gold. A world of things she couldn't write. Like her doubts that riches would change him, and the way her stomach felt when she thought of spending the rest of her life with him. *Till death do us part.* An ink splotch fell on the paper and spread all over "California." She grabbed a pinch of sand, sprinkled the spot, shook the paper, and wrote:

> *Your sister, Elitha.*

She sighed, hoping the carpenters would come by ship. Otherwise they'd wait until next May before heading across the prairie. "Finished," she sang out.

Perry lay like a corpse.

She folded the letter, laid it on the window shelf and went outside to fetch the venison roast from the spit. Gay-Gay, her headstrong white mare, looked up.

Back inside, Elitha made her voice light as she cut the meat. "I bet the newspapers in the States got wind of the gold out here, with all the emigrants writing to home."

Silence.

"You alright?"

"I could eat a horse."

"Supper's ready."

He rolled from the bed, sat with his head in his hands, then shuffled to the table with glazed eyes. Thirty-eight. Old.

She kept her tone cheerful. "You get good gold this week?" He'd buried a bag.

"Aye. But diggin deeper now, we is, a big trench. Broke me bleedin shovel." He glanced at her over the meat. "God's bones, had to ride to the fort for a new one!" If she had known, she could have sent her letter sooner.

He sawed his meat with his hunting knife and speared it with the point. "Twelve dollars, that rascal Sam Brannan asked fer it. A plain spade!" He put the meat in his mouth, chewed. "Keeps his fingernails long, that one does, to get a fat pinch."

"Pinch?"

"Pinch o' dust counts for a dollar." Chewing, he shook his head. "Fort smithy's crankin out shovels like salt at the bottom o' the sea, 'e is."

She recalled the tale of the magic handmill that never stopped grinding salt, making the sea salty. "How does the fort look now?"

Bits of food came out with the s's. "Fort Sacramento, they're callin it. Hub of the world, it tis. Men from all lands, and a colorful bunch they is. Stealing what they can't buy. Brannan's sellin supplies so fast Sutter leased him that building outside." He stabbed the air with his fork, "That one you stayed in."

Wiping damp debris from her face, she remembered the sawdust beds and the useless waiting for Pa and Tamsen, and couldn't imagine it as a store.

"Made doors between the rooms," he said clanking his fork and knife on the plate and grabbing the bucket. He tilted his head and drank, water running from both sides of his mouth, down over his shirt. "Ahhh." He poured the rest on his hair, dark points of it streaming water over his face. It would make mud under the table, and she decided to press pebbles into it to make a floor.

How did he endure the sun? Paint was looking bony too, after riding back and forth so many times to the diggings — thirty miles one way. Perry banged the bucket to the floor and eyed her across the table.

"Keseberg set up a store too," he said, "Stocked it rich, 'e did. But never did give me the time of day." He grabbed a piece of gristle and gnawed viciously.

It was obvious to her where Keseberg got his money, but she was through tormenting herself with that. A hot shaft of sun came through the window glass; still it was cooler inside than out, adobe having that advantage over wood. Aloud she said, "Maybe the best kind of house would be made of adobe with a covering of wood on both sides, to keep the rain from melting the walls and to keep the dust out of the inside."

He used his knife to work a string of gristle from a back tooth.

She waited, wanting to say: I can't believe there isn't a single man in California who could build for us. But repeating that made him angry. The trouble was, the Illinois carpenters would probably disappear into the mines the moment they set foot in California — if they came at all.

He grabbed another piece of dripping meat, gnawed it, spoke through his full mouth. "Neptune's bones, the trappers from Oregon territory is swarming to the mines, and a rowdy bunch they is! Shooed em out of our diggings, we did."

"Did you hear anything about my stove order?" She didn't want to cook outside another rainy winter.

He shoved a whole biscuit in his mouth, stood, loosened his belt, lifted a hip and cracked a loud one. As he stepped to the bed and fell back, staring at the ceiling, a fecal cloud sickened her. "Like I said," he muttered, "clerks has left the stores in San Francisco. The bay is full 'o ships. Deserted. Stacked like cordwood. Yer wee bit o' paper is in the pocket of some bloke up to his knees in mud. Nay, more'n likely floated out t'sea by now. Ate by a whale."

There was no end to discouragement. She sighed. "We live like Indians, Perry." With a king's ransom buried out back.

With startling suddenness, which made her flinch, he leaped from the bed. But instead of threatening her for what she'd said, he shoved a cup under the barrel and yanked out the cork. The amber liquid gurgled out.

He gulped half a cup and placed it on the table and, to her amazement, did a quick-stepping jig, slapping his thighs and waving his arms as he sang:

Oh the times was hard and the wa-a-ge-s low.
Leave her, John-ny, leave her!
But now once more asho-o-re we'll go,
for it's time for us to leave her.
Leave her, Johnny, leave her.

He stopped suddenly and narrowed his eyes to thick dark fringes, the dimple deep in his cheek. "No ma'am, this old tar ain't totin wool atwixt his ears!"

She almost hated to ask, "What're you planning?"

He danced a quick step, slapped his thighs and placed his hands on her shoulders, all but singing, "Those trappers? Outa the Colombia River? Blokes I chased outa the diggins?"

She nodded, having no idea what had got into him. "Are they carpenters?"

He howled, and when he had recovered, said, "No. But it's rich claims they be wantin, and I gots me a sweet little idear where they can buy some." He went to the window, stared out, gulped the liquor.

"I'll show them nigger bastards. Sheldon too. Dollar a day me arse!"

"What are you going to do?"

He turned, his eyes steel points. "Me business, lass. Me business."

Reaching for the soap-plant bulb, she took the bucket of dishes to the river, a weary dread weighing her down.

The red sun peeped across the hills, the air too dry for dew. Birds filled the morning with chattering and piping as Perry shoved Elitha's letter into his saddle-pack. Patting the bundle, which was fat with gold bags — she knew — he smiled at her, still mum about his plans.

"When you coming back?" She'd decided to stay home and train Gay-Gay. Besides, she was getting easier about being alone. Indian Mary had taught her some tracking tricks — following small animals through the grasslands and river bottom, learning how they spent their days. It was a cross between a puzzle and a story. Once she'd seen an Indian boy tracking the same fox, and, smiling at him, realized this was the Indian equivalent of ABCs. And if she got too restless, she could always go to Rancho Omuchumne. If Gay-Gay wasn't too headstrong.

He squinted, finger-combed his dark hair and replaced his stained hat. "Few days?" Clean-shaven, he grinned. "Hell girl, you know I don't know. Maybe one of Daylor's niggers'll git word to you."

At least that was honest.

He jabbed the points of the spurs into the pinto. It jumped forward, but before it had gone three steps, he yanked on the Spanish bit and the animal sat on its tail. "Hear 'ny more about Sheldon's greaser wantin' to buy me land?"

She'd assumed Perry had lost interest. "No."

Watching him go, she frowned. He was taking a lot of gold to the fort. More than usual. And just what did he mean, showing up the Indians and Sheldon? Knowing him, it wasn't likely to come to any good.

55

Some men had too much land, Pedro reflected as he sat astride Chocolate watching the herd graze on land belonging to Don Guillermo Hartnell. The former Englishman owned the south side of the river — from *Nueva Helvetia* to the flats across from McCoon's rancho — a long series of grants on the Cosumnes. Señor Sheldon, whose north bank holding was small by comparison, knew Señor Hartnell quite well. Said Hartnell had done paperwork for the Governor and got paid in land. Ay, ay, ay, Pedro wished he could read! It was hard to earn land by the sweat of one's brow. But he had María, and, yes, certain amusements.

Resting his forearms on the saddlehorn, he chuckled at her story about McCoon failing, again, to get the Sacayak Indians to wash gold for him. Paying Sheldon's Indians a dollar a day! It was *cómico*, when he realized all the man had to do was treat them with respect. He wiped his sleeve across his brow.

Dios mío, it would be nice to have the Omuchumne home again. Four vaqueros couldn't keep up with the emergencies — grizzlies on the prowl, wolves and coyotes after the calves — much less the routine chores. Pedro longed for a whole night's sleep. Besides, *Indios* made life pleasant. He liked their dry humor. María missed her women friends. They both missed the Big Times.

But Sheldon said the Indians took too much gold from the diggings to let them stop now. "Geniuses," he called them. They no longer winnowed it in blankets, but washed it in water they fed through a flume that they'd dug for miles and lined with wood. Indian ingenuity was as endless as the gold.

Pedro saw Quapata coming, smooth as a song on his black stallion. Yesterday the Indian had joked: *Easier to feed out rope now*, though the stub of his finger was barely healed. Typical. His smile dropped. Quapata was riding low and hard.

The lathered stallion pounded up beside Chocolate. "Señor Valdez. No like *hombres* at Señor Daylo's. Señora no like too." Quapata's face twisted with urgency.

"What men?"

"Strangers. Wear animal skins."

Walla Walla hunters wore such garb. "Indians?"

"*Americanos.* Two."

Pedro tightened the bead on his sombrero and spurred Chocolate. Quapata, who was not one to overreact, rode beside him. Pedro guarded more than cattle during the absences of the *patrones*. Señoras Sarah and Catherine he would defend with his life. He splashed across the shallow river, Quapata in stride, his brown heels gripping the stallion's belly. At Mill Ranch he waved at María, who looked up from her work, and continued pounding the mile up the trail to Daylor's adobe. As he rode he felt down to the stock of his new Allen pepperbox four-shooter, reassuring himself. Gold was drawing adventurers to Sutter's camp, and they all stopped at Daylor's store.

Unsure what lay ahead and not wanting to alert the bad men, he signaled Quapata and jumped off Chocolate. "Wait here." Handing the rein to the Indian, he quickly pressed four balls and four packets of powder into the grooves of the stubby gun barrel, then crept around the last bend of the trail to the adobe. Two saddle horses and a pack mule nibbled blackberries in the shade of cottonwood, picks, shovels and tin pans strapped on their backs. He jumped to the porch, spurs jingling, and pushed open the door.

Inside the trading room Señora Daylor was backed into the corner between a barrel of beans and a pile of tumbled blankets, her gown intact and buttoned, but he'd never seen her blonde upsweep unraveled like this. Her eyes locked with Pedro's and he read gratitude.

Within an arm's reach of her, a strongly built young man in buckskins and a wide felt hat, two turkey feathers nearly scraping the ceiling, turned cold blue eyes on him. Beside the man a rifle stood propped against a crate. A taller, thinner, older man, also in long-fringed buckskin, cradled his gun in his arms. The rifles were the percussion type, barrels shorter than some. But Pedro's Allen was faster, accurate enough at short range. Both men wore knife holsters in front, horn hafts angling toward their right hands.

The younger man drawled, "My stars, the Mexican niggers is crawlin all over this here country, ain't they?"

Pedro felt his nerves tingle like when he lassoed grizzlies. He looked at the Señora and asked her, "What's happening here?"

The younger man purred, "Wall whaddeya know, Daddy? This here spik in a monkey suit kin talk English!" He parodied amazement as his eyes ran from Pedro's sombrero to his vest, the sash holding the four-shooter, down to the goatskin spats over his *pantalones.*

"Were they bothering you, Señora?"

She swallowed and glanced from one stranger to the other. "Well, first they was lookin at the goods — "

The older man nickered.

Wild men without principles. Some *Norteamericanos* would kill their own mothers. Pedro was glad he'd come in time. "Have they bought something?"

As she shook her head, the *Norteamericanos* exchanged an amused look.

Pedro looked at them and said quietly, "It is time for you to go, *señores.*"

The older man spoke for the first time, "Suh-un, peers this here greaser's fixin to throw us outa the store. Now don't that beat all." His rifle lay loose in his arms.

"Sure do, Pa. A body'd think the niggers'd crawl home to Mexico after they got their butts whupped." His tone was flatter, deadlier than the older man's, as if the additional generation had drained out every human quality. "Mebbe they ain't even smart as monkeys."

Sarah squeaked, "Please go."

The younger man purred, "Darlin, we'll throw the Mexican out fer ya."

"No, I mean you." Her hands moved over her apron.

The man's lips twitched in a smile as his hand closed around the standing rifle. "But we ain't bought nuthin ye-et." Stepping back, flat blue eyes shifting to Pedro, he brought the rifle stock up to meet his trigger hand, the round dark hole coming around.

Pedro drew and fired, a flame licking across the short distance, smoldering at the edge of the round hole in the buckskin shirt. The man jerked back with the impact and fell.

At the same instant Pedro threw himself at the older man's knees and heard the rifle discharge. His sombrero jumped back on his ears. Adobe flakes rained down. Sarah screamed.

The older man dropped his rifle and had his knife out before he hit the floor, Pedro on top — lengthwise over him. He held the wrist holding the knife.

The man kicked like a downed bronco. He flopped across the floor with

Pedro on top. They crashed into barrels, overturning them. Glass beads spilled across the floor. Sugarcane fell on Pedro's head as he strained with his left hand to hold the man's knife hand down.

The old arms were sinewy whipcords, strong as *el Diablo*. With a sudden flip the older man was on top, thrusting the knife downward, the shaft honed, shining in the light from the window.

Cabrón! Pedro pushed up with both hands, teeth clamped, his back pressed into something painful. The slightest release would leave him pinned through the neck. His arms were about to burst when light flooded the room. Quapata, he hoped and prayed.

A brown elbow locked beneath the gray beard, jerked the man's head back in an open-mouthed grimace. Pedro seized the knife from the loosening fingers. "Gracias, señor." He said to the *Norteamericano* as he jumped to his feet and glanced around, breathing hard.

Sarah cowered in the corner. The man he'd shot twitched in a widening red pool, blood jerking from the hole in the buckskin. Quapata's powerful bare legs were braced wide as he maintained his choke hold on the writhing, kicking old devil.

Pedro slipped the old man's skinning knife beneath his own sash. "Don't kill him, Pata," he said, recovering his Allen from the floor, nosing it under his sash opposite the knife. He grabbed the legs of the old man, who no longer resisted, and nodded for Quapata to help him carry him out the door.

They swung him off the porch and dropped him beside the saddle horses.

Massaging his throat, the man rasped and croaked, "Lemme git my son. I'll leave peaceable."

Pedro exchanged a look with Quapata, pulled out his Allen, turned the barrel a click, and pointed with his chin. "Pata get the *hombre*."

Quapata left.

"Mount your horse," Pedro ordered.

In a minute or two, the wounded man lay across the saddle of the other horse and the old man was leading it westward toward New Helvetia, drops of blood beading in the dust of the trail.

Pedro's joints suddenly loosened. "He will die," he said to Quapata and the Señora, who stood on the porch watching the retreating horses.

Quapata's black eyes flickered agreement. Sarah shut hers.

"Maybe I should have killed the old one," Pedro said.

Quapata kept his eyes on the trail. "Dead man no talk, but I sure Señor Valdez no killer."

Sarah said, "I gotta sit down." She turned into the Daylor's living room.

Pedro watched the place where the trail mounted the hill out from behind the trees. When the horses and mules appeared, still heading west, he went back inside the trading room. Among the beads and blankets and sugarcane were two rifles, a wide-brimmed felt hat and Pedro's sombrero with a hole through the crown. Then he saw a piece of paper in the blood.

Putting on the sombrero, he carefully lifted the paper and took it outside to wipe on the fresh grass where Sarah threw the wash water. The slanting black lines were smeared, but it was legible, had he been able to read. He blew it almost dry, folded it, and put it in his pocket.

Aware of the Indian — the wide, dusty feet beside him — he said, "Gracias, Pata." He embraced the powerful brown man, felt the return hug, then turned and glanced at the hill where the *Norteamericanos* had disappeared. Even the dust had settled.

But nothing would ever be the same.

56

In the yard of the trading post the following day Sheldon narrowed his eyes at Pedro as Sarah Daylor told of the shooting. Señor Daylor had stayed at the diggings with the Indians. Sheldon got quickly to the point.

"Did they shoot first?"

"My gun is small. I pulled it faster."

He pondered that, then turned to Sarah, asking gently, "You sure they didn't touch you?"

She smoothed her apron, then held her elegant nose high, every hair now secure in her bun. "Well, no. But Jared, they would have if Mr. Valdez hadn't showed up."

Sheldon nodded, overbite parted in thought, then dipped his head at Pedro as if to say good work.

Pedro reached in his pocket and gave Sheldon the scrap of paper, rusty with blood. "I found this on the floor."

Smoothing out the wrinkles, the *patrón* scanned, eyes swinging back and forth in the shade of his hat. When he looked up, the stubbled wedge of face was hard, yellowish eyes staring into the distance.

"What does it say, Jared," Sarah asked.

He read aloud:

"July 15, 1848. New Helvetia.

I, William Perry McCoon, being of sound mind, do hereby sell the following gold mining claim to the undersigned, Henry Pidd, for Two-thousand *dollars ($2,000.00). The location and boundaries of said claim are depicted on the map below the signatures.*

Perry McCoon
Henry Pidd."
Witness: Philosopher Pickett

He handed it to Sarah and she looked at it.

When it was Pedro's turn to look at the scrawl, he studied the map, saw a circle around a place in the river. Now two men owned the land where he wanted his rancho. McCoon was selling little bits and pieces of it and keeping the grazing land.

Sheldon mounted his horse and clipped. "I won't have it."

"Señor?"

"The selling of claims."

Perhaps this was a good time to ask. Removing his sombrero and clutching it to his chest, for he had a great favor to ask, he said, "I am afraid this is a bad time, after the trouble at Señor Daylor's."

"*Qué?*"

"You remember I spoke to you about buying Señor McCoon's rancho?" With his dream slipping away, he was reaching out to grab its coattail.

"Sí?" The horse stepped away. Sheldon brought it back.

"Now I know that is impossible. I was wondering if you could talk to Don Guillermo Hartnell for me. I'd like to buy the piece of his land that lies across the river from McCoon." He had the impression something was afoot between Hartnell and Sheldon. Maybe a sale, or a lease of the land across from the gristmill. Maybe land for Pedro could be discussed in those talks.

Sheldon cocked a fierce eyebrow. "Wanna be McCoon's neighbor? With the likes of those trappers coming in?"

"I want to live near Captain Juan's *ranchería.* The Hartnell land is flat. Has good grass." Maybe the miners would leave when they learned the *Indios* had taken most of the gold from that part of the river.

Sheldon looked like he could eat nails. "Those Indians don't seem very cooperative to me."

Pedro knew the *patron's* anger wasn't directed at him. "They'll work for me."

Sheldon's knuckles whitened on the rein and he talked through clenched teeth. "I'd sure as hell'd rather have you on Rancho Sacayak than the son-of-a-bitch that's there." His yellow wolf eyes sparked fire. "Leading the dregs of humanity right through my place!"

Pedro thought of Señora Catherine and the baby, a half mile away.

Sheldon snorted as if expelling the thought of McCoon. "I'd hate to lose you, Pedro."

"*Gracias, patrón.*" He appreciated compliments, but there came a time when a man needed to be on his own.

"I'll see what I can do. You've done a fine job. Quapata could take over here."

"*Otra vez gracias, patrón.*" Watching Sheldon ride toward Mill Ranch, Pedro thought about the wounded *Norteamericano* and knew he would be dead by now. Soon more trouble would come.

A few days later Pedro saw Señor Sheldon, who had stayed at the rancho, riding toward him. "We got visitors," he said when he came close.

By the scowl Pedro knew what it was about.

"Sheriff McKinstry and that Oregon trapper."

They shared a glance. Then, signalling Quapata, Pedro rode alongside the *patrón*, glad he was so well respected in California. McKinstry had been appointed Sheriff by the United States Army, replacing Alcalde Sinclair as justice of the peace, Sutter's bid for his old job having been ignored. Pedro didn't know McKinstry.

At the sight of the old trapper's horse, Pedro felt his blood curdle. The events of that day stayed with him like a nightmare that wouldn't fade. Dismounting, he followed Señor Sheldon to the door.

Inside the living room, Sarah Daylor was at the stove offering chicory coffee as Pedro and Sheldon removed their hats. Pedro locked eyes with the man he'd wrestled with, then shook his head at Sarah, declining the outstretched cup.

Florid-faced McKinstry, red-bearded, tin star pinned on his shirt, nodded at Sheldon and continued his questioning of Señora Daylor. "You say you weren't attacked?" In a comical semblance of fear, his thin reddish hair stood up where his missing hat had pulled it.

Handing a steaming cup to the sheriff, she wagged her head. "But they said things." She avoided the old man's eyes, turned her elegant nose to Sheldon, nodding at two vacant chairs, meaning they should sit.

McKinstry persisted. "Mr. Pidd here says they didn't touch you. Atall."

"No, but — "

The old man interrupted. "Sheriff, we was aganderin at the goods as peaceable as a couple a cut-jacks, when this here Mexican run in and kilt my boy. Woulda kilt me too ifn I had'na whupped im." He leveled a dead look at Pedro.

Should have. Señor Daylor would have broken every bone in the *desgraciado's* body. Pedro looked at the weathered claws in the man's lap and remembered the strength in those wrists, and the close-up smell of him. A gun handle parted the long buckskin fringe in the slats of the bent-willow chair. Pedro's voice came low. "It is not true."

He glanced at Sarah, gracefully seating herself on the side of the bed, and felt proud of protecting her honor against this filthy dog. But she was saying nothing.

McKinstry sipped coffee, then cleared his throat, resting the cup on his knee.

"Jared, before this here goes any further, I just wanna say you and Bill got a fine place, and everbody in the territory praises that gristmill a yours. With men of your caliber, Californy's bound to be a fine country."

Sheldon pursed his lips. "Thanks, Sheriff. But let's git to business. Mr. Pidd here is lying through his teeth. My *mayordomo* is innocent."

McKinstry glanced at Sarah, the ankles of her high-top shoes primly crossed, a cup in her lap. "With respect sir, you heard what she said. They never even touched her." His fleshy jaw quivered as he leaned down and placed his cup on the floor. He sounded like he'd rather be doing anything else. "Jared, this here man has buried his son. Now I gotta take your Spaniard to the fort for a trial." He avoided Pedro's eyes.

Sheldon clipped, "Any trial will be held right here. On my property." He trained his wolf stare on McKinstry. "You don't need none though. Cause my foreman was defending Mrs. Daylor and himself at the time of the shooting. It was a case of self-defense."

"Lie," the old man snarled.

Pedro tensed as Sheldon scraped his chair back and stood. McKinstry heaved his bulk between Sheldon and the old man, a palm on each chest. "Now Mr. Pidd, you didn't mean that, did you. Not that lie part." Turning to Sheldon: "Jared, he doesn't know what he's saying. Outa his head with grief." In the light that angled from the small window, beads of perspiration glistened on the sheriff's brow. His pale eyes pleaded. "We'll have the trial here if that's what you want. Maybe I can do that."

Sheldon looked at Pidd's hand, which rested on his buckskin-covered thigh near his gun, then at McKinstry. "Like I said, there's no need for a trial atall. My man is innocent."

"Sit down, Jared, please. Please." McKinstry followed Sheldon's eyes, then addressed Mr. Pidd, whose hand hadn't moved. "Hand over yer gun."

"Ain't givin it up while that murdering spick's got aholt ahis."

"Both of you," McKinstry said, "hand over your guns." He turned to Sheldon. "Tell them. Please. We'll talk this over without guns."

Sheldon, who wore his pistol and knew how to use it, looked at Pedro and nodded in the sheriff's direction. He barked at the man in buckskins, "You too."

Pedro extended the Allen. Seeing that, the old man did likewise. McKinstry took the identical guns into the adjoining room and laid them on an open bag of beans, in Pedro's line of sight. When he returned, he sat and fingered the threads of his trouser knee. "You see, Jared, there's a powerful lot of talk around the fort. We gotta have a trial."

Sheldon leaned toward him. "George, you been here in California a piece now, and you know damn well Pedro Valdez wouldn't shoot less he had to."

The Sheriff threw up his palms. "I know, I know. But you haven't seen the fort fer a spell, Jared." He nodded at the old man, whose cold eyes Pedro watched. "The whole damned place is run over now. You got any eye-dee how they hate Mexicans?"

"Well now," said Sheldon, clipping off whatever the old man was trying to say. "You hold a trial over that, you better haul me in too. Cause I'm a Mexican citizen."

The man in buckskins took advantage of the lull: "Ifn you don't find that thar nigger guilty a murder, at's fine with me." He jerked his stringy beard at Pedro. "Me and my friends'll take care a the sumbitch."

McKinstry ignored it. "Aw come on, Jared, you're not a Mexican the way he is." His eyes flicked at Pedro and back. "Besides, with McCoon stirrin things up . . . " He inched forward on his chair, rolled the brim of his hat and lowered his voice confidentially: "It's all I could do to keep a whole shit load a men from riding out here with a hangin rope. They're screamin fer his scalp." He glanced at Pedro.

The top of his head tingled. He'd heard of scalping east of the Sierra Nevada, knew *Norteamericanos* favored this method of counting dead Indians.

McKinstry added, "They won't take kindly to me either, if I let him off." His face was white, freckled, his erect red hair adding visual effect to his fearful tone.

Pedro had heard all he needed to know. Not that men of Spanish descent and California birth had ever had equal respect under Captain Sutter, but Pedro had always imagined they understood his sense of honor, regardless of whether they liked him. Now his life hung by a thread because of his birth. He couldn't win a trial at the fort or anywhere else, judged by such men. Señor Sheldon would need all his Indians to protect Pedro from the mob that would come, and he wouldn't dream of causing the *patrón* that trouble. He had no choice in what he must do.

Sheldon picked up his hat and stood. "You do your job, George. I'll do mine. Any trial will be here. And it's my partner who's most beholden to Señor Valdez for what he did." Yellow sparks lit his eyes. Every man in the country knew of Bill Daylor's courage. The legend had grown. Now he was supposed to have whipped fifty or sixty Indians, all coming at him at the same time.

Beads of sweat coalesced and ran down the lawman's red face.

Fortunately, the Rancho Omuchumne partnership of Bill Daylor and Joaquín Sheldon was like a law unto itself, a separate country on account of its remoteness and the reputations of its owners. It had taken courage for the sheriff to ride out.

After they rode away he stood with Sheldon on the porch. "I'll continue as your *mayordomo*, but no *Norteamericano* will find me." He lifted his chin. "They can come and hold their trial, but without me. Even you will not find me, *patrón*." He sensed rather than saw Sheldon glance at his profile.

Sheldon shifted to Spanish, his voice soft. "You wouldn't be able to buy land." He paused. "I meant to speak to Señor Hartnell for you."

A man outside the law couldn't put his name on papers, couldn't live across the river from Perry McCoon, couldn't arm a tribe of Indians and fend off *Norteamericanos* forever. Pedro sighed, his dream slipping through his fingers. But submitting to a trial was the same as admitting guilt. He'd hang. Men didn't stand trial for self-defense. That was the unwritten law impressed on the heart of every man on the frontier. Besides, Señora Daylor apparently hadn't seen the rifle stock come up, the gunbarrel swing toward Pedro the way he had seen it. Her story wouldn't silence the trumpeting for his scalp and he would never ask her to change her story. He gazed across the lush green of the river ranch.

"I'll ride to New Helvetia and sort things out," Sheldon said. "Maybe I can help get a good jury together, the Rhoads boys. Men who owe me." He avoided Pedro's eyes. Something in his face said he didn't believe he could succeed.

"Don Joaquín, *muchas gracias*. You do me much honor, but I know you must go to the diggings and check on the *Indios*." His heart brimmed with gratitude, but even Sheldon couldn't guarantee a favorable majority in a yard full of clamoring *Norteamericanos*. Nevertheless, he would not dishonor his *patrón* by expressing such doubt aloud.

"Got my own reasons for going," Sheldon clipped. "This McCoon thing," he swung his wolf eyes to Pedro, "Sellin claims, has got to be stopped."

57

Pedro lay staring at the planks of the ceiling, head pillowed by his interlaced fingers, as María slept beside him. She wanted to go to her home village. Before the lovemaking they had argued about it. Pedro knew several more *Norteamericanos* had traveled the trail toward Rancho Sacayak. Quapata had warned him to stay out of sight. He hated hiding. Hated feeling like an outlaw, a foreign outlaw in his own country. He'd done nothing wrong, yet his action affected everything he did. Even caused the argument with María.

The golden light no longer fell across their naked bodies. Night was coming, a warm night, Billy asleep on his mat. She lay on her side in the freshening air from the open door, a small hand under her cheek like a baby. Sweet María.

Pobrecita! An Indian runner had brought the sad news that miners had killed her three cousins, who had been searching for Salvador's body. Young men about her age. They had played together as children. Cousin-brothers Indians called them. *Madre de Dios*, the damned condor swooped around in his mind. What else explained all this bad luck?

Startling him, she opened her eyes and said, "I will be gone six sleeps." She sat up and smoothed back her hair.

"I still don't understand why you must go."

She leaned down, grazed her lips on his forehead with breath like a summer night, her blunt-edged hair sweeping across his face. "I must."

The words pierced him. Reaching for her, gentling her *suave* breasts to his chest, her fragrant hair around his face, he was close to tears. "Stay here with me, María." It came out choked. He couldn't go to Rancho Sacayak without attracting a murderous mob.

She pulled up. "I cannot."

When she talked like that it was like trying to make the river flow backwards. He sat up and looked at her. "Among my people a man is not a man if he allows his pregnant wife to wander out into the dangerous world."

She answered in kind, the black pools of her eyes drowning him with love. "Among my people a woman who does not attend the singing to the dead is herself not worthy of burial."

"I'll go with you." Piss on the danger. "But wait until I can speak to Señor Sheldon. He might be back tomorrow." Indian funerals lasted a week. Surely a day or two wouldn't matter. It would greatly impose on the *patrón* — probably force him to stay home with the vaqueros — but Pedro would request the time off. He sighed, gazing out at the rapidly darkening sky. He'd never asked for special privileges. It was as distasteful as hiding.

But her chin was up. "I go in the morning."

Mid-stride, she stopped, cocked her head, listened. She couldn't place the sound. A distant pop. She shifted Billy's sling to her other hip and resumed walking toward the home place. His weight and the burden basket on her back added heat to the stifling day, and though her pregnancy would not show for some time, her breasts felt heavy. With every step she felt the burden of sadness for Crying Fox and her three cousin-brothers.

Another crack, like a sharp clap of hands, followed by a slight echo. But she was alone. A cottonwood splitting? Sometimes they grew too heavy. But she was far from any cottonwood stream. And it seemed unlikely that two would break in succession. And oaks were generally too wise to overburden themselves. Only strong wind broke them. She glanced at the blue oaks on the hills. Not a dusty leaf stirred. Oblivious meadowlarks fluted brilliant arpeggios in the grass, always social at the end of the day. She walked on.

She was closer to the home place and Father Sun was behind the hill, when she heard another pop, only louder. And another. Like the guns at Sutter's Fort, she suddenly realized, as they would sound from a distance. She quickened her pace, ignoring Billy's moaning, his attempt to climb out. The sounds came again, ever louder. He was fussing when she reached the crest of the last hill. Heart pounding with exertion and fear, she touched her amulet and heard Angelica Root's warning: *Hide. Be careful.*

She put her hand over Billy's mouth and crouch-walked into a buckeye tree, brown leaves hanging low all around her. Through an opening she saw the ti-kel field far below. The sunset cast a reddish tint on the roughened dirt, softening the depressions. No boys and girls ran on the field. Nothing moved.

She looked across the field to the green thicket that marked Berry Creek, the u-machas behind it. Smoke from the supper fires should be rising behind the trees. Where were the voices of the people? Where were the children? The quiet chilled her. She heard only the whisper of her heart in her ears.

Something moved on the field. She blinked, trying to make it out. An ear-cracking explosion threw her off balance. Momentarily senseless with fear, she caught herself on her hands and knees and saw a familiar shape jerking on the field. Arms, legs. A person.

Her eyes unveiled. Slowly, as she looked around the ti-kel field she made out other human shapes, one here, one there, sprawled, as motionless as the lumps and shadows upon which they lay, the color of the clay from which Coyote had made them. Some very small. Her people. Many voices stilled. No one helping. Poison burned in her throat. Her arms and legs felt limp, her body empty, except for her heart — awakened and galloping in its cage.

What was happening? Where were Father and Mother? She pressed her hand on Billy's mouth and moved quietly forward to peek through the foliage, searching for the origin of the thunderclap. Leaves moved below her. A stone's toss down the hill. Something dark in the elderberry. A raccoon tail in the branches — dangling from a fur cap. Leather-shirts. *Americanos*! Like the ones who tried to kill Pedro. Raccoon-tail stepped out of the elderberry, and stood looking down — a hide-bound foot propped on a boulder, using the long gun like a staff. *Hunters.*

A man's voice made her jump in her skin. "Spose more's in the bushes?"

"Mebbe."

Two more leather-shirts emerged from the foliage and stood looking over the playing field.

"Seen one hightail it over yonder." He raised an arm toward the north trail, fringe hanging halfway to his knees. Her people were like quail to them.

Her mind screamed for Father and Mother, all her people.

A leather-shirt was leaving, thrashing down through the brush and boulders. The others followed. *Hunting*. She eased onto a hip and elbow, hand still on Billy's mouth, remembering to breathe while her heart flung itself at her throat. The leather-shirts got to the playing field and walked through it, gunbarrels leading. They swiveled in all directions and kicked bodies. Earth-colored bodies blending with the earth.

Spirits hovered dangerously, stealing her strength, weakening her and pounding her temples. Were Mother and Father on the field? She waited.

The *Americanos* disappeared around the green wall at Berry Creek, heading for the village center. Slowly she released the pressure on Billy's mouth, looking into his frightened eyes, telling him not to cry. He didn't. She patted him thankfully and reached into her burden basket for jerky. It would quiet him while she circled the field on the river side. She would approach the u-machas under cover of the dark and willows along the beach and see what the hunters were doing. Maybe Father and Mother were hiding too, and she would find them.

Soundlessly she stepped down the hillside through rocks and bushes toward the mossy scent of the river, shifting her weight only when nothing was loose beneath her feet. Twilight was rapidly fading, and she hoped the rattlers were watching for her. At this time of evening, human eyes were weak.

Quietly she stepped past Great-grandmother Dishi's power place. Deserted. It was dark when she reached the sand of the beach. A sickle moon would rise later. Covering Billy's mouth, she stepped carefully across the gravel and up the incline toward the village, the path her feet knew so well. Ahead barked harsh *Americano* laughter and the clatter of metal implements and wood being split and piled. She heard the crackling of a fire and through it all, the babble and coo of the river.

Her foot hit a shadow. Something big, warmer than the still-warm sand. She bent to touch it. Human flesh. Father's scent, and the acrid smell of blood. She kneeled, turned his face, brushed particles from his nose. He didn't seem to be breathing. *Father!* Her heart labored. Pain pinched her chest. He had power. This couldn't happen!

She took Billy from the sling, sat him aside — quiet with his jerky — held her breath and lowered her lips to Father's nose and mouth, waiting for the wind of his life. Something moved in the gravel and Billy squealed. She jerked up and clapped her hand over his mouth, smelling a dog in the darkness.

One of the village pets had stolen his jerky. Had the *Americanos* heard the cry? She waited, tensed to run. But their laughter continued. No boots crunched toward her.

Quaking in her bones, she dug into her burden basket and found Billy a flat wheat cake, this time sitting him beside Father's face, knowing that when the dog returned, it wouldn't dare steal from under her. Again she lowered her lips to Father's nose. A faint stirring of air touched her lips. She waited, felt it again. Joy mingled with grief and terror as she hugged his quiet form and rested her head on his big shoulder. He must have been crawling up the path for his bow and arrows when he lost consciousness.

A gun fired. She jerked up, fear flashing to her toes. A yelp came from above.

Sensing Billy gathering himself, she swept him to her arms and covered his wail just in time.

"Wahoo!" came from the village. More laughter. Then another gunshot, and another.

Terrified, she listened, but no footsteps approached.

Loose souls darted about the black, silent beach. They howled in her mind, stood her hair on end, shook her bones. Yet she must hide Father. *Mother, where are you?* She put Billy in the sling and took Grizzly Hair's wrists — large for her hands — and began to drag him to the willow thicket. He was a heavy man, and despite the cooling breeze over the river, perspiration stung her eyes. Mournful owls in the cottonwoods gave voice to the souls. Her feet gave way in the noisy gravel and she listened over the pounding of her heart.

"Be damned if that thar ain't a fortune."

A night bird shrieked.

"You cut, I choose."

"Who made you boss, Wildcat?"

She had to get Father under cover before they quieted for the night. Please don't leave, she whispered to his soul, though she knew she shouldn't ask it to linger.

Loud yells.

" . . . more where that come from."

" . . . Injun mine."

Her foot bumped something big and cool. Reaching through the dark, she felt a face, hair singed across the brow. Mother? No. Bikoos on her back. A cousin-sister. She groped and found the baby. Stickiness matted its hair, a hole in its skull the size of her finger. The home place was the land of the dead. Numb to the taboo, she took her cousin-sister's dead hand and dragged her out of the way so she could continue to drag Grizzly Hair. The known world was gone.

Inside the thicket she probed and found two holes in Father's back, near his backbone. No exit holes. His shin was also splintered. Lead balls must be removed from his body, but she had no experience carving into living flesh, and her obsidian knife was too broad. She would stop the bleeding and restore him as best she could. Then later get the Wapumne healer to cut out the evil.

She crawled up the path, the medicine she needed hanging from the rafters of the u-macha. But the slim light of the sickle moon revealed sleeping murderers outside the family house. Four, maybe five. They snored, their upper faces white.

Gripping her blade, she stared, entranced by the thought of cutting their throats. But before she could get to all of them, they would wake and kill her. Father needed her, so did Billy. She must find healing plants in the dark.

All night she crept around the riverbank and grasslands, remembering where the plants grew, using her nose. She struggled from silent task to silent task, hampered by Billy, afraid he'd wake and cry if she left him. She cleaned Father's wounds and stopped the bleeding. She sang to Angelica, dug a root, and cut milkweed stems to twine together. She filled her watertight basket in the river, brushing every track behind her.

Splinting Father's leg with a branch and twine, she wondered if she would ever hear his voice again. Finished, she pulled the feathery willows around the three of them.

"Daughter?" His croak brought happy tears to her eyes.

She leaned to his mouth, indicating he must speak quietly.

He rasped, "Your mother. Dead."

Her spirit momentarily left her. Then a painful hole opened near her heart. A wail surged to her mouth, and she scarcely had the strength to push it back with her hands. Mother!

He was struggling to say more.

Trembling, she lowered her mouth to his ear and whispered. "Rest, Father."

Mother was gone. Would he want to live? She put body-mending herbs in his mouth, her whisper as shaky as her hand. "Mix this with mouth water. I cannot make tea." *Mother dead.* Sweet Etumu. She of quiet strength. Of deft fingers. Of bottomless pride in her man. Gone. Part of a moan escaped.

A bubbly sound came from Father, then a rasp. "*Americanos.*"

She found his cool dry hand, held it between hers. "I know. In the village." She now felt like a spirit herself, hovering off the ground, disbelieving.

Weakly his hand squeezed hers. "Go." Then it went limp.

She bent forward, relieved to feel air from his nose. Go? Surely he didn't expect her to leave!

He whispered, in the voice of a child awakening from a dream, "Bad here. Go now. Far away," then fell unconscious.

She cradled his big head, rocking gently, her face wet with tears. Soon the sun would come from his eastern house and the *Americanos* would awaken. She would not go. Could not leave Father.

He needed her. The *umne* needed her. Mother must be buried, and the others. She had no idea how she would do this with the murdering *Americanos* present. Perhaps they would leave. She would wait, healing Father by night. Angelica Root would help her know what to do.

When the first shred of gray sky came through the willows and she lay on the coarse sand, Grizzly Hair on one side, Billy on the other, the fringed branches arranged to hide them, she heard the whisper of animal feet in the gravel. Then came the crunching crackling, smacking sounds of an animal devouring flesh and bone. The roots of her hair moved.

The horrible sounds continued and she couldn't stop the gruesome scenes in her mind. Billy slept beside her and Father's breathing continued, barely detectable to her lips. Dew fell, intensifying the medicinal smell of willow and the thick odor of blood.

Suddenly she remembered Elitha and Perrimacoo had planned to return to Rancho Sacayak. Perhaps after the sleep. They would help, possibly alert the Omuchumne, many of whom were related to the dead, and Pedro would come.

Steadily the sky brightened through cracks in the willows, but morning as she had known it was gone. In none of the stories since the time of the Ancients had anything like this happened. Here in the home place there would be no banter, no bathing in the river, no praises to the spirits. Or was this a dream of terrible power? She felt like a rabbit alone in the universe under the cold eye of Molok.

"Shee-it! These niggers'll stink up the place good by t'morry." Five *Americanos* moved around the beach among the gnawed bodies.

Lying loosely over Billy, a stone's toss from the bad men, Maria held his mouth closed and barely breathed as she strained to see. Scorpion Trail, Singing Grass and Falls-off-House lay at grotesque angles, the others hidden from her worm's-eye perspective. Any motion would be seen. She lay as still as a deer, narrowing her eyes to hide the whites — the color that attracted attention. She wanted to inch back to Father — all night his breathing had been too shallow for sleep — but could not move. She must trust the plant people to help him.

A leather-shirt bent over and grabbed Scorpion Trail's man's parts, sliced them off and kicked the next body. The head lolled her direction. Sun-through-the-Mist. The storyteller's face looked taut, shiny, resigned to his fate.

As the murderers moved among the bodies, clouds of flies rose and descended. *Half the village.* Other bodies lay on the field, and she had stumbled on Grasshopper Wing in the bushes just outside the circle of houses. Would the killers remember Father in the path? Would they search for him?

A leather-shirt grabbed something she couldn't see and with a ripping sound pulled free a big white cloth. She held her breath. It was the *Americana* garment Mother had worn so proudly. Tossing it aside, he bent over and worked with his knife.

Nausea curled up her throat. She swallowed back bile. Even if the proper songs were sung, mutilation confounded the spirits of the dead. Mother might never find her way to the happy land.

Straightening with his trophies, the man called to the others, "Gots me a good pair a titties." He stepped to the stand-up mortar rock, the smooth greenstone where Mother had pounded meal all her life, and laid out the breasts to dry in the sun.

She squeezed out the sight, tears running from her closed eyes. The bad luck, even death that would come to her unborn child as a result of witnessing this shrank beside the sharpness of the larger horror, the emptiness. She had looked forward to the closeness with Mother during the Cry, needed her quiet strength. *This is a dream.* She blinked, tried to make the scene vanish. But it would not. Then as she looked across the bodies, a welcome numbness descended like fog, the murderers' movements seeming to slow, their voices receding and unreal. Surely now this was a dream.

"Hell, just throw 'em in the river, git 'em floatin in the current." A leather-shirt tossed the long-awaited infant of Scorpion Trail and Singing Grass into the water, the tiny backside floating in the sun-sparkled water. They reached for Singing Grass, then Etumu.

Numbly she watched as Mother and the friends of her childhood were dragged by the hair and thrown into the river — was it red with blood? A leather-shirt lifted what seemed a child, but the head lolled as he swung the body back and forth for the toss, and in the instant the face turned her way, she saw it was Great-Grandmother Dishi.

A witch's spell. Why hadn't she thought of that before? An unknown enemy had paid a powerful doctor to make her see what wasn't there. In reality her people were bathing and eating their nu-pah. She blinked hard and reached for the power to make the vision vanish.

Dishi splashed into the water and the river-baby opened her liquid spirit to the softness of the Old One who had sung to it for so many seasons. If this were a spell, she was powerless against it, watching as the body drifted toward a gentler resting place than this beach of carnage. She felt herself drifting with it, but caught her spirit, held it in check. She must stay strong for Father and Billy. Only strength counteracted a magic spell. But if it were real —

"Looky thar. The bloat keeps em afloat, movin down the river."

"Naw. The biguns'll jam up like logs."

"Mebbe. Down at McCoon's place." Laughter.

"Wall, caint think of a finer roost." More laughter came and she continued to smell blood.

Leather-covered thighs were slapped. "Serve him right fer sellin us claims in a nigger nest."

A man lifted his hat and scratched his head. "Fergittin the gold is yah? Why ifn McCoon hadna — "

"That sneaky old tar done sold us these here claims fer one reason and don't chew forget it. Cuz these varmints was takin out the gold. Fer him! We wasn't sposed to git none." The bearded chin jutted like a weapon. "We was damn lucky to figger it out atall. Wouldna, cept fer dispatchin these here Diggers."

"Wildcat's right. Serve ole McCoon good to git stank out!" Laughter.

"Ifn he don't git t'home fer a week or two, won't that smell purty!" Loud guffaws. He grabbed a cousin-nephew. "Gitcher self one bout like this, and see if ya can throw fur as me."

Bile welled up again. Maria covered Billy's eyes as he struggled to see his best friend. She shut her eyes and rested her chin on the sand, willing the vomit back down. *The umne slaughtered.* She and Father might be the only ones left.

When the sun had travelled west she heard a horse. Then from the village center, a man's call. "Ahoy!"

Perrimacoo. Strange to hear his jauntiness. Surely he would help. Billy began to say "Da — " She clapped her hand over it.

The *Americanos*, who had been washing sand and gravel, stood along the shore facing the village, water streaming from the baskets the women had coiled.

Perrimacoo yelled again, "Where's me herders?"

Wildcat cocked his head. "He talkin bout them thievin savages?"

Gravel crunched nearer.

"Mebbe we orter tell him how much we 'preciate buyin claims chock full of Injuns. Bought dear too." Loud enough for him to hear.

"Yeah. Injuns washin out the gold afore we cud git to it."

Stepping closer, Perrimacoo shouted, "Where's me niggers?"

"Cleaned out the EN-tire nest."

"Ever one," Wildcat echoed, cocking his hairy head. "Saved ya the trouble."

A leather-shirt pointed at the sand. "Come see the blood fer yerself. Thar, and thar, and thar." He looked up proudly. "Floated em on down to yer place." Smiles stretched their lips.

An arm's length from where she lay with her chin on the ground, Perrimacoo's boots stepped by. The dark *pantalones* on his hips shifted toward the leather-shirts, his small gun snug in its holster. *Make them leave*, she said to his mind.

He stood over Scorpion Trail's blood, then glanced around at other dark spots, squinting toward her, but not seeing. *Shoot the murderers,* she told him from her mind.

His voice cracked. "Ent got no right."

"T'liminate varmints? On our claims? Hell we ain't!"

Wildcat added, "They'da turned on ya, sure as shootin. Jest 'ike they did them missionaries up in Oregon territory. Heared about the Whitmans? Butchered with tomahawks."

"These Indians was peaceful." He sounded choked.

Wildcat widened his stance like he expected a fight, his beard jutting toward Perrimacoo. "Ain't no sech thing as a peaceful redskin. Now the sooner you Californy greenhorns larn that, the safer we'll all be. Look, we left ye most of the scalps. Send em on in to the agent of the You-nited States gov'ment. Pays five dollars apiece bounty. Good fer it too."

Perrimacoo shuffled back toward Maria, then stopped, turned toward the five leather-shirts, his scratchy voice betraying lack of power. "Me niggers was savin me gold, they was. Any you found in their shanties, hits mine. It wasn't on yer claims."

They exchanged glances, Wildcat assuming a big-eyed, innocent look. "Wye, we ain't found nuttin like at, have we boys?"

"Hell no."

"Uh-uuh. But let's show him the way outa here." The speaker dropped his basket and started toward Perrimacoo, the others following.

Swiftly Perrimacoo walked away. *No. Shoot them.* The thump of her heart sounded loud. Then hooves pounded away, and the *Americanos* laughed.

The gray-green willow leaves fluttered against her cheek, an evening breeze coming to life. Shovels in hand, the *Americanos* poked around the boulders and rocks of the swimming hole, looking for gold. Overhead, vultures flickered in and out of her wedge of sight, circling. She pushed backwards to Grizzly Hair.

His shallow breathing hadn't changed. "I cannot leave you," she whispered. He lay unconscious.

She felt the numbness begin to lift, exposing the raw surface of her mind. Every thought stung. Her people were dead. Why couldn't she accept this fate? It was Molok's dream. Still, she couldn't shake the thought of flinging herself at the men as they squatted by the river's edge with the baskets, or stabbing them in the back when they made water. Molok was not to be mocked. She'd known that, but she had expected to be stoic when the end came. Yet her mind burned on.

She would go to Bear Claw. He had spells that killed. She would need something belonging to each leather-shirt. But that was easy. Like infants, they made no attempt to scatter their urine. But even the thought of vengeance didn't quench the burning in the raw tissues of her soul.

She must get Pedro to avenge the murders. And yes, Pedro must help find any of her people who had fled. Together they would bury the dead. And he must help her protect the home place, for it was more than people, she realized now. It was the dancehouse, the ashes and bones of her ancestors, and spirits who lived in the boulders, and the animals and plants, and Grandmother Howchia watching from the oak. Ignorant murderers had defiled everything — a defilement that started with the condor robe. Perrimacoo must go. The baskets of gold were gone, but she knew how to get a thousand dollars so Pedro could pay him to leave.

But even as she thought that, she knew fate must eventually be accepted. Molok's unblinking eye encompassed the world. *Be quiet my soul. Accept what is.*

Coyote laughed on the hill.

58

"Bloody bastards!" Perry shouted, kicking the bucket across the room. It ricocheted off the wall in a shower of water and dry adobe flakes.

Elitha flinched. He'd been raging for half an hour, ever since he came back from finding the mutilated bodies. She feared his anger would reach to her.

"Butchered a cow too. Like to skin em alive and keel haul em, I would!"

Devastated at what had happened, she kept her eyes down. She couldn't stop thinking about Indian Mary walking home yesterday. Was she dead too?

"Shot the babes along with the mums," he'd railed, shaking his lowered head. His head came up and he glared at her. "Have ye nuthin to say?"

"I, I — " Nothing came.

"Glad be ye Billy's dead? And now ye have no other babe before yours? That it, is it?"

"Perry, I like Billy. It's sickening what happened. I — "

"Oh shut yer blatherin trap!" He kicked the bucket to the ceiling. She flinched as it clattered down with a big chunk of dry mud. "Not a herder left to work me cattle. And every pinch of gold gone too!"

She kept her face a mask of placid concern, recalling that he was the one who invited the Oregon trappers in. "Maybe some of the Indians are hiding."

He eyed her. "Oh clever! Married to a dolt, do ye judge? Think I didn't look?" He swung his leg back. With a crash the bucket went through a window. "Now look what ye made me do!"

She stepped toward the door, planning an excuse about collecting greens. She needed time alone to absorb what had happened. She would go to the elderberry trees, where an Indian might hide. She knew other places. And the tree where the old blind Indian grandmother sat. She reached the doorway.

He bellowed, "No ye don't!" and yanked her arm, flung her like a sack. She stumbled against the table, knocked his rifle to the floor. Her hip bone hurt.

"Fuck ye, then kill ye, their kind would."

When dark fell he slept with his pepperbox revolver on his chest. Elitha wept silent tears for the Indians. For Pa and Tamsen. For herself and the baby inside her.

Maria tossed a pebble through Perrimacoo's broken window, then crouched behind the oak.

Dry grass rustled behind her. She spun toward it. In a sliver of moonlight she saw the backside of a skunk waddling past. She turned back to the window. She would ask Elitha to care for Billy. Even in the bad house he couldn't be in more danger than with her. She felt for another pebble, found a piece of wood, threw it.

It thunked on the door she had helped make. Under the brooding oaks the house looked ghostly.

The door moved, the barrel of a gun nosing it open.

She lunged behind the tree as a thunderbolt exploded. A tongue of red flame died. She stifled Billy's cry, knowing the gun would bring bad men who were a short walk away.

Perrimacoo called, "Who goes there."

"Mary."

"Mary? Come here." He stood in the open doorway.

She approached, stopping well before him.

Elitha appeared at his side in a long white gown, dark hair to her waist. "You're alive!" she whispered excitedly. "We thought you'd been killed."

Maria extended Billy toward her, still covering his mouth. "Keep Billy here, *por favor*."

Elitha came out and took him, replacing Maria's hand over his mouth. "Have you been hiding?"

"Sí." She stroked Billy's cheek with the backs of her fingers. "Gracias. Keep him silent."

Perrimacoo, who was resting the gun beside his foot, said, "Is Captain Juan alive?"

"Sí." When she left him, he'd been breathing.

"I needs him to help herd me cattle out of here."

"His death is near. *Por favor*, tell Señor Valdez." Pedro wouldn't know what had happened unless someone who had escaped ran that way. Perrimacoo was her best hope.

He scratched his head.

She heard horses. Knowing she might never see her son again, she darted into the shadows. But now, if she got caught, he wouldn't die with her.

Before breakfast Perry uncorked the *aguardiente*. By mid-morning he was staggering. The sun blazed higher and Elitha's agitation intensified. She rocked Billy on her lap. He hadn't eaten a thing, mewling softly, saying things she didn't recognize. She mustered the nerve to speak her mind to Perry. "I think you'd better go."

He raked his fingers through his hair, forming clumps. He lifted the cup and swallowed. "Ent goin."

She stopped rocking and looked at him. "You could get there and back with Señor Valdez in two hours. I'll mind Billy."

"Girl, I SAID no!"

What was the matter with him? Indian Mary and her father needed help.

"Put yer damned eyeballs back in. I ent riding into no nest of vipers with no . . ." glance darting around the room, "greaser!"

"But — "

"But nuthin. Shut yer flappin mouth!"

She stood with Billy, thinking he wouldn't hit her while she held his son. She must appeal to his vanity. "You are SO good on a horse, Perry. You and Mr. Valdez could clean those men right out of here."

"Oh sure. Ride up to the five men I sold claims to and — " He bowed, made his voice sweet. "If ye please, sirs, be so good as to vacate yer claims."

"They killed our Indians, Perry. Your vaqueros!"

"So?" His eyes were steel points in red mazes.

"You could send for the sheriff."

He shouted, "Daft ye be! Killin niggers ent against the law."

"It's not?" These were ranch workers, different from the Indians punished by the militias back home.

"Hell no! But going back on a bargain is. Philosopher Pickett wrote those claims up legal like." His hands were on his waist and he thrust his face toward her. "Read law in the states, that one did, so quit looking at me with cow eyes."

Mr. Pickett came to her mind — one of the hard drinkers at the fort. She softened her voice, trying not to rile him, afraid he'd hit her despite Billy. "But it's wrong to kill Indians in cold blood when they're friendly." She couldn't bear the sight of his flared nostrils, the stubborn drunkenness of him. Or was it fear? She studied his belligerent face and suddenly knew that was it. He was afraid to do the right thing. In her heart she couldn't help but think how different John Rhoads would be acting.

She sat down on the stump stool, rocking, knowing she must fetch Señor Valdez. But how could she get out of the house? "There, there," she soothed the whimpering child, "Your mother will come back."

Perry took another swig, glared at her, then took the cup to bed and curled around it, facing the wall.

Not against the law to massacre Indians. The thought cut into her like the sun fracturing through the jagged shards of window-glass, a puzzle of light reflecting over the floor and half the table. It crept slowly across the table, Perry silent, Billy sobbing quietly. She couldn't imagine living here without the Indians. Ranching would be impossible. She moved out of the encroaching sun and sat lightly on the edge of the bed.

He got up, stepped outside the drape and peed by the door — a disgusting habit that brought flies and acrid odor. He looked old and tired, buttoning himself. "The buggers'll kill all me cows." He uncorked the barrel and the liquid splashed into his cup.

"Wouldn't they run off first, being, being so wild and all?"

"Oh that maiks it better now, don't it." His dream of being a country squire had died with the Indians. He gulped from the cup, and she realized he was like a cornered animal, frustrated and angry, lashing out at the nearest person.

How would she sneak out? Watching his boots, fearing a kick, she patted Billy's hair and murmured, "I'm so sorry, Perry." For the Indians, though he deserved some pity too.

With a mad glimmer in his eye, he stepped toward her, liquor breath blasting.

Eat, she thought. That's what cock turkeys did when beset by hostile males pecking and jumping on their heads. She nibbled the salt pork she'd been trying to feed Billy.

Like a turkey, Perry backed away.

"Here Billy." She put the pork to his lips. He jerked his head from it, hazel eyes wet from weeping. "Poor thing," she murmured, "Hasn't eaten a thing."

"Oh fer Chrissake, he won't starve!"

Quietly she rocked to and fro. "You're right. He's only been here overnight."

Suddenly the lines of Perry's face softened. He stood looking at the wall. Then, as if they'd been playing tiddlywinks, he said, "I'll be ridin to Sutter's camp." He picked up his gun. "You go to Daylor's with Billy."

Scheming something, but she wouldn't ask. Soon Señor Valdez would be there to help Indian Mary — if it wasn't too late.

59

The sun was at their backs but still high when Pedro and Quapata tied their horses at McCoon's vacant adobe. Pedro had suggested the Indian stay at Sheldon's ranch, but his dark face had hardened and he said, "I help Señor Pedro. My woman's people are dead." Every inch a man.

In the dead heat beneath the canopies of lichen-encrusted oaks, they walked up the hill between boulder outcroppings, Pedro gripping the Allen pepperbox revolver before him, stalking the *desgraciados*, the stinking human trash, the cowards who killed women and infants. Quapata, arrow on bowstring, walked quickly and quietly, rolling off the sides of his heels, full otterskin quiver slung across his bare back. The missing finger made no difference. He could get a second arrow off faster than Pedro could turn his chambered barrel.

Nearing the crest of the second hill, Pedro touched Quapata and nodded toward a clump of buckeyes. They ducked under the branches and kneeled. "The

Norteamericanos are probably at the river," he said, "looking for gold." He tilted his presidio hat, pointing down the hill toward an unmarked route through the rocks. Quapata, eyes quiet as a snake's, nodded in agreement.

Maybe María would see them from wherever she was hiding. *Gracias a Dios* she had asked Elitha to care for Billy. In McCoon's house! The instant he'd heard that, he'd known the full extent of the danger. His heart tripped at the thought of being too late. He tried to walk like the barefoot *Indio*, but the grass stalks were dry, the fallen leaves crisp. Everything crunched under his boots. *Five men.* Elitha had been sure. If he could get close enough —the Allen was accurate only at close range — he could finish two before they knew what happened. Quapata could too. That left one. Were there more? Was the old *Norteamericano* here? He should have killed him when he had the chance.

He crouch-ran to the mounded blackberries, blinking through stinging sweat to see the huts on the other side. The call of a distant quail pierced the heat and he realized an alert woodsman would have heard the tunnel of quail silence across the hills, would notice the screaming jays, the whistle of a ground squirrel sentinel. The old *Norteamericano* and his ilk hunted beaver. Men like him learned from Blackfoot and Apache. Cunning, brave, brutal.

The village was deserted, two houses torn apart for firewood. No sign of the enemy. Lying in ambush? He motioned with his gun for Quapata to circle the other way, and ran from hut to hut toward the river, noticing bedrolls and saddles. Good. They were still here. He sprinted across the open space on his way to the beach. Over the soft hiss of the river he heard a man's voice.

"Company."

He stepped behind a dense thicket of willows, kneeling to see through an opening, relieved that they had been complacent.

A gun cracked. Dead ahead.

No ball thudded in the sand or came through the trees. *Aimed for Quapata.* Knee-high buckskin moccasins stepped on the path before his nose. The feet moved uncertainly, toes pointing the other way. Turning this way and that. Large feet, bigger than the old man's.

Pedro raised the Allen, pointed to where the chest would be, fired. One. He turned the barrel a click and jumped into the sunshine, stopping the man's forward pitch, using him as a shield as he fired at four men running at him, the old *Norteamericano* not among them.

Two went down, one gripping an arrow in his chest, the other diving. Two balls. Pedro let the wounded man, who had absorbed his friend's ball, slouch before him and clicked the barrel to number three.

Something buzzed against his shoulder and he saw a sixth man eyeing him down a smoking barrel.

Firing, Pedro flung himself across the trail. A puff of dust rose where he'd been. A wounded man crawled toward him like a lizard, leading with his pistol, grimacing in pain.

Pedro turned and squeezed. Four. The man's mouth opened wide in his beard.

He scrambled deep into the willows, a hand in his pocket for four more balls and powder packets. Whirling to watch his back, willow branches in his eyes and face, he unlocked and opened the barrel with trembling fingers and stuffed the balls and packets into the grooves. Something moved in the willows. He closed the lock. It was María on her hands and knees! Wild-eyed. She pointed at a mound shrouded in leaves, black hair showing. Captain Juan. He looked dead.

He had made them a target! Giving her the down signal, he squirmed to the edge of the thicket. Chin on the sand, he lay searching the brow of the gravel, the water's edge. Nothing moved in the beach clearing, no larger than a big corral. Where was Quapata? He felt pain in his shoulder and saw his vest torn, blood on it, but it was a slight wound. Bugs were suddenly crawling all over his face, and arms — tiny purple iridescent beetles streaming down from the willows.

He squirmed forward, blinking beetles from his eyes.

A gun reported from behind. He whirled and saw willows thrashing. A man reloading, María out of sight. He fired. Hit the gun arm. The *pistola* fell to the ground. The man dropped to his knees, reaching for the gun.

He turned the barrel a click, aimed and squeezed. The man's head jerked back, the bushy beard up, a hole singed in the exposed white neck. The gun dropped again. Wiping beetles from his face, he pushed through the willows and saw the man was finished. He stuffed the extra gun in his sash, saw María rising from a pile of spent branches, and crawled back to the edge of the thicket.

Quapata stepped from the bushes near where the sixth man had appeared. With a bare foot he rolled a body, signaled Pedro the man was dead and pointed his stub at an injured man a short distance from away. Alive but harmless, moaning, an arrow in his side.

Pedro pointed the barrel between his pleading eyes and said, "Now I give you more mercy than you gave women and children." He squeezed off number three.

A piece of the head chipped off, pink matter oozing.

He stepped cautiously from the willows, looking around. Four men lay sprawled on the sand. Another dead in the willows. Watching the bodies, expecting gunfire from the bushes, he joined Quapata, whose next arrow was ready, and asked, "Any more?"

"One went that way." He pointed his stub past the brambles on the creek.

The first man Pedro had shot moved, touched his gun. Pedro walked over and stood over him. Too weak to lift his rifle, the man looked up, terror in his face. *Like shooting a wounded horse.* He fired number four, making a dark hole in the white forehead. He turned away.

As Quapata cut the throat of the last wounded man, María crept out of the willows, curly leaves all through her hair. Pedro went to her, the strain showing in her face, and pulled her into his arms.

"Pedro. Oh Pedro. Gracias," she said into his chest.

"*Amapolita mía*, Thanks to the Virgin I came in time."

"You are hurt," she said drawing back, looking at his shoulder.

"It is nothing. We go now, *rapidamente*." One man had escaped, but he would come back, possibly with others. He scanned the bushes, seeing nothing, and told her to go to her father. "We'll bring horses."

He and Quapata quickly saddled one of the *Norteamericano* horses and a mule, and led them to the willows. María scrambled on with her carrying basket while Quapata and Pedro gently laid Captain Juan — still breathing — across the mule's saddle. There were leaf compresses on his back.

They took a circuitous route toward McCoon's cabin, far off the trail through the blue oaks, Quapata leading the mule with Captain Juan, Pedro leading María. The animals broke sticks and kicked rocks. His heart was in his throat to see her sitting tall in the saddle. Easy target. He walked before her, swinging his four-shooter from side to side.

Ahead, a man yelped.

Quapata gave Pedro the rein and signaled him to stay with María. Positioning an arrow in his bow, the *Indio* crouch-ran ahead.

In a minute or two he called, "Come señor." Calm, assured voice.

Pedro led María to where Quapata stood with his drawn bow aimed at a man in a buckskin shirt and torn canvas trousers, light gray except for a large dark spot in front. He had wet himself. He was on the ground clutching his wrist, a rifle an arm's length away.

"Monster rattler got me." He made an exaggerated face of pain. "Don't mean you no harm." His eyes darted from Quapata's arrow, the point of which would drive into an eye, to Pedro's gun. "Palaver English?" His voice quavered.

"You killed the Indians."

"No. I warn't thar," he whined, "Honest." About Pedro's size, younger, silky brown beard.

"Where are your *compadres*."

"Don't have none." He glanced at his wrist. "I needs to suck the pison out, sir." His eyes pleaded.

Dipping his hat at Quapata, who hadn't slackened his draw, Pedro looked at the *Norteamericano* and said, "That *Indio* speaks no English and he is not happy. His relatives were murdered." He picked up the rifle and shrugged as if he couldn't do a thing about it. "*Indios* believe in revenge."

"Please sir, tell him I didn't kill no Injuns." Pitiful.

Squaring his shoulders, Pedro ordered, "Give me your other gun."

He fumbled with his good hand, tossed a four-shooter to Pedro's feet. The other hand hung limp and pink, already swelling. He'd been sneaking around, crawling in the rocks, to get bitten on the wrist. But Pedro was tired of killing, and the fear on the young face was giving him an idea. "Do me a favor, señor."

"Oh yes sir. Anything you say sir. Yes sir."

"Tell everybody you meet that a Spaniard named Joaquín will kill any *Norte-americano* who sets foot within five miles of this *ranchería.* Will you do that?"

"Oh yes seenyer." It rhymed with meaner. "You Wakeen?"

"Sí. And tell them my vaquero here — *Tres Dedos* — can shoot a tick off a coyote at half a league. Do you know what *Tres Dedos* means?"

"No, seenyer."

"Three Fingers."

He looked at Quapata's maimed hand, still pulling the bowstring, and swallowed. "Yes sir. I'll tell ever man I see."

"Is that your mule?" Pedro pointed with his eyes to a grazing animal.

"Take him, seenyer."

"Gracias. Pata, *no lo mate.*" Slowly the Indian slackened his bow.

"Oh seenyer! Thankee kindly for my life." The coward was weeping.

"*De nada.*" For nothing.

When it was clear they hadn't been followed, Pedro sent Quapata ahead to Rancho Omuchumne, where he was sorely needed, then rode beside María. Progress was painfully slow because of Captain Juan's injuries and his obvious pain.

The sweet-wise aura of María, her bearing proud as she sat tall in the teeth of tragedy, her breasts swaying with the horse, her body streaked with pale dirt, made him swallow a hard lump. *Madre de Dios!* No Spanish woman could do that.

They were halfway to Rancho Omuchumne when Pedro remembered the baskets of gold. But he couldn't leave María, and couldn't ask her to turn back with him. Captain Juan was more important. Besides, what good was gold now? Even if Señor Sheldon got the land for him, the Indians were dead. And he had to be the most wanted man in the territory.

But outlaws needed gold too. He exhaled, vowing to ride back tomorrow. The man with the rattlesnake bite would probably live, and could identify him. To protect the *patrón* he must leave Rancho Omuchumne, maybe live in the wilderness. But for now María and her father needed the sanctuary of the room above the gristmill.

60

Dew fell heavily in the mornings now, two moons after the massacre. It sweetened the bleached grass before the sun rose behind the browning trees, but Maria moved from task to task like a cold-blooded creature, wiped clean of joy. Already she had collected herbs for Father's morning tea, and was on her way up the millhouse stairs.

Perrimacoo's brown and white horse suddenly stepped around the corner. "Where's your hair?" he said with a grin.

"My people are dead. Where are you going?"

"Came to see you."

"I am here." Standing halfway up the stairs, higher than Perrimacoo on his horse, she adjusted the burden basket and looked up to see Pedro in the window. She was anxious about every man who came to Sheldon's mill, worried about avengers coming for Pedro.

"Elitha me wife says to me one day yer boyfriend was saving gold to buy me rancho. And I says to meself, Perry, says I, go see about it."

"We have no gold now." The morning after they had arrived, Roberto galloped in with news of a grizzly killing a cow. After tracking the animal half a day, Pedro had gone back to the home place, but found no gold. Several new pairs of *Norteamericanos* had been panning in the area, and she'd been relieved he hadn't tried to kill them, despite his threat. Before the sleep she had made him promise not to think of the lost gold. They were already sad.

Under the leather hat Perrimacoo's eyes were nothing but blue glints in twin thickets of dark lashes. She turned and climbed the stairs.

"I might could make ye a bargain."

Wishing he wouldn't make her say things twice, she stopped and looked at him. "We have no gold."

His jaw shifted and his eyes took on a different cast, though his relaxed posture remained. "You could get rich in a few days if you came with me to Sutter's Creek." He smiled like a man who thought himself wise.

"You want me to couple with Captain Sutter and you would take most of the money."

"You bitch." The smile remained, insolent now.

She turned and climbed two more steps.

"All right then, you taik TWO hundred dollars a night."

She opened Pedro's door and shut it behind her.

Several mornings later soft footsteps sounded on the stairs, barefoot. Pedro was out with the cattle. She opened the door. It was an Omuchumne man she knew, home from Dry Diggings. His pained, steady expression told her he knew of the massacre of her people. "My people are on their way home," he said. "Today they will arrive. We will dance the Yumeh."

He left. She turned to Father, gaunt and motionless on his mat, eyes closed. Knowing he had heard, she said, "I will go and wait for my friends in their village."

It had taken more strength than she had to stop her mind from revisiting the bloody scenes of the home place. She had begun to feel adrift, even from Pedro. It had been too quiet around Mill Ranch with all the Omuchumne away. She longed to see Blue Star. Taking Billy, she quietly closed the door behind her.

Wind — the kind that might bring rain — moved through the stubble of her hair as she walked along the path cushioned by fallen leaves. With the trees and vines molting, the Omuchumne houses and granaries were visible from a greater distance than usual.

The empty u-machas looked forlorn with a dust devil dancing around them. Outside Blue Star's house, Maria put Billy down. He played with the leaves drifting from the large oaks, and she sat watching the leaves, unaware of passing time.

By twos and threes the Omuchumne arrived, men followed by women and children. Tomaka, shuddering with extra flesh, embraced Maria with her expression before she wrapped her heavy arms around her. "We are sad about your people," she said into her hair, her breath warm, her huge breasts comforting.

Hugging Tomaka in return, Maria blinked tears away, and felt sympathy pouring into her from the hands that rubbed her back and shoulders. This was the Omuchumne birth-helper. She turned to Blue Star, thinner after toiling at the diggings, tears streaming down her face. Blue Star's parents and younger brothers were dead too.

They shared sorrow though embrace, and Maria murmured, "It is good you married Quapata and moved away from the home place."

Blue Star stepped back as Omuch approached and spoke to all of them:

"We are home for the Anniversary Cry," he said. "You and your father are invited to celebrate the dance of the dead with us. We dance in eight sleeps."

That soon. She doubted Father would be well enough. And the Omuchumne must hurry to gather and hunt for the feasts. They must weave new baskets, and decorate the dancehouse, and repair the costumes. No dance was more needful of careful preparation. But she looked forward to helping her friends with these tasks, almost glad for the rush. It would steer her mind from the river of blood.

Four sleeps later her fingers were flying over a new cooking basket when barefoot steps sounded on the wooden stairs. She opened the door and saw to her great joy two cousin-brothers — Spear Thrower and Stalking Egret, neither of whom she ever expected to see again. She couldn't stop staring at their strong young bodies, unharmed. "You're alive," was all she could say. Then she remembered her manners and invited them in.

Grizzly Hair woke from a nap and rose on an elbow, the corners of his lips turning up in a smile. "Where are you going?" he asked politely, but his tone was high and weak. His singed hair poked awkwardly from his scalp and the flesh hung loose from his upper arms.

Though their eyes betrayed deep sorrow for the loss of the people, they were clearly relieved to find Maria and her father. They sat on the floor beside his mat, telling how they and their wives and children had been living with the Wapumne, east from the home place. "We buried the dead," said Spear-Thrower.

Grizzly Hair nodded approvingly, then looked over their heads.

"We made a platform fire and burned them and what was left of their belongings. We sang their spirits away. We buried the ashes at the back of the roundhouse." *Beneath Grandmother Howchia.*

Grizzly Hair exhaled, a burden visibly lifting from him. He said "Omuch invites your families to his Anniversary Cry, beginning after the sleep."

"We will attend," said Spear-Thrower.

Stalking Egret added, "We go now to bring our women and children from the Wapumne village."

"Are there others?"

"We are the only survivors, hy-apo."

"Where will you live?"

They exchanged a glance. Then Spear-Thrower spoke. "Now that we have found our esteemed headman, we will ask Omuch for permission to build houses in his village. We want to live near you."

The cousin-brothers left and Grizzly Hair closed his eyes, arms at his sides. A strong man, Maria thought, returning to her basket-weaving. She recalled how he had endured the cutting into his flesh. She had been frightened watching the doctor from the southern river slash into his back, hunting for lead balls that pained him so terribly. The blood gushed, but he made no sound. The doctor pulled out one bloody ball, and said another was lodged too near his spine. It must remain. He had stitched the holes together, and she put healing herbs on the wounds.

But when she had brought baskets to pay the doctor, he stopped her with an upraised palm. "I owe your father. Today I pay."

"What debt?" Grizzly Hair had never sent dunning sticks to be tossed into their u-machas.

"All *Indio* people owe your father. He was war chief against the black hats."

Now, she proudly regarded Father's unmoving face. Here lay a man of knowledge, one who had defeated many enemies. Now he was conquering the evil within.

Eight days had passed. Pedro came in from the cattle early, and Grizzly Hair announced. "I will dance."

"Can you walk?" Maria asked. She had seen him struggle to stand.

The sunken eyes glittered with determination. Slowly he pushed up from his mat, steadying himself on a bent knee, then pulled himself to his full height. His rib cage protruded from his once-fleshy form, jutting from the concavity of his stomach. Skin hung in folds from his inner thighs and draped over his bony knees. He looked worse upright than on the bed.

Shocked by his shaking, and sensing the pain from the evil ball inside him, Maria put his arm over her shoulder and helped him to the door. "Come Billy," she called. Determination like this was to be encouraged.

A step at a time they descended the staircase, him towering over her, Billy trailing. She helped them both bathe and cleanse themselves in the river, rubbing their skin and hers with soaproot and cleansing herbs. She replenished the wormwood bundle hanging with Father's amulet, gave him some for his nostrils, and tied on her skirt. On the path to the Omuchumne roundhouse people passed, turning to look curiously at the three as they walked painfully slow.

Near the roundhouse the dance doctor pushed his shoulder under Grizzly Hair's other arm and helped him down the ramp through the low door to the northwest pole, where the ill would receive special strength from the ceremony. The doctor spoke to a family seated in the pine boughs. "The esteemed hy-apo of the eastern village will join you."

They moved aside, the mother holding a small boy with blistered skin, giving the post of honor to Grizzly Hair. He crossed his legs and sat impassively, eyes unfocused, preparing to receive the spirits.

Maria inhaled pine scent until it tingled and cleansed her internally. She patted the boughs beside her to show Billy where to sit, the earth's cool breath washing away the anguish of the last two moons. It was time to speak the names of the dead, to commune with the spirits of Crying Fox, Etumu, Dishi, Singing Grass, Scorpion Trail, Running Quail, Grasshopper Wind, Sunshine-through-the-Mist and many, many more.

As the roundhouse filled with Omuchumne, the ceremonial fire was lit between the four posts. Light from the doorway dimmed with nightfall, the orange flames leaping brighter. Spirit food was brought by the women — oo-lah, acorn soup, and peppermint tea. A buzz of conversation came from the hundred or more people seated around the wall, but Grizzly Hair never spoke.

The deep heartbeat of the drum started. In a floor-length black feather robe,

Raven stepped from the shadows, hopping toward the snapping fire. The dance doctor shook his magic bundle in each of the four directions while the bird flitted around, and addressed the congregation in formal, sing-song tones.

Although Maria had attended a Cry every year, never had the magic words gripped her so urgently. She would embrace the spirits of her lost kin. Their names would be spoken, sung, and wailed. Although she and Grizzly Hair and the two cousin-brother families were not of this village, they were included. This honored her. Beside her, Billy watched the dancing spirit-impersonator, his giant shadow looming on the encircling wall as he moved around the fire, facing all the people.

The dance doctor pointed his purple obsidian knife at Maria and others. She joined the women forming a circle outside the circle of dancing men, nearer the fire. Tomaka's full, rich singing filled the dancehouse to the beat of the sacred drum. Her soulful calling of the spirits vibrated inside Maria, moving her feet as she bounced in the women's line past the men, stomping on the earth in heartbeat with the mysteries of life, shaking the dead, rousing them. The first spirits swooped. Goose bumps shivered down her spine. She barely noticed the scuffle by the door.

She glanced at disruptive *Americanos*, trying to shove their way inside. A flash of fear. They looked drunk. Did they have guns? No. No guns. The people nearest the door pushed them out, and she heard laughter. She prayed the spirits would not be angry. These were white men, like so many others who followed Captain Sutter to his eastern gold mining camp — noisy, dirty men. But mostly friendly to Indian people.

The drum continued to move her around the fire, one foot, then the other. She felt herself blend with Tomaka's song, with the man-dancers passing by, and with all the people. Then the dance doctor raised his feathered arms. The singing stopped. It was the signal for intimate remembering. She returned to Grizzly Hair.

A flute player took his place beside the drummer, opposite the door. As pairs of mourners sat facing each other at the four poles, the flautist put the instrument to his lips. The otherworldly melody pierced beyond the present world. She went with it, ignoring the laughter outside the dancehouse, entering the magic.

Sitting before her on folded legs, Grizzly Hair placed his warm, dry hands on her shoulders and looked directly into her eyes. "Etumu," he spoke the name aloud. It crinkled the flesh on her back and arms.

"Etumu," she repeated, searching his black eyes. She saw the depth of his loneliness. Etumu had meant everything to him, and had needed him, calling on him to notice her when she was still a girl, after her sister Oak Gall died in the mission. Mother had done countless small things to enlarge him in the village. She had always looked at him with respect. Now Maria saw that the love Mother had for Father was matched by his for her. Maria stroked his bony chest, then wet her fingers in the streams running from his eyes, allowing her tears to flow unchecked as she too remembered Mother's face, the eye folds, the proud glances at

Father. She drew him to her, put her face against his big cheek, loose now, mingling tears with memories as they unlocked normal restraint.

Etumu's quiet soul enveloped her and she opened herself to it like a child sucking milk.

"When do we get to the fuckin?" An *Americano* yelled into the dancehouse.

Fear shot through her, but Father only closed his eyes. When he opened them, they shone like damp stones. Then, quickly, his expression softened, then dimmed. He seemed to shrink as he gazed downward, shoulders slumped.

She understood. He was a guest in another hy-apo's dancehouse, dependent on the generosity of others. He had no people left, except her and Billy and the two families seated near them. He felt he should have protected the *umne* from the guns of men like those yelling into this sacred place. But the ambush had been perfectly timed, when he and others were bathing before supper. The people had been shot as they emerged from the water and ran to their wounded children. Had she been alive, Etumu would have reminded him of that.

Proper revenge had been carried out by Pedro, a family member, but that didn't bring the *umne* back. She looked into Father's eyes. He locked her in his gaze, and she saw more than grief for Mother. More than grief for the people.

Etumu said: *Be strong. As long as any people are left, they must live where their ancestors lived. The mortar holes must be visited again. Sing to our river-baby spirit. These things will make Grizzly Hair hy-apo again.*

"Thank you Mother," Maria murmured.

Grizzly Hair was clearly listening to Etumu's secret words for him. He gripped Maria's elbows as she gripped his. His eyes were deep, solemn, trusting. He and she were more than father and daughter. They were allies. Her strength was to be used for him. His strength, when it returned, would be hers. She must get Perrimacoo away from the home place and remove his bad luck house. She would need power, and gold. It was time to go to Captain Sutter's camp. Pedro would understand.

61

Pedro shouted, "María, you are beyond control!"

What did that mean? She wanted him to hold her, kiss her, murmur of love.

His fists clenched at his sides. "Mother of God, think!" His eyes shot gray flashes at her, then at Billy — a frightened rabbit glancing from one to the other.

Think lingered in the wooden walls. Hadn't she spent the last two days and nights thinking? Far more than four times. His stare knifed her. Before she met Pedro, she would have said his look hurt her stomach, but he insisted love came from the heart. If so, hers was bleeding. She didn't know exactly how, but she would match her powers against Sutter's, and learn his secrets. If she came home with the gold, it would be a sign. Gold would buy the home place back and placate the spirits. But she couldn't explain it in Spanish, except to say, "I go find knowledge."

"Carnal," he growled, eyes sparking fire.

Carnal? She didn't know the word. Unable to bear his face, she glanced at Father on his mat, the lines of his face sorrowful, but his sunken eyes held understanding. It took some of the ache from her heart.

Pedro opened the door. "If you go to Sutter's camp, you are a *puta*!" It came out like spit. "Don't expect me to rescue you." He strode out without breakfast.

She turned to Father. "The spirits told me to go."

"Then you must. I will talk with Pedro."

She put Billy into the care of Elitha, who was staying with Señora Catherine, then swam the river. On the opposite bank the trail led east. Repositioning the burden basket, she walked fast all morning. It would be a long uphill trek to Captain Sutter's Creek. She hoped to arrive before the sun entered his western house.

Walking stamped down the memories of the dead, who tried to surface in her mind. It dimmed the flashes of bloated people, once whole and dear, stuck in the river shallows. The thump of her feet quieted the alien voice inside her, which said at odd moments, *You invited Perrimacoo to stay in the village and you looked upon the condor robe when you were impure. You should be dead like your people.* Walking helped. She was on the trail to knowledge, the only trail.

Nevertheless, the fight with Pedro lingered inside her. *Beyond control.* It meant nothing, but the way he said it tore through her. Already weary with sorrow for her people, now she was battling her man. She had never seen him so angry. She had trusted him to understand.

Her eyes flooded and she saw everything as if under water — the parched hills wavering, the powdered trail where many horses had run. By now Pedro would be in from herding cattle, back in his room for siesta. Could Father explain it all?

His Spanish wasn't as fluent as hers. But even she found it difficult to voice her love for the home place — a home spun into her thoughts and memories from the moment of birth, interwoven with the lives and spirits of the ancestors, boulders, earth, hills, river, trees, animals — and tamped into her being. She was facing her worst fears for all of that, and for her man so that he could live there freely as a *gran ranchero.*

Moisture dried on her cheeks. Bitter indignation welled in her throat as she remembered his red face and clenched fists. Amulet bouncing with her breasts, she walked rapidly, oblivious to the sun's journey above her, uncaring that she was watched by antelope and mountain sheep, and passed by riders.

A rider wearing a red shirt overtook her. *Americano*. She kept her eyes forward as he walked his mule alongside, watching her. The pan and shovel in his bedroll and his high boots into which his *pantalones* were tucked indicated he was a miner, no doubt headed to Sutter's camp. After a time she felt safe and wondered if he would offer her a ride. He rode on.

She had conquered fear. It was a sign. This was the way to face Sutter and his men. Some might be vicious murderers, like the old man who wanted to kill Pedro, all sucking power from Captain Sutter — hadn't Elitha said that? But Maria had learned magic. She would draw it to her, thus preparing for the chaos of the changing world.

The heat of the long dry was lessening and she sensed First Rain would soon come. The earth needed it. Everything was dusty, old, hot and weary. She felt the sameness of the rolling brown landscape, and for the first time her feet slowed. The gullies held no memories. The spirits were unfamiliar, silent, dry. Birds and small animals napped out of sight. She wiped gritty perspiration from her eyes, and walked on.

Walking was like the Cry, when people danced to keep their souls from flying apart. Oh, but she wanted Pedro to gallop his horse to her and hold her in his arms. She longed to see his face without anger, to feel his pride in her for undertaking this frightening journey.

But Pedro would not come.

Puta. A woman who received gifts in exchange for coupling. She had tried to say she sought something of greater importance, but his ears had been deaf. And what if a woman was a *puta*? Did it give a man license to be impolite? To refuse to help her? Pedro was unreasonable. All people exchanged gifts. To live in the world was to reciprocate kindness for kindness, food for care, money for work, pleasure for pay, doctoring for food. Men hunted and shared. Women gathered and shared. A woman coupled with her man when she didn't feel like it, to give him pleasure, but also in exchange for the hides and meat he brought, and the house he built. Wasn't every woman a *puta*?

So why was he angry? She knew, oh she knew! And it made her feet fly. He was blinded by jealousy. He feared she would prefer Captain Sutter. Ridiculous! And he didn't even try to defeat that fear. Pedro was like a young child who hadn't learned the first thing about life. Until he did, his vision would be clouded. *I must be patient.*

Father would make him understand. Oh, she hoped. The sun was low at her back, Sutter's camp nearby. She could smell it.

At the crest of the hill she looked down on the largest town she had ever seen, scattered among the dusty green oaks. A forest of smoke columns rose, flattened into an elliptical black disc over the narrow valley. Pale cloth houses, some round, some square — perhaps two hundred — crowded along a stream that flowed from steep hills. In the midst of the cloth houses stood a circle of wooden u-machas, steeply pitched, and a roundhouse like the one at home. People meandered among the structures like disturbed ants. At this distance she couldn't tell if any were *Indios*.

Were the bad *Americanos* among them? Pedro had allowed two to survive. The one with the rattlesnake bite had seen her. They could have friends and relatives down there. The *Indios* who called this their home place might have been murdered, as her people were. She might be shot on sight, mistaken for one of them. Hand on her amulet, she sat on a rock to renew her strength.

Later, thanking Angelica Root, she headed downhill toward knowledge. The stench of human waste grew worse. Then came the textured aroma of boiling grains and broiling meat. She heard the men's voices. Her stomach told her it was supper time. But too many people occupied this narrow valley. Little food would be found along the stream.

Approaching the first fire — *Americanos* by their clothes — she held her head high, gaze forward, toward where she sensed Captain Sutter was. She felt eyes on her, heard talk and boisterous laughter. Whistles and exclamations pushed her along. She let out her breath, relieved that no guns pointed at her. Her power was strong. She saw *Indios* camping at the far end of the little valley, at the foot of the hills, and felt relief that they were alive. She walked tall, glad her journey was over.

Some of the camps were unoccupied, the ground littered. Cooking pans, buckets and candles spilled from boxes and bags. Pantaloons, stockings and blankets hung from low limbs. She headed into the most crowded part of the buzzing town, drawn by Captain Sutter. Why did so many men travel without women? So far from their homes? It unbalanced nature's harmony.

Aware of being followed, she turned toward the stream where hatted men squatted, swirling pans. Despite the long dry, plenty of water ran in the stream, but it was pitted and opaque with silt. No fish would swim here. She slogged over a hillock of mud and, from the corner of her eye, saw that men still followed, without guns. They appeared curious. She stopped beside a man digging a deep hole, perspiration glistening on the black hair covering most of his face.

"Where is Captain Sutter's house?"

The man's bird-like eyes moved down her length, then up, as he leaned on his muddy shovel. His beak was sharp and long. He turned to another, who sloshed dirty water back and forth in a wooden box as one might rock a baby. They spoke.

Not recognizing the talk, she started to leave.

Fingers gripped her arm. She turned.

The man had quit rocking, and stood, unbuttoning himself with his free hand. Beak Nose grinned, babbled something.

She twisted in the grasp, having no wish to couple with smelly strangers. "I go to Captain Sutter!" Remembering that white-skinned men shouted when they meant to be heard, she yelled, "No!" and yanked her arm.

Beak Nose whipped the cloth from her hips. It fluttered to the ground in a heap of red and yellow. The men who had followed her stood staring at it, and her, and Beak Nose was pulling her to him.

From a neighboring campfire an older man rose from a pot he was stirring, and with a raised hand, stepped toward Beak Nose. "Gentlemen, gentlemen. Is that necessary?"

Americano. In his middle years. Broad and solid with bushy gray beard. No hat on a thinning gray head. She felt his power. So did Beak Nose, for his grip relaxed.

More men came from their fires, forming a growing spectator circle.

She jerked free, grabbed her skirt and turned to leave.

The older *Americano* caught her wrist in a stronger grip. Her heart pounced. She scanned for guns in the hands of the crowding men, saw none and reached within herself for calm, for dignified expression, for the magical power she knew was hers.

The *Americano* looked at her as he gestured up and down her length with his free hand, speaking to the crowd in the oratorical tones of a headman:

"Gentlemen! Before us trembles the very wildwood flower whose existence has provoked, lo these many nights, so much skepticism of late. I implore you. Cast your eyes upon this rare dark loveliness, and you will see our princess, our Pocohantas, our own Cleopatra of the wilderness." It was *Americano* talk, yet only a few words sounded familiar.

He paused to survey the men, who were devouring her with their gazes. "Look beneath the mark of barbarism, which so unfortunately mars her perfectly formed chin. My friends, she alone among the hideous females of her race is worthy of elevation upon the pedestal of Diana." His voice resonated, penetrating, but the alien talk made no sense. Did he mock her?

"Observe the rich color flashing in and out of the dusky cheeks, the natural grace and dignity of her bearing." He stood stiffly, gesturing. "Beneath the crudely cropped hair are a pair of magnificently lustrous eyes — large and black, yet soft — so prevalent in novels, yet rare in real life. Who among you has witnessed such perfection of nut-brown limb? Among females of any race?" As he ran his thumb and forefinger down her arm to her to wrist, his bulbous blue eyes stopped on her breasts, swollen with early pregnancy. "Or such graceful mounds of femininity as heave before us."

Terrified, she didn't struggle. Escape would be impossible. All eyes bored into her, rude and frightening. Her heart raced, told her to run. No, she said silently, and faced the men directly.

"My friends, let it not be said that this rarest of wildflowers was tarnished with frowns, that our Cleopatra of the California wilderness was ravaged by animals." Chinning his fuzzy gray beard into his ample chest, leveling his bulging blue eyes at Beak Nose and Rocker, "Or her petals bruised." He released his grip. Pedro had talked of her petals. It indicated love and respect. She breathed easier.

Cheers. Whistles. Scraps of talk came through the noise: ". . . Counselor's right," "Look at them heavenly curves!" ". . . Ifn her skin war white!" ". . . Perry McCoon's mistress," a miner said. She'd seen him before, a man with a slightly feline face.

A man fell to his knees before her, looking up into her eyes, palms pressed together in supplication. Half the crowd kneeled, some snickering, some gazing at her with the faraway look of men communing with the spirits. A few placed their foreheads on the ground, arms outstretched toward her muddy feet. Slowly retying the skirt around her hips, she watched the quieting men.

Her heart stopped as a young one grabbed her. Other hands did the same and she was jostled and lifted until she sat on a platform of arms, six men carrying her. Shouts hammered her ears as her porters bumped and pushed their way through the laughing, babbling men. She shut her eyes and squeezed her amulet, beseeching *oam'shu* for the calm to understand what was happening so she could meet and outmagic any evil.

With a flurry of activity, men arranged barrels and boards before her. Then she was deposited on a raised platform, standing head and shoulders above the tallest, a heap of bottles at her feet.

The resonant voice of Counselor penetrated the din. "What is your name?"

A yell: "Squaws don't never tell their names."

She looked at the questioner, seeing no malice, and said, "Mary." It didn't matter. That was only a nickname. Besides, she had power.

A few shouts stood out from the others. "She done said som'm."

"Shut yer traps."

"Cleopatra spake."

Counselor raised his arms for quiet. Slowly the crowd hushed, front to back. He asked her to repeat the name. She did.

The men chanted: "Mary, Mary, Mary, Mary."

Looking over their heads, she knew these were not the faces of killers. Those in front kneeled as they chanted. Bottles were passed. A few Indio and Kanaka men stood quietly in the back with their women. Had Bohemkulla visited the camp, seduced the men? Her mind was functioning again. Fear hovered in the distance, ready to embrace her at the slightest invitation, but for now she glowed with power.

Something white moved at the back of the crowd. A broad white hat making its way toward the front. Under it was Captain Sutter's pink face, his red shirt tucked into brown pants, straps over his shoulders. His surprised voice came through the roar of loud talk.

"Mary, mine chile." Sutter turned to Counselor, who was a head taller. "Vhat goes here?" Sutter's nose was rounder, purpler than she remembered, his belly fleshier, protruding over his pantaloons. But the sight of him invited no fear. Magic flowed through her limbs.

Counselor cleared his throat. "If I may . . . " When the noise lessened, he continued. "We were saying, Captain, before you so kindly joined us, that this unaccompanied barbaric princess ought to have the freedom of the camp. She should choose her swain."

Men shouted approval, swiveled their hips, licentious grins on their lips — like men at the Second Grass festival, hoping to be chosen. *She should choose* bespoke power.

Sutter seemed confused in the midst of the laughter and excited talk. "Iss no princess. Iss one of mine Indian girls." He flushed.

A roar answered, men outshouting each other, fists raised.

"He has enough."

". . . ain't fair."

"Ain't MERican!"

He puffed out his chest, nearly losing his balance, and reached for her hand. "Zee iss mine."

She raised it out of his reach and announced to the crowd: "I trade one sleep with Captain Sutter for thousand dollars gold."

Smiles touched the men's lips. Those in front told the men behind, and when the talkwave hit the back, even the *Indios* whooped with laughter. Sutter's face grew redder than the cloud on the western hilltop.

A person never knew how power would align things. Even the gold-seeking men of the camp were under her spell. She smiled inside, trusting that she would return to Pedro in four or five sleeps with knowledge, and gold.

She pushed away the memory of his face when he'd said *puta*, needing all her power as she accompanied Captain Sutter to his tent.

62

Captain Sutter lifted the canvas flap and told two *Indias* to bring meat and "*kartofeln*."

They walked out, looking at Maria's singed hair with sympathetic expressions. In the muted light of the cloth room, blankets trailed from the bed, empty bottles littered the floor and a metal trunk disgorged clothing. Against the far wall, two barrels supported a shelf on which lay a large open book, a heap of papers, a sombrero and two baskets. Crossing to where the slope of the canvas met her head, she saw golden sand in the baskets.

"Today you walk far?" Sutter's voice was pleasantly quiet.

She turned. "Sí." He jammed one boot over the other, levering it off with the toe. She braced herself for the stench that sickened her five years ago.

"Eat first." His tan mustache parted like a rabbit's over big teeth. It was too dark to see his red eyes.

The women — young as Maria had been the first time she visited Sutter — returned with two baskets of food. After they set them down, he shooed them out and pulled plates from underneath the bed, handing one to Maria.

She sat against the cloth wall next to the bed, ignoring the venison and took two fleshy roots. What made his feet stink so?

He sat on the side of the bed wiggling them toward her, eating with his hands, as she did. "Iss dark," he said wiping his whiskers on his sleeve.

He leaned down and selected two long-necked bottles from the floor, cracked them on the trunk, detaching the bottoms, and jammed the necks into the dirt, one near her, the other on the opposite tent wall. He lit candles and pushed them into the bottlenecks, where the flames would be protected.

She watched him carefully, as he watched her, but he sang no songs nor indicated in any way that power came from the candles. She saw no hint of self-purification, heard no discourse with any object that might contain an ally. Equally discreet, she kept her powers secret, calm while he eyed her swollen breasts.

He felt beneath the bed, brought out a bottle of the candle-holder type, poured, gulped the liquid, poured a second cup, extended it to her and said, "Trink."

She accepted the cup, but kept her eye on the half-empty bottle, which he set beside the candle. Tiny bubbles rose from nothing inside the glass. It was magic, beautiful in the candlelight, bubbles continuously replacing themselves. Sutter was sharing his power with her!

Unafraid, she drank, thrilled by the sparkling spray on her nose and lip. But immediately her bones weakened, as when she drank *aguardiente*. This surprised her. If she drank more, her thoughts would weaken too. She had learned that brandy was a thief of power. So was this. Captain Sutter must believe he had power to spare. She pretended to swallow, then lowered the cup to her side away from him and poured it on the dirt. She needed all her wits to walk among the supernaturals who once populated the earth.

Sutter swallowed and gazed over his cup, lids flat across the crescents of his eyes. "Come." He patted the blankets beside him and fumbled with the buttons on his trouser flap.

Coupling would weaken him further. But she had told Pedro she wouldn't. "Trink," she said back, pouring the sparkling liquid into his cup.

He smiled. "Ya ya, iss plenty of time. The night is young. Ve finish what ve start a long time ago, *nicht*?"

Her shadow on the tent wall enlarged, flickered wildly and dimmed. She looked beyond the snoring figure of Captain Sutter and saw the other candle had gone out. The one near her was low in the bottleneck. Soon it too would drown in a pool of wax. The soot-blackened bottle tunneled the light, projecting it to the cloth ceiling, a circle as large as the tent, moving, breathing with the flame. Darting insects appeared on the canvas as monstrous birds swooping chaotically. This was the world now, as it had become, with power flying loose and the Immortals in swift retreat. It was a time of transition, unpredictable. New animals. New people. New drinks. New plants. To survive she must reach beyond the boundaries of herself.

The last of the camp's revelers had quieted. Owls whooed. Shrieking night birds imitated laughing women. Captain Sutter had taken no herbs, canted no songs, wore no amulet. He said the *champagne* "fortified" him. That meant strength, but he had fallen to sleep after drinking one bottle.

Now he coughed like he was gagging, then rolled over and bolted to a sitting position, blinking repeatedly. "Ahhhh. Mary. You here still. Goot. I haff sleeping!" He rubbed his eyes and stared at her.

She sat, quiet in her strength.

"Come." He patted the bed, branchlets and rushes springy beneath woolen blankets.

She rose, stepped from the low canvas to the center of the tent where she stood taller than herself, enlarging. She was Deer Woman, no longer small, no longer young. She was pregnant, not with one man's child, but the world. She was tall, old, huge of girth and hips, ponderous of breasts, heavy. She stepped toward him, flesh shuddering, feet drumming the rhythm of eternity. Men were compelled to follow no matter how they squirmed and tossed their antlers. Deer Woman enveloped all. She, the wisdom of the earth.

Sutter's eyes were like plates. Fear bled from his pores, stank up the tent as he sagged back on his elbows. "Mary, is it you?" A whisper.

"I come to learn of your power." Her voice was round, full of the world's harmonics.

His was thin and quavering. "I dream, ya sure. I dream now."

"Yes. Dream. I walk with you to your power place." She would enter his inner sanctum without fear, meet his spirits. She, the earth's all. "Show me the sources of your strength."

"I sleep now, ya sure."

He had no intention of displaying his power. "Follow me," she said.

Timidly he rose, for man cannot resist Deer Woman. She led him through the sleeping camp, past the camp of *Indio* workers, past a second camp where Don José Amador and other *Españoles* slept, and across the ruined creek of the world.

Morning Star beckoned. Maria led up the hillside, dimly lit by the thousand pricks of light from the campfires of the supernaturals. Even the night animals slept. Sutter's steps were halting, stumbling in his stockings; he whined about stopping to rest but she was patient, and when they crossed a creek that talked, their feet left the ground.

Now they walked rapidly in the air, climbing mountains and traversing valleys, passing the many-branched tree of life. Captain Sutter begged to stop, but each time, she turned, showed him her awesome female flesh, and he followed.

She came to a cave in a mountainside and pulled back rocks, opening it. Inside a glowing peach light illuminated a scene of plenty. Smoke from sacred fires scented the air where hundreds of people prepared for a Big Time, many in feather robes and headdresses. Full baskets of delicious-smelling food were laid out over a field of tender green grass. Sutter stood open-mouthed.

She smiled at him. "Come. Meet my uncle."

He followed her up a small canyon until they came to a little u-macha beneath large shade trees, the peach light the only indication of anything unusual. An old man sat overlooking a green meadow. His skin was soft as buckskin, his hair hanging in long gray bunches. He was age itself, eyes sparkling like polished onyx from the dim folds of his face. He engaged Captain Sutter in pleasantries, and when they were done, cocked his head, smiled slyly and asked, "You like my niece?"

Sutter, who had responded politely, seemed increasingly at ease. "She is very beautiful. But . . . ."

"But?" The old man inclined his head curiously.

"Her feet . . . ." Sutter glanced at Maria's feet and stammered, "On the way here, I looked at them when she was climbing some steep rocks and her feet seemed . . . . round, small. Pointed."

Hooves. Her magic was strong.

The old man smiled indulgently, well pleased, she knew. "Perhaps you would like to join us in a dance before we eat?" He had judged Sutter as worthy.

But she must purify herself. "Uncle, first I will bathe."

"Run along then. Captain Sutter and I will talk."

The next time she saw the captain he was dancing in a men's line, hands on the waists of the men on either side. Thunder rolled through the canyons when she approached. It rocked through her and prickled the backs of her arms as she stepped in time with the drum beat. She was light and springy.

Her deer sisters came from the dance doctor's corner and pranced with her in the center of the circle, surrounded by people stomping to the drum, the rhythm of eternity. The men watched her and her sisters, who had enormous brown eyes and long lashes, which they batted coquettishly as they lifted their headdresses. Their hair was softly tan with pale spots on their cheeks, blended into the tan. Moving suggestively, the dancing men gave Maria glances intended to arouse her. But she and her sisters pranced alone.

Afterwards she cleansed herself in the stream and returned to find Captain Sutter seated on the grass, feasting with the others.

"Do you want to stay here?" a woman asked him, apparently also seeing him as worthy.

He glanced around, smiling at the people. "It is very nice, but I must go back. My son comes from Switzerland. I must be at my fort vhen he arrives."

They nodded understandingly. Then before Maria knew what was happening she awoke with Sutter, halfway between sky and earth, their legs entangled in a thicket.

He rubbed his eyes "Where haff been ve?"

"The Land of the Immortals." She too was in awe. "Now we walk to your creek."

It seemed they had been gone a long time, at least a sleep or two, but everything in the tent was as they had left it — the rumpled blankets, champagne bottles, baskets of gold. The coral-pink color coming through the canvas was all that remained of the land of the Immortals. It made the tent beautiful.

Captain Sutter lay down, groaned, turned to his side and almost immediately snored. She left her skirt in the tent and went to bathe.

Emptying her mind of trivia, ignoring other *Indio* people doing the same, she waded to her thighs in the deepest part of the creek and turned to offer gratitude to Father Sun. Then she willed her thoughts to fly to those who had admitted her to the happy land. She was thanking them when a loud voice interrupted: "The wildwood Cleopatra! She bathes in light!"

She turned to see miners, one standing with a pan of water, the other on a knee, dipping. Tents flew open. Scuzzy-headed men in strange white clothing — tight-fitting to their wrists and ankles — peered out. They relieved themselves outside their doors and teetered across the rocks on bare white feet, beards wild, hair in clumps. Clowns. Soon she was surrounded. Some smiled, others bowed their heads before her as they had before the sleep.

"Oh beauteous creature!"

"Oh paragon of womanhood!"

"Oh fer a heavenly poke in that poon!"

"Gitcher ugly sticker outa here!" The speaker threw up a hand to defend himself from a blow, and soon they were laughing and rolling in the mud like puppies at play.

Slipping away, she opened the flap of Sutter's tent.

He sat up. "Mary!" Scowling toward the sounds of the mock battle, he seemed surprised, befuddled.

She had spent the entire sleep with him. The sun was up and it was time to leave. She walked to the baskets of gold, waiting to be paid.

He looked from the tops of his pale eyes, underscored by puffy half-moons. "Come." He patted the bed beside him.

She reached for her skirt, began tying it around her waist. The noise outside dwindled.

"No. *Komm mal. Wir machen noch verkehr.*" He opened his square flap, his pink man's part small and rising.

Sickened by the smell, she said, "The sleep is finished."

He stood, stepped toward her, his man's part bouncing.

She moved back.

He grabbed for her, but she slipped to the side and darted out into fresh air. Hearing his footsteps at her heels, she hurried through the camp, passing men at their breakfast fires. Some smiled and followed.

Howls, laughter, the banging of metal pans told her Sutter was behind and losing ground on his tender feet.

Someone yelled in sing-song mockery, "She's tired a you."

"Peers she don't like the old goat."

"Want a young stud?"

She circled the camp and stopped at the tent next to Sutter's, where a man she recognized stood in her path.

Eyes crinkled with amusement, thumbs in his waist band, he said, "Perry McCoon's mistress, I belief." He looked her over. "Remember me? Heinrich Lienhard?" The dense brown-gray fur on his face was closely trimmed, and his nose was small. Then he smiled and she remembered the feline face, and his politeness.

"Sí. At the fort."

Counselor joined them. "Out for a morning constitutional are we?" He winked at Lienhard.

Uncomfortable with Counselor's speech, she looked toward the distance, over the men crowding around. Then she heard Sutter's gasps, watched his stricken face as he passed by into his tent.

A wall of hirsute faces smiled after him.

They belittled their captain. It had been different back at New Helvetia, where he had been feared by all men and coupled at will with their wives. Even Pedro had done his bidding. She recalled the twenty-five cannons and the racks of long guns fired by men when he raised his hand. She looked at Heinrich Lienhard and Counselor and said, "I come to learn of Captain Sutter's power."

Lienhard's whiskers moved in a cat smile. "Captain Sutter's power?"

Chuckles rattled through the crowd. "Power" popped out several times.

"I got more in my pinky."

"You wanna see power, darlin? Try ole Tennessee."

Counselor was talking too.

She shook her head. She couldn't hear over the disorderly talk.

Counselor held up a hand. The crowd quieted.

"Do I hear misplaced hilarity in our fair wilderness camp? Rumors that the esteemed Captain Sutter lacks manly endowment? Indeed, gentlemen, think for a moment. He hath bedded this beauteous creature all night then run a footrace for her in the morning. Hardly a mark of weakness, my dear fellows."

"You old men sticking together, huh?"

"Let her try me!"

Heinrich Lienhard regarded her kindly, a glint of teeth where the cat smile parted. "You men, go to your digs before Herr Sutter's Indians pick out all da gold. They work the creek now an hour."

Half the crowd drifted away, including Counselor. The remainder stood back in twos and threes, within earshot.

Ignoring them, Lienhard opened his palm toward the fire. "Join me Mary?" A pot of coffee steamed on a flat rock and a pan of simmering meat emitted the aroma of *puerco*. She smiled acceptance.

A man of middle years, Lienhard turned his attention to the meat, tossing the pan until all the slices were reversed. His furry chin moved as he spoke. "I too haff interest in Herr Sutter's power." He didn't laugh.

She said, "He has little strength now."

Lienhard glanced at her and cut his eyes back to the meat. "You play to his veakness."

"I do not understand."

"Females and trink are his veakness."

Drink. "*Aguardiente* and champagne?"

He nodded. It was as she had suspected. Thieves of power. "Where did he find his power when he had it?"

Lienhard sat beside her, looking at the meat. "His power? Mmm." He gave her his quiet feline smile. "Imagination and style, *mein schatz*. And confidence in what he can make. No fear of cost." He chuckled. "Herr Sutter was zo intent on making civilization, he tinks not at all about paying debts. Dot iss strength, and ya veakness too." He swallowed a chuckle. "Understand?"

Not really. She approached it differently. "Does he have helpers who give power?"

"Helpers? Mmm." After a moment he whispered, "He took it, my dear. Simply took authority." He lifted a brow at Sutter's open tent door and pressed a finger across his lips.

Puzzled, she lowered her voice. "Took it?" Power came slowly — after long, exacting discipline and dangerous encounters with the spirit world. Some never grasped it, no matter how long and hard they tried. Power wasn't there to be plucked like a berry from a vine.

"Ya. He pretends to be a captain." He smiled at the meat.

"Pretends?" Either a man was headman or he was not.

The feline smile spread. "He had imagination to fool the Mexican government." He held the pan toward her, indicating she should take a piece of meat. "He plays the big important man, with confidence for the future. Men want to be part of it. Zo maybe he deserves his rank, and landt, and attention." He put the pan down on a warm rock.

Style. She had much to learn. Chewing the tough *puerco* meat, obviously dried hard before the cooking, she mulled over what he'd said. In the American tongue many words meant power. Strength, authority. *Imagination* was new to her. Fooling others certainly was a mark of power. Still, no one could pretend to be a headman. It baffled her.

Sutter came from his tent, casting a hooded glance at all the men within earshot. He lowered himself on a crate opposite Maria, avoiding her eyes, and poured warm coffee from the pot into a tin cup, much of it sputtering on the firestones. As if it might fly away, he gripped the cup with both hands and let steam rise into his tan mustache, listening as Lienhard spoke in German.

They exchanged utterances, the pitch and volume rising. While Sutter was talking, Lienhard glanced at Maria, pointing his cat's chin at a pile of biscuits in a basket, indicating she should take one.

"Zo," said Sutter, suddenly giving her a level look, "you ask after mine power." The red zigzags in the whites of his eyes looked painful as he rolled his eyes up at the men standing around them.

She nodded, mouth full of biscuit.

"You stay mit me. Ya. Denn you see power." He sipped.

"First, pay for sleep."

Over the cup Sutter's pale eyes locked into hers. "I owe you no-sing."

She didn't hesitate. "Thousand dollars for sleep." The listening *Norteamericanos* talked rapidly among themselves. She heard:

"He ain't paid up."

"We all done heared the terms."

"I'll say."

"Shore did."

"Ever man in camp."

The cat face followed the speakers, then looked at Captain Sutter's balding head and the pink tops of his cheeks as he stared at his cup.

Wishing she understood the deeper currents of the tongue, she added: "Two thousand dollars I stay next sleep with you."

Sutter lifted his pale eyes to her, rabbit mouth tight. "As you perfectly goot know, I haff not pay because you. . . . because ve . . ." The irises floated higher on the red and white as he scanned the listening men. His volume decreased. "Because you didn't . . ." His chin quivered beneath his square-cut beard. "I didn't . . ." The men stepped closer.

He was weak before her power. "You pay two sleeps," she said, "then I come at suppertime."

Coffee sloshed over the rim of Sutter's cup as he set it on the blackened dirt by the fire. He stood, hiked back his shoulders and strode into the tent. Immediately he returned like a tom turkey, chin back, breast feathers fluffed, carrying a basket of gold. Gasps came from the spectators.

"*Momento*," she said rising. From her carrying basket she retrieved the soft deerskin bag she'd brought for this purpose, extended it, held the sides open.

He scooped a hand into the gold, forming a careful, mounded pile, waited until it stopped slipping, then poured it into her bag. Nine more times he did it, counting, "*zwei, drei, vier*, fife, sex, seeven, eight, *noin*, ten." From the tops of his eyes he watched the hovering men and said in a loud voice, "Tousand dollars. Paid. For last night."

"No," she said. "That was ten."

The eyebrows arched over humorless eyes. "Mine chile, one handful iss a hunnert, ten hunnerts a thousand. Und now for dis night." He dipped his hand into the half empty basket.

Lienhard hissed through his teeth, "I cannot belief!"

Sutter's hand paused. "You tink I am a poor man, hmm?" He put the gold in her bag.

"Zo much, Johannes! We yust agreed. Every flake must go to the teamster." Seeing Sutter ignore him, he spat out: "*Sacrament! Nichts mehr!* Ve be partners, Johann!"

Sutter made a dismissive gesture. "Not to vorry. Mine *Indios* and Kanakas strike big today. You see." He put the gold in her bag and said, "Fife," then scooped another handful.

Lienhard poured the remains of his coffee on the fire, where it sizzled. Then he delivered a fierce German harangue, and went into his tent.

Sutter finished the ten handfuls, speaking more to the surrounding men than to her. "Und Now!" He stood, tossing his empty basket like offal toward the tent. "Cleopatra iss mine yet another night." His chest puffed out between the suspenders, belly tight in the red sling of his shirt.

The miners exchanged awed glances as she lashed the thong around and around her fat bundle of gold, and dropped it in her carrying basket. She positioned it on her back, and the men stepped back as she passed. She would spend the day in the *Indio* camp resting. Because, once again, when the campfires of the Immortals pricked the sky dome, she would need all her wits.

63

Hooting and hollering sounded in the distance.

Maria opened her eyes and thought she was a child again, with Crying Fox outside the u-macha playing with his friends, Etumu preparing food. She shook the bad omen from her mind. She was here, beneath the willows of Captain Sutter's creek, waking from a sound sleep. Etumu and Crying Fox were dead, along with Great-Grandmother Dishi, uncles, aunts, cousin-sisters, cousin-brothers and all their children. Father was slowly recovering.

Immortals had sent her to this place of gold gathering. She was like Red Cloud, who long ago recovered the people after they had been won in a game of chance and herded to the northern land of ice. She would win back the home place. Her medicine had been strong, and she was not finished.

It was late in the day. Shadows pointed east. A breath of air cooled her hairline. She rose and walked a few steps to check her carrying basket, which she had stored inside the brush shelter of a friendly family working for Captain Sutter. *Nisenan* they called people. She crawled under the brush, reached down to the bottom of her basket and felt the fat doeskin bag, safe. Then, squeezing her amulet, she walked toward the disturbance across the creek.

Miners teemed around a wagon and oxen. She waded the stream, shading her eyes from the glare, nodding greetings to the *Indios* and Kanakas who continued to wash gold along the creek.

As she entered the crowd — boxes and barrels passing hand to hand over hatted heads — a man grabbed her breast and leered at her with the face of a demon, hissing with foul breath, "This handful's gotta be worth a hundred."

She pulled back in horror.

A voice: "Keep yer dirty paws offa Cleopatra!" A fist reached across her, rammed the devil-face. Bone cracked. Bright blood spurted to her chest. He fell back, two red streams from his nose soaking his black beard.

She cringed, turned toward the creek to wash. A flame-haired man pushed her out of the way and smashed his fist into the jaw of the man who had hit devil-face. The crowd surged forward, trapping her in a chaos of yelling, shoving men. Before she knew what was happening, she felt herself picked up and carried forward as if by a many-handed centipede. From behind came grunts, hollow thuds, smashing bottles. The centipede deposited her in the wagon bed, where she watched in safety.

In a cloud of dust, fists flew, hats sailed, bottles smashed into sunbursts of glass and liquid. Hatless men rose from the ground, only to be pounded down again. Others whirled and rammed their fists into anyone within reach. Men on the outskirts pushed forward to join the fray.

Captain Sutter climbed to her side, his expression a mix of consternation and pride. In the penetrating tones of a herald he announced: "All trinks on me. Each man a full bottle!"

Men turned mid-punch. Others gaped at Sutter with bloody lips. Several rose to all fours, then swayed to their feet staring. From a hundred throats a cheer rose: "Hurrah!

"Drink to Captain Sutter!"

"A fine old gentleman."

This was power.

But the teamster wasn't enchanted. He squinted up at Sutter through bushy brows, yelling over the din, "'At's twenty pinches apiece comin to me. And I ain't forgot the thousand you owe." Bloody men were yanking out corks with their teeth, handing out bottles.

Sutter smiled benignly at the teamster. "Join us, mine goot man. Trink and be merry!" Loud cheers.

The teamster elbowed his way to Heinrich Lienhard, who gave him the flat look of a cat ready to hiss.

"To Princess Cleopatra!" somebody yelled.

"The most beautiful female!"

"To all females!"

"To beauty!"

The dirty men raised bottles, clacked them together and swilled the contents as Sutter hung his hand on her shoulder, his eyes sliding down her breasts. He opened his mouth to speak when the teamster leaped into the wagon shouting, "I'm staying right here till I gits every pinch comin to me!"

Two heads shorter, Sutter scowled up. "Mine goot sir, can you not see this iss not za time." He nodded fondly at Maria.

"Time my ass! I'm campin in yer damned bed till I gits paid!" Pistol raised over his head, black beard blanketing a red shirt, he jumped off the wagon and stalked through Sutter's tent door. Titters purred through the crowd. Bursts of ribald laughter.

With a pat on Maria's behind, Sutter tried to imitate the jump from the wagon and caught a suspender on a peg. He dangled before falling to the dust. A roar of laughter met him as he pulled himself to his feet and followed the teamster inside.

Again Maria puzzled over the rude treatment of the headman. Even if *Americano* drink had stolen his power, he was hy-apo. Then, glancing through the crowd, her heart stopped. A Spanish black hat. Familiar gray eyes. Severe.

Eyes more wont to smiles and warmth. Eyes she thought she knew. He disappeared behind the crowd.

Drawn like a bird to flight, she turned, foot over the side, toes feeling for the protruding hub of the wheel, but strong hands stopped her.

"I go now to my man."

"I'd say yer man's got some rough comp'ny."

"Ain't a looker like you, though." Roaring laughter.

"No. My man is there." She pointed, but saw no sign of Pedro.

A nasal voice: "We's needin s'more looks at yer beauty."

A louder voice: "Cap'ns got her all night."

"Yeah. Leastwise I git a nice long look."

She would not struggle. Drawing upon her strength she stood quietly in the wagon bed gazing at the surrounding hills, pushing away the voices, the feel of eyes boring into her. Pedro had ridden all the way from Rancho Omuchumne. If the distance were to be closed, he would come to her, if not, she must accept that.

She stood at the wagon's edge, trying to plan her night with Captain Sutter, but couldn't forget the anger in the gray eyes. *Accept.*

A sudden tumult of horse hooves pounded near. She turned. Startled men leapt back. In a blur of speed a horse exploded past, Pedro standing on the saddle, whisking her into the air, the horse galloping beneath. Frightened miners stumbled to get out of the way. At her back, Pedro's manly odor, the excitement of his strength as he sat her down before him, surging, legs goading the animal. The yelling receded: ". . . Cleopatra!"

Pursuers followed. She turned to see horses, far behind, losing ground. Pedro's face was like iron. She looked ahead. With breathless speed Chocolate galloped down a cañon filled with evergreen oak, then up a sloping gorge along a dry creek bed, rocks clattering.

Pedro said nothing. She had nothing to say. Her sense of being wronged mixed oddly with the pleasure of her bare back pressed to Pedro, his arms fencing her. They rode on, long after sounds of pursuit faded. At last the horse slowed beneath a spreading oak. Pedro reined to a stop, never having spoken.

Jumping off, he paced, avoiding her eyes.

Chocolate snorted and blew. She slid down the frothing animal and stood watching Pedro. What could she say to a man who lacked understanding? Her heart went to him. He was like a spotted fawn she'd seen chased by a dog, swimming to exhaustion up the river, bleating for help, losing ground to the relentless pursuer, only to be caught on land. She wanted to hug him.

When he finally turned to her, his eyes were wild, crazed. He whirled away as if she sickened him.

An arrow to the stomach couldn't have pained her more. She closed her eyes and touched her amulet, praying for calm. He came to me, she reminded herself.

Choked sounds: "Any other man would beat you."

This caught her by surprise. Except for Perrimacoo and Captain Sutter, men didn't hit women.

He paced away and stood staring through the trees, one boot forward. "You must hate me." He breathed hard as if he and not the horse had been running.

Hate. A strong word, opposite from what she felt. "*Te amo*." It came out rich and full, for he was her life, all that was left of it.

He bent forward, placing his face in his hands, shoulders moving. The fawn bleating.

She went to him, rolling her weight from the sides of her feet, not wanting him to hear, afraid he would wrench away. Softly she touched his back.

He jumped in his skin, but did not turn, or leave.

Gently she embraced the curve of his back.

He wiped his sleeve across his face and straightened, staring through the trees, allowing her to hold him, to lay her head against his shirtback.

She closed her eyes. The source of his love — his heart — spoke to her and she opened herself to it the way she listened to plants, the way she had done so often when this same heart spoke of love in the early mornings and at siesta. She pressed her ear to its muffled thumps, her hands caressing his chest through the fabric, feeling his man's nipples. She heard the low, steady undertone beating for her.

His voice came through his ribcage. "Why, María?"

There was no why, that he understood. She lowered her hands to his sash, below.

He tensed.

She felt her way back to his chest, speaking to his heart. "You are my man. *Te amo*."

He expelled air, his shoulders loosening.

She massaged him. "I love only you."

Slowly he lay down on the matted grass where deer had slept beneath the branches.

She went down with him.

"No," she answered flatly.

"But you took his gold." The tightness lingered in his voice. His black hat lay beside him, the band faded to pink, as he sat against the trunk of the oak, his wavy auburn hair curling around the collar of his pale shirt, which bloused around him, the sash in a heap where he'd dropped it.

"I did not couple with him. I hate his coupling."

The hawk nose was proud, the brows troubled. "I believe you, María. But Captain Sutter was my superior officer and you are my woman. He will think . . . . You must give back the gold."

Kneeling before him, she studied the endless facets of his gray eyes, fractured, deeper than she could see. "I have not injured him. I owe no retribution." She wanted to understand Pedro's way of thinking.

"You deceived him."

Deceived? "He paid me for staying a sleep with him. I did. Now, tonight, I stay the second sleep with him."

"Don't do it. Give the gold back."

It was an order. She struggled against rising anger, reminding herself this was the way he talked. As a dog barks, an egret squawks, one cannot blame them for using their tongues. If disrespect lay behind the order, that was beyond Pedro's understanding.

Leaning forward, he took her hands from her knees, held them in his. "María, María, María. I am so afraid you will be hurt. Killed. Please, give him the gold and come home with me. This afternoon." The depths of his eyes seemed to connect with the spirit world.

He wanted to protect her. This she understood. It was as he'd said before, *Españoles* did not allow pregnant women to walk into danger. She returned the pressure of his hands and studied the kind lines of his face between the auburn sideburns, the curve of his hawk nose. Once again she would try to make him understand her way of thinking.

"I went to Captain Sutter's camp in full light. I walked among many strange men and was not killed, not hurt at all. My power is strong, Pedro." She returned his gaze, which was the *Españolo* way of talking deeply.

"You were lucky."

"Sí," she said, relieved he'd begun to understand. "I have luck now. Many seasons ago when you took me to Captain Sutter's bed . . ." he looked away, "I had little luck. Captain Sutter had big power. He wanted what I did not want to give. Now I have no more fear of him and with the help of my helpers, I have big luck. I took from Captain Sutter only what he gave with his own hand." It made no sense at all to return the gold.

Pedro had followed every word. Seeing his brows moving in concentration, she added, "The gold is for you, to buy the home place." She paused. "What is the meaning of deceive?"

He lifted her hands, closing his eyes, kissing one palm, then the other. "*No importa.*" He looked into her eyes and his voice vibrated with its normal purity of tone, the gravel gone. "Little Poppy, you must have a guardian angel on your shoulder. But do not stay with Captain Sutter tonight. Give that half of the gold back. I do not want it."

She wanted it all. Perrimacoo had recently implied he was interested in selling his land papers, as Pedro well knew. "Will you not help me remove Perrimacoo from the land?" Her voice sounded tight, and she fought to keep her expression from shattering. For so long their bond had been sealed by the desire for Pedro to live in the home place. Had he changed his mind?

"I am a wanted man, but I have my honor."

She frowned, looked away. He'd said this before, but it didn't explain anything. He had protected himself from a killer and taken the lives of those who killed her people. Both *Españoles* and *Americanos*, he'd said — and she wouldn't forget that — believed it was proper for those who took lives to forfeit their own. Vengeance was the way of the world. "You were brave," she said. "You restored balance. Who would prevent your buying land papers because of that?"

He examined her hands, which he continued to hold, and exhaled. "I don't know. It's not certain, but whoever reads my name on a paper could come after me. No. I don't want to talk more about this now. Just promise me you will give Captain Sutter his gold — whatever he paid for tonight. Then come home with me."

He looked at her with such intensity of longing, she melted. Peace with Pedro was as necessary as power. That much clarity she had gained. With bravery she had faced his anger, and learned that his love for her ran very deep. But she saw that he needed to believe he guided her, as a mother guides a little child, and that he would grow weak and angry if he felt she was beyond his guidance. Therefore she would appear to be controlled by him. "*Bueno,*" she said.

He pulled her to him, kissing her and massaging her scalp beneath her short hair. "*Gracias, Amapolita.* I thought I would die without you."

Between kisses she murmured, "My spirit dies without you."

He stood, tucked in his shirt and said, "We go now. Soon we lose the sun." Proud Hawk.

"But you are *bandido*. Maybe they shoot you."

Tying on his sash, he said, "Last time they were too busy looking at you."

Her power had saved him too. "But next time," she said, "they might see you."

He inserted the gun and knife in his sash, on opposite sides.

64

Pedro knew, as he cradled María's softness before him and rocked with the rhythm of the horse, that life was nothing without her. Last night as he lay sleepless in the room with Captain Juan, that bright knowledge had flamed in his heart. So he'd ridden to Sutter's camp ready to die, just to see her. It was almost funny, when he thought of it like that.

But on the way he'd imagined scenes so wrenching — her with Sutter — that he considered ending her life along with his, so they would die together. *Loco* he was. Crazy in love. Then her denials, her sweet attentions to him. *Madre de Dios*, his poor overworked heart had climbed from the bottom of hell and soared higher than the angels of heaven. *Amor!*

He put his chin in her soft short hair, glove tight with her. She was magic. A flower of a girl with a pull on his manhood like no woman he'd ever known. He felt the odd desire to absorb her through his belly where she would lie safe and close to his heart. She and the unborn baby were his family, his purpose in living. It surprised him, this tenderness of longing to hold the infant in his arms. And he believed everything she had said. She never lied. Helping Chocolate pick his way down the dry creek, he vowed to make a greater effort to understand her Indian ways.

"I smell a village," she said turning to him.

"Amador's. Sutter is over that ridge." Reining to a huge boulder, he flicked his hat back on its strings, kissed the nape of her downy neck and inhaled the peach-like aroma of her skin. Man was weak. "Wait here with Chocolate. I'll be back in a few minutes. And María?" He dismounted.

"Sí?" Ever calm, ever dignified.

He left his hand on her thigh. "*Te quiero.*" More than he could say.

"*Te amo.*" The vanilla voice.

She waited while Pedro borrowed disguising clothes from his *Españolo compadres* in Don José Amador's camp. The sun's yellow light pushed long shadows up the hill, the shadow of a boulder creeping up over mounds and gullies and oaks and pines.

As Chocolate cropped the dry grass in rhythm — lipped a mouthful, bit it off, chewed four times, took a step, lipped the next batch — she sank into thought about the gold miners. They cared only about gold and liquor. They had no respect for the spirits or the *Españolo* priests or their headman. Captain Sutter's imagination worked no magic on them; only drinks and liquor did. Theirs was a different kind of power — the power of blackbirds lifting as one from the earth, banking, turning as one across the sun, landing as one. Blackbirds fed in a frenzy, as the miners hunted for gold, pecking one another without remorse, yet always ready on the slightest whim to fly together.

Chocolate ranged too far and she nudged him back to the boulder, his black eye rounding from his head, seeing her on his back. You are my man's woman, he said. I will humor you. A powerful alliance, man and horse. One of the few helpful aspects of the changing world.

She recognized Pedro immediately, striding across the dry grass, a floppy leather hat darkening his face. He wore a checkered shirt and brown trousers tucked inside his boots in the *Americano* manner, no sash or bolero. But his proud walk gave him away. Nevertheless, clothing disguised. From a great distance she would have recognized any of her people, before they were killed, by the nuances of their bare bodies. Legs, torsos and hips varied more than faces, which had to be seen close up for recognition. Yet *Americanos* relied solely on faces. Pedro would blend with the crowd in Sutter's camp.

They climbed the ridge, Chocolate's haunches pushing powerfully, then wove a careful route down through the trees, to the camp of Sutter's *Indios*. Pedro hobbled the horse while Maria greeted the men, women and children who sat around supper fires. Unable to understand their tongue, she spoke Spanish.

"Your things are safe," they said, eyes watchful in the way of strangers.

She pulled her basket from the little house and returned to the deepening shadows of the trees where Pedro waited. They sat dividing the soft golden sand into two equal amounts, half in the doeskin bag, half in the old pigskin bag she'd brought. She handed the doeskin to Pedro to tie on the horse and put the pigskin in her basket, positioning the thong on her forehead. A prickly feeling of being watched made her turn around and examine the trees. The toyon bushes were dotted with red berries, the forest of *tules* green at the creek. No one.

Pedro said. "I'll be near you at all times, with my Allen." He patted the stock of his gun, which jutted from the waistband of his trousers, and drew out his horn-handled skinning knife, giving it to her.

"I have a knife," she said. "In my basket."

"This one is better. Put it here." Carefully he tucked it inside her skirt, tying the cloth tighter around her waist.

The freshly honed shaft felt cool on her hip. "But you might need it."

"I want you to have it. Do not hesitate to use it if Sutter tries to force you and for some reason I am not there."

That struck her as funny. "You want me to return his gold but not hesitate to kill him." She chuckled, having no intention of stabbing the headman of Sutter's Fort. Just look at all the trouble Pedro was in because of the necessary killing of lesser men. "I am not afraid of Captain Sutter," she said. "*Aguardiente* and champagne have stolen his power and my power is good now. My husband, you are in greater danger."

"I'll take care of myself. I pray to the Virgin you won't need the knife." He studied her. "Use your power."

He had acknowledged her, and she smiled in thanks.

He took her hand. "One sound from you and I'll be at your side. Tell the captain you are ill and must move your bowels. Leave the gold in the tent and walk out to the trees behind it. I'll be there with Chocolate."

He turned in a half-circle, gazing intently at everything until he pointed up the hill. "Leave here when the sun is gone from the top of that big, dead pine. I'll take Chocolate around first." The scraggly old giant had two upright spires bisected by shade and light. The floor of the narrow valley where they stood was growing cool and dark more quickly than at home, yet the sun shone on the mountainside.

"María, I am proud of you." He swallowed. "Keep that angel on your shoulder." He kissed her mouth and left.

She called on Angelica Root and gathered her calm. Wading the creek toward the *Americano* camp, she heard a distant violin weaving a sad thread through the twilight. In the shadow of a toyon bush she saw a coyote. He stood smiling at her with slanted amber eyes, tongue lolling. Coyote the Trickster. This was the gaze she'd felt earlier. She stood still until he sauntered away and she wondered about the omen.

"Thar she be," a miner sang out. Staring at her, he rose to his feet as she walked toward the camp. "Hel-LO DAR-lin!" He cupped his mouth and hollered to the other side of the camp, "You men from New York owe me two hundred and fifty dollars!"

The violin stopped. The camp stirred, men talking and yelling all around. They watched her progress. Some groaned to see her, others slapped their thighs and whooped. "Cleopatra!" Ahead, Sutter came from his tent, the backs of his hands on his hips, waiting. Grinning.

Beneath the dark pines, Sutter's tent glowed from the candlelight within. Men crowded around as she approached, Pedro at the back beneath his leather hat. She feared only that he would draw attention to himself without cause. His *Españolo* honor demanded she not stay the night with Sutter, though her *Indio* honor would have her keep a promise. Power was diminished by untruth, but she needed Pedro's love. She would follow his plan though it diminished her power. He didn't understand that things happened of their own accord, often turning plans against their framers. Was that the meaning of Coyote's smile? A tremor of fear passed through her as she looked squarely into Sutter's pale eyes. *Be calm.*

Liquor breath blasted. "Mary, mine chile! Goot girl." He took her by the nape of the neck and steered her to the doorway, where she stood, dumbfounded, looking inside as he turned to the men outside, flapping his wrist, shooing them away.

Perrimacoo was looking at her — the last man she expected to see — an unfriendly smile hollowing the ghost of a dimple in his cheek. He was seated at the trunk opposite the hairy teamster, each holding a fan of cards. A cloud of murky smoke hung over them, rising from *cigarritos* balanced on the edge of the trunk. The teamster twisted toward her, his mouth a red o in the blanket of his black beard. She had forgotten about him. The young *Indias* she'd seen before looked at her from the opposite corner.

Perrimacoo said softly, "Blow me down if it ent about time you got here, with the Captain thinkin he'd been bamboozled and all." Several empty champagne bottles and one that was half full stood on the trunk. Her eyes watered from the smoke.

Sutter snaked an arm around her, his plump trousered hip hard against her skirt. "If you men be zo goot as to leaf us, hmm?" He steadied himself on her.

The o in the black blanket was replaced by the tip of a pink tongue and white teeth flashing. "Like I said. I ain't leaving this tent till I gits ever pinch comin to me." He turned back, slapped down his cards and looked at Perrimacoo. "Two-hundred smackers to ya. Three-hundred all told."

Perrimacoo hadn't lost his smile. "Just walked in the door, it did." He looked at her, then at Sutter. "Captain? If ye please, I'll taik me share now."

Sutter took his hand from her waist and staggered across the tent, waving the women out of the corner. "Later. Go girls. Git! Dots right." He gave Perrimacoo an intimate smile and shooed the women out the door. "Now, if you please, my friends, outside a half hour or zo. Hmm?" He tilted his head at Maria, his red eyes watering in the candlelight.

"Nope," said the teamster, manipulating the cards in his oversized hands. Two stacks whirred thrillingly and became one. Magic. Anything could happen.

Perrimacoo lifted a brow at her burden basket and said to Sutter. "A man's pay comes afore the delivery of goods." He seemed to know what was in it.

Heavily, Sutter grabbed her waist again and swayed as he stood with her. "Dot iss between you and she. I giff golt to Mary. What you say, *liebchen*?" Liquor fumes. "He iss arrange your coming? You giff him eighteen hunnert? Hmm?"

Things were twisting, but power lay in straight talk. "No. I give you half the gold back." She remembered she wasn't supposed to talk about it before leaving the tent. She hadn't thought it over four times.

Sutter seemed to melt, his eyes slippery. "You come to me with luff denn."

"I smells a rat, I does," said Perrimacoo. "I heard you gave the nigger bitch two thousand dollars, includin me eighteen hunnert. Now what's she tryin to pull?" He looked at her with the slant-eyed, deceitful expression of Coyote.

The teamster, who had been shutting one eye then the other as he looked between her and Sutter, thumped down the cards, drew himself up — the top of his head lifting the canvas off the teetering tent poles — and boomed: "If thar be gold in this here tent, it's mine! Ever pinch!" He glared at the basket in Maria's hands.

"Me gold it tis sir," said Perrimacoo looking at his cards. "I see your three hundred and double it. Six hundred to ye."

The bushy black brows writhed like caterpillars. "You gittin it off that squaw?"

Perrimacoo tilted his head at Maria. "Me girl she is. From me own rancho. She'll hand over ever pinch, cause she knows what's healthy." His blue stare leveled into her. "Her Spik pimp makes no never mind." Her neck prickled and he spun his words as soft as a spider weaving a web. "And you teamsters, God knows you have gold aplenty, bleedin the mines as yer wont to do. Sit man, play monte."

The teamster seemed to think it over, head high in the canvas. She wanted to slip out of Sutter's grasp and run from the tent, but his fingers dug into her arm. She dropped the basket at his feet hoping it would distract him.

"Ve haff ya goot fortune," Sutter said, eyes riding up on the white half-moons as he looked at the tall teamster. "Mary brings me the golt, men. I say, vinner take all, but play outside? Hmm? Here take light." He released her, pulled a bottleneck from the dirt and extended it to Perrimacoo.

She stepped back toward the door. Perrimacoo was ignoring the candle. "First give me my gold," he said.

The teamster leaned across the trunk and grabbed Perrimacoo by his shirt and lifted him from his stump, nose to nose. His hat fell back. "Like I said, man, any gold here is mine." He had him off the ground. Sutter stared at them and she stepped back almost to the door.

"No no no fighting in mine tent," Sutter shrilled. "I holt da golt. You two go outside. Go!" He turned and looked at her and she froze, forcing calm into her face as if she were only politely stepping back from an argument. Never taking his eyes from her, he put the candle bottle back in the ground and without straightening grabbed the wide mouth of her basket and jammed in his hand down to the armpit, bringing out the pigskin bundle. "Ya iss golt. For da vinner. Outside now, both you men!"

She took another step but in an instant he was behind her with his free hand on her buttock, pushing her back in the room. "I pay big for you, *liebchen*," he said in her ear.

She would watch for a better time. The teamster, who had dropped Perrimacoo, wrenched the pigskin bundle from Sutter's hand and hefted it up and down. He unwrapped the bag and pinched the contents, his bushy black brows wiggling with interest. She didn't breathe.

"You gave all this to a filthy mahala when you owed me?" He looked at Sutter with undisguised hatred.

Perrimacoo, down on his stool again, said softly, "Hit's mine, but yours if ye wins."

The teamster sat down and looked at him and laid the open bundle between them. He picked up the cards, divided the pile and fluffed and ruffled them with magical dexterity.

"No, outside, gentlemen. Please," Sutter said.

"Fer Crissake," the teamster growled into his wagging *cigarrito*, "fuck the goddamned mahala and shut up." He sucked hard on the *cigarrito* then jerked his chin at the bed. "Want me to take the first poke?" Smoke blasted angrily from his nose.

Looking confused, Sutter snaked his arm protectively around her waist. Perrimacoo upended the bottle and drained it, then lifted half the cards and set them aside. The teamster picked up the remaining cards and placed them on the first stack. She knew it was time to go.

Trying to remember exactly what Pedro had told her to say, she used the only *Americano* term she knew. "I go shit now." She wrenched away, the lie sucking away her power, and ran headlong out the door. The baby wouldn't be born breech, as it would have if she'd backed out, but that was the least of her worries.

She rounded the corner and ran alongside the tent, toes digging in the dirt. It was darker than she'd thought, but in the candlelight coming through the canvas she saw Pedro by a pine at the back of the tent, beckoning wildly with both arms.

"*Liebchen*!" Sutter screamed a few steps behind.

Pedro's hand connected with hers and he ran pulling her toward the horse, a solid black shape in the dark.

Heavy bootfalls crashed close on her heels. She glanced back. The dark forms of men loomed in the light from the glowing tent, Sutter hopping, pointing, yelling to the gathering miners. "Cleopatra stolen! Kill the bastard! Men to arms!"

She tripped and fell over a log. It knocked her breath out. Pedro lifted her in his arms. She was trying to breathe when he pushed her to the saddle.

The teamster pounced on Pedro and they fell wrestling on the ground, the horse stepping nervously.

Perrimacoo ran up and seized the bridle, growling, "You little cheat," and tried to pull her off.

She kicked but he only laughed and kept grabbing for her leg. Miners swarmed through the trees like hornets and an ominous sound came through the noise: Droom, droom, droom-droom-droom. Bohemkulla? The Spanish Devil? Angry spirits? Her heart thumped a swift beat.

The swarm of men yanked her off the horse and held her from all directions. She saw Pedro surrounded, guns bristling. Captain Sutter pushed through the crowd with his rifle over his shoulder, marching and making the sound. "Droom,

droom, droom-droom-droom." Men snickered at him, the stench of their unwashed clothing pressing in on her.

Perrimacoo, having taken the doeskin bag from the saddlebags, held it over his head. "The idol-worshipper was makin off with our gold."

"Stealin Cleopatra too!"

"Second time!"

"Don't peer to be no Mexican."

"March the rascal to light and we'll see."

Within moments they were in front of Sutter's tent, his supper fire rekindled. Men threw branches on it and stomped crates apart, cracking slats over their knees. Fear buzzed to the extremities of her hands and feet and she hardly dared breathe. Facing her own death would be nothing compared with watching Pedro's.

His head was up. *Proud Hawk.* She tried to go to him. The men held her back.

"Hit's a Mexican all right," a man yelled.

"Hang him!"

Knowing what that meant she kicked, bit, scratched, gouged with her elbows, aimed high with the heel of her foot — whatever came within reach.

"Reglar she-devil," said a man snickering and dancing out of range.

"Spitfire!" said another.

She peeled skin down the side of a face.

"Ooo-we," he yelled, dancing back. Men wove in and out all around her, smiling, and she didn't know what they intended, but she continued to yank and kick and scratch and writhe. She reared her head back and caught somebody on the chin.

Captain Sutter was yelling, "No killing at mine camp. Dot man iss mine lieutenant."

Listen to him. He is headman. Out of breath, she paused to listen.

Perrimacoo's voice came clear, "I say flog im with is own lariat. Teach im a lesson!" She saw him in the firelight, holding the doeskin bag.

"Yeah. Teach him good."

They shoved Pedro at a young pine, face first, lashed him to the tree, a rope around his waist and neck. With a loud rip, his shirt was torn open.

"Give it to him," a man cried.

"You, teamster. You got the muscle."

"Show the monkey who won the war."

"Mebbe it's Wakeen. The one that massacred the Oregon men!"

"What's yer name?" A man jammed his gunbarrel at Pedro's face. She heard the thunk of bone. *Don't tell them.* All the men holding her were staring at him.

"Pedro Valdez," he said clearly, and she felt her legs weaken beneath her.

"He IS a spik!"

"McCoon was right."

"Dressed up MERican!"

"Punish the Mexican or none a our gold'll be safe."

"Our squaws either!"

The shouts melded into an unintelligible roar, the fire coloring the men's eyes orange and the lower branches of the pines around the clearing.

The teamster came from Chocolate with Pedro's lariat, whipping it overhead. It snapped like a heavy limb breaking. Men shouted approval. Black against the firelight, the teamster looked even bigger than he was, and the men of the camp were of one heart. Her skin prickled. Still breathing rapidly, she tried to find her calm.

"Give him what he deserves!"

The huge arm jerked. *Crack.* The braided leather curled around Pedro's back. She strained toward him, immobile in the strong hands. The leather was drawn back, but a dark stripe lingered in its place. The skin crawled on her own back.

The big arm waved and the riata whirred and cracked again. Pedro writhed. Two lines crossed his skin.

She closed her eyes. She had lured him here. *Crack.*

A faint moan. She couldn't look.

Men cheered. "Teach im!" *Crack.*

"Teach im!" *Crack.*

Counselor's voice came over the crowd. "Gentlemen, gentlemen." She opened her eyes, saw the big *Americano* standing near Pedro with his hands spread wide. "What crime has been committed here?"

Stop them. The arm swung back. She looked away. *Crack.*

"Stand back sir," said a voice. "We caught this here greaser ahightailin it with gold. In the dark of night."

"At's right. Pimpin fer this here mahala."

Crack. She looked. Giant bird tracks overlapped his back, his face turned away against the tree.

"Inflicting punishment outside the scales of Lady Justice," Counselor said, "hardly bespeaks of civilization."

With jarring suddenness she remembered the knife. If she had pulled it when fighting the men, she would be dead. It was good luck her memory had been stopped. The knife was to be used with cunning. Power was shifting; she felt it inside her.

Crack. With her elbow she felt the horn haft. Counselor was babbling his strange talk: "If you can't wait for the light of day, hold a trial now. I'll be state's advocate."

Crack.

A man with a very white face jumped before the teamster. "He's right. The whuppin oughta come after the trial." Squeezing her amulet she silently beseeched Angelica Root to give her power. Only last night she had been Deer Woman.

The whip settled softly behind the teamster, a snake at rest in the dust. "Mebbe we don't need no trial," he growled. "Mebbe the Spik's got the idee now."

White Face said, "Sides, we got the gold."

"Whose is it?" Counselor demanded.

"Mine," said the teamster, handing the riata to White Face, who began to coil it. *Yes, finished.* She felt calm, ready.

"Mine," Perrimacoo said, but a man grabbed for it and the bag fell open, half-empty. He stared at his feet. All the men stared, pointed. In the firelight sprinkles of gold glittered on his trousers. He hugged the bag and tried to run, but stumbled. The bag flew up in a showering arc as he went down.

"Spilt all over. Looky thar!"

The teamster dove at Perrimacoo and they wrestled on the ground.

"It's alla ours!" shouted a miner, diving to the gold.

"Yeah! Divvy it."

"It's the MERican way!" Men fell to their knees, grabbing.

A frenzy of loose power swirled and shifted, and in the maelstrom of chaos the hands left her and she stood alone. Counselor picked up a pot and banged a gunbarrel on it. But every man was scrambling for the glittering dust. Men who only moments before had been of one heart, a unison cloud of blackbirds, now shoved and kicked each other, grunting and snarling, "Son of a bitch!"

Swiftly and calmly she went to Pedro and slashed his bindings. He whistled, and moments later they were on Chocolate, pounding away, Pedro behind in the saddle. A few surprised shouts mingled with the roar of the fight. The horse splashed across the water and she looked back to the fire, small and bright in a black world, and the writhing heap of men. No one followed.

She slumped back against Pedro, who trusted the galloping animal to see in the dark, and felt the rise and fall of his rapid breathing. How long could he survive with *Norteamericanos* flocking into the gold camps along every stream?

"*Desgraciados y cabrónes*!" He gnashed his teeth and urged Chocolate with his legs. From the stiff way he sat in the saddle, she sensed his pain. At Rancho Omuchumne she would apply healing herbs.

But now it was time for clarity. She had faced Captain Sutter and come away knowing he was less to be feared than the blackbirdmen. Theirs was a different kind of power. They turned at the slightest whim and attacked those of another feather, or each other. Yes, she had walked in her strength among them, nearly returning with two bags of gold, but she had seen them torture Pedro and knew they would kill him next time.

His chest warmed her back, and as she narrowed her eyes to the cool night air flowing past, she vowed to stay out of danger, for that endangered him. But Coyote's warbling laughter rang out, and the forest trembled with foreboding. Her plans and Pedro's had been turned on their heads. What more did fate have in store?

IV

Coyote's World

65

JANUARY 1, 1849

"Now you git." Catherine shoved Elitha toward the door. "Outa here!"

"I SAID I'm helping with the dishes." She loved pushing against the warmth and giggle of her best friend, laughing and shrieking as the advantage shifted back and forth. Little Will toddled in a circle clapping his hands, keeping a wide berth from the dish-piled table they danced around.

Sarah, tall and queenly at the dishpan, as much at home here as in her own house, added to Catherine's gits, "Four hands is more'n plenty. You're just in the road."

Catherine grabbed a hank of muslin and snapped it at Elitha's rear.

She squealed and dashed to the tallest thing in the kitchen — Sarah — and crouched behind her, hands on her slender ribcage. *Still not pregnant.* The towel zinged around Sarah and stung Elitha's upper arm. "No fair!" She was about to fall over laughing when pain stabbed through her, melting her grin.

Sarah, sudsily disengaging Elitha's hands from her waist and catching the towel mid-whip said, "Us two is washin the dishes and that's that." With authority conferred by her twenty years, her blue eyes locked into Elitha. "You're in no condition."

She sighed and touched her protruding belly. She and Catherine were sixteen-year-old married women acting like children. Still it was the most fun she'd had since —

She let them march her into the front room past the five men, who had been toasting the new year, Catherine triumphant on her left arm, Sarah on her right with her wet hand soaking through Elitha's sleeve. She smiled meekly at the bearded faces around the fired-up stove. Catherine pushed her into the rocking chair and turned and shook a finger at Mr. Sheldon. "Now don't let her git up, hear?" A smile crinkled his eyes as he blew *cigarrito* smoke and nodded at his wife. Love. Elitha could almost smell it. Catherine and Sarah bustled back to the kitchen.

It felt good to sit, she had to admit, even though she'd already dined like royalty through the whole New Year dinner while Sarah and Catherine served her and the men and eight children. Now, embarrassed by the men's attention, she smoothed her apron over her frock — buttons a foot from closing beneath the green print. Perry was in San Francisco speculating on gold mines, and she'd been staying with Sarah and Mr. Daylor, the three having come the mile in the wagon.

The men resumed talking about gold. " . . . Mormon Island . . . boundless quantities . . . the Mormon Battalion getting a head start on it." She liked Mr. Daylor's cheeriness, yet felt oddly uneasy in his presence. In the evenings when she excused herself to go to the cot in the trading room, he looked wistfully at her belly. Speaking in Perry's quirky English-sailor fashion, he seemed unnaturally gentle or polite when he addressed her. Maybe she didn't know how to be friends with the husband of a friend. She often found herself blushing in his presence. *Easier to be a child than a woman.*

The three Rhoads men couldn't have differed more, yet they were father and sons. Father Rhoads stood with his hands clasped behind his back, wiggling his fingers at the stove — a Biblical patriarch of blockish build, slicked-back white hair, untamed brows and severely downturned mouth. John was strong, resolute and bearlike even in his Sunday clothes. Every glance of his deep-set eyes brought back what they had shared on the tramp across the mountains, and the way she'd begged him to go back for Tamsen. She hadn't dreamed there was a limit to his strength, that he'd been about to collapse from water on the lungs. Beside his dark hulk, Sarah's twin brother could have been a European nobleman, slender and blue-eyed and blond like Sarah. He didn't drink spirits, nor did Elder Rhoads — they being more dedicated Mormons — but John drank along with his brothers-in-law.

With *aguardiente* loosening their tongues, Mr. Sheldon and Mr. Daylor were in fine fettle, then suddenly Mr. Sheldon was talking at Elitha: "I'm buyin three hundred acres across the river from you and Perry. Hartnell land."

"Why?" spilled out before she realized how childish it sounded. Men bought land all the time. Still, he had more than eighteen thousand acres here at Rancho Omuchumne.

"Cause in eighteen and forty-nine even more *dinero's* coming our way in the shape of hungry miners, that's why. If we're smart, we'll be ready to feed em more'n beef — vegetables is what they want." He sipped from his glass, the stemware being among the Sheldon articles Elitha admired, and turned to the men. "Most every man can shoot game, but they don't know one wild plant from another. Why, I heard of men offerin twenty pinches for a single potato. Not for eatin, mind you. To cure scurvy. Your business," he looked at Mr. Daylor, "has been boomin, but you haven't seen nuthin yet. Men'll keep swarmin in from every land." His slight overbite was parted like he was picking up a good scent.

Row farming didn't seem suited to Mr. Sheldon — a man who ran more cattle than Perry ever would. Besides, Elitha knew Catherine would want him closer to home. "We'd be proud to put you up while you're working across from us," Elitha said, pleased to sound a little more adult, "but wouldn't it be easier to grow vegetables around here?" The bottomland was rich; his wheat grew as high as her head.

She detected something in the men's expressions and thought they might have said the same thing to him. But Mr. Sheldon looked like he had something up his sleeve. "Well, I got a good price on it," he said, "and a man never knows, could be good growin land up there. Oh, tell Perry I might need to dam the river after a time, if it's alright with him. I'll need to back up the water to where I can get it up outa the river bed."

She nodded, thinking that at Rancho Omuchumne he not only had the river, but Deer Creek flowing parallel, so it didn't make much sense, but no more was said because the door flew open and the rosy-cheeked children — hats and cloaks speckled with rain — poured in with cold air and the smell of wet wool. Señor Valdez came in last and shut the door.

Catherine dashed into the front room shaking a cloth behind the children. "Git along to the kitchen now. Alla you." Soon, chatter came from the other room and lamplight spilled from the doorway. It had grown dark, the days short. Elitha removed the glass from the hurricane lamp on the sundries table and started to get up to fetch a match, but Mr. Sheldon stopped her.

"You'll git me in trouble." He fingered a match from his shirt pocket and lit the wick.

Señor Valdez, who stood in his sarape with his hat in his hand, his auburn hair damp and flattened, said, "*Patrón*?"

"Sí," Mr. Sheldon said.

"The children have named all the leetle horses. I teenk you will like the names." He smiled but she saw that the Spaniard had more on his mind.

Mr. Sheldon nodded him on.

"More men at the river, *patrón*, swimming their animals across. Trouble maybe."

"They see you?"

He shook his head and smiled. "Deeferent trouble. High water." Elitha knew he was in hiding after the incident at the trading post, and she didn't doubt that he had killed the Oregon men at Rancho Sacayak — after all, he'd rescued Indian Mary and her father. But was he the mysterious Joaquín who rode with a vicious Indian? Killing white men right and left? It didn't seem possible, but she never wondered any of it aloud, because Mr. Sheldon protected the Californian. Señor Valdez looked friendly, but it was frightful the way retaliation fired men to violent acts. The good thing was, Indian Mary was safe here at Rancho Omuchumne. Captain Juan wasn't looking so very grand any more. This afternoon she'd seen his frail form limping up and down between the mill and the house.

The men were reaching for their coats, but Mr. Daylor stopped them. "Pedro and I'll see to it. John, you'll catch yer death." Putting on his coat, he turned to Mr. Sheldon. "Jared, we needs a ferryman, we does. I been thinking our brother-in-law Sebastian will do." He opened the door. "Do us all good to get him and Elizabeth out here on the Cosumney. Done ferryin work, 'e 'as."

Sheldon said, "Maybe another improvement for eighteen-forty-nine."

As the door shut behind Mr. Valdez, Elitha felt a jolt of happiness to think Elizabeth Keyser from Johnson's Ranch might come here to live. Then there'd be three girls to visit. But then she thought about Mary Murphy married to that dreadful Mr. Johnson.

"Well now, Father Rhoads," Mr. Sheldon said, "what are you plannin for eighteen-forty-nine?"

"Be headin to Zion with the Saints."

For a stunned moment Elitha thought the old man was planning to die, then remembered Zion was that bleached desert where Belle and the other oxen had labored so hard to pull the wagons. Before —

"When?" Mr. Sheldon asked.

"Brigham wrote to wait till the first crops are in. They can't feed any more'n what they got there now. We'll head over the mountains with what's left of the Battalion. Follow their wagon road." He wiggled his fingers at the kitchen. "Up over Kit Carson Pass." The crease deepened between his wild white brows. "That's a mite higher than where the Donners got bound in, so we won't leave till June, to miss the snowmelt." Elitha and John Rhoads exchanged a glance.

Sarah's twin brother said the first thing since Elitha had come into the room. "I was hopin you'd change your mind, Pa. With the mining so good at the diggings and all."

The patriarch said back, "Son, some things is more precious than gold. Riches ought to be used in the service of the Lord." Directing his words more to Mr. Sheldon and Mr. Daylor he added, "Our gold will help build the grandest tabernacle on the face of the earth."

"Is it true Brigham Young wrote the Mormon Battalion to offer their wages for building the town?" Mr. Sheldon asked.

The white head jerked down, then up. "And their gold besides. Mark my words: Salt Lake City will shine." By the downward pull of his lips, Elitha saw he wouldn't change his mind about leaving.

The room grew uncomfortably still, wood shifting in the stove, a surge of wind rattling the window. No doubt Mr. Rhoads hoped all of his nineteen children, and their children, would accompany him to Zion. But Sarah, Catherine, and Elizabeth were married to non-Mormons and not about to go. John had built a house about two miles down-river and was settled in. Maybe that's what kept Brother Billy so quiet, considering whether to go.

The door opened and Bill Daylor stamped in with a great show of rubbing his shoulders and gritting his teeth. "Right brisk it is." He hung his coat on a peg and pushed in between Sheldon and Father Rhoads at the stove. "Greenhorns negotiatin the river. Got acrost, they did." Whenever he came into a room, things perked up.

He turned to Mr. Sheldon. "Jared me man, ye got more up that long sleeve of yours? For forty-nine, I means." He grinned ruefully, "If ye don't mind spillin it to yer partner." Maybe the three hundred acres had been news to him after all.

In a smiling lack of hurry, Mr. Sheldon strolled to the demi-john barrel on a shelf near the kitchen and released the amber flow into his glass. Reinserting the cork, he stuck his head into the kitchen, from which giggling and high-pitched talk bubbled, and made a roundhouse gesture. Moments later Catherine was in the crook of his arm being brought into the room, little Will trailing. Mr. Sheldon leaned down and kissed her forehead, then bowed, sweeping his hand toward the bent-willow chair. With an impish grin she plumped into it, snuggling little Will into her lap. A child holding a child. Elitha hoped she'd look older than that when her baby came.

"Folks?" Mr. Sheldon orated, "Forty-eight was the best year of my life." He tousled his son's hair. "Got William Chauncy Sheldon here. A loyal band of Indians bringing in gold. The mill and cattle doing good. Thinkin to fix up Slough House for a road stop. Add the vegetables to that, and looks to be a right prosperous year." He gazed at Catherine. "Maybe git another young'un."

Pregnant! Elitha opened her mouth at Catherine, who nearly bounced from the chair. "We're not sure yet," she said, crimson hitting her cheeks. Mr. Sheldon smiled down at her with such love it almost hurt. Perry never had looked at Elitha quite like that.

Refilling his glass at the barrel, Mr. Daylor strode to the center of the room, his shelflike shoulders topping a wiry frame, eyes twinkling over the buttressed architecture of his nose. "A bad year forty-nine is shapin up to be for Sir John Sutter Esquire."

Wondering why got lost in the pain flashing through Elitha. *The black-eyed peas.* Beans really, brought around the Horn. Supposed to bring luck on New Years Day. Gas.

Mr. Sheldon looked at his partner. "Got som'm under that hat a yours?"

Through the ebbing pain she saw the mischief in Mr. Daylor's raised brows. "Been hatchin it for some time, I has."

Mr. Sheldon's eyes cut to Catherine, then back to Daylor. "You sneaky old tar. Think it's aged enough to let er out?" The pain eased and Elitha settled back to enjoy the funning.

Mr. Daylor glanced up at Sarah, who was coming from the kitchen wiping her hands on her apron, every hair neat in her blonde bun. A flicker in their mutual gazes told Elitha they shared the secret. But Catherine looked steamed. "William Daylor I vow!" she demanded, "Tell it straight! What ARE you doin to Mr. Sutter?"

Was he about to take his long-awaited revenge? He was said to be the strongest man in California — violent and unstoppable. But Elitha had formed another impression. She doubted if he'd harm a fly. Now he looked like the coyote who ran off with a stolen piece of pork. "The old fool is nigh about to meet 'is match, he is."

Catherine rearranged her face to haughty. "You can right well stop teasin, Brother Daylor, cause I don't give a fig." She flounced toward the window, where the sky was rapidly darkening.

Mr. Daylor's free hand rotated out. "As ye please." He lifted the glass to his lips, his long cheeks streaked with color.

Catherine jumped up, sat little Will down, and stood thrusting her chin at Mr. Daylor — an amusing sight, her being about two feet shorter. "WHO is this match for Mr. Sutter?" She turned to her husband, but Mr. Sheldon had his foot on a stool, arm resting on his knee, *cigarrito* hanging, overbite parted — enjoying this as much as his partner.

Another pain rocked through Elitha and she put her hands on her belly, willing it to stop. *No more black-eyed peas, ever.*

Mr. Daylor was saying, "Recollect all the inquiries about a loan for the vain-glorious captain, does ye?" Mr. Sheldon nodded sardonically. Even Perry had been approached by Sutter's son, but the boy was a greenhorn, Perry said, bamboozled by the men at the fort. So who was this match for Sutter?

" Well, *I* loaned him the money," Mr. Daylor said, the streaks of color intensifying down his cheeks.

"What?" barked Mr. Sheldon, straightening, apparently as surprised as Elitha.

"Why-y?" Catherine sang out. Mr. Daylor was probably the wealthiest man in California, thanks to the gold, the store and the cattle, and he didn't gamble. But why would he of all men loan money to his old foe?

"Hads me a talk with young Sutter, I did, and he tells me his mum fancies sailin to California, and he's borrowing the fare money." Still smiling, Mr. Daylor sipped from his glass. Elitha hadn't imagined Mr. Sutter as a family man, though he had a grown son who had come from Switzerland. Why hadn't he sent for his wife before now? It had to beover ten years since he'd come to California.

Mr. Daylor was warming to his story. "And I says to young Sutter says I, what kind of laidy might yer dear mum be then? And he says to me Mr. Daylor says he, this woman can row her own boat. Mind ye, not in them words, but I begins to fathom Frau Sutter I does, and the more we jaw, the more I sees an iron-plated man-o-war acuttin through the foam with all guns firin."

Mrs. Sutter didn't sound like the refined wife of a European squire.

Helplessly Mr. Daylor lifted the tufts of his brows. "And I says to young Sutter says I, does yer dear mother know what lechery abounds in this California wilderness?" He looked left, then right. "'Ave ye no care, says I, for her delicate female constitution in a locale such as this? And he looks me in the eye like a man — not a day over twenty-one — and says to me, sir says he, she'll NOT ABIDE the drunken debauchery me daddy's been awallowin in. And I turns to Henry Lienhard, who's sitting right there tuggin young Sutter past the shoals o' the language and arrangin the money, and gives him me hand."

With a snort of comprehension Sheldon tossed back his head then stared at his partner. "How much money."

"Twelve thousand dollars, for the passage of Frau Sutter and a grown daughter with a tongue to match her mum's, and more relations to boot — the lot of em to moor theirselves to the so-called king of Californy. And gittin a right smart fee is Lienhard, to escort the lot."

"You ready to lose twelve thousand dollars?"

Mr. Daylor shrugged helplessly. "Wot could I do? Why, not a soul in a thousand miles would make the loan, and them beyond the less likely." His eyes sparkled. "And worth every penny it tis. But, partner mine, I gots me a sterling rate secured by blocks of land in what they're laying out to be the City of Sacramento." Daylor chuckled and sipped. "And Sutter gawpin over our shoulders, knowin he can't say a word to stop the deal, makin out to 'is boy 'e's overjoyed at the approachin appearance of his beloved wife who he's been missin so hard these thirteen years." He guffawed, a man nearly forty and brimming with life.

"Well, you better build yerself an ark," Mr. Sheldon said, "cause that town'll be under water." His smile faded and he stepped forward with his glass extended, "I'd like to make a toast." He raised his glass. "To John Augustus Sutter, pioneer of California. Man of vision — Now William Daylor, put your eyeballs back in and think a minute on what he did here. Built a civilization outa nuthin. Ever time somebody needed something, he'd hire men to figger out how to make it. He tamed the Indians and trained em to work. Why this very minute he's got men making hats and barrel hoops and shingles up at the springs, ferry boats down at the waterfront. He's sawing timber in Coloma, tannin hides, dryin meat, makin boots and shoes from the biggest herd a cattle this country ever saw. Helped me get started, if you haven't forgot. And did it all with a gentleman's style — keepin the Mexican authorities fairly happy. Now this son comes along, and just cause he's been taught to do sums and Sutter wants to brag on him, he hands him power of attorney. The boy sees the size of the debts, panics, sells the entire fort for what? Seven thousand dollars? Money you and I — "

"Trash heap now," Mr. Daylor cut in, "camp for rascals thievin their way to the mines, and ye knows damned well why Sutter gave 'is affairs to the lad. Dodging creditors."

"I heard they're hauling in a pile of rent for the booths in the fort. But that's not my drift, William Daylor. You are. You makin the loan. It's a damn fittin end — pardon my language — to that ridiculous episode, never mind your schemin brains. John Sutter will fade from history along with his fort, and that's sad. So here's to him. For old time's sake." He lifted his glass. "Captain Don Juan Sutter, a man I'd say earned the title of gentleman."

A cockeyed smile twisted Mr. Daylor's face, but he raised his glass. Drinking to Mr. Sutter, Elitha was amazed to see. John Rhoads quelled his coughing and raised his glass. As the glasses clinked, Father Rhoads added, "He won't fade from history." Sheldon and Daylor turned to him and waited.

"Where I come from, Mr. Sutter's praised as a friend to Uncle Sam. A good and generous one at that, and a benefactor to every overland immigrant. Good to me and Mother Rhoads, rest her soul. He scowled around the room. "If Latter Day Saints used spirits, I'd drink to John Sutter." His mouth bowed all the way down to his jawline. The men raised their glasses and swallowed.

In the silence that followed Elitha felt inspired to contribute, "I won't forget the supplies he sent up to the mountains."

John Rhoads added, "A lot of people wouldn't be alive to remember, without his generosity."

"Well," Father Rhoads said, "we'd best be on our way. She's about to blow good." Out the window the sky was black and the wind was trying to upset the snug house.

"Fore you go, Pa," Sarah said, "I want you to know that this year we'll be hiring a storekeeper." Stunned, Elitha looked at the Daylors, Sarah moving into Mr. Daylor's arm.

"By thunder, that's overdue," said her father.

Where would the shopkeeper sleep? On the cot Elitha used? Could the Daylors put her up after this man came? She doubted it, and didn't want to impose on the Sheldons, who had a child. With so many miners roaming the country, she didn't want to stay home alone when Perry was gone, which was often.

John Rhoads had his head in the kitchen, "Younguns, time to hightail it."

Children dashed into the room, pushing for space beneath John's arms as he headed for the cloaks. Elitha felt sad the visit was over. She and the Daylors would be leaving next. Still, the cot would feel good tonight. Maybe lying flat would straighten out the kinks in her insides.

"Happy New Year!" the children called as they paraded out — twins belonging to John and Matilda, who'd felt too ill to come to dinner. Some of the children called a different Rhoads pa back in Illinois, others the younger brothers and sisters of Catherine and Sarah.

"Happy New Year," Elitha sang out. Wind flattened the apron over her belly.

As the door closed, a harsh jab cut through her. Worse, much worse than before. A moan escaped and it was all she could do to stay on her feet.

Sarah, who was reaching for her cloak, turned. "You look peaked."

The Sheldons eyed her too — Catherine's smile gone. She put little Will down on his feet.

"It's not what you think."

"Well, you better lie down anyhow." Catherine took her hand and pulled her into little Will's room, Sarah following. They made her lie down on the bed.

Looking up at her hovering friends, she felt foolish. "It's only gas. The baby won't come for two, three months yet." The boy needed his bed. She tried to rise, but Catherine held her down.

66

Rain streaked the dark window, glistening in the light from the front room. Elitha squeezed her eyes shut as pain stole her breath. When she opened them, the sisters were whispering in the corner, Mr. Sheldon a black shape in the doorway.

She hated putting the Sheldons out and holding up the Daylors. It was time they headed for home. She got to her elbows, but Sarah and Catherine stopped her. Something felt warm on her thighs. Wet. Like a pan of warm water. Bringing up a wet hand, puzzling over it, she felt another pang starting deep within, held her breath and clenched her fists as it mounted. Turning from the worried faces she pulled up her knees, then stiffened her legs and drew them up again. Nothing helped.

Maybe it was happening. They knew more about this than she did. Hard behind the thought came the memory of her real mother's death. "Childbed fever," people had whispered of Mary Blue. Indian blood in her, but still she died. Tamsen's screams floated back. Tamsen, the bravest woman in the world.

In the back of her mind, on the dark sea where dreams formed, a horror began to rise, something she had forced aside, refused to acknowledge. She had lived in a make-believe world, telling herself all along it wasn't her time yet. And now pain and fear sailed at her in terrifying proportions, a two-headed monster looming down on her with sharp fangs and death-dealing tentacles, sucking her into a grip of fathomless agony. Terror made boards of her legs and arms. She balled her fists and gritted her teeth, willing the monster away, the pain to subside. But it tore through her with white-hot keenness.

" . . . too soon," Sarah was saying. "Something's wrong."

" . . . git brandy down her."

God, help me! A squeak came out as she bit her lip, determined not to scream and embarrass herself. *Something's wrong.*

Sarah looked down from lofty heights and seemed to speak from another world. "Poor thing, she's shakin like a leaf." She laid a cool hand on her forehead.

Teeth chattering and clammy with sweat, she couldn't control her body.

Catherine put a tin cup to her lips. The fumes burned her nose and the liquid seared down her throat. "Put more wood in the stove," she told Sarah. Skirts rustled from the room.

Elitha was choking on the *aguardiente* and couldn't say no to more wood, more heat. Fear, not cold was shaking her. The stove lid clanged, wood thumped. The monster stirred again. "Oh, no," she whispered, lying back with the cup, willing the thing away. But it muscled slowly through her. She moaned, cried out. Later, in excruciatingly slow stages the pain loosened its vise, and she lay sweating, rigid, afraid of the next one.

"Here, git this in you." Sarah forced more *aguardiente* past her clacking teeth.

But the invigorated leviathan rose again and again, its spikes tearing and grinding relentlessly through her. She couldn't take more. Nobody could. If she was going to die, she wanted to get it over with quick.

Between attacks she opened her eyes. Rain slashed the window and wind keened around the eaves. The shadowy figures of willowy Sarah and shorter Catherine remained at her side. In a timid voice Catherine asked, "You all right?"

She shivered so hard her jaw felt wired shut. She couldn't say yes and was too polite to say no. Had it been like this when little Will was born? No one could know. Pain wasn't like comparing scars. She barely breathed, swallowed brandy, but the enemy welled up again and again, worse and worse each time, crushing the shame out of her.

"Outa her head," she heard — a scream lingering between the wooden walls. She saw her own terror in Sarah's hovering face, heard Sarah's whisper to Catherine, "Hope it don't go thirty-five hours, like yours."

Thirty-five hours! Frantic at the thought she threw her head from side to side on the pillow, wanting out of her skin. *Let me die now.*

"You'll be fine," Catherine said.

The brandy fogged the spaces between the agony. A lamp was lit, her shame illuminated. Cool cloths were laid on her head. She thrashed, threw them off, screamed in crescendos, knowing sound passed her lips.

A child's voice: "Lady cry."

Someone at the outer door: " . . . don't need Indian plants."

Indian Mary's voice! A door closing. She felt the cooler, damper air. Soaked in sweat she tried to rise, to say that Indian Mary could help. Herbs helped.

"Never you mind. I sent her away."

"No I . . . " But the monster attacked and she fell back into a screaming void.

A whisper woke her. "It was for the best."

Heart beating in her loins, she opened her eyes. Four sharp squares of sunlight came through the window and blanched the bedclothes, which left no more sensory impression than if they were painted on. *For the best?* Catherine sat in the rocking chair beneath the daguerreotype of a fierce old woman, the chair crammed into the space between the bed and the door. Pink calico stretched across her shoulders as she twisted around to where Mr. Sheldon stood in the doorway, little Will in his arms. Sarah was gone.

Mr. Sheldon gave her a look and stepped away. Catherine whirled back to Elitha, smiling weakly. "You all right?"

"Guess I lived." Did she have a baby?

"Oh poor, poor Elitha. It was bad." She leaned over the bed and smoothed her hair, then brought a tin cup from the floor. "Here, water will do you good."

Was it dead? Deformed? She tried to edge up on her elbows, but had no more strength than a rag doll. Catherine lifted her shoulders, helped her drink. She swallowed tentatively, unsure whether her insides were intact. The water cooled downward. The aching in her privates she wouldn't call pain, nothing she had identified by that name would ever be pain again. Even the air felt doubtful, uncertain as the expression on Catherine's face. No baby in the room. Anxiety edged her heart like a crisp border of tatting. Maybe the whole thing had been a hideous trick, a test of her grit. "What day is it?"

Catherine studied her, hazel eyes intelligent astride her substantial nose, and said, "January second, eighteen and forty-nine."

She shut her eyes and breathed the fragile air, held it and exhaled. Slowly, beneath the quilt, she lifted her amazingly heavy arms from her sides to her abdomen and felt the emptiness. The baby was supposed to relieve her loneliness. "Not a good way to start the year was it?"

"Nope." Not even a moment's hesitation.

Dead. She closed her eyes, saw in her mind the place of the baby's conception, the adobe, the bed by the wall, the broken window she'd tried to make Perry fix. Bad luck house, Indians called it. Cursed. "Boy or girl?"

Almost a whisper. "Boy. Never did take a breath. So tiny and all, and the birthin so — " She patted her through the quilt.

Dead. Did she want to see him? No. That would make him real. Probably buried anyway by now. She thought forward, to the coming year without the child, and felt a looseness float through her sorrow, a sense of not being tied down, like she might levitate over the bed with the quilt trailing from both sides. "Perry'll be sad," she said. He genuinely cared for Billy, and she'd hoped his love for their baby would change things between them.

Catherine raised a skeptical brow and gave a shrug that said she didn't think much of Perry. They knew he had women in San Francisco and in the floating town at Sutter's Embarcadero, and in hotels where the town of Sacramento was being built. Even after a day of riding home in the sun, his shirts gave off the essence of rose water.

"You ever wonder why you're here?" It came unbidden.

Catherine cocked her head. "With you? Here at the ranch?"

"No, in the world."

Catherine reached beneath the quilt and took Elitha's hand and squeezed it. "You poor girl. You got friends here. You know that, don't you? Alla us Rhoadses, and Jared and Mr. Daylor."

It must have seemed she was fishing for attention but couldn't think how to undo it.

Catherine leaned over the bed. "God put every one of us here for a reason." Her eyes were a foot away yet she inhabited a different world — a respectable house with a loving husband and adorable child.

"Tamsen, my Ma, would of said that. So why is she dead? And her babies living with strangers? Not even going to school? Living with people who don't even speak English. People who won't even answer my lett — " Sobs erupted and racked her overworked muscles. She pulled back her hand and meant to roll over to hide the emotion, but her body was too weak. Only her head turned.

"It's natural you're upset. Get some more sleep." Gentle pats came through the quilt. Then the wooden sound of the door shutting.

Did God spare her only to watch the family disintegrate? Why did He let her marry a man who lacked the respect of his neighbors? One who frequented bad women, gambled his money and made it hard for her to care for her sisters? Why did He make her suffer in childbed only to give her a dead baby? What was the purpose? She moaned, suddenly realizing as plain as anything that she was feeling sorry for herself. Pa would shame her. What kind of pioneer stock was she anyhow? "Catey!"

The door flew open and intense concern showed in her face — a girl who'd gone thirty-five hours. "Elitha?"

"You're the best friend I ever had. Thank you ever so much for helping me through my time."

"Course we'd all help."

Still, eighteen-forty-nine looked to be a bad year.

67

APRIL 29, 1849

Black with mud except for the whites of her wild eyes, the mired cow bellowed and slashed out with her front legs. Every move sank her deeper in the mud — up to her shoulders now. On the first try Roberto had settled his lasso around the far-flung horns and pulled so it slid down tight around the horn stems. Now he looked like a fisherman with a surprising catch. In a loincloth and a red bandanna anchoring his long hair, he braced his powerful legs and kept the rope taut on a thousand pounds of crazed stupidity. Quapata stood waiting to help.

Past time to get the herd to safer pasture, Pedro chided himself while knotting the end of his riata around the groove atop the windlass pole. A treacherous time, when the spring floods receded, leaving the land between the river and creek a slough, but the hot wind had browned the high ground, so the cattle turned to the marsh grasses.

"Now?" Quapata asked, his brown face intent.

"Sí." Pedro and Quapata upended the pole, slanting it away from the cow, driving the point deep with their combined weight. Then Pedro secured the free end of his riata around the base of a willow clump, as one would anchor a tent peg. Not even a crazed cow could uproot a plant that chose to live in the path of violent floods.

Reaching for the iron bar, Pedro motioned Roberto and yelled over the trumpeting of the cow, "*Está bien*. Pull her out."

Within moments Roberto had the braided leather around the pole. Pedro inserted the bar between pole and leather, and the rest was easy. Roberto walked the bar around the pole, each revolution winding the rope, cinching it up. Slowly the cow would rise from the bog. "*Silencio señora*," Pedro told the frantic animal.

"Good work," came from behind.

Pedro turned to see Señor Sheldon sitting on his horse, reins in hand.

"*Gracias patrón*, for the iron cinch." Oak often crushed under the pressure.

"We need to talk." Trouble showed in his face as plain as the turkey feather in his sombrero. Was Pedro the cause? Weaving through stumps of bunchgrass toward the *patrón*, he thought back. He'd offered to leave the rancho, but Sheldon had insisted he'd be safe here. And indeed, no mob had come. Too busy mining. Even the Sheriff had gone to the mines. Strangest of all, the reputation of the vicious "Joaquín" had a way of protecting Pedro. At Daylor's store miners told chilling stories of the desperado Joaquín — raiding camps, shooting men point blank, stealing their gold. Meanwhile Pedro was peacefully running cattle. Furthermore the description of the outlaw and his accomplice, "Three-fingered Jack," kept changing. Now the killer's hair was black! So was his horse, and the accomplice had become a brutal *Norteamericano*! Quapata, of course, was a mild Indian.

Stranger yet, Quapata's hand didn't necessarily identify him, particularly in a country where so many vaqueros had lost fingers. But the confusion went deeper. *Norteamericanos* didn't count the "thumb" as a finger. To everyone else it was the *primer dedo*, the first finger. So *Cuatro Dedos*, a four-fingered killer rumored to be preying on the mines, had all his God-given fingers in English, but not in Spanish. In Spanish, Jack had lost two fingers. So depending on who named the bandit and who counted fingers, Pedro had explained to María, the accomplice of Joaquín could have anywhere between two and five fingers. "Coyote," she'd said, smiling.

Now, following the *patrón* away from the bawling cow to where they could talk, Pedro had to smile too. He had joked that he and Quapata could stand on Daylor's Road and confess to the killings at Rancho Sacayak, and nobody would take them seriously. All resemblance to "Joaquín" had vanished, and besides, men lost interest in what happened last month. They weren't interested in the killers of men they didn't know. All they cared about was rumors of "color" in this or that stream. California had become a land of strangers unbound by the normal rules.

Señor Sheldon turned and said, "We gotta get the Indians home pronto. Daylor said men are pourin outa the saloons in Sacramento City, cleanin their guns and riding for the hills. Trappers from the Columbia River, most of 'em."

Oregon men, the worst kind. "After me?"

"No. The Indians. I want you to send word to the diggings. Tell them to hurry back. And Pedro?"

Already heading for the windlass, he glanced back. "Sí?"

"The trouble is on the Río Americano — middle and north forks. Seven white men killed, some say in retaliation for a whole village being massacred. White men are on the warpath. My guess is they'll go back to the saloons once they get their vengeance — God help the Maidu. Our Indians will have plenty of time to get home while that mob does its dirty work to the north. I just don't want to take chances." His yellowish wolf eyes bored into Pedro. "Not after what happened at Rancho Sacayak."

"*Comprendo, patrón.*" Trotting through the bunchgrass, Pedro calculated. The middle fork of the American was five or six leagues north of Dry Diggings — Weber Creek as it was now called, after a friend of the *patrones* who had joined them. The town that had sprung up there was named Hangtown for ominous reasons. It didn't make sense for Pedro or Quapata to go, not with *Norteamericanos* camped all over the cañons and María expecting the baby. That left Roberto or one of the two younger vaqueros.

He explained the emergency to Roberto, leaving out the part about it being a precaution. He didn't want to slow the messenger or delay the Indians' return.

These were people who would hold a Big Time at the slightest provocation. "Want to take Chocolate?"

Roberto was running toward his mount, Quapata taking over the windlass. He yelled over his shoulder, "Gracias no. I take five, ride fresh. *Por favor*, Ramón should care for my boys." His wife and daughter and parents and grandfather were at the diggings, but his two sons had stayed at the rancho.

Pedro called after him, "*Vaya con Dios, amigo.*" The Indian leaped gracefully onto his horse, slapped the haunch and turned to wave, hair flying. He would string four extra horses and cut the spent animals loose as he used them. Thirty miles. Six miles per horse.

Pedro mounted Chocolate and trotted him to Ramón and Locklock, who patrolled the edge of the herd. "Two or three days and everyone will be home," he said. "Then we'll get some sleep." The vaqueros smiled.

He had to smile too. *Gracias a Dios* the Indians were coming home! Movement caught his eye, another *vaca* breaking from the herd. Wheeling, he slapped his hat on Chocolate's haunch, and turned the cow so fast she flopped on her side. She scrambled to her feet and he trotted her back to the herd.

Galloping back to Quapata at the windlass, he felt pleased. It wasn't just that manpower was on its way home. María would get her midwife. For weeks she'd been adamant that every woman needed a birth-helper, that no birth was safe without women singing in the birth house. She had asked, "Who will massage me with herbs? And pacify the spirits? And bring the baby down?" Tomaka was the Omuchumne birth-helper. Good fat Tomaka, who had once warmed his bed. Never had he wanted to see her as much as he did now. This morning María had announced that she wanted to go to the diggings. The Omuchumne had worked on Weber Creek so long and so many women had become pregnant that they had erected a birth hut. "Take me there," she had begged, her black eyes tugging at his heart. Right then and there he should have said no. But he didn't, and now she probably had her hopes up. He had agonized over it all day.

But the Omuchumne would soon be home. With fear pushing them — a touch of bad conscience pricked him — they could arrive by tomorrow night. And the *patrones* might keep them home for good. Or was it wishful thinking to assume the gold was playing out? Millions of pesos had been taken from Weber Creek.

He hobbled Chocolate and walked down to where Quapata continued winding the riata around the pole. *Norteamericanos!* The bastards had whipped him for one reason: his Spanish blood, the fact that he was a native *Californiano*. His back had healed but his pride never would. They were invading dogs. Except for his duty to the *patrones* — ay, ay, the bloody scenes that teased his mind! How easy it would be to become Joaquín and step from the bushes and punish them, and take their gold. The way a coyote snatched food and sped to safety.

But now he turned his full attention to cutting loose this bellowing beast, more dangerous now that she was getting her footing. He must judge the perfect moment as Quapata walked around the pole, the rope tightening, shortening.

68

It was the noon meal in Pedro's room above the gristmill, two days after Roberto had been dispatched. Maria was relieved that the Omuchumne women would soon be back at their home place, and she told the baby inside her to wait. All too well she recalled Elitha's long suffering; her magic double had lacked a birth hut and the proper procedures of birth. Of course her child had been born dead. She set the salmon nu-pah before Pedro and Grizzly Hair, Billy eyeing the basket from his Grandfather's lap. She had no lap, the baby having dropped.

Pedro dragged a corn cake through the hot nu-pah and said, "*Norteamericanos* treat all Spanish-speaking men like filthy cholos." She heard his emotion. The night of the flogging, when he had returned the clothing, Señor Amador had told of other whippings of Spanish-speaking men, from Mexico and Chile. Pedro muttered, "A reputation can be powerful."

"What is reputation," Grizzly Hair asked, still thin and hardly able to walk. Another word for power? Maria wondered.

"It is what men think of you."

Father looked at him and spooned his fingers into the salmon mush.

The door latch lifted. No boots had sounded on the stairs. *Indio!* Maria's soul soared. The Omuchumne were home! But no. It was Quapata's maimed hand pushing the door open, and his face. "Señor Daylo want you at his house."

"Is something wrong?" Pedro asked.

"Maybe." Strong talk for Quapata.

Pedro reached for his sombrero and kissed the tip of María's nose, then he tucked his short gun into his sash and left, boots drumming a fast descent.

Father stared at nothing, intent on everything. Hair moved on the back of Maria's neck as she listened to the horses pounding away. In the silence she heard a prickling rush of power. Loose. Billy felt it; she saw the alarm in his face, and he whimpered.

Her heart beat strangely and she saw that Father was sensing trouble too. "I go see," she said. "Keep Billy here." He nodded.

The mile to Señor Daylor's house seemed long with her big belly leading. Twinges of pain stung her groin from the pressure of her steps. Her swollen feet padded more slowly than she wanted on the river trail — a damp, narrow corridor between leafing cottonwoods and oaks, the birds strident overhead. Power crackled. Anything could happen. *Norteamericanos* here? She feared that Pedro's lingering anger would leach away his power and endanger him.

At a small riverbank clearing near Señor Daylor's adobe, she saw the heads and shoulders of Ramón and Locklock protruding from a deep hole, dirt flying from their shovels. Quapata stood watching at the side. She stopped to watch. What did it mean that vaqueros were digging a hole? "Where is Pedro?" she asked Quapata.

He nodded up the path toward the adobe.

She continued walking. If *Norteamericanos* had attacked, vaqueros would have bows and arrows, not shovels. The danger was different.

At the house she saw Señor Daylor kneeling in the hard-tamped yard, hammering a lid on a wooden box. Three women stood on the porch — Elitha, her little white horse still perspiring at the rail, and Señora Daylor, who had her arm around Elizabeth Keyser, the new *Americana* whose husband was building a house. The three pale faces looked sorrowful, Señora Keyser's eyes swollen and red. She stared fearfully at the box as if it held awesome magic. Her small son was nowhere to be seen. In the box, Maria suddenly realized.

She recoiled, knowing it was unsafe for a pregnant woman to be near the dead. But then she remembered all the maimed and dead people she'd looked upon, even touched, at the home place. It didn't matter any more. Even if she had a birth-helper, her child would probably be born dead. She calmed herself and looked around for Pedro. Not seeing him she asked Señor Daylor if he knew where he went.

"Be back in a minute, 'e will." No fear in his voice.

Good. The loose power must be here then, swirling around the wooden box. She faced it and stayed to watch, for she was curious about *Americano* death rites.

Chocolate nudged Pedro between the shoulder blades as he peered through a small aperture in the wall of blackberry brambles. Before going farther he needed to know whether any of the encamped *Norteamericanos* could identity him as a killer. He counted eight men exactly where Señor Daylor said they'd be — a hundred and fifty yards from the adobe, about twenty-five yards from where he stood in the brambles. They sprawled like logs around a dead fire, horses saddled, bedrolls packed, rifles handy — what kind he couldn't see from this distance. Some wore buckskins but the old man was not among them, nor the *cholo* with the rattlesnake bite. He recognized no one from Sutter's camp.

The Sacayak-New Helvetia trail, now called Daylor Road, intersected with the north trail just over the rise. That meant the *Indios* would pass by the camp on their way home. But Señor Daylor had thought these *Norteamericanos* might be friendly, and had asked Pedro to inquire about their business, he being the only man for the job. Señores Sheldon and Keyser were in Sacramento trying to raise a posse to help the Maidu people, and Señor Daylor was burying Señor Keyser's child.

"Me guess is, resting on their way to the southern mines," Daylor had said. "Those racks they're ridin look a wee bit windbroke. See if they need horseflesh or anything else." Raising the tufts of his brows he had added, "Don't shoot anybody."

But just in case, Pedro had loaded his rifle and Allen pepperbox revolver.

Now he mounted, placed his sombrero string beneath his nose and reined the horse around the berries and up the road as if just arriving. "*Hola!* Can I help you?" His friendly tone. The filthy dogs had defecated on the open ground, with an outhouse only a stone's throw away. Some of the eight were sitting up. Others stood, leaving their rifles on the ground, oiled, reflecting sunlight.

Straight-backed, he reined the horse off the trail and approached the camp. "I am the *mayordomo* of the rancho of Señores Sheldon and Daylor, " he said. "I would be honored to help you, if you are lost." The rifles were the new fast-loading kind that made his musket an antique.

One of the standing men hitched his *pantalones* and narrowed his eyes, already small within the pocked and lumpy landscape of his face. "We ain't lost." A flat tone.

"Perhaps you go to the southern mines. I would be happy to assist your animals across the river."

The dead eyes didn't blink. "You call that pitiful piss trickle a river? Us Columbia men"— he ran his eyes slowly down Pedro, lingering on his fancy leather stirrup holders — "are real men. We could walk acrost an never feel nuthin damp." Neither lashes nor brows softened the scarred face, which resembled an alligator lizard, a foot-long beast that clung to your boot when you tried to kick it away.

Pedro glanced at their skinny mounts. "Perhaps you would like to purchase new horses. We have some three-year-olds for sale." Chocolate quivered with flies, which had no doubt visited their shitpiles.

"We don't buy horseflesh from Mexicans." He leveled his lizard stare. "Kill us a beef if yer so all-fired set to please. We been ridin hard two days now."

Rage warmed the back of his neck, but he kept his voice soft. "Señores, this is Rancho Omuchumne, where guests are fed and treated well. I will speak to Señor Daylor about a bullock. But if you have no wish to buy goods or pay him a visit, you should camp some other place." A whole beef!

"We like it here."

"Then I must ask, señores, what is your business?"

From a man with a fleshy nose came a nasal drawl. "Tell him, Pockface. Or I will."

Pockface shrugged. "The boys and me met up with some redskins. Up thar at Hangtown? We got the notion they lived hereabouts." He scratched his head with a forefinger, nudging up his stained hat. "See, we's ridin with the biggest posse you ever seen."

"Posse?" These couldn't be men Sheldon had found.

"Yup. Settin out to clean out the Diggers. Mean to give em a right warm reception." His thin lips pulled back in a lizard grin.

Virgen en Cielo, salva a los Indios!

Flesh Nose was getting to his feet, extending wrinkled newsprint. "Says right here these here Diggers in Californy is the most worthless bunch of cutthroats on the entire continent. Go ahead, read." He shook the paper at Pedro.

"No, gracias." One more instant with these excuses for men and he'd pull his Allen. He turned Chocolate and said as congenially as possible, "Adios."

It took strength to refrain from spurring the powerful stallion, especially when he heard the thunk of leather and the exhalations of men mounting horses. Looking casually back he saw the riders facing inward, talking. He called, "Wait here, señores, I ask about a bullock."

Pockface cut his eyes to him and back to the riders.

Señor Daylor's yard was deserted. He took the millhouse fork, heading up the narrower trail where the vaqueros had been digging the grave. Heavy vegetation flanked the path. He looked back through the trees and saw, about fifty yards back, the *Norteamericanos* following. Alarm intensified, and he nudged Chocolate to pick up his pace without changing his gait.

Señora Daylor held an open Bible and stood reading over the gaping grave. All other heads were bowed — Elitha McCoon, Señora Keyser and Señor Daylor. On the other side of the grave, behind a mound of dark earth stood the vaqueros, shovels in hand, and — *Madre de Dios*, María! What in heaven was she doing here? His mind had almost refused to recognize her pearlike physique and trimmed black hair.

Knowing the *Norteamericanos* couldn't be far behind and wanting to appear casual in the saddle, he rode to the grave and hissed a loud whisper, "Indian killers. Hide María! Quapata. You *Indios*. Go!"

All the faces jerked up. The three señoras looked at him as if he had yelled an obscenity in church.

He pointed his head back up the trail at the *Norteamericanos*. "Run and hide — María, Quapata, Ramón, Locklock! Go!"

They stared like startled deer. Confused by his easy posture? His casualness?

He hesitated. Would even *Norteamericanos* shoot ranch workers beneath their employer's nose? In the middle of a funeral? It was plain from the dirt on the *Indios* and the shovels in their hands that they worked here. Besides Señor Daylor had a reputation as a strong man. He had implied Pedro was hot-headed. Maybe he was. María was crouching behind the dirt mound, her big black eyes on him.

He heard galloping, turned and looked back. The riders were coming up three abreast through the trees, rifles in hand. Maria screamed, "Run Pedro!"

"You run!" He leaned down to unstrap the musket from its saddle holder, the Allen worthless from a moving animal, even more worthless at long range.

Unarmed, Señor Daylor walked toward the oncoming riders, arms extended in a halt gesture. They didn't stop but parted and galloped around him. Shots popped.

Pedro yanked the musket free. María lay on the ground, legs protruding beyond the mound. Hit? The *Norteamericanos* jumped from their horses for truer aim at the fleeing vaqueros, one drawing a bead on María.

Pedro leveled the big gun and pulled the trigger, but Chocolate moved and the ball drilled harmlessly through the crown of the hat. Shots exploded in quick succession. Quapata and Locklock sank to their knees. No, dear Virgin!

María was squirming toward the grave. An easy target. He aimed his Allen and fired at the man aiming at her. Missed. Turned the barrel and fired again. The killer turned his gun from María to Pedro, and María dropped, thankfully, out of sight. Pedro didn't need to think. He turned the barrel and took out his knife, a weapon in each hand, and spurred the horse hard at the man. One way or another this was a dead man.

Señor Daylor, who was in the midst of the *Norteamericanos*, stood shouting at them, "Get the hell out off my property! Stop, Pedro, don't shoot!"

Every nerve and fiber in him rebelled. It broke his concentration, changed the flow of his blood. Then he was past the man and neither of them had fired. *Don't shoot!* It made no sense, like a dream going nowhere.

Norteamericanos hugged their rifle stocks to their cheeks. He turned Chocolate toward them and spurred. They jumped out of the way, shots going wild. Horses whinnied. Women screamed.

Pockface shouted back at Daylor, "Indian slaves gittin all the gold. Ain't Merican Mister Mexican rancher."

Coming to his senses, Pedro sat the horse back in the trees and stuffed the wad down the barrel of his musket. This gun had aim. *Don't shoot!* He hurried with the wad.

Flesh Nose was yelling, "Them's murderin redskins!"

"Not these Indians," Daylor yelled back.

Pockface stood up, looking down the grave at María, where she lay on the coffin, and started to raise his gun.

In a flash Chocolate was between them. Pedro leaped off — the horse trotting out of the way — kneeled and aimed the musket pointblank at Pockface, who stood aiming at him.

"Put those guns away. Get off my rancho," Daylor yelled.

The *desgraciado* turned and went to his horse. They all did, and in a moment the last coward was thundering away, turning out of sight on the leafy trail. Escaping!

It was so quiet Pedro heard his breathing. He went to María — sitting up — and stepped down beside her on the little casket, which was smeared with blood. The back of her leg was bleeding above the knee. Blood beaded on the fresh pine. The bone seemed alright. Relieved that she was not more seriously wounded, he removed his shirt, tore off a strip and tied it around the wound. In a few seconds the cloth reddened.

She looked at him with that same glazed, distant look she'd had after the massacre of her people. Accepting fate? Thinking of the condor curse?

But condor feathers hadn't done this! Anger erupted in him like a volcano. White-hot hatred for *Norteamericanos* swelled in his chest and threatened to break through. "I will have you taken home," he told her as gently as he could. He would follow the bastards and kill them. *Don't shoot!* What was wrong with the *patrón*? Had he lost his senses?

"Go help the others," María said, holding the wound, blood running through her fingers. "I will heal." She looked utterly calm.

Silently thanking the Virgin, he stroked her hair and hoisted himself out of the grave. Señora Daylor was holding Locklock's head in her lap. As he approached, she looked up and said, "Looks like a goner." She rocked the boy like a baby. Blood jerked from a ragged hole in his neck.

Pedro ground his teeth. The killers would pay. Elitha, looking like she'd seen the Devil, came and kneeled down beside Sarah.

Pedro headed toward where Quapata lay, the scowling *patrón* standing over him. But Ramón stepped from the trees, ash-faced and shaking but unhurt, not more than thirteen *años*. They looked at one another and Pedro put his arm around the trembling boy, glad to feel him in one piece, and asked. "Where are Roberto's boys?" Five and six years old.

"Fishing I think."

"*Gracias a Dios.*"

He went to Quapata, kneeled. Blood seeped from a hole in his upper chest, too high for his heart, maybe a lung.

"Shot before me very eyes," the *patrón* said. "Help me carry him to me house. Sally'll see to him." Señor Daylor bent down, took Quapata's ankles.

Pedro put his hands beneath Quapata's smooth, muscular shoulders, but realized the strain would pull the injury. "Wait," he said letting him settle back, "María knows the healing art. My rafters are full of her medicines, and she is only hit in the leg. Ramón should take Quapata and María to my room." Quapata's head dropped to the side. Dead? Unconscious? *Vipers!* Putting his ear to his chest, he was relieved to hear a steady thump. "We can put them both on Señora McCoon's horse." It was saddled and tied to the porch of the adobe.

"What's wrong with your horse?"

It took a moment to register. "*Patrón*, we must ride and kill the cowards who shoot unarmed men and pregnant women at funerals." The man's courage was legendary and he had a fast-loading rifle in his house. They both knew every hidden passageway through the junglelike vegetation. They could kill the snakes before they got too far.

Señor Daylor looked down his nose, his large nostrils flaring pink. "White men ye be talkin bout, Pedro."

"White men?" Confused, he looked at him. "We could pick them off like roaches."

"Pedro, is it a war on me rancho yer lookin to start? Think man! Men such as those is wantin to drive us ranchers off our land. Give em a damned good excuse, ye will." He breathed through his nose like a winded horse. But his eyes looked kind.

"They shot my woman and the vaque — "

The warning look stopped him. Hot-headed, it said. Spaniard. As that sank in, a sick spot began to spread beneath the rage, like a spoonful of poison in a water-gourd.

"Taik Quapata to your room on your horse. I'll handle the white men, I will." He walked swiftly toward his house, a tall man with confident strides.

Trembling inside with the frustrated need to ride for the killers, Pedro helped Ramón lift Quapata and hang him face down over Chocolate's rump, then they put María in the saddle, blood oozing from the soaked cloth. Pedro led the horse to the millhouse, praying to the saints that Señor Daylor was riding after the *Norteamericanos,* but knowing he was a poor horseman. *Gracias a Dios* the rest of the Omuchumne had not appeared while the murderers were camped on the trail.

White men? How could Pedro not act? What were the requirements of honor?

69

Back in his room, Pedro sat on the side of the bed looking at María, who lay groggy with herbs, her leg bound with a clean cloth, a fringe of green leaves poking from the sides. The ball had passed through without breaking bone or severing an artery. Quapata was in far greater danger. Numbed by her tea, which Pedro had brewed under her direction, he lay bandaged in the corner opposite where Captain Juan sat staring at nothing.

Feeling an unquenchable rage for *Norteamericanos*, Pedro looked into the black pools of María's eyes and gave voice to a piece of it. "I cannot live here any longer."

Her face was impassive.

"I am not free here. This is not my rancho. I must be free to avenge the deaths of my friends. *Comprendes?*"

"*Indios* are not free," she said. "Not since the pale skins come."

It caught him off guard, made him think. If he'd had his own rancho, her people would have worked for him. That was the Spanish way. She had breached an unspoken truth, something that had been niggling at the back of his consciousness. Ranches were established at Indian villages so *Indios* would work for the rancheros. Pedro recalled the difficulty of helping Captain Sutter subdue the Indians — Sutter wanting an empire with hundreds of villages in his employ. Under Sutter's orders he had led the troops in surprise attacks against rebellious villages. Now he cringed to remember the innocents slaughtered. When Rafero, headman of the Mokelumne, tried to avenge the death of his relatives, Sutter had ordered him hung. Pedro had carried out the order and left Rafero's head to rot on the gate as a warning. No, *Indios* were not free to avenge deaths. Or leave Sutter's fields at harvest time. And having less food stored, they became dependent on Sutter for their food. The *patrones* at Rancho Omuchumne never killed *Indios*, and they encouraged them to store their own food. But nevertheless, the pattern had been set by Sutter. Every *Indio* in the countryside feared guns and cannons, and no doubt feared disobeying their *patrones* no matter who they were. A tendril of guilt crawled through Pedro.

But wait. Back when he and Sutter first landed on the Río Americano, *Indios* had outnumbered them hundreds to one. Why hadn't they banded together and fought for their freedom? The way they did in 1829 against the presidios? God knew, whether or not the *comandantes* admitted it, the *Indios* had crippled the missions and stopped the abduction of laborers from the valley. So why hadn't they regrouped against Sutter? If they had, Pedro wouldn't be sitting here on the edge of the bed wondering. Was it because of the plagues of illness that had devastated them and broken their villages?

Glancing at Captain Juan, who was sitting wraithlike, and trying not to think of his part in luring *Indios* to work for Sutter, he asked, "Why do *Indios* work for rancheros?"

Captain Juan raised his chin — short black hair poking out of his head at all angles. "Inyo been here a long time. We want to see *Españoles* and long-horns and guns. Inyos like to ride horses and get easy food. We like shovels and buckets and knives and guns. We will have these things when pale skins go to their home places far away."

Waiting for us to leave. But with gold lying all over the place, when would that happen? And what of Pedro? Why did he work for ranchers? He'd left Monterey Presidio for adventure, curiosity, hope of a land grant, the security of a position, and, *sí,* easy food and horses. The very same reasons. But the adventure had soured. The Mexican regime was in disgrace, and no land was in sight. Now he felt the yoke of the patronage system on his shoulders and was beginning to feel something else. The shootings hadn't outraged Señor Daylor to the same extent as Pedro. Indians were being exterminated. Would people of mixed Spanish and *Indio* blood be next? Did Señor Daylor consider Pedro a white man?

"When do we leave?" Maria asked, apparently accepting his decision.

"Not until after the baby comes and you and Quapata are well." He glanced at Quapata's sleeping face. *Like a brother.* He was strong. Surely he would survive.

Reaching for his sombrero and sarape, he turned to Captain Juan. "Keep the Allen. Shoot any stranger who comes up those stairs uninvited." To María he said, "I go check the cattle."

"You cannot herd them alone." She looked through him, rejecting the lie.

He went to the bed, leaned down and kissed her lips. "I may be gone all night." He patted her big belly.

"Protect the Omuchumne," she said, knowing his heart.

"*Sí, Amapolita mía.*"

It was child's play tracking the *Norteamericano desgraciados*. He followed the hoofprints in the damp earth, most of them continuing up the trail out of the bottomland, heading toward Sutter's Fort. But to his amazement, two circled back toward Daylor's adobe. Pedro followed them to where they'd camped the previous night. They picketed their horses and removed the saddles and bedrolls, planning to stay. The arrogance! He felt a bitter smile twist his lips. It would be their last camp.

Shadows were lengthening, moisture cooling the air. He stood in the same blackberry thicket, ready with his musket, knowing the Daylors must have seen the bastards.

Señor Daylor came into view, rifle in hand, walking toward the two men, apparently not having seen Pedro. The *Norteamericanos* watched his approach, guns in hand. Pedro braced his musket on a sturdy, thorny cane, eyeball down the barrel, the dark nub of the sight squarely in the center of a buckskin shirt.

Señor Daylor talked — too far away to hear, but his voice sounded firm and final, and he shook his rifle at them. *Talk*. With men who had killed and wounded defenseless people beneath his nose. Pockface, unmistakably Pockface, stood before the *patrón*, gesturing and wheedling.

The sunset was at Pedro's back, his gunbarrel hidden in the shadows of the berry canes, his finger on the smooth tongue of the trigger. Flesh Nose spoke in a nasal tone that carried fifty yards across the open. It would be easy. The two of them could finish them, except that Daylor didn't know Pedro was there.

Daylor turned and — *Madre de Dios* — walked back toward his house! The *Norteamericano* vermin went back to their fire-making and unpacking. It was beyond comprehension, the *patrón* allowing them to stay. Now these two snakes were guests of the ranch!

White hot fury seared up around his heart and his finger twitched on the trigger as he kept Flesh Nose in his sights. If he fired, Daylor would return, but whose side would he be on? Never having been as close to Daylor as to Sheldon, he moaned aloud and withdrew the gun. He couldn't risk shooting it out with Señor Sheldon's best friend, Sheldon's partner and brother-in-law — a man whose life he had saved on more than one occasion. If only Señor Sheldon had come home! He would have exterminated the killers.

He decided to wait until the Omuchumne people came down the trail — no matter how long it took. The first shot from Pockface or Flesh Nose would unleash him from any obligation to Señor Daylor. Where were those people anyway?

It grew dark, the *Norteamericanos* nursing their cups around the fire.

Knowing *Indios* refused to travel in the dark — they thought all sorts of spooks would get them — Pedro settled back, head pillowed on his arms, staring at the brightest rash of stars he'd seen in a long time, and tried to understand. Here was the bravest, strongest "tar" ever to set foot in Sutter's Fort, a man who had defied his sea captain and walked the plank, then had his way with Manu-iki in Sutter's own kitchen. A man who had held off twenty Indians and Kanakas with his hard fists and rode to Monterey in chains, a man Captain Sutter feared to this very day. Yet he allowed the murderers to camp in full view of where the Omuchumne would pass.

No, he couldn't call William Daylor a coward. What then? A white man? One who feared losing his rancho? Yet the man enjoyed the absolute, untrammeled trust and admiration of the *Indios*. He bought barrels of sugarcane for their children. It didn't feel honorable.

In the chill before dawn, coyotes started up their weird falsetto warbling. Pedro got to his knees, looking at the camp. Moisture soaked through his *pantalones*. Barely enough light came from the eastern horizon to see the sleeping *Norteamericanos*. His head ached with sleepless frustration and he prayed that if it came to shooting, he and the *patrón* would be on the same side. It was one thing to be wanted by lawless *Norteamericanos*, and another to anger the men he had worked for and respected.

He lay back resting his eyes, unable to stop his mind. The *desgraciados* said they'd seen the *Indios* more than twenty-four hours ago. They should have been home by now. Could it have been another band? A few rancheros from Mexico had come north with their *Indios* in search of gold, so maybe — But no. He would have heard if they'd gone to the Hangtown area. He must not fool himself. It was well known that Sheldon and Daylor sent their Indians to Dry Diggings and that was the reason these vermin were camping here. Lying in wait! Nearly sixty *Indios* were on the trail. Totally unarmed. Sheldon had insisted they leave their bows behind to show their peacefulness, and so far they hadn't been molested. Did they know these vipers lay in wait? He had been over the futility of going out searching for them in the dark. He would be more useful here, with his sights on the enemy.

His thoughts drifted to the plump brown faces of the children. Nothing was more beautiful than an *Indio* child smiling in that open way. They were never beaten, never yelled at, unlike the children in San José. Maybe that was the secret. He tried to imagine his own child with María's magnificent eyes — black fathomless pools. He had sorted through *Indio* and Spanish features, moving them around like puzzle pieces, trying to imagine what his child would look like. He couldn't wait to be a father. And with thirty-seven *años* under his belt, it was about time.

A woodpecker whickered like a woman clearing her throat. *Indios* called it laughing. Clown birds. He got to his knees again. The sky was lighter, pink up the Sacayak trail, the hills taking on color. He positioned his gun across the spiny canes — excellent support — the berry flowers giving off a sweet fragrance all around him.

A door slammed. He turned to see the Señora emerge from the foliage surrounding the adobe and walk toward the outhouse. Her blond hair swung freely at the waist of her dark frock — tall, thin, still not pregnant. She stopped a moment, head toward the sleeping men, then disappeared into the small structure. The door thunked.

She came out and went to the corral, opened the gate and shut it behind her. The cow bawled impatiently as she tied it to the snubbing post. Clattering the bucket and stool down from the posts, she hunched over the bucket, milk pinging in a rhythm he heard fifty yards away.

Señor Daylor came out rolling in his shipboard gait to the outhouse. A tall wiry man in long underwear and boots. Pedro looked east toward the junction of trails, the bright glow of the approaching sun in the aperture. No sign of people. A thousand birds were bursting into song. Soon the bees would swarm over the blackberry flowers.

Both *Norteamericanos* sat up and stretched. Pockface urinated and went to the saddled horses, returning with a cooking pot. Sarah stood a moment looking at them, then carried her pail of milk to the adobe, to which Daylor had returned.

For his gun? Through the burgeoning new growth of leaves he saw the señora come back out and shoo chickens from the straw-filled crates beside the house.

He looked east. A shadow moved across the glow of the coming sun. A deer perhaps? Another and another moved. A herd? No, slim, upright shapes. *Indios!*

He looked at the *Norteamericanos*. Pockface was pointing east. They exchanged words, grabbed their guns, and ran for their horses.

To scare them, Pedro pulled the trigger and braced against the kick. The explosion rang through the still morning. Señora Daylor screamed. He was reloading, fingers fumbling with the hurry, glancing through the aperture. The *desgraciados* stood with their hands on their saddles looking around in all directions, beginning to understand, he hoped, that this would not be easy.

A single black shape grew rapidly larger in the brilliant sliver of rising sun. Running directly into the guns of killers. Trusting the safety of the *patron's* yard! Pedro opened the lock as the two horsemen trotted across to intercept the runner. A gun popped. Theirs. His signal. Slamming the lock closed, he put his sights on Pockface and moved them with the galloping horse.

The *Indio* swerved off the trail, running a zigzagging course at full tilt, the horsemen hard at his heels trying to aim their rifles. The Indian's legs were a blur, weaving one way, then the other, baffling their aim as the weaving horses baffled Pedro's. The *Indio* passed through his sights.

He waited and fired at Flesh Nose. The horse screamed and fell. *Cabrón!* The rider jumped free and Pedro grabbed a new wad. Pockface was looking all around as he galloped after the running Indian, who was nearing the corral. The shot had worried him, Pedro saw as he reloaded.

Suddenly Daylor was out in the open waving his gun. "You gave your word you'd leave me Indians be! Now git, if ye likes livin."

Pedro rammed the wad down. Daylor turned and saw him for the first time, and so did Pockface — slowing his horse. The *Indio* dove into the bushes near the adobe and Pedro was almost ready to fire again.

Back up the trail more Indians were approaching. Seven or eight shapes already large against the rising sun. The first man had drawn attention from the others. Pedro leveled his musket at Pockface, who was wheeling his horse about thirty yards away, but as he squeezed, the horse jumped into a gallop toward the oncoming Indians and the ball grazed the back of the saddle. The horse kicked out and continued. Double *cabrón!*

The *Indios* wove in and out like the first man had, dodging the fire of the fast-loading rifles, but as Pedro jammed down his next wad, an *India* bent over, gripping her middle. Shot by Flesh Nose, who was down on one knee aiming again. She staggered and fell not far from Señor Daylor's feet, and he still wasn't shooting! The gun hung in his hand. The other *Indios* parted, three diving in beside Pedro, the others zigzagging toward Daylor — Pockface galloping on their heels and trying to aim.

Daylor looked paralyzed. Flesh Nose was calming his animal, which had jumped to its feet, apparently not seriously wounded, and was about to mount.

Slamming his lock closed, Pedro stepped into the direct path of the Pockface's horse and fired at his chest. But at that instant the horse tossed its head and took the ball in the neck. It jerked and Pockface catapulted off, rifle flying. The horse fell on its side, pinning the man's legs.

Pockface tried to reach for his rifle, his lizard face registering fear — the first emotion Pedro had seen on it. Pedro was working the lock ten yards from the man's head, keeping an eye on Flesh Nose, when Daylor stepped between them with his gunbarrel inches from the lizard skin.

"Get on down the New Helvetia Road if ye value yer ugly face," Daylor said.

Pockface squirmed free of the horse and grabbed his rifle and hat, and got to his feet. "Someday you'll thank us for riddin the country of these here Diggers," he said, glancing back at Pedro. He forced an alligator smile and hooked an arm toward Flesh Nose, who was on his nervous animal approaching alongside. Pockface jumped up behind the saddle.

Daylor, his gun now hanging at his side, watched the departing horse.

Stunned that he was letting them go again, Pedro, who still had them in his sights, pulled his trigger finger, but not all the way. He let out a moan, feeling like a man torn apart on a torture rack.

The double riders walked the horse past the bushes of the adobe and disappeared into the trees, heading toward the fort. Pedro lowered his gun, both arms shaking with the need to kill. He glanced at the *Indios* in the vines.

They were dirty and haggard, like all the moisture had been siphoned from them. He hardly recognized them. They looked fifteen years older than when they'd walked away last month — having returned for a Big Time holiday. Their bodies were streaked with pale sweat that had once been moist. Never had he seen *Indios* in this condition. A quarter-mile run wouldn't do that. What had happened?

Señor Daylor was staring at them too.

Pedro glanced up, wondering why the rest of the Omuchumne weren't coming down the trail. The first *Indio* — the one who had diverted attention from the others — was walking toward him, as if slightly unsure of his footing. He was the one who enacted Coyote Man at the ceremonies — Pedro knew, though *Indios* professed not to know.

Daylor spoke in their language, "Where are the other Omuchumne?"

Coyote Man made a tired gesture. "Only us."

"But where they?"

"Dead."

Pedro's jaw dropped as the shock of it slammed into him. Fifty dead. He went to the fallen girl. It was Blue Star, Quapata's wife, María's best friend. The *Indios* were gathering around. Five men and two women, counting her. He felt lightheaded, the buzzing of bees and shrieking of the birds momentarily fading. No Roberto. No Tomaka. No birth helper. No Omuch. No village. No vaqueros. No smiling children. Blue Star lay curled in the dirt, clutching her middle. Flame licked through his own gut and up around his heart like a sacrificial font. His *sangre* surged.

Coyote Man was saying in pigeon Spanish: "We run. Horses fast. Americanos catch us. Stand Inyo in line, shoot all. See how many ball pass through." He looked at the survivors. "We run. Run again."

The bloody scene exploded in Pedro's mind — children lined up. His stomach was on his tongue. A throaty Indian song came from the girl squatting by Blue Star. The death song. Coyote Man joined the singing; they all did. The naked, strangely aged people lifted Blue Star and slowly — singing the dirge — carried her toward the village. Roberto's two boys stepped from the trees and followed the procession. Did they know they were orphans?

Pedro went to where he'd picketed Chocolate. He untied him and rode after the killers. They couldn't get far with two men riding double. Two hearts lined up.

"No!" Daylor yelled.

"Sorry, señor." The first time in years he hadn't called him *patrón*.

70

Pedro circled ahead and found a perfect blind about a mile from Daylor's adobe, far enough to dull the gun's report. He lay on his belly in the bushes beside the trail, which ascended from the river bottom. The vegetation here was thinner but adequate. He braced the musket. His stillness and the branch he'd lain behind would conceal him — an *Indio* trick he'd played as a child.

The horse walked into view, each step bringing the killers closer into his sights. Livers being more painful than hearts, he lowered the barrel a hair, and waited with exquisite patience. They still didn't see him.

It was an easy shot now, no more than twenty yards. He whistled, saw the startled shift of the lizard eyes to his, and braced for the recoil as he pulled the trigger. The two ejected from the saddle. A perfect shot.

He ran forward. They lay writhing. Pockface tried to raise his revolver. Pedro kicked it from his hand. Flesh Nose curled into a ball. By the smell he knew their bowels had loosened. He saw the wet stains on their pants.

"Your mothers are whores and your fathers are cowards. You are shit-faced vermin who kill women and children and unarmed men. You don't deserve to die this easy."

Pockface, pressing his hand to his shirt, blood running through his fingers, hissed, "You fuckin filthy half-breed! Them war animals. Like you!"

Pulling his knife, Pedro knelt and told him in a soothing tone, "If I could kill you ten times, I would." He slit his throat, silencing the flapping tongue. Realizing that Señores Sheldon and Keyser were overdue and that he must hide these filthy dogs, he turned quickly to Flesh Nose.

Pedro knew his face betrayed nothing when he told Señor Daylor the two *Norteamericanos* had escaped. But they lay beneath a pile of brush with horror and shock stamped on their dead features. Later he and Ramón would bury them.

Awake during the night, the anger not even slightly quenched, he heard Señor Sheldon's horse in the courtyard. He got up and told him what had happened to the Omuchumne, and was glad it was dark so the *patrón* could not see his face when he told about Señor Daylor letting them get away. He turned and left Sheldon standing there at the stairs of his porch.

In the morning it was time to ride up the northward trail with Sheldon and the Rhoads men to dig a mass grave for the *Indios*. He was glad Daylor would stay at the store. María lay on the bed propped on her rabbit blanket. She wanted to visit the survivors in the *ranchería*, wanted to take herbs to Blue Star. "*Por favor*, take me that far."

"*Amapolita*, my sweet little poppy, only the grandest of miracles will save your friend. She is in a sleeping death."

Her black eyes were more persuasive than her voice. "On your way you will pass by the *ranchería*. Please take me there. You can pick me up when you come back from the burying."

Closing his eyes, he rolled his head to relieve a hard knot in the back of his neck. She should stay here and let her leg heal. *Norteamericanos* would never expect to find *Indios* above the mill. Pedro glanced at Captain Juan sitting against the wall, his hand on the Allen pepperbox. He wouldn't hesitate to shoot. She was safer here.

Virgin save us! The room was an infirmary. Quapata lay bandaged on a mat against the wall. And the ranchería was empty except for a handful of people who had run thirty miles before killers who saved their powder for desolate stretches, then carried out their business.

Why was it so hard to say no to María? A simple word? He leaned over the bed and wrapped her in his arms, cradling her soft face against him. Her tears unknotted him and his legs weakened. As she wept steadily, her hard belly against him, his insides melted. Her relatives and friends had been slaughtered like sheep, leaving his precious flower alone in the world — pregnant and without a midwife. *Indios* needed their people.

Sobbing erupted from his heart as he clung to her and no force of will could slow the rockslide of emotion. He remembered the riotous fun the *Indios* had at their Big Times and ball games. All night he'd remembered how, as Sutter's instrument, he'd helped make them vulnerable. He squeezed her tightly, unable to halt the raw emotion. The thought of those men forced to watch the murder of their women and children hurt the most. *Hearts lined up.* Oh Virgin! He hadn't cried like this ever, not even as a child.

At last his throat loosened enough to rasp, "*Amapolita.* I will take you there." The six *Indio* men at the *ranchería*, including Ramón, would have their weapons at the ready. And if the baby started to come, the three women — the one Omuchumne and the two who had escaped the Sacayak massacre — could help María to the birth hut.

The shaft of sunlight coming through the window wavered before his wet eyes. Billy stared, no doubt stunned to see a grown man weep. Pedro wiped a sleeve across his face. Captain Juan sat impassive, a stick man against the wall. Quapata's eyelids twitched. Waking up? Pedro swallowed, blinking away the moisture, and went to the corner and picked up the helmet, dusting it in his hands. Some of God's angels bore swords and girded for battle. In the eyes of the Moorish invaders of Spain, El Cid, too, had been an outlaw.

His vision cleared and his heart felt washed of doubt. His destiny was to protect the survivors, and, yes, avenge them. He returned the helmet to its corner and knelt beside Quapata, his eyes now open.

"*Amigo*, your children are dead and your wife is dying." He grabbed the hard, four-fingered hand — the right one, the left shoulder being shattered, and saw in the slits of the black eyes that Quapata had suspected the worst, or accepted fate more quickly than Pedro could.

"Almost all of your people were killed," he continued. "I go now to bury them." He squeezed the strong hand. "*Hombre*, you and I will avenge the deaths."

Comprehension flickered in Quapata's eyes. His hoarse whisper cracked. "They will pay." His eyes flooded and he turned to the wall.

"Sí, they will pay. Make your body well, *amigo*, for revenge."

Hearing the strength of his own voice reverberate within the walls, Pedro lifted María from the bed so she could select herbs from the rafters, then put her over his shoulder and went out to bury the dead.

Ten yards from the edge of the piled corpses — the skin starting to stretch with bloat — Pedro stood drenched with sweat and resting with Señor Sheldon, both leaning on their shovels. Only two days had passed. The smell was a noxious mixture of sweat, urine, vomit, defecation, but only the early hint of decay. About a hundred vultures skirmished over the entangled limbs and backs and heads where Pedro and the others had piled the bodies, small children on top. The vultures had already pecked out the eyes and made ragged holes here and there. They scuffled like chickens, taking brief flights then settling on other portions of their feast. The constant whumping of the huge wings beat like a war drum in Pedro's soul. Missing were the corpses whose skulls had been smashed with crowbars as they knelt over their baskets washing gold for their *patrones*.

Sheldon's wolf eyes penetrated. "Pedro, I need you. All I got left is Ramón and Roberto's two boys, and a couple of old men." His week's stubble dripped with sweat. He'd returned from Sacramento without a posse. The law was helpless, he had said. Men poured from ships and lingered at the embarcadero only long enough to outfit themselves for the mines. Merchants in the tent stores couldn't keep help, much less join a posse. "Most of the miners think Indians ought to be eliminated."

This morning, before they left the rancho, Coyote Man had announced to Sheldon: "Home place bad spirits now. We go hills. Make bows and arrows. Eat acorn, rabbit." His face could have been carved brown stone. Sheldon, who needed them so badly, had wished them all well. No doubt Captain Juan and María would want to go with the others, probably hoping to return to Sacayak. But mortal danger lurked in every streambed. Pedro would help them find a safe place to live.

Now, looking at the *patrón*, he couldn't explain all his reasons. The best he could say was, "Sometimes a man knows he must go another way in life."

Sheldon swung his eyes to the wide, shallow excavation — John Rhoads shoveling at a steady pace, throwing out rocks the size of grapefruits and melons, a breeze fanning the dirt. Billy Rhoads threw dirt at half the pace. Old Señor Rhoads left his sons and stepped out of the hole, joining Pedro and Sheldon.

"Looky up yonder," he said wiping his brow. He extended a palm as if beseeching the white-capped mountains. "Snow's about gone." A man might just make it through now." His mouth clamped down.

Pedro, glad for the interruption, stepped back into the excavation. It felt good to exhaust himself against this godforsaken earth, to make his arms and back hurt. His anguish for the *Indios* needed the release. Digging beside him were Coyote Man and one other *Indio*, who, despite his poor condition, had insisted on helping.

Some of what Señor Rhoads was saying came over the thunk and scrape of shovels. " . . . pack the wagons . . . Salt Lake — "

Pedro stomped his shovel blade down the side of a rock and pried, nearly breaking the handle. Sweat tickled down his back. His mind was clear. He knew his purpose. He was, as the *Indios* said, a warrior. Back at his old profession.

A gigantic shadow knifed across the pit. He looked up and saw a condor four times the size of the other vultures swooping over the corpses, scattering vultures in every direction. The low, concussive whump-whump-whump of their wings stirred his sombrero as they lifted their heavy bodies above the gravediggers. The condor lit on top of the human heap, a bird that to *Indios* represented the power of the universe. It seized an arm, and like a chicken eating a worm, hawked down great hunks of it. The diggers paused from their shoveling and stared.

Then the *patrón* stepped down into the pit and dug beside him. *I need you Pedro* hung between them. Hurling dirt, Pedro said, "Maybe some of the young *Norteamericanos* can herd cattle. You said the saloons are full." Boats had been converted to saloons, and permanent establishments were being built on lots laid out by Captain Sutter's son.

"Cesspool scum," he hissed, squinting briefly across the golden hills.

Sorry, señor, Pedro thought. It was all he had to offer.

The *patrón* closed his eyes, then opened them and dug, and after two more shovel loads said, "Maybe you're right. Most men aren't washing gold enough to keep em in boots." He glanced sidelong at Pedro, "Not all *Norteamericanos* are bad, you know."

"I know, *patrón*. You are *Norteamericano*." He felt the tug of their bond, the years of struggling together with the cattle, the sting of letting go, but that didn't dim the shining light of his destiny.

Señor Sheldon spoke Spanish. "You know that three hundred acres I'm buying across from McCoon?"

"Sí."

"I wanted it for you. Maybe someday you could run cattle on it. Pay me back over time. That still holds. Never mind where you go between now and then."

"*Patrón*, you do me great honor. Thousand times gracias." He gripped the shovel handle and muscled it into the hard earth to vent the emotion — where did it all come from? — but he would not be seduced by the old dream. What he had in mind left no room for future plans. If he hedged now and failed to be a man, he couldn't live with himself later. His voice came steady: "I will always be your friend. If you ever need help — you or your family — send word and I will ride to you in a moment."

Their gazes locked and Sheldon said, "*Amigos*."

They went back to digging, Sheldon not asking questions. But something in the cut of his jaw said he never forgot how it felt on the other side of the law.

"I must ask, *patrón*, if I may herd your cattle until María is well enough to travel."

"*Naturalmente*. It will take that long to round up some new vaqueros. And Pedro?"

"Sí?"

"If you need anything — a place to stay, anything at all — send word, understand?" He propped the shovel under his arm and extended a hand. It was dry, calloused, his jaw set, his eyes understanding. "*Siémpre.*" Always.

He squeezed the hand and smiled. "Maybe I have a request very soon."

"Sí?"

"Señora Catherine helped Elitha McCoon when her time came."

"Sí?"

"Maybe you would speak to her about helping María, if she doesn't mind, her being *India* — "

"She'll be glad to help."

71

A woman went alone to a birth hut. That much Maria remembered. She insisted on crawling the distance herself, dragging her wounded leg through the drying grass. The three surviving *Indias* — the last of her people — waited for her. Even Señora Catherine and Elitha were there to honor the birth.

The tiny earth dome stood apart from the Omuchumne village, most of which had been properly burned to the ground. No belongings were left to lure the spirits of the dead. Looking up at the rounded hut beneath the outspread arms of a protective oak mother, Maria thought of nothing but what her belly promised. Glad the wait was over at last, she crawled through the low doorway into the dim interior.

During her pregnancy she had looked upon dead children. Could she give birth to a living child? It was a bad sign that Elitha, her magic double, had a dead child after an agonizing birth. Waiting for a sharp pang to stop, Maria dragged herself to the fur pallet and emptied her mind. Bad magic must not be entertained in this dark womb of female power.

The bear rug felt luxurious and had the sweet animal smell. It too had been washed, sprinkled with pine tea and dried in the sun. Elitha came crawling inside behind three *Indias*. Señora Catherine remained at the door, looking in.

Bent-Willow-Reflected-in-Pond, a cousin sister who had escaped death at the home village, offered Maria the wormwood tea mixture. Accepting the small basket, Maria swallowed. The tea would distance her from the sensations of her laboring body, but she was careful not to drink too much. She had no birth-helper to pamper her through the ordeal, and even Bent-Willow-Reflected-in-Pond, though she'd given birth twice, was uncertain of her knowledge. Maria must give direction.

Feeling the hard pull on her insides, she was glad she had paid attention to the actions of the home place birthhelper when Billy was born. The big woman had embraced her from the back, her fleshy upper arms covering her like a blanket, and crooned in singsong fashion: "The strong power in your belly is health. The baby comes. Don't mistake it for pain or the baby will fear the world. Fear is the enemy. The baby comes to joy. Little child, come to the world. As I hold your mother, so shall you be held. Come quickly. We welcome you." She crooned this as she massaged herb paste into Maria's abdomen and the small of her back, reminding the child to come headfirst. She hugged and rocked and crooned and circled with her hand, steadying Maria over the sand basin, which had been scooped out for the baby's short drop to Earth Mother. Maria's soul had floated above her laboring body as the women around the walls talked of happy births and sang joyful songs. Now she must recreate the magic of that birth.

"More tea," she said at the end of the spasm, and Bent-Willow-Reflected-in-Pond put the basket to her lips. She had also instructed her about the paste herbs, though she hadn't been entirely sure of the mixture. Tomaka's knowledge had died with her.

Bent-Willow-Reflected-in-Pond joined Hummingbird Tailfeather against the smooth, mud-plastered wall. The two sang with Broken Salmon, the only surviving Omuchumne woman now that Blue Star had died. Their voices halted uncertainly. They looked at one another for help with the words. None of them had been birth singers. Maria couldn't remember the songs either, but she knew the spirits recognized good intentions. "You sing very well," she said. "Sing it again, a little louder so the baby can hear."

At the women's insistence Elitha had removed her clothing and sprinkled herself with pine tea, but her large eyes looked confused. Señora Catherine, at the door, hadn't undressed, but it was good to have these *Americanas* present. Normally the hut wall was packed with celebrating women, but these five would do.

She closed her eyes and let the herb people draw her beyond the mounting sensations in her body and, as she opened her breathing, her mind's eye opened the internal passageway. "Help me to the basin," she said to the women.

Quickly the three *Indias* and Elitha moved her to a sitting position at the edge of the pit. Broken Salmon kneeled beside Maria's legs, which were straight, spanning the pit. Elitha sat close by, watching.

Broken Salmon massaged herb paste into her abdomen while Bent-Willow-Reflected-in-Pond hugged her from the back with thin arms, but they felt strong and good. Hummingbird Tailfeather brought more tea, and she swallowed it gratefully. The birth was peaking, almost continuous, the infant holding fast, threatening to pull her apart.

She moved further beyond herself and heard herself gasp, "Come to us, Little One, nothing to fear, come down to us. Come. Now. Now. Now." The sensation split up through her core, violent, severe, no talk possible, all breath behind the infant.

"I see the head!" cried Broken Salmon.

Head first. *Thank you Mother Oak.* She sucked air and bore down, "Come now." She gritted her teeth and pushed every shred of strength behind the slow, reluctant movement of the infant.

"I've got the shoulders," Broken Salmon said excitedly.

With a sudden sense of a fish slipping through the fingers, the hard sensations let up. She opened her eyes, blinked back stinging sweat. Broken Salmon was on her knees reaching into the sand basin. Bent-Willow-Reflected-in-Pond craned her neck to see around her legs, and Hummingbird Tailfeather kneeled over Broken Salmon — the three young with laughter. The first smiles since —

A soft wa-aaa-aa. Alive! Thank you Oam'shu. Thank you, Mother Oak; thank you Wormwood and all the plant people. Thank you Spirit that Lives in All Things. She stared at the white-sheathed, blood-streaked infant squirming in Broken Salmon's hands. No penis, a twisted blue cord trailing. Even Elitha and Señora Catherine laughed at the baby, who was gasping.

Maria reached over her knees and took the warm, slippery little being. "I will suck out the matter." Normally it was done by the baby's grandmother. The baby was heavier than she expected, and it felt strange to place her lips, which seemed so huge, over the tiny mouth, and to suck out matter that had come from her own womb and spit it to the side. The infant's eyes were wide, looking directly into hers. Oh, thank you spirits!

The perfect little features brought tears to her eyes. What kind of changing world would this little girl see? Would death continue to come in whooshing blasts? Or would this child live long enough to give life from the folds of these tiny genitalia? Five small fingers on each hand, five toes on each tiny foot. *Alive* despite the omens and portents. What did it mean? A new person for a new world? The baby wrenched into a puckery cry, and she marveled at the strength of the sound. Her joyful tears splashed down on the small chest, still covered with mucus and blood.

She cuddled her to her breast, hardly aware that Bent-Willow-Reflected-in-Pond was kneeling before her, biting through the cord. Etumu would have done that, had she lived. *A child almost without relatives.*

"I take her to the river," said Hummingbird Tailfeather.

Another task the grandmother normally performed, that and burying the afterbirth. She handed the infant to her and bore down again, entrusting her cousin-sister with the small bundle of life, whose hair, she noticed, had a certain reddish tint. "Bring her back."

Laughter erupted and she smiled through the twinge of afterbirthing. Elitha and Señora Catherine smiled too, though they couldn't know the foolish thing she had said. Of course the baby would be brought back for the four days of recuperation and spiritual cleansing. She pushed out the slick lump and lay back to be washed with yarrow tea.

Pedro sat with Billy on the fallen trunk of an oak which the *Indios* had used for how long? A hundred years? *Won't be needed now.* He heard what seemed the soft cry of a lost fawn, but decided it was his imagination. No screams had come yet from the birth hut, the worst of the birth — he crossed himself — still ahead. Then he saw a naked *India* hurry toward the river with something in her arms.

He stood up, peered through the trees, stopped breathing to listen. A muted cry. Yes. Already! His heart vaulted. *Gracias a Dios*!

He grabbed Billy and rushed across the tangle of vines toward the river beach. The woman was up to her knees in the water dipping the infant. She turned, held a palm toward him. "No."

Was something wrong? He must see the child. He tore off his boots, told Billy to stay on the shore, and splashed out to the woman, to the sound of a crying, sputtering baby.

The woman hunched over and wrenched away. "No. Bad luck. Go away. Men wait four days."

Damn the *Indio* rules! He grabbed her shoulder and pulled her around. Cradled in her arms lay a baby girl crying mightily, water streaming from her auburn hair.

He stared as if paralyzed, seeing nothing amiss despite the woman's stricken expression. The baby's face puckered in self-pitying distress, her lower lip quivering. Her narrowed eyes seemed to blame him for the dunking. He threw back his head laughing and continued to laugh as the woman waded away upstream.

"Wait," he called, suddenly alarmed. "Is María all right?"

The woman, who was again dunking and rubbing the infant, turned and smiled. "She is well."

Thanks be to the Virgin!

The name he'd been turning in his mind fit this strong-willed infant. Isabella. The Spanish queen who had sent the first explorers to this new world. He smiled.

Señora Sheldon approached him at the river beach, her face alight, her gold watch bumping on her bosom. "It was as easy as pie! Golly, I guess Indians don't feel the pain." Her face beamed satisfaction.

Looking down into her wide smile, he said, "I will go with you to tell Señor Sheldon." It was about noon. The *patrón* would be coming in from the corral.

That afternoon, still in a festive mood over his daughter's birth, Pedro rode three leagues downstream to help the Rhoads men maneuver a barrel of gold into their wagon. He worked between John and Billy Rhoads pushing the barrel up a ramp, rolling it on the bar cinch. Señor Sheldon and Father Rhoads steadied it with ropes.

"Well, Pa," John said as he grunted the barrel into place, "I reckon you'll git plenty of help unloadin this thing at the other end." He lashed it to the side of the wagon bed.

The lips of the white-haired man straightened to a line, a smile for him. "Plan to deliver it to Brigham's doorstep."

"Well, someday I'll go see that tabernacle."

"It'll be a dandy all right."

Pedro helped bring furniture from the house he'd helped build for the patron's in-laws. John Rhoads' little brothers and sisters scampered back and forth with boxes and bags, jumping into the wagon bed to pack them.

The old man turned to Sarah Daylor's twin, "Git yer things, Billy, and come with us."

He shook his head and smiled quietly as if the matter had been settled.

"No womenfolk around here atall," said the father. "You'd have yer pick in Salt Lake. More coming in there all the time." Pedro sensed a secret pain behind the gruff exterior.

"I like it here, Pa," said Billy, checking the grease of the wagon springs on the tip of his finger.

Later, on the trail back, Sheldon trotted alongside Pedro. "Got som'm to show you."

On Sheldon's stoop, so near yet so far from the birth hut, he couldn't help but pace back and forth while the *patrón* retrieved the *Placer Times* from the house. Sheldon came out and sat on the step, shaking out the paper. Pedro felt too jumpy to sit. He was thinking about where to hunt for quail eggs, which María liked so well. The *Indias* would take them to her. Could he stand waiting for four days?

Sheldon read: "May 12, 1849. The letter below was received at our office shortly after our own prepared account had been published. In many particulars it will be found to differ materially from the one referred to. We readily give it a place."

He glanced over the paper and said, "Mr. Daylor wrote two letters on the killing of our Indians. This one he took down to the publishing office. They printed it word for word. The other was about the same. He put it into Sheriff Bates' hand."

Reminded of the massacre, Pedro felt the song leave his heart.

"I want you to hear what Mr. Daylor wrote. And remember, this here newspaper is delivered to every mining camp in California. It's read in San Francisco too." The *patrón* looked at him hard, perhaps knowing there was a secret grave on his property.

He wondered how Daylor would describe Pedro's part. But before Sheldon started, he remembered. "Señor Daylor can't write."

"Sally wrote it for him. I smoothed out a few things."

So this was Sheldon's letter too; that anchored Pedro's attention more firmly.

"On second thought maybe I'd outa read this other letter first," Sheldon said. He turned the paper over and read "White Man's Revenge." It was a very short account of an entire "tribe" of Indians being gunned down. The writer congratulated himself for his part in it. The scene was so vivid in Pedro's mind, he couldn't utter a sound.

Then Daylor's letter: "On or about the 20th ultimate, I left my rancho with a party of Indians in my employ, for the mines . . . " It went on to say that in his absence, a party of armed white men attacked and killed Indians while they were working on their knees. " . . . brains were beat out with rocks and stones." A group of white men heard the "alarm" and ran toward the spot, meeting the armed party. The killers warned them to go no farther because the Indians were on the warpath. Paying no "mind," they proceeded to where they found the bodies of the Indians, the remainder having fled. The killers pursued the Indians, overtaking most of them about ten miles from "my ranch."

Pedro found no fault with the accuracy. It told of the men camping, "150 yards from my house. Myself, wife and others out to bury a member of the family deceased and previous to leaving the ground, I was informed the party of men were at the house about to kill the Indians there." No mention of Pedro. So far so good. The less attention to him the better.

Sheldon continued, ". . . Captain of the Company" requested a beef, and "I refused." He read about the massacre, giving the correct number of dead and injured. Did the brazenness come across? Men asking to be fed while lying in wait? " . . . The next morning I was called by my wife to see two men who were riding rapidly to the south, in a few moments they wheeled and galloped hard back. Then I saw Indians running to take shelter in the brush."

Pedro replayed the scene in his mind, his role unmentioned, and Sheldon ended with a sentence about the mass burial. "Signed Wm Daylor." Slowly Sheldon folded the paper, his lips parted as he gazed at the green river behind the cottonwoods, the birth hut about twenty yards from the bank.

Pedro spoke in Spanish, a language suited to intimacy. "I think it said there that some *Norteamericanos* came to help the *Indios* when they were attacked. What will those men think when they read this? Won't they whisper that it is a coward who fails to shoot murderers who camp on his property?"

The silence between them had a sharp edge, Sheldon watching the river, the point of his jaw moving. Then he spoke in a controlled tone. "Mr. Daylor is a smart man even if he can't read. He knows this is a damned war of extermination and a lone white man can't dent it with a gun." He gave him a look, and Pedro knew Sheldon was aware of the graves and wanted Pedro to think well of his friend.

He didn't.

Sheldon got to his feet, speaking Spanish. "Many stories in these wretched papers," he smacked it with the back of his hand, "tell of white heroes killing Indians. The *malcriados* print every dirty lie from the mines." His wolfish gaze pierced. "Ours is the only one, Pedro," he struck the paper again, "the only one that tells the truth — the Indians are murdered whether they are guilty or innocent!" He examined his boots, then pursed his lips at the paper. "This letter will do more good than guns."

"A letter?" Pedro must have sounded skeptical because Sheldon strode into the house and returned with another paper, whipping it open.

"Listen to this in the *Alta Californian.* A 'correspondent' writes that the California Indians are 'a degraded and brutish class . . . the nearest link, of the sort, to the quadrupeds of any on the continent of North America.'"

"Quadru — "

"Four-legged animals." Sheldon's eyes flashed across the page. "Here's another. `The Diggers graze in the fields like cattle, and their tough, cold, oily skin evokes a feeling of repulsion just as if one had put a hand on a toad, tortoise, or huge lizard.'" He looked hard at Pedro.

Pedro closed his eyes. María's soft skin came to mind. Listening to these lies was torture. "The holy *padres* came to Alta California to save the *Indios*' souls. They loved them. They touched — " His voice cracked and he swallowed.

"To miners they're a blight, see, competition for the gold. So they write this trash to justify the slaughter." He looked down at Pedro with an expression of pure pain. "Not long ago I read an editorial crowing happily that within a few years not one Indian will be left."

Pedro jumped up scowling at the newsprint, half expecting his anger to scorch it. "I'm glad I cannot read." He turned away.

"Odds are that part about the skin comes from the pen of a man in some fancy hotel in San Francisco thinkin to clear out the mines for a water ditch he's sellin shares in. You gotta understand, Pedro. This here's a lot bigger'n we are. And there's nothing we can do about it till California gits to be a state. *Comprendes?* It took courage for a merchant like Mr. Daylor — " He stopped himself and swept his gaze over the trees. "A man has to hope when this is over, there'll be a few Indians left."

"I tell you . . ." It exploded too harshly, and Pedro lowered his voice. "María and Isabella will live."

The *patrón* nodded solemnly.

"Now I go break that bay stallion," Pedro said, heading for the corral. That four-legged lightning bolt would wring out some of this anger. And very soon Pedro would be a clear-eyed, uncompromised warrior again.

72

The first time Ben Wilder saw Elitha McCoon up close, it was late August. She was sitting in the shade before her little adobe house reading the *Placer Times*. Already that put her on the uphill side of the great divide separating females — those who could read and those who could not. The Lord knew a man didn't need schooling to succeed; plenty went on to make their fortunes and marry refined ladies. Oh, men with schooling like Ben might romp with the downhill females, but he had a whole different set of feelers out for girls who could read. And he hadn't expected to find one here, not after what he'd heard of Perry McCoon — a gambler who played poorly and spent his few sober hours practicing rope tricks.

In heavy block letters the backside of the paper proclaimed: "Indian Murderer Dies Like a Man" — a hanging Ben had read about this morning. As her dark, neatly parted head lifted over the newsprint, he connected with the biggest, saddest-looking brown eyes he'd ever seen.

His tongue wouldn't move. Not since Rhode Island had a girl affected him like that.

"May I help you?" she asked in a rich contralto. Was that breeding or natural grace as she laid the paper on her lap?

He remembered his hat and dislodged his tongue. "No thank you, ma'am. Just paying a neighborly call. Resting from what you might call the most peculiar way to earn a living man ever invented. Sorry to startle you." He nearly drowned in those eyes. What secrets dwelled there? He finger-combed the roostertail his shadow told him stood on his head.

"I'm a married woman." Out of the blue. She'd read his mind.

"Oh, I know that," he stammered — not his smooth self at all — and I surely didn't mean to unsettle you, ma'am." Still she didn't wear a ring, and the speculation had it . . .

She smiled, that is her full lips did. The brown eyes kept their secrets. "I don't make this a habit, but you look like you could use some shade." Folding the paper she nodded at a stump near the firepit, indicating he should sit. "How long you been in California?"

Not Californy — the only way he'd heard it pronounced in months. *Good family.* "Two weeks come Sunday, and they tell me I'm a native."

Her lower lip widened as she smiled, and he saw she liked his little joke. "Come by ship?"

"Nope. Hoofed it the whole way."

Her brows lifted a notch. "But it's only August!"

He appreciated the opening. "My brothers and I had a notion to beat everybody to the gold. And we did a pretty good job of leaving that whole mess of wagon trains in our dust — a man can outdistance any four-legged critter hitched to a load — so we weren't prepared for the mob of humanity that got here first." When the sun came up it still felt peculiar not to start walking, pulling that infernal mule.

"Did you cross over at the Truckee Pass?"

That puzzled him until he remembered it bore the name Donner now. "No ma'am. I doubt anybody'll use that trail after what happened to those starvin fools." Every paper in the East had run the gruesome details of the Donner Party, and though nothing of the sort could have happened in August, most overland emigrants agreed the route was jinxed. Her fascinating eyes seemed to reflect the whole suffering world, yet she was so young! "We came over the Carson Pass. Ran into a bunch of Mormons going the other way. They said it was a good road. My hunch is all the emigrants will come that way."

"Sounds like you might have run into Mr. Rhoads — "

"That was it! By thunder, Rhoads was the name." Marveling at this coincidence — a link between them — he recalled the meeting in the sagebrush, just beyond Salt Lake. The Rhoads wagon had creaked about as slow as any Ben had ever seen.

"They're friends of mine."

That stopped him cold, and his voice betrayed it. "You Mormon?"

She grinned and shook her head.

He cocked his head sharply to the side, dismissing with a relieved chuckle the barbaric images that had crossed his mind, then took a turn at the questioning, which is what he'd come for. "How long you been in California?"

She hesitated. "Let's see. Forty-seven, March. I guess that makes it two years and about six months."

Before the gold. Rarely did you meet anybody who'd been here that long. "Married a while?" The direct approach — an intrusion, but a fifty dollar bet said she was leaving McCoon and Ben had been delegated to investigate, which was the story of his life. When anything needed to be checked on, figured out, or explained, Ben Wilder got appointed. This time he had to admit it was a pleasure.

"Forty-seven, June."

He calculated. Married immediately after arrival. Couldn't be much over seventeen now. He waited for contingencies, caveats, a wedge to get a toehold in.

Hearing none, and seeing her struggle to avoid his face — did she find him attractive? — words drained from him. *Firmly married.* Not what he'd dared hope.

A prairie grouse — those gray birds pecking all over the gold country — called a three-syllable cry as if speaking for him. He turned his hat between his knees, which poked a long ways up and out, and realized that after two thousand miles in the company of argonauts, he was overdue to see any girl, never mind which side of the divide, never mind how married. When he finally found his tongue, he said, "Got family hereabouts?"

Those eyes could have melted stone. She swallowed hard and murmured, "The family's back in Illinois." Something very sad there.

He followed her gaze as it swept down the swale away from the house. Motion caught his eye near the river ford. Her cheeks went slack. She stood up, tall and slender, the folded paper in her hand mutely screaming: Joaquín Strikes Again!

She said, "My husband is coming. I don't mean to be unneighborly." A rider was heading up the hill.

He jumped up. "I didn't mean to impose. Those brothers of mine'll be riled, being left with the digging." He put his hat on his head and saw the dust advancing rapidly, its source soon to emerge over the hill.

She was saying, "I enjoyed the company, but I don't — "

"Make it a habit."

Her smile showed apprehension, as if she wished he would vanish.

He left for the Wilder claim, which was half a mile upstream and across the river, reasoning that McCoon might have seen him but was too far away to recognize him. *Jealous.* He passed an interesting split boulder and walked swiftly up what he judged to be an old Indian trail.

A shout froze him in his tracks. A man's voice, words running together. Looking back, he saw only the thatch on the adobe roof, the house beneath the fall of the land. More shouts — McCoon's. Something crashed. A washtub against a tree? The Englishman was crazy. Ben turned back; she might need help. Then the shouting quieted and he stopped.

It could be worse for her if he showed his face. You didn't get between a man and his wife, especially if you were the cause. Maybe she had denied having company. It would have taken an eagle to see much. Better leave it alone. He continued up the path.

But when night came and he lay in the tent with his brothers — three tall men laid out like fish in a tin, tent flaps open to a triangle of bright stars — he imagined those brown eyes looking at him in a more than neighborly way.

73

Maria sat with her legs hanging over the lip of the cave as she nursed the baby and gazed over the brown hills above the dry gulch of French Creek. She felt warm in front, cool in back, from the cave. She couldn't see the flat where the trickle called Big Creek joined French Creek or the town called Spanish Camp in the bottomland. If she went down the trail, just around the hump of the hill she could see the white tents and frame houses, tiny in the distance. For three moons she'd lived in the cave with the survivors, too far from purifying water to submerge wholly. Her heart felt lost.

Isabella released the nipple and smiled, milk on her tongue. Maria smiled back and lifted the baby's fat little belly to her shoulder. Growing fast. Pedro had named her too soon, just as Perrimacoo had named Billy the day he was born — foolhardy. One should wait until a child was walking. She sighed. Pedro seemed different now — a subtle change. More inclined to give orders. More secretive about his activities. For a moon he'd lived in the cave, but now he left for days at a time, trusting the people would be safe near Spanish Camp.

Below the cave mouth she heard the prattle of the children — Billy, two boys of Bent-Willow-Reflected-in-Pond and the daughter of Hummingbird Tailfeather. They were pretending Billy was their baby. Amazing how children awoke each morning alive with the excitement of new things. They didn't think about the past and didn't care where they lived. Often she wondered what lay ahead for Billy and Isabella.

Pedro and Quapata were gone, tonight the fourth sleep, and she was impatient to hold her man in her arms.

Grizzly Hair appeared around the hump on the trail, a jackrabbit hanging in each hand. The low sun on the west ridge illuminated his painful walk, the lead ball still hurting his back. She knew he wasn't calm in this strange country where one could not bathe properly or hear the river-baby spirit.

He glanced down at the four children standing beside the trail, laid the rabbits beside María, then slowly climbed into the cave and settled himself against the wall. No joy came from him any more, though people still looked to him for wisdom.

The children dashed back to their play and Maria wondered if Isabella would ever know the fullness of Grizzly Hair's knowledge. He needed the home place. Pedro said it was safer here. But what was a safe body without friendly sprits?

Broken Salmon appeared on the trail — a woman with no family, her husband and son buried in the mass grave. She carried a load of acorns on her back, but no joy came from her either. Often she and Grizzly Hair sat on opposite sides of the cave, staring across the firepit past one another. Coyote Man and the other four Omuchumne men had camped somewhere near Wapumne's old village, also deserted — a band of troubled men without women.

Isabella burped and Maria put her to the other nipple, hoping she'd get a belly full before —

A pop sounded. In the distance. Gunfire. The sound identical to —

Two more. The baby looked up, questioning, sensing her rigid posture. Grizzly Hair stepped from the cave, listening. "Maybe shooting targets," he murmured unconvincingly.

Often the men of Spanish Camp held Big Times, sometimes shooting guns in the air. But these shots came from a different direction. East. Up French Creek. An *Indio* village lay that way. Her heart thudded. Grizzly Hair stood in the orange sun, which blazed from the far ridge, looking toward the village. Recently he had made friends with those people through sign language.

The baby stopped sucking. Too much bad power crackled. The popping continued, and continued.

Later, after the gunshots had stopped, Maria humped her hand down over another grasshopper. In the lingering twilight she cracked the insect's neck and tossed it in her burden basket. She hadn't been able to bear another idle moment in the cave. The heat of the long dry brought great numbers of grasshoppers, and it was a pity too few people were left to hold a proper round-up. These stragglers would only whet the appetite; this season there would be no grasshopper paste balls, no baskets of roasted hoppers for crunchy snacks and spicy seasoning.

Stalking another one, she heard footsteps. She grabbed Isabella, her bikoos propped on a rock, and hid behind a toyon bush.

Spear Thrower came up the path, without game. Stalking Egret followed, also without. Something short moved between them. As Maria stood to greet the hunters she saw a young child — about seven *años* — staring at her, long hair falling over her shoulders. Stalking Egret took the girl's hand, and pulled her forward. She dug in her toes and tried to break free. Terror glittered in her eyes, but the hunters were stony-faced.

Stalking Egret lifted the writhing child over his shoulder and continued walking. Maria fell into stride beside him asking, "Where are her people?"

"All dead."

Horror jangled through her. "I will care for her," she said.

Clearly relieved, he set her down and went on with Spear Thrower.

She knelt beside the slender girl with a chubby baby face, as if an infant had been elongated. The child made no sound and her eyes were dry, but too wide — a silent scream. Maria started to hug her, but the girl jerked away and ran back down the trail.

The poor little thing wanted her people, her mother.

Dashing after her, Maria wondered who had done this. *Españoles* from Spanish Camp? Pedro had assured everyone they were friendly. She thought back. Broken Salmon had gone to the town more than once to exchange gold for beans. She'd said *Indios* walked about freely. Had things changed? If so, everyone was in danger; the *Españoles* knew people lived in this cave.

Maria overtook and grabbed the child. "You must come with me," she said lifting the twisting, kicking girl from the ground. "Billy," she called. "Bring the other children. Come quickly."

In moments the four trotted down from the cave entrance, agape at the sight of the thrashing child, her long hair flinging into Maria's eyes. The daughter of Hummingbird Tailfeather, who was only a little younger, asked the girl where she came from, and that had a calming effect. She turned and stared, her black eyes snapping with silent emotion.

Carefully Maria set her on the ground, but she didn't try to run. Slinging her carrying basket from her back, Maria reached in and pulled out a grasshopper for the girl, but she jerked her head away. The others licked their lips and shouted, "I want it. Give it to me."

"No. I will roast them at the supper fire. For now we will take our visitor to the cave and show her where we live. Here, take her hand. That's right, you on this hand, you on the other. Show her the way." The looks of disappointment over the grasshopper faded as the children brightened to the task of leading an older child.

Maria fetched Isabella and walked behind the children, who escorted the child slowly up the trail as a mother would walk a toddler. They cocked their heads solicitously toward her as if she were the most precious thing in the world.

And she was, Maria realized — a tender survivor in a world out of control. The hair on her scalp moved to think of the massacre the child must have witnessed. Her own slaughtered people flashed to mind before she could squelch memory. All the children padding up the path were in grave danger. When would Pedro return?

Most of the twilight at the cave entrance had faded by the time supper steamed in the baskets. The little girl stood upright in the cave — as only children could — gazing out into the dark. Bent-Willow-Reflected-in-Pond handed Spear Thrower, her man, the nu-pah basket and cocked her head quizzically at him. Neither of the hunters had said anything about what had happened.

They sat cross-legged in their places and their eyes were unmoving black stones in the firelight. Still not ready to talk. Supper had been prepared in a limbo of cautious respect, and though the hunters surely would have advised the people to leave if there had been immediate danger, Maria wondered if they should flee anyway, and leave a scent trail of skunk for Pedro to follow.

Grizzly Hair broke the silence. "Was it *Españoles*?"

Stalking Egret shook his head. He spoke in a detached monotone. "*Norte-americanos*. With fast-shooting guns. They killed all the grown people. When we got there they were putting the children in a wagon — all but babies. They shot them. They took the children away. This one slipped away." He nodded at the girl.

Maria knee-walked to the girl and ran a hand down her smooth back, gesturing to a place where she should sit and eat. But she made no effort to speak or acknowledge that she was spoken to.

Maria spoke slowly and patted the dirt between her and Billy. "Come. Sit down." Still, she stood as if deaf, her face darkened by flickering shadow.

"Eat," Hummingbird Tailfeather told Stalking Egret, pointing at the rabbit nu-pah.

He blinked back moisture, which shone in the firelight. "No food tonight."

Grizzly Hair spoke in the sing-song of a headman's oration. "You are welcome here, child. We are your new family."

She neither moved nor ate. All night she sat at the cave entrance, refusing kindnesses, never making a sound.

Watching to make sure she didn't run away, Maria slept little herself. She heard the muted whispers of the two married couples and listened to the coyotes yipping across the hills. Sinister owls hooted from the trees, and she longed for Pedro.

When morning grayed the cave mouth, the girl remained sitting, facing the trees. Spear Thrower and Stalking Egret squat-walked toward the entrance, bows and quivers slung across their backs. As they disappeared down the trail, Maria took last night's nu-pah to the girl, sprinkling it with the two roasted, crushed grasshoppers she'd saved for her.

With a trembling hand the child scooped a fingerload of the paste and placed it on her tongue. *She will live.* Maria hugged her, and she did not wrench away. A sharp moan came from behind. Broken Salmon was twisting her head from side to side. Trying to shake away memory, Maria knew. Sometimes it took more strength than people had to refrain from thinking the names of the dead. There were so many, and the girl's presence reminded them, and warned them that the killing of *Indios* had not stopped.

"We must hold a Cry," Grizzly Hair declared, then left on his morning trap check.

Maria watched him go, realizing a Cry must be performed in a dancehouse, or an outdoor consecrated circle. The wailing and singing would be heard a long distance, and people must be thoroughly bathed before meeting the spirits of the dead. That meant — and it gave her a thrill — that Father was planning to return to the home place.

The young girl left the cave and made water near the entrance. Then she stood a moment following the flight of a flicker, the bright coral of its underwings flashing as it swooped from pine to oak.

"Little Flicker," Maria named her.

She turned to Maria as if the word had meaning in her tongue. "Little Flicker," Maria repeated, pleased to have drawn response.

Then suddenly her little chin quivered. Her eyes squeezed shut and tears flowed down her contorted baby face. The first tears. Maria pulled her close, wishing she could wring the bad memories from her, just as she sometimes wished Pedro could squeeze her own memories away. If she were killed, she hoped some woman would care for Billy and Isabella as well as she intended to care for Little Flicker.

That afternoon when Maria was pounding acorns in the stone bowl, she heard the jingle of spurs. She looked up and saw Pedro hurrying to her, bolero flapping, his face stretched in a smile beneath his black hat.

She flew into his arms and buried her face in his man smell. She couldn't stop the tears of relief and joy. Billy darted from the trees, hugging their four knees while his three playmates grinned in a polite row. Quapata came up the trail with a leather bag.

Every time Pedro returned — always without warning — it was the same. Her heart burst with sudden happiness. Each time, he and Quapata left their horses in a different place and came by secret routes to the cave. The other people were glad to see Pedro too. In some ways he had become their headman.

When she and Pedro entered the cave, Grizzly Hair nodded a greeting, but Little Flicker shrank back.

"She is afraid," Maria said, sitting against the wall. "A terrible thing happened to her people." Quapata crawled past, pushing a leather bag ahead of him to the dark tail of the cave — the gold Pedro was storing for a safer time. The three women, who had been outside, came in and assumed their places. Ready to listen.

Pedro nodded at them. "Where are your men?"

Bent-Willow-Reflected-in-Pond said, "Not back from hunting."

Maria sat tight against Pedro. How did one tell of such horror? She started, "Before the sleep —"

A shadow flashed across his hawk-like profile. He knew. He glanced at the fearful figure of Little Flicker, her eyes wide with terror as she looked at him, and explained.

"We were building the brush corral when we heard the shots. By the time we got there everyone was dead. We followed the wagon tracks — did you know they took the children? Seeing nods, he continued. "We followed them to Hangtown. I asked questions."

The women edged closer to hear, for his voice came low and grave. Maria knew that when he went among *Norteamericanos* he removed his black wig and left Quapata in hiding. Still, she feared for him constantly.

"They sold the children," he said. "To a barber, a merchant, a banker, a whorehouse and several saloons. Some to ranchers for farm work, and their women for housework."

"Sold them?" She had never heard of selling people.

"Two-hundred dollars for boys old enough to work and pretty girls, down to twenty dollars for the youngest." He looked at the girl. "Does she speak Spanish?"

"She does not talk."

Grizzly Hair cleared his throat, and Maria saw the renewed power in his posture, the light catching the angle of his wide cheeks. He said, "I take my people to the home place."

She caught her breath. Grizzly Hair meant what he said, but Pedro had been adamant that they must stay here. Would she be asked to choose between husband and father? It would feel like lariats pulling her in opposite directions.

Pedro looked him in the eye. " No. You cannot. *Norteamericanos* continue to wash gold at your old *ranchería*. It is dangerous there." It came so direct, so like a parent to a child, she cringed inwardly.

As if fixed on a spot over his head, Grizzly Hair's eyes sparked as in old times. "*Norteamericanos* come here now. Shoot Inyos."

Pedro was suddenly tactful. "There you would need to hide every minute."

"Here we hide every minute."

"I have *amigos* in Spanish Camp." It was true. He traded for the goods in their stores.

"Storeman give Inyos bad trade." That was also true.

Pedro lifted his nose. "You have gone down there?" He had told them not to.

Grizzly Hair drew himself up, sitting taller. "Every man must find his own way." That was also true. Pedro watched over them like a mother quail watched foolish chicks.

"It is the same everywhere," Pedro said in a softer tone, "not just here. Storekeepers have two sets of weights. *Indios* get little for gold. Let me buy all the food. There is no need for you men to hunt, to expose yourselves. I'll get what you need."

"Hunt makes men strong."

Pedro leaned back, closed his eyes and exhaled. He said nothing more. Neither did Grizzly Hair.

Maria felt sure Stalking Egret and Spear Thrower would follow Grizzly Hair, their old headman. Their women would follow. Fearless in her bereavement, Broken Salmon didn't care where she lived as long as it was with others. But if they all left, surely Pedro wouldn't ask Maria to live in the cave alone with the children. She could not.

A sudden longing for the scenes of her childhood filled her — the village center as it had been, the u-machas and cha'kas standing about, the roundhouse and the cheerful river babbling from its green channel, the plant people whose growing places she knew as well as she knew Isabella's face.

Pedro crawled to the entrance and glanced back at her in his special way.

She handed the cradleboard to Broken Salmon and joined him. The children knew not to disturb them. The setting sun tinted all things the color of clover blossoms — the hills, his pale shirt, the lichen-splotched boulders. In their secluded place the slick dry grass lay flattened, though they had not been there for five sleeps.

He kneeled in the circle of boulders and removed his hat. Damp auburn curls stuck to his forehead. She kneeled before him looking into his gray eyes, and touched a curl at his collar. Isabella had such hair.

"*Amapolita*," he said, cupping her cheek. "Have you been well?"

"Sí, but my heart needed you."

He wrapped her in his arms. "My heart missed you too. But it is full now. We talk later." They rolled over together and rocked back and forth, his smokey man's aroma mixing with the clean smell of the straw beneath them, his clothing falling away. They connected — two halves of a lightning bolt. The magic of it brought tears to her eyes as she lay on him, afterwards, never wanting to separate.

Pensively he stroked her back, and she knew she would never tire of the feel on her skin. Coyotes yipped, out hunting for supper, and she heard the rustle of a small animal stepping into the twilight, careless of the whispering grass. Free of the hot sun, the earth released whiffs of fragrant moisture from deep within. She inhaled it and it almost seemed the world's harmony was restored.

His hand stopped. "He is determined, no?"

It broke the spell. She became aware of the absence of a running stream, the poverty of a communal bucket for washing. "Father's luck returns."

"His *suerte?*" Quiet, disbelieving. After a while his hand resumed its stroking and he murmured, "Once you said a woman lives in her man's house, in the place of his choosing."

"In the home place of her man's people," she corrected. But *Españoles* wandered far from their homes. Breaking the connection, she rolled to the side and nestled her head on his shoulder. Was he asking her to stay in this place of his choosing? Could she stay without the others? It felt like a snare, and she couldn't say more.

His hand circled absently on her shoulder and after a while he spoke as if to himself. "My home is where I put my helmet." Rising on an elbow, he kissed the tip of her nose, his eyes dark in the fading twilight. "And, *Amapolita*, my helmet will be where you are, wherever that might be."

Joyful at the concession in his voice, she rose on an elbow and rubbed his furry chest in longer and longer ovals. Maybe he remembered that none of the old ways applied in these changing times. All was in flux, all power scrambled, hers hibernating since she had yielded to him. But Father's sudden strength gave her a sense of awakening.

"The home place gives good luck," she said. "And we hide well. We can bathe at night when no one sees."

"Often they kill the men and take the women for themselves."

"We are wary as mountain lions," she assured him, loving the contours of his chest. "And Perrimacoo is there. He and Elitha might help us."

"Don't count on it." The undertone of acceptance came through the whisper.

The first stars winked in a deep purple sky. She leaned down and kissed his thickening, lengthening man's part. His groan sounded in her depths. In his trembling and her voraciousness for him the future floated away and their nexus obliterated all.

74

"Mrs. McCoon. I gots a letter." It was Mr. Packwood's voice.

Elitha dropped her knife, wiped her hands on her apron, and hurried outside. Sure as anything a dollop of civilization had come to Rancho Sacayak. Every other day Mr. Packwood carried letters from the gold camps to Sacramento, then rode back the other way. And every five days a teamster came with supplies.

She reached up for the letter, executing a reflexive curtsy with her "Thank you."

He touched his hat, his smile lingering longer than necessary, and kicked the horse up the trail. Tearing open the envelope she sat on a stump. It was from Catherine Sheldon.

March 20, l850

Dear Elitha,

Just a note to say I'm still planning to come with Mr. Sheldon on Easter day! That's April 3. Remember? We said we'd have tea like real ladies? Well let's do it! The Mister says there's a new eating house over in Cooks Bar! Sally and Elizabeth want to come too. So don't forget! I'll be there helping Mr. Sheldon decide where to build our new cabin — someplace on that 300 acres across from you. The Mister does not want to leave me and the babies alone with all these bad men roving the countryside.

Elitha looked up. Not in a hundred years would Perry build a place so she could be near him while he worked away from home. Heaven knew, it might be a hundred years before he got around to working at all. No. That wasn't fair. On his better days he went down to the river and charged for helping men get their animals and supplies across the river. But the Indians had spoiled him for hard work, and now they were gone. She looked back at the slanted handwriting.

We know you have to cook breakfast for the miners, so we'll be there mid-morning! Love, Catey.

Post Script: Isn't it dandy about Mary Murphy!

All she knew was that she'd run off with a Frenchman, who bought a ranch up on the Yuba River. Mary had done the unthinkable, yet by all accounts was contented as a bug. Where was the pain? The everlasting suffering that befell such women? You stayed with a man until death —

She shoved back the weight crashing down from the attic of her mind and penned a happy note to Catherine, saying how much she looked forward to the tea, and how glad she was that Sarah and Elizabeth were coming.

EASTER DAY, 1850.

One by one the miners pushed back from the table, or, if they ate outside, stood up and held out their pokes. From each open bag Elitha took a pinch of gold and dropped it into her can. Twelve men this morning, in three shifts. The last said "good-day," jammed on his hat and headed for the diggings.

She transferred half the dust to her secret can and stacked the plates. Taking the leftover biscuits and a pan of clabbered milk into the oak forest, she laid them on the flat rock for Indian Mary. A chunk of a boulder had split off and fallen before the mother rock. It reminded her of the stone tablets of Moses, one leaf upright, the other flat as an altar.

Yellow and purple flowers bobbed on either side of this wilderness table, and she admired the spring beauty all around, half expecting Indian Mary to step from the trees. A ground squirrel piped his alarm from another boulder. "It's only me," she told him, loving these moments with nature.

The food seemed an offering on this Easter morning, and suddenly she heard in her mind the voices in the tent under the snow: Low in the grav-y lay, Jesus my Savior — The wrong words to an Easter hymn. But a grave it had been. And about this time of year, when Ma and Pa had finally died. *Spring death.* She shivered, though the breeze contained hints of the summer to come. When would she see her little sisters again? Not very soon if Perry could help it. Lately he'd lost all self-respect and lay in bed most of the time. He didn't even ride much or practice rope tricks. The adobe was an unfriendly place, no place for children.

Pushing away the uneasy thoughts, she hurried back. Indian Mary would return the pan to the rock, still not daring to come to the house. The Indians hid like deer. How did they eat now that the river vegetation had been demolished? And relentless hunters cleared out the game to sell to miners. The old village was full of bad women, and the roundhouse was a hotel, with blankets partitioning the spaces. What dark things transpired within those walls she didn't want to imagine. Sometimes Perry took the can of gold and came back smelling of rose water. But it didn't matter much to her.

Back in the adobe she lifted the drape. He lay half off the bed, one leg on the floor, odors of spilled liquor and his unwashed body strong. He'd gambled in Cooks Bar until late, hadn't been home even in the wee hours when, by moonlight, she had finished preparing today's dinner and hoisted it into the oak.

The dishes could wait. It was almost mid-morning and Cooks Bar was a quarter of a mile away. What fun it would be to see Catherine and Sarah, she thought as she undressed to wash. She hadn't seen them since Mr. Keyser's burial in February, and a burial was no time for a proper visit.

Unable to use the river any more, she sponged herself from the bucket. Snuffling sounds came from behind the curtain. She held her breath, hoping Perry would not wake up. Snoring followed. Good. But when she lifted the corner of the curtain and reached for her new brown frock, his eyes opened. She whisked the dress from the peg and dropped the curtain.

"Goin someplace be ye?"

"I told you. To the Eating House — with the Rhoads sisters." She slipped the frock over her knickers and camisole.

"That were Easter."

"Today's Easter."

He groaned.

She buttoned her bodice.

"Expect me to cook dinner for the rascals do ye?" A threatening tone.

She had two kettles of stew already simmering over the fire. "I'll be back in time."

"Ye better, or I'll smack yer backside."

Swallowing humiliation, she combed her hair, ducking and bobbing to see in the small mirror. Some of the fine hair evaded her as she tried to turn it into neat rolls around her ears. *Haste makes waste.*

"Bring me the morning taik!" he yelled.

She jumped, dropped the hair. Now she'd have to start over. Hurrying in with the can, she gave it to him and turned back.

He grabbed her hand. "Kiss fer yer man." He puckered his lips, not having shaved for two months.

Lightly kissing the bristles, the stench of his breath turning her stomach, she tried to pull free.

"Not so fast, lassie mine. Me thinks a little pokin would feel good about now."

"Oh Perry, please not now. I gotta hurry, so I can get back and wash the tins in time for the noon meal."

But he was stubborn and his physical state was such that it took him an eternity to satisfy himself.

Angrily she made her way over the half-dug ditch, which was intended to divert the river from its channel. Gummy clay stuck to her shoes. She was late. She'd had to sponge off again, and redo her hair. Furious at Perry, though she had no right to be — it was her duty — she threaded her way through pits and mounds.

Men doffed their hats and said, "Howdy, Miz McCoon." They watched her struggle to lift her shoes, which grew heavier with each step. How they dug in this muck she'd never know. It didn't fall from the shovel. They had to scrape a boot down the face of it, then scrape the boot on the shovel edge. When the ditch was finished, she'd need a bridge to get to the river, but then again maybe she could use ditch water, if the mud ever settled.

"Top o' the day," said the grinning red-headed Irish boy named Vyries Brown. "Fine vittles they was this mornin." His name rhymed with diaries.

Preoccupied by the fear that her friends would think she'd forgotten them, she forced a smile and made her way around Vyries' rocker and between the staring men. Wasn't there flesh enough in the old roundhouse to go around? she asked herself in vexation. They acted like they'd never seen a female.

The river ran brown now. It amazed her how quickly all the trees had been cut. Scraping her shoes so she wouldn't stick to the planks, she crossed the water on a teetery, makeshift bridge balanced on boulders. On the opposite shore, equally barren of vegetation, she dodged pits, longtoms and cradles, all manned by miners who suspended their digging as she passed.

"Hello, hello," she repeated as she slogged by, trying to hurry. As she climbed the bank, the footing improved, but her shoes seemed to weigh forty pounds apiece. The tents were thick, long underwear strewn over the guide ropes. What had been an open meadow less than a year ago was now a town pockmarked with hoof holes to trip the unwary. The town backed up to the oaks, which continued to recede as new wooden structures were built.

She arrived at the plank building that bore a large cloth banner across its front — COOKS BAR EATING HOUSE — and scraped a shoe on the bottom step.

She almost didn't see the tall man smiling at her, the corners of his blue eyes slanting downward across his generous cheekbones. Ben Wilder. She caught her breath.

He removed his hat. "How do you do, Mrs. McCoon."

"Why, Mr. Wilder, I haven't seen you in the longest time." The surroundings came into focus — the precise lines of the tents against the blue sky, the oaks with pale green halos. The Goddess of Spring had touched the world with her wand.

He stood before the steps gazing down. "Been gone since November."

She liked looking straight into his eyes, though she stood on a step. Few men were that tall. During his brief visits she'd appreciated his gentlemanly manner. Schooled, she recalled, in Rhode Island. Twenty-eight years old, ten years younger than Perry. Suddenly uncomfortable in his gaze, she went back to adding curls of clay to the pile beneath the step. "Tried your luck someplace else?"

"Luck?" He threw back his head and barked a laugh. "Why I'd believe Lady Fortune had retired altogether if it weren't for the beneficence she bestows on others." The corners of his wide lips lifted.

Forgetting her hurry, she asked, "Just where was it that Lady Fortune failed to bless you?"

"Downriver. Near Daylor's Ranch." He continued to look at her, but not rudely. "Didn't have much time to prospect, for all the politicking."

"Politicking?" She smiled. He WAS just the kind of man who could speak easily to crowds. Abe Lincoln. That's who he brought to mind — Pa's young friend. Ben Wilder was much handsomer, but he had that same loose-jointed lankiness and amused confidence. But California wasn't yet a state, and no counties had been organized, so what was there to politick about?

"Keeping the masses from rising up." His easy manner invited questions.

Looking anxiously at the door, she forced herself to end it. "I'm having tea with my friends this morning. Good to see you again. Maybe you'll . . . stop by? Like you did? I'm cookin meals now." Feeling her ears burn, she nodded, lifted the brown fabric, and hurried through the door, hearing: "Be a privilege." She turned and smiled.

Inside, her steps echoed on the wooden floor, the room empty except for the three sisters sitting near the kitchen. Sarah raised a hand in greeting. Catherine twisted around. Walking between the rows of tables and benches Elitha heard her heart thudding. She'd been anxious to see her friends, but now a delayed surge of excitement coursed through her, and the Rhoads sisters had nothing to do with it.

"We thought you'd fallen in a pit." Catherine said, her familiar grin helping quell Elitha's unthinkable thought.

"Sorry. Perry was sick." She felt as rattled as the dishes clattering behind the kitchen door. "Did I ruin our tea?"

Catherine's lips blurred in an exasperated buzz. "Silly goose. Course not." She pointed to the bench across the table. "We're just glad you could come at all, with all that cookin yer doin."

Settling next to Sarah, she felt her cheeks redden. A woman cooking for a living was to be pitied. Sheldon and Daylor's Indians were gone too, but they got by without their wives selling meals. Nicely dressed in new frocks, the three smelled of good soap, every hair of Sarah's blond bun in place.

Elizabeth looked cheerful as she scolded in a mocking way, "Now look, you made her feel bad. She's to be admired for keeping house and home together." She had a delicate attractiveness, but had never been as prosperous as her sisters. Her husband had drowned two months ago ferrying men and animals across the river. Elitha had sensed the Rhoads family hadn't taken it very hard, the drowned Austrian having had Indian wives and nobody knew how many "pickaninnies." The thought brought Johnson's Ranch to mind.

She leaned forward on her elbows. "What's this about Mary Murphy?"

Catherine beamed a grin. "You didn't see it in the *Times*?" Seeing the wag of her head, she continued, "Her Mr. Covillaud is dividing his ranch into a town and it's to be named Marysville. Isn't that grand!" Her smile was infectious.

"He must love her very much." Fire and brimstone would come later.

"Ever so much," Elizabeth was agreeing. "Good thing she up and left that low-down excuse for a man she married the first time! But Mr. Covillaud is a Catholic and they're saying she won't be accepted in their church."

Watching the kitchen door open Elitha realized she'd never met Mrs. Gordon, the proprietress. Out came a frightfully skinny woman with a face like an ancient lava flow. Her eyes sparked beneath apelike brows, like the witch in Pa's Hansel and Gretel story. The line of her mouth widened in a lipless smile. "You girls ready for my famous brandied peach cobbler?" A younger version of Mrs. Gordon came from the kitchen.

Everyone nodded for cobbler and told Mrs. Gordon how they wanted their coffee and tea. The two women whisked their black skirts out and shut the door.

Amusement flashed in the three pairs of eyes and Catherine's gold watch bumped on the table as she leaned her bosom into it, her whisper threatening to explode into laughter. "Mr. Sheldon says," she nodded at the door, "she brought six daughters to California to find husbands." She pressed her lips together until they quit quivering. "They all, even the youngest, is — " she paused to gain control, "WAY past marrying age."

Feeling fortunate to hail from a family of comely women, Elitha learned that the Gordon women had come from Missouri, having spent the winter in Drytown and Amador. "Do they all work here?"

"Most of em work up at Willow Creek and Forest Home." The best hotels around, Elitha knew. Musicians played there and she longed to go hear them.

Elizabeth whispered, "I'll bet ever one of em gits a man afore summer." A sudden flush rose on her neck and she looked down.

Catherine and Sarah stared at their sister, her pink cheeks flanked by twists of honey-hued hair. With men outnumbering white women so heavily, she'd likely had offers during her two months as a widow, living as she did near Daylor's busy store. Even the shopkeeper, Mr. Grimshaw, was a fine young man. Ben Wilder had been there too, and that brought to mind his mysterious statement: *trying to keep the masses from rising up*.

The homely women returned and set flowered china around the table. Straightening, smoothing her apron, Mrs. Gordon announced, "I gotta meet the supply wagon. Lorena here'll take care of you."

As the older woman marched out the front door, Lorena fetched plates of cobbler and poured clotted cream over each. "Is there anything else you'd like?" Schooled accents. Seeing the shakes of their heads, Lorena Gordon picked up a broom and began sweeping around the other tables.

Elitha lifted her creamed tea and looked at Sarah over it. "One of the miners said you had trouble down near your place."

"You ain't heard?"

She shook her head, sipped.

Catherine jumped in. "Squatters are running rampant, burnin everything in sight for firewood, even the planks off the outhouse! They butcher the cattle and hold big feeds at our expense. Steal horses too. The Mister had the worst of the thieves hung and sent a petition down to the sheriff. It declares we hafta protect our property." She shook her head, the impish grin replaced by a troubled look, the brown bun frayed with all the head movement. "There's too blamed many miners."

Elitha knew of the hangings, and was surprised they hadn't served as a lesson to squatters.

Sarah continued. "A couple weeks ago there was a showdown. Mr. Sheldon ordered the squatters off. We was afraid there'd be shooting."

Glancing at Lorena Gordon, who was vigorously sweeping, Elizabeth lowered her voice. "The ringleader's here. We seen him when we come in." She pointed to the floor. "Right here! Him and his brothers."

Sarah pronounced with distaste, "Ben Wilder," then forked cobbler into her mouth.

Elitha rattled her cup down into the saucer and realized she'd elevated Mr. Wilder in her mind, imagined him as a civilizing influence.

"It's bad for Captain Sutter too, up at Hock Farm," Sarah said. "The Mister says the Captain's lost thousands of horses and cattle. Havin a conniption fit about the squatters too, when he's not drunk." She and Catherine exchanged a glance.

Mr. Sutter had been at his Hock Farm since the arrival of his wife and family. Elitha had heard the jokes from Perry, the gist being that the befuddled gentleman was firmly under the thumb of a shrill "fish wife" — one who slammed the door in the faces of his old drinking cronies. And young Indian girls were not to be seen on the place.

Lorena Gordon dragged the broom to the table. "Can I bring you anything more?"

"Not me," Elitha murmured, knowing she should invite Lorena to call on her, but was of no mind to just now.

Lorena's craggy face brightened. "You can't imagine how AGREEABLE it is to meet young women of GOOD character. My sisters and I are starting a Christian morality group to discuss how best to bring the PURIFYING female influence upon this WICKED country. We'd be obliged if you all COULD join us."

The Rhoads sisters exchanged a glance.

The rail-thin woman continued: "We might invite the Reverend Fish here to Cooks Bar. He HAS been preaching temperance in the southern mines. Men WILL listen to a speaker of such persuasion." She pursed her lips and furrowed her prominent brows. "This community needs a man of his character."

"We'll think on it," Catherine said reaching into her pocket.

Elitha displayed her thimble of gold dust, wrapped tightly in a length of cloth. "Yes. I'll think on it too. What do we owe?"

It was decided that each would pay her own two pinches — the brandied peaches having been dear. Lorena headed for the kitchen to fetch her pay can.

A nerve-shattering scream shocked Elitha to her feet. The benches toppled back as all four rushed toward the kitchen.

Captain Juan stood between the work tables, naked but for a loincloth, horror stamped on his dusky face. His arms hung limply from his hunched frame. Lorena swayed, then slowly sank to the floor.

75

Maria waited behind an oak, the bikoos weighing heavily on her back, Isabella being nine moons now. Father had allowed plenty of time after the last *Americano* eater left before he entered the big wooden house. She had come with him, hoping for a glimpse of Bad Face, who regularly filled Father's basket.

Every three sleeps he went to the house and returned to the boulder hideout with a full basket. "The new people are many," he had said. "We must make friends with those who live in the place of our ancestors."

"How?" Broken Salmon had asked.

"The same way we befriend wild dogs. One at a time." Maria was proud of the way he was adapting to the changing times. Not all *Americanos* were bad. Many smiled at *Indios*, and she never forgot the admiring way they had looked at her in Sutter's camp. Spear Thrower reported that he had been approached by friendly *Americanos* who talked with hand signs. But Stalking Egret had been fired at by white hunters, as if he'd been game.

She felt torn. By conquering fear, Father was healing his soul. Pedro warned him every day, but Grizzly Hair declared, "Every man must find his own way." Besides, bringing supplies to the hiding people made him more of a headman, no matter how much food Pedro brought in his saddlebags. Hadn't Etumu's spirit directed that Father should be in the home place? He was courageous and wise, but Pedro looked at him with tight lips. The tension between them upset her.

A woman's scream shocked her, jerked her back to the present. Isabella whimpered, awakened. Had the scream come from the wooden structure?

Grizzly Hair lurched out that very door and headed toward her, faster than she'd seen him move since the lead ball lodged in his back. He limped along in his loincloth, which he wore in deference to *Americano* ways. Why was he hurrying? What was wrong?

In a short time a fringe of shovels and picks spiked the air, then hats, as a swarm of miners came up from the river and rounded the tents and buildings. Diggers, she called them, enjoying the joke that *Americanos* called her people Diggers — because the women dug for bulbs. But anyone could see which group did more digging. They poked their heads in the eating house, then, to her shock, stampeded after Grizzly Hair, who was in the open coming toward her, though he didn't know she was there.

Fearfully she stepped back from tree to tree. She must protect Isabella. Father started to run then stumbled and fell. A gun exploded. Her heart stopped and she squatted with her back against a tree and hurriedly pulled the bikoos off, to quiet Isabella.

The shouting came no closer. Preparing her spirit to see Father dead, she rolled to her hands and knees and peered around the tree. He was alive! On his feet, being herded toward other trees by the Diggers. Señora Daylor and Señora Keyser walked behind. Then she saw Elitha and Señora Sarah coming. They would help. Where was Bad Face? She would help too. Pedro had ridden away this morning, telling them all to stay hidden. He wouldn't return until late in the night.

The crowd stopped beneath a tree. "Git a rope," she heard.

"Hang the Digger! Hit'll be a lesson to others."

"Hangin's too good! I say whup im to death."

Her bowels felt loose. These were the blackbirdmen.

"He didn't do anything," Elitha said, but her voice was drowned out by the shouting. Barely breathing, Maria reached for her calm.

A narrow-faced woman in high shoes ran toward the men with skirts gathered. Her hair was pulled tightly back from prominent brows. Bad Face. "Let that pathetic Indian be!" She had a voice like a screech owl, elbowing her way through the crowd.

Every man turned.

"I give that old beggar scraps all the time. Why he's tame as a pussycat. Lorena just didn't know. She fainted to find him in the kitchen, is all."

A jumble of overlapping talk roared. A tall man spoke calmly. People listened, then shouting started again, blackbirdmen chirping. Maria made out: "Not on yer life . . . rope . . . Injuns'll cut him down." Again they were herding him, back toward another building.

Bad Face yelled. "Leave that Indian be, I tell you!"

They took him inside. After a long time Bad Face, Elitha and Señora Sarah came out and disappeared behind the tents. Most of the *Americanos* went back to the riverbottom with their shovels and picks. Feeling as if she were nothing more than skin stretched over a huge beating heart, Maria waited. She heard nothing.

"Perry, please go and have them cut that Indian down!" Unable to watch as they strung him up by the thumbs — the "lenient" punishment settled on — she had hurried back to the adobe. Perry knew these men. He gambled with them all the time. Surely he'd made friends despite the fact that he, as he jokingly said, was a "Mexican rancher."

He sat on the bed and finger-combed his dirty hair, which was beginning to be flecked with grey. "Expect me to risk me neck, do ye, fer that 'eathen what shot me pigs? Forgot that, did ye?"

"But he — "

"I'll tell what he did. Refused to wash gold for me — his whole bleedin tribe. Wye, if I ent had to pay Jared that fifty cents a day extra fer every Indian, we'd a had a pretty penny by now."

"Perry. It's Easter. Where's your pity? His people were massacred. Everything they eat is trampled under the mud or killed by the white hunters. He only wanted a few biscuits."

"Hangin by the thumbs ent so bad, not fer an Indian. They don't feel pain like whites do. Hit's done all the time — five days at a stretch." He looked up at her. "Yer Easter miracle is they didn't kill him on the spot, or cut off his balls." In the sunshaft, the pinpoints of his eyes were surrounded by red, white and blue.

Did he ever think how many times she'd looked into those eyes for help only to know it wasn't to be found? Did he remember what Mary Murphy did? But Captain Juan was the important thing now. After serving the noon meal — she must start on it now — she would locate Ben Wilder. He had turned miners around before, maybe he could do it again.

A freckle-faced boy stepped part way down the bank, boot sliding in the mud. "Mr. Wilder, Miz McCoon's looking fer yah." Like a happy terrier he pointed up the bank.

Ben scattered his shovelful of gravel into the upper end of the Wilder rocker and followed the finger. There stood the angel of the adobe cabin, seeking him out personally. To Asa and John he said, "Be a minute," and hurried up the bank.

Her contralto voice was demure. "I'm ever so sorry to disturb you, Mr. Wilder, but, well, I couldn't help but notice how the men listened to you over there." She pointed with her head across the river. "And I — " She stared at her clasped hands, a flush creeping up her cheeks.

"Did you think we should have killed the Indian?"

"Oh no!" She looked up sharply, confusion falling away. "He's a poor old man with a bad injury in his back. And it was true what Mrs. Gordon said. He couldn't possibly have hurt Lorena. I was there the moment she screamed. He must be cut down immediately."

"But what if no one else had been there, and Lorena hadn't been able to scream for help? That's what worries the men. They feel responsible for protecting you women." He gazed into her huge brown eyes and remembered somebody had said eyes were the portal to the soul. He wanted to know what lay behind them, but she was married and reason must prevail. "I had the feeling Lorena wanted him killed."

"You won't try to get him cut down?" A hard edge.

Disagreeable sensations crawled up his spine. Lack of conviction rarely afflicted him, and he'd felt certain until this minute that justice had been done in the matter of the Indian. The savage could have raped Lorena, but even if he was only begging, Cook's Bar was a growing community. That kind of behavior wasn't to be tolerated. "What do you care about a Digger?"

"He was the chief of the village that used to be here."

"Chief?" He couldn't help but smile. Men claimed to have spied naked Indians living in underground dens and eating bugs. Such primitive beings didn't have the organizational sense to designate chiefs. They weren't like the warriors of the plains.

"Yes. And he was grand, like Chief Delaware."

"That skinny old wretch?" He recalled the beautifully beaded and befeathered Sioux. Was it possible a tattered loincloth denoted authority among beings naked as jays and proportionately lower on the chain of life? Her interest in the Digger interested him.

"His people were all killed, and," her cheeks colored, "his daughter is a friend of mine." She looked at her muddy shoes.

Such a girl admitting such a thing! His heart went out to her. Before the gold discovery no one else lived around here. She must have been lonely beyond reckoning, with that gambler husband of hers riding off to distant card games. Maybe she'd nearly lost her mind. Now she looked young and vulnerable, yet a certain stubborn dignity showed in the tilt of her chin. Strange, the way the courage of her admission attracted him all the more. He found himself saying what he wouldn't have believed five minutes ago. "I'll go over and see what I can do."

A heavenly smile stretched her lower lip. It was the first time she'd looked her age — only seventeen years old, and the sight of her standing there hit him like liquor hits a drunk, every fiber craving more.

She curtsied. "I'm obliged, ever so much. I'd come with you but — " She looked back over her shoulder. "I gotta get back."

To McCoon, he knew. "I'll do my best."

A few minutes later he was glad he hadn't made any promises. Looking through the open boardinghouse door, he saw Jared Sheldon, that son-of-a-bitch who had thrown him off the Slough House digs. Ben had nearly smashed his flinty jaw. Now, assaying the drift of the conversation in the building, he realized Sheldon also wanted the Digger cut down.

The proprietor retorted, "You'd better git on outa here Mister Sheldon. Who d'ya think you are anyhow? Tellin us to go soft on Diggers! We got ladies to protect, and businesses."

A plump young girl stood beside Sheldon, gripping his arm. What was the man doing here in Cook's Bar anyway? Just like those highfalutin so-called Mexican ranchers to think they owned the whole damned countryside. This one had the nerve to point to a distant peak and claim it was his property line. Not an inch fenced! Why, he'd even hung white men. By thunder, these throwbacks to the Spanish Empire lived like kings, and contrary to United States law — a hundred and sixty acres being a normal limit. Not till hell froze over would a United States court allow these huge tracts to stay intact. This grandee would have been history too if Ben hadn't calmed the mob, and no thanks had come his way either. So now, was he about to jump into this argument on Jared Sheldon's side? Damned if he would!

He was out of there before the bastard turned around.

Helplessly, Maria watched Bad Face leave the building. Then Señora Sarah and Elitha left. A tall man left. Next Catherine and Señor Sheldon walked away. But Grizzly Hair remained inside. She would wait for dark, then look in. The first coyote howled. Isabella fussed. She put her to her breast. No gunshots had sounded. No cries came from the building. No sounds of whipping. They could have cut his throat; they didn't care that he was a man of knowledge Her milk didn't flow, though the baby was pulling hard.

Later, cold descended with the dampness and she shivered. Loose spirits moved about in the dark. A warm trickle ran down her back from the bikoos, the baby wetting through the oak moss. She got to her feet and walked quietly toward the wooden building, careful to avoid the dried holes horses had punched into the clay in time of rain. A squashed moon had risen over the tents and houses and hung awkwardly at the side of the sky. Coyotes yipped near and far. Oil lamps glowed inside most of the tents and winked from the windows of the big wooden houses. Occasional shouts of muted laughter came from throughout the town.

Squares of light fell out both sides of the wooden building. She crouch-walked along the moonless side, only about two body lengths from a neighboring tent. Fortunately the miners in the tent were busy. She saw their shadowy figures playing with cards and lifting bottles to their mouths. Beneath the window of the building she slowly raised up until her eyes were over the sill. Men sat playing cards and smoking. Others slept. She swept her gaze around the lumps of blankets, to the shadows in the back.

Her heart stumbled. Father hung by his thumbs, stretched thin, toes just off the floor. His ribs jutted above the concavity of his belly, the thong loose on his hipbones. He looked dead, thinner than ever — thumbs big and round, head forward, long hair over his face. Then his head came up, hair parting. *Alive!* Their eyes locked, and she felt his absolute helplessness. Her vision swam with tears.

She sent her thought. *Maybe Pedro can help*. How late would he return? Too late?

Go quietly, father said in his thoughts. *Now*.

She circled through the dark forest upstream of the town, shadows startling her. Grizzly bears and mountain lions hunted at night, and Bohemkulla, the fearsome road spirit who attacked lone travellers and scrambled their minds. She stepped across the Sacayak boulder and swam the stream above the boulder falls, paddling like a dog to keep Isabella's head above water. The river-baby spirit touched her and she began to feel the pull of Grandmother Howchia calling to her.

Ashore in the moonshadow of the oaks, her feet recognized the familiar path to the old village, the ridged boulder cresting the trail like a turtleback. Danger lurked about, not only from unpredictable spirits. *Americanos* camped in the old village. She could smell them. In a torment of conflict, wanting to hurry to the boulder hideout in hopes Pedro had returned, but knowing he would be very late tonight, she stood still. The safest route was straight back into the forest. But when she looked up through the tracery of branches, moonwoman told her to heed Howchia's call. She moved toward the tree.

Gone were the u-machas and cha'kas, dark *Americano* tents pitched in their places. Light spilled from the dancehouse, flooding the small amphitheater before the doorway. It beamed up from the smokehole into the branches of Howchia's tree. As she approached the light, all else darkened around her and she bumped her toes on the tongue of a wagon.

Laughter stopped her in her tracks. A man and woman came to the dancehouse door. Naked. Chalky white. The man was prepared to couple. She hunched down into the semblance of a rock. The river had awakened Isabella, but she rarely made noise. *Stay silent.* Men's voices muttered, and she saw the red tip of a *cigarrito* moving in the darkness, back in the trees. Blackbirdmen. Waiting to take turns with the women who lived in the house of spirits. The woman pushed the eager man away and squatted to urinate. They didn't know this was a place of sacredness, that their actions placed them in danger.

They went back inside, embracing as they walked — the erratic spark scribbling in the darkness — and she continued her careful steps to the rear of the dancehouse, one foot before the other, already beneath the outstretched arms of the tree, which flourished in the mound. Out of view of the blackbirdmen she stepped up the familiar soft earth, toes sinking, the pull of Grandmother Howchia intensifying. She stopped at the trunk and let herself merge with the tree. Fear dropped from her shoulders. She embraced the healer she had never seen in life. Her arms reached only partway around, but she pressed her cheek and breasts into the furrowed bark and felt Grandmother's spirit.

Father hangs helplessly, she said without words, *though he went in friendship to the strangers. They could kill him. My strength has waned and I cannot help him. I will send Pedro, but I fear for him too, Grandmother. They could both be killed. I am ashamed the condor robe was stolen. We suffer much because of it.*

The tree spoke. *Molok's robe cannot be retrieved. Do not be sad over it in this time of upheaval. You have power, Granddaughter, but follow your man. He is a warrior. He faces danger for you. Trust him now. Keep your children under his protection as long as possible. Learn from my son. Keep the knowledge of our people. Pass it to your children. Better times will come.*

Trust Pedro. Gratefully she leaned against the sculpted bark. She had done right to follow both Pedro and Father — though their ways were different. This cataclysm would end. "Thank you, Grandmother," she whispered aloud.

Feeling rested, she left for the boulders where she would wait for Pedro.

76

Pedro considered himself a soldier with a holy mission. On his way to the boulder hideout long after dark, he recapitulated. Three of the killers of the Omuchumne remained alive. But dispatching them wasn't his sole mission. He stole gold from the miners, who destroyed everything the *Indios* ate — miners from all lands, except those who spoke Spanish. Some of them were *malcriados* too, but he had limited daylight hours, and plenty of others were willing to part with the gold in exchange for their lives. Singlehandedly Pedro was keeping large numbers of *Indios* alive.

Not only did he keep Captain Juan's group fed, but he made the rounds of others in hiding — starving, filthy women with singed hair reduced to prostitution in exchange for crusts of bread, and once-proud men, now walking skeletons brave enough to beg from those who had destroyed the waterways and annihilated fish, game and food plants. *Indios* were routinely shot for begging. Men who had once hunted deer by stealth and cunning now stole food in the night, though massacres were the common punishment. These people were dying of disease and privation, but considered of no more consequence than insects.

Ay, ay, ay. A bandit. Not long ago he'd been a good soldier, though a little independent. But he couldn't help but think, as he picked his way though the dark, that if Mexico hadn't lost California, he would be heading for his hacienda, and some of the *Indios* dying in the hills would be his grooms and herders. As a people they would have been a large and useful labor force. The sons and grandsons of Spain knew the souls of the *Indios* were beloved by the Virgin, equal in the Church, knew that one harmed them with trepidation. Spanish law was the sword of the Church. But in this barbaric land Pedro was the sword — a lonely *bandido* living a dangerous life, one who would have taken his family to Mexico long ago, except that every day he saw more *pobrecitos* who needed help.

A crooked moon provided little light as he approached the boulder-crowned hill. He let Chocolate find his way. As he dismounted, María surprised him. Not asleep. She told him Captain Juan was hanging by his thumbs in a big sleeping house! Ay, ay, ay, why didn't he stay in hiding?

"*Por favor*, go cut him down and bring him home," she said.

"You think I have magic, *Amapolita*, to walk into a lion's den and ask the beasts to hand him over?" He threw off his black wig.

"You are a *bueno* warrior, *mi hombre*."

No man could refuse that tone. He kissed her full warm lips, then woke Quapata and the two other *Indios*, and rode toward the boardinghouse, still wearing his *Norteamericano* disguise. His auburn hair was distinctive, different from the black *bandido* wig. He would scout the place and figure out a plan. Quapata, Spear Thrower and Stalking Egret trotted alongside, bows in hand, quivers full. Each of them could take two men before anybody knew what happened, and with his new Springfield rifle, Pedro could hit a running rabbit through the eye. But that was only a start on the twenty to thirty men in the boardinghouse. You never knew how many. When they were "flush," miners paid to sleep inside. He would use cunning, the *Indios* serving as backup.

He waved them into the shadows of the trees, draped the reins over the limb of an oak and crouch-ran to the building. Peeping through the window he saw the floor strewn with men. Four groups sat hunched over cards, four oil lamps. Haloes of *cigarrito* smoke tied the groups together. He made out the shadowy mounds where the hips of sleeping men pushed up the blankets. Barely visible all the way in back hung Captain Juan — skin-sheathed bones, but clearly alive. What had gotten into him anyway, to walk into the Eating House kitchen like that?

He studied the card players — *Gracias a Dios* no familiar nose and beard combinations. The color, curl and trim of beards made men easy to remember. But like flies to horse dung, miners moved around after gold strikes and he had to be careful his former victims didn't recognize him. *Señor Cuidadoso*, other *bandidos* called him. Nothing wrong with being careful, the two full pouches pressing on his belly told him. That gold was the mainstay of the plan forming in his mind. The greed of miners could be counted on. He would stake his life on it.

He returned to his horse and took three monte cards from his saddlebags and slipped them into his sleeve. Swinging the bedroll over his shoulder he walked toward the front door and pushed it open.

Heads jerked up. *Bueno*. Nobody familiar.

He smiled and glanced around, and when he located the proprietor, said in his accent, "Howdy. Got room for one more?" His eyes met Captain Juan's. The *Indio* looked down, motionless as a crucifix. Seeing his swollen, blackened thumbs, Pedro cringed inwardly, but *Madre de Dios*, he was lucky to be alive. Maybe this would teach him.

A rough-complexioned man of middle years, who had been reclining with his jaw cupped in his hand, pushed to his feet and sauntered toward Pedro. "One pinch, up front. No vittles."

Pedro untied a purse. The man extracted a huge pinch, then nodded toward the wall. "Drop your roll over there."

The card players watched from hooded brows as Pedro stepped over and around sleeping men and lowered his bedroll beneath the window. Rifles lay scattered around the room, and most of the gamblers had handguns in their belts.

A big blond card player spoke in singsong, "You dona talk alike a Yankee."

"Transylvanian," Pedro responded without hesitation. He remembered a hair-raising ghost story Captain Sutter told about the place, and hadn't met anyone who knew the accent. "I play monte," he said brightly, as if just thinking of it.

Men beckoned from all four groups.

Bueno. He joined the nearest game, and with a great show of concentration made foolish mistakes. Miming the stunned greenhorn who couldn't believe what was happening, he lost steadily. One by one players from other games drifted to his circle, dragging their blanket rolls. The other games folded.

"You find a goot vein, ya?" asked a man offering a bottle of whisky.

Pedro took a slight swallow and almost saw their ears perk up beneath greasy locks. "Yup." He knew that game. Get him drunk and pry the location out of him.

Two men removed their boots and happily wiggled their toes. The stench of unwashed feet thickened with the smoke.

Briefly lifting the corners of his cards, Pedro glanced around with an expression of one who thinks himself wise, and emptied his purse onto the pile of gold dust, turning it inside out, shaking it, patting the dust from the folds.

A needle-nosed man with rat's eyes in a scooped out face turned over his downed cards and revealed a matched pair.

Angrily Pedro threw in his cards and exploded, "Thunder weather!" A comical oath Captain Sutter used — Transylvania being somewhere near Switzerland, he figured it would work.

Needlenose laid down the edge of a newspaper and swept gold onto it with tender strokes of his little finger. Finishing he said, "Guess I'll turn in." He rose, hitched his pants.

A grizzled *viejo* offered Pedro a bottle of brandy, asking, "Your claim in the neighborhood?" He stretched out a leg, bending it as if to see if it still worked.

"Yup." Pedro said, taking a taste and handing back the bottle with a pained smile. "Hoped to double today's take." He sighed and jerked a thumb at Captain Juan. "What's he done?"

"Skeered a decent woman half to death," said the proprietor.

"Beggin pervert," muttered the *viejo*, rising painfully. He cocked his head at the *Indio* and said, "Ain't they sum'm. Don't never make a peep. Whup em, hang em, don't make no never mind. Nary a peep."

Pedro shrugged and smiled, then drew out his other purse — the big one — opened it, yawned and said, "Men, I'm tuckered, so all this stands on the next hand." He tilted it so all could see what he'd lifted from Big Bar this afternoon — maybe ten thousand dollars. As they settled in their former places, suddenly wide awake, he set the rules:

"If any of you wins, the winner gets half, the rest split the other half. On the other hand, if I win —" He glanced tiredly around the room, stopping at Captain Juan. "If I win, you cut him down. He walks out, and I get the gold." Looking at the surprised mouth holes in the array of beards, he shrugged. "I can use him in my digs. Besides, it's Easter."

Men bolted from their blankets to join the game. The proprietor shuffled and dealt, and now Pedro played monte in earnest. Those tedious years at the Presidio hadn't been entirely wasted. Perhaps Lady Fortuna would smile on him as she sometimes had done then, and he wouldn't need the trick.

The Swede shuffled, setting his bottle before Pedro. Needlenose cut. The proprietor dealt four down, one up. Needlenose checked his hand and squeezed out a handful of gold on the floor, where the cracks between planks were packed with sparkling dust. Pedro leaned down to the floor and peeked under his card. *Cabrón!* No luck tonight. And slipping cards past these hawks would be tricky.

Something — he didn't know what — made him turn around. He looked up and met Captain Juan's gaze for a stunned instant. It almost seemed he was trying to speak without words — María said they talked "from head to head" all the time. Pedro heard nothing, but read intensity in those dark eyes. Men were making little thinking noises as they considered their cards, and he turned back to the pensive faces around him, several sucking on *cigarritos.*

"Mebbee the Digger won't walk," said a man eying the card he had just drawn from the bottom of the pile.

Pedro took a card from the top of the pile. With his breath coming shallow, he reclined on his elbow, jiggling the hidden cards down in his sleeve, and looked at the worthless card while positioning his wrist for a quick transfer. A muscle twitched in his eyelid. *Dios del Cielo*, the things he did for María!

A piercing, inhuman cry reverberated in the room. He jerked his head up. Everyone was looking at Captain Juan. With a single move he swept the cards in his shirt and replaced them with a new set. His heart kicked like a horse in his ribs and he looked calmly at the men as they turned back to the game.

"He done peeped," Needlenose observed.

"Yup," *el Viejo* admitted, smiling at his cards.

But Pedro was not smiling. Perspiration felt clammy on his forehead. His cards lay badly askew. Casually he pushed a corner of the worst one, straightening it a little. Did they suspect? Poker faces were part of the game, and not even a maddened grizzly was more dangerous than a roomful of cheated gamblers.

But the proprietor added gold to the pile and Needlenose dumped half his poke on the heap and guzzled brandy. Pedro slowly released his breath. *Gracias a la Virgen!* In the aftermath, his arm felt trembly as he extended his heavy purse to the center of the circle and plopped it on the plank beside the loose gold.

Their eyes slid over the gold, over Pedro. Willing his runaway heart to quiet, he slowly turned over his cards. *Cabrón!* The colors were faded! Deciding whom to shoot first and second and third — by then the arrows of the *Indios* would be flying — he forced a surprised smile.

"Hit cain't be," said a man who had until now been quiet. Hostile stares lifted to him.

His accent came ragged. "At last I have good luck." Alert to every move in the room, he put his feet under him, squatting, concentrating on the exact locations of his Allen pepperbox four-shooter and his skinning knife, beneath his belt on either side. "Now we cut the Indian down," he said, reaching for the gold.

"The hell with the Injun, I say som'm stinks." Nobody moved.

El Viejo squinted at Pedro, his eyes hidden beneath tangled brows, "This here worked out jest right fer ye, didn't it, Transylvanian."

He withdrew his hand. "Most of you finished better than I. No?" He spread his hands, trying to look reasonable. The accent sounded wrong. His eyelid twitched.

"Yah knows?" said Needlenose looking around at the men. "This here sounds like a Mexican to me."

A knot tightened in his innards. Blood tingled in his legs, telling him to run. About this time he'd normally be leaning over Chocolate's mane, hooves digging distance between him and his adversaries. But normally he had their gold. Now they had his. His purse sat before him on the floor and he didn't dare reach for it. And they still had Captain Juan.

The proprietor eyed him. "I don't do business with Mexicans."

"Thunder weather!" Pedro exploded, leaping to his feet. "I'm no Mexican." He was a lion mid-spring, not knowing where to land. Ay ay ay, soon he'd be hanging beside Captain Juan, and not by the thumbs.

Something moved. He turned to see a Colt in the proprietor's hand, aimed at him. The men on the floor reached for his purse. In the poor light the proprietor's pitted complexion added menace to his voice. "Why don't we all jest loosen up a mite and play us another hand."

The miners sat back, leaving the gold where it was. "Sounds fair to me."

"Me too."

"Yup."

"Ya iss goot."

But it was not good. Ignoring the gun, he gestured dramatically around the room and the lion in him roared, "Another hand! I thought you were gentlemen!" Raising his nose and bracing his feet, he welcomed the torrent of rage that broke the dam and let him speak with passion. "I am an honorable man. I came as a friend, to patronize this establishment and maybe find an honorable partner for my rich claim." Several faces relaxed into eyebrow-cocked interest. Greed.

His words echoed within the plank walls, resonating with the force of a practiced singer able to project to a thousand head of cattle. "You won a big purse from me." He looked the proprietor in the eye, lowered his gaze to the Colt, "And now you pull a gun on me because I win one lousy hand. Now cut that Injun down!" He pointed like the accusing finger of God.

The Colt nosed into its home under the belt. Outside the light of the oil lamps men sat up in their blankets, rubbed their eyes and grumbled obscenities. A number of gamblers stepped back from Pedro, exchanging glances. No one moved for a weapon.

Seeing the calming effect of his outrage, he roared one last volley. "You men have no honor!" Reaching down, he snatched up his poke and jammed it into his shirt, silently praying to the Virgin the cards would not dislodge and fall. No one moved. He pointed at the piles of gold dust on the floor. "Keep your own filthy gold. I would not touch it."

From the blankets came a sound like a wounded bear followed by: "Fer Crissake, cut that fuckin Digger down and let me sleep or I'll carve somebody's liver out!"

The proprietor hurried to the corner, whisked a chair beside Captain Juan and stood on it. He slashed a strap, Captain Juan's weight swinging to one thumb. The *Indio* winced, trying to stand on the tips of his toes.

The Swede drew the chair to the other side and sliced through the other thong. Captain Juan's knees buckled as he hit the floor, but he regained his balance and stood working the nooses from the stems of his ballooned thumbs.

He seemed taller. Had he stretched? His eyes spoke to Pedro: Gracias. Pedro acknowledged the look and nodded toward the door.

"Here," said the proprietor taking a pinch from the pile of gold the squatting men were dividing. "This is for your trouble. Stay here tonight, on me."

"I have no wish to stay," he said, proudly turning his back to the outstretched hand. With Captain Juan he walked swiftly toward the door, keenly aware of rapid footsteps scurrying in the room, following him. Not breathing, he continued without turning — feeling his back like a target.

"You'll need this," said Needlenose.

He whirled, took a breath, and cuffed his own head with the heel of his hand, then accepted his bedroll and rifle. "Thank you."

"I can dig with the best of em. Make ya a damned good pardner." The rat eyes pleaded from his dished-out face.

Captain Juan went out the door and Pedro looked over the men in the room, their easy posture. He smiled at the ugly man. "Maybe I come back. Maybe we talk tomorrow." He swung the roll over his shoulder and gripped his Springfield.

Crouch-running along the moonless side of the building, afraid they'd come for the gold — as he would have — he joined the four shadows. Not until they crossed the river did he breathe freely. Captain Juan sat behind him in the saddle, the *Indios* trotting alongside.

Turning, Pedro said, "It must have been very painful."

Captain Juan hesitated only a moment. "First time in many moons back no hurt."

77

Pedro pulled María to him. Her lips moved with his, the sweetness of her breath feeding his appetite, making him want to stay. He shut his eyes, wondering what Joaquín Murieta wanted with him. Jesus Gonzales hadn't said what the meeting was about, only that Murieta's closest associates would be there. He pushed her away, holding her by the shoulders. "I will be back in two days, *Amapolita*."

Her black eyes glistened in the morning sun. "I will wait for my warrior."

He loved that. This child wife of his was a diamond in the gravel of his life, and, no Señor, he was not too proud to bask in her adoration. He had finally learned how to read past her *Indio* mask. Last night he'd seen her joy when he brought Captain Juan to the hideout.

Kissing her one more time, he mounted and waved at Quapata, who was staying to see that Captain Juan didn't try anything foolish in his absence. In the high grass before the cathedral-like boulders crowning the hill, the children — strangely silent Little Flicker among them — waved to him. *Indios* didn't believe in saying good-bye; they'd learned it from him. He reined the horse and rode away.

The day was warm but pleasant along the flank of the hills, big swathes of yellow and purple flowers in the green grass. Giving wide berth to the mining camps and the trails to his prime "hunting" grounds, he made his way through thickets of live oak, a hawk circling and crying high overhead, and reflected that Murieta must have a joint raid in mind, something really big. Pedro's own reputation had grown and some said he rivaled Murieta for the title of the "real Joaquín." Other "Joaquíns" tried, but didn't measure up in horsemanship, or careful planning. He loved nothing more than leaning against a porch in some boomtown listening to stories of his own raids, his machismo wonderfully exaggerated.

Like the hawk, the wisp of an old story seemed to follow him, lurking at the edge of his remembrance. Something about a young man being drawn into a forest and the ground opening up and swallowing him. No fire or devils greeted him, but instead pleasant men whose skills he admired. They taught him their tricks and secrets. He couldn't remember how the story ended, and wondered why it came to him now.

Puzzling over it as Chocolate picked his way around rocks and fallen limbs, it suddenly occurred to him that Murieta was an antiquated word for death. An omen? Death for all who stood in his way? Murieta taunted death and was young and brave enough to get away with it. A Castillian, *bonito* in the way a flattering artist would paint a young man, he was light-haired, almost blond. An angel of death. He dressed liked a true *caballero* too, and he had more machismo than any twenty-year-old ought to have. Pedro thought back over Murieta's exploits. Warfare it was actually, like in the forests of old Spain.

Many *Norteamericanos* coming to the mines didn't seem to realize the war with Mexico was over. Nowhere had the trouble been more heated than around the hills of the mining camp called Sonora. Murieta and his brothers and sisters had been among the thousands of Sonorans to come north to try their luck. They had staked a family claim not far from where Pedro rode now.

Experience gave the Sonorans a big advantage over farm boys and bankers. They knew how to read color and trace it to its source. It was they who removed most of the millions from this area. Jealous *Norteamericanos* whipped, hung, and shot them, even passed a law that "Mexicans" — by that they meant anyone who spoke Spanish — could not own mining claims. Pedro smiled to recall the furious merchants, no longer able to gouge the "greasers," having the law repealed. But *Norteamericanos* trailed the Mexicans and jumped their claims like eggers following quail to their nests. That was why, on that fateful night, they attacked Murieta's camp. And when they violated Joaquín's Rosita, they made a very big mistake.

Rumor had it Murieta had been lashed to a tree and forced at gunpoint to watch. That was one reason Pedro didn't want María travelling with him. She and the children were safer with the other *Indios*. Quapata had the Allen pepperbox and knew how to use it.

It was evening when he rode into the secluded camp, open on all sides beyond the copse of trees. Good visibility and escape routes in all directions. He dismounted and hobbled Chocolate near the other horses. Murieta came across the inner clearing to hug Pedro, one side then the other, his dark blond hair luxurious on his shoulders. "Bueno, *Señor Cuidadoso*," he said, not hiding his pleasure. "Gracias for coming to my humble camp." He even smelled young, beaming his hundred-candle smile at the other men as though to have them admire his prize.

The six men came forward to greet him. He already knew Jesus Gonzales. The other five spoke on cue, signalled by Murieta's subtle nods. Most were even younger than the young lion. Pedro unloaded his bedroll and positioned it by the fire as a backrest, and made himself comfortable while the two women, disguised as men, offered meat and beans from a still-warm pot and a stack of tortillas wrapped in muslin. Rosita and Teresa.

The food was piquant and *sabrosa*. Gonzales playfully pinched Teresa as she stacked wood by the fire. Her black eyes snapped with fun and she slapped him and ran away. Pedro liked her, liked the fire he saw in both women. The feel in the air was expectant and fresh, men on a dangerous mission, and he realized that El Cid and his men so many centuries ago probably camped at such fires with such a feeling in the air.

Across from him, Murieta reclined with catlike grace, his eyes somehow directing everything that happened — the serving of food, the placement of the men, even the story-telling. Everything fit into his scheme, except Pedro. It had been a long time since he'd fit anybody's mold. But it pleased him to be here, and he was happy biding his time until the lion revealed his purpose. As the spring night dampened and chilled around the friendly fire, he realized he was the *primo* guest, the one whose presence in the lair pleased Murieta the most.

Murieta nodded at Valenzuela, a Chilieño with an Aztec nose torqued to one side. "Tell my friends about your escape near Hornítas."

Valenzuela pushed up his hat, hanks of inky hair falling from it, and told of a night attack by a posse. His close-set eyes glinted as he described how he had jumped into the branches of a tree and swung out over a cliff. He and two *compadres* found themselves barely able to stand on a narrow ledge high on the wall above a steep cañon.

"The *Norteamericanos* searched for us and we heard one say, 'Look, the branches are broken. Let's go get them.' They were braver than we thought, *muchachos*. We heard the branches crack and knew they were coming. So we shot at them in the dark and tried to hurry along the ledge. They shot back — four times as many of them. I was hit. We all were. Bullets flew around us like bees, and tree bark, and chips of rock from the cliff. We lay down and slid down the steep gorge, praying we would not die. I almost did. Doña de Guadalupe! It was the closest I ever came to heaven." He hoisted his *pantalones* to show a scar on his calf. "I gashed that on the way down. Cracked my skull so hard I didn't wake up till morning." Murmurs of appreciation circled the fire.

Murieta all but whispered, "Ah, but you had a hundred horses stashed in the next cañon." With a smile on his lips, he narrowed his eyes at Pedro. *Pay attention to my man*, he was saying.

Pedro told how he'd gambled for Captain Juan and what he'd said about hanging being the only time his back didn't hurt. The men slapped their knees and chortled. Gonzales tipped up a bottle of whisky, ahhed as it went down, and said, "You never know what is funny to an *Indio*. Once I heard Apaches laugh while they slowly cooked the brains of a man hung upside-down over a small fire." Back in the shadows the women paused, listening as they prepared bedrolls, only their eyes reflecting firelight. Gonzales continued, "To the *Indios* it was funny, like a rabbit caught by an eagle. 'He was careless,' they say. 'He offered himself. And now the joke is on him.'"

After a deep silence, Joaquín Murieta raised his head and the fire highlighted the streaks in his mane. "Did I tell you about my friend who fought with General Santana?" Hats wagged and lips turned up in pleasant anticipation.

"My friend he was very brave and much admired by the women." Murieta was soft, like the paw of a mountain lion. He stalked his enemies with the same concentration as he charmed the *pantalones* off women. Now he all but purred and Pedro struggled to hear him over the crackling fire.

"One night he was on his way to Texas. He and his men camped near the Río Grande to wait for ammunition. It was about nightfall and they looked down the hill over a small village. My friend saw some señoritas walking to the cantina." His lips curled up at the corners and he glanced around the fire. "My friend, he can see a señorita five leagues away."

Smiling, Pedro leaned back on his saddle and sipped the cup of whisky-spiked chocolate that Rosita had made him. The fire felt good and he enjoyed Murieta flattering him with solicitous looks.

"About twenty soldiers slipped away and went down to the cantina to make the acquaintance of the beauteous flowers of the desert. Before long my friend had the prettiest one, and she took him to her house." He surveyed the expectant faces. "That is true, *amigos*. My friend, he always has the prettiest girl. And what I tell you next is true also."

The purr softened and all breathed quietly to hear, Murieta extracting subordination from his disciples. Or was it only that he didn't want the women to hear?

"Suddenly shots rang out. *Norteamericanos* shooting in the plaza. For my *amigo* this happened at a most embarrassing moment and he could not find his *pantalones*. So he ran outside in his shirt, and he was outraged at the bad manners of the dogs who would steal Texas. His friends joined him, but the bad men were already galloping away. My friend, he says, 'These are worse cowards than I thought!' His *compadres* looked down at his naked front and said, 'No *amigo*, they fear your cannon.'"

Laughing, Pedro realized how much he missed the company of men who had learned Spanish at their mother's knee. He'd been something of a loner at Sutter's Fort and at Sheldon's rancho, straddling the worlds of *Indios* and *Norteamericanos*. But in childhood he had run with a lively group of boys, close as brothers. He saw that same closeness now, around the fire. It touched him, tempted him.

Murieta's brother-in-law Claudio was telling about some men who got into a fight in an old adobe in Mexico. "They threw each other against the wall and the plaster broke, and Spanish coins fell out, very old. The kind brought over on the galleons from Spain." Eyes gleamed around the fire and Pedro recalled that Grandfather Valdez had sailed to Mexico on such a ship. Anything from old Spain fascinated him, maybe because he'd always felt like a far-flung son, a seed trying to root in these hostile northern rocks. Claudio leaned forward.

"Let me tell you what else was found behind the plaster of a wall. This happened at Alamos, an old silver mine not far from La Colorada." He told of a brother and sister separated when they were very young. The girl grew up far away, but returned to Alamos. Not knowing one another, the two fell passionately in love, and when their father found out, he put her in the wall and sealed it, because they were brother and sister. For many days the people of the pueblo heard her cries, muffled and strange. "It was her bones those miners found. And it is true. Her bones are there to this very day. No one will go near that old house." Claudio looked around at the men. "Every night her ghost moans and shrieks. You will hear it if you go there."

Wood shifted on the coals and the glow from the waning fire barely lit the shadowed men. Pedro was contemplating the sin of incest when Valenzuela said, "I thought you said the mines around Sonora were closed because of fighting and revolu — "

"Some *vecinos* remain there," Claudio said, "They scratch around in the slag left from centuries of mining." He looked at Joaquín Murieta. "Some of our family."

"Señores," said Murieta, sitting up, "I have been thinking."

Now it comes.

"You are all brave *bandidos*, and our enemies ride stiff-legged on mules. They cannot shoot straight." He glanced around at the smiles. "Every one of you can ride circles around them." He told of his home in Mexico and said that working as a disciplined army they could drive large *caballadas* down there, and his family would sell the horses at a big profit, and convert gold dust to coin. "In a short time we could have a million dollars each. For the rest of our lives we would live like Spanish grandees."

"Kings," Valenzuela amended.

Pedro suddenly realized how tired he was of riding alone and how much he enjoyed this brotherhood. Though he often felt close to Quapata, *Indio* language and superstition divided them. With María it was different; a man enjoyed mystery in a woman. But mostly he was tired of hiding her and the baby. He was too old for that. He no longer wanted land in Alta California, where he wasn't wanted, and he knew that he could grow old stealing gold for the *Indios* and still not come close to what they needed. The thought of ending this dangerous and frustrating life thrilled him. He could just as well have his *rancho grande* and beautiful hacienda in Mexico, and put María in it. And he wouldn't need to look over his shoulder every time he stooped for a drink of water. He dipped his hat at Murieta and said, "We would live like kings."

The young lion lounged back on an elbow with his mane caressing a shoulder. He smiled, eyes slit in contentment.

But there was a limit. "Each man keeps his own gold," Pedro added, doubting if any of these men did as well as he.

Valenzuela's back stiffened in the shadows. "No Señor. We divide our profits equally. We always do." The other five nodded vigorous agreement. Somebody said, "Share and share alike."

Before he could respond, Joaquín Murieta beamed a smile at Valenzuela. "Of course. You are right, my friend, about the horses — those we help each other herd. That is natural. Our friend Señor Valdez speaks only of the gold which we take from the obliging miners, no?" His hundred-candle-power smile turned on Pedro.

The supreme confidence was fascinating, disarming. "Sí," he said, "And if four of us cooperate, those four divide the gold."

Murieta nodded at the reluctant men and extended his hand toward Pedro. "We have much to learn from Señor Valdez."

The men exchanged glances but grunted approval.

Silently chuckling, Pedro couldn't help but give Joaquín Murieta an admiring snort and wag of his head. Later as he sank toward sleep, rustles and moans of lovemaking came from Murieta's blankets across the coals, and he reflected on the oddity that a man so young and vigorous would bear the name Death.

With coyotes laughing across the hills he floated into dream and rode with shadow men through the underworld. Weaving among the hooing owls and shrieking night birds, he suddenly found himself apart from his fellows, imprisoned in a strange crystal palace. People peered in but he could not see out. Terrified, he opened his mouth to yell for help, but no sound came out.

78

LATE SEPTEMBER, 1850

Summer still blew relentlessly across the destroyed land and up the hill to the adobe. It could have saved its hot breath, Elitha thought as she dipped beans from the sack. Everything had withered six months ago, including her young apple tree. She looked up at the oblivious vultures gliding across the dusty blue, apparently deaf to the clank of picks and shovels in the riverbottom. The incessant sound of digging grated on her nerves. And that wasn't all.

Ben Wilder had been avoiding her. He hadn't eaten at her table even once, and she knew it was because she had been forward. He hadn't done the favor she'd asked either. Hadn't said a word on Captain Juan's behalf, a customer told her. Well, he was nothing but a selfish Forty-niner out for himself. Yet she dreamed about him — long sensuous dreams that left her stunned.

Angrily she dashed a half bucket of water into the bean pot, then singed her rolled sleeves — eyes narrowed against the wind of the flames — as she struggled to lift the pot shoulder high, finally pushing the handle over the hook. She went inside. It was cooler, the only good thing about adobe. She unwound the newspaper from the seven-dollar-a-pound beef she'd bought from the teamster. And to think she'd once been surrounded by cattle! But she had to offer more than wild game if she expected to compete with the eating houses. The four-pound slab of meat stuck to the paper, quivering as she pulled it off. Her stomach bucked. Gulping hard, she took the honed knife and cut the flesh.

The maroon halves parted smoothly behind the blade. A warm animal odor rose from it, a smell deeper and fuller than blood alone. She dropped the knife and ran outside, bent forward, spewing chunks of brown and pink, the salt pork and biscuits of breakfast. Connected by strings of mucus, it draped over the parched grass. Again and again she heaved, crying from her mouth, retching from her soul — sick of the scorch of fires, the clank of shovels, Perry gambling away the gold, sick of knowing, yes, knowing she was pregnant again. Knowing she couldn't leave him and that she had been stupid and piteously self-deceitful to think Ben Wilder would whisk her away like Mary Murphy's Frenchman had. She heaved out the truth with the last strings of spit. Even if he had, she wouldn't leave a husband and run away, because Donner women didn't do that.

Feeling weak and trembly, she wiped her mouth with her apron. The bean pot hung too low in the flames. Straightening the tripod, she headed inside, but the meat-smell turned her back. She went to the shelter of the split rock where, three years ago, she had buried a gold nugget, and sank to her knees. The boulders stopped the worst of the Devil Wind and twigs cracked beneath her.

As a little girl she'd never thought life would look bleak, hadn't imagined being pregnant would feel like this — the birthing fearful yes, but not the sickness of wanting a man to know her secret heart. She scraped back a rich accumulation of decaying vegetation. Perry was as oblivious as the vultures. She knew he would laugh at the girl she'd once been, sitting in the apple blossoms, and she believed, clawing in the dirt, that he had deliberately stood between her and her little sisters. Two years had elapsed without a word from them, the house as crude as ever. She pulled the nugget from the earth, exactly where she'd buried it.

It lay heavy in her palm. She brushed off the encrusted earth until rich glints of gold shone through. Someday when she found her sisters, she would have lockets made for them, with Donner inscribed on the inside, and they could carry a lock of hair or some other small hidden treasure.

Horses approached. She looked out and saw Perry, who had shaved and combed for the first time in weeks and ridden away early. He and another man dismounted. Perry stuck his head in the house, then yelled around the yard, "Elitha, hit's company."

She dropped the gold in the hole and patted the earth in place. Wiping her hands on her apron, she walked dutifully toward the house. The meat was seething, boiling with layers of small yellow and black striped bees, so thick they held the smell in.

Perry pointed at it. "Seein how much the yellow jackets can eat, be ye?" It was a tone meant to amuse a guest, but it perturbed her to have him talk to her like that in front of a stranger. Perry looked old. Not just weathered like a woodsman, but aged. His eyes swam in a permanent film and his nose had grown lumpy and purple-veined. The missing tooth made him look ruined and simple-minded.

The other man removed his hat, displaying reddish hair on a thinning pate, and she recognized him as one of the men at the fort; he'd been there when she and Perry returned from San Francisco. Embarrassed to forget his name, she looked at the insects.

"George McKinstry," said the man. "We've met before."

"Elitha McCoon." She gave him a hint of a curtsy. "At Captain Sutter's table." In rough clothes then, he now wore dark broadcloth like an Illinois banker. "You still the sheriff?" He didn't wear a badge, and she hoped Perry wasn't in trouble.

"No. I prefer to get paid for working." He smiled. "A pleasure to see you again. Perry and I been talking about the news." As if seeing her confusion, he continued, "You haven't heard? California's a state now."

"Is that a fact!" She was truly surprised. The papers said Congress had been stymied for more than a year debating the slavery question.

"That's right. We're in the Union now. The thirty-first state. Word came yesterday. Like I was telling Perry, the newspapers came on the *New World*. She's a paddlewheeler, come out of New York only two weeks ago. Can you believe? Cut the record in half I heard. You should have seen it! Men running all over town and galloping around on their horses waving the papers and hollering, 'California's admitted and Queen Victoria has a baby!'" He chuckled. "Shootin off firearms to beat the band."

"Are we free or slave?" she asked. The South had supporters in California.

"Free."

She released her breath. "I'm so glad for the Indians!"

He looked at her funny. "Has nothing to do with them. Just Negroes."

"I don't under — " A glance at Perry slowed her down. Very peevish. He didn't like her speaking up about men's affairs.

"Indians are a different situation," Mr. McKinstry was saying. He looked at Perry. "Mrs. McCoon takes to politics I see. You tell her what the Legislature decided?"

With his eyes on McKinstry, Perry wrinkled his nose her way like this was too complex for her poor mind and said, "She don't need to know. Clean up the table, lass. We got important business."

That vexed her. "Perry, I've heard Indians are bought and sold all the time and I want to know if ours are still in that kind of danger, that's all."

Perry started to open his mouth but the ex-sheriff was saying to her, "The only time Indians can be auctioned is if they're found to be loitering and strolling around or being immoral, you know, unemployed. They're arrested as vagrants.

But they're not bought and sold outright, so the laws of slavery don't apply."

Seeing that Perry looked resigned, she continued, "Who auctions them?"

"Towns, counties, after they're in custody."

"Do they get paid? Can they leave if they want?"

With a look at Perry, McKinstry assumed a concluding tone, "Well now, they're getting their keep and learning the arts of civilization and that's pay of a kind, and no man wants his workers to up and leave. So no, and no." He looked to Perry as if to say, let's get on with business.

Giving the man a grateful glance for talking to her, she took the broad side of the knife and scraped the meat, insects and all, onto the newspaper, carrying it at arm's length with yellow jackets swarming all over and bouncing off her wrists. But she was thinking about the Indians. They could all be called vagrants, except those who were employed. And most people thought they were immoral. So it sounded like an excuse to get free labor and for towns to make money. Why didn't the anti-slavery laws apply? Glad not to be stung, she placed the meat on the stump by the firepit. The black men she'd seen mining didn't have to worry about being captured and forced to work for somebody else, but Indian Mary and her father did.

She took the pot to the ditch for water, deciding to boil the meat whole and cube it when it was done. Nobody would know, and the muddiness didn't matter; the grit sank. She'd learned not to scrape the bottom of the gravy. And there was something else she wasn't scraping the bottom of either. Free. What did it mean? She sat down and waited for the water to simmer, then dipped the floating insects out. Was she free? She worked hard and felt trapped, even though her customers paid her. Perry took what gold she couldn't hide, and played with it. That's what gambling was, playing. He didn't gather wood or fix the house, and of course men didn't cook or wash the plates. In the beginning he'd worked with cattle and mined gold. But not since he lost the Indians. Yet he wouldn't be arrested as a vagrant, or be auctioned like a workhorse. He was white.

Perry came outside with Mr. McKinstry and they shook hands. Putting on his bowler hat, Mr. McKinstry nodded at Elitha, mounted, and rode away. Something flew into her eye and she was rubbing it when Perry said happily, "Lass, it's on the road to riches we be now!" He extended a poke filled with gold for her to see. "Twenty-five thousand dollars it tis! And a fraction of what I'll win when the speculatin's done." It was the first time in weeks she'd seen his dimple.

She blinked at the gold dust. What on earth had he sold? What did he have to sell? Then like a slap, she knew. She couldn't bring herself to speak, knowing he'd lose the gold quickly and soon she wouldn't even have a house to cook in, to make a living in, never mind how crude.

"Well ent ye going to congratulate yer man?"

"You sold the ranch."

"Not too feebleminded of ye!" He held the purse before him, admiring it. "But only the ground up there at the road."

"Not the house?" She heard her uphill tone of hope.

"Not daft entirely is this man o' yours." Despite his pleased expression, she detected a heaviness behind it, like even he didn't believe in future riches.

Relief didn't cancel the despair or the hot wind. She wilted, sank down on a stump in the shade. "Oh Perry, I was so afraid for us, and — " she made herself say it, "our child. We need a place to live."

With a sudden "Wahoo!" he threw up the purse and caught it. "A babe is it!"

She couldn't even smile, and at that moment caught sight of Indian Mary in the trees, holding up a bundle of herbs. For the retching.

Several months later Perry slid down from his horse, dragged himself into the adobe and announced Bill Daylor had died. He threw himself on the bed.

Stunned, Elitha stood by the bed though a yard full of men waited outside to be fed. Perry hadn't been nearly this dejected when he'd lost the gold. But then, he'd lost it by stages, every night having expected to come home with it doubled. The trip to San Francisco to speculate with the "big boys" finished it. Now he looked nearly dead himself. "What of?" It didn't seem possible anything could fell a man so full of life.

Perry turned toward the wall. "Cholera morbus."

Cholera. Brought on the steamship carrying the news of statehood. The newspapers screamed with stories about rampant sickness in Sacramento City, the scarcity of doctors, the lack of hospitals. Disease was reported in the mining regions too. Poor Sarah!

Early the next morning she drank Indian Mary's tea, which stopped the nausea, hung out her NO EATING TODAY sign and pulled the brown frock over her head for the first time since Easter. The waist buttons couldn't be coaxed together. With a sigh she counted. July, August, September, October. Four months pregnant, going on five. She slipped a clean apron over the gap and sadly tied the strings behind. Even at the funeral she'd look like a woman who had to cook for a living.

Perry gulped the last of his whisky and went for the horses. He'd been drinking worse since he'd lost the money. She ducked to see herself in the tiny mirror, pinning her hair, and heard his call, "Elitha, damn it to hell." As if Daylor's death were her fault.

"I'll be right there." She must be careful with him today. Daylor had been his best friend.

He muttered as she rushed to mount her mare, and didn't get off Paint to give her a hand up. It was a bright autumn morning, the last cottonwood left standing flashing yellow leaves against a blue sky. Soon they'd cut it too. As they rode past Mr. McKinstry's new plank store and house, which he'd built near his bridge, Perry grumped, "Taiks me land for a song 'e does, then builds a bridge to steal me customers!" Ferry customers.

Mr. McKinstry's bridge spanned the river at the narrowest place, and every time a heavy supply wagon went across, the timbers bounced like rubber. On the opposite bluff Mr. Sherwood had also built a store, on Mr. Sheldon's new ground, and next spring Mr. Sheldon might build a cabin over there. Civilization was springing up all around, yet it seemed to Elitha that she would live in that crude adobe forever.

The eight miles to Rancho Omuchumne were long, and Daylor Road was crowded with wagons and teams and riders with picks and shovels jutting at odd angles from their saddles. Many men tramped by on foot, pans dangling. Perry barely nodded to them. Celestials in peaked straw hats and cloth slippers trotted with odd jerkiness. Daylor Road was busy, but Daylor was dead. The first time she'd seen the road, it was nothing but a faint pair of wagon tracks leading to what seemed the end of the world. Only three years ago.

And it didn't seem fair that Mr. Daylor was dead twenty-four hours after acting the Good Samaritan. He had gone to Sutter's Embarcadero for supplies for his mercantile, and on his way back stayed the night at the old fort, which was nothing but a derelict sleeping place now. Hearing a moan, he discovered a sick man on a pile of old straw. He gave him a drink from his cup and tried to make him comfortable, but the man died during the night. At his store the next day, Mr. Daylor felt ill as he unloaded the supplies. Sarah put him to bed, and he was dead in two days. By a fluke Perry had been there.

Now as they approached Daylor's store Elitha saw the long wooden box in a wagon. Sarah stood beside it, tall and elegant even in grief. *Not pregnant*. How many times had Elitha thought that as she looked at her? Now she would never have a child by Mr. Daylor.

Mr. Sheldon raised a hand in greeting. His wedge of a face looked older, stricken. At his side stood Catherine, visibly pregnant, toddler Will at her knee and little Sarah in her arms. Dismounting, Elitha nodded a greeting to John and Matilda Rhoads, who were keeping their children in tow. Also in the yard were the new neighbors — the big Wilson family, who had built a bridge and Wilson's Exchange on the other side of the river. She saw the Pattersons, Elders, Cummings and others. Old Rancho Omuchumne was well populated — a white settlement around the Daylors' expanded store and a big blacksmith shop across the road. John Rhoads was building a school over by his house. The very last remaining Indians stood by the trees — two boys and a man. Perry and Elitha tied the horses to the porch rail.

Mr. Grimshaw, the young storekeeper came over, his slicked, side-parted hair so straight and blunt below his ears it seemed a shiny brown fabric. Mr. Daylor had made him a partner in the store. "You're the last," he said, "so we'll head down to the grave in a minute." He and Sarah were partners now.

Poor Sarah. She'd loved Mr. Daylor so much. Elitha went over and hugged her. Struggling visibly to keep from crying, Sarah patted Elitha's belly, her swollen eyes betraying envy. It wasn't fair at all, Elitha thought, wishing they could swap places. With a stab of guilt she stopped the thought, and said, "If there's anything I can do, just say."

Elizabeth brought a man over on her arm. "Elitha, this here is Mr. Gunn." Both sisters were widows now. In two years.

"Sorry to have to meet you at such a sad time," she said with a curtsy.

Catherine looked over at her middle. "You too." They shared a commiserating look.

Mr. Sheldon called, "Let's go."

She gave Catherine a parting squeeze and returned to Perry, still sitting on Paint, and mounted Gay-Gay.

Women loaded their families into wagons and Mr. Sheldon helped Sarah and Catherine up beside the coffin. Mr Sheldon stepped up to the driver's seat and flicked the reins, starting the procession. Elitha and Perry rode in the middle, behind the Cummings' horses, in front of the Wilson's wagon. All proceeded slowly. Elitha leaned toward Perry and asked, "Where's the grave?"

"At the old Indian *ranchería.*"

She knew the place. She had searched for grass nuts with the women and girls of that village. All dead now. She had been pregnant then. Maybe this baby would die too; maybe she would. The Grim Reaper pointed his bony finger at random.

The procession stalled at the foot of the mound that had stood behind the vanished roundhouse, people stopping the wagons and getting out. People ahead on horseback were riding up, Perry and Elitha waiting their turn. She looked up the road at the town of Slough House, the Inn's shed roof arching over the road at the far end. Mr. and Mrs. Quiggle were walking toward them, as were some of the other business proprietors. They ran the Inn profitably, though it was a rowdy place, drawing from the heavy travel between Sacramento City and the southern mines, and they paid the Sheldons good rent. Over a shop this side of town stretched a limb of the hanging tree, where Sheldon had been judge and executioner to horse thieves. The grass beneath it and along the road was green again with the recent rains, the air musty with fallen, rotting leaves. It seemed a particularly eery time for a burying, the day after Halloween.

Gay Gay pushed up the hill on strong haunches. Elitha dismounted and tied her to a tree with other horses, and walked to the pile of dirt — shovels bristling from it — that marked the open grave. The aroma of earth was strong. The Hicks family and others were waiting. She stood beside Perry while about fifty people gathered, the cheerful birds sounding disrespectful. Then the men slipped ropes around the coffin and lowered it into the hole.

Mr. Sheldon started to speak in a voice slightly frayed at the edges: "Mr. Daylor's the first white man to be laid in this Indian burial ground." Elitha had assumed it was only a hill. He continued, "No man was more beloved by the Indians than William Daylor." Glancing at the two Indian boys, Mr. Sheldon said, "No man was more respected by any of us." He swallowed and looked at the sky, blinking — Elitha wondering if she'd ever heard the name Sheldon without Daylor close beside it. He paused long and Sarah and Catherine could be heard softly weeping.

Elitha glimpsed Señor Valdez through the trees on his magnificent dark horse. He sat tall in the saddle, his hair glinting a rich auburn in the sun coming through the branches, his sombrero over the horn. Paying respects to Mr. Daylor.

Mr. Sheldon resumed: "Mr. Daylor was born in England about 1810. Didn't get any schooling at all. Except on board a commercial brig, but that was an education of sorts, and he was smart as a whip. He built the first trading post outside Sutter's Fort right here on this land. He was brave," he swallowed. "and honest." Moisture appeared in Perry's eyes, and he rolled the brim of his hat.

"He was the first to see this beautiful Cosumnes valley and convinced me it was the place I'd been looking for. And he was right about that. I gave him half and we, we always, always — " He gained control of his voice, "worked it together."

Sarah sobbed louder, half a head taller than Catherine, who supported her on one side while Elizabeth held her on the other. Mr. Sheldon pulled out a piece of paper, unfolded it and read:

> *"Last Will and Testament.*
> *Daylor's Ranch, October 31st, 1850.*
>
> *Know all men by these presents, that I, William Daylor, being attacked with cholera, as my friends think, and to carry out, and to fulfill my last wishes, I hereby appoint Jared Sheldon, my only administrator . . . as I wish him to arrange and settle all of my affairs truly and honestly.*
>
> *I, therefore, leave him in possession of my effects and property to administer — "*

"And a pretty penney 'e 'ad too," Perry whispered too loud.

People turned to look. Sheldon shot him a glance and continued to read,

> *"My wife is to have a provision made for her first. . . . My two Indian boys are to be taken care of by Mr. Sheldon according to his judgment. I being in my right mind and senses approve of the above and do so by my signature.*
>
> *Signed William Daylor, his mark.*
>
> *Witness to the above: the signatures of John Connack, Perry McCoon, Thomas Coburn."*

Mr. Sheldon folded the paper, slipped it in his pocket, looked up at the blue autumn sky, and said, "Lord, help us fathom your ways." He grabbed a spade and jammed it in the dirt and threw the first dirt in the hole. It sounded hollow on the box. "Ashes to ashes," somebody said. Other men picked up shovels.

She went to Gay-Gay and leaned her forehead on her back, the strong, warm smell of horse life in her nose, and pressed her hands over her ears to stop the sound of dirt hitting the coffin — men trying to cover up the hole of death. Death fooled a person. Before she'd left the tent under the snow she'd thought life was tougher, more tenacious. But Mr. Daylor breathed a miasma too thin for the eye to see, and even he — a strong man — was gone. She must not waste time pining after fantasies. She would walk this trail. With all her heart she would love this baby growing inside her, and maybe Perry would change.

79

One more Indian killer lay dead. Punished. As Pedro aimed the flat of his hat into the rainstorm, trusting the horse to pick his way to the boulder hideout, he thought back to the morning, when he'd roped the man's arms to his sides and run him behind the horse. He had turned in the saddle and said:

"Now it's time to think of the little children you killed. And women, and unarmed men. You remember them?" Running hard with his mouth open, the man gasped. Pedro continued, "Remember their faces when you shot them? Talk to me, *Cabrón*. Or maybe you want to run faster?"

"No, no," the man barked, wheezed and said, "I 'member. But they was only Injuns."

Nudging Chocolate a bit faster, hearing the breath coming louder, he turned back and said, "And you are only a dead piece of goat shit."

He'd used his spurs. Chocolate dug into a run, dragging the man half a league across a rocky slope. Pedro left what remained of him for the vultures. The wind had started then, and the rain.

He'd been lucky to find the man, he thought now as lashing rain stung his knuckles and trickled down his neck. Only three of those eight killers still drew breath.

He was wet to the skin. *Madre de Dios*, it was cold, and coming from the southeast again. At this angle rain drove beneath the overhanging boulder where he and María normally slept. Tonight they'd have to crowd in with the *Indios* under the lintel boulder. His guitar had been ruined long ago. He envied Joaquín Murieta and his men, who wintered in the dry cave above Spanish Camp. Ay, the things he did for María!

But his purses were full. The German outside Bedbug had promptly handed over his take. That plus the sack he and Valenzuela removed from the store made Pedro flush. And satisfied, getting the killer. He felt invincible, almost bored with danger.

Near McCoon's cabin, half a mile from the hideout, he smelled cooking meat. Pulling on the reins, he sat looking at the drenched adobe. The fire outside steamed and smoldered beneath a metal tripod, a pot over it. Señora McCoon did well to keep the fire going in this weather. She needed money, he knew. Everyone knew. Everybody pitied her for being married to McCoon.

The aroma was mouth-watering. On a whim he headed for the adobe.

Elitha rubbed her swollen belly — seven months along now — and stared out the window at the brimming brown river, wondering how she would ever get money ahead to fix the house. They still used the same slatted door; and the cross section of an oak still teetered on its stump and served as the table. At least she had four nice chairs now — a skilled miner made them in exchange for food. But with supplies so dear, she needed more customers, and with the weather so bad, and the high water, most of the miners were wintering in Sacramento City, or San Francisco.

Perry was back from the river. With his drinking curtailed by the inflated cost of liquor — she thanked the Lord for that — he ferried a few men across the water and made a little money. Mr. McKinstry's bridge had washed out, and Perry had acquired the raft Mr. Keyser had drowned on. Perry wasn't a swimmer either, but she knew he wouldn't take chances with cattle after what happened to Mr. Keyser — the animals shifting all to one side, the man's body never even found.

Perry yanked off a boot. "Neptune's bones, a gully washer she is!" He rubbed his foot. "What's fer dinner?"

He knew perfectly well. "The usual."

"No potatoes?"

"Ten dollars apiece." She gave him a level look. She couldn't even afford a newspaper. For all she knew the people in Sacramento City were still dying from cholera. Five had died in the Slough House area. Not having a paper made her feel isolated, poor.

Over the drumming of the rain on the packed yard she heard a horse whinny. She peered through the veils of moisture moving crosswise over the window, and saw a man in dark clothing tying his horse.

Perry joined her at the window. "Well if it ent the greaser."

Señor Valdez walked boldly to the door and knocked. "*Buenos dias*, Señora," he said when she opened the door, "and Señor McCoon." Perry's eyes widened. In fear? Anger? There was bad blood between them — Perry once pulled a gun on him. But the Spaniard smiled and bowed. She was sure he meant no trouble, and it wasn't civilized to leave a man standing in the rain.

"Come in," she said.

He entered like a king, smelling of wet wool. His black hat nearly touched the damp ceiling. He seemed to fill the room, the tails of his red-striped sarape streaming water. Sometimes she wondered if Mr. Valdez was Joaquín, the dashing gentleman bandit. The outlaw never struck Cook's Bar, Michigan Bar, Slough House, or any of the nearby camps. Could that be because he lived around here?

"I hope you are well?" Valdez asked warmly, carefully removing his hat and balancing the water until he pushed it out the door to shake it off.

"Git to the point," Perry said.

Elitha cringed, but Valdez merely elevated his hawklike nose and said, "I understand you serve food to travellers. Perhaps I could buy a plate."

Perry exhaled, and she hoped he'd treat Señor Valdez like any other customer. "We'd be obliged, sir," she said.

"SIR!" Perry glared at her then snapped at the Spaniard. "Five pinches to ye." He reached for the pay can.

"Perry — "

He thrust the can at the man. "I said five pinches." Normally a meal cost one.

"*Está bien.*" Señor Valdez pulled a fat poke past his Colt revolver and opened it to Elitha. "Go ahead, Señora. Take five."

She took a pinch and didn't want to take more.

The Spaniard acted fast, placing five more pinches into the can. He smiled. "One extra, for the Señora."

Maybe he was the bandit. The one that paid over-generously for meals and was gracious toward women. She set a plate and cup before him and lit the spermacetti lamp, it being dark with the weather so bad. Perry hooked back the divider curtain and sat on the bed as if to keep the man under surveillance from behind. Pulling her cloak over her head, she went outside for the stew.

When she returned, Mr. Valdez had removed his sarape and folded it over a chair. "That smells *sabrosa*," he said with a smile, eyeing the steaming pot. "Men say you cook *bueno*. Taste good."

She shrugged and asked after Mary's health. He answered politely, dipping out a plateful, not mentioning the baby.

After several minutes of eating, he twisted in his chair and looked back at Perry. "I will be pleased to buy thees rancho."

Stunned, Elitha sucked in air. The aftermath of the sale to Mr. Sherwood had been disastrous and Perry had sunk to a new low. But he rose from the bed and came to the table where he could see Mr. Valdez' face.

"Sold part of it, I did."

"Sí, and I weel buy the rest."

Dread crawled through her veins as Perry seated himself across from the Spaniard. Gold flew from his hands faster than birds flushed from a bush. Would she wind up living in boulders like an Indian?

Pedro was having fun. He'd planned none of this, but rumor had it McCoon wanted to sell land at inflated prices. Pedro didn't believe he owned a proper title to sell. Moreover his sights had shifted to Mexico, where he would live with honor. But this was too amusing to pass by. While McCoon's fortunes had gone sour, his own had blossomed. He had helped drive another five hundred horses across the border and buried a hundred thousand North American dollars in a secret place in Mexico. *Indios* talked of power. Gold was power, when you had it to play with.

He told McCoon, "I will pay thirty-thousand dollars for the remainder of your rancho." That and McKinstry's money would give the *desgraciado* a total of fifty-five thousand dollars for land he'd acquired for nothing. He bit into a warm, flaky biscuit dripping with butter and stifled a smile as McCoon labored visibly with his emotions. He would hate doing business with a "greaser," but temptation showed in his eyes and he licked his lips. He was sober and out of liquor or he'd be drinking. Once he had dressed like a grandee, but now his clothes were badly worn and the boots, which were thrown into a corner, gaped like the mouths of dead men.

McCoon jerked his head up and narrowed an eye at him. "Come next Sunday we'll have ourselves that ridin competition, we will. Or has ye forgot?"

Long ago Pedro had concluded McCoon was too much of a coward. He had never set a date. Filling his lungs, he said, "I do not forget *nada*."

"Ride then we will by Jove! Up behind the Bridge House store, where all can see and ye can't cheat. If I wins, I gits yer thirty thousand and keeps me land. If you wins, ye gits title to me ground."

As if any real vaquero would cheat, or need to, to defeat the likes of him! Pedro gave back, "I think you have no title, señor, and I win nothing."

"Yer afraid to lose, is all." He went to the bed and pulled a leather bag from underneath. "Show ye the front end of a 'orse, I will." As he fumbled through the bag, Pedro filled his stomach. Elitha stared out the window, tall, with child, dark hair swept back from a lovely pale face. She would appeal to any man. After a few minutes McCoon came back and sat in the chair across the table, extending a yellowed, dog-eared sheet of paper.

He lay down his fork and took it. Documents from Mexican governors had an eagle stamped into a glob of wax. Only Captain Sutter's swirling scrawl marked the bottom of this. Knowing McCoon couldn't read either, he pretended to follow the writing from side to side, while McCoon looked one way and then the other, glancing between the paper and Pedro's eyes.

He held the paper at arm's length as he'd seen others do, and said, "*Capitán* Sutter has written this, not the Mexican governor."

McCoon jumped to his feet. "Callin me a liar, in me own 'ouse is ye!" He jerked his head south. "Mexico ent worth a hill of beans, or 'as ye forgot? Cap'n Sutter's an official in the new gov'ment, 'e is, and a damned sight more consequential than a beggared Mexican!" His defensiveness gave him away. He owned nothing.

After he disgraced the *desgraciado* on the field, maybe he would throw the supposed land title back at him and inform him how worthless it was. "Captain Sutter, he counts *Indios, sólamente*. He represents *nada*."

McCoon put the paper on the table and slapped his hand down on it. "Good enough fer me and McKinstry, it tis, and it's damn well good enough fer a greaser!" He glowered like a tomcat.

"*Está bien.*" Suddenly he was impatient to show McCoon how to ride a horse. "The Sunday that comes, when the sun is high." By then the ground would be drier.

He rubbed his full belly and smiled at Elitha, pitying her as much as he despised McCoon. "*Sabrosa*," he said. Delicious.

80

JANUARY 5, 1851

It was a sunny spell between the California winter rains. Elitha went outside, tugging her cloak around her shoulders. Perry stood leaning toward the small mirror, which was tacked on the doorframe, the stretched wool of his longjohns sagging badly at the knees and drooping from two rear buttons. In a sudden breeze, the loose square of it luffed like a sail.

The ground was damp, the packed clay of the yard firm underfoot. "Looks like a good day for riding," she said. Droplets of moisture sparkled on grass as fresh as salad. The sun and breeze would dry out the footing even more.

"Aye, lass." With his face stretched to the razor his voice was distorted, but happy.

She headed down the path, getting an early start on the quarter-mile to Bridge House. His cheerfulness stopped her.

"Ent seemly fer me wife to walk in like that, big in the hold 'n all."

She turned to him, the honed knife dropped to his side, his face soaped white. He grinned a mouthful of teeth to match — except for the one that was missing. "If ye don't be wantin to saddle the mare, wait. I'll ride ye up." His dark wavy hair gleamed in the sun. She had helped him wash it, and his clothes, the shirt hanging over a branch with its empty arms waving. With each passing day his humor had improved, until now he seemed as saucy as the day she met him.

She nodded she would wait. Not for a long time had he shown off his expert riding, and nothing pleased him more than being the center of attention. If he won the money, he'd be drunk and dangerous for weeks. If he lost — She wouldn't think about it. For now he was the old Perry, an attractive man proud of his abilities, a man who could charm the birds out of the trees. Despite everything, she felt, what? happiness for him? a certain tenderness? She would enjoy the moment and cheer for him.

He cocked his elbows, pushed out his rear, and bent toward the mirror. How he could disdain the Spaniards, yet desire to be hailed as a great vaquero was a mystery to her. But he didn't seem to notice the contradiction. Men were like that; most admired the fancy-riding of the Californios and, like them, accepted riding competitions as a test of manhood.

"Howdy do neighbors," came a call.

She turned to see about thirty men, the remnant of Cook's Bar, swinging down the old Indian trail. The die-hards, the ones with winter claims, all on foot and crowded together.

One sang out, "Looky thar. He's gittin all prettied up."

Perry splashed water over his face and, chin dripping, beamed a dimpled grin. "On your way to Bridge House be ye?" He reached for the towel.

"Ain't a man fer miles around would miss this here buckeroo contest."

"Female neither," chirped Vyries Brown with a freckled smile. They stood a respectful distance from Perry as others appeared on the hill, including the tall figure of Ben Wilder.

"At's right," said another of Elitha's customers. "Even the Ladies of the Roundhouse'll be there."

She watched Ben Wilder's long-legged, loose-jointed walk and something about his smile raised her spirits a notch higher. He would see Perry at his best, maybe wouldn't think her entirely daft to be his wife. Somebody was saying: "Mrs. Gordon and Lorena went on up with the Hays women in their wagon."

Up the south side of the river, she knew, Bridge House being over there. Mr. McKinstry had rebuilt the bridge for the event, so she and Perry and this half of Cook's Bar, and all the people from Slough House and Cosumne would use it. If he charged for single riders and pedestrians, he'd make a pretty penny.

The crowd would be large. Earlier the Gaffneys — an Irish family Perry let build on his land — had waved as they rattled by in their wagon. Perry had invited everyone he knew. He'd posted a handbill at Daylor's, now called the Cosumne Store. Mr. Grimshaw had helped him write it. Elitha had been excited to receive a note from Catherine saying all the Rancho Omuchumne folks were coming. She hadn't seen them since Daylor's funeral. Today she would hold up her head. Perry was the star attraction.

"Go on ahead," Perry said with thrilling authority. "Taik a minute 'ere, I will. Get yerselves good places to gander from." He was a changed man.

The men started down the swale, one calling over his shoulder, "Ever one of us's got a bundle ridin on ya, McCoon." A playful threat.

"Good lads! Ent plannin to disappoint ye." His clean cheeks shone brightly in the high sun.

She couldn't help but smile.

Pedro combed Chocolate's mane with a salmon-rib comb, smoothing in bear grease between strokes. The mane and tail glistened black as the eyes of the children. They stood to one side, their brown skin a shade lighter than the horse's coat. He saw them admiring his clothing, the best from Mexico. His black trousers were decorated with silver brads. His vaquero hat was new. He'd let his hair grow long because it was auburn, different from the black wig of his bandit disguise. He doubted any of the men from the boarding house remained from last Easter. Miners were transient, but no matter the risk, a vaquero answered a challenge. This one was long overdue.

"We want to go watch," said the seven-year-old daughter of Bent-Willow-Reflected-in-Pond. The children nodded in unison, including Little Flicker, who never talked.

He glanced at María, sitting on a small boulder holding the baby. She was upset because she wanted to go too. All the *Indios* did, the children parroting what they'd heard the adults say. María said he was being too careful. Hardly a day went by without her saying, one way or another, that times were changing, that it was safer now for *Indios*.

Billy said, "My *padre* rides with you, señor. *Por favor*. I go too." His light eyes marked him as McCoon's, and he was nearly five years old.

Pedro reconsidered. In his own way the Englishman loved his son. Every once in a while Pedro still heard the boy practicing his name in English. With him there, McCoon wouldn't want trouble. In truth, it would probably be safe. Word of the contest had generated a fiesta mood. All Pedro's friends were coming — Murieta and his men in disguise, and the Sonoran miners from the Río Calaveras, and the vaqueros from Don Andrés Pico's rancho, every *Californiano*, every Chilieño and Mexican within thirty miles. The *Norteamericanos* would be matched, maybe outnumbered. That in itself was security. Maybe five thousand people in all would attend, vaquero contests being a favorite pastime, especially when the streams were swollen and mining was difficult. Men put aside their quarrels at entertainments. Many times he had seen that. And when he and McCoon were finished, others would show off their skills. No one would want the fun spoiled by violence. Least of all the merchants, who had set up tent stores near the arena — one selling cloth, buttons and sundries for women.

Women. They were another assurance. The wives of Pedro's friends were coming, including Rosita and Teresa. The Gaffney women, Señoras Gordon and Hays and their grown daughters would be there. Ramón had sent word that the women and children of Rancho Omuchumne were coming with Señor Sheldon. Now there was a man who could stop trouble. If *Norteamericanos* shared one trait with all others, it was the protection of their women. And yes, Pedro had to admit, he rarely heard of *Indio* massacres any more. The killings tended to be random and isolated. Maybe the sheriffs were putting more pressure on the slave traders. Those maggots crawled in the dark. They would not raise their filthy snouts in this crowd.

María's gaze weighed on him as he anointed and combed Chocolate's hock-length tail. He had to chuckle at himself. Fearless in encounters with desperate men, he could never could say no to her.

He turned to the children standing solemnly in line and gruffed his voice. "*Está bien*, but you stand exactly where I tell you, and stay there." He would put the *Indios* with Joaquín Murieta and his men, who would know what to do if trouble started, or if a bucking horse came too close.

The children's mouths fell open, their eyes widened. Then they squealed with delight, joined hands and jumped up and down. The *pobrecitos*, he realized, had been holed up under terrible conditions, living more like foxes than human beings. He threw back his head and laughed at the jubilation.

María came over with shining eyes. She embraced him from the back and kissed his neck, her breasts amazingly soft through his shirt and bolero. "Gracias," she murmured. To Captain Juan she called, "Come."

The big *Indio* had been watching from the other side of the boulders. Now he stiffly made his way through the rocks and green grass. "It is well, my son-in-law," he said approaching. "Big Time make friends." Speaking to the children and anyone else within earshot, he pointed to his genitals and added, "Cover up, wear cloth, *Americano* way."

Self-conscious to be pregnant in front of the huge crowd, Elitha rode side-saddle before Perry as Paint walked into the large arena defined by crowds of people. A roar of approval went up. A one-sided blizzard of hats flew skyward. Men yelled, "Show him, Perry! Give him hell!" Bottles flew high, then plummeted.

Perry turned back to her and said, "About to see an old tar trounce a Spaniard at his own game, they is." Even he didn't know all the events that would be performed. Mr. Valdez would start every other one. But Elitha knew Perry would do standing rope tricks. He'd been practicing all week.

The quiet side of the arena was crowded with more Spaniards than she knew lived in the country. Many stood in miner's clothing and sombreros. Others sat astride fine animals, the men attired in the Mexican manner. A few of their women sat on horseback too, lace mantillas draped over high combs, but most sat with children in wagons. Among the Spaniards, Indians stood wrapped in blankets — mothers and children, men in tattered shirts. She saw Indian Mary's brown face, the straight cut of her shoulder-length hair slick and shining, the baby in her arms, Billy at her side. Elitha raised a hand. Mary waved back.

Perry stopped Paint before the Sheldon wagon where Elitha was to watch. Catherine's impish grin welcomed her as Mr. Sheldon stood in the wagon to guide her transfer, Mr. Grimshaw helping. She felt big and awkward stepping into the crowded wagon.

Catherine patted the boards beside her and bubbled, "This is such fun!" Beyond her, Elizabeth leaned forward and smiled an excited welcome, as did Mr. Gunn, her new husband. Mr. Sheldon sat little Will on his lap. Beyond him, Sarah Daylor held her plump infant niece on her lap. Not even three months since Mr. Daylor's death, Sarah and Mr. Grimshaw were already betrothed; working together in the store had acquainted them. Still, she found it hard to look over there and see them holding hands.

Flouncing her frock she whispered in Catherine's ear, "We're both ladies in waiting." Pregnant. Catherine giggled at that, and Elitha smiled toward Perry, who was riding around the arena.

He looked grand in his white shirt and dark trousers tucked inside his blackened boots. His coiled riata hung from the saddle in the Spanish manner and his wavy dark hair glistened in the sun, not grayed or receding. He was proud of that, and hadn't wanted to cover it with his stained hat.

She caught the eye of John and Matilda Rhoads in the next wagon, and smiled at them and their numerous children, including twin boys named for presidents — Andrew Jackson Rhoads and James K. Polk Rhoads. With them were Sarah's twin, Billy Rhoads, two Indian boys and a man Elitha didn't know, all clapping and shouting for Perry. The eldest Rhoads boy stood and raised both fists. "Go git'em," he shouted. She saw they all admired the way Perry rode. Not a soul gave her a pitying look, and she felt happier than she had in ages.

She looked around the crowd. Men sat on horse and muleback, but most stood in large joshing clumps, well lubricated with liquor. She located Ben Wilder, a head taller than most others. He was listening to the men of Cook's Bar, who were talking up at him. It was clear they prized the attention of the tall man. She turned away before he saw her look.

Beyond the American section stood about fifty small Chinamen in peaked straw hats, long black pigtails down their backs. "Look at all the Celestials," she said to Catherine.

"Pourin off the boats, the Mister says. Got the patience of Job. The only ones who'll take the time to sift out the flour gold after the others move on." Her voice rose in excitement as she pointed at the store and waved. "There's Kate."

Fifteen-year-old Kate Beale had come from Illinois with her parents and before you could shake a stick, married Mr. Sherwood, who had built a store called Bridge House opposite McKinstry. Elitha had attended the wedding about a month ago. Now Kate was teaching in the school her husband built for her. Having organized it, he named the community Katesville — the second town named for a good friend. Kate sat waving from her chair on the porch. By the looks of the miners tramping in front of her, streaming in and out of the store, Mr. Sherwood was inside doing a brisk business in spirits. Waving back, Elitha sensed Kate's admiration for Perry's good riding. Newcomers were quick to catch on to California traditions.

A flock of women in brightly ribboned frocks and pushed-up breasts sashayed across the arena before the crowd. Their glances lingered on the men as they lifted their skirts, showing calf. As if mud were a problem!

"Brazen," Catherine breathed.

"Advertising," Elitha said. Perry would know their names. But he didn't even look at them as he floated around the arena in a graceful sitting trot, proud as any Spaniard. She could tell Paint felt the tension too. A sheen of moisture rippled on his large brown spots and his eyes were wild in his controlled head.

On the opposite side, a thunderous cheer exploded — Señor Valdez entering the arena. He sat straight-backed and motionless on his magnificent chocolate-colored horse. Neck arched, the horse slowly pranced around the circle, stepping high, its long black tail gently flouncing. The silver gear winked in the sunlight. The perfection of horse and rider sent chills up her spine. Californios were all but born on horseback, and Perry hadn't learned to ride until he was full grown. Still, even lacking the Spanish clothes and silver trim, he was the best trick rider most men had seen. She knew he would give his all to keep the Spaniard from winning.

While the two men circled the arena half a lap behind one another, an eerie thought entered her mind. Perry was like a man rising from a long sleep. A mythical man. Seeing the starch in his posture, she somehow knew the ranch and the gold had nothing to do with it. He had slipped beyond caring about such things. Even when he wasn't drunk he sometimes lay in bed for days. And now, from this low state, he had risen. Readied himself to compete with a youthful vigor he no longer possessed. It was a miracle. Did anyone else see it?

Valdez stopped his horse before the Spanish section, removed his black, stiff-brimmed hat — red-banded, red-tasseled — and bowed to his audience. The roar deepened. "Vaquero! Vaquero! Caballero!" Sombreros sailed up and down, up and down. The Celestials were cheering too.

Isolated in the quiet American section, Jared Sheldon clapped his hands together — a dry sound. Heads turned toward him. Feeling hurt, Elitha looked away, toward the wild horses and cattle being driven into a brush pen. Had Mr. Sheldon clapped for Perry? The trouble between them was a long time ago, and it seemed to her this new, risen Perry McCoon deserved everyone's applause.

The Spaniard put his hat on and his horse stretched into a smooth lope. Perry watched from the side, sitting on Paint. With an economy of movement Valdez took his lariat from the rear fender of his big saddle and began feeding it upward into the air where it opened into a larger and larger loop. He turned the loop vertical before the horse and ran the graceful animal through it. Again and again he repeated the trick as the horse cantered in even strides. Cheering from the Spanish section never let up as he completed two laps. A few admiring oohs came from the Americans.

Stopping the horse, Valdez coiled the braided leather and nodded at Perry.

Perry spurred Paint into an even stride. He took his lariat, which he had oiled with bear grease, and swung it overhead. Effortlessly he ran the horse through the loop. Twice around the arena. Once the rope touched the back hooves and she held her breath, but Paint recovered without breaking stride. Perry finished to tumultuous clapping and shouting. Elitha and Catherine stood and drummed their heels on the boards. Bottles sailed as high as men could throw. Perry had done well, and Elitha felt mild surprise at how good he really was.

Señor Valdez tipped his hat at Perry, appreciatively, she saw. Perry galloped Paint his fastest and drew himself up in the saddle, kneeling, then standing, balancing a moment before he began whirling the lariat. Elitha had seen this before, but it never ceased to amaze her. Now he looked more mythical than ever. Gooseflesh pricked her arms as he again tilted the whirling tremendously large loop and — she hadn't seen this before — ran the horse through it. Knees flexing with the gait, he regained his balance and brought the huge whirling loop overhead. On the second lap he repeated the trick without a flaw. The yelling and stamping hurt her ears. Perry retrieved the lariat, sat down in the saddle and reined Paint to the side. Running his fingers through his hair, he smiled around the boisterously cheering crowd, then nodded at Valdez.

The Spaniard's dark horse galloped until its tail drew a black line and its hooves only ticked the ground and tucked beneath its belly as it circled the arena, the rider still — straight-backed in the saddle. Spectators stepped back. Señor Valdez was keeping the area open. Then in one graceful move he was on his feet standing proudly, chest out, one boot before the other. The lariat was in his hand and he fed it upward where it lifted and widened and widened and tilted, and with the fluidity and timing of a dancer he ran the horse through the loop again and again without pause, the harmony of the rope keeping time with the drumroll of hooves. Perry had run the horse through only twice. On the second lap, without altering the rhythm, Valdez raised a hand toward the Spanish crowd.

The crowd responded with a report like a lightning strike. Even on the near side she heard clapping and, "Never saw the likes!" Mr. Sheldon stood and shouted, "*Bravo caballero! Bravo Vaquero!*" Maybe he shouldn't be blamed, she realized, for cheering for the man who had once been his *mayordomo*.

At the end of the lap, Valdez sprang to the ground, coiling his lariat and bowing to the spectators as his riderless horse slowed, circled and stopped beside him. Señor Valdez bowed toward Mr. Sheldon.

No one would mistake the winner of that event, she knew. Even Perry nodded graciously toward the Spaniard. Valdez beckoned a group of Mexicans. They ran into the arena and positioned themselves about three horse lengths apart, their sombreros like pale mushrooms in a row.

With a handspring into the saddle, Señor Valdez melded with the horse and flew to the end of the line. Then he wheeled and rode hard in and out between the men, digging sharply into each turn, sliding a little in the damp ground. He circled and repeated the dodging course on the way back. At the end of the line he ran the horse full tilt at the Rhoads wagon. The animal never flinched or slowed, but slid to a sitting stop inches away. Cheers drowned the screams and the relieved laughter of the women and children.

The sombreros remained in place as Perry ran the same course. The pinto lunged and strained and slid at the sharp turns. At the end Perry ran Paint full tilt to the wagons, sliding and sitting him perfectly. Who would guess Perry had been a sailor? He was superb.

He trotted the horse back to the center of the arena where the mushrooms were scattering to the sidelines. Perry reached for his lariat and was circling it as he sprang out of the saddle. Beneath the whirling loop he slapped the horse away and stood alone, starting his rope tricks. He excelled at this. He traced a series of figure eights — overhead, side to side, dancing through it. He added twists and flourishes she hadn't seen before. She watched in silent awe. Ooohs and aahhhs sounded around her, and sporadic clapping — even before he was finished. Then Perry bowed and applause boomed. It was Señor Valdez' turn.

María had never seen Billy in such a trance. As Pedro danced with his *reata*, the boy's mouth fell open. He had yelled and clapped with the *Españoles*, then cheered for Perrimacoo.

Longhorns were driven across the field. First Pedro, then Perrimacoo lassoed a flying hoof, expertly tripping the huge animals then, after they whumped to the ground, deftly tying their thrashing feet. Both men made it look easy, but she knew the souls of cows — powerful, vicious when they were restrained. A careless man could be gored, or get his head kicked off.

"Bravo! Bravo!" people cheered, and Maria wondered at the strange magic that had made both these men her husbands. But her heart was swollen with love for Pedro.

Then Pedro and a crowd of men went to the brush corral. Many people stood between her and them and for a time she saw only moving hats, Pedro's red band and tassel distinctive among them. She knew they were struggling with a dangerous animal, jerking back from it, then approaching again.

Suddenly Pedro burst into the clearing on the back of a leaping horse. It kicked and twisted like it would break itself in two, but he held on.

She held her breath. Beside her, Joaquín Murieta murmured, "*Ah, que bronco*!" His companion said, "*Muy bruto*!" Her heart beat rapidly. It would be nothing for that horse to kill him.

Holding the saddlehorn with one hand, Pedro flapped violently up and down, the attached coil of the lariat waving with his spread legs. In the silence of the crowd she heard the horse's gasping, snorting, grunting breath and the trumpeting farts with each leap, and the punk punk of its landing.

He flew loose! Somersaulting over the animal's lowered neck with his legs following his shoulders, hat flying wide. She stepped forward, winced at the thump of his landing. In a twinkling he rolled away from the crushing hooves, and jumped to his feet. Hands up, smiling. Uninjured! The horse continued to buck away from him.

Her voice caught in her throat as she squeezed Billy's shoulders and said, "He defeated the horse." The crowd was screaming its relief and appreciation as mounted vaqueros swung their lassoes and chased the bucking animal. Women and children stood in the wagons stamping. "*Bravo, caballero*!" Men shouted, Joaquín Murieta among them.

Pedro waved his hat at the spectators, his private smile locating her across the distance. "*Bravo!*" she called, but her voice was lost in the roar.

Another horse was being prepared. Hats seethed in the corral.

Perry flew into the open on the back of another bucking devil. Elitha stood in the wagon. The crowd quieted. Catherine stood and took her hand. Where did they find such animals? The horse hovered airborne like it weighed nothing, twisting as it kicked out one side, then the other, then landed — ears laid back, eyes white, teeth bared, snorting like a dragon in old-time stories. The furious horse was bent on murder and Perry held the saddle with one hand as it humped high, mane flying. A big piece of daylight showed between him and the saddle, his legs wide over the neck. The horse wrenched away and Perry fell to the ground. She heard his back thud and saw his legs up in a V. The hooves thrashed down, around and around. Perry writhed as if trying to curl himself, but one foot stayed up, caught somehow. He was under the hooves. She was paralyzed by the violence, unable to breathe. Not a sound came from the crowd.

The horse continued to buck, Perry jerking with it. Oooh pushed like a monster's breath from thousands of throats. Her heart banged on her ribs. Señor Valdez was running on foot across the field circling his lariat.

Men converged. Valdez lassoed the animal's neck. It sat on its haunches, then reared and flailed its front hooves at the onrushing men. They shrank back. The horse wheeled and dug into a furious run, jerking the Spaniard and pulling Perry. Valdez let go of the rope. Mounted men came whirling ropes, but the horse had parted the Celestials and was digging for open ground, dragging Perry behind. The riders galloped after.

She scrambled down from the wagon and hurried with the crowd after the runaway horse. A shout came. "They got him!"

She pushed through the people, pleading, "Let me pass, please. I'm his wife. Please."

The horse was being led away, kicking and fighting a dozen ropes. Perry lay on his back surrounded by men. She squeezed between them, excusing herself, and knelt at his side.

His eyes were open, his cheek torn and bloody. He looked up at her and his old sidewise smile formed on his lips, the dimple almost in his cheek. "Caught me damned boot in the lariat, I did." A thin line of blood trickled from the corner of his mouth and he made no attempt to move.

Her hand trembled as she smoothed back his hair, barely aware of all the people peering down. "You hurt bad?"

His voice came whispery. "Knocked the wind out 'o me sails." He started to smile, but winced.

Above, a familiar voice said, "I wanted to treep the horse with *la reata*, but he might fall on heem." Señor Valdez, looking as pained as Perry.

Voices yammered. Is he dead? Back broken? Reg'lar thrashin! Poor girl. Bout to burst. Tongues clucked and heads wagged. She didn't know what to do. Suddenly Ben Wilder was beside her saying, "Better get him off the damp ground. Asa and I'll carry him to a wagon." They reached down, took his arms and legs.

"No. Let me — " Perry's voice trailed off. The tall men stood back.

Alarm jumped through her, followed by an odd calm. She knew what was important. "Perry, you were splendid. I've never seen such riding in my whole life. Honest, I never have."

The wrinkles on his brow smoothed and the corners of his mouth twitched into a faint smile. The way he looked when he cared for her. He closed his eyes.

"You were WONderful!" She said, taking his hand. His head fell to the side and pink bubbles slid off his tongue and out the side of his mouth. A man knelt, took his wrist.

"He's hurt bad," she said to Ben Wilder. "Please take him to the Sheldon wagon." She stood with her knees trembling and pointed the way, but the man with Perry's wrist said, "B'lieve he's a goner," and removed his hat.

She stared at Perry and kneeled awkwardly beside him, leaning over her belly to put an ear on his chest. It caved in with sickening ease. She jerked back. Then listened again. Silence.

81

Walking with the children and other *Indios*, Maria followed the crowd away from the field of the vaquero contest. Pedro led his horse, walking beside her. Ahead, about a hundred *Americanos* snaked down the swale and up the curving path behind Señor Sheldon's wagon, in which Perrimacoo lay. They were returning him to his bad luck house, his spotted horse tied behind.

"His roping was good," Pedro said suddenly. He had been quiet, acknowledging with silent nods the compliments of people passing by.

"You won," she said.

He nodded and by his face she saw he was more sorry than proud. She understood. Among her people, before the *Americanos* came, arrow-dodging champions had sometimes been fatally injured during ritual wars. Not in her lifetime, but the stories of sadness on both sides stayed in her mind. Men preferred their opponents to live; it made winning sweeter.

For a long time she had known magic would snuff the life from Perrimacoo. She looked down at Billy, and saw his face pinched with thought. He hadn't said a word after his outburst of questions about death. He had been too young to understand when his *Indio* relatives lay massacred on the river bank.

They arrived at the top of the hill and she pulled Billy and Little Flicker into the trees, back from the house, back with the other *Indios*. Pedro came too. Perrimacoo lay in the open. Unpurified *Americanas* knelt around him, dabbing cloths on his face and hands. Touching the dead. Elitha was out of sight. Crowds stood around the yard, but Joaquín Murieta and his friends hadn't come.

She shook her head sadly and told Pedro, "Elitha is in the bad house." Perrimacoo couldn't force her now, so why didn't she stay out of it?

Pedro said nothing. He didn't like her to talk about power. She watched

Americanos take turns digging with the shovel, Billy watching too. She squeezed his hand. This man had been his father. And Elitha — her magic double — would continue to have bad luck. Maybe that's what drained it away from María. She hated the thought, but she and Pedro had argued too often about magic. She would speak directly to Elitha about the bad house.

With a rattle of harnesses, Señor Sheldon whipped his team to a gallop down the hill. Señoras Catherine, Sarah and Elizabeth bustled in and out of the house preparing huge amounts of food, apparently intending to feed the crowd. No *Americanos* went to the river to purify themselves, though a dangerous spirit was about to spring out among them. Instead, they stood in solemn groups, or sat in wagons, whispering.

Taking the children, Maria followed the other *Indios* to the river. After bathing, she plucked purifying herbs from the scattered surviving stands, careful to leave some in each location. It worried her that no pine tea could be made. Not a single gray pine was left. That endangered everyone.

When she returned, the hole in the ground was deep. A man stood to his waist throwing out earth. Back with a wagonload of wood, Señor Sheldon was building a wooden box. *Americanos* and *Españoles* sat in their wagons and stood perilously close to the dead.

She stepped to the fire and placed herbs on it to purify the smoke. Eyes followed, but nothing was said. Back in the trees, she sat beside Pedro.

Billy asked, "Spirit come out?"

"I have not seen it yet." Until the ghostly veil lifted from the body and floated to the sky, danger abounded. Anyone might become the host of a lost, angry soul. "We must sing the spirit on its way," she said.

"When?"

"When they put him in the ground." She remembered the *Americano* rite of death.

Every once in a while one of the children strayed too close and Bent-Willow-Reflected-in-Pond or Hummingbird Tailfeather snatched them back. Isabella fussed.

Putting her to the breast she asked Pedro, "When will Elitha give you the land paper?"

Pensively he scooped up a handful of decaying oak leaves. "Señora McCoon is grieving and about to give birth. I cannot ask her now." He had decided that if Mr. McKinstry considered the grant legal, he should not dismiss it lightly.

"She must leave the bad-luck house."

Glancing up from the leaves, he studied her. "That's the only shelter she has."

"Her friends have big houses."

He expelled air from his nose, which meant he was impatient, "María, Perry McCoon is dead." He spoke under his breath. "It was the horse, and my failure to trip him, that killed him, not the condor robe. *Ay Madre.*"

Didn't he realize that everyone who entered that house had died? Including María's people, who had built it for Perrimacoo. Even Señor Daylo, who had only visited briefly, died mysteriously. "Elitha's first child died. Her second will die too if she doesn't leave. Maybe she will die." But silently she knew that something was keeping Elitha alive.

He crumbled the leaves, letting them fall to the ground. "That is pure superstition." He stood, slapped his hands clean on his trousers. "Even if she gives me the land paper, I will tell her to remain in the house as long as she wants."

The Rhoads sisters helped Elitha from bed, and led her to the grave, which was on a little rise behind the house. Behind their solicitude, she saw they all judged Perry's death to be a blessing. She didn't know what to think about that, but she was glad she had praised him at the end. She felt as though a rope binding her to a post had been cut.

Many people had gone on, but about a hundred sat or stood in the winter sun. Perry lay in the open coffin, which Mr. Sheldon had made from wood intended for his Bridge House cabin. It was a neighborly thing to do, and she felt grateful to him. She kept expecting Perry to move, his hands stacked on his caved-in chest.

"We thought you'd like to say your farewell first," said Sarah, stepping back. Elitha stood alone before Perry, watched from all directions.

The blood and mud was washed from his face, his hair combed. He still wore his best clothes. They hadn't been able to get the mud out of his trousers and the shoulders of his muslin shirt.

She kneeled beside the coffin. "Well, Perry," she murmured, truly saddened at the suddenness of his death and not wanting anyone to hear, "it's good-bye. I'm sorry you won't see our baby." She couldn't imagine him in heaven, but maybe God would take pity. Feeling self-conscious, she began to get up — so bulky and clumsy now.

An arm shot around her, helping. Vyries Brown's freckled young face creased with concern. Thanking him, she looked around. Where was Ben Wilder? Then she remembered the trouble between him and Mr. Sheldon. He and his brothers hadn't stayed for the burying. She stepped back beside Catherine.

Mr. Sheldon took the hammer and nailed boards over the coffin. A loud hollow sound rang across the hills. Then John Rhoads, Billy Rhoads, Mr. Grimshaw and Mr. Sheldon lowered the box into the grave.

An awkward silence. No one had a Bible. The Gaffneys offered to go home for theirs. "No, that's all right," Elitha said. "He didn't believe in it anyway."

Mr. McKinstry removed his hat and stepped forward, leaving Kate behind.

All the men's hats came off. He cleared his throat and spoke, "William Perry McCoon will be remembered as one of the first California pioneers. And Perry, you were one damned fine buckeroo. We lay you to rest here on your own rancho." He stepped back with Kate.

Mr. Sheldon looked around, but before anyone else could speak, strange singing started in the trees. The Indians, singing their death dirge. Mournful but oddly soothing tones rose in long progressions across the quiet hillside and up the river bottom. The singing seemed exactly right. The sounds floated heavenward. Maybe God would hear, would forgive this wayward sheep his weaknesses.

A long time later the singing stopped, and in the silence that followed, Perry's son stepped to the edge of the grave, naked and pot-bellied as any Indian child. He looked down at the box and said, "Me nime is Billy McCoon."

82

After two weeks with Sarah Daylor, Elitha was ready to go home to the adobe, anxious to give it a good cleaning. She also wanted to start saving gold. She caught a ride with Mr. Sheldon, who was taking a load of lumber to his cabin at Bridge House. He had the Yankee knack for neat construction, and would put in a plank floor today.

The first thing she did inside the adobe was pull off the blankets to give them a good scrubbing. They weren't quite dry when dark fell, but she slept well anyway. Even with the big baby kicking inside her. The next morning she was sweeping out the spider webs and pack rat debris when a man's voice called, "Howdy neighbor."

She pulled back the leather drape. Ben Wilder stood there, tall and lanky, smiling through his crinkled, sloping blue eyes. "Howdy," she said back, smiling.

He was dressed in typical miners' garb — suspenders over a red flannel shirt tucked into brown trousers, which were tucked into knee-high boots. His shapeless hat made a wavy frame for his bearded face. "Thought I'd pay my respects."

"Surely." She led him to the grave, the perimeter marked with white quartz stones, which she'd found around the diggings.

He removed his hat and stood silently, then replaced the hat. "There's a marble quarry some twenty miles south and east. If you'd like I'll get you a block delivered here, to mark the head."

"I'd like that very much."

He stood looking at her. She felt embarrassed about being so pregnant, but it couldn't be helped. "I'll be serving food again," she said, "starting tomorrow morning, and I'd be obliged if you spread the word in Cook's Bar."

He raised his brows. Surprise or admiration, she couldn't tell which.

The next morning he and ten other miners ate in her yard. It was his first time. As she took a pinch of his gold dust, he said, "I've made arrangements for the stone to be delivered."

Two days later he arrived pulling a mule with the stone strapped on its back. It had been nicely squared, about a foot long, eight inches wide, and four inches thick. With a comfortable smile he said, "I'd be happy to letter it for you."

"Could you?" She heard her own enthusiasm.

From his pocket he took a crevice tool, a tough little implement for prying gold from rocks. Squatting, he scratched one of the rough sides. "Yup, this'll do the trick."

"First let me think what to put on it."

"Think till tomorrow afternoon." He touched his hat and left.

The next day he sat at the table and told her the gossip of Cook's Bar as he scratched at the marble. "Won't do to rush this," he said nodding at the stone.

She was glad to have him come for an hour or two each afternoon. He said it rested him after shoveling mud. The next afternoon as he etched, she sat across the table and penned a letter to her three youngest sisters, Leanna having written that she was hired out to a farmer in Calaveras County.

January 20, 1851

Dear Georgia, Francis and Ellie,

Are you well? Are you going to school? I hope so. I have sad news and happy news. Perry died of a bad accident and I am about to have a baby. I am cooking meals for money and my house isn't any better than when Ellie was here. Still, I would like you all to come visit, if you would. I am the more lonely since Perry died, and would so like to have our family back together.

Do you get my letters? Please write. It would be such a welcome sight to be handed a letter from you. Did I tell you? Mail is delivered by stage every day to the Bridge House Post Office."

Love as always, your big sister, Elitha

Several days later it was pouring again, but supper was cooked. At the table Ben worked the marble, the familiar scratching sound soothing to Elitha. The clouds were so dark outside, she lit a spermacetti lamp, wicked with a spike of dry horehound flowers.

Sorting through the things in Perry's big leather bag, she came across the letter from Captain John Sutter and suddenly realized Señor Valdez hadn't come by for it. She opened her mouth to ask Ben's advice, but remembered he believed in squatters' rights. And if there was a doubt about Perry owning this land, as Mr. Valdez seemed to think, it wouldn't do to advertise that to the miners.

She lined up her words. "How would I go about transferring Perry's land to Mr. Valdez?" Everyone had known of the bargain.

Ben stopped scratching, looked at her, then went back to his work. "Well, since the forty-nine Convention, women can own property in this state, so I'd say you inherited Perry's title, if it's legal. You could just sign it over, right on the front side of the paper. Get three witnesses to sign." He scowled at the marble. "He didn't come for it then? The Mexican?"

"Nope."

"If I were you I wouldn't be too quick to hand it over."

"I haven't exactly been quick, have I?" She grinned. It had been over three weeks since the contest. And somehow she didn't expect Mr. Valdez to throw her out of her house.

Ben continued scratching.

"I heard you Forty-niners don't think the Mexican ranch titles will stand up in court." In no uncertain terms Sarah had informed her of this, and advised her to keep all squatters off.

He raised his brows at the RIP, the P of which he'd been lengthening. "Way I understand it, anyone living on land can challenge title, so it's up to the ranchers to prove their property is legal. They got to show a proper survey was conducted under the Mexican government." He looked up, his eyes kindly. "Maybe he won't come for it."

He seemed well informed. "You think my title would be challenged?" Perry had let squatters camp everywhere — the Gaffneys, for instance, down near the old Indian village. She knew Mr. Sheldon had told the Wilder Brothers to get off his Cook's Bar land, now that he was here working on his dam.

The carefulness of Ben's tone matched hers. "First, the U.S. Land Commission has to rule on your title. If the Mexican government granted legal title, the U.S. is supposed to honor it. But I've heard of cases where Sutter gave land he didn't own, and didn't have the authority to grant. That's the kind of thing Uncle Sam's commission looks for."

Elitha sat heavily on a chair next to Ben, the baby kicking inside her. "Why would Captain Sutter do that?"

His lips twisted in a wry smile. "Power."

Indian Mary's favorite word. "It doesn't seem powerful to me, more dishonest. Or stupid. People can find out he hadn't the authority."

"That's how the feudal lords of Europe operated."

"Feudal?"

"A knight consolidated power by making the surrounding knights beholden to him. He rewarded them with land. Then they would defend him in battle." He glanced up at her. "Empires got established that way."

"But the Mexican governor would have stopped Captain Sutter from doing that." Wouldn't he?

He flicked away marble dust and raised the block on edge, examining his work. "In a fort that well defended? Forty cannons? All those men ready to fight for their supposed property?"

Suddenly she didn't want to hear any more. What did he know? Captain Sutter had gone to war for a Mexican governor, Perry told her. Ben was just a Forty-niner, a greenhorn, with notions. Anyway Mrs. Sutter was turning the Captain's old friends away at the door. He was no feudal lord, more like a pathetic old man. She wouldn't mention it to Ben again.

But one thing he'd said she agreed with. She would wait to hear from Señor Valdez, and keep it quiet that all she had for a land deed was Captain Sutter's letter.

On a cloudy afternoon at the end of February, Ben finished the last numeral on the stone. He set it on edge at the head of the grave, packing dirt around it. Elitha stood back to see the effect. Her own quartz rectangle looked primitive, the stones jagged and veined with orange and gold. The headstone gave the grave dignity.

William Perry McCoon
RIP
Native of England
Died 1851

She said, "I wish there'd been room for California's best vaquero."

He gave her a funny look. "I can't spell it."

That made her chuckle. "Me neither."

Seriousness crossed his face and he looked over the green hills. "Maybe it isn't my place, but I've been worrying about you. Out here alone and all." He glanced at her belly.

She looked down, felt heat in the tips of her ears.

"I heard of a doctor in San Francisco. Maybe I could get him up here."

Astonished that he would suggest such an expensive and doubtful thing, she stared at him. It was something a husband would say — a husband unlike Perry. Again her face burned. She'd often caught herself wanting to hold Ben, wondering how he would feel against her, but such thoughts were unseemly in her condition and she couldn't imagine any man would find her attractive. Yet if she could choose one, it would be Ben Wilder. Embarrassment tangled her tongue.

"You ought to have a doctor." He spoke with the self-confidence she so admired. "When will your time come?"

"A few weeks," she murmured.

"Few?"

Her face was so hot she turned away. "Maybe two or three." The baby had dropped. That was a sign. What she couldn't say was that she'd arranged to put herself into Indian Mary's care. Indians had an easy time with birth, but she couldn't say that either. Forty-niners thought Indians were animals, and being part Indian herself she didn't want to talk about it.

He laid a hand on her shoulder. "I'll see what I can do."

"Oh, please don't trouble yourself. I'll be fine."

"By thunder, you're a brave girl." His look melted her. "Mind if I ask how old you are?"

"Seventeen." He looked to be near thirty.

Elitha felt like she'd participated in a strange fairy tale. After four days in a tiny brush hut made for her by the Indians, she now lay on her own bed, her sweet baby girl beside her. Very much alive.

Elizabeth Cumi, she'd named her, after Aunt Betsy and her own real mother. Everyone had loved Aunt Betsy and Elitha hoped Elizabeth would be like her. The baby had Perry's dark lashes and a thin wash of dark hair on a perfectly round head. She never tired of staring at the sweet little face. She knew Perry would have loved her.

"Anybody home?" It was Ben.

"Just a minute." She finger-combed her hair and straightened the blankets, making a neat fold below her chin and the baby's. "Come in."

Too tall for the house, he ducked inside, hat in hand, and came to the bed. He stared at Elizabeth. "Well I'll be, I don't believe it!"

"Told you I'd be fine. Pull up a stool."

He reached back and pulled it to him. "What is it, I mean a boy or — "

"Girl."

"Well, I've never seen two more beautiful young ladies. I thought you'd dropped off the face of the earth!"

"Went to a friend for help." She looked away from his steady gaze and hoped he wouldn't probe.

He didn't. It was one of the things she liked about him — quick to pick up on her feelings. Discreetly he inquired after her health, then told her about the Wilder claim, about how he and his brothers were tunneling into the riverbank, finding gold that had been deposited there centuries before. "Coyoting, it's called bec . . ." The sound of a horse stopped him.

They both listened. A man's voice called, "*Hola, señora.*" It had to be Señor

Valdez.

"Come in," she called.

"Shh," Ben whispered, hunched over and stepping toward the door. "Sounds like a Mexican. You gotta be careful with bandits running rampant."

Señor Valdez opened the door and stepped in. "Señora McCoon," he said, standing half a head shorter than Ben, "You have company. I return later." He made no move toward the bed.

"Nonsense. Come and see my baby." She shifted the infant to face the men. "Isn't she pretty?" She thought a moment and said, "*Bonita?*"

Valdez stepped hesitantly toward her, eyes on Elizabeth. "*Muy bonita*, like my wife said."

Ben echoed, "Wife?"

Elitha cut in, "They live nearby. She helped with the birth." She jumped to the point. "Come for your land title?"

Señor Valdez bowed slightly. "I return later."

"Good idea," Ben said.

"Señora, have no fear," Valdez said backing out the door, "The house I do not want. Stay here all the time if you weesh. A mother needs a roof over the head."

"I appreciate that."

His head was still inside. "Other thing. I pay for the land."

"That wasn't the agreement. You won fair and square."

He looked a moment longer, then was gone. Ben seated himself at the bedside, and suddenly she didn't want to hold anything back from him. She would tell him who she really was, even tell him about her Indian blood. If he didn't like it, better to find out now. But first the title.

"Ben, I'm afraid Perry was one of those who got his land from Captain Sutter. All I have is his letter. But whatever it's worth, I'm going to sign it over to Mr. Valdez. I want you and your brothers to be the witnesses."

His sloping eyes looked friendly in the dim light. "River property is valuable, you must know. If I thought you had a chance in Hades of proving up, I'd do everything in my power to stop you."

"A bargain's a bargain." She couldn't live with herself if she didn't sign over the letter, whatever it was worth.

"Yes, but these Mexicans . . ." He trailed off and started again. "There are bandit gangs around, and I'd sure hate to see you give anything to criminals." He frowned at the baby.

"It doesn't sound like I'm giving up anything."

"You never know. Possession may be nine-tenths of the law. I hear squatters are getting big blocks of land that used to be John Sutter's, down in Sacramento City."

She smiled. "Well then, I'm squatting here in the house, then maybe I'll own the land it sits on." Soon she could cook again, and keep all her wages. She would save for improvements and collect her sisters. They could help with the baby. It didn't matter who lived on the rest of the land.

Ben looked troubled, but it seemed the right decision. She would wait and see what developed.

He reached out and petted the baby's head with two long fingers, then shook his head. "You really are a brave girl, Elitha. Most females I know would have headed straight for home. Did you say your folks were in Illinois?"

Nobody around Cook's Bar knew her story; that had been clear for a long time. The miners were transient, they knew her only as Mrs. McCoon. "There's a couple more things I gotta say, Ben."

He gave her a playful look. "You weren't married to Perry McCoon?"

She chuckled, then took a breath. "My maiden name was Donner."

His eyes flew open. "You don't mean the — "

"I'm the daughter of George Donner."

"The mountain tragedy?" He looked flabbergasted. "Why didn't you say? All that time I was carving on the — "

"Why do you think? With me cooking meals and all?"

Comprehension spread slowly across his face. "But Mr. McCoon. I don't mean to speak ill of the departed, but he didn't seem the kind to keep a secret from the whole damn — forgive me. I've been around men too long."

"I guess he got tired of the jokes too, like, well, 'Be careful what goes in the pot.'" Immediately she regretted that.

"People say — "

"Ben, I didn't — " Tears clouded her eyes and she turned her head away, appalled that time, which was supposed to heal all wounds, didn't.

He touched her shoulder through the blanket. "By thunder, I said you were the bravest girl I knew, and I didn't know the half!"

She dabbed her eyes with the edge of the blanket and turned back to him. Not a trace of disgust showed in his face. She waited, but he didn't say Pa was stupid for taking the cut-off, or the Party was foolish for not knowing how to live off the land. All he did was look at her like she was the most precious thing on earth, the way Mr. Sheldon looked at Catherine, the way Mr. Daylor had looked at Sarah. Tears blinded her again, but they had nothing to do with the past. It was plain as the crumbling adobe that he cared very much for her, and she was happy.

Indian Mary had said strong power abided in this cabin. But once she'd said power could mean good luck as well as bad. Ben Wilder felt like the luckiest thing that ever happened. She reached for his hand and squeezed it. Then out of the blue and not so happily, she recalled the trouble between him and Mr. Sheldon. Why did things have to be so complicated?

83

June 20, 1851
In care of Mr. and Mrs. Brunner, Sonoma
Dear Frances, Georgia and Ellie,

Do you get my letters? I would ever so much like to hear from you. Leanna writes often. She is betrothed to Mr. App in Jamestown. If you were here we could all go to the wedding on the stage. What fun that would be!

I think of you often and wish you would come and live with me. I could arrange to have you picked up. I am making enough money now to rebuild the house. The school in Katesville is only a mile away, and the teacher is very nice. I hope you are attending school.

Tomorrow I am going to a dance in Fiddletown. It will be such fun! My best friend, Catey Sheldon, will care for Baby Elizabeth. Catey's husband built her a cabin nearby, so she could be with him for the summer. She has a new baby too.

Please write. Love and hugs to each of you,
Your Big Sister, Elitha.

To show them how fine the dance would be, she enclosed one of the many invitations she had received — embossed with pale pink roses. Ben said the men who organized the dance had the printing done in Sacramento City.

Folding the letter, she sat a moment staring across the table, out the open door. Mr. Sheldon had ordered Ben off his land and said he would round up a posse to throw him off if he and his brothers didn't leave immediately. Ben was riled. Elitha hadn't known what to say about it, except that she declined to attend the dance with him.

She had arranged to go with Sarah and Mr. Grimshaw. But if Ben went, she hoped to dance with him. Maybe Sarah and Mr. Grimshaw would get a chance to hear his side of things.

Elitha peered into the mirror, dark hair securely pinned, the lace collar on her brown frock fresh. She pulled up her skirt to check the shine on her old shoes, bear grease a marvel — and the lightest of cooking oils. She went outside tying on her brown bonnet, feeling as carefree as the silly woodpeckers that swooped and cackled in the oak. Her sign proclaimed: NO MEALS SERVED TODAY OR TOMORROW. That in itself was enough to set her feet dancing. She was ready to take Elizabeth to Catherine, but the baby was taking an unexpected morning nap and she wanted her to rest as much as possible before going to a strange place.

With her brown skirts billowing like she was in a Viennese dance hall, she whirled to the imaginary beat of waltzing violins — the chink and scrape of shovels adding percussion from the riverbottom. The baby cried.

She hurried in. Elizabeth's face was twisted, and she writhed on the bed. "Poor little sugar," she said, reaching for a fresh square of muslin. "You didn't eat much this morning. What's the matter?" Her diaper was stained with pale green liquid. Colic?

Quickly she tied on a clean diaper, then took a blanket and made a handy sling like Indian Mary had shown her. The walk quieted the baby.

As she crossed the bridge, Mr. Sherwood rose from his chair on his porch and said, "My but we're in fine feather today, Miz McCoon. Headin to the dance are you?" The new sign on his porch said BRIDGE HOUSE STATION AND POST OFFICE.

"Yup. Going with the Grimshaws. Looks like they got here already." She nodded toward the wagon in front of the Sheldon cabin.

"Come up about an hour ago."

"You and Kate going to the dance?"

Mr. Sherwood petted back the hairs on his pate. "Aw, she's been needlin me nigh onto a month now. Even hired a boy to take toll. I'm startin to weaken."

She laughed. "See you there." She adjusted the blanket and hurried on as a six-mule team crossed the bridge, the planks bouncing and creaking like they would break. "Six bits," she heard Sherwood yell at the teamster.

Catherine called her in, the scent of the new walls and floor like walking into a pine forest. Catherine sat in her stylish rocking chair nursing her newborn daughter, whose tiny face made four-month-old Elizabeth appear gigantic by comparison. Sarah and Mr. Grimshaw perched on the extra chairs, Sarah pregnant at last, but not so it showed. She looked angelic in a blue satin frock, every hair of her blonde bun in place. Mr. Grimshaw's brown suit matched his slick helmet of hair and his clear coffee-colored eyes. He rose, nodding formally.

She complimented Sarah's dress and said she was "obliged" to them for taking her to the dance. "Where's little Will and little Sarah?" she asked Catherine.

"With their pa. He's workin on the dam."

Pleased she wouldn't have the older children pestering her for a while, Elitha said, "The baby's got a loose stool this morning. Sure you want to take her?" A whisker of hesitation and she'd stay home.

"Silly goose! Just lay her on the bed."

That done, she leaned down and kissed her forehead. "Give yer ma a big smile now, Precious. Come on." She tickled the fat under her chin, but the baby seemed listless. "Her dimples are so darling when she smiles," she tossed over her shoulder.

"From Perry," said Catherine like she'd tasted something sour.

But Perry had been uncommonly handsome and Elizabeth was lucky to have his looks. "Does she feel warm to you?" Elitha asked. Catherine was only seventeen too, but three children gave her a world more experience.

With the newborn over her shoulder she struggled to her feet, stepped to the bed and felt Elizabeth's brow. "Feels fine to me."

Relieved, she looked into Catherine's hazel eyes. "How can I ever thank you?"

"Easy. Next time, I go to the dance and you watch my THREE. Now go on, git! Have a good time." She shooed them out the door.

She was on the buckboard with Sarah, Mr. Grimshaw checking the gear on the team, when Mr. Sheldon rode up with the two children. Dismounting, he took them from the saddle and stood with his hands on his waist staring at nothing. His jaw twitched beneath his whiskers. The children went around the house holding hands.

Timidly Sarah asked, "Something wrong Jared?"

"Those damned Wilder boys like to git their derned heads blowed off, that's what." He looked like a starved wolf eyeing prey. Elitha closed her eyes and inhaled quietly.

"What they done now?" Sarah asked.

"Fer starters, built a fence around their gal derned tent. Right there on my property! Can you believe that?" He breathed like a winded horse, through his nose, his eyes fierce. "And that tall one?" He turned toward the trees as if knowing the hatred in his eyes was scorching the wrong target, "got together a damned so-called Miners Committee!" He shook his head and muttered, "Scuse my French ladies." Reaching into his pocket, he drew out a piece of paper. "Gave me this. From the so-called committee." He gave it hard shake. "Oughta feed it to the dogs."

Catherine came out with a baby on each shoulder asking, "What's wrong, Jared?"

"Later. Better send these people on their way. They got a five- six-hour drive."

Mr. Grimshaw climbed up to the springed seat. "Jared, if there's anything I can do — "

"Thanks, but this here's my fight." His hard jawline showed through the whiskers, his yellowish eyes leveled on Elitha. A tremor edged her stomach. It almost seemed he knew about her friendship with Ben.

Mr. Grimshaw gentled the reins on the twin brown rumps and the wagon lurched over the lumpy ground back to the road, harnesses rattling. Wishing men could get along better, Elitha held onto the rail. The Grimshaws said nothing, but that was normal. They were quiet people.

The wagon creaked and rattled eastward with the ruts, past the shanties and hovels of Live Oak, past what looked like a funeral at St. Joseph's Church. The reminder of death spurred Elitha's resolve. She would explain her friendship with Ben Wilder. One thing she had on her side was plenty of time.

Mr. Grimshaw was a calm, reasonable sort of man, not swashbuckling and colorful like Mr. Daylor, or ingenious and hardheaded like Mr. Sheldon, but a born mercantile proprietor. His prosperous business depended entirely on the patronage of miners, so Elitha thought he might be a little more sympathetic to a Forty-niner.

"Oh," Sarah said reaching into her pocket, "before I forget." She handed Elitha the teardrop earrings she'd sent for. "I owe you two dollars back. Pretty, huh?"

"Oh yes, and I'm so glad they got here in time for the dance." Thanking Sarah, she slipped them into her pocket, and a few minutes later found herself thinking momentarily of Tamsen and how she would have liked painting these golden hills dotted with wide-spaced oaks, pruned by deer across the bottom. But the pigments were lost in the snow, and so was Tamsen. Life was tenuous enough without men fighting.

"You know," she started, "I am acquainted with Ben Wilder. He was the one that bought the marble block for Perry's grave, and carved on it. He was very nice about it."

Sarah turned her bonnet, her blue eyes pale, her prim nose slightly downturned. Mr. Grimshaw kept his eyes on the road.

She continued, "He's an educated man." That drew a glance from Mr. Grimshaw, an educated man himself. Reading and writing separated people more than anything else. "And there's something more about him," she paused trying to put words to it. "Men listen to him. Sarah, remember when Captain Juan was about to be hanged, out back of the Eating House?" Sarah nodded. "Well, Ben Wilder was the one who calmed everybody down, got them to settle for hanging by the thumbs."

"Mmm," Sarah said noncommittally.

"I think he's a good man, at heart, and if he's at the dance, I guess I'll dance with him." There. She'd said it.

The Grimshaws were quiet for a time, then Sarah said, "You sweet on him?"

She felt herself blushing. It had been only four months since Perry's death, and with Mr. Sheldon feeling so angry — "Maybe," she admitted.

The Grimshaws were quiet. Every mile or so they passed a road stop — some with huge hay barns and watering troughs catering to teamsters, others eating houses catering to stages and riders and men on foot. But no matter what they passed, the golden grass stretched out beyond in a seemingly endless tapestry, the white-capped mountains of death in the distance.

Mr. Grimshaw cleared his throat and started a new subject, or so it seemed at first. "You know, I heard there are more than six hundred men for every white female in the mining regions. Some calculate more like a thousand to one. Isn't that something?" It was like him to think in numbers.

"Is that a fact!" Sarah exclaimed at him, slapping her satin-sheathed knee. Elitha could almost hear: So why pick Ben Wilder?

Innocently she said, "I don't think that's surprising. Ladies don't want to risk everything coming across the plains or sailing and walking through all that pestilence in Panama. I don't think they like to leave home, the way men do." Pa had been the one bound and determined to come to California.

"Mmm," said Mr. Grimshaw.

Then the Grimshaws were quiet, the late morning air heating up unpleasantly. At Forest Home, the large rock hotel built by the Castles of Michigan, they stopped for water — both horses and people. She and Sarah visited the four-seater outhouse. Miles later they had dinner at Willow Creek House — as busy and almost as elegant as Forest Home.

The closer they came to the Fiddletown turn, the more clean men they saw heading for the dance on mules, horseback and foot. The wagon had joined a parade of rigs coming from the junction of Bedbug — the sign crossed out, "Ione" written above it — then from Drytown, Sutter's Creek and Jackson, then China Camp and Pokerville. The dust seemed almost as bad as on the great migration across the plains. Then at last they were climbing a steep grade, pine trees mixing with the oaks the higher they got, until the trees were dense enough to shade them from the heat of the late afternoon. But at the first huts and shanties of Fiddletown, most of the trees were cut.

Fiddletown was a city in a mountain gorge straddling a stream. The Chinese section came first, some of their buildings resembling adobes, the squiggly lines of their signs making neither words nor pictures. In the doorway stood men with long black pigtails, piles of peaked straw hats and other strange goods at their feet, sides of pork hanging from trees in front, celestials scurrying back and forth. After that came large buildings, many brick, with upper-story balconies. Fiddletown certainly looked like the commercial hub Mr. Grimshaw said it was.

They stopped before the Sign of the Star Hotel — a large white star blazing on a blue placard. Blue bunting was draped all around the upper-story balcony. Mr. Grimshaw ushered Elitha and Sarah into the dining area, the horses being led to a hostelry up the road.

Inside, a mob of people, mostly men, milled around the half-filled tables, which were set with white linen, stemmed glasses and silverware. Tinsel and ribbon hung from the stairs and upstairs balcony. Along one wall stood a table heaped with platters of steaming food. Elitha hadn't seen such a grand place since Springfield. She didn't see Ben, but with a couple of hundred people in the place and new arrivals coming every minute, that wasn't surprising.

They joined a table with two men, who stood and helped with Elitha's chair while Mr. Grimshaw held one for Sarah. Everyone was in a festive mood, and it was infectious.

As Mr. Grimshaw went to pay, Elitha followed Sarah in search of a woman who could tell them where the privy was. "Mr Grimshaw is such a gentleman," Elitha said as they wended their way through the buzz of talk and the press of bodies. She looked for Ben, realizing it was possible he had brought somebody else, or hadn't come.

"He's from a real good family in New York," Sarah replied, clearly pleased Elitha had noticed. "His father's in shipping." A beaded dowager with clown-red cheeks told them the privy was upstairs on a bridge.

They exchanged a shrugging look — on a bridge? — and pushed their way through the crowd. With queenly posture Sarah led up the stairs. Near the top Elitha turned and looked down at the crowd. There, in line with Mr. Grimshaw, she saw Ben, half a head taller than any other. He had come! And the way he smiled at her, raising his poke in greeting! He had been watching her. The night opened like a blooming flower.

She caught up with Sarah, who was down a short hallway opening a door. They stepped outside onto a long narrow span of rope and wood, which connected with the rest of the hotel across the stream. The bridge swayed beneath her feet, and she looked down, waiting for Sarah to finish inside the canvas cubicle marked "ladies." She had the odd sensation that if she didn't hold the rope handrail, she might float away. Maybe it came from being away from the baby for the first time, or the thought of dancing with Ben, or just the heat lifting. It was late June and the days were long — probably about eight-thirty now, guessing from the red sunset in the gorge. The dust suspended in the air looked like spun gold. Red gold.

When Sarah lifted the canvas flap and came out, Elitha avoided the eyes of the men who were waiting for the next cubicle marked "Gents," and went in. An oak seat teetered on a bottomless wooden box, the stream rippling far below, and she felt the sway of people walking on the bridge. After a good inspection, she concluded that no men were below in the stream, though the possibility was unnerving.

Later, in the Powder Room inside the building, she and Sarah studied themselves in a large brass-framed mirror, a profusion of red wallpaper roses behind them. Their hair had jarred loose. Road grit hung in their eyebrows and dulled their cheeks. Pouring water from the ornate aqua pitcher into the matching basin, they washed and used an embroidered cloth smelling of lavender. After three years in the adobe, Elitha felt like Cinderella in Prince Charming's palace.

Realizing this was the only quiet time they would have to talk, she said, "I saw Ben Wilder downstairs."

In the glass Sarah looked at her, then at the earrings she was screwing on.

"I'm going to talk to him, and tell him how ranchers feel about men moving onto their property and putting up fences." She put on her own eardrops.

Sarah's pale eyes were noncommittal.

Back at the table Mr. Grimshaw handed them each a folded card with a pink ribbon threaded through it and a tiny pencil dangling from a string. The front said, The Walker Cotillion. Embossed in the upper corner were three pink roses. The numbered lines puzzled Elitha, having danced only in barns and in the front rooms of houses. She was glad Sarah asked what the cards were for.

"Like this," Mr. Grimshaw said holding the ribbon to her wrist. It hung like a bracelet. He pointed at the lines and said, "Your dance partners write their names there." He wrote his name on Sarah's card and said, "I'd like the first dance, and the last, and every other dance you want me to have." He was not the least chiding of her for not knowing the manners of a cotillion, and he whispered into her hair loud enough for Elitha to hear, "Ladies are in short supply, so the polite thing is to dance with plenty of men."

"May I have a dance?" blurted both men at the table, ignoring their filled plates. A crowd was gathering, men with water-slicked hair and trimmed whiskers. They formed a line. She saw Ben come over and stand at the end, looking at her in that solid, easy way she liked so much.

She went to him, the face of each man she passed brightening, then falling in disappointment. She felt like the princess in the fairy tale, with men lined up outside the palace gates hoping to marry her. That princess had married the only man who could make her cry. But with Ben smiling down at her with his sloping blue eyes, crying was the last thing on her mind.

"May I have a dance," he asked.

She handed him her card. "The first one."

"Honored, ma'am." He used the proffered back of another man to write his name, asking, "Any more? It's a long night." The sound of hope. She could tell he wasn't upset she hadn't come with him.

She wanted to dance every dance with him, but thought he might like to dance with others. Then she saw the mob around every female, never mind how old or ugly or married, and said, "How about every fourth dance?"

"Including the last?"

She smiled yes, and within five minutes her entire night was planned, "Ben W." on every fourth line. Other men wrote in their names until she got to the bottom, and the crestfallen line melted away. Ben also disappeared through the crowd.

Feeling like singing, she picked up her plate and followed Sarah and Mr. Grimshaw to the food line, where the breaded oysters made her ravenous.

"Griz," a man called, craning his neck around the line. A man digging into the scalloped potatoes looked up.

"Didja hear bout the Joaquín gang strikin here?"

"Warn't that som'm!"

Elitha took a roll and wondered again if it was Mr. Valdez. But that wasn't fair of her, just because he was the only Spaniard she knew. She dipped brandied peaches on her ham and went back to the table. Still, it added excitement to think Fiddletown had been struck by the famous outlaw. She couldn't wait to tell Ben.

A waiter poured champagne and she spread the linen napkin, suddenly thinking about the mouse suppers in the mountains. *God reminding me to give thanks for this feast.* She closed her eyes and was halfway done with her little prayer when Mr. Grimshaw said:

"You men hear about the Joaquín attack?"

The man with a large bony nose wolfed oysters and talked through them: "First thing we heard when we got to town, wadn't it Zeke?" Bobbing his head, Zeke chewed enthusiastically. She had read about the bandits stealing tens of thousands in gold dust from miners all over the mining regions — places far apart. It was a wonder the same men got around so fast.

The two men competed to tell the story, raising their voices to accommodate curious listeners at the next tables. A gang of bandits had been playing monte in the card room at the back of Mr. Erauw's mercantile, when somebody recognized the leader and accused him of being Joaquín. The "fancified Mexican" threw down his cards and jumped up on the table, "spurs ajinglin." He brandished his gun over his head and yelled, "I am Joaquín!"

Then he leaped from the table and raced through the mercantile, where ladies screamed. Men followed as he ran out the door and jumped on his horse. But the pursuing cardplayers yelled to the men on the street. One grabbed the bit of Joaquín's horse and the bandit shot the man "dead between the eyes." By this time the whole town was chasing after, but the Mexicans, being superb horsemen, dodged a hail of bullets. Then they jumped off their horses and wriggled into the brambles west of town, "jist like a bunch of snakes."

"Why, no white man could git though it!" Zeke supplied.

"What color was Joaquín's hair?" Elitha asked.

"Black as midnight, is my guess," said the man with the big nose.

"No one mentioned the color?"

"No ma'am. But Mexicans all have black hair."

No they don't, she thought. People at the surrounding tables had gone back to eating. In the middle of the room men lowered the candelabra by means of ropes. With the heavy wheel suspended over the heads of diners, a man lit all the candles — tiers of them, maybe forty, and the huge fixture was raised. Elitha joined the cheering, and the room brightened. She itched to be dancing in Ben's arms.

More champagne was poured, and by the time everyone had finished eating, she felt-light headed. Words tumbled easily from her mouth. She almost floated as she carried dishes to the kitchen, the men taking the chairs and tables out to the yard. She and Sarah visited the bridge again — it was twilight now — and the

Powder Room, where women chattered happily and patted their hair. One told the story of the town's founding by the Walker family, who, coming down the mountain from the Carson Pass — having left Missouri in the spring of forty-nine — had broken an axle. Instead of repairing it, they sat and fiddled, the story went. They found "color" in the stream and stayed right where they'd broken down and never moved again. They started their hotel business and the town sprang up around it. By the time Elitha and Sarah returned to the dining hall, it was cleared for the dance.

The four Walker men — three grown sons and their father — stood on a table with violins in hand. They helped their sister up with her Irish tin flute. Beside the table stood the dowager, apparently Mrs. Walker, with a washtub made into a drum and a scrub board bordered with bells and metal cups. Bringing their fiddles to their chins, the men moved their shoulders in silent rhythm, then a spritely waltz jumped from their bows.

A hand touched Elitha's waist.

She turned and looked into Ben's blue eyes. Before she could introduce him, he swept her across the floor. It was thrilling. Magic. She felt transported to a ball in Vienna. But she didn't want to be anywhere else. She whirled in Ben's arms to the fast one-two-three, one-two-three, skimming the floor with her toes, whirling like a star in the heavens, her heart and spirit sparkling with the tinsel. He was tall enough to look over her head, but he looked down, only at her. And she looked up, locked in his gaze, loving the feel of his arms and the warmth of his breath.

She almost moaned in disappointment when the waltz ended. A smiling man appeared at her elbow. Consulting the card, she saw it was Mr. Tom Richards. The music began and they both struggled to recall the steps of the gavotte. Stumbling through it, she asked all the obligatory questions, "Where are you from?"

"Cornwall." "Where is that?" "Not far from Wales." An accent. "What did you do there?" "Me two brothers'n me were miners." "It's lucky you knew something about mining before you got here." "That it tis." "Havin any luck?" "Fair." A careful tone. Probably finding good color. "Where's your digs?" "Amador, over by Drytown."

The next man was a lawyer from Massachusetts who said with a twinkle that he could make more money shoveling sand in San Francisco. "Why don't you then?" "And miss this!" Apparently having the time of his life, he said he was on the dance committee and similar events were to be held on a regular basis. "A civilizing influence, don't you think?" "Sure is," she agreed.

Back in Ben's arms for a quadrille, she felt like she'd come home. With him teaching her the steps, she twirled easily beneath his arm and paraded up a corridor of dancers, noticing Kate Sherwood, Miss Orten and the Hays girl in the arms of smiling men, even Mrs. Hays. Most men danced with each other. Then she connected with Sarah's icy eyes, and lost the beat.

"Would you like to go out for a breath of air?" asked Ben, reading her mind.

The street was dark, oil lamps glowing from windows high and low. She smelled pine wafting down the mountain. The slight breeze cooled her cheeks. From the open door came perky music and the rasp and stomp of shoes. Ben went to a pump at the boardwalk and cranked it up and down until water shot from the spout into a tin cup, which was chained to the pump. Offering it to her, he asked, "Something on your mind?"

"Yes." But first she took the cup from him and drank.

"Well, I guess we got till the next man comes for you." He worked the pump and guzzled two full cups while she sorted her thoughts. "Is it something I did?" He wanted to know.

"Oh no." Then she realized in a way it was. "Do you know Sarah Daylor?"

"No."

"Mr. Grimshaw?"

"The proprietor of the Cosumne Store?"

"Yes. Well they're married now, and she's one of my best friends. The one I came to the dance with."

"Pretty blonde lady, in a blue frock?" His tone was cautious. She winced to see dark spots on the front of her dress, her breasts leaking, visible even in the half light. She had missed two feedings. She told Ben about the Daylor-Sheldon partnership and explained that Sarah and Catherine Sheldon were sisters.

The music stopped. Immediately an older couple came out the door, the woman fanning her dance card as Ben said, "I think I'm getting the gist. You feel traitorous being seen with me."

"Well, they've done so much for me that — " Embarrassment stopped her. She couldn't see his face, couldn't tell if he was nettled.

A man appeared at the door speaking in the gentlest, humblest tone she'd ever heard. "Ma'am, I guess this is dance number five."

"I'm coming." Turning to Ben, she whispered. "I don't mean to be rude, but I guess I had to tell you." She hoped he would dance with her again.

He put his large, warm hand on her shoulder and said, "Three dances from now we'll talk some more."

The night whirled by in disjointed chunks — chatter with strangers about their digs and occupations, interspersed with increasingly personal talk with Ben, conversation softened by the excellent music and the warm embrace of this long loose, wonderful man.

First she explained that Catherine was minding the baby, and that Ben and his brothers were considered the ringleaders of the squatters who had threatened Mr. Sheldon down at Cosumne about a year ago. Four dances later she described the difficulties Mr. Sheldon was having raising cattle, now that the Indian herders were gone and so many outlaw miners were stealing horses and butchering cattle.

She had to wait four dances to tell him how angry Mr. Sheldon had been this morning about the fence and the Miners Committee. It was a slow waltz and Ben held her closer than before. It seemed unreal, feeling that good while telling him what a nuisance he was.

His breath was warm on the part of her hair. "There's a few things that need to be straightened out, that's all," he said. "Let's us have a talk with the Grimshaws during the intermission." His tone resonated with the confidence she loved.

Relieved, she looked up. With his mouth so near, his breath so fine, she would have kissed him if he'd wanted. Surely a gentleman like this would win them over. And maybe, through him, she could help stop the awful conflict in the river bottom.

84

She sat with Ben's long arm around her and they drove like that down the mountain in a little trap he had rented. Dawn was spreading across the immense valley, tinting the distant coastal mountains. Silver reflections twinkled from a river snaking north to south. The chittering of the awakening birds might just as well have been wedding bells. She and Ben were moving toward a bright new future. Despite dancing all night and eating a wonderful breakfast, she didn't feel one bit drowsy. He had asked her to marry him.

The way she'd smiled, he must have seen the *yes* in her eyes, but she was a proper girl, and said she'd give him her answer before the week was out.

He had handled the talk with Sarah and Mr. Grimshaw like a diplomat, erasing any reservation in her heart; she knew they saw him for the gentleman he was. She couldn't wait for him to speak to Catherine and Mr. Sheldon and explain to them that he had actually stopped the squatter mob, and that if he hadn't, Mr. Sheldon could be dead now. In the confusion, nobody had realized that. Far from a hothead, Ben Wilder was the most reasonable and kind-hearted man she'd ever known. She would be proud to call herself Mrs. Wilder. The thought made her believe in miracles.

She chattered about Fiddletown. "They sure hauled a lot of brick up there to make all those buildings. Must have been Mr. Zins' bricks."

He tugged her closer. "Mr. Zins?"

She explained that he had married Mrs. Wolfinger, who had been rescued with Elitha, and that he had started a brick kiln in the clay pits of Sutterville.

He grinned down at her. "I sure do admire the way you know all the old-timers."

"Old-timers!" she said with a playful jab of her elbow. "Just cause I got here two years before you!"

"Two and a half," he corrected with a crinkle-eyed grin.

She snuggled into him and said, "It's a wonder they built that city so fast."

"Don't ever underestimate the argonauts, or the power of Manifest Destiny. The optimism I heard crossing the plains would float an anvil. Nothing can stop these men."

Other wagons and riders travelled the road, many leaving the dance. Elitha waved at Mr. Richards and his brothers on their way back to Amador. She felt married already, her earrings in her pocket, her loosened hair tickling her neck as the rig bounced forward. She didn't even mind Ben's glance at her front, where rings of white had dried on the brown fabric. A married man needed to know about such things.

At the thought of the milk, a powerful surge swelled her already engorged breasts. The fantasy of the baby hungrily sucking, relieving the pressure, made the milk well up like stoppered geysers. The frock was too tight. The pain cut clear up under her armpits.

Too slowly the wheels ate the long rutted miles, and it became harder to enjoy Ben's arm around her. She squirmed on the seat until he asked after her comfort. As if it were a small thing she joked, "I hope I can last till we get to the Sheldons." The bumps nearly tore her apart.

He was quiet for a time, then said, "Mind if I ask you a question?"

"Go ahead." Anything to take her mind off the pain.

"Well, maybe since you understand how ranchers think, you can explain why a man who purports to own more than," he paused, then emphasized each syllable, "eighteen thousand acres down at Slough House, would come nine miles up to Cook's Bar to grow vegetables where he can't even irrigate without flooding the place with this — dam thing! And that's not profanity, though it tempts me sorely." Something different in his tone — hard and masculine — alerted her to the depths of his feelings, and though she worried about the frightful quarrel in the river, it interested her to see this new side of the man she would marry.

As to the why, she had asked the same question the first time Mr. Sheldon mentioned it, so it was to be expected from a Forty-niner. "Well, like I said, it's real hard to make a living from cattle now, with almost no Indians left to protect them. Some of the miners think the stock is there for the taking, just because there aren't any fences. I know for a fact Mr. Sheldon has lost many thousands of animals. So I guess he decided to try his hand at crops."

"By thunder, then why the devil doesn't he grow his beans or whatever it is down on the land he threw us off of, the first time? A bee gets under his bonnet and he takes a notion to waltz up there and throw us off again!" He took back his arm, holding the reins with both hands.

She realized it might seem like Mr. Sheldon was just trying to bedevil him. She tried again. "Catey says there's too many brambles near the slough to grow vegetables down there, and with no Indians to help clear brush, I guess he thought it was easier to buy Mr. Hartnell's land across from me and — "

"Back where I come from, a man clears his own land." A voice like granite.

But if she was to be married to a miner, she must try to see things the way he did. "What is your Miner's Committee doing?"

"Held a meeting yesterday." He turned to her. "See, Sheldon claims to own the riverbed." His lips spread back as if cleaning his clenched teeth. "Showed us a property deed from the Mexican government. See, it's like if your pa and his neighbors were growing crops on their homesteads back in Illinois, when all of a sudden somebody comes along and says: I can make money by running cows over your land, so, sorry boys." He waved a flippant hand. "Backed up by nothing more than foreign writing on a piece of paper! And like we talked before, it's not likely to stand up in the U.S. courts."

"And your claims could be honored by the courts?" Now she had an interest in the Wilder claim, which would be in the backwater of the dam.

He dipped his head in sharp agreement. "Seems like Mr. Sheldon's got the notion he can part men from their gold." With a dry laugh he looked over at her, "men who walked across the continent to get it. He's planning to flood the claims of about a hundred men. Course at the moment, with the water diverted into the ditch, everybody's happy scraping up color from the main channel, but the minute he pulls out the wing-dam, the water'll back up. And not a man on the river believes he has the right."

"Including you?"

"Yup." No hesitation. "A couple of the boys read law in the states." She felt the granite, the futility of trying to push the two sides together, and began to feel tired.

He turned to her. "Men are killed every day for less.

"Killed!"

"I'm not saying it's right, just a fact. Those of us on the Committee had our hands full."

Killed. Softly, she almost changed the subject. "It's been nice having Catey at Bridge House."

He sighed as if to clean out his mind and reached his long arm and pulled her to him. "That's enough of that. We'll get it all settled. Don't you worry about it." The confident, reasonable, fully-in-charge tone was back. She didn't let on that the squeeze hurt her taut breasts.

Three hours later when the buggy stopped before the Sheldon cabin, she felt crazy with pain. Climbing down with Ben's help — the front of her dress soaked

— she prayed the baby was hungry. No doubt she would be, Catherine having had too little milk for both babies. Elizabeth would suck hard and pull out the pain and restore her to her former cheerful self. Nothing else mattered as she approached the door, not even Ben beside her, ready to face up to Mr. Sheldon.

The door opened. Catherine stood there with a blank expression, hair straggling from her bun, little Sarah gripping her wrinkled skirt. She seemed ill. Behind her, Mr. Sheldon stared at Ben.

Elitha looked from one to the other and realized this would be harder than she'd thought. "Catey," she said, "I'm about to burst. Ben here talked to Sarah and Mr. Grimshaw up at the dance, and he'd like to talk to Mr. Sheldon. I hope you don't mind if I come in and get the baby fed while you're all talking, maybe outside?" Seeing hollow stares, she laid a hand across her breast and added, "It's REAL bad."

Mr. Sheldon came forward and gently pushed Catherine from the door. "Come in Elitha." To Ben he said, "You stay outside," and closed the door.

She looked at the bed, where a lump was covered by her pale green blanket. "Where — " She stepped over and reached.

Catherine grabbed her hand and said, "We did all we could."

Mr. Sheldon added, "Musta been cholera."

She jerked her hand free and threw back the cover. Elizabeth lay still, eyes closed. Collapsing at the bedside, she drew her to her aching bosom and pressed her nose into her sweet baby neck and said quietly, "Ma's come back to you, Precious. Wake up now." What was the matter with these people? Moisture raced from her nipples. Elizabeth felt cool, but not — *I was having fun while —*

Catherine tried to pull her up.

She shook her off and hugged Elizabeth.

"Breathed her last a little while ago," Mr. Sheldon was saying.

"Don't say that!" Panic and anger blinded her as she jumped to her feet with the baby and threw open the door and ran to the rig. Ben joined her with a surprised look on his face.

"Take me home," she said, trying to scramble up the wheel. She missed the foothold, nearly falling on Elizabeth. Ben caught her. A cry sounded. But Elizabeth hadn't moved.

Ben stayed the night rocking her in his arms as she rocked the baby. Blazing color bursts exploded in her mind whenever she allowed herself to step out into the black void, then she would lurch back to solid refusal. In her embrace the baby also refused. All night she refused to nurse, refused to move, refused to make a single sound. Her little arms and hands grew cold and firm, though Elitha warmed her with her body. Outside, bitter gray light outlined the trees. Day. Something nudged her toward the void, and at last, trancelike, her mind made the leap and she stood in the emptiness. A harsh scream scraped out of her throat.

Implacable silence responded. The first sobs pushed up and exploded from her, then long wails. Water poured from her eyes and nose, milk from her breasts, anguish from her heart. Her baby was dead. Oh God no! Ben held her tightly as sobs rocked her, and over and over she told Elizabeth, "I wasn't there to hold you when you cried."

After what seemed hours, her strength wilted, dissolved into whimpers. Slowly Ben disentangled the baby from her arms, laid the small body on the bed, and covered it with the blanket. Taking another blanket he led Elitha from the adobe and, beneath the oak, lay on the ground holding her length to him, petting her hair, murmuring, "There's nothing you could have done. Cholera's bad now. Lots of men have died. Whole tribes of Indians. It's a blessing she went so fast. She's in God's arms now. Sleep, dear Elitha. You must rest."

Closing her eyes seemed a betrayal of Elizabeth, but she finally forced her lids down. Brilliant orange and yellow shapes careened at her from her throbbing head, shocking her to alertness. Thoughtless birds screeched as if Elizabeth had never existed.

Much later, how long she had no idea, Ben took the slats from the door, telling her he'd make a better one, and fashioned a little coffin. Then he dug a grave, and together they buried Elizabeth next to Perry.

"She was so sweet," she said.

"Would you like me to get another marble block?"

Kneeling, touching Perry's block, Elitha said, "No. Just carve Elizabeth's name on the bottom. Here." The hot sun stabbed her swollen eyes and she felt faint, worn-out. Her breasts still cried for Elizabeth, but her eyes had dried. Ben helped her up and supported her.

Asa Wilder appeared on the path, hat in hand. "My condolences, Mrs. McCoon." He had to have been watching.

She couldn't speak.

He cleared his throat apologetically, "Ben, I gotta talk to you a minute. Something's come up."

"I'll see her back inside. Wait by that split rock."

As Ben steered her across the threshold, a sensation pressed into her, something formless, dark, sinister. She made a frightened sound, and backed out. He looked her a question.

"I can't go in." There was a curse.

"What do you mean?"

"I'll lie down over there." Everyone had died.

He helped her to a flat spot where Perry had once penned hogs. She lay straight and still, hands over her womb, her thoughts compacting like a clock wound tighter and tighter. She had known the baby was sick when she went to the dance. She had enjoyed herself while her baby was dying. She had neglected her.

"Elitha," Ben called after a minute or two, "I've got to go over to Cook's Bar. There's a problem. Will you be all right?"

She sat up. A hard shiver passed through her, though the day was warm. Her head was muddled and she couldn't answer.

He came and kneeled beside her. "I'm sorry to say this now, but the men are up in arms down at the dam."

"I'll come with you."

He looked at her a long time with his blue eyes sloping down from the outside corners, then took her in his arms and said, "I'm sorry but you can't. It wouldn't be safe."

She sighed. Men thought they were immortal. They fought over unimportant things. But life had to go on. "I'll be fine here."

As his lanky frame disappeared up the path, Indian Mary stepped from the trees holding a handful of vegetation. She had been waiting. At her knee, Little Billy's dimples cut into his chubby cheeks. Mary looked up.

Elitha looked too. Coming up the trail from Bridge House was Catherine and her baby with little Will helping little Sarah toddle alongside.

Remembering how rude she'd been, she staggered to her feet.

They met in an embrace, the baby between, Elitha's voice shaky. "Forgive me, Catey." Her cheek felt plump and smooth, and wet.

She sniffed back tears. "I was afraid you blamed me. Oh, Elitha, I'm so grieved. We tried so hard. Did everything we could think of." She swallowed hard, the live baby squirming in her arms.

"I never should have gone to the dance," she said trying to control her sobs. "But I'm ever so grateful for all you did." How pathetic words were! She hugged this best friend with every ounce of feeling she had.

Indian Mary's voice came from behind. "I bring sleep tea."

They both turned. Mary laid her hand on Elitha's shoulder and seemed to see into her, though in the Indian way her gaze missed its mark. They formed a three-way embrace, the newborn in the middle, the older baby on Mary's back, Billy and Sarah and little Will at their knees.

85

Joaquín Sheldon stood before his Bridge House cabin, wolf eyes leveled at Pedro. "Gracias for coming so fast."

Pedro dipped his hat. The *Indio* runner had found him in Spanish Camp, and he had not hesitated.

"Needed you to help get this cannon in position." He tilted his hat toward his wagonbed, where a big lump pushed up what looked like a heap of moth-eaten old mission *Indio* blankets.

"Cannon? From the fort?" Had it come to that?

Sheldon nodded. "There's a dozen of em left down there, no use to anybody. Figured I might as well help myself. It'll show those miners I mean business."

He had a team hitched to the wagon, but Pedro and Sheldon sat on the stoop smoking and talking of old times until a man rode up. Sheldon introduced him as James Johnson, a friend from the Slough House area. Then Pedro and Mr. Johnson were positioning planks around the cannon to further disguise it, then riding ahead of Sheldon's wagon up through Cook's Bar just as cool as you please, Mr. Sheldon clucking his team and nodding to acquaintances as if he were hauling nothing more than the next load of lumber for his dam. People seemed accustomed to the sight.

They passed the Eating House and the thickest bunch of tents and started up a hill through the live oaks. Mr. Johnson looked over at Pedro and said, "You working fer Jared?" He wore an amicable smile under his hat, blue eyes, pale complexion — an ordinary *Norteamericano* face like the men Pedro routinely relieved of their gold.

"We are *amigos*. And you, señor? You work for him?"

"No. Jared's gonna cut me in on the vegetables, for my work on the dam. I wrote to home fer the missus and the boys to come out and join me. Plan to make a new start out in this country, maybe buy some of Sheldon's land down around Slough House."

They left the trail and headed up an incline, the ground rough with rocks and scrub trees, easy for the saddle horses, but difficult for the team. But in a very few minutes Sheldon called ahead to stop. They had arrived near a high rocky bluff overlooking the empty river channel and the uncompleted dam — another marvel of Yankee ingenuity, an amazing structure sixteen feet high, horizontal slabs of split oak fitted between uprights and wedged into the boulders for support. The center portion wasn't finished, but when it was, the dam would back the river to a height where water could flow into Sheldon's channel at the base of this outcropping, in a natural ravine, and back to his vegetables. Miners on both sides of the dam were squatting with their paraphernalia, looking down.

Pedro helped slide the cannon down a wood ramp that Sheldon had laid by for that purpose, and took down the wheels and tongue piece. Sheldon set to putting the fieldpiece back together while Pedro and Mr. Johnson stood lookout. But no man showed his face. It took all the strength the three had to pull the heavy brass piece up the tiered rocks to the wide, flat top, like pulling it upstairs. When they positioned it, they saw that every man down below was standing looking up.

"Good," Sheldon said. "Give 'em something to think about."

They went back for the canisters of grapeshot, carrying armloads from the wagon, and stacked them beside the cannon. Still no one came. Johnson mopped his face with a bandanna and said, "Well, that's about it."

"Yup," said Sheldon.

Pedro was looking at the cannon, realizing it was the same type as *La Pulga Vieja*, as they had called her — the eight pounder General Vallejo had used in the Indian war. Captain Sutter had collected it along with many other unused field pieces.

"Which one of you wants the first watch?" Sheldon asked. "I gotta go down to a meeting at the Eating House." He had men lined up to keep a round-the-clock guard.

"I will guard *la señora*," Pedro said. It looked familiar.

Señor Johnson stuck out his hand. "Peers we're pardners."

Pedro shook the friendly *Norteamericano* hand, and it gave him a peculiar sensation, like the sand was shifting under his feet.

But after the two men rode away, he felt an even stranger feeling when he examined the brass nozzle and found the foundry mark. He stood looking at it, amazed to think he'd fought against Captain Juan with this very weapon. He remembered well having gone to the shop with his companions and checked the marks to make sure they got the one that had been repaired. This very cannon had given the presidios their so-called victory over the Valley Indians. And here he was twenty-two years later, positioning it to kill *Norteamericanos*. How quickly the world changed! Missions in decay, the war with the United States lost, the rush for gold sweeping all before it. His former enemy was now his father-in-law. He shook his head in disbelief at the tricks life played.

Ben Wilder stood on a crate and banged two shovel blades together over his head. The packed Eating House quieted as the agitated men looked up at him. Handing the shovels to brother Asa, he slipped Sheldon's proposal from his pocket and read aloud from the paper:

"July 6, 1851

Proposition of Jared D. Sheldon. I wish to use the water upon my farm long enough sufficiently to irrigate it — which will probably require from 6 to 10 days, after which I expect to leave the water run, as usual, and pledge myself through my Committee that the river shall not be interfered with, under this arrangement.

Second — it may be necessary to use the water once in 2 or 3 weeks after this, if so, I shall use the water but one day in the week and that on Sundays. The miners reaping the benefit all the rest of the week.

Committee (James Breen, Henry Waddilove, A. W. Lewis)

This proposition to be accepted or rejected before 6 o'clock this evening."

Talk erupted. Pointing to the wall Ben raised his voice and cut off the clamor with: "For those who can read, I'm nailing it over there. For those who can't, here's the gist: Mr. Sheldon," he waved the paper toward the window where Sheldon and his dozen men stood, "will finish out the dam with a sluice, a four-foot gate."

He chose his words carefully. This was no time for inflaming the men. "Then he'll back the river up for 6 to 10 days, or as long as it takes to give his ground a good soaking. After that he'll pull up the sluice and let the water run. He doesn't think the vegetables will need but two or three more soakings after that, depending on the heat. And at those times he'll lower the sluice at sundown Saturday and let the water rise till it reaches his race, then raise it Sunday night." Most men soused themselves on Sundays anyway.

He glanced at Sheldon's intense stare. "Is that fairly stated?"

Sheldon dipped his hat.

Ben concluded, "Now we'll discuss whether to sign this proposal. We on the Miner's Committee want to hear all sides — whether your claims are down under the dam or back behind it. Who'll speak first?"

As the Counselor came forward, Ben stepped down, gesturing toward the crate. He felt torn. Much as he despised Sheldon's attitude and felt that no man had the right to flood mining claims, never mind how long, his love for Elitha moderated his sense of justice. Through her, he now had a personal link with the Sheldons, and had to admit that in presenting this written proposal, the rancher had shown a measure of self-imposed restraint. Ben would listen carefully, weigh what others said.

Balancing on the crate with an almost comical show of caution, the heavy, gray-haired speaker leaned back on his heels and made himself comfortable before the crowd. Then came his stentorian tones:

"Gentlemen, verily I say unto you, the granting of this proposition will set a dangerous precedent for years to come. As many of you know, my claim is below the dam and I stand to benefit for a time from the absence of water. But the Interests of Justice for the Majority must, in this case, override personal gain. I warn you against the placement of signatures upon any document penned by a man of agriculture, and hereby set forth my reasoning." He moved his feet farther apart. Ben listened attentively, though he'd heard the Counselor speak on this subject before.

"At this juncture, we in California find ourselves hoisted on the horns of a dilemma. As we speak, the Legislature has commenced to consider disputes arising between the interests of mining and those of agriculture. Farmers claim to own the streams and riverbeds and that means, my good friends, if it be found to be true, they control all the water in this dry territory — the very substance of life, the crucial element in mining. Yet they are few, and we are many. The Majority possesses the right to divert water as befits its needs, when and where it wishes. This is the American way. Furthermore, our Creator endows each of us with the inalienable right to work our claims without interference!" A cheer exploded, the Counselor waiting.

"And so, gentlemen, you miners stand on the profoundly opposite and repulsing pole from the so-called ranchers, who are the direct beneficiaries of the defunct Mexican government." He made eye contact around the room, finishing with a look at Ben. "If you sign any document that can be construed as GRANTING Mr. Sheldon the right to control the river, as sure as day follows night, it will weigh on the rancher's side of scales when the Legislature acts. Do not wait until it is too late to recognize your folly."

Ben thought through the complexity of that as, beneath the Counselor's furrowed gray brows, his glance shifted around the crowd. Then the man cocked an eye to the ceiling and proceeded like a storyteller. "Two men are wrestling." He turned to one side, put his heels together and bowed slightly. "The smaller of the two asks the other: If you would be so good, sir, please allow me to lock my arm around your neck before the whistle is blown."

He raised his voice. "That, gentlemen, is the request before you today. If you wish to continuing mining in California, do not kowtow to Mr. Sheldon. Insist on the dam's removal. We are the Majority."

As the older man stepped down amidst shouts of approval, Ben raised an arm, pointing at the head of James Gallogly, known as Corky, who was coming forward. In the moments before Corky spoke, Ben reviewed the merit of the Counselor's argument, different from his usual *the United States government owns the nation's streams, not the Mexican ranchers.* And he had a flash that the resolution of this dispute could affect all areas of the arid West, which would no doubt follow California into becoming settled territories of the United States.

Corky, a spokesman for the Irishmen who had flocked to the mines via New York, observed in bemused humility: "Would that we were all blessed with such a tongue!" He bowed low toward the Counselor, drawing a laugh. Many regarded the potato famine refugees as little more than monkeys. But they constituted about a third of the mining population in this area now, and that was a measure of power. Ben wanted their opinion.

"In me County Cork homeland, ye understand, I had me perfect fill of the outrageous claims of the landed. And a wonder it tis to come to America — all these distant fathoms to the farthest shore — only to find another o' that ilk bedevilin the mines of Californy. I, for one, will swim back before I sign that paper." A roar came from the Irish, supported by claps from others. "As for the dam, laddies, take up yer axes!"

More than the Irish yelled approval. "Axes to the dam!" "Axes!" came from many throats. Mr. Sheldon leveled a wolf-like stare from one to another, mouth slightly parted. Good for him to hear this, Ben thought.

Others spoke in succession. Jim Breen, Sheldon's man — also an Irishman — tried to speak, though miners interrupted with shouts, especially when he declared, "A perfect gentleman is Mr. Sheldon, and a better friend we couldn't find to represent us in the Legislature." Breen's claim was beneath the dam, so few took him seriously.

"Give him the floor," shouted Cody. "We need to hear all sides of this." Had Cody changed his mind?

Breen continued, then Ben called on Cody, a tough breed of man with a good education.

"We've heard Mr. Sheldon called an imperious and callous landowner," said Cody. "Yet I've been standing here amazed to see a landowner willing to curtail his self-perceived rights to satisfy men who might be termed squatters." An angry rumble rose, and Cody raised his voice to be heard over it.

"Men, men, you have every right to establish claims along the river, you know I believe that. All I'm saying is, put yourselves in this man's place." He pointed to Sheldon. "Give him credit for backing down from where he started."

As he spoke, Ben handed Asa the paper, pantomiming nailing it to the wall. Cody's points were well made. Sheldon had, indeed, come in the spirit of compromise. Cody finished:

"You've won your point, men. Most of you take the day off on Sundays anyway — sewing on buttons, reading Scripture and — " Laughter stopped him and he smiled, then resumed. "So go prospect somewhere else during the first flooding, then, when the water recedes, it'll do some of your work for you, washing out dirt you'd have to dig otherwise. Sign the paper, I say. Mr. Sheldon proposes a fair deal."

Ben respected Cody, and he noticed by the nodding heads in the audience that others did too. But young hotheads who relished violence were peppered among them. "Ain't fair," they shouted.

"We'll lose more'n a week's take!" Another yelled.

Jared Sheldon came forward without waiting to be invited. When he stepped on the crate the hooting and shouting seemed about to lift the roof. Ben raised his arms. "Let him talk, boys."

"That cannon don't look like no negotiatin!" Somebody yelled. Ben had been notified about the cannon — Sheldon's backup strategy, he knew. The rancher stood hard-jawed, taking in the men's reactions. Angry shouts continued, and it looked like the meeting might splinter into a fight. Men were fingering revolvers. Sheldon started speaking, but the shouts didn't stop.

The word "compensate" stood out from Sheldon's drowned speech. It softened the faces of those in the front. They turned to those behind. "Listen to him!" " . . . pay you . . . " "Compensate" hissed back through the crowd.

At last even those in the back quieted, all men looking at Sheldon. He narrowed his yellowish eyes around the crowd, the point of his jaw twitching. "I will compensate every man in the backwater for every lost day of mining."

Shouts: "How much?"

"I've been told the average take here is fifteen dollars a day." He hurried on through a growing rumble, "I'm prepared to pay twenty." That would make the vegetables dear, Ben thought.

Silence. Then a shout: "To each man in every claim?"

"Yup." A clipped, New England sound. Reading the mood-shift of the crowd, Ben recalled Cody's words, *a fair deal.* It was the most they could have hoped for, a deal to stop violence.

He climbed the crate Sheldon vacated, and the crowd silenced. "Men, I've heard enough. As Committee Chairman I think we'd better take this offer. Do I hear a motion?"

"So move," Cody called.

Ben was quick. "All in favor say aye."

A chorus responded.

"All opposed say no." The hotheads shouted no.

"Ayes have it."

Sheldon and his men beelined through the parting crowd. Ben reached for the shovels, clanking them overhead. As men looked back over their shoulders he said, "If Mr. Sheldon doesn't honor the agreement, we meet here and talk." But he hoped Sheldon was an honorable man.

The outcome of the meeting seemed too pat, too easy. The ornery cusses in the corner gave him a dose of skepticism.

86

SUNDAY MORNING, JULY 12, 1851

Señor Sheldon had been in his field since dawn, clearing the little ditches from the main channel to the crop rows. The corn had begun to wilt; however, the river had backed up all night and the water was starting to flow. Sheldon's son worked with his own little hoe, which the *patrón* had made for him. Three *años* now. Pedro smiled at Little Will from Chocolate's back, hoping someday he too would have a son working beside him.

But his heart was not smiling. This morning, waking up to the flooding for the first time, the miners had demanded more compensation. Sheldon had refused. That was an hour ago, and the *malcriados* had been drinking ever since.

"Will you still pay twenty dollars a day?" Pedro asked the *patrón*.

"They terminated the deal." His lips pressed shut.

He rode back to where he could see the cannon and check on the guard. Downstream the other scout waved his hat — the signal that all was well. But it was not. Trouble could erupt at any time. All his senses felt honed.

Feeling disconnected, as if she had been severed from the earth's gravity, Elitha finished washing the breakfast tins. Since Elizabeth's death, the only thing she'd looked forward to was driving through the southern mines with Ben and planning their wedding. They were supposed to leave after the noon meal. But it was frightening, the things the miners had muttered over biscuits and gravy this morning. Some seemed to hate Mr. Sheldon, despite his agreement to pay them for lost time. She looked out over the full ditch and the empty river channel, too muddy to cross, and felt drawn to Ben and his side of the river. She walked up to the bridge and around toward Cook's Bar.

Fifteen minutes later she saw Ben in a circle of tents, standing in the midst of a very noisy crowd of men, many putting bottles to their lips. He saw her and tried to pull himself away, but every time he did, a man would shout something and he would turn back and speak to them. With a look of desperation, he looked over their heads — like it pained him to tear his gaze from her — and finally waved her on. He'd talk to her later.

Knowing Ben was sorely needed there, glad — oh so glad he was there to make these rowdy men stick to their agreement — she went beyond the town to the high rocks, curious about the cannon, and found Vyries Brown sitting beside it, rifle over his knees. He raised a hand in greeting. "What brings you out here, Miz McCoon?" His cracking voice betrayed his youth.

"Nerves, I guess." Never having seen a cannon, she gathered her skirts and climbed up the rocks. Beside it stood a keg stamped: GUNPOWDER, McCallister & Co.

"Makes the skin prickle don't it?" Vyries' pug nose and red hair made him look even younger. Worry showed in his moss-green eyes as he looked at a group of men in the riverbed.

But she had faith in Ben. "Do you know how to fire it?" Catey had said it was only to show the men Mr. Sheldon meant business, and it certainly had got their attention.

"Sure. Mr. Sheldon showed me. One shot of these'll level a crowd of men." He patted the stack of open canisters filled with round, gray balls.

"Well, I hope it won't come to that." She changed the subject. "Did you come out to California by yourself?"

"Me and me big brother came round through Panama," he said, chewing on a long yellow straw. "But it's dead he is now, lying up yonder." He jerked his head up river.

"I'm so sorry."

"There be a lot of dyin in these lonely hills, missus. Many a poor man lyin down before his Maker without so much as a proper prayer said o're him." His copper curls flamed in the sun and flakes peeled from his nose. He knew about Elizabeth because he often took his meals at Elitha's, but they had never really talked.

"Some are afraid to help the ill," she said. "Did you know Mr. Daylor was stricken after he helped a dying man?"

"Aye. And that's a story comin round. T'would make a man feel forsaken to be shunned at his own dyin." Looking over the dam, he worked on his straw.

"I wish men wouldn't fight. Why are you doing this, Vyries?" She touched the tarnished brass muzzle, hot already in the sun.

The straw wiggled and he shrugged.

"If you end up firing it, you'll kill your friends. Have you thought of that?"

He sighed and stared down at the river, empty below the dam, full above. "Me friends is all back in the old country."

"I know better than that. You've got friends here all right, and it'd be a terrible sin to kill them."

He blinked his glistening eyes. "Me dear old mither woulda said such a thing." Pensively he added, "And t'would be a wonder if she's eatin atall, over there!" He let out a sigh, no doubt thinking about the famine.

"Do you believe in sin?"

He crossed himself. "Aye." It came out deep, a man's voice.

"Then how could you fire at living men?" She touched the neat bunches of iron balls, like big seeds in open pods.

He threw down his straw. "Sure and tis what I've been thinkin since sunup!" He stood up with his gun, his voice cracking high. "And me own dear mither limpin down to Saint Paddy's to pray fer me soul all those many miles away." He wiped a sleeve across his peeling nose and walked away, his tattered trousers disappearing into the brush.

She stayed there, feeling the intensifying heat, expecting him to return from a call of nature. Below the weeping dam, a few miners shoveled madly in the mud. Others hurriedly rocked sand and gravel in their cradles, as if expecting the river would soon spill back into its bed. She heard drunken shouts. Perhaps Lorena Gordon was right that Temperance was the answer to the wickedness of mankind. Liquor had certainly made Perry nasty, and a lot of it was being consumed this morning. But that was no different than other Sundays. Fights were common. Fortunately, most men appreciated Mr. Sheldon's deal.

She heard footsteps and looked up, but it wasn't Vyries. Three men came up the rocks, one who regularly ate dinner at her table. They returned her nod and smile, but she felt awkward beside the cannon, so she stood and brushed her skirts and was leaving as they opened a little lid on top and positioned something in it. One of the men pounded with the side of his pick. They had to be Sheldon's men, no doubt sent to spell Vyries, and he'd been too upset to bid her a polite good-bye.

She went back to the adobe, passing Ben, who remained occupied. But she couldn't let it rest. She walked up the path to where she could just see the dam from her side of the river and was about to sit on a rock, when she saw a large rattlesnake coiled on it. She backed up and tossed a rock. Its tail buzzed and she found a different rock. Shuddering — rattlesnakes were so thick — she sat tentatively, and hadn't been there more than a few seconds when Indian Mary stepped beside her, Isabella on her back, Billy alongside. "My man says maybe trouble." Mary's face showed worry — a rare sight for her. "Your tall friend too?"

"Maybe." Their men would be on opposite sides. She patted the big stone beside her.

Indian Mary sat and nodded toward the cannon. "Big gun broke big walls in war of black hats," she said. "Many people die."

"It's only to scare the miners. They won't need to fire it."

Then she noticed men crashing down the bank to join those already in the riverbed. Other groups of men were joining them. She watched in comprehending shock as they converged and headed up the channel toward the dam, lifting their feet slowly from the mud like men in a bad dream, axes and guns in hand. Three tall men were among them. Lord no! Would Vyries fire at them? She looked toward the high outcropping, but couldn't see the cannon. And though the miners arrived at the dam and raised their axes to it, no explosion sounded. Her stomach tightened in anticipation; but then with sudden and absolute clarity she knew that the men working on the cannon had not been on Mr. Sheldon's side.

Had her talk with Vyries upset the balance of threat?

A rider appeared on the crest of the opposite bluff — Señor Valdez looking down at the miners. He turned his horse and galloped away, dust rising. Mary stood up, staring after him.

Pedro spurred Chocolate through the corn. He and the other scout arrived simultaneously. "Jared," Señor Lewis yelled, "they're axing the dam!" Sheldon threw down his shovel and scowled toward the river, which couldn't be seen from there.

"It is true, *patrón*," Pedro said.

Sheldon's yellowish eyes drilled him. "Then why don't I hear the cannon?" Instructions were to fire at anyone who touched the dam. To Señor Lewis, he said, "Ride to Sacramento, get the Sheriff." It would take hours.

Nodding, the man offered his rifle. "Here, Jared. I won't need this. You'd better take it."

Sheldon took the gun, picked up Little Will and ran for his horse, which was tied to an oak limb. He put Will on the saddle, mounted and pounded toward the river. Riding smoothly, he yelled over at Pedro, who galloped alongside, "I thought that boy on the cannon was a good kid."

They rode beside the main ditch, past scattered tents, Sheldon shouting, his *amigos* dropping what they were doing and trotting behind. When they pulled the horses up at the bluff, about a hundred armed men stood below the sluice, many with picks and axes, all looking up at them. Sheldon's nostrils flared in angry disbelief.

On the rocks, the cannon dozed in the sun with its top open. The boy was nowhere to be seen. Across the river Maria and Elitha sat at safe distance downstream. From the riverbottom came a thunk. Then more thunks. Axes on wood.

Señores Johnson, Cody and the others arrived, panting, rifles in hand. "Why ain't that cannon blasting 'em all to hell?"

"Yeah! What the dev — "

"It looks spiked, *patrón*," Pedro said. "I will go see." He started to dismount.

"No," Sheldon said, "Tex, you do it." As Tex dismounted, Sheldon turned to Pedro and said, "*Por favor*, I trust you with what is most *importante*. Keep my son safe." He lifted Will from the saddle and held him, short legs walking in the air, toward Pedro.

With foreboding — the child would hamper his ability to help — he sidestepped Chocolate and took the boy to his lap, but spoke from his heart. "Those men look dangerous, señor, like a stampeding herd. The dam, he is not so *importante*."

"A man's gotta draw a line. This here is my property. If I back down now, pretty soon I'll have nothing left."

Pedro glanced down at the angry mob and felt as if the grapeshot, which should have been felling these *desgraciados*, were churning in his stomach.

Tex was peering into the cannon port with the posture of a man discovering a broken axle. Looking up, he said, "Spiked." More thunks came from below.

Sheldon dismounted and gestured with his rifle. "Come on boys, follow me." He strode down the bank, boots skidding, gravel rolling ahead. His men followed, rifles in hand.

"Virgin help him," Pedro murmured, crossing himself.

The boy looked up asking, "What?"

"It was a prayer, *niño*."

Outnumbered ten to one, Sheldon walked toward the miners. It flashed in Pedro's mind that he could leave the child and help, but no. The boy might follow, and Pedro was too far away for a good shot. Besides Sheldon's men would be in the way.

The *patrón* stood face to face with the miners and his voice carried up the bank: "You men are trespassing. The next one touches that dam dies!" In a line behind him, his friends raised their rifles.

A shot exploded. The boy flinched.

A man collapsed and fell over a rock. A shout: "Give it to Sheldon." Pedro held his breath.

Multiple reports echoed up the river. Men fell, Sheldon face down in the mud. Sick in his stomach and gripping the child's hand — *más importante* — Pedro watched helplessly as men scrambled into the rocks. Shots rang off boulders and thudded into the wood of the dam. Men ducked in and out as they fired. The boy was urgently asking a question — indistinct as if underwater.

"Hold your fire!" somebody yelled.

Slowly men crept into the open. Some of the miners toed up the bank, guns in hand, hat brims down over their faces. It had happened in less than a minute. The shooting was over.

Sheldon's men stood over the wounded. They squatted and turned Sheldon over onto his back.

Very sick now, Pedro said to the child, "Can you sit on those rocks by yourself? And not move?" The boy nodded. Pedro dismounted, quickly hobbled the horse, and sat the boy down, giving him a stern finger. He looked like he'd never move again.

The *patron's* eyes were open but blood ran from a large hole in his right breast and from his left armpit, a single ball having torn through him. Señor Johnson was badly wounded, blood pumping through his shirt from an opening over his heart. Señor Cody writhed and moaned, bleeding from the abdomen. Others grimaced and gripped their wounds. No miners that Pedro could see were dead or wounded.

Armed miners remained in the river bottom; men with axes watched from the sluice. They had won. Pedro could hardly breathe and his heart boomed with pent-up, futile pain, wishing he could turn back time. What had gone wrong? So terribly and irreparably wrong?

Looking down at Sheldon, his vision blurred with moisture.

Weakly the *patrón* whispered, "My son?"

"He is well, señor, up there." He pointed, blinking. "Now I take you to your house." It looked like a miracle was needed to save him; Señora Catherine would want him near her. As he lifted Sheldon's feet, another man his arms, a splintering thunk came from the dam. And another, and another.

"You bastards!" a man yelled. "At least wait till we git the wounded outa here." The axing stopped.

When they had Sheldon halfway up the bank, the sounds resumed. Pedro rode with the boy alongside Señor Sheldon, who hung face down over his saddle. Others were taking Johnson and Cody to their tents. The ride from the dam to the cabin, which had always seemed short, now took an eternity, but he couldn't rush it, with the *patrón* bleeding.

Still trembling with shock and rage and the need to turn back time — *Madre de Dios*, he still couldn't believe it — he helped carry Joaquín Sheldon into his new house and laid him gently on the pine floor, at Señora Catherine's feet. She stared down, the youngest infant in her arms, then kneeled beside her husband. No man could afford to lose so much blood. It was pooling around him. Sheldon's eyes were rolled back in his head, but his lids fluttered. Little Will and his younger sister stared. "Pa dead?" asked Will, his innocent face troubled. Pedro turned away and gulped back emotion. *Más importante.*

The Señora put the baby on a chair, tore a strip of the baby's blanket and pressed it into the wounds. Then, hands trembling, she took her husband's hand and put it between hers, and leaned down and kissed his face. A girl really, even younger than María.

Unable to tolerate another instant, Pedro said, "I will ride for María. She knows herb medicine." But he knew it was hopeless. On the floor lay the most honorable man he had ever known, killed by gold miners. He had the feeling, as he went out the door, that his last link to the civilized world of reason had been severed.

Watching for snakes, Elitha stepped down through the rocks, the dam drawing her like a magnet in a nightmare. Maria was running up the path toward Bridge House, no doubt looking for Señor Valdez. They had been too far away to see the shooting, and it happened too fast. Men were being carried out. Who? Mr. Sheldon? "Couldn't be." Ben? "Couldn't be" kept time with her steps, competing with the gunshots still ringing in her ears.

The mud was deep in the river bottom so she made her way along the side, over humps of dirt and around the "coyote holes." Were those thuds axes? Or her heart? She couldn't tell. Questions jumped in her mind. Had men died because Vyries left the cannon? Who fired first? Was it her fault?

When she got there Ben wasn't among the men chopping at the dam. No men lay among the rocks, though blood covered a round boulder, like a bloodied bald head poking out of the mud, and she saw the mud reddened in places. A man cried, "Stand back!" The men with axes dashed for the south bank. She climbed the bank, realizing she should have crossed the river when she had the chance.

Water spouted from an opening in the sluice, spilling as if from a giant faucet. Then with a noisy crack, a timber broke and the rush of water thickened, breaking loose another timber. It poured smoothly, washing the blood down the river, rising up around the bald red rock, long fingers of water rapidly probing their way downstream. Miners pulled back their tools and rockers.

Elitha gathered her skirts and broke into a run back toward the bridge. She had to find Ben.

But the sight of lathered horses outside the Sheldon cabin stopped her, including the one belonging to Señor Valdez. The saddle on Jared Sheldon's horse was unnaturally red. With a gathering sense of dread she knocked, gasping for breath.

Catherine opened the door and stared as if blind, the white of her face as shocking as the red sheet of blood on the floor behind. Mr. Sheldon lay in the middle of it, still as stone, his face blank. The brightness of the blood dulled all else in the room — the baby fussing in the chair, little Will staring and little Sarah staring. *Three babies*. Indian Mary and Señor Valdez passed by, leaving. Two miners squatted beside Mr. Sheldon, their hats off as if in prayer.

"Oh Catey!" Elitha stepped toward her.

"You'd better go," Catherine said in the distant voice of a stranger. "Ben Wilder did this."

Slowly Elitha backed out as Catherine shut the door. Feeling as if she were melting apart, she stood staring at the door. Oh dear God in heaven, no. Jared Sheldon was dead or Indian Mary wouldn't be leaving. She had to sit — out of sight of the cabin. Out of sight of Señor Valdez and Indian Mary, who were mounting his horse, out of sight of the ogling driver clucking his team across the bridge, and the Chinese miners trotting beside, and the curious men coming down from Cook's Bar. She couldn't talk to Ben or anyone until she could breathe. Until the pieces of her firmed up and came back together.

Shakily she went down the steep rocky incline and sat under the bridge watching the recently pent-up river, muddy as it came, hurl itself through the bottom boulders. The splash of it swirled with the tempest in her mind. Overhead, the rumble of wagons and hollow tattoo of hooves and boots drummed with her confused heart. The cursed adobe and condor feathers came to mind, hung over her. The world had gone crazy. Was she responsible for Jared Sheldon's death? She had slept outside the adobe after Elizabeth's death, but, having no alternative, convinced herself it was stupid superstition and resumed living inside. She had been blinded by her love for Ben. Now her best friend had shut her out, a girl with three babies and no husband. For all she knew Ben was dead too, but she hadn't the strength to go see. She felt limp, paralyzed in the shade of the noisy bridge.

Later — she felt completely unaware of the passage of time — Pa's words came to her. *You got Donner blood. Nothing can stop you.* Just go down the trail. But it was a path littered with death, heads like signposts along a road, beloved people buried to the neck staring at her as she passed by. How many? She didn't even know. But she had to go find out if Ben was among them.

She climbed the boulders up to the bridge. No horse was at the Sheldon cabin, the wagon gone. No doubt they had taken him back to the mill house and would bury him in the Indian mound beside Mr. Daylor. Sheldon and Daylor together again. In the space of two years she and the Rhoads sisters — Elizabeth, Sarah and Catherine — were all widowed. She yearned to be included in the circle of their forgiving arms, to ease the guilt scraping through her, and to help Catey with her babies. But the door had shut in her face. Perhaps deservedly so.

The sun had moved across the sky and the river had quieted to its normal summer flow, miners washing dirt as if nothing had happened. She arrived at the Eating House and looked over the heads of the eating men, Ben not among them. She walked swiftly to the Wilder claim, beyond the dam.

She came over a rise and saw the crude fence, but no tent. A square of packed earth marked where it had been. The Wilder longtom lay on its side. Her heart pounded as she approached the river's edge where a man was rocking a cradle. He looked up, touched his hat and smiled. "Ma'am."

"Howdy. Would you know where I might find Ben Wilder?"

"Nope. Them Wilder boys abandoned their claim. Looked awful keen to clear out, I'd say." Watching that hit her — every man in Cook's Bar knew she and Ben were to be married — he pushed the upper box back and forth over the lower box, sand and gravel dropping, rolling against the screen, dirty water leaking from the spout at the bottom.

"Thank you," she managed, part of her leaking out too. *Cleared out.* Alive. Maybe he had tried to find her, but she'd been under the bridge. She returned to the Eating House, walked up the aisle between staring men, opened the door and went into the kitchen. *Cleared out.* Like a guilty man.

Three women turned from the counter, Mrs. Gordon's sleeves rolled up on hairy arms. Elitha collapsed on a chair beside her.

Mrs. Gordon furrowed her too-prominent brow. "You're not cooking supper over at your place tonight?"

"No. I was wondering if you knew where Ben Wilder went?" It hurt her pride to admit she didn't know.

Mrs. Gordon wiped her hands on her apron and pulled up a chair. Lorena went out the door with a stack of plates and a steaming pot hanging at her knees, "All I know is what I'm about to say." Her manner, sympathetic and motherly, increased Elitha's alarm.

"I got dinner done and set out by noon, but the men came in late. By then the grease was clabbered over. And my, what a sorry lot they were!" She glanced away, frowning at the memory. "Their chins hung right down to their chests. You could just see the — " She stopped as if searching for a word, and settled on, "remorse."

Narrowing a dark eye, she continued, "Ben Wilder took one look at the food and ran outside. He retched good and long out there. In the meantime his brothers said, over and over, 'If only we hadn't done it. If only we hadn't done any of it.' Just like that. Over and over. Finally Ben comes back in and says to me, 'Mrs. Gordon, I can't eat.' He slumped down on one of the benches for the longest time. Then, when most of the men had gone, I came over and ladled the stew so he could see all the goodness in it, but he shook his head. Then he settled his bill and says to me, 'I'm done with mining, for good." Just like that. He went out the door, and I haven't seen hide nor hair of him since. Would've asked about you, but he was heading out so fast — " She gave Elitha a pinched expression of sorrow — a woman who had brought six daughters to California to find husbands. "He didn't talk to you?"

"I wasn't home." She needed to escape the pitying eyes. He had to be guilty.

"Mr. Johnson and Mr. Cody died too," Mrs. Gordon said, adding to the horror, "and more bad wounded."

"Any miners hurt?"

"Nope."

One-sided. She forced out a thank you and left.

Outside, men were talking to a young man in a gray suit, who was busily scratching notes on paper. He raised his chin and said, "Excuse me, miss. I'm with the *Sacramento Union*. Did you happen to see the riot this morning?"

"No." She hurried toward the bridge, knowing the reporter had gotten an earful. *Riot.* Would all of California soon read that Ben Wilder had led a murderous mob? And that Elitha Donner had been his intended?

Dread slowed her steps as she crossed the bridge. Ben could be hiding at her place, expecting her to protect him. Could she tell him to get out? Catherine's face kept coming at her, the way she'd looked shutting the door. It brought to mind the expressions of certain people when they had called her a cannibal, expressions that said she occupied the other side of an important divide. Passing by, she saw the door of the Sheldon cabin open, as if men had gone in to see the blood on the floor — a place as empty as her heart.

Her adobe was equally empty. She searched, but found no note. The sun was going down. Elizabeth was dead. Perry was dead, Pa and Tamsen, Uncle Jacob and Aunt Betsy, her cousins and all the others. And now Mr. Sheldon. People picked themselves up after a barn burned or a loved one died, but this was more. Her betrothed had killed a good man and left her to live with it. Her friends had turned against her. She was alone on this trail.

87

Long hours of work and talks with Indian Mary kept Elitha going. She hauled water up from the river and brought in loads of oak limbs, chopping the wood. She dickered with professional hunters who brought long strings of birds — fifty to a hundred at a time. She singed and plucked feathers and cooked meals for larger and larger crowds. She spoke little with her customers and declined many invitations to sings, stage performances and other events. And she slept in the adobe with a knife and Perry's gun.

Then the Bridge House Dance Hall was completed and she began accepting invitations. Music and dancing helped put Ben out of her mind, and she was glad she hadn't married him. She was also glad the turnover of miners was so great that most had never heard of him. Nevertheless, she couldn't forget the "horrible riot in the Cosumne" — as the *Sacramento Union* called it. She felt driven to learn every detail of what had happened.

On the shelf with her dishes she kept the folded newspaper containing the lengthy article, re-reading it often. Forty to a hundred miners had been involved, it said, Ben the only one named.

> *. . . we are informed that a man by the name of Wilder, who had settled upon and built a sort of brush fence around a small piece of land in the immediate neighborhood of the selected location of the dam, objected to his (Sheldon) building the dam at that point, and claimed, by settlement, the property. Mr. Sheldon took immediate steps to eject the man . . . and commenced preparation to go on with the work. In a short time, however, he was informed by a body of miners who were working in the river some distance above and with whom Wilder was engaged, that he could not construct a dam at the point alluded to. . . .*

The story told of the event in bloody detail, but the account seemed one-sided. It named fourteen men who worked for Mr. Sheldon or were his friends; clearly they had provided most of the information. Nevertheless the writer did not directly accuse Ben.

> *We have since been told that the mining party charge Mr. Sheldon's men with having first fired. Sheriff Harris has informed us that the miners engaged in the riot are willing to put themselves into the hands of the law, and abide by the results of the trial. We forbear to express any opinion in regard to these scenes of blood and inhuman conflict as far as the respective parties are concerned, because we know that an adjudication of the case by law will be the only true guide that can be used in forming a conclusion, and because our feelings are too deeply and profoundly affected by the strong prejudices of friendship towards some of the parties on one side to speak with impartiality.*

Six weeks passed without mention of a trial in the paper, and without word from Ben. She thought it for the best. What would she say to him? Perhaps he had gone back to Rhode Island. But it cut terribly that she could not help Catherine, who would be grieving so, and tell her how sorry she was.

One day a bespectacled stranger appeared in her yard, a young man with an air of unusual vitality. She judged him to be in his early thirties. "They say the fare is good here," he said in a schooled Southern accent, doffing an elegant gray top hat in one hand and gripping a carpetbag in the other.

"Room for one more," she said ladling out beans and pointing at the ground. "If you don't mind sitting there in your fine clothing." It was noon. Sweat soaked the sides of her dress and trickled from her temples.

He pulled a handkerchief from his pocket and dabbed his face. "Maybe I can squeeze in over there, if those gentlemen in the shade don't mind."

Within a few minutes she noticed half her regular customers were listening to the stranger and answering his questions. As she cut squares in the pan of corn bread, she heard snatches about the prospects around here and mining techniques. Stepping carefully through the seated men, she extended the pan toward him, asking, "Where you from?" The first time in weeks she'd roused herself to wonder about any of them.

His face was smooth, oval, and alert, his spectacles thick. "Louisiana. Name's Oliver Wozencraft. Lately of Washington, District of Columbia."

"The Capitol." What was he doing here dressed in a gray pinstriped suit, asking men about mining? "I am Elitha McCoon." At his gentlemanly acknowledgement, she turned to start another pan of coffee. His voice stopped her:

"I've talked to some people down in Slough House and Cosumne who say you've been here a long time, Miz McCoon." She turned. He continued, "and they say you know the local Indians. I'd like to speak to them, if you could arrange it. I understand they are in hiding."

She felt the link with Catherine and Sarah, no matter how fragile. But what was this about Indians? The surrounding men seemed equally amazed to hear this from a man in an expensive suit and top hat.

"I'm a federal Indian Agent," he continued, eyeing her through his thick lenses, "setting up reservations for the California Indians."

She didn't know what that meant, and began to wonder if he was one of the unscrupulous men swarming all over the hills looking for Indian "vagrants" to sell as "apprentices." It was a brisk underhanded business that made some men rich. She told him she'd talk with him when she was through with the meal. He ate, probing the men the whole time about the frequency of the rains and other topics. Then after everybody else left, she suggested they walk up the river path.

He put on his hat and they strolled toward the old Indian village while she told him about the people who once inhabited Rancho Sacayak. She told about the massacre, but withheld the fact that some Indians still lived nearby.

Mr. Wozencraft shook his head sadly, and said he had come to negotiate treaties with the surviving Indians, to provide them with reservations where they would be safe. So far, he had been north to Mount Shasta and all through the valley. He and two other agents were arranging more than four hundred separate treaties, but he was hindered by the fact that so many Indians were in hiding.

This was, she thought, too elaborate a ruse for an Indian trader. As they ambled toward the remains of Sheldon's dam and — he claiming to be a trained medical doctor and personal friend of President Fillmore — she realized that what he proposed would certainly be a blessing to the Indians. But something about him bothered her. Why would such a man settle for work with Indians? "Would they be put on good land?" she asked, thinking to draw him out on the details.

"I'd see to it. The President means to tame the West in every respect, and that starts with the Indians. They must learn to farm, and farming means good ground. They must learn to plough and sew and — " he broke off and stood staring at the river. "Say, that looks like the remains of a dam down there." He pointed at the protruding uprights and horizontal oak planks, water eddying and swirling around the broken sides.

Briefly she explained what had happened.

"Well, I'll be." He stood admiring the dam's construction, the backs of his hands on his waist, topcoat threaded through an arm. "Just what this country needs! The first time I came out West here, in forty-nine, I traveled the Santa Fe Trail. Ever since, I've been telling Congress they must invest in dams, water being the most critical element to the development of the West — that and railroads." He slung his coat over a shoulder and pointed at the dam. "And here I find somebody else had the same idea." He wagged his head in pleased wonderment, perspiration trickling into his sideburns.

It occurred to her he was a builder looking for free labor. "You've spoken to

Congress about dams and railroads?" she said. It didn't fit.

A smile pushed his glasses up on his cheeks. "They haven't responded."

Not wanting to challenge him directly, she said. "I'm right worried about the Indians, and I can't help but be surprised an Indian agent would be speaking to Congress about dams."

He studied her through the thick lenses, but showed no anger. "And I wouldn't have thought the lovely young proprietress of an eating establishment would take such an interest in Indians. I have papers."

"I'd like to see them." She led the way back to the adobe where he'd left his bag. Inside, where it was cooler, she sat him on "Ben's chair," sat down herself, and studied the stack of papers he fished from his carpetbag — all related to treaties with Indians, including some that chiefs had signed with Xs. Two letters addressed to Mr. O. M. Wozencraft were signed by President Fillmore and bore the seal of the United States government.

"Looks all right," she said as he returned the papers to the bag and buckled the clasp. "But a bag like that could be stolen."

He eyed her through the lenses, then smiled like he admired her being so cautious. "I invite you, Mrs. McCoon, to write to the President of the Mechanics Institute of San Francisco — a friend of mine and a man of excellent character, known by everybody from Sam Brannan on down. He'll vouch for me. Meantime, I'll stay at Forest Home till I hear from you. Word is, that hotel is as fine as any in these United States."

Only three days later Elitha received her reply. A letter redolent in praise of Mr. Wozencraft, attesting to his veracity as a federal Indian Agent. What surprised her most was the speed of the mail. Steamboat sidewheelers churned from San Francisco to Sacramento in six to ten hours now — a voyage that had taken her and Perry over a week one way. Times were changing fast. Maybe the Indians would finally get some help.

She sent a note to Forest Home, offering to arrange a meeting between Mr. Wozencraft and Captain Juan.

88

Beneath the strange but friendly dark-needled pines of a type not found in the home place, Maria sat beside Grizzly Hair, covertly studying the smooth face of Señor Wozencraft. They had come a day's walk up the river from the boulder hideout, to where Wozencraft wanted the *Indios* of all six remnant bands to live.

She could hear in their questions that they doubted the *Americano*, despite what Elitha had said about his trustworthiness.

The round lenses enlarged his eyes as he talked to the six men, Maria repeating each utterance in her own tongue. Three *Americano* "witnesses" stayed aloof down the slope, tossing pebbles in the river.

"When you sign the treaty," Señor Wozencraft was saying, "you promise to be under the control of the United States government. You promise not to steal or kill, or injure United States citizens, and promise not to return to your old lands. In return, you live here." He opened his arms to the beautiful valley — only a small part of the "reservation."

Skepticism laced Grizzly Hair's tone. "Would *Americanos* hunt and fish and wash gold here?" They were the killers, and she had seen miners shoveling and panning along the river and all its streams.

"No. Only the Indians of the six bands here represented would be allowed on this property."

Grizzly Hair lifted his brows just enough to let the doubt show, then turned to talk quietly with Mi-ony-quish. During the pause in translation, she recalled Pedro's scorn about the reservation. Nevertheless, he had agreed to escort them here, but had lingered back at the river fork, having spotted a particular group of miners. Billy had stayed at the hideout with Salmon Woman, and Isabella sat on Maria's lap. "They believe miners no leave this place," Maria explained to Wozencraft, as Grizzly Hair and Mi-ony-quish talked briefly of what had happened to Señor Sheldon when he interfered with gold washing.

Wozencraft inflated his chest. "I speak for the big chief President Fillmore who lives in Washington. He will make them leave."

She feared Wozencraft lacked wisdom. Grizzly Hair voiced a discrepancy in the talk. "Captain Sutter is Inyo agent. He speaks for the big chief."

His face remained smooth. "The State appointed Sutter to count Indians. He only — " He changed directions, "I am from Wa-shing-ton Dee Cee." Many times he had mentioned that place — clearly a place of power.

"This place is good," Grizzly Hair said, pleasure showing in his eyes as he glanced around. "Water clear." The others nodded. Maria had seen they were all well pleased with the land and the river rushing noisily over the rocks. The survivors of the six bands were few. The land would provide plenty of food. Too good to be true, Pedro had said.

Poltuk of the Loclumne leaned forward, meaning she should translate: "We need guns. Big Chief give us guns?" Sadness glimmered in Father's gaze at the mention of guns, and during her repetition for Señor Wozencraft.

Stiffening, he said, "Absolutely no guns. That's the whole point. No hostility toward the people of the United States."

The sad look lingered in Grizzly Hair's face. He wanted no killing. He changed the subject, asking to hear what goods would be received in exchange for the people moving here for all time.

Señor Wozencraft reached inside his cloth bag and drew out a paper. After each item Maria translated:

500 head of cattle, averaging 500 pounds apiece

200 sacks of flour weighing 100 pounds each

75 brood mares and 3 stallions

300 milk cows and 18 bulls

12 yoke of work cattle

12 work mules or horses

25 plows, assorted sizes. This prompted questions. "What is a plow, what it is for?" As Maria translated the surprising answer, the ripping of the earth, she saw the puzzlement in their faces, reflecting her own. Why grow strange plants where food is abundant? Unfazed, Wozencraft continued:

200 garden hoes

80 spades

12 grindstones

1 pair of strong pantaloons and 1 flannel shirt to each man

1 linsey gown for each woman and girl

4000 yards of calico and 1000 yards of sheeting

40 pounds of Scotch thread

2 dozen pairs of scissors. From the bag he pulled out a snapping instrument, and used it to cut a thin curl from the bottom of the paper. Maria and all the headmen stared in wonderment at the clever device.

8 dozen thimbles

3000 needles

1 Mackinaw blanket for each man and woman over 15 years old

4000 pounds of iron

4000 pounds of steel

"I cannot bend it," Grizzly Hair said.

Santiago said quietly. "I learned how in the mission."

Wozencraft finished by saying: "None of the stock — that means animals — are to be killed, sold or exchanged absent the consent of the agent. That's me."

"Animals belong to you?" Grizzly Hair asked.

"Yes. That is, they belong to the government, but you would have the use of them. The Big Chief, President Fillmore, wants them to bear many young for you. You take care of them."

Hin-co-ye, the dance doctor, said, "We like to eat animals."

"Only with my permission," said Wozencraft. "Milk the cows. Use the mules and horses to pull the plows. This is the beginning of a big farm for you Indians."

"Farm?" Maria asked.

"Ranch." He looked around at the men. "You must learn to live like white men."

Why, she wondered, picturing the wandering, homeless hordes. Why should they live like that? She saw the same question in the eyes of the men, but they asked about the goods, each question answered by Wozencraft in a friendly, straightforward manner. She could tell they trusted his good intentions but doubted his knowledge.

In the golden light from the setting sun the dark pines looked beautiful and the ripe red berries on the toyon bushes hung in inviting clusters. The spirits of the place seemed peaceful. She glanced around for Pedro, not seeing him yet. Only about six miners were visible in the river bottom. Señor Billy Rhoads and the other two *Americano* witnesses were talking with them.

Grizzly Hair spoke to the other men in their own tongue. "What harm comes from marking the paper? If too many *Americanos* come, Wozencraft and Headman Fillmore will ask them to go. Maybe they have the power. But in the meantime we can hunt and fish again. Trees live here and food plants. Many deer, many rabbits, many birds. This land paper is a big honor. Good luck. I will mark it."

His talk was right. Maria felt the magic of the place as she told the oval-faced man, "He marks paper." The other men were nodding agreement. "They all mark paper."

A smile pushed up his glasses, and he called Señor Rhoads and the other witnesses. Fumbling in his bag, Wozencraft brought out a quill and a bottle of dark fluid, demonstrating how to make the proper mark.

Grizzly Hair took the quill and drew a big strong X where the man pointed. When all the others had marked the lines, Señor Rhoads and the two other *Americanos* added squiggly marks. "Now," Señor Wozencraft said, "Each Indian must tell me his name." He dipped the quill and held it expectantly beside the first X.

The men were prepared for this rudeness. Each gave the next man's name — Hin-co-ye carefully saying Grizzly Hair's name, Mi-ony-quish giving Hin-co-ye's and so on. When Wozencraft was finished scratching, he pressed a clever round device beside each mark. It left a round black track — the mark of Headman Fillmore, he explained. Then he produced an identical paper, and the ritual was repeated, each step exactly the same. The second paper he presented to Father.

With a formal nod of his topknot, Father accepted it, then pushed slowly to his feet — his back still hurting, the torn trousers loose on his hips though he had fleshed out some in recent moons — and shook his land paper in each of the four directions, each time declaring: "Our new home place."

To Maria he said, "Tell Señor Valdez to ride back for Spear Thrower, Stalking Egret and the others. They must come immediately." He extended his hand to Wozencraft, who seemed surprised, perhaps not knowing *Indios* had often seen this *Americano* custom.

They clasped hands. Then Grizzly Hair told Maria to ask when the food and other goods would arrive.

"When President Fillmore and the Senate ratify, ah, mark the paper."

Grizzly Hair scowled and pointed to the round tracks. "Mark already here."

"He must see your names, then write his own like this." He pointed at the tangled nests of lines scratched by the quill. And the Senate must sign too." Maria didn't know who that was, but she translated for the other men, and felt a thrill of pride to see their unspoken agreement that the land paper should remain in Grizzly Hair's possession.

Father's gaze swept over the new home place. She felt his strength. A true headman. She glimpsed Pedro in the trees and was suddenly anxious to tell him Father owned a land paper. It was a proud moment. Father had been right about making friends of the new people. The Americanos had honored him. Now Pedro had a home here and, it occurred to her with a flash of joy, he no longer needed to go to Mexico.

Back by the river fork Pedro had spotted one of the eight Oregon men who had massacred the Omuchumne, one of the three left. After scouting and deciding to kill the man in the morning, he had returned to the *Indio* camp for supper.

María's eyes sparkled as she said, "Now we have land paper."

He saw her pride, heard her hope, and hid his disdain. "I have a land paper too, Little Poppy, but it is worthless. Maybe this one is too."

The shadow of displeasure crossed her face, but he would not mislead these people whom he loved and respected. "*Norteamericanos* do not honor my land paper. I think they honor one of *Indios* even less."

Captain Juan sat stonily, perhaps weary of their disagreements. María brightened. "Show your land paper to Señor Wozencraft. He can mark it with the power of the Headman in Wash-ing-ton Dee Cee."

Suppressing a mocking ay, ay, ay, Pedro passed the basket of acorn mush to Santiago and glanced at the separate fire where Wozencraft ate with the *Norteamericano* witnesses.

"You are not happy for us?" María said, cocking her head in her heart-melting manner.

He reached and pulled her closer, holding her chin so she would look into his eyes. "*Amapolita*, I want you to think how happy we will be in Mexico, where no *Norteamericanos* will come. We will take all the people of these headmen who want to come." He had completed another trip with a big *caballada* of horses and a large bag of gold — a fifth of it his — and hid it with his helmet in a secret place. Mexico was his home now.

"But we have good luck now. No need to live in a faraway place. You can build your hacienda here."

Ah *qué malo!* A new argument about where to live.

Captain Juan sat as if he'd negotiated a grand bargain. Like Montezuma's with Cortéz? At the other fire a shadowy figure in a top hat was rising, coming their way.

Pedro stood, alert and ready. Señor Wozencraft leaned back on his spread legs and said, "Mr. Valdez, wasn't it?"

"Sí, señor."

"What are you doing here?"

Even blinder than he looks. "Eating with my woman."

"Are you aware this is to be an Indian reservation?"

Pedro jerked his head in María's direction. "I said, this is my wife." Maybe he thought they didn't talk.

"I must inform you, Mr. Valdez, that no Mexicans may dwell upon these grounds, or benefit in any way from the largesse of the American people."

Pedro narrowed his eyes at the man — the round lenses blank in the twilight. "I am a native Californian, señor."

"Californios are excluded from the reservation."

"Are you telling me to leave?"

"Not this minute. But I must advise you that if you are seen here with the Indians, I'll be getting letters of protest. It could ruin the ratification process. It would be advisable for you to take your wife to your hacienda." He seemed pleased to know a Spanish word.

Holding back a furious retort, Pedro glanced down at the *Indios* around the fire, polite in their silence. The last thing he wanted was to pour cold water on their "good luck," however slim its chances, even if it conflicted with his plans. "No one will see me live here. I give my word."

Señor Wozencraft nodded and left for his fire. María searched Pedro's face. "You will not live here with me?"

"I said no one will see me. We talk later, *Amapolita*, when we are alone."

Captain Juan spoke in their guttural language. María explained. "Father says we will hold a Big Time when the other people come. The men are happy about dancing."

Hin-co-ye, a spirit doctor, represented his remnant band. *Indios* admired his kind of leader more than the other kind. No doubt this one would plan the details of the fiesta. Tired, Pedro yawned and stretched. "I go to sleep now."

"I listen to the talk," she said.

That was fine with him. Morning would come early, and he had an Oregonian to visit.

"Yes. A Big Time with a Cry," Grizzly Hair continued, laying another branch across the fire. Orange sparks rose into the pines, illuminating the broad lines of his face. Glad the difficult talk was over, Maria sat in a restful manner and watched Pedro head back to the shadows and crawl into his blankets. She checked Isabella in her bikoos, saw that she was fine, and turned toward the energy of the men around the fire.

Her interest flared with the sparks when Poltuk talked in a realm where her thoughts often wandered. "*Americanos* come like flies to dead meat now," he said. "They did not come in the time of our fathers."

The dark heads bobbed. Perhaps they wondered, as she did, why gold had lured the new people at this time, but not before.

"Our Condor Robe was stolen," Grizzly Hair stated simply, driving a pain into Maria's stomach.

Mi-ony-quish glanced past him in surprise. "You had a condor robe?" Seeing the nod, he exhaled an ahhh, and intoned, "A powerful vestment."

"Yes." Grizzly Hair said, "It was stolen from us and sent to Russia, a land far beyond the western sea."

Poltuk said, "Bad luck to the people of Russia."

Mi-ony-quish asked, "When was it stolen?"

"When Captain Sutter lived in his *castillo*."

Hin-co-ye cleared his throat to speak, and all the men looked toward him with respect. "Molok's wings stretch from the western sea to the eastern sea and to Russia and the campfires of the Immortals." He glanced up where they twinkled. "But now people everywhere are ignorant of him."

Maria couldn't understand why her life, or Elitha's, had been spared, when so many who had visited the bad house had died. Even *Americanos* who mined at the home place were dying all over the hills, no one singing to their spirits. With the proliferation of loose spirits, the suffering was spreading. Worried that it would catch Pedro, she glanced at the dark lump of his sleeping form.

Hin-co-ye spoke in a monotone. "Power is fractured now, very loose. But it started before your condor robe was stolen. In time of the big sickness in the Valley of the Sun too few were left to bury the dead." Goose bumps rose on Maria's scalp as she recalled disease flashing like fire through the valley when she was a child. It happened mostly to other peoples, and she had tried to put it from her mind.

Hin-co-ye continued, "No medicine could stop the evil from entering the people. Their urine turned black. Their faces were spotted, and they went crazy. But even that was not the start of the trouble. Before that, we fought the cannon and guns of the black hats. You," he nodded at Grizzly Hair, "led the peoples in a war and many died in fire."

Grizzly Hair, whose face bore a stony look, said, "Yes. We have lived with loose power a long time." She was relieved to hear he didn't blame her.

Hin-co-ye said, "It started when people closed their ears to the world. Now twisted power is whirling upon us. Molok's robe is only a part of it."

As everyone sat watching the dancing flames, Maria recalled Bear Claw saying a time of total chaos would come. Grizzly Hair said, "But when power is loose, people can catch little pieces, and get new kinds of luck."

Hin-co-ye nodded toward the coals, cheeks sucked in thought.

"Land paper is a good piece," Father said.

89

The *Indios* were asleep when Pedro rode out. Later Señor Wozencraft would lead them around, pointing out distant landmarks defining their supposed new territory. Meanwhile Pedro rode downstream past the fork in the river until he came to the camp. He waited in the willows where he could see the blankets of the five sleeping men through the branches.

Bright color spilled over the ridgetop where the sun would rise and birds rioted in the oaks and willows. A noisy company. A man crawled from his blankets, unbuttoned his long underwear and urinated. The wrong man. At the fort Pedro had met men from every land, and knew such underwear was not worn beneath buckskins. Trappers wore leather next to their skin, and slept in it. He waited.

A man in buckskin rolled to his knees and staggered to his feet, wiping sleep from his eyes. The long fringe hung still as he shot an arc into the willows. Chocolate stepped nervously, sensing Pedro's alertness. Patting his neck, he whispered, "He is my man, but *El Bandido Cuidadoso* he is patient." The man's friends slept with their guns.

The *Norteamericano* returned, the other four waking up. Their horses grazed so far away they didn't whinny or pay any attention to Chocolate. After eating, the miners went down to the stream and began shoveling. But all men had to shit. Pedro nudged Chocolate to a spot where he could see the tops of their hats. About an hour later, he saw Buckskin trudging up the bank alone, heading into the willows.

With a slight touch of the sides of his boots, he walked the horse slowly toward the willows. Gravel rolled. The miners in the river looked up. He dipped his hat in casual greeting and proceeded behind a wall of brambles as they looked back to their shovels. The babbling of the stream and the cacophony of birds covered the soft hoof sounds. He stopped a distance away.

Good luck. Through an opening in the willows the *cabrón* was squatting, faced the other away. Pedro reached for his lariat, realizing this would test his skill. The clearing was narrow. Trees and bushes were the enemy of a lasso. It would be like threading a needle. *Está bien.* He could do that.

With a glance to be sure the others hadn't followed, he snaked out a small loop, circling, feeling the weight of the braided leather, judging the distance. "Son of a whore," he called softly as he let fly.

The man's head jerked toward him as the loop settled around his neck. He and Chocolate were one, backing and tightening the noose. "Remember the little *Indio* children you killed, and the women."

Then he let Chocolate feel the spurs, just the tips, as he wound the lariat around the saddlehorn. The horse bounded into a gallop, the leather snapping tight across his thigh. He turned back to see the man dragging behind, gritting his teeth, trying to dig his fingers in between his beard and the leather. His *pantalones* trailed from his boots. Pedro called back to him, "Now you can shit good."

Shots whistled by. He leaned down to the mane, spurring southward, and the shots stopped very soon. They didn't want to risk their lives for this one, he realized. Besides, he was flying away on the fastest horse in California. He didn't look back.

Later as he reined down a boulder-strewn cañon and picked his way through poison oak and piled rocks, the lariat suddenly tightened on his thigh. He looked back. The head had come through the rocks, but not the shoulders. He touched Chocolate. The horse pulled, then stopped and turned a questioning eye on him.

"Go *muchacho*," Pedro urged without looking back. The big animal threw his weight into it. He felt the strap cut into his thigh, then pop slack.

He rode on and waited for the anger to lift, as it always had before. He coiled the lariat and hung it on the saddle pin, but nothing changed. He knew he was finished killing.

90

For five moons the people had lived in the strange place. Not trusting the gold diggers, who seemed more numerous all the time, the men had built the u-machas on the hill where intruders could been seen from every direction. Maria and her children slept in the house with Grizzly Hair and Broken Salmon, Pedro visiting at night. Not a day went by without someone wondering aloud when the goods and animals would come from the big hy-apo, President Fillmore.

Billy and Isabella were gathering mushrooms with Little Flicker in the pine forest. The intermittent rain had stopped and the sky was blue as a robin's egg. The fragrant pines and green grass were washed and sparkling.

Little Flicker, who still didn't talk, pointed to a mass of cream-colored fungus. Maria pronounced its name and tore the heavy prize in half. Billy pointed at a stand of hooded gray fungi pushing out of a rotten log. Delighted, she plucked all but four and tossed them in her burden basket. "Always leave some of the mushroom people, so we can have more next time."

"They come again in time of rain," Billy filled in. She smiled at him.

As Maria and Little Flicker skirted the hillside, Billy called, pointing. "Grandfather goes to the river."

Maria stopped beside Billy and looked down. Grizzly Hair, Stalking Egret and Spear Thrower were walking toward about ten *Americanos*, who stood beside a wagon piled with goods. Hope soared out of its hiding place.

"Children," she said, "I go to talk for Grandfather. Go to the u-macha." She saw the hope in Grizzly Hair's stride — not as bent and halting as usual.

"We stay and hunt mushroom people," Billy declared.

She shook her head at the little man, six *años* now. "Children do not collect mushrooms alone. Go to Salmon Woman."

Before she reached the river, she saw disrespect in the *Americano* faces. She heard it in their talk as they looked at Grizzly Hair. Hope sank again as she joined them, her stomach knotting. Two *Americanos* had taken a long-toothed implement from the wagon and stood on opposite sides of a generous pine, pulling the blade back and forth between them, chewing into the soft flesh. She went to them and touched the cold metal. "No. Not to cut. This is a good tree."

One of the sawyers shoved her so hard she fell back to the ground and lost her wind. She slowly rose to her feet, inhaled and said, "This tree is a strong healer. Gives food and medicine."

Grizzly Hair added in English, which he had been learning, "Help *Americano* too." They continued pushing and pulling, the flakes flying.

The tree cried shrilly and Maria felt the cut as if it were her flesh. It took her voice away. Grizzly Hair gestured around at the distant boundaries. "Inyo home place. Inyo tree."

"Jed," said an *Americano*, "What's that Digger yammerin bout?"

"Land paper," Grizzly Hair said, pulling the tightly folded square from his loincloth thong, where he always carried it. "We sit. We talk." She saw that he avoided looking at the suffering tree and tried to ignore the wet squeak of the saw and pine essence spilling around them. She would never understand how *Americanos* could burn the friendliest medicine trees for firewood.

The man nearest Grizzly Hair yanked the paper from his hand, shaking it open. "Well, I'll be. Whar'd this old buck Digger git a thing ike this. Got the

President's mark on it! Looky here." The others looked.

Relieved they recognized the sign, she saw Grizzly Hair's dignity as he opened his hands at the new place. "Inyo share land," he said. "We talk." Many times he had stated his belief that the diggers would never leave, as Señor Wozencraft said they would, and that the people must befriend them. All must share, he had said. Power was realigning itself.

The *Americanos* eyed him with amused hostility, except for those cutting the tree. They never stopped working.

Father sat down, as if to show them how, and folded his legs. He patted the earth, indicating they should sit.

Maria explained: "He says, we will share with you. Land and water and trees. Sit and talk, *por favor*."

One man erupted in laughter, slapping his thigh. Others laughed and chuckled with him, but the sawyers continued their work. Then the man who started the laughing wiped a finger across his cheek and said, "Rich, ain't it? He'll share the land with us." His hand went to his belt.

Stalking Egret whipped an arrow from his quiver.

Two explosions split the air. A smoking hole showed in Father's chest. Paralyzed, she watched frothy blood ooze out. He sat stiffly, his face unchanged, then slowly toppled. Stalking Egret folded at the knees and fell forward. Spear Thrower gradually released the tension on his bow, eight men pointing guns at him.

An *Americano* yanked the bow from him and another gunshot made her jump. Grizzly Hair jerked on the ground. Pink matter pushed up through his shiny black hair above his ear.

"Now let that be a lesson. You Diggers stay outa our way. Hear?"

Her heart lurched in her throat as she stared into the small black circles of their gunbarrels.

A rippling, crackling shriek came from the tree, followed by a swishing sound and deep boom that shook the ground and traveled up her bones. It boomed again as the tree bounced on the resilient earth.

91

During the fall and winter the population of Cook's Bar turned over two or three times — a thousand men, Mrs. Gordon estimated at the peak. Now it was in decline, though the business at Bridge House increased as travellers came through. Few of the men who courted Elitha had heard of Ben Wilder, and none knew where he was. They virtually stood in line to squire her to dances all over the gold region and at Bridge House. The only places she wouldn't go were Saunder's Hall at the Mill Ranch bridge and Slough House. Sarah and Catherine could be there, and Elitha didn't want to upset them. Men spoke gallantly of protecting Elitha's honor, and claimed she needed only say the word and they would "take care of" any who bothered her. They watched the adobe when she was away, and she felt safe.

In the Counselor's company she went to Volcano to see Shakespeare's Richard III, laughing when the audience, well loaded with "ammunition," hooted at the overwrought portrayal of King Henry dying from stab wounds and pelted him with rotten cabbages, pumpkins, potatoes, a sack of soot and a dead goose. The next week Counselor took her to an all-night dance in the Gaffneys' barn and asked her to marry him. But he seemed more of a pompous uncle than a husband.

A South Carolina gentleman took her by stage to see Lola Montez in Sacramento City — the theater tickets costing a hundred dollars apiece. The spider dance intrigued her. Afterwards an actor named Edwin Booth, from a famous family of acting Booths, recited from Hamlet. The whole six-hour return trip she parried syrupy compliments and rejected marriage proposals.

Vyries Brown returned to Cook's Bar and invited her on a horseback ride. He had been captured, he said as they rode, and "gagged and tied by the men who spiked the cannon." She was grateful to him for telling her, and felt easier knowing she hadn't contributed to Mr. Sheldon's death. But when they stopped to rest in a grassy place, he too asked her to marry him. She was no more interested in Vyries than the boys in Kate's school. She quickly mounted her new horse, Gay-Gay having been stolen.

At every dance men held her too tightly. They pulled her to them on the homeward drives, and she would push them away, saying, "No, please. Have you heard of Ben Wilder?" That usually worked. They would twist their whiskers and mumble, "Can't say as I have."

The "forthcoming trial" mentioned by the *Sacramento Union* never occurred, or, if it did, wasn't mentioned in print. But though she wondered where he had gone, she was glad she hadn't married the man accused of killing Jared Sheldon. Someday, she hoped, Catherine would come to heal the rift, which stung like an open sore.

Flaunting all reason, Ben still visited her dreams — his easy manner, his length lying with her as he never had in life. She would awaken with a luxurious, sensuous feeling and a desire to find him. Sometimes it took three hours of cooking and serving meals to banish it, and she worried about her mind.

In December she caught the stage to Jamestown, a booming camp in the southern mines. There she hugged Leanna, praised her fine good looks — she'd been so skinny — and witnessed her wedding to Mister John App, a good and decent man, who was starting a farm and prospecting on the side. When the newlyweds climbed aboard the stage for a San Francisco honeymoon, Elitha felt her childhood receding. She wiped tears and waved until she could no longer see the bouncing coach.

Back home she made an effort to socialize with the local women. With Lorena she heard a lecture in Ione City on the Water Cure for Females. In Michigan Bar she heard a woman from the National Temperance Union speak on the Evils of Drink. One Sunday she accompanied Lorena to her church in Ione, but though Lorena tried to shame her, Elitha wouldn't return. "I have to cook," she said. Nothing in church roused the sense of God she felt in an unspoiled place. A pink streak on the horizon of a winter's sunset brought her closer to prayer than Reverend Fish in a building filled with judgmental women.

In Amador she and the Hays sisters heard a female speaker in blowzy pantaloons denounce the Male Principle as the cause of all corruption and praise the power of the True Woman. But these outings failed to deepen friendships. The women were inclined to talk in exaggerated accents about trifles. They made Elitha yearn for the old ease with Catherine, Sarah and Leanna.

Meanwhile a steady stream of women flowed into California. Most married within weeks. Even Lorena Gordon had been married for some time. St. Joseph's at Live Oak turned out Irish brides and grooms every Sunday, many of the men settling on open land. There were plenty of funerals too. Ten thousand people were said to live, at least temporarily, between Michigan Bar and Slough House. Men came and went in waves, following the latest rumors. But all knew the easy gold was gone. The growing number of small weekly or monthly papers, which Elitha tried to buy, bemoaned the increasing lawlessness, called for more schools and praised the beautiful countryside.

In this stew of strangers Elitha felt sealed apart. She hardened herself when people bantered about the cannibals of the Donner Party, and was glad when they turned to the only other story known to everyone — the dashing exploits of Joaquín. It came back to her that she was called "that quiet McCoon widow." Fondly she remembered tracking animals for the enjoyment; it didn't seem possible that was only four years ago. The wilderness was gone now, and at eighteen, she felt old.

She missed Indian Mary too. But the reservation was a blessing, especially now that a company of men were blowing away the hillsides with water cannons and silting the waterways so no fish were to be had. Prospectors at her board had been replaced by teams of company men. The water was so bad Elitha let it settle for days before using it, and even then it caught between her teeth with a gritty alkaline taste. But despite having a place reserved for them, she heard Indians were still living in the hills, and were treated badly.

Why, she often asked herself, when righteous people lectured about wickedness, did they fail to see the evil of their actions upon the Indians? At the very mention, most women's faces wizened like they had sucked a lemon. But injustice didn't happen only to Indians, as she learned from a man who called himself Jimmy Buetler.

Buetler worked on the hydraulic crew, claiming to have been a carpenter in the States. Elitha gave him a can of gold to buy lumber and other supplies, which were very dear. He was to start adding two bedrooms to the house, a fireplace and chimney for an indoor kitchen, a wooden roof and porch across the front.

Two weeks later he came to dinner without the lumber, but said he was "in line" for it. Instead he asked her to accompany him to a fiddler's contest at Willow Creek. "The Walker boys'll be there," he said, sweetening the pot.

She smiled. "Pick me up at noon." Music was balm to her soul. Sometimes she felt better for two whole days.

The next day she hung out her "NO EATING" sign and climbed on his little rig. At the Willow Creek establishment, fiddles flew. Like puppets on a thousand strings, miners hopped around the room dancing jigs, all elbows and knees and beards. Then men became drunk and a fight escalated into bottle throwing. When the ruckus was over, Elitha crawled out from behind the bar and joined the singing of Old Dan Tucker and Get Along Home Cindy. Jimmy tried to kiss her, but she pushed him away and, thankfully, he stayed pushed.

A miner with a sweet Irish tenor all but made her cry with, "When the Work's all Done this Fall" — a song about a man working on a rancho in the southwest, longing to return to his mother in the East, and being murdered on the way home. Had Ben gone home to Rhode Island? Did he have another name there? As the popular ditty went: *Oh what was your name in the States?/ Was it Johnson or Simpson or Bates?/ Did you kill with a knife and fly for your life?/ Oh what was your name in the States?*

They left at dawn, Jimmy clucking the horse to a trot. "They say you're sweet on a man 'at hadn't been seed in these parts nigh onto six months." No mention of the riot. Lordy, it was like it hadn't happened.

She felt exhausted. "Ever hear of Ben Wilder?"

He scratched under his hat. "Tall string bean?"

Fatigue vanished and she bolted up straight, staring at his face, dark with the dawn at his back. "That's him. Where is he?" She hardly noticed Indians coming down the road at the Dry Creek junction.

"Last I heard, haulin freight from Stockton to Sacramento."

So near. And no word, no explanation. Relieved Jimmy asked no more questions, she sat quietly as the horse trotted past a line of Indians. What was wrong with her? She didn't care a fig about Ben Wilder. She looked at the Indians, aware of not having seen so many since before the massacres. Men and women and a few children, all walking swiftly in twos and threes, mostly men, many old. At the

Ione junction more joined the parade. All headed her way. It was like a dream. Maybe she would wake up and they would be gone, along with Jimmy Buetler and what he'd said about Ben. Maybe knowing Ben was in Sacramento City would exorcise him from her mind.

Passing the camp of Chinamen, who worked for the hydraulic company, Indians came toward them from Bridge House, all converging and heading down the road to Michigan Bar.

"What the devil." Jimmy pulled the horse to a stop. "Injuns is crawlin outa the rocks. And ain't they the funny bunch!"

Elitha caught sight of a young woman's back with a big baby in a cradleboard, a light-haired boy at her side. Her head was a black ball, singed in mourning, but her figure looked like Mary. "Wait here," she said, and jumped down from the buckboard.

She made her way through Indians of every description — most wearing cast-off clothing, a few in torn top hats, men in tattered jackets and no pants, some in loincloths. Around their necks hung strings of buttons, shells and the bottoms of glass bottles with holes drilled through.

"Mary, Mary," she called, hiking her skirts and running up the rutted wagon trail past something long and shrouded, carried by Indians. On both sides the denuded hills had been reshaped into strange, washed-out angles and ugly gashes, as if a monster had devoured the earth and belched out the remains. The girl turned.

Seeing the pitch and ash on her face, fear needled her. "It's really you, isn't it Mary?" She caught her breath. "Who died?" Somebody close.

The moist black eyes rimmed in white glanced from her blackened face, while the baby with auburn curls grinned peek-a-boo — the child whose birth Elitha had witnessed. "Father," Mary said.

Captain Juan! She watched the shroud passing by, "How did he die?" He'd been terribly crippled, maybe mortally.

"*Americanos* kill him with guns."

Elitha sucked in breath. "Where?"

"New home place."

Outrage and anger slammed into her. "Mr. Wozencraft said it would be safe there!"

"My father want *Americanos* to share land."

"No. It wasn't to be shared. It was for you Indians alone!"

A tremor quivered through Mary's lower lip — brown against the black. "Señor Wozencraft go. No come back." Her gaze followed the men with the load.

He had abandoned them! Guilt gripped Elitha. She had been too trusting, too hopeful. She should have left them hiding in the boulders. And now they were having a funeral for a fine chief, and all she could think to say was, "I didn't know so many Indians were left."

"Come far away — many peoples." Mary swallowed hard.

Elitha touched her shoulder, wanting to comfort, but not knowing how. She felt dirty, filled with blame. "Why here?" Michigan Bar was a tent town less than two miles from the old village.

"Last dancehouse here, close by home place. We put ashes in old bone place."

"Then go back to the reservation?"

Her black ball head turned from side to side. "Bad place." She laid her hand on Elitha's forearm. "You are friend. Come cry with us. Big honor to Father." She conveyed no accusation.

Elitha blinked back tears, remembering the supply wagon she had to meet this afternoon. "It might take me a day or so, but Mary, I will come and honor your father." Indian dances lasted five days or more. There would be time.

As Mary continued up the road, Elitha turned back to Jimmy's rig, her thoughts racing. Yes. She would return, but she would ask Catherine to come. They had shared an intimate time in the birth hut with Mary, and though Catherine had shut the door in Elitha's face, nothing in the world said Elitha couldn't open it.

92

That afternoon Elitha bought flour, sugar, pork and a slab of beef. The young driver was about to flick the reins when she said, "Wait." Maybe haulers knew each other. "Do you happen to know Ben Wilder? He has a route from Sacramento to Stockton." Why couldn't she just leave it alone?

"Yes ma'am, ran into him yesterdy."

She could hardly breathe.

He raised his brows. "Want I should give 'im a message?"

"No." She turned to the house hearing the "hah!" and the creak and rattle of the wagon. Putting things away, she tidied up, hung out her "NO EATING" sign, and walked up to Bridge House in time for the evening stage. "Slough House," she told the driver, giving him half a half-pinch.

She wedged in between three smelly miners and looked across at four more, one with a splinted leg, which made her sit a little sideways. All doffed their hats and stared in the unabashed manner she'd grown to expect. "Slough House did I hear?" the splinted man asked.

She nodded. They spoke all at once. "At's where I'm headed." "Goin thar myself." "to the dance." "Well I'll be . . . "

"Mill Ranch," she clarified, "Sheldon's place." They looked skeptical, not knowing the name. And he'd been in the ground only seven months. "It's near the roadhouse." She felt the strangeness of living in a world overrun with people entirely ignorant of what came even weeks before.

"Wall, a looker like you orter shake a leg. Heared the Walker boys'll be there. Be right proud to squire you."

"Alla us," chimed the man in the splint.

Serving meals these two and a half years had made her easy among men. "I expected you'd be headed for Sacramento City," she said.

"Fer a chance 'ike this, we'd frolic a spell and catch tomorry's stage." The indentations around their hairy mouths spread in smiles as they nodded to each other.

"I thank you kindly, but my friend is expecting me." Knowing they would think "male friend," she looked out the window.

The stage stopped before the enlarged Cosumne Store and Post Office — barrels and crates stacked around the yard. Elitha kept her eyes down, not ready to see Sarah and Mr. Grimshaw. Last time they'd met, Ben had acted the peacemaker, only to be accused later of murdering Sarah's brother-in-law.

The thought of him aroused an unwelcome sensation — part pain, part aching emptiness. Time was supposed to heal it. Out the other window was the blacksmith shop, expanded to include a stable and second forging shed. Her mind was as disordered as the yard was littered.

Men thumped onto the roof, boots scrambling up over the window, the wood bowing under their weight. The coach rolled forward. A mile beyond the driver called, "Slough House — supper and team change."

Lamps glowed beneath the shed roof arching the road. Several hostlers rose from chairs where they'd been tipped back against the wall. The coach door opened and, faintly through the walls, she heard fiddles, laughter and stomping feet. Horses neighed from the big commercial barn. The driver made a beeline for the roadhouse door, and she hurried into the gathering dark.

Passing the "hanging tree" and a new mercantile store, she slipped in the mud and skated before catching her balance. Her shoes echoed on the improved plank bridge across Deer Creek, which rushed noisily in the berry vines below. Lost in the dark was the mound where Mr. Sheldon and Mr. Daylor lay buried with centuries of Indians. She shivered, realizing she'd neglected to bring her cloak. The day had been warm, as many February days were in California, but the nights were cold.

Leaving the lamplit windows of Slough House, she hugged her arms and continued up the narrow road flanked by tall trees, the spiny tips fading into the gloom. An owl glided close to her head, startling her. Dogs barked. Indian dogs? Did they feel the spirits of their dead masters lurking about?

The stars gave little light. She stumbled on a root and fell, hands into cold mud. As she stood and straightened her frock, she saw the millhouse looming blacker than the night, but light spilled from the familiar house across the yard. She picked her way toward it.

Quietly she scraped her mud-caked shoes on the bottom stair and stepped up to the door. Now, she thought, I will end this one way or the other. But first she wiped her hands on her petticoat then brushed down her outer skirt. She poked her hair into place and felt the good times she'd known in this house rising around her like ground fog — the first time Perry had brought her here, Catherine's impish grin as she rounded the corner, their talk beneath the walnut tree, the outhouse, the cookout with the Rhoads family, Mr. Valdez playing his guitar, the excitement over gold, the New Year's dinner in forty-nine when the baby was stillborn and Catherine said: you're not alone, you know that, you always got us Rhoadses.

Bawling wouldn't do. Again she pulled up her underskirt, using the warm tears to wipe away the mud. The door opened.

She threw down her skirt and faced the dark shape of a man. Liquor breath blasted: "Well I'll be. Look what them dogs been abarken at."

Catherine's plump silhouette joined him, lamplight at their backs. Unable to see, she felt the absence of smiles. Who was this man? She had hoped to see Catherine alone. Sarah appeared in the light behind, very pregnant, Mr. Grimshaw at her side, and little Will, grown taller. Inwardly she groaned. Too many people, all staring. Sarah's white face and small downturned nose seemed, what, haughty? angry? cold? She must look a sight and almost wished she could drop through the porch. But she'd come to do this, never mind who else could hear. She took a deep breath and said:

"Catey, I'm just plumb tuckered at our not being friends. I don't know if Ben Wilder killed Mr. Sheldon, but I haven't seen him since before it happened. And I've never felt so down in my life as I've been thinking I almost married a man that, well, helped kill him. Now you can shut me out again if you like, but I came to say my piece." Her voice betrayed her, turning gravelly. "I've sure been missing you, and Sally." She willed the tears to stay in her eyes. All she could see was Sarah's strange expression and Catherine's shadow-dark form.

Catherine said quietly, "Well you sure pick yer times."

What did that mean? Who was this man breathing liquor?

"Sorry to bother you," she said, feeling unwanted. It was pointless to mention the Indian funeral. Maybe the Quiggles had room for her at Slough House. Then tomorrow she would talk to Billy Rhoads about the Indian treaty and leave for home. Sadly she turned to leave. A hand stopped her.

She turned, bumped into Catherine. With a rush of relief and joy she felt herself being hugged, and laid her cheek on Catherine's head, squeezing back.

Tears spilled over the dam. "Oh Catey, I'm so, so grieved about Jared. He was the best man in California."

Catherine nodded, but her crying was alarming. It wasn't joy. She seemed about to collapse. And the look on Sarah's face was pain. Could they still be mourning so hard for Mr. Sheldon? She turned Catherine toward the light to see her face. She looked like she'd been crying for hours. "Why — "

The strange man stepped forward and circled an arm around Catherine's waist and helped her through the door. Over his shoulder he said, "We pulled her baby outa the river this mornin." He hooked an armful of air. "Come in."

The image of the Grim Reaper loomed in Elitha's mind — bony hands and a long curved scythe. She couldn't move. People were being cut down — Indians and whites alike. Hoping she wasn't adding to the grief, she stepped gingerly through the door. The man sat down with Catherine on his lap, rocking her like a baby. That started to answer the *who*, and Elitha hoped he was worthy of Catherine. But which baby had drowned?

Shutting the door behind her and feeling excluded from Catherine, she went to Sarah and touched her arm. She looked about to give birth.

"It was my fault," Sarah said. She looked rigid, her eyes rimmed with red.

"Stop it, Sally," Mr. Grimshaw said. "That's not true." He took Elitha's elbow and nodded toward the kitchen.

His skin was smooth beneath the brown helmet of hair, and he looked almost boyish in his agitation. "Little Sarah," he said, his coffee-eyes clear. "We found her in the river behind the store. A stageload of customers came in. We were busy and Sarah asked the hired girl to watch the baby. She thought the Patterson girls were with her." He looked down. "She loved that little tyke — named for her, you know."

"Have you had the burial?" Elitha whispered.

"In the morning. The baby's laid out in the back room."

"I think you got enough on your minds. I'll stay the night at Slough House." She nodded toward the front room. "Who is that man?"

"Mr. Mahone, Catherine's friend. Came with the Mormon Battalion."

Sarah entered, rolling from side to side in her pregnancy, a pale woman all washed out, the only color her red eyes. "Elitha, we had no idea you wasn't seeing Ben Wilder."

"He left. I never saw him after the shooting."

Reaching an arm around Mr. Grimshaw, Sarah sighed like it was too complicated and leaned on him. "Elitha shouldn't have to sleep at a roadhouse. Catey says to drive her on over to John's." She turned her pale eyes to Elitha. "We're staying the night here and there's no extra bed."

"I hate to put you to any trouble." But Mr. Grimshaw was already reaching for a coat, which he gave to Elitha. He put on Mr. Sheldon's old one.

Mr. Grimshaw let the horses pick their way in the dark.

"Is Mr. Mahone a good man?"

"Oh, I think so. Built the new bridge across the creek. Did you notice?" Before she could answer he added, "Does good work, and she needs a man around."

"A nice bridge," she allowed. She sat quietly wishing she'd had Catherine to herself. The poor girl! She knew how it tore you apart to lose a baby. And Mr. Mahone would never take Jared Sheldon's place. Maybe Catherine would listen to her. Don't marry a man unless you're sure, she'd tell her when she had the chance. Living alone was easier than people said, and a lot easier than living with a drinker.

Dogs barked a ruckus when they stopped before the Rhoads house and she felt bad to rouse everybody. Mr. Grimshaw felt his way up to the porch, Elitha following. A couple minutes later she saw, through the window, a tiny flame illumine a long-fingered hand. Then a lamp wick burst to life, lighting a sundries table and Billy Rhoads in his nightshirt, straightening the lamp glass. The witness to the Indian treaty.

He opened the door, clearly surprised to see her. From back in the house came coughing and a tortured croak, "Who's there?"

Billy called over his shoulder, "Stay abed Brother John. Only WR and Elitha McCoon." He lowered his voice. "Sufferin bad ague and chills. Noomony, the doctor calls it. Water on the lungs." Ushering them in, he shook his shoulder-length blond hair. "Gits it whenever the rain starts. I vow it hangs on longer ever time."

As Mr. Grimshaw explained her need for a place to stay, she saw herself pleading with John to go back up the mountains for Tamsen. Would that scene follow her to her grave? She felt the magnetic pull of the robust man who had rescued her, who had kept everybody moving even when the food caches were found plundered. It seemed three lifetimes ago that she had joked to Mary Murphy about becoming his second wife. But John hadn't been a Mormon polygamist after all. He was a good solid man devoted to one wife, a man who provided for so many children she couldn't keep track.

Meeting Billy's pale eyes, she said, "I don't mean to put Matty out, with John sick and all."

"You don't know?" He glanced at Mr. Grimshaw, whose downcast eyes announced he was only a bystander.

"Know what?"

"Matty passed away, long about two weeks ago."

The Grim Reaper. People were dropping on every side. And with John so poorly! "Who's caring for all those youngsters?" These poor men! How were they getting by?

"We sent 'em to Brother Dan and Amanda, in Gilroy. Matty made her wishes known before she went. Sent the girls too, to help raise the younguns. So all we got here is Thomas and Jonathan. Big strong boys, good help on the farm."

Feeling a load lift to know they hadn't been fussing with children, she asked, "Who gets your meals?" Men couldn't do that either.

Billy shrugged. "Oh, we throw on beans in the mornin, pry the crust off at night. John feeds the stove when we're out, though I vow he oughta stay abed. We're still cogitatin on how to make biscuits. Catey sends a few, but she's got the babies and Sally's got the store."

God must have sent her! Besides cooking, these men had clothes to wash and mending to do and cows to milk and chickens to raise. No farm could run without a woman, and there weren't nearly enough to go around. "Well now," she said, "I can make biscuits with my eyes closed. John saved my life and now I'm going to take care of him and the rest of you till you throw me out. And that's final." She pointed at the sofabed. "I'll sleep there."

Mr. Grimshaw's glance said he'd hoped for this. Billy stood grinning like he'd never heard anything so fine. "No need for that. Two upstairs rooms is empty. You're heaven-sent, Miz McCoon."

"Tomorrow I'll tidy up here and cook enough for two days, then go back for my things. And I have something else to do too." She removed the coat and handed it to Mr. Grimshaw, looking Billy in the eye. "I'll talk to you about that in the morning."

93

In the morning she rose before dawn, lit the stove, dipped two buckets of water from the river, set them to heat on the stove, made up a batch of biscuits and had them in the oven before the amazed boys came from the back bedroom. As they pulled up their suspenders she explained why she was in their kitchen.

They exchanged a happy look. "Mighty bliged, ma'am," said one. After she got them to say which was Jonathan and which was Thomas, they headed for the outhouse. Billy came in combed and clean.

"Mornin," he said, reaching for the coffee pot.

With a smile she removed his hand from it, sat him at the table and poured him a cup. "What do you think women are for anyhow?"

His pale blue eyes connected momentarily with hers and suddenly he was blushing like a girl. Realizing she should have thought before saying that, she turned back to the stove and peeked in the oven. The biscuits needed a minute more. "I've got to go up to an Indian funeral this afternoon, up at Michigan Bar. For Captain Juan. Remember him?" She turned around. "He was shot by miners up at that place where they were supposed to be safe." She couldn't keep the bitterness from her voice.

He looked at her with his water-colored eyes. "Lord that's a shame!" A witness to the treaty, he might be feeling guilty too.

"I need to speak with Mr. Wozencraft, and hoped you'd help me find him."

"Heard he's hung out a shingle in San Francisco. Don't work for the government any more."

He really had abandoned them! "Well, who else has taken responsibility for those poor Indians?"

He sighed. "It just wasn't to be, that's all." The two boys came back in and sat at the table, looking from Billy to Elitha like secrets were being told. "I'll drive you up there," Billy said.

"I can take the stage."

"No sense paying fare. Sides, I mean to give my condolences to that Indian girl."

Maybe he did feel guilty. Anyhow it felt good to know that at least one other white person in California cared about the Indians.

Billy and the boys had gone out to the field when the sound of coughing came from John's room. Elitha pushed open the door.

His dark eyes looked dull, sunken in the bottom of their pits. His cheeks were hollow, the corners of his lips pulled down like Father Rhoads, the blanket up to his chin. He bore no resemblance to the bear of a man she had known. Struggling to keep shock from her face, she brought the chair closer to the bed, explaining that she was here for as long as they could use her.

His sunken eyes came to life, the kindly, intelligent look transporting her back to that afternoon when he had appeared at the Donner tent to take all who could walk to the fort. "You're an angel of — " He broke into a fit of coughing, rising on an elbow, and when he was through blood-streaked sputum lay on his lower lip.

She glanced around for a cloth, but he wiped it on the bedclothes. "There now," she said. "You rest. No need to talk. But I'm warning you, I'm going to wash every stitch on that bed. And make you a pile of handkerchiefs."

His lips straightened in a smile. "Angel of mercy."

"What do you think YOU were? Up there in the mountains? It's the least I can do, and I don't want to hear one more word about it."

Did she imagine more than gratitude in that craggy face? Four years ago she would have rejoiced to see it. Now she wasn't sure, but it felt good to help the man who had saved her life.

In the afternoon she was seated on the buckboard beside Billy, heading past the Cosumne store and up Daylor Road. They talked about the reservation.

"I shoulda known politics would interfere," Billy said.

"What do you mean politics?"

In profile his small nose turned down and he screwed up his eyes at the road ahead where a line of jackasses swayed under huge burdens. "Well, John says that passel of drunks in the California Legislature got riled up about not bein consulted and sent a smokin resolution to Washington. Right high and mighty it was — full of whereases about how our miners got the right to pan wherever they da . . . good and well please, and no redskins should be allowed in the Mother Lode." He looked over at her. "Had strong words for Mr. Wozencraft too."

"But the President wanted the reservation. Isn't the federal government more powerful than a state?"

Billy shrugged. "California's sposed to be the richest state in the Union now. Maybe they don't want to tangle with us."

Fresh anger fired her. "Well, I read the Legislature is meeting in Sacramento City now, and I'm going to give them a piece of my mind!" The Indians had been deceived.

Billy looked at her skeptically, then dipped his hat to the trader pulling the line of jackasses.

She was already making plans. She would catch a stage in a week or so, when John and Billy could spare her. The anger wouldn't lie still until she had done her best to get to the bottom of what had gone wrong, and try to rectify it. The thought quieted her mind as they fell into silence, seated far apart on the buckboard. Chinamen trotted alongside on cloth-covered feet, shouldering sticks, big covered baskets dangling from both ends.

Billy was a puzzle. She'd never felt the slightest spark of male interest from him, though most men seemed ready to fall at her feet. Nevertheless, she was glad for it. He lived with John, and her work there would be easier without that complication. A tall handsome man of twenty-two years, Billy held himself with spinsterish dignity.

And John. Poor John, weakened in the lungs because of rescuing the Donner Party. Come hell or high water she would bring him back to health. Maybe her woman's touch would help with his grief over Matilda too. She'd been pleased to learn of his relief that her standoff with Catherine and Sarah was over. "Never did cotton to it," he'd blurted out between coughs. She'd made him a mustard plaster from the seed she could find in the mildewed pods in the field, mashed them in an old Indian mortar with vinegar and water. Indian Mary knew a tea that loosened phlegm but she couldn't remember the herbs. If the right moment presented itself at the funeral, she'd ask.

"Mind stopping at my house first?" They were approaching the tents and buildings of Bridge House and she needed to make a sign: No cooking. Inquire in summer. She also had to leave a note for Vyries Brown asking him to watch over her place. Billy was turning the horses up the old McCoon trail.

A saddled sorrel mare — one she didn't recognize — stood grazing near the house and tugging a rope tied to an oak branch. Thinking Vyries must be there, she jumped off the wheel and started toward the door of the adobe, where the wildflowers she'd planted stood so prettily. Then her heart jumped to her throat to see the tall lanky frame of Ben Wilder sauntering toward her from the backside of the house.

The sloping folds of his blue eyes crinkled in a smile across his cheeks, the easy manner straight out of her forbidden dreams. As he looked back and forth between her and Billy Rhoads, she felt the spark flaming across time, across the chasm of betrayal and violence. And Billy would think she had lied about not seeing him. Her voice stuck in her throat.

"Howdy," Ben said, a little scratchy. "Heard you asked after me. Thought maybe . . . " Studying her face — did he see the wild confusion? — he changed direction, "A teamster — " What stopped him? Her silent accusation?

He swallowed and looked across the hills, turning his hat in his hands. A tuft of dark hair stood on the top of his head. She used to love that, a part of him never under control. She'd learned there were other parts.

At last she found her voice but it came out rusty. "I didn't think I'd see you again." She remembered her manners. "This here is Billy Rhoads, Sarah's brother. You met her with Mr. Grimshaw, at the dance in Fiddletown. Billy, this is Ben Wilder." Billy seemed unfazed, hiding very well the shock he must be feeling.

Ben displayed the gentlemanly warmth she'd often admired. "Your sister is a fine lady, Mr. Rhoads. I can see you favor her."

"She's my twin," Billy said.

Elitha saw a question flicker in Ben's eye as he glanced from Billy to her. Part of her was glad, wanting to dismiss him or say something about how they had to be going — sorry Ben, maybe I'll see you around sometime.

He seemed to be digging in his heels, adjusting his long legs. Looking her in the eye, he said in a level voice, "I'm glad if you found happiness, Elitha. I'll rest easier knowing." He nodded approvingly at Billy, the breeze moving the tuft of hair across his forehead.

Before she could speak Billy was saying, "It's not what it looks." He held his hat toward the adobe door. "Why don't we set a spell, make a pot of coffee. I'll get water and start the fire."

Grateful, she nodded. Billy was right. They needed to talk. He went inside, got the buckets and headed for the river.

Ben's puzzlement was obvious. "You mean you're not — "

She shook her head. "I'll make something to eat too." Michigan Bar was only a mile away, but Indian fare gagged her.

They went inside and he put his hat on the table and pulled up a bent-willow chair to "his" place, where he'd sat carving, and said, "You're not married yet, or promised?"

She reached into her crate cupboard and shook her head. Was he? But now that they were alone again, the other question was trying to take shape on her tongue.

He was already answering it. "I left to save you heartache, Elitha. After all you'd been through, the last thing you needed was to be hitched to an accused killer. Even be friends with one."

Unable to look at him, she sliced salt pork. "You didn't send word."

"I shot Mr. Johnson. It was self-defense pure and simple. Then all hell broke loose, but I never fired again. I knew how you'd feel — your friendship with Mrs. Sheldon and all. But by thunder, I've been waiting all this time to get my name cleared, not wanting to see you till it was. You see, I couldn't ask you to take my word for it." The last came out so rough, he cleared his throat.

She didn't look up. "You could have told me."

He swallowed and sounded almost boyish. "I wanted you to take me without reservation." His voice regained its normal timbre, its old confidence. "I knew I'd stand between you and your friends until I was cleared. So I went directly to Sacramento City and gave myself up, told the sheriff my whereabouts, and kept hoping the trial would be held. Every day I expected it. But time went by and I needed work, so I started a hauling business. Got real busy, but not busy enough to stop wondering if you forgot about me, maybe found somebody more suited, somebody not implicated in — "

"You went down to the dam with a gun."

Their eyes locked. "That I did." He looked down and all she saw was the top of his dark head. When he looked up, the tuft of hair fell between his eyes. "I'd probably do it again. Things were hot that day, in more ways than one. The deal blew up. Sheldon was flooding claims without compensating the men. With tempers so high, some saying it was my fault for trying to negotiate, well, I don't think any man woulda been without a firearm that day. I felt like I'd brought the men that far and I'd better stick with them. Suppose I even imagined I could stop trouble." He shook his head like he'd heard a not-so-funny-joke.

"Mr. Johnson was going to shoot?"

"Had me in his sights. I saw the muscle move in his hand." He whooshed out air and looked away.

The cold thing in her kept pushing out questions. "Why didn't the sheriff put you on trial?"

"Now there's a good question. First off, Catey Sheldon didn't accuse me. And I've spent some time thinking about this. Back where I come from, things are set up to clear a man of false charges. I get the feeling out here men don't care. Everybody's heading for the next bonanza, the sheriff right along with the rest. And the miners I made go to town with me?" He shook the hair from his eyes. "To a man they said, forget it. I think what this state needs is good men to see that courts of justice get established. Without that, there can't be a real civilization." His eyes pleaded.

Did she trust him? That's what it came down to. Whatever trial there was, was happening right here in her adobe.

"You musta had a million offers." She could hear that he still cared.

Thrill and suspicion mixed badly. She managed a careless shrug and arranged pork strips in the frying pan. "Now I'm cooking for the Rhoads men down at Slough House." For all she knew John —

Billy came in. "Got the fire going, water on. Here's another bucket." He set the water beside her.

"Thanks. We'll be a minute." She grabbed the coffee can, handed it to him. "If you don't mind starting it?"

She and Ben watched him go back out to the fire. She palmed flour into the bread pan, white dust clouding between them. "We're going to an Indian funeral over in Michigan Bar. You know, my Indian friend's father? Well, he's been shot and killed by miners." It felt like a test.

He frowned and made a clucking sound in his cheek and shook his head.

She added a pinch of salt, three pinches of saleratus and a splash of water from the bucket, stirring with her hand. Blindfolded she could whip up a light batch of biscuits. Lord in Heaven, what was this sensation in her insides? It felt wonderful to have him sitting here. She liked the way he watched her hands fly as she pinched out dough, folded it, and swiped the balls through the grease in the old coffee can. She enjoyed the feel of his eyes as she whisked the pans out to the fire. Why did her heart race so? He could be lying.

He joined them for the meal. She watched him charm Billy, talking about how Sacramento City was booming. She wanted to trust this man. His education showed in the way he talked, and she knew for sure he hadn't made up the part about going down to the sheriff. That much had been reported in the paper.

"I'd like to go to the Indian funeral with the two of you, if you don't mind," he said.

Guilty pleasure infused her. She got out her roll of used brown paper and made her sign, also writing notes for Vyries and Jimmy Buetler — "Go ahead with the rebuilding, even if I'm not here" — then climbed onto the buckboard between the men. What would she say to John? What was Billy thinking?

With Ben's illicit warmth beside her, she sat primly. The sun was low when Billy pulled the team to a stop overlooking Michigan Bar. At least a hundred campfires were strewn across the shattered hills. Indians didn't look extinct here, though the morning paper had predicted the "imbecilic race" would be gone in just seven years, "crushed beneath the iron heel of progress."

How would Ben see the Indians? The trial started in the adobe, she realized, had many facets.

94

"Eat. Eat before we dance," urged Hin-co-ye, the *temayasa*, dance doctor. "You will need strength. Eat before we cry."

Maria had eaten her fill. At the fire with Broken Salmon and Pedro and the children, she looked around at the large assembly that had gathered in the former home place of the Wapumne. It still amazed her how widely respected Father had been. Bent-Willow-Reflected-in-Pond, Spear Thrower and their children sat at the next fire with Hummingbird Tailfeather, her face and bald head blackened as so many were. On all sides people were eating oolah, which Maria and the other women had made from the acorns packed on their backs. The ceremonial food would keep them dancing all night.

Father would have been proud, she knew as she looked around at the people. From as far away as Monterey and the home place of Ts'noma they were still arriving, though tonight would be the second night. All were dressed for the celebration, many in the skirts and trousers of *Americanos*. Shell money hung around their necks with other *Americano* trinkets they had found. Feathers decorated their hair, the few who had hair.

Most of the diggers and their tents had disappeared since the water cannon ate the hills. However several sat leaning against the old roundhouse. She controlled her fear as they tipped up bottles and laughed coarsely — men apparently drawn from upriver by last night's ceremonies. With them sat the men from the house of the water cannon. She hoped the rituals of the Cry would snuff out her awareness of all of them.

Last night at the orations Hin-co-ye had said that if the people were meant to die, nothing could be done about it. If they were to be captured and forced to labor, it was not important. More important was the proper conduct of the Cry — purification and wormwood in the nostrils, the right food. For those prepared for death, the time of dying didn't matter. "Eat. Eat. Eat. Eat," he called now as he walked among the fires stamping the tail of his plumed walking staff. "So we are ready to cry."

Several fires away, Maria saw one of the men who had orated so well about Father. She had thought she had known everything there was to know about him, but last night she learned he was the most admired headman in the wide place called California. She heard details of how he had galvanized warriors from many villages to fight the combined Mexican garrisons. Coordinating with Estanislao, who led hundreds of mission people to join the battle, he organized arrow runners, food suppliers and medicine women to move in and out of a network of underground trenches leading to a three-tiered stockade — a huge spider's web to lure the black hats. *Indios* had won the first two battles, and both sides left equally discouraged after the last. She knew Father had been a war chief back then, but as the orations progressed, she appreciated for the first time the extent of his departure from tradition, and how eloquent he must have been to persuade two thousand men to leave their villages and fight side by side with strangers. No such thing had been done before.

"Except for the Departed," one of the speakers had said, "all of us would have been forced from our homes and into mission labor. The Departed, who now goes to the Happy Land, helped make the missions wither. The black hats stopped coming to herd us away. Some people say it was a bad thing the missions withered, but I say to you, they did not suffer the *azote* on their backs. They were not locked in the wooden trap to stand in their own water and defecation."

As Maria listened to the orations, she imagined her father as a brave young warrior, so different from the father she had known — a man convinced that the sorrows of fighting could not stop the changes in the world, and that *Indios* should make friends with the new people. She realized now that he could have chosen a path no *Indio* had walked — war chief of many peoples fighting to expel *Americanos*, for the speakers made it clear they would have followed him. But Father had defeated the temptation of worldly power — the strongest and most seductive of human enemies — and had been rewarded with higher wisdom. Few in life had the opportunity of meeting that enemy, much less defeating it. It occurred to her now that Captain Sutter had failed where her father had succeeded. Grizzly Hair, Captain Juan, had been a man of knowledge.

She noticed a line of pale-robed people just arriving. Their shoulder-length hair indicated they were women, but their bare faces looked male. What did the costumes mean? They looked like spirits. Leaving Pedro, she threaded her way through the campfires, walking toward the robed people, nodding greetings to the men from the Lake of the Tulares, and from Estanislao's River.

The robed men came to a halt before her, maybe twelve or thirteen. "Where do you come from and where are you going?" she asked of the first — clearly a man, and not young. The flesh stretched tightly across his wide cheekbones and was creased around his eyes. Even his feet and hands, which protruded from the woolen robe, looked emaciated.

"We come from Mission San José. We come to cry for our friend."

That surprised her for two reasons. She had imagined that place a crumbled heap, and the man's way of speaking sounded like her *umne*.

"We are hungry." The ritual statement in the nuances of her tongue.

"Come and eat," she responded, intrigued, looking from one robed man to the other, sure she didn't know any of them.

They followed her to where women dipped out baskets of oolah and peppermint tea. As they received the ritual food, the robed spokesman said in the warm, wonderful accents of a cousin-brother: "We will sing at the Cry and play our flutes."

"Your talk sounds familiar."

"Your home place is mine." Stunned again, she saw how his flat nose fit in his face — a trait of her people. A ripple in his wide, mobile lips displayed emotion as he said, "The Deceased went to the mission with me. I stayed. He was the best friend of my childhood."

Bowstring! The long-lost Bowstring whom Father had praised as the best flute player in the world, the one who married a mission woman and played *Españolo* instruments under Padre Duran. Bowstring's mother had never given up hope of seeing him again, and now she was dead — killed by *Americanos*. Honored by his presence, Maria extended the traditional: "Thank you for crying for my father."

"Your father!" He stared a shade too long at her pitch-blackened face. "You are my cousin-niece then." He glanced around at the people, who were preparing themselves for the dancing. "Is your mother here?"

Closing her eyes, she looked down and shook her head. "All gone. Your mother too. We dance for everybody." Politely she looked past the shock in his eyes and saw a team of horses pulling a wagon to a stop. On the seat were Elitha and Señor Rhoads, with them the tall *Americano* who had been good to Elitha at the time of her baby's death. Maria must greet them too, and offer food.

"Eat," she said to Bowstring and his men. "And bathe. Soon we will cry." She gestured to the barren shore and brown river, now filled with silt from the destruction of the hills. Not even Chinamen washed gold here any longer. Leaving Bowstring, she threaded her way through the people, many adorning themselves with beads and dance feathers, and heard Hin-co-ye announce in ceremonial tones: "All here very sad. All cry. Last time to be sad."

That landed like a thunderbolt. Her feet stopped. *Last time to be sad* — the traditional statement that everyone knew meant *until the next Cry*. But it might actually be the last time. When would people hold another Cry? Her *umne* were all dead except for the husbands and children of Bent-Willow-Reflected-in-Pond and Hummingbird Tailfeather. Could so few hold a Dance for the Dead? Not likely. They didn't even know the words. Could any of them safely rouse the spirits of the dead? Those camping here — mostly older men whose common tongue was Spanish — would leave when the Big Time was over. Most would creep back into their hiding places in rocks and caves, many to die of disease and shootings, some to starve in the plundered land. Bowstring would return to San José. Hin-co-ye and the others from the reservation were looking for a new hiding place. They wandered homeless as bears, sleeping in a different place each night. She could not depend on anyone to hold another Cry.

Strength drained down from her shoulders and out the tips of her fingers. *Last time to be sad.* She might never again freely picture Father's eyes as he looked lovingly at her, or remember the old strength of his body before he was injured, or recall the lines of wisdom of his face. She might never again commune with his soul or the souls of Etumu and Dishi and all the dead loved ones. *Last time to be sad.* A spiritual desert stretched before her. But she remembered that Grandmother Howchia still lived in the oak. The fire that destroyed the roundhouse might have burned the leaves off a strong oak, but could not kill it. The thought moved her forward, toward Elitha.

After a brief visit with Indian Mary, Elitha remained on the buckboard between Ben Wilder and Billy Rhoads, looking across the twilight expanse of Indian campfires. Mary had said that earlier in the day, the Indians had tamped out a dance floor — a huge rectangle — and swept it clean. In its center stood a platform of dry brush upon which the body of Captain Juan had been placed. Last night there had been speeches about him, and singing in the roundhouse. Tonight only dancing and singing were planned.

Four Indians with flaming sticks moved across the open ground and knelt to ignite the brush. Another — wearing a torn top hat and cape — walked with ramrod posture around all sides of the rectangle calling in guttural tones. From the corner of her eye she saw Ben smile, and realized the Indian did look a little clownish, but she tried to ignore that and the drunken miners who laughed coarsely within earshot of the ceremonies.

Indians from all sides began to move onto the dance floor. They threw baskets, blankets, hats, and smaller things on the funeral pyre. Then suddenly a piercing female-sounding wail came from the top-hatted Indian. Eerie, mournful beyond anything Elitha had ever heard, it jangled her nerves. The miners stopped laughing and watched.

Silence followed. Then the top-hatted Indian tilted back his head and emitted a second unearthly wail. Another voice joined him, and another, and another until slowly the wailing entered her and teased out every sorrowful emotion she had ever felt — all the deaths that she had suffered. The sound of sorrow blended into her soul. It rose in pitch, even the dogs howling, until it seemed to come from the very landscape — the lacerated hills, the upside-down earth, the dead fish and animals, the dead Indians who once populated this region more numerously than these visiting hundreds. Goose bumps prickled her arms and she almost felt the ghosts. Then suddenly the wailing ceased.

The death-like silence stood her hair on end. She glanced at Ben, whose expression had changed to awe, and whispered, "I bet that lasted half an hour." He nodded, and for a moment she thought he would take her hand, but was relieved he didn't.

Another wail started, followed by a new chorus of cries as penetrating and lengthy as the first. Then again the sudden, far more terrifying silence. As if Hell had swallowed all but the snarling dogs.

The Indian with the flapping high hat strode around the dance floor gravely orating, the feathers on his staff flouncing each time he pounded the butt end on the ground. Elitha could tell he repeated phrases three and four times. After about twenty minutes of this, he stopped.

Shadowy Indians moved onto the tamped ground, young women forming a circle nearest the fire, men standing in a large group nearby. It looked like Indian Mary went out to dance, though it was hard to see at that distance, the firelight and shadow darkening them all, making them all look alike — so many without hair.

Wooden flutes were raised. Strange, hollow music floated across the hills, joined at intervals by a dirgelike chorus of men. Beneath, steady as a heart, thumped the mournful drumbeat. Wails and wild ululations interrupted the chorus as the Indian women leapt around the fire, pouncing twice on one foot, then twice on the other. Their high leaps forcing air from their lungs as they landed, the rasping heh, heh, heh, heh grinding like one monstrous voice. Blood tingled in Elitha's veins and a nameless terror infused her along with the stench of burning flesh and the sight of the dark frenzy of elbows, knees, feet and flying hair black against the orange firelight. It seemed a likeness of Hell.

"A savage spectacle. *Walpurgisnacht*," Ben said.

Grandma Donner had used that term for the night the earth belched up witches, some riding on farting goats, others on flying brooms. But it was more than a "spectacle." Elitha knew such violent dancing would have helped her pour out her grief for her own dead. Maybe Ben thought it was more like a circus. But why care what he thought? She didn't really know him. He could be a murderer.

The first hour of the wild dancing held Pedro entranced. Then he thought ahead. Tomorrow he and Murieta's men would herd the last of the huge *caballadas* down to Mexico. He had told María and she was sad. Ay, but he worried about her and the baby while he was gone — it could be two months. But he had seen a wagon arrive and it looked like Señora McCoon with two men, one of whom looked like Señor Rhoads. They might help.

It was out of the question to take María with him. The dangers had quadrupled. The so-called state lawmakers had hired a desperado named Harry Love and twenty of the most vicious killers in *Norteamerica* to end the career of the "Joaquín gang." Salaried to hunt for five "Joaquíns," the rangers were combing the hills and streams, and bribing the weak. Pedro couldn't expose María to that.

He had convinced Joaquín Murieta they should bypass the big valley, take the herd through San José, then down through Santa Barbara and Los Angeles. Don Cristóbal and other rancheros would hide them at night. The native sons of California were *simpatico*.

Even in the dark he could see that the wagon was still there. He left Isabella in Spear Thrower's arms and, in the flashes of firelight spaced by lurching dancers, stepped carefully around masses of clay that had been dislocated by the water cannon. Then suddenly the singing and dancing ceased.

He looked back and saw María and other young women collapsing where they stood. He shook his head. *Ay Madre*, where did she get the strength? He couldn't jump up and down like that for two hours straight. The medicine man was making an announcement, speaking in the stiff way of *Indios*. Then he shifted to Spanish: "The men of the mission now sing to *Dios* and María.

Without the dancers, the firelight was more constant as Pedro proceeded. A sound stopped him — a pure voice cutting through the night like an angel. Other voices joined the first — sweet, interwoven, a sound as ancient and sacred as the cathedrals of Spain. The Latin Requiem — he knew it from his boyhood. He looked back at the robed *Indios*, and from habit picked out a few words that sounded Spanish.

Dona eis Requiem. Give, rest.

"Yes God," he said aloud. "Grant the *pobrecitos* rest." But do not wait until they join You in heaven. Pedro wouldn't be here any longer to help them.

The exotic tones threaded around one another like angelic knitting needles shaping an otherworldly fabric. The music transported Elitha to another realm.

Ben exclaimed, "Well I'll be hornswoggled. Latin! They don't sound like monkeys now."

That brought her back to earth. She knew perfectly well that people commonly called Indians monkeys, but she didn't want to hear it from him.

Billy Rhoads leaned past Elitha to speak to Ben. "Do you know Latin?"

"My old schoolmaster gave me a little credit for poking through all those books of Cicero and Heroditus. Listen."

In exquisite harmony the voices hung suspended, then one by one peeled away and tripped down a delicate ladder, regrouping at the bottom in a new, enchanted harmonic. Like disembodied spirits moving through the night, neither male nor female, they repeated phrases, each time flowing in reshaped harmony. Ben translated:

"Lamb of God, who taketh away the sins of the world, give us rest." Staring intently at the singing Indians, he echoed the Latin as they sang: *"Agnus Dei, qui tollis pecatta mundi, dona eis requiem."*

He knew these were no monkeys, she could tell. And she had to admire his education. Far beyond hers. This was an exceptional Forty-niner.

A man's voice startled her. "Señora McCoon. *Por favor*, may I talk with you?" It came from beside the wagon, the resonant accents of Señor Valdez. She hadn't seen him since she had given him Captain Sutter's letter about the ranch.

She started to rise, but Ben put his hand on her. "Do you know who it is?"

"Señor Valdez." She stood.

Ben whispered, "Don't get out of the wagon."

For months she had yearned to be cared for and looked after, but now annoyance pricked her. After leaving her alone for seven months, Ben Wilder was telling her what to do. "Señor Valdez is an honorable man," she said more coldly than intended. Pushing past Ben's knees, she climbed down the wagon wheel.

"I only mean to keep you safe, Elitha. It must be midnight."

It was indeed dark. Indians continually tossed fresh branches into the flames, but the fire was too distant to illuminate the Spaniard's features. She sensed him drawing himself up, and knew he liked being called honorable.

"I must go away for a leetle while, Señora. My wife and *niños* need a safe place to stay for two months. I am sorry but I must ask if you can help them find a place."

"Gladly. I'm staying at the Rhoadses now. Maybe they wouldn't mind." She raised her voice toward the dark figures on the buckboard, "Billy, Indian Mary needs a place to stay, and I could use help with chores. Do you suppose she could stay at your farm?"

"Sure," Billy said. "And we could use a couple of bucks to clear brush in the new field."

"Señor Rhoads?" Valdez said. "I thought maybe it was you. *Buenas noches*. I hope your family is healthy."

"John's under the weather, but Elitha here'll bring him back. Say. Stop by sometime and tell us what you're up to. We lost track of you."

"I have been working and saving *dinero* for a big rancho far away. I weel return and take María with me in two months. We talk then, no?"

"A pleasure."

"*Muchas gracias* for taking her. I will find you hard workers for the brush. Go with God and say hello to your family."

Elitha said to Señor Valdez, "Tell Mary to come when the funeral's over."

Billy said, "I'll send Ramón in the wagon to fetch anybody who'll come."

"A thousand times gracias, Señora, and Señor Rhoads." With a bow in the dark, he was gone.

First light was graying the sky. Maria's legs wobbled to the drumbeat. She had been dancing since Bowstring and his troupe finished singing. All night she had pounded her grief down through the soles of her feet and wrung herself inside out, indulging her sorrows together with the hundreds who had known Father. She had shouted his name and pictured him. She had remembered and remembered and remembered, and wailed out her last spark of strength. Now, sleeping people littered the dance place. Her legs moved erratically as she staggered past them toward Pedro's bedroll. She felt like a dying animal, too exhausted to think, struggling to reach that destination, though it was only a stone's throw away.

She lifted the cover, fell in beside him. Heavy sleep rose up from the earth and sucked her down.

95

"María. María." It was Pedro, kneeling beside her.

Gradually she surfaced, disentangled herself from dream and realized the sun was bright and high. Isabella was crying, dogs barking, people stirring all around.

Pedro peered down at her. "Are you well, Little Poppy? I am afraid you danced too long." Despite the sunlight a light haze sat on his head and shoulders.

She blinked and rubbed her eyes. "I am well. Did Isabella eat?" Pushing hair from her face, she sat up. She felt stiff.

"Sí, the *niña* ate acorn mush. I don't know why she is crying." The strange fog around him defied the sunshine.

She blinked again and looked at the surrounding people in the large, sunny encampment. Her vision was crisp except when she looked at Pedro. Passing a hand over his face she felt nothing. Then she knew.

NO! She closed her eyes and trembled, unable to accept it. Too many had died. She couldn't lose Pedro. She wanted to shout *peligro*! But he was speaking.

"Señora McCoon says you can stay with her at the rancho of Señor Rhoads while I am gone." He scowled with concern. "You are shaking, *Amapolita*."

"Stay, Pedro." She looked at him in the direct *Español*o manner, repeating what she had begged of him, not caring that she had chided him for repeating talk and now did it herself.

He put his hands on her shoulders and spoke forcefully, "María, *Te amo*. You are *la dueña de mi corazón*, owner of my heart. Understand? I promise you, this is my last ride with Joaquín Murieta. I will return in two moons, with horses enough for all your people who want to come to Mexico with us. We will travel by a secret route. I have hidden four hundred thousand dollars in the knot of a tree down there." She had agreed to go with him to Mexico, now that evil had struck her father. He continued, "It will buy us beautiful land and build us a big comfortable hacienda. Our children will wear fine clothing. Our *mayordomo* will escort them to church and school. They will read books. Picture that life, *Amapolita mía*, and stay safe with your friend Elitha until my return. I ask this from my heart."

Absently, she glanced to where Elitha's wagon had been.

"They will send Ramón for you and the others when the fiesta is over." He took her hands and forced a smile — the haze remaining — and explained that Señor Rhoads needed the help.

Hardly able to breathe, much less feel gratitude about having a temporary home, she said, "Do not leave before the Cry is finished." If he would stay just one more sleep, she could live a lifetime cherishing each additional moment.

He made a vexed noise in his throat. "Joaquín says we leave today from the cantina of Señor Seymoures. I have already delayed our departure, Little Poppy, and Joaquín is restless. He is afraid Captain Love comes north." He shrugged. "I must go, now."

Señor Seymoures dwelled a short ride away, the "Portegee" leaving his wife and four young boys to ride with Murieta, not intending to return. And though Pedro had told the story in disbelieving tones, Maria feared he wouldn't return either, not because he didn't want to, but because of the men who hunted him — circling, sniffing like wolves. *Indios* from the Calaveras River had reported Murieta's movements to them. If she warned him about the shroud of danger, he would call it superstition. She rose to her knees and started to say, "*No. Por fav* — "

He pulled her to him, pressing his face into her breast, his voice cracking as if he might cry. "Little Poppy, this one time I must say no to you, and I will not change my mind."

She swallowed a lump the size of an oak gall and laid her cheek on the top of his head, the brown-red curls he had given Isabella. Would she ever embrace him again? Inhale his leathery *cigarrito* scent? Gently she lifted his trimmed beard and rubbed his face with her tears, his mustache, his slightly downturned hawk nose, but she could not look at his eyes. She murmured, "I wish I had the power to shrink to cricket size and ride in your pocket."

"I cherish you, *te quiero*," he breathed, closing his eyes.

"*Te amo*," she said back. She had begged him to stay. No more could be done. She ran her finger across his cheek, collected a tear, put it into her mouth. "You are *el dueño de mi corazón*."

He pushed up to his feet and stood looking down a moment, the gray facets of his eyes mysteriously unending. Quapata was in the saddle nearby, holding Chocolate's rein. Hundreds of people moved about them, but all faded as she reached out and ran her hand down Pedro's buttoned trouser leg, down the soft goatskin around his calf. Sitting beneath him, she left her hand there — the last touch.

She heard his effort to lighten his leaving. "They will not catch *el Bandido Cuidadoso*, my love. I will hold the memory of your beautiful face and black eyes here." He closed his fist over his heart. "*Hasta la vista*." He turned, the goatskin pulling from her hand, and walked toward Chocolate, hips shifting from side to side in his black *pantalones*.

"*Vaya con Dios*," she managed to say as he mounted in a fluid move. *Great Spirit of the Españoles, protect him!* Maybe the aura was nothing but superstition. Fervently she hoped so as she watched the horses gallop away and disappear behind the deformed hillside. Then her ears and eyes opened. She heard the baby cry, saw Little Flicker and Billy staring at her, the nearby people politely averting their eyes. The *Españolo* custom of saying good-bye cut to the heart.

Father's death had weakened her. She must go to Grandmother Howchia. Maybe Grandmother could restore her. Maybe she would say the fog around him was not Death.

Spear Thrower agreed to accompany her to the home place, and to leave immediately, in order to return before the evening ceremonies. As she put the children in the care of Bent-Willow-Reflected-in-Pond, he slung his bow and quiver over his torso, and they headed up the old Wapumne path.

Every step stretched the distance between her and Pedro, and hurt more. She walked downriver; he rode up. Without the willows and cottonwoods, birds lacked perches. The sun felt naked, the breeze unfriendly. She had walked this trail often as a child on the way to the Wapumne Big Times, skipping beside Grizzly Hair, Etumu, Crying Fox, and her cousin sisters. But now the place was unrecognizable. The silt-choked river ran straight where it had turned. Pits and trenches scarred the shores. Noticing that Spear Thrower walked like Crying Fox, she choked back a sudden sob. At the dance tonight she would let her mind dwell on her brother, his muscled calves, eaten by *Americanos*. A sound buzzed in her ears. A threatening spirit?

Only a few hairy-faced *Americano* diggers were in the rocks along the river. When they glanced up Maria held her gaze forward. The rush of sound grew louder as they neared the home place. Now and again violent shudders racked her at the thought of Pedro being caught by Captain Love. *I will return*, he had said. She would cling to that. And remember that she owned his heart, the place where his love came from. Rounding the river bend near the old walnut grove, she stopped beside Spear Thrower.

The once-wooded hillside where she had played as a child and gathered as a young woman gaped open. At the top, three men with braced legs controlled the long snout of a water cannon, which ejected a powerful stream. Pale clay and rocks rushed down in a torrent, a mountain eroding. Only two trees were left in the deepening muck, soon to be buried. Below, mud boiled into a wooden trough bisecting the trail, numerous *Americanos* poking shovels into it. At the end of the trough, cream-colored water made a waterfall into the river.

Spear Thrower signaled Maria. She backtracked with him and headed around the other side of the hill. Had Grandmother's tree been buried too? Or cut down? Maybe Howchia had gone to the happy land at last, her soul released from the dying tree. What was left to look at now? The tiny remnant of her people were in mourning. Few babies were born. The dance places gone. Pedro — She forced her mind away.

Approaching the home place from the north hills, the village center looked desolate. Even the diggers were gone. Nothing remained of the dancehouse, not even ash. But the mound still rose beside the wide excavation, and on it stood the magnificent oak, taller than the two other oaks on the denuded creek bank. The tree spread her arms over the area where the u-machas and cha'kas had been, green buds were swelling all over her flourishing twigs. Grandmother was here!

Spear Thrower went and stood at the river's edge watching the pale torrent, perhaps speaking to his private spirit ally, perhaps respecting Maria's privacy. Looking at his strong back and sloping shoulders, his acorn brownness, his hip slung to one side, she realized he was the last man of her people, and she the last woman.

She climbed up the mound, toes sinking into the softness, a cloud of yellow finches scattering from the twigs above. At the wide trunk she closed her eyes, inhaling the tannic aroma of the bark. *Grandmother, I come in fear and sorrow.* She tried to empty her mind. *Once, I slept in this place without noticing the smiles of my uncles and aunts, the caring of my parents, the sounds of children playing, women pounding. I went willingly to Señor Sutter's place. I married men not of our people, one who stole Molok's robe. Another whose life vengeful men would take. I wanted them, Grandmother. I liked their different ways. I said I will go to Mexico with Pedro, but* — She moaned and clung to the trunk with outstretched arms, trembling, wanting but not daring to ask if Pedro would die.

A rumble came from deep in the ground and reverberated up the trunk: *I am rooted. In time of rain I wear the mist rising from the earth. In the long dry I wear its dust. I do not ask if there is a better place. I am what is. I am rooted. Older than the finches, younger than the rocks, I am not immortal. Granddaughter. Where are you going?*

Her soul was quiet. She knew the question was as important as the answer she had come seeking.

96

Elitha stood in the doorway looking at Indian Mary as she washed the breakfast dishes, and felt a momentary pang of regret. Mary had refused Matilda Rhoads' clothing — insisting bad spirits would kill her for touching the belongings of the dead — and now wore Catherine's once-green frock, faded to gray. The oft-mended underarms revealed brown skin, and the frayed hem hung like fringe about her calves. The rags of civilization had transformed a lovely wild girl into a barefoot scullery maid.

About to leave for Sacramento City, she said, "Mary, you've been working hard these two months. Let the other girls wash the bedclothes. Take time with Billy and Isabella. Go for a walk." Two other Indian women had come with Mary to the Rhoads farm. They also wore rags. If she hadn't given Jimmy Buetler all her gold, less the little needed for the stage and sundries, she would have been able to buy material to sew them all new frocks. But working for board and room didn't give her any extra. And she hadn't heard a word from Buetler. Apparently he had taken the gold and run.

Mary turned and looked at her, black hair framing a face no longer plump, cheeks flat beneath prominent bones. "Work makes wait short," she said. "Work makes forgetting. Billy is happy with men. Go. No think about clothes washing." She turned back to the dishes.

"I mean to do what I can to get the reservation back."

"No matter. Bad place." She didn't look up.

That was Mary's attitude. She would go to Mexico with Mr. Valdez, but all the other Indians needed a safe place. And it made Elitha furious the way they'd been tricked. They had let down their guard. And yes, work made forgetting. How well Elitha knew that! Mary's wait for Señor Valdez had made her withdrawn, hard to talk to. Elitha turned and left, hoping Señor Valdez would arrive today. The girl deserved a little happiness.

She climbed aboard the eight a.m. stage, immediately making it clear to the men inside that she didn't wish to chatter. Not only would she speak to the law-makers, but she intended to locate Ben Wilder's place of business. This could be the most important day of her life, and she needed to think.

Last evening after the supper dishes were put away she had gone to the porch for a breath of cool air. John Rhoads joined her, the hot dry air having healed his lungs. He was fleshing out again and working in the fields, almost his old self, except for his eyes, which looked thirty years older than when she'd met him five years ago.

"When you gonna cook us some bad grub?" he had asked.

She gazed over the field of golden wheat. "Well now, maybe you'd like some rock biscuits. I used to do those up pretty good. Or maybe some hornet grubs, fried just enough to stop the wiggling." She turned a sisterly smile at him, to tell him Indians ate that. But he was standing too close. Her smile faded.

He laid a bear paw on her shoulder. "You've brought this household back together, Elitha. Made us a family again." His voice was thick.

She knew where this was leading. Reason said she should grab him while she could. It also said her cooking days at the Rhoads farm were over. She would not mislead this man, this greatest of California heroes.

"I appreciate that." Swallowing, she tried to explain. "But I've been thinking . . . about Ben Wilder." She struggled onward, stumbling over words. Since the Indian funeral Ben had visited once, but after a strained buggy drive, she had told him she needed to think alone. People around here said he had been the ring-leader in Mr. Sheldon's death, even if he hadn't pulled the trigger. For two months he had stayed away. It boiled down to trust. And somehow over the months of helping the Rhoads men, disentangling dreams of Ben from the daylight world, and appreciating his respect for her feelings, she had decided to trust him. Like the "leap of faith" Reverend Fish talked about.

As she fumbled toward explanation, John stepped back, listening quietly in the shadow of the house. Only a slight crack in his voice betrayed his feelings. "'Preciate your tellin me." A vise had tightened on her heart. Never had it felt so bad to speak her mind. And now, as Perry used to say, the die was cast.

The driver cried, "Walsh Station." She went to the outhouse while a four-horse team was watered, and soon they were racing full tilt down the old road to Sutter's Fort, bouncing over the ruts. The occupants of the coach continued to leave her alone, and silently she practiced her speech: Gentlemen, my name is Elitha McCoon. I have lived at Rancho Sacayak since before the discovery of gold and am here to object to . . . No. A friendly touch would work better, like the way Abe Lincoln opened when he spoke to the farmers in the Donner yard! Good afternoon, gentlemen, esteemed Legislators. I feel privileged to speak to you, and I must say I applaud your great wisdom in deciding that the heat in the fair city of Sacramento is insufficient to . . . No. The *Sacramento Union* said the majority of

Legislators wanted the capitol in Vallejo or Benicia or San José. Gentlemen. My name is Elitha McCoon and I feel honored to speak to you today about the plight of the Indians, the wise and wonderful people . . . No. Even the Spaniards from the coast thought Indians had childish minds and were born horse thieves.

How could she explain the Indians as she knew them? Slow to anger, as much at home with nature as the sun and rain. She looked out the window at the flat grasslands, the large oaks standing every few hundred yards. But thoughts of Ben intruded. She hadn't been very nice to him that last time. The coach slowed and stopped at Perkins Station. It felt good to stretch her legs and join the other passengers in a bowl of soup while fresh horses were hitched.

Back in the coach she could almost feel the miners' spirits lifting the nearer they came to the steam-driven floating palaces that plied the rivers between Sacramento City and San Francisco.

"Where'd ye say you was headed?" one man asked another.

"New York." The man smiled. "Older and wiser."

BRIGHTON, announced a sign as the coach passed through a small town at the junction of roads: Sutter's Fort to the north, Stockton to the south. She glimpsed the racetrack where the paper said two thousand people had watched "thrilling combat" between a bull and a large grizzly bear. The coach rattled and bounced west down a new road bypassing the old fort. These days everything bypassed the fort. It seemed sad, the adobe walls crumbling, people hauling off the remains. In her mind she saw it as it had once stood, isolated on the plain, the end of the trail for weary travellers, none wearier than she. Now Captain Sutter was in disrepair too, occasionally brought down from his farm on the Feather River to march in a parade, or sit in the front row of an entertainment. A relic of another time. "Disgracefully drunk," one reporter had written.

Tables, chairs and pitched tents began to appear beneath the oaks, which were leafed out despite cavities burned in their trunks. People used them as windbreaks and fireplaces. She'd seen that six months ago, on her trip to the theater with the Counselor. Blackened spires stood as reminders that even these large trees would eventually burn through. Frame houses flanked the road. She craned her neck to see flowers behind a whitewashed fence, then jerked back as a wagonload of men whizzed by, too near, too fast, about fifteen men gripping rifles.

At regular intervals roads intersected J Street, down which the coach flew. Square blocks had been laid out far beyond the actual town, she recalled, but now houses had sprouted on them. The growth was startling. Then two-story buildings stood between the houses and gardens, and all manner of buggies and rigs passed by in clouds of dust. The driver slowed the horses to a more stately pace. Some of the houses were as grand as Springfield's best. She tried to see the names of the commercial establishments, but before she knew it, the stage stopped in a confusion of men and conveyances.

The driver opened the door. Across the transportation yard, over the heads of the milling men towered a three-story structure with UNION HOTEL painted on it. Two-story buildings lined all the surrounding streets, many sharing walls.

"After you," said the New Yorker.

Stepping out, she turned and asked, "If you please, have you the time?"

He pulled out a watch, flicked it open. "Eleven o'clock."

The twenty-mile trip had taken only three hours. "Thank you, sir. Have a pleasant journey. Your wife and children will surely be glad to see you." He touched his hat.

Stepping into the dust, she jumped as a heraldic voice yelled, "Leaving for Marysville. Five minutes." Only four feet away, the man pointed a finger at a freight-sized wagon, where men sat on rows of benches. *Marysville*. She felt a pang of desire to go see Mary, but realized as she made her way through the melee that the return ticket to Slough House would cost all her remaining coins.

Hawkers yelled over the blare of voices, the rattle of harnesses: "Departin fer the southern mines. Big strikes in the Calaveras." "All points to Nevada City. Make your fortune." "Stockton, Sonora, Columbia. Ten minutes." "Bound for the famous Folsom mines. Don't git left behind."

She dodged men with rifles and bedrolls scurrying frantically and uncertainly from one wagon to the other. A driver reached down and grabbed a man's elbow, a hawker boosting him from below, deciding for the undecided. Six-bit teams stamped impatiently, jangling their harnesses as they shook off flies. A passenger in a wagon yelled, "Git the hell on the road! We been sitting on these hard benches for an hour." Guns bristled over shoulders.

The driver drawled back, "Not rollin till I gits four more."

"Yer on my foot," yelled a passenger, shoving the man next to him, causing the others to lean like angry dominoes.

It was the oppressive heat, Elitha decided, that made the men so surly, the transportation yard so unpleasant, that and the stench of human waste clinging to the city air. Too many cesspools, too many people using outhouses too close together.

She stepped inside the cool, quiet lobby of the hotel. An old clerk put his finger on a line in a leather-bound volume and looked up as she asked where the Legislature met. "Go up Fifth to China Slough, that's I Street, then take a right to the Court House. You can't miss it. About the size of a three-horse livery stable, Greek pillars and dome the size of St. Peter's." Almost smiling, he went back to Shakespeare.

She passed many people. Nodding at a woman waiting on the buckboard of a covered wagon, she nearly collided with a man staggering from the Miner's Supply Store with a heavy box. The flies and stench thickened the nearer she came to I Street. Then it opened before her, the Chinese sector on her left — a string of crowded stores backed up to a wide slough — clearly the city dump. Celestials bustled around the stores, plucked chickens and meat hung outside, and stacks of pointed straw hats were displayed with pans, boots, shovels and picks. Behind the stores brown cattails poked at odd angles through the garbage and she could almost see the rank odors rising in the heat.

On her right, beyond the huts and Chinese men tending green leafy vegetables, she saw the unlikely dome, an enormous red, white and blue flag draped tiredly over it. Hoping the Legislature was in session, she went up the stairs between the pillars and pushed the lettering on the door: SACRAMENTO CITY AND COUNTY COURT HOUSE.

With relief she saw the chamber benches filled with men. At a table in front, a white-haired gentleman with muttonchop side whiskers fondled a mallet and gazed at her while a speaker orated about rampant crime. Men of all descriptions stood crowded in between the last bench and the back wall, turning to look curiously at her as she shut the door.

The air was close, warm, and smelled of unwashed bodies. She was the only female. Her heart raced at the thought of speaking. Where would she stand? At the front? How would she signal her desire to be recognized? Would she fall in a faint? She squeezed in beside two men, one in a top hat and tails, perhaps a banker, and leaned against the wall, as others did.

After paying twenty dollars to come all this way, she would say her piece, just as she had at Catherine's. But first she'd watch how others did it. A legislator stood beside his bench gesturing broadly, his stentorian tones overwhelming the chatter of the spectators. He finished with: "I propose we amend the bill to expel every Mexican from the interior of the state." Men shouted and stamped approval, others clapped. Some sat stonily.

The chairman recognized Assemblyman Philemon Herbert from Mariposa County. In common trousers and shirt, the young man leaped on the bench. He pivoted often as he spoke, so all could see his face. His speech was clipped, slightly southern, his vocabulary large — he mentioned he'd come from Texas. With a flourish he whipped a newspaper from his pocket and read a list of crimes committed by the bandit Joaquín.

"My fellow lawmakers," he shouted, "Are we going to take these outrages lying down? Or are we men? The time for action is long past! Captain Harry Love and his twenty rangers have done nothing but dispatch a few common horse thieves. Meanwhile the five Joaquíns listed in this petition run free. It's high time to support Governor Bigler's resolution and post a five-thousand-dollar reward for any person or persons who capture the robber leader. Dead or alive. I move we send the Governor's resolution to MY committee. From there, I promise you it will be approved and signed before the sun sets."

"Second," came a shout as cheers exploded. Hats hit the ceiling. Elitha's heart pounded all the louder. How could she match such fervor? These men had no fear of public speaking. Would they laugh at her? Behind her fear niggled an old disquiet. Was Señor Valdez one of the five Joaquíns? She hadn't realized so many existed. His means of support remained mysterious.

Assemblyman Catlin was recognized. "Mr. Speaker, my fellow lawmakers," he said as he rose to his feet, "there's another bunch of thieves you should be worrying about. At this very moment they are pilfering the State Treasury. I speak of none other than Captain Love and his gang of rangers. They are no doubt laughing through their teeth, to be put up at nice hotels and fed fine meals while they pocket a hundred and fifty dollars apiece each and every month. I ask you, why should they ever catch Joaquín? Any Joaquín? Why, it would be downright contrary to human nature! Now I don't mean to denigrate their abilities. We all know of their fame as bounty hunters, scalp collectors, Texas border fighters and the like. But my fellow legislators, if we're going to catch Joaquín, we've got to stop spending public revenue to keep those twenty men in spending money. Support our colleague from Mariposa County. Issue an honest reward. Then see how fast the villain is caught!" More clapping and stamping.

The chairman recognized Señor José Cavabarrubias, a tall, dignified Spaniard with a face as white as any European. He spoke in the distinctive accents of a native Californian. "The *bandidos* must be stopped. All honest men are in agreement. But none of the five Joaquíns named in the petition are known criminals." He went on to say Carillo and the other listed names were common Spanish surnames, and Joaquín was an extremely common given name. Furthermore, no photograph of the bandit existed.

"Gentlemen," he said, "my Military Affairs Committee rejected a reward, and properly so, because it is an eenvitation to murder. A reward would tempt unprincipled men to attack eennocent men. Native Californians would be in great danger. If a Mexican is brought to this chamber, who among you would know he is the *bandido*?" He paused only a moment. "We do not even know hees full name! We do not know if he is one man or five, or ten. Gentlemen, for the sake of humanity and ceevilization, join me in defeating this bad measure." Polite clapping followed as he resumed his seat. No doubt he came from the coast or the southern part of the state, Elitha thought. Native Californians still out-voted Americans in those regions.

A legislator stood rattling a newspaper. When recognized, he read from an editorial in the *Los Angeles Star*: "Many men of veracity assert positively that Joaquín Murieta and his band are now somewhere between San Juan Capistrano and San Diego, bound for Lower California." He let the paper drop to his side and turned around, looking nonplussed. "That was two weeks ago, gentlemen. I could read from a whole string of papers from Santa Barbara south, men asserting they saw the bandit, OUR bandit, passing through, helped out by his countrymen. A regular newspaper trail." He shook the paper in the air. "These men know his name. They know his face. He was well known in Los Angeles before he ever came to the mines. He was wanted for murdering General Bean." He twisted his face into a mask of wry amazement. "Esteemed colleagues, the whereabouts of Joaquín is no state secret. So what in heaven's name are the California Rangers doing on their posteriors in Mariposa County? The representative from Sacramento is correct. Only a substantial reward will net us the robber chief." Much clapping followed, men stamping as they sat, some mopping their brows.

She felt the arms of men on both sides dampening her all the way through their broadcloth and her worn gingham. So far, only legislators had spoken and the subject of debate hadn't changed. No one standing in the back had raised a hand. She knew nothing about procedures, and what she had to say seemed out of place. Light-headed from the heat and odors, she knew she must wait and observe longer.

"Dinner break," shouted a legislator from the floor. A rumble of agreement followed. Another shouted, "Men can't think starved." Another struggled with a window, grumbling, "White men can't think in this heat!"

"Order!" The chairman's mallet rang like a pile driver. When the room quieted, he said in a reasonable tone, "Somebody pass those men a drink." Bottles appeared, passing overhead, hand to hand along the benches with frequent stops. As the liquor was imbibed, the debate continued. Until a crash and the sound of falling glass silenced all. The man at the window had kicked out two panes. He growled in a threatening tone, "This is the worst damned hellhole I ever got trapped in. I move we go back to Benicia."

"Out of order," thundered the chairman, banging his mallet. "There's a motion on the floor, and we're not leaving the room until the matter's settled. Do I have to remind you that men all over this state demand an end to the reign of Mexican terror? I'll accept a motion on the question."

Immediately a vote was underway, men circulating bottles and calling aye or no after each name was read. The chairman banged again. "The ayes have it. Thirty to nineteen. Do pass. Meet back in chamber when you're done eating. Session adjourned." He tapped the mallet lightly on the table, whisked his top hat to his head and pressed forward into the rising crowd.

Elitha floated out the door and across the porch like a boat on a tide, shoes barely touching. The air smelled worse outside, but she was relieved when the press of bodies dispersed down the stairs. She almost welcomed the broiling sun drying her damp frock and was glad for her poke bonnet. She hurried up the dusty street overtaking the banker. "How much time do they take to eat?" she asked.

He was rushing after the legislators who were already turning down J Street. He stepped aside to let a spray wagon pass, Down with Dust, City of Sacramento, gaily painted on a huge perforated barrel. He looked at her like a fond uncle and said, "They get back to work whenever we can get them rounded up." He touched his hat and waddled across the dampened street, elbows pumping, long coattails flapping.

Wondering where she should eat, she fell behind and watched until the flock of dark-suited legislators disappeared into a building. She looked beyond, to where J ended at the river, the tops of paddlewheelers and sail tips of sloops and fishing boats visible over the bank. Men were unloading heavy bundles on the levee, though it had to be well over a hundred degrees.

Then it came to her. She should go find the chairman in his eating place and ask, before his food came, how a citizen went about being recognized. She hurried up J to the corner of Third and stopped in her tracks. The simple wooden sign said: KESEBERG'S RESTAURANT: Inquire about Hotel within.

It kicked her stomach, forcing up the image of the murderer's scraggly beard ticking denial. She had attacked him, then endured the long river trip by looking past him as if he didn't exist. He had done likewise. Would that happen here? Or would he tell people she was a Donner and make a sideshow of her — a cannibal in a cannibal's restaurant. A man in tails stepped around her to hold the door for his fellows. The last one quipped, "Good eating here, if you like meat." They guffawed as they entered.

The jokes never stopped. She turned to find a shady place to calm herself. Maybe she should forget about the Legislature. But that would give that vile man a victory. No, his name on a sign wouldn't stop her from trying to help the Indians. If she saw him, she would ignore him like the offal he was. If he told people her name, she would face it.

She stepped into the cave-like interior, much cooler than the courthouse. Glancing warily around the dim room, the only windows in front, she removed her bonnet, heard the clink of dishes, the hum of conversation. As her eyes adjusted to the dark, she saw a long table in the back filled with legislators. A dark-suited waiter, too short for Keseberg, was setting down glasses before them. In the light of the oil lamps on the table, she picked out the muttonchop whiskers of the chairman at the head, took a deep breath and went to him. The banker, she was surprised to see, sat at the opposite end.

"Well, well," the chairman said as she stopped near him. "Here's the pretty little thing I saw in chambers." He reached, encircled her waist and drew her to the side of his chair, glancing at the other diners like he'd caught a large fish.

She hadn't anticipated feeling like a child, men chuckling at her. She tried to step back but he secured his grip. A man was joking, "That's why I want your job. Better view of the back of the room." Men howled.

The chairman sipped from his glass and gave her a squeeze, asking juicily, "What can I do for you, my dear?" With a nod he dismissed the quizzical waiter, who stood with a white towel over his sleeve.

She cleared her throat to dislodge her voice. "I came to bring your attention, that is, the attention of the Legislature to a matter, and I was wondering how to go about it. I'd like to speak this afternoon, if I could." It seemed incongruous, embarrassing, to be standing in this man's embrace.

Within the brackets of his side whiskers, his pudgy cheeks tightened into a big-lipped smile. "Depends on what it's about." His grip never lessened.

Not wanting to be drawn into the particulars within the hearing of only a few legislators, she kept it simple. "About an Indian reservation."

"Which one?"

A man came from a swinging door behind the table, a flash of light from the steamy kitchen briefly illuminating his face — filled out now, the blond hair neatly tied behind, the beard still long and stringy. Louis Keseberg stood three feet away, eyes registering recognition. The chairman was saying, "Which reservation, little lady?"

Her voice shook. "Ah, up around Spanish Camp." Without thinking, aware only of an instinctive need for freedom and mobility, she jerked out of the chairman's grasp.

"Spanish Camp," he echoed, clearly disliking the way she'd jerked away. "Must be a dozen by that name. Be specific."

Under Keseberg's glare she was trying to think when a sandy-haired legislator at the side of the table said, "Up on the Cosumnes River?"

"I think so," she said weakly, knowing she didn't sound like a girl who could address an assembly of men. But Keseberg towered in the shadows like a ghoul, opening his hairy mouth to speak. Heart drumming, she gave him her fiercest look and willed him to silence. He swallowed back the words.

The sandy-haired legislator was explaining to the chairman, "She must mean that idiotic Wozencraft scheme to give half my district away."

Keseberg cut in, "If you will, gentlemen. May I tell vhat we haff for eating today?" She released her breath. He was sticking to business.

"Yes, by all means," the chairman said at her.

"Liver and onions," Keseberg began.

Liver. Men tittered. She backed up, bumping a chair. Men at another table looked questions at her. "Sorry," she murmured, seeing Pa's empty breast in her mind, and Tamsen hanging upside down like an animal being bled. Keseberg continued, "Fried chicken and meatloaf."

"No brains today?" asked a smirking legislator. They loved eating at the famous cannibal's table, she realized, and even with his back turned, she could see Keseberg welcomed the notoriety. It probably gave him an edge over other eating places. She felt unstable, like she was standing in a boat. But, thankfully, he kept to business.

After an eternity, he returned to the kitchen. She stepped to the chairman's side, weak with relief but feeling better for having faced down Keseberg. The chairman buttered his roll. She waited. After a long time he jerked his head at her like he was dismissing a bothersome bug, and bit into his bread. Rude. Or was she rude to interfere with his dinner? Or was it that she had pulled away from him?

She stammered, "About my speaking to — "

"No Indian reservation is subject to debate." He looked ahead, the flesh of his eyelids flat across his marble eyes.

"I only meant to — "

"Miss, " the sandy-haired legislator said, "you're talkin about gold country. Hasn't been any Indian trouble there. No need for a reservation."

"But the Indians — "

"Take a tip," snapped the chairman still looking ahead. "You'd rile the members." He leaned toward the banker at the other end of the long table, "Now about those securities . . . "

Hot with humiliation, she turned and walked to the door. *No need for a reservation.* There was a great need, and she'd spoiled her chance to tell them. If one location wasn't good, another could be found. How could she get them to listen?

Sunlight slammed into her. Tying on her bonnet she walked the two blocks to the busy riverbank. A steamer blasted. She should have played it coquettishly, kept her subject a secret. Keseberg had thrown her off. No, she decided on second thought, she had failed to ignore him. There was a difference, something to do with the kind of power Indian Mary talked about.

Her breathing returned to normal as she watched an auctioneer among the piled goods rattling out numbers and stabbing his finger at the gathered men. Two young women dressed in lovely frocks and modern face-framing bonnets chattered beneath parasols as they entered the high-arched SACRAMENTO CITY MARKET. Horse-drawn rigs of all kinds rattled up and down the dusty levee — Front Street — people stepping out of the way. She had done her best. Now she would find Ben. Maybe he could suggest what to do next. After all, he had worked here for a year, and might be familiar with the procedures.

A Wells Fargo stage left the boardwalk at the large corner-building where J met Front. Three men in tails and high hats stood talking beneath the sign: PAGE, BACON & CO. BANKERS. Waiting for a pause, she asked for directions to Wilder's Transport Company, and felt a pleasant thrill that these gentlemen, the first she asked, knew of Ben's place of business.

97

Seventh and M was a long, hot walk. The Sacramento Iron Works disgorged black smoke, adding haze to the outhouse smell. But the air cleared a little as Elitha passed a row of hotels and the Stanford Brothers Wholesale Provision House, where a freight wagon backed up to a landing and iron doors opened against brick. One man handed crates down to another in the wagon. Then came modest houses with gardens and barking dogs, and Rowe's Olympic Amphitheater and Circus. She stopped to read the posted bill:

MASTER RAFAEL
Little Rising Star
To Perform Daring Equestrian Feats:
Leaping Whip, Garters and Hoops,
Riding upon his Head with Horse at Full Speed.

Not even Señor Valdez rode upon his head.

She turned up M Street past intermingled houses and commercial establishments. Weedy empty lots appeared between unpainted buildings of fresh lumber, some half built. Several blocks farther she stopped.

A hostelry and foundry stood beside a small frame building with a sign painted over the door: WILDER TRANSPORT AND HAULING COMPANY. Behind the structure lay a freight wagon on its side. Sensing Ben's nearness, she almost couldn't breathe. *Wilder.* Tamer was what she needed. But she had told John Rhoads she would tell Ben he could come calling, if he wasn't spoken for. After a time they would decide if they were meant for one another.

The unnaturalness weighed on her. Only a bad woman went to a man. He could turn her away on that account. No matter what else he was, Ben was a gentleman when it came to manners. The door was open a crack. She pushed it inward, peering inside from her poke bonnet. A young clerk looked up from a table stacked with paper.

"I was looking for Mr. Wilder."

"He's out." He removed his pinched spectacles, twin indentations marking the bridge of his nose, side-parted hair hanging in brown sheets like Mr. Grimshaw's.

"Out of town?"

"No ma'am. If you'd take a seat?" He nodded at two wooden chairs against the wall. "Your name please?"

She told him and he went out a back door. She lowered herself to the edge of a chair, hands folded, telling her heart to quiet.

Moments later the door opened and Ben ducked through it. He stood staring at her as if thunderstruck, dark beard shaved back from his mouth, red shirtsleeves rolled up on grease-streaked arms, a towel in his hands. Perspiration glistened on his high forehead and streamed down into the side whiskers connecting his unruly hair with a wide frizzy beard. The only thing that moved was a lock of dark hair falling over his nose.

She swallowed and stood up, aware of the clerk waiting at the doorway in the sun. "Ben," she managed, "I'm sorry to bother you at your work. Could we talk?"

He stared at her left hand, then her right, then lifted his gaze to her eyes, his wide mouth twitching into a ghost of a smile. He wiped his hands on the towel, the strong smell of him — grease, perspiration, an elusive scent of excitement combined with memory — dancing with him, sitting beside him on a buckboard, the way he held her when Elizabeth died. No matter how married he might be, she would never forget that.

The clerk cleared his throat. "Excuse me, sir." Ben blocked the door.

His electrifying gaze never left hers as he stepped to the center of the small office, the clerk shutting the door and resuming his seat behind the little table. Elitha couldn't stop looking into Ben's sloping blue eyes.

"You're not married?" he asked.

That was her question. "No, Ben. I . . . came to talk to you."

Suddenly he sparked to life, whirling to the clerk. "Tell Leland Stanford an urgent matter came up. I'll see them — " he turned to Elitha asking, "Two hours? Three?"

She smiled and shrugged.

"Two and a half," he boomed, telling her to sit and wait a minute while he washed up. He walked briskly out the back door.

Tickled it had been so easy, and he so pleased — any fool could see that — she felt about to burst with energy and couldn't sit still. She went out the front door and peered around the side of the building. Ben stood at a horse trough by the hostelry, wriggling his shirt over his face. He threw it off, widened his stance, bent his knees and dunked head, shoulders and half his lanky torso under water. In a few seconds he popped up in a brilliant sunburst of spraying water. Furiously rubbing the towel over his hair, face and armpits, and scrubbing hard on his blackened arms, he saw her and froze, then stepped to an open lean-to, threw in the towel and pulled out a pale shirt. He flung it over his head, thrust his arms into the sleeves and walked, smiling, toward her. His wet hair stood up like Indian feathers and his beard dripped.

"My toilette," he said jabbing the muslin shirttail into his trousers, shifting from hip to hip. "How bout wetting our whistles on some soda water?" Smiling into her unabashed grin — she loved the loose-jointed way he walked — he said something about a hat, took a giant stride up both steps to the front door, and in a second was back, combing his hair, the hat under the other arm. "Seen J Street?"

"A little. I came in on the California Stage."

He stopped mid-comb. "What time?"

"Eleven this morning."

He resumed combing. "See my passenger wagon, Stockton bound?"

"Yes," she sang out, overjoyed to recall that. This was a respectable businessman, not a murderer. She liked seeing dirt and grease on him. She understood work.

Looking pleased, he tilted his head and extended his elbow. "Ma'am?" He led her into the hostelry — straps, barrels, tools and harnesses all arranged neatly, several rigs parked close behind one another — and helped her into the seat of a small trap, more like a bench and footrest between two large wheels. It was cunning, with its seat newly painted black and its spokes red. He shouldered it outside, and hitched a horse.

Soon they were clopping down Seventh Street with the sun frying them and Ben finger-combing his damp beard. His hat hung loose and wavy around his face and he turned every other second as if to see whether she still sat beside him. Or was he waiting for her to say her piece?

Happiness pushed it out of her. "You got a sweetheart?"

He squinted ahead, his sloped nose pointing to the horse, the silence unhitching her heart. The sun seemed to melt her words and they slid down around her feet and dripped behind in the dust. At last he answered, "Maybe."

That meant yes. She tried to swallow the darning knob in her throat, and it hurt. He reined left on J Street. Visions of women loomed before her like dust devils — young beauties touring with their families, captivated by this man of the Golden West. Brazen actresses of the entertainment stages. Painted lips, whaleboned waists. Maybe a fine lady, one of those she'd seen entering the Sacramento City Market. SHE wouldn't know of the trouble on the Cosumnes, and Ben would like that. No doubt he'd been man about town since she last saw him, and women weren't in such short supply here. With his tall good looks, enterprise and education, Ben would attract everything in skirts. She blinked tears, felt the hot air drying them in her eyes. He didn't look at her the way he had at the beginning of the ride.

The road was crowded. He reined to a stop, waited behind several other rigs, then steered the horse around an enormous pit in the middle of the street. "They dug out a really big oak," he explained as if she were a bare acquaintance. "J Street's got to be straight and clear." A little further up the road he pulled to a stop at a hitching ring.

All the excitement and anticipation she'd brought to Sacramento City had oozed out with the perspiration. Feeling dried up, she stepped down. He lifted his elbow to her, and she clung to his arm, damp and sinewy beneath the muslin, a muscle twitching as they walked beneath the porch overhang and through a door marked: JENSEN'S SODA PARLOR. The most she'd seen of his body was at the water trough — except in dreams. And now those dreams must stop.

It was much cooler inside. Several groups of men and three young women sat at tiny round tables. Ben removed his hat, hung it on a rack and pulled an iron filigree chair for her. Then he went to a man behind the counter, spoke to him and produced money from his pocket. The man went into action at an elaborate machine, pumping a handle up and down. It hissed as he held a glass beneath the spout.

Ben returned and sat opposite her, his knees jutting out both sides of a table designed for shorter people. She could hardly look at him for the darning knob, the pinch in her chest, the disappointment. But she forced a smile. "I'm glad for you, Ben." She'd always been a poor liar.

Elbows on the table, he leaned forward, interlocking his long fingers and resting his bearded chin on the platform. "You wanted to talk to me." His eyes were a foot away.

She looked down. The door banged as others entered. People at other tables spoke quietly over drinks. She told him the easier thing, how she'd fared so miserably with the Legislature. The proprietor brought two shapely glasses of pink, fizzing liquid, ice clinking. Ice. An icehouse must be near. Ice from the lake now called Donner. That's where she'd heard they got it.

She wrapped her hands around the cold glass and explained about Keseberg. She held nothing back. Ben knew her secrets. Most of them. The berry-flavored soda cooled a path to her stomach and cleared her head. The confession loosened her, gave her heart to face Ben as nothing more than a friend.

He guzzled his entire drink, set the empty glass down with an ahhh, and called to the proprietor to bring another. "Tell you what," he said, his blue eyes lively, "I know Assemblyman Catlin. Helped pay for his flyers when he got elected. The stage for Slough House leaves too early. Why don't you stay in town tonight, and I'll get us an appointment in the morning."

She realized it was his vitality that attracted her so powerfully. No doubt his lady friend liked it too. Still, he had said *we*. She savored it like the crumbs of that first biscuit up in the mountains. "How would that help?"

"Well, he's your representative. Mine too. He's bound to pay some attention to us. We'll go talk to him."

We. Us. And he was right. A woman wasn't viewed as having important ideas. But it would be excruciating to spend the night in the same town, knowing he might be around the next corner escorting his lady friend to the theater, or visiting her —

"Would you like that?"

"Yes. I'll stay. I appreciate your help, Ben."

"The least I can do. We'll go by his office when we leave here, and see about an appointment." The soda man removed Ben's empty glass and set down a full one, pink bubbles foaming over the top and sliding down the side.

She took a cooling swallow of hers and said, "Ben, I don't think for one minute you did more than defend yourself, back at the dam." It graveled her voice, but relieved her to get it out.

He sucked down more soda, set the clinking glass on the table and gazed at her in his unsmiling, direct manner. "Thank you, Elitha. I appreciate that." He moved a finger down the damp glass, pushing beads of moisture. "But I'll go to my grave thinking if I'd done something different, Mr. Sheldon would be alive. He had some admirable qualities."

Men got up and walked out the door, the soda parlor emptying like her heart. Ben was in pain too, she could see, but for a different reason. Wanting to reach across the table and take his hand, she said, "Terrible things happen all the time, and it's not to be explained. Sometimes I think the Indians are right about their Coyote. Do you know about him?" He looked blank. "It's sort of a god that mixes everybody up and laughs at us when we're trying to do our best and everything goes sour. I guess he's supposed to teach us to laugh at ourselves. I know you did what seemed right, but things got out of hand. Not because of you, in spite of you."

His gaze shifted from her left eye to her right, then back. "You really don't hold it against me?"

She shook her head. "No. And I think we gotta go forward in life. Just like I can't dwell on Mr. Keseberg. I'll never excuse what I think he did, but still, I don't really know he did it, do I? And I guess I'm proud of myself for not letting that stop me from trying today, with what I wanted to do for the Indians. Maybe it's a little like the Bible says. Turning the other cheek." It was a poor comparison.

Ben's wide lips twitched upward at the corners. "Now there's one fellow I'd keep all my cheeks turned away from." His tone was soft, amused.

She found herself grinning, half embarrassed, smiling at a Keseberg joke! No other man could do that to her. And the way he looked! Lord in heaven, she must have been in hibernation two months ago not to know her feelings for him went all the way down to her roots. It hurt to keep swallowing back the knowing he belonged to another.

He reached across the table and suddenly her hand was inside his warm, long-fingered hand. "You asked if I have a sweetheart." Something clamped in her chest. She couldn't hide her feelings. Was he deliberately torturing her? She started to pull her hand back.

He squeezed it. "I hope so, Elitha. I've hoped it for a long time. But I didn't want to rush you."

You. She stared at him, wondering if she'd heard right. The pained smile on his face confused her, but if she'd heard right, she wanted to jump up and hug him. "Me?" She couldn't keep the surprise and joy from her face.

With a scrape of his chair he came to her and pulled her up, wrapping her in his arms, his big hand pressing her head against his shirt. Her lips touched the crisp, damp hair in the open V of his shirt and she inhaled his scent. Through the muslin his heart thudded rapidly. For her! Her tears wet his shirt and she didn't care who was looking. This was how it was supposed to feel.

His voice rumbled from the muscle-padded echo chamber of his ribs. "You want me then?" He still didn't know.

She pulled back an inch and looked up past his beard, swallowing, blinking. It squeaked out. "I want you, Ben." She'd meant only to have him court her, but her heart had spoken. It broke the dam all the way through, smashing the darning knob to splinters and she sobbed openly, clinging to the beat of his urgent heart. She felt a tremor in him, a slight earthquake of the bones.

"I need you, Elitha." His voice cracked. "There are women. But it's you I think about." He swallowed. "Dream about."

She wrapped her arms around his tall wiry frame, wanting to care for him as one would a child. She knew now why the princess in the fairy tale married the only man who could make her cry.

He pushed her back to arm's length, the blue of his eyes pooled with tears, the folds at the corners crinkled all the way across his cheeks. His voice boomed with the self-confidence she loved. "By thunder, this calls for a celebration!"

98

After all these months of wanting her, Ben couldn't let go. He pulled her to the counter and dug in his pocket for coins. Jumpin Jensen wiped a tear off his cheek and said, "Git on outa here, Ben Wilder. Ain't ever day a man sees sum'm 'ike 'at."

"You're a gentleman. This here's going to be my missus." As if he didn't know! But Ben was bursting with happiness, afraid he'd wake up and find her gone.

He couldn't stop looking into her beautiful brown eyes weeping with joy *for him*. Never mind Jumpin Jensen, he pulled her to him — full bosomed beneath the threadbare blue gingham, tall for a girl, slender, the satin cushions of her lips tentative at first, then eager for him. The hunger of pent-up love thundered in his ears, exciting a part of his anatomy he had to control. "Come," he said forcing himself away, "we've got places to go."

Time flew in a happy whirl. Leaving the rig in front of Jensen's, he escorted Elitha to the first of three stores offering ready-made women's clothing, and refused her protests. "It's for our meeting with Assemblyman Catlin," he lied. That stopped her.

Viewing her in a variety of frocks, he grabbed his beard and leaned back, considering how this or that color set off her fresh complexion and dark beauty. A goddess. It was all he could do to keep from dancing a jig and yelling, ELITHA MCCOON WILL MARRY ME!

Seeing her in an aqua-colored, drop-waisted frock with embroidered roses all over it, the unctuous proprietress said, "Ahhh, she has a midriff like a wasp." She grabbed a handful of loose material at the small of her back. "See, the style shows it so beautifully! I can stitch it up in minutes." But the frock was excessively ornate, unharmonious with Elitha's natural dignity.

He thanked the woman and escorted Elitha up J toward the City of Paris, a place women crowed about. But passing the cluttered porch of Warren's New England Seed Store — everything for the farm and city garden — she wanted to go in. He liked that.

Bags were stacked high. Ox yokes and hay rakes hung from the rafters. A planting machine stood beside a barrel of seed potatoes. She felt the shiny leaves on a row of unfamiliar potted plants. A voice came toward them, "Camellia Japonica." A youngish man of obvious energy appeared from behind a center aisle of shelves. "Bought those off a boat from China. My guess is they'll grow in this climate."

The smell of dirt and seed affected Ben in an interesting way. He felt nostalgic, sentimental, and loved the man's New England accent. He introduced himself and complimented Mr. Warren on his store, wondering about his sudden desire to cut and plant potatoes. He saw himself showing them to Elitha. Farming was in his blood.

"This camellia," she was saying, "does it bloom?"

Mr. Warren made his hands into a large circle. "Pink blossoms this size. He grabbed a flyer off a shelf, "Grows to the size of a small tree." He handed it to her.

Back out on the boardwalk, she said she wanted an ornamental garden to work in some day. He loved that. Some women viewed dirt as a disease.

In the City of Paris she tried on a gown beribboned in every possible place with small green bows. Looking down at it she murmured, "I can see this at a dance, but I think something more suitable for day wear would be best."

"Hmm," said the vampirish proprietress, a woman of indistinct age and false eyeteeth of a darker hue. She dashed to the back of the room and disappeared through a curtain. Moments later she reemerged shaking out a cloud of brown and white taffeta, thrusting it to Elitha's neck. "What do you think?" She bared her teeth at Ben.

The rich brown exactly matched Elitha's eyes and the checkered pattern was big and bold. No gewgaws or froufrou. Yet dramatic. "Good," he nodded.

After several minutes behind the curtain with the vampire, Elitha emerged in the frock, floating toward him with the dignity he loved so much, more beautiful than ever. Pleasure showed in the natural sadness of her eyes, the crisp white of the blouse setting off the peach glow of her cheeks. At the sleeves the pattern was slanted at a graceful bias, hanging wide at the wrist. The front opened in a V to the waist, revealing the white blouse.

"Do you have a brooch?" Ben asked the woman, "and half-gloves in the same brown?"

She flew behind the back curtain.

Elitha whispered, "It'd be dear, Ben."

"What do you think money's for?" He saw she liked the dress. Everything he'd ever worked for was standing here before him. Without a doubt he was the luckiest man in California. For once in his life he had done the right thing to wait and hope. By thunder, the number of times he'd stopped himself from riding out there! The stacks of wadded letters! "A parasol too," he called to the woman. "Same brown if you have it. Oh, and one of those little white bonnets that just frames the face and hair." He smiled at his goddess.

"Ben, the cost!" She gave the taffeta a friendly shake.

He liked her frugality, a virtue plenty of women lacked. "Elitha, this is the grandest moment of my life." His business was booming. He could have hired men to do it all, but he needed to work with his hands and wasn't the kind to sit speculating in hotel lobbies and saloons while the sun was up. He winked down at her. "An engagement present." Later he would pick out a ring, surprise her with a diamond set in pure California gold.

Before long he was parading up J Street with parasoled Elitha on his arm, a box with her old dress in his other arm. She had insisted on taking it back to her Indian friend, Mary. Most people just tossed their worn clothes on the boardwalk for the Indians. Passing men tipped their hats, getting an eyeful before their gazes slid enviously to Ben. She was magnificent.

"Oh Ben, look!" She stopped at Nahl's Art Shop — a narrow space roofed over between two buildings. The artist, a slight acquaintance whom he greeted with a nod, sat before an upright canvas within his open doorway, reaching out, tickling the canvas with the tip of his brush.

"Such lively work!" she said. "Look at the color, the faces!" Nahl smiled at her and continued working.

"I didn't know you appreciated the arts," Ben said, guiding her inside. But of course she liked the arts. She was a goddess.

"Tamsen was good at it," she said, surveying tiers of canvasses and standing before the likeness of a Mexican galloping a black horse up a cliffside trail, a knife raised in defiance.

Ben liked the paintings along the floor. He didn't share the popular taste for languid scenes. "Look at this," He chuckled. "Charlie, I see you been in a gold camp."

She came to look. The more he examined the details of "A Live Woman at the Mines," the funnier it got. A man was leading a demure woman from a tent, gesturing proudly at her. A frenzied crowd of miners faced them, hair and beards askew as they jumped, trying to see over heads. They stamped their boots, threw up their hats and fired pistols in the air, one being boosted by another who made a stirrup of his hands. In the background men raced down a hillside, skidding and sliding toward the viewing. "You ever feel like that?" he asked, recalling the first time he'd gone up from Cook's Bar to see her.

She shot him a secret smile. Charles Nahl asked, "You are an artist, madam?"

"No. But I'd like to take lessons."

"I giff you lessons." He smiled at Ben.

Suddenly awkward, Ben was still seeing those potatoes. Marrying Elitha somehow went with farming. He didn't understand it entirely but maybe it had to do with children.

She seemed to understand his dilemma. "But first we need to talk about where we're going to — "

"Charlie," he hurried to say, "this is my betrothed, Elitha McCoon. I'll contact you about instruction." The German nodded and went back to his canvas, Ben feeling maladroit.

On their way out she asked Nahl, "Did you name that oil of the Spaniard, the one with the knife?"

"Joaquín."

"Is that really what Joaquín looks like?" She opened her parasol and twirled it prettily behind her head.

Nahl grinned like a schoolboy caught copying. "Well, Mexicans haff Indian bloodt. So I paint him wit black hairs, black eyes." He smiled. "Very white teeth."

"I know a Mexican with auburn hair and gray eyes."

"I paint da image dot folks carry here," he tapped his temple.

Ben steered her up the boardwalk.

She glanced at the Placer Times building and said, "I can hardly believe this is such a big city. Only five years ago it was nothing but cattails and oak trees and ducks and Mr. Sutter's embarcadero."

"Didn't I tell you?" He loved the opening. "Never underestimate the men who come for gold." Slyly he added, "Or the men who haul their supplies." He turned back and opened his arms. "This town is a huge capital T, the top of it along that levee. J Street here the stem. Some of us are fattening the stem." Continuing up the boardwalk he added, "I agree with those who say it was a brilliant stroke of democracy to give the streets numbers and letters instead of naming them after supposed highfalutin men. Here we are." He pointed up a staircase over a hattery and followed the rustle of taffeta up the dark stairs.

He knocked at the door that said: AMOS CATLIN, ATTORNEY, MINING AND WATER LAW.

"Enter," a man's voice called.

Catlin was alone, the clerk's desk closed for the day. The legislator rocked forward to all four chair legs, smiled across his table and rose to his feet. He had once assured Ben that Jared Sheldon shouldn't have dammed the river, even if laws weren't in place yet. Now any structure impeding the flow of a stream had to be proven for the public good. They shook hands across the table.

"This is Elitha McCoon, from the Bridge House." Ben noticed Catlin's surreptitious survey. "We're to be married." She curtseyed like a princess.

"You lucky old block, no wonder that light's in your eye."

After perfunctory questions about the transportation business, Catlin signaled with his eyes and Ben told him about the Indian reservation. "I thought you might be able to help." Feeling the intensity of her eyes on him, he added, "A reservation sure looks to be needed." Women often devoted themselves to society's unfortunates and though it was out of the ordinary to care about Diggers, she was no ordinary girl.

"Well now," Catlin said, leaning back on his hind chair legs, hands behind his head, "as I recall, the boundary of that reservation was to go from the Sacramento County line out the Cosumnes River to Yoemet on the river forks, then south, taking in twenty square miles, including Drytown, Amador and Sutter Creek. That your recollection?"

Elitha said she didn't know the boundaries, but Ben had heard all he needed. He was glad it was Catlin explaining instead of him.

"Miz McCoon, wasn't it?" She nodded. He rocked to the level, hands folded on the table. "You're talking about proven mining regions. The commercial segment of this state is laying the groundwork to break that area into a new county — Amador it's to be called. Pushing El Dorado north, Calaveras south. Now these Amador mines are going to be extremely important for a long time. You see, that federal reserve would have gobbled up the best half of it." He wagged his head in dismay. "That Wozen-something left his brains to home when he wrote that up. Of course the Indians won't like it. But they just as well try to get New York City back." It interested Ben that Catlin talked to her almost as if she were a man.

Elitha sat tall, her opaque half-gloves folded in her lap, her voice low and ladylike. "If the federal government can't locate a reservation, perhaps the state should." Not only did she speak well, she knew government was conducted at different levels. Ben was bursting with pride.

Catlin put his elbows on the table and knuckled an eye like he'd had a long day, then looked up. "I'll say this. The locals understand the economic potentials better. But I doubt — " He looked away, the window illuminating the curve of his cranium through the thin hair. "How many Indians you worried about?"

Ben said, "Not many."

Catlin leaned forward. "Take 'em in as apprentices. Train them to tend your horses. Fix your wagons."

A flicker of consternation skittered across her eyes. "Those people used to eat plenty well living along the rivers and streams," she said. "They took care of themselves. Miners killed them. They don't need employment, they need protection."

"Times have changed, my dear. They've got to change with it." Ben heard the shift to indulgence; it was time to go.

But she continued, "Do you think it would do any good for my friends in the Slough House area to write up a petition? The Rhoadses, Grimshaws, Mahones might help. They see the plight of the Indians. Maybe we could find an out-of-the-way place and bring it to the Legislature to consider." Magnificent, Ben thought. Legislators needed to have solutions pointed out.

Catlin scowled and nodded. "I'll think on it. Those are fine people you mention." He rose to his feet. So did Ben.

She stood immediately. "I appreciate your taking the time."

On a sudden impulse, Ben put his arm around her and said, "Amos, I've got to say, would you believe she survived the Donner Party?" As surprise registered in the man's eyes, her shoulders stiffened slightly, but now he had to plow on, "In fact she's the eldest daughter of George Donner."

"CAPTAIN George Donner!" he exclaimed. Elitha nodded meekly and Catlin said, "Well, I'll be. What a courageous pioneer your father was! And your sainted mother. Ma'am, I am honored to make your acquaintance, and it would be my privilege to help you in any way I can." He extended his hand. She lifted hers, but he took her in his arms and patted her back. He pushed to arm's length, looking into her eyes, his own glistening. Ben saw her bewilderment and wished he'd kept a clamp on his tongue.

Showing them to the door, Catlin slapped Ben on the shoulder and said, "You ugly bounder! I should've known you'd pick a famous girl, and it's about time you settled down." Opening the door, he added, "Stop by sometime and tell me what's going on in Stockton." The Natomas Company being his major client, he had his ears cocked for anything related to water supply for the mines. He looked at her. "Come in any time, my dear, any time, and we'll see what we can do."

Then they were back on the street and Ben was thinking about a place to eat — he needed a quiet setting to find out if she was peeved at him. But unfortunately the best food was in brothels. She was working her parasol open, the sun blazing hot though it had to be well after six o'clock.

Remembering the Bay State Oyster House, he asked, "Could you eat now?"

"Well yes, but Ben, don't you have some men to see?"

God Almighty! He touched his forehead as if to restore his mind. The Stanford account! It had been over three hours. She would think him a dolt! The shock in his face must have been as plain as the oversized cut-out of a beer pitcher across the street — he'd meant to take her in the Zins and Weiser Brewery, her being acquainted with Zins.

Pleased how fast she hurried and scrambled into the trap, barely holding him back, he snapped the reins on the rump of the startled horse. The animal stretched into a full gallop and they bounced up the rutted street, elbows linked, her hugging the frock box and laughing like a happy child. And a funny sight it had to be — him grimly leaning forward with the reins, clearing man and beast from the road. Worried as he was about the account, he was worrying more about being too quick to tell Catlin she was a Donner.

Sharp angles of sunlight slanted across the floor of the Oyster House and laid a bright wash over Elitha's dark head, the linen tablecloth, the flower in the vase, and the dish of oysters on the shell between them. It was hot as Hades. The waiter had propped the door open with spittoons to catch the delta breeze if it happened to come up the river. So far not a breath stirred the lace curtains at the windows. Ben leaned forward and spoke softly, though the other tables had few occupants.

"About my mentioning your being a Donner. It just fell out, before I remembered you like to keep it secret. I'm sorry. Will you forgive me?" He'd lost her once. What had gotten into him?

Her sad eyes were moist, her voice soft. "He spoke of Pa with respect."

That startled him. "He doesn't grow wool between his ears. The better element hold your father in high esteem. His story — yours — will be told and retold as the great tragedy of this state. You ought to be proud of your part in it."

She looked down. "A lot of people blame him, and they think I ate —."

"Like I said, Amos Catlin's among the better element. Are you grieved with me?"

"No. I wouldn't have done it myself. But now that it's done, I'm glad. I'm proud to be the daughter of George Donner. I just took it inside. Guess I didn't want to have to defend him. He doesn't need defending. But knowing your friends see him the way I do, I can hold my head up, even if people joke. So I have to thank you for that, Ben." Her brown eyes brimmed.

Suddenly afraid he'd get teary-eyed in a public place, he reached, patted her hand and changed the subject. "Did I tell you my people were farmers?"

She nodded.

It was time to get this out. "Well, I miss farming. Oh, there's a certain verve here in the city. Nice for a single man, but I like the way the sun looks in the morning when it comes across a tended field." He couldn't read her face.

Something bothered her. With a pronged tool she pried an oyster off the shell. "I thought you liked the transportation business." She slipped the oyster into her luscious mouth.

He swallowed. Oysters were supposed to be an aphrodisiac. "I like the money," he admitted, "but I guess I've seen it as a way to get by, until my actual life starts." He looked at her through the steam from the potatoes, onions, carrots and kale, which the waiter was setting down, unfortunately adding to the heat. "At first, when I came to California, I figured I'd make a fortune picking gold nuggets off the ground like hen's eggs." He loved her little smile.

"Then came the trouble over the dam." Not one to pussyfoot around, he said, "I'd like to buy a farm." He noted her equanimity and remembered what she'd said at the soda parlor, about going forward in life. He liked that. "What do you think about farming? We're to be a team, Elitha." He picked up his prong and worked at an oyster. He'd live in Hell if she wanted.

"Ben?"

He looked up to see her put the prong down as if about to make a confession. A firebell rang in him. Women were notorious for changing their minds. He'd better make himself good and clear. He squeezed her hand beside the bud vase. "To me, where I live isn't half as important as who I live with. Understand? I just want to be with you. Go ahead, sweetheart." Her word; she'd used it that last dance in Fiddletown. If only he could fathom those eyes!

"I made a promise to Ma and Pa, up in the mountains." He held his breath. "When my little sisters got to Sutter's Fort, they told me again, I was to care for them until my folks got through. Well, that meant for good." She looked him in the eyes. "I promised God. I want to find them and care for them."

He waited for worse, then asked. "Where are they?"

She was fighting to control her emotions. "I don't know. Sonoma I think. I write to Mrs. Brunner in care of the post office, but nobody writes back. They're getting along in years, and I guess the girls are helping with the farm work."

"But Sonoma. How — "

"The Brunners were at Sutter's Fort, then they went to Sonoma." Her eyes told him this was more important than farm or city. "Perry didn't want them."

She hadn't changed her mind, and he could have whooped for joy, but restrained himself to match her mood. "I insist they live with us." It gave him deep feeling of satisfaction.

She started to sob — strange little laughing, crying noises — and covered her nose and eyes with the spread fingers of her half-gloved hand. He felt something coming up from the basement of his soul. He was thirty. He wanted children around him, wanted a son to carry his name, wanted to right some of the wrong life had handed those poor orphans. He envisioned all this on a farm, with milk cows, clover on dewy summer mornings, and a dog named Bowser. She looked so grave he feared there was something else. "I mean it, Elitha. I want you AND your sisters."

He reached for her other hand and held it in his. "I can hardly believe this but I love you even more now than I did five minutes ago. I admire your convictions, about your sisters, and the Indians, helping John Rhoads, though it like to've killed me." His own eyes were filling up. "We'll go get your sisters. You and I. The two of us." The people at the next table were looking and he smiled to let them know this was private.

"Thank you, thank you, Ben." A look close to reverence.

That bothered him. Any decent man would take those girls in.

The lace at the windows lifted slightly, and the meal passed in animated discussion about the Donner girls, their names, their traits, the way they'd come through the ordeal and Tamsen's high hopes for them. They discussed the fact that Sacramento City had no school yet, though at least fifty children were roaming the streets, and those who could afford it sent their girls down to the Dominican nunnery in Benicia, via paddlewheeler.

"The girls come back Friday night. Excellent, I hear, if you don't mind papists and having them gone Monday through Friday."

Her brows drew together. "There's Rhoads School near Slough House and Katesville, but they're primary. I could teach as much. The girls need more. Benicia sounds right, that is, ah, if we — "

"Speaking of the Cosumney," he jumped in, rescuing her, "what's going on at your place now? Is Valdez settled out there?"

"Oh no. He's going to Mexico. Vyries Brown lives in the house, with a mining partner named Delaney. They're watching over things for me."

The rocky hillsides came to mind, passable for grazing, but useless for real farming, except for the bottomland claimed by the Gaffneys and McKinstry's road-front. Those titles would be clouded. Ben intended to purchase surveyed land, and it was funny how the thought of a farm turned him around on the squatter question. In fact, it would be prudent to charge Brown and Delaney rent, but that could wait.

She was saying, "I paid a lot of gold dust to a man to rebuild the house, but never saw him again."

"Wouldn't you know! Sometimes I doubt if there's a thief left in the rest of the world. California sucks 'em in." The only thing for it was to elect good men to run the government.

The future was taking shape, and he wasn't one to stall once things came clear. "Elitha. Here's what I think we should do. You go back and settle your affairs with Rhoads. Write to the Brunners. Say you're coming for the girls. Then come back to Sacramento and we'll get married. By then, I'll have some time cleared and we'll go to Sonoma and find your sisters. Just take them if we have to." He gave her a look she wouldn't mistake. It infuriated him that those people hadn't written back.

"Would we live in your building?"

The narrow cot and miniature stove came to mind, a room designed for a midget. "No. I'll rent a place, maybe out about 18th and K. Cottages are going up there. Your sisters can start the fall term in Benicia." He felt enlivened, the hauling business a key part of the future. "Unless you don't want me to, I'm going to look for a farm to buy. I don't see any reason why we can't have both places, town and country. What do you say?"

"I'd like that. I'm a farm girl at heart." Her smile was succulent, her dark eyes suddenly sparkling with mischief. "But I'm warning you, I've got to have an apple tree."

"Apple tree? I'll plant an orchardfull. We'll have apple pan dowdy, apple strudel, apple pie, apple cobbler, apple cider, apple — "

Her laughter bubbled in full rich contralto, then her head tilted. "You'd leave me live in town while you're gone?"

Alarm shot through him. She thought him uncaring. "I wouldn't be far, close enough to get back in a couple of hours. See, the river land near town is spoken for." Could he explain? "You're not like the hothouse flowers from the East, or the girls that fall over the traces at the first setback and grab for the easy money. You cooked for a living in a gold camp. Alone. In a mud shack. A day or two in a nice house in Sacramento City would be nothing. In no time you'd have friends among the better women, go to church if you wanted." With sudden inspiration he added, "You could take art instruction. Then when the girls finish with school, or a good school is built near the farm, we'll be together all the time."

She looked at him with those wondrous brown eyes.

"Want another reason why I love you?"

She almost covered her smile.

"Perry McCoon, may he rest in peace. Every man in Cook's Bar knew what kind of a man he was. But you stuck by him, and earned the living. With grace and dignity."

"I didn't always want to stay with him." The wisdom of the world was in her beautiful nineteen-year-old face.

"That's the point. You did anyhow. You're a natural-born pioneer." She had no idea how well she would be cared for. Oh sure, life on a farm was work and you had to expect setbacks, but by thunder, this girl had survived the Donner Party! That was the kind of mother he wanted for his sons; yet she had a cultured bearing to impart to girls.

Although the waiter came to light the candle, he helped her from the chair, anxious to show her the city at night. His California gold was on his arm.

99

Father Sun came through the windows of the Rhoads kitchen. Elitha had been back for two sleeps with a ring on her finger, a spectacular crystal on a gold band. It sparkled as she sat at the table reading the paper that talks. Maria saw her new strength. She would soon marry the tall *Americano* and move to an unknown place — understanding at last that the house of Perrimacoo was bad luck. But Maria worried that when she was happy and lucky, Elitha had little power. And now that Elitha's luck was improving, Maria's was waning. They were magic doubles.

Maria would go to a strange new home too, when Pedro came — any day now. She clung to that despite the aura. She had also been thinking about the meaning of home. He had said it was where he put his helmet, and where she was. Now his helmet was in Mexico and she was on the Rhoads rancho poking cloth down into boiling water with a stick. Mexico would be lonely without parents or relatives. Not even Spear Thrower and his family would come. A woman went to live in a man's home place, but that was familiar ground with familiar faces, a place where Big Times were celebrated. Now everybody was dead and she would go to a place so strange the plants had sharp spines. She wouldn't know their souls. How did people live so far from their earth places? The new people pulled up the stakes of their cloth houses every few sleeps and moved on, looking for better luck in the ground, the streams, everywhere but within. Pedro, too, looked over the horizon for a more *simpatico* place.

She stirred the heavy clothing and waited, feeling like a leaf drifting in a backwater, waiting to be swept away. Every move she made, she waited, and listened. All day, all night she listened for the sound of his horse. Her ears felt sore from listening. She longed for his touch. She looked up and Elitha was looking at her over the paper.

"Have you heard from Señor Valdez?" she asked.

She wiped her sleeve across her brow, the sleeve of the old blue dress Elitha had given her. "A runner says he comes soon." Remembering how joyful she'd been to hear he was alive and how disappointed to learn he was still far away, she started to heave the huge pot from the stove.

Elitha rushed to her side and pushed her hands. "Just leave it be. Let it cool on the stove." With a puzzled look, she said, "Where was he when he sent the message?"

"In the southern mountains."

"Coming this way?"

"Yes."

She picked up the paper and stared at it. "It says here Captain Love killed Joaquín Murieta. About a week ago."

Her breath caught. "Where?" Her heart beat no, no, no, no in her breast. She could hardly hear.

"Cañon Cantua. In the mountains, down at the far end of the valley."

The messenger had come from there. "Other men killed too?"

"Murieta and Three-Fingered Jack. No one else is mentioned. They've pickled Murieta's head the other man's hand in brandy."

She released her breath and steadied herself on a chairback, although it didn't mean Pedro had escaped. Men who would cut off a head would do anything.

"But over here it says they got the wrong man. Some people say it was just innocent Mexican horse herders that got ambushed on their way to Mexico."

Wrong man. Head cut off. The horrific thoughts collided and she stared out the window over the withering corn stalks. But *horse herders on their way to Mexico* helped her breathe. Pedro was coming the other way. "What color is the hair on the head?"

Elitha scanned the paper, pursing her lips. "It doesn't say. Only that Captain Love will display it in Stockton next week — preserved in a pickle jar. He wants anyone who knew Joaquín Murieta to come and identify him. He's positive he got the right man." She looked at Maria. "You said you met him. Maybe you should go. I could arrange for you to ride on one of Ben's freight wagons."

"Go see a head?" Bone-deep dread chased her out the door and across the packed yard. Big danger would lurk around a severed body part. She stopped beneath the black walnut tree, hoping the babble of the river baby spirit would calm her. *Americanos* had no understanding. They played with strong power.

But no calm came. She remembered the aura.

More sleeps passed and she lay awake listening. When Father Sun was high, her eyes felt like they had been sanded. Isabella's fussing bothered her, though it was rare, and she felt grateful to Ramón and the two boys — young men now — for taking Billy with them when they worked. He rode well, helped herd cattle. "I will be a vaquero like Pedro and my father," he had said in English better than hers.

To take her mind from Pedro, she lay remembering happy days. Being Grandmother Dishi's eyes, telling her the exact shade of the sky and river. She remembered hot days when all the people swam together, contented as fish in a hole, and the excitement of sliding down the Sacayak boulder for the first time with her cousins. She remembered Father's fine orations and the way people looked up to him as he stood on the dancehouse roof.

Since then she had lived in many places — Sutter's Fort, Pedro's room above Sheldon's mill, the cave near Spanish Camp, the hideout in the boulders, the reservation, the Rhoads rancho. Mexico would come next. And yet the home place pulled her. She decided to go back and visit it. The clarity helped her sleep.

The next day as they kneaded big lumps of dough, Elitha asked, "How long will you be gone?"

"I say good-bye to my home. Maybe one sleep."

"I thought Indians didn't believe in saying good-bye."

Maria folded the dough, pressed the heels of her hands onto the softness. "In old time *Indio* did not say good-bye." Bent-Willow-Reflected-in-Pond, who was learning English, looked up, then went back to kneading at the end of the table.

Elitha nodded. "That's fine. You go. But do me a favor. I have a gold nugget this big buried in the dirt between the split rock by my house." She held up her flour-white fingers, and explained where it was. "Would you dig it up and bring it back to me?"

Later, when the first loaves came from the oven, others inflating near the stove, it was time to prepare meat and potatoes. Hummingbird Tailfeather was outside supervising her daughters as they took turns churning. Whenever bread came fresh from the oven, the Rhoads men wanted large quantities of butter.

During the men's meal the sound of horses clattered outside. Holding her breath, Maria set down a pan of rolls and ran to the window. But it was only Ben Wilder in a small rig. Elitha hurried outside and down the steps and into his arms. They kissed in the sunshine — two tall, slim people, with love in their hearts.

Hand in hand Elitha brought the tall man into the house, her face glowing with energy and power. Maria put a plate and fork on the table for him. Maybe today he would take Elitha away. The Rhoads men ate in strained silence, Elitha hardly eating at all. Mr. Wilder rarely took his eyes from her. "Heard from the Brunners?" he asked.

Elitha shook her head.

"Well, I've got some news." He slathered his steaming bread with butter, closed his eyes at the first bite and made a mmmm noise. "John," he said, "I smelled this bread all the way to Sacramento. Wouldn't blame you for chaining that woman to the bread pan, but I'm afraid you'll lose her real soon now. I've found a place — my brothers and I — out by Katesville. Rancho de los Cazaderos. Heard of it?"

John Rhoads nodded his shaggy head like a thoughtful bear. "Sold to a conglomerate, wasn't it?"

"Yep. Think we might buy it from them, my brothers and I. Thought I'd go on up there and take a gander. You heard anything about the title?"

"Nope." He forked a piece of meat and chewed, holding bread in his other hand. "Thought you was plannin to live in town a spell."

"Oh, I got us a little cottage lined up, 18th and K."

"Ben," Elitha said suddenly, "Mary needs a ride up to Bridge House, if you're going that way." She nodded at Maria. "Could you give her a ride?"

"Be glad to." He went back to eating.

She began collecting the dishes as Mr. Wilder said, "One of my teamsters went to see Murieta's head, down in Stockton." He pushed back from the table. She froze.

The men began standing up, holding their hands over their bellies as if in pain. John Rhoads said, "I hear it ain't Murieta."

Mr. Wilder cocked his head like he'd heard something very strange. "They got sixteen signed affidavits to prove it was. Musta been hundreds lined up to see it. Captain Love'll get the state reward all right."

In fear of missing something she hardly breathed.

Mr. Rhoads spoke in a restrained tone. "Well, I heard the mining camps are refusing the rewards, saying they got the wrong Mexican. There'll be another showing. In San Francisco."

Another showing. They weren't burying the head! The horror and ignorance continued. While the men ambled into the front room like nothing was wrong, Maria could almost hear the whir of air, the click of a condor beak. Where was Pedro?

She walked the old, familiar path from Bridge House, and easily located Elitha's gold nugget in the split rock near the adobe house. Feeling the weight in her pocket, she walked the ancient trail down into the gully, then up the hill to the place where Pedro had sat on his horse so long ago looking down on Father's people. She looked upon a very different scene, the playing field now a fenced pasture for strange, hornless cows with white faces. The trees and vines along Berry Creek were gone, the vacant village center visible. Howchia's oak still flourished, with no dancehouse beneath it. On the right flowed the river, the color of yellow clay, a fringe of gray-green willows growing happily alongside — hardy, deep-rooted souls.

On the left the Gaffney house and barn marked the far end of the playing field, where goals had once been scored. Two mules stood head to tail, flicking flies. White cloth hung at the windows of the wooden house, and a young child in a yellow frock stood in the yard, chickens pecking around her.

She descended the hill and went to the tree, slipping the bikoos from her shoulders and leaning the sleeping child against the pungent trunk. Big green acorns studded the branches. No people to harvest them. She slipped the frock over her head, then pressed against the warm bark. *I am here, Grandmother.* Silence.

She sat at the base of the tree, glad for the shade. Soon it would be Cos time, but how would salmon find their way through this murky water? They must; they always had. Isabella fussed and Maria released her from the bikoos. The little girl stood on her chubby legs smiling at her in Grandmother's shade.

Wanting to show her daughter the home place, Maria took her to the old bathing place. A small sprig of peppermint grew near the water's edge. "See," Maria said pointing, "Some of the plant people live yet." She swam with the baby, pointing out the familiar rocks and finding more plants — brave survivors. For the first time in more than two moons she forgot to notice the sun's movement across the sky, and Pedro's face never haunted her.

When she took Isabella back to the tree, her dress and the bikoos were gone. Strange. But she felt no fear as she sat in the eastward slanting shadows, enjoying the warm air. Beside her, Isabella poked twigs in the soft black earth where generations of her ancestors had played, and been buried. She extended an acorn cap to Maria.

"A gift of Eagle Woman," she explained. "Your great-grandmother lives here. See?" Maria patted the bark.

"Home," Isabella said with a twinkly smile.

The earth rolled beneath them. Leaves rattled overhead, the giant turtles awakening beneath the tree roots. Maria tingled. Hair bristled at the base of her neck, as in a lightning storm. She stood up, felt power enter the soles of her feet, travel up through her body. It sizzled in the oak-smelling air and shimmered over the hillsides. She stretched her open arms to gather it and felt power enter her body.

"Home," Isabella repeated.

She swept her up, hugging her. "Home," she said, spilling with emotion.

A small voice said, "What did you say?"

Turning to see the young girl in the yellow frock, Maria spoke English. "You finish your supper?" Many times she had heard *Americanas* say that to children when the sun was sliding behind the western hill.

"Cleaned my plate," the child said sweetly, running her gaze over Maria's naked body. Then she arranged her unlined face into a scowl. "Did you feel the ground move?"

"Yes," Maria said, setting Isabella down, her feet moving toward the little girl as they made contact with the ground.

The rosy-cheeked little girl stroked Isabella's hair and looked up at Maria and said, "Was that your tattered frock?"

"Yes."

"Don't you have another?"

She shook her head.

"Well, I didn't know it was yours." She beckoned Maria to follow, adding, "You ought not to be naked."

At the Gaffney house lamplight glowed through the lace curtains and spilled through the open door. In her power, Maria entered, amazed to see a man jab his fist into another man's jaw. The two *Americanos*, whose hands were wrapped thickly in wound cloth, both stared at her as two women jumped to their feet, thread falling from their laps. Strangely, the men didn't seem angry with one another.

"Saint Paddy save us!" a woman said, "What have you brought us, Mary?" Her hair was the color of iron rust, and she had no lashes or eyebrows. The other woman had tawny coloring like Joaquín Murieta.

"She wants her old frock back," the child said, taking Maria's hand and pulling her into the kitchen. The dress hung on a peg behind the door, the bikoos on the floor beneath.

As she slipped the dress over her head — feeling the weight of the nugget — all four people came into the kitchen, their eyes very blue. One of the women helped Maria fasten the buttons on her back, then gently pushed her down into a chair at the table. "Sure and we're awondrin where you come from."

"My home place is here," she said, gesturing toward the river.

"A wonder a body niver laid eyes on you then." Turning to the others the rust-haired woman said, "And it's fine English she speaks." She cocked her head at Maria much like the child had. Maria saw that she had lashes and brows after all, but they were extremely pale.

The other woman said, "Have ye family hereabouts then?"

"My people are dead."

The women exchanged glances. "And you, my dear, how be ye keepin flesh to the bone? And with a babe to boot?"

She had to think about the meaning.

Before she could tell them about the Rhoads ranch, one of the men said, "Mither, ye been aprayin after a hired geerl." He gestured at Maria. "Methinks the Lord provides."

The rust-haired woman crossed her arms beneath her bosom, narrowed her eyes and laid a finger on her jaw. "Wouldja be willin to work here fer us then?"

"Maybe," she said, surprising herself. "But maybe my man comes and we go to Mexico." She had the power to think *maybe.*

"And it's a man she's got!" She opened her mouth and turned to the others.

The woman with honey-colored hair said, "You men could use the help of a strong young Indian." They nodded, their wrapped hands hanging at their sides.

Pedro had a land paper for this land, but it lay with a bag of gold coins under her bed at the Rhoads ranch. It seemed a Coyote joke, these people inviting him to work here, but now he wanted to be his own *patrón* in Mexico. Not speaking for him, she accepted the offer of tea — a poor quality, and had a stray thought that someday she would make them better tea.

She and Isabella stayed the night in the warm Gaffney barn, nesting in hay. She slept well with bats whirring about, picking mosquitos from the air. Friends from home.

100

Seven sleeps later, still feeling her power and waiting for Pedro, Maria entered the Rhoads kitchen and was surprised to see Elitha up so early. Her packed bags stood at the door, and she wore her brown and white checkered gown with an apron over it. She had a fire in the stove and was making coffee and biscuits.

"You leave now," she said to Elitha. To meet Mr. Wilder, she knew. The two of them would find Elitha's sisters.

"Yes," Elitha said with a glance at Isabella, who gripped Maria's frayed skirt and stepped flat-footed on chubby feet.

They had talked. Elitha wanted Maria to live with her in the white "cottage" in Sacramento City, where she and Little Flicker would wash the clothes of Elitha's sisters. Maria had said no. She would wait where her man could find her. Besides, Billy would be sad to leave Ramón.

But now, seeing Elitha ready to go, Maria thought about the men who displayed the severed head and hand in the jars, and decided her power might be strong enough to repel the bad magic. "Captain Love," she said, "Is he with the head of Joaquín Murieta?"

Elitha cracked the oven door and peeked at the biscuits. Shutting it, she said, "I don't know. Maybe. Why?"

Maybe. "I go ask how many men were killed." Sixteen people had sworn that Captain Love and his men had killed Joaquín Murieta and Three-Fingered Jack, but had they also killed Pedro?

Elitha searched her face, then came around the table and put her hands on Maria's shoulders, her large brown eyes filled with kindness. "Mary, I know how worried you've been about Mr. Valdez. Sometimes we have to force ourselves to do what we don't want to, so we won't be wondering forever. I think you'd be doing the right thing to go ask."

"You tell me how to go on boat?"

"Maybe Ben and I can go with you. We're heading to Sonoma, and that's a stop along the way. But hurry. The stage leaves in a half hour."

"I go talk to Billy and Little Flicker. How many sleeps to San Francisco?"

Elitha looked at the ceiling then back at her and said, "Better figure one night in San Francisco, and another night in Sacramento City on the way back. Two nights."

She continued to feel her power. Billy was glad she wouldn't take him from what he called his "work." Hurrying to the river for herbs, she packed them with dried meat and nu-pah in the bottom of the bikoos, along with a purse of gold coins.

She hardly had time to realize, as a Rhoads boy drove her and Elitha to Slough House, that she would see a very new world. She would ask the men in San Francisco if they had seen a man with hair the color of the red-tailed hawk.

On the hurtling ride to Sacramento City, Elitha looked stronger than Maria had ever seen her. Color glowed in her pale cheeks. She mentioned everything they passed. But Maria kept her strength inward. As the distance from the home place lengthened, she unfocused her eyes. Isabella seemed to understand. Sitting quietly on her lap, the child stared out the window, then fell asleep.

When Mr. Wilder helped them from the coach, Maria hardened her shell around her strength to protect against the quick movements of strangers and the shouting. She was shocked to see structures encrusting the earth like fungus. Only a few large trees remained in an area where many would have grown old and happy. Too many people — she could smell their excretions — lived where sedge and redbud would have grown. The walls of the *Americanos* were reaching out, capturing more and more space, changing the world to what they called *indoors*. Only small dusty lanes remained between the buildings.

Elitha spoke to Mr. Wilder. She saw in his manner he didn't want to go to San Francisco. Elitha whispered, "She's been like this the whole way." They didn't know her senses were keener than ever, that she heard even the overlayered words of people across the lane.

She followed Elitha and her man down a canyon of buildings, then up a man-made slope to a wide brown river crowded with huge boats, some with tooth-like railings. The shore had been made straight and sterile. At a big ticket house, more crowds made her heart race — everyone staring rudely at her. But she stood with Elitha and Mr. Wilder and regained her calm.

With it came clarity. As Mr. Wilder extended a handful of coins toward a man in a cage, she touched the elbow of his shirt and said, "I go alone." Their presence, their love for each other, his yearning to be with Elitha alone and Elitha's anxiety to get quickly to her sisters would tug at Maria's power. He pulled his hand from the cage.

Elitha leaned her head around him and said, "You might get lost, Mary." Her pale, high brow was creased with worry.

"Many people go. I ask the way."

They exchanged a look. Elitha asked, "You sure?"

"I want to be alone in San Francisco." It had once been called Yerba Buena and that gave some comfort.

A man behind said, "Hurry it up, up there in front." Many people in the line muttered.

Mr. Wilder thrust his hand into the cage and said, "One round-trip ticket to San Francisco. Two one-way to Vallejo." He turned to Maria and explained they would travel on the same boat, but he and Elitha would get off before she did.

They walked on a wooden pathway — a bridge laid from the man-made bank to the top story of an enormous floating structure with two layers of toothed railings. Beneath her dry feet she felt the movement of the water and marveled at the cleverness of the new people. Father would have enjoyed this.

The boat filled with people and the wooden pathway was withdrawn. The boat shuddered and roared, belching black smoke from a tall pipe. A gigantic wheel at the side turned, slap, slap, slapping the water, faster and faster, the spray flying to the rail where she stood. It startled her at first, but she saw it made the boat swim, and welcomed the cooling spray.

A blast screeched. In fright she lurched toward the benches where Elitha and Ben sat. They smiled and called it a "whistle."

Recovering, she realized she must expect the unexpected and control all fear. She must retreat deeper into herself. Digging a coin from the bikoos, she handed it to Mr. Wilder. "It is the gold of Señor Valdez," she explained. "He wants me to use it for the journey. You take."

He looked at her oddly, then, seeing Elitha's nod, accepted the coin, but handed another back.

"No, you take." She repeated, refusing it.

"I already did. The fare was only fifty cents," he said. "Put that back in your purse." He smiled kindly.

Wondering if she would ever learn the secret language of coins, she put the gold beneath Isabella's feet. The baby wriggled and thrashed, not wanting to be laced up.

With a happy look Elitha said, "Let me walk her around."

She gave the baby to Elitha and returned to the rail at the front of the boat. The sun was high and the trees along the banks stood motionless as she cut through the wind, racing through the wooded river channel on the giant grinning fish. Here the miners hadn't destroyed the huge sycamores and oaks, the ripening vines hanging in great veils from the green heights. Clouds of birds flitted through them. Life remained abundant. Around her and on the deck below, people talked and laughed.

Seven hours, Elitha had said the journey would take. Many channels ran outward, the driver skillfully guiding the boat through the watery maze. Sometimes, rounding a bend she saw a fence, a house, or waving children running toward the water. The boat whistle screeched its greeting. She inhaled the fecund aroma of the backwaters, her power intact, and flew toward Father Sun.

The roar and vibration stopped. The whistle blew, a bell clanged, and a man yelled, "All out for Vallejo."

Elitha came to the rail with toddling Isabella gripping her finger. She had eaten. Bits of food clung to her smiling cheeks. "Maria," Elitha said, "I'm going to miss you terribly." She hugged her, her breath smelling of coffee, her hair of *Americana* soap. "I'll send you things, for you and the children." Mr. Wilder added, "When I finalize things at Rancho de los Cazaderos, we want you to come live with us there. If you're still in California."

"Maybe I go to Mexico," she said, sorry tears prickling her eyes at the *maybe*. "Good-bye," she said, glad that Elitha would soon be reunited with her sisters.

Elitha picked up Isabella. "You sweet thing, I gotta go now. Take care of your mother now, hear?" She kissed her cheek and handed her to Maria, "She's so beautiful. I love those auburn curls." She fluffed them. "She's got Señor Valdez' eyes too." She smiled wistfully at Isabella, then rustled away after Mr. Wilder — a bag in each of his hands, the checkered fabric of her gown melting into the throng on the wooden pathway.

Maria sank back into her power.

The boat erupted into life. She picked up Isabella. "See. Father Sun goes to his house in the west." The water was streaked with fiery gold. Isabella fussed to return to the bikoos, having had a tiring day. Maria laced her in and hung her on her back. Then, she continued to stand at the front of the boat, racing toward the sun, toward knowledge. The trees and water were dusted with gold, the sun bloated and red. But after a while the colors faded and the shores moved apart.

A salty aroma permeated the wind as the boat churned into a wide, flat, silvery world. This was how it was before the creation of land — Raven, Coyote and Turtle on a boat drifting endlessly in a watery world. Turtle conquered his fear of the depths and dived all the way to the bottom, bringing up mud in his claws. Raven shaped it into earth, the home place of all creatures. Maria knew how Turtle felt, alone and fearful in the deep water.

An island loomed indistinctly in the darkening mist, then fell rapidly into the dusk behind. She heard only the slap, slap, slap and the roar of boat. Ancient and new times lived together. Turtle had conquered fear and brought land. What would come of her journey?

She hardly noticed that most of the passengers had gone below and the air had turned chill. A man moved from lamp to lamp along the rail, lifting glass shells and lighting wicks. Like a many-eyed monster, the boat forged through the young night, the lamp glass protecting the flames from the wind.

Ahead, a mountainous silhouette came toward her — black against the twilight lingering in the sky, a mass of twinkling lights along the shoreline. As the boat approached, the pinpoints of light separated and shadowy buildings appeared. The roar in the boat's bowels stopped abruptly, as did the slapping. The silence jolted Isabella awake. People emerged on deck. A woman pointed, holding back her blowing hair. "There it is. The City!" San Francisco.

The grinning fish monster glided silently through the restless black water. With a thud that threw her forward, the boat stopped. Her head spun with the lack of motion. Voices shouted. People thronged toward the wooden pathway. The journey was over. After the sleep she would conquer fear rising like mist from uncongealed thought, a nameless horror lurking like a dark island apart.

All night she huddled in an unlocked portion of a sprawling waterfront building, lying between pieces of iron smelling of rust, grease and salt. Rodents scurried in the blackness. Dawn jabbed slivers of light through the walls, but she ate none of the food she had packed. Like a young man on his quest, she would hold onto her power and enhance it by fasting.

San Francisco was like Sacramento, but without sunshine. Men and animals rushed up roads lined with brick and wooden structures. She shivered — not expecting cold in this season — and glanced both ways at an intersection. She saw many men, but no women or children. Three men in tall black hats stepped from a coach, the driver whipping the horses onward.

Approaching, she asked, "Where is the head of Joaquín Murieta?" She gazed politely past them.

"Well, I'll be damned," said one. "First squaw I've seen since the mines!" He smiled down at her torn blue frock and bare feet as one would smile at the antics of a child. "Even they're flocking in to gawk at that atrocity."

Not understanding, Maria repeated. "Where is the head?"

The man pointed to a building higher than the intervening buildings. Turning to leave, she heard: "Amusing the way they ape the whites." She didn't understand *ape*, but it didn't matter. She knew where she was going.

Hills rose vertically behind the town, the peaks concealed by clouds. Shivering, she realized the truth of the old wisdom, that clothing provided little warmth. Only acceptance warmed. In time of rain she could stand naked in sleet and frost with less discomfort, because she expected and welcomed the cold. Now as she walked beneath the overhanging porches of the stores, wind blowing her hair and plastering her skirt on her legs, she thought of the home place. Father Sun would be heating the morning air. The sky would be deep blue.

Approaching the building, she slowed. About a hundred and fifty people —

men, women and children — crowded around the door. But they parted as she passed through, staring at her and Isabella in the bikoos.

Talk crackled. *Filthy feet* hissed on their tongues. But nothing mattered except talking to the men who had killed Joaquín Murieta.

The cold metal doorknob moved in her hand, but the door held fast. Turning to a woman hugging herself in a woolen shawl, Maria said, "I come to see men who show the head of Joaquín Murieta."

The woman lifted her nose and said, "This show ain't fer Injuns."

"Squaw, you got a dollar?" said a man standing stiffly near the door, a ring of keys rattling in his hand.

"Yes."

People within earshot turned to repeat what she'd said to those behind, and stared with eyes like fried quail eggs. But she was prepared for anything, glad to be alone, and glad for the strength fasting had enhanced. "You can see the show," he said, "but git to the back of the line." He flicked his hand the way Elitha shooed chickens. "And let the whites go first."

Relieved not to be excluded, she asked, "You ride with Captain Love?"

"I ain't gabbin with no Squaw."

From the back of the crowd she watched the line slowly move, boots and shoes shuffling forward. The door had been opened. As new people arrived, she nodded for them to go before her. In a strange place one followed the rules of courtesy. People who had viewed the head hurried the other direction, speaking in excited tones: "Grotesque . . . vicious . . . Joaquín for sure . . . loathsome hand."

Warming to the spirits swirling off the waters of San Francisco, she waited. Isabella seemed to enjoy the brisk wind and strange sights. Maria prepared to face the fearful possibility that the men had not seen Pedro, that she would never see him again, and would never know why. Yet an even darker island lingered in the mist.

At last the viewers moved faster, the sun slipping in and out of the clouds. It blazed brilliantly as she stepped toward the threshold, slanting through the windows inside a cavernous room, and she saw people ahead of her bunched before two tables — a large jar on one, a smaller jar on the other. "Lord amercy!" "Ooooh!" echoed within the walls. Beside the large jar sat two men in chairs. Men she had come to talk with.

"One dollar," said the man at the door.

She handed him a gold coin, unsure if it was a two dollar or five dollar piece. He dropped it in a metal box and waved her across the threshold.

The room went dark, the sun hiding. She fortified herself as she neared the jars, prickling at the feel of angry spirits hovering. She grew taller in her power.

The place lacked air — all houses did, but this was worse. The smells of many people mingled. The room grew darker yet, the door being shut, new people being kept out. Periodic flashes of light washed across the room as the door opened and closed, viewers leaving.

Without looking she saw the amber fluid in the jar. She didn't want to see Joaquín Murieta, who had been a vibrant man in life, reduced to a head. Instead she focused on the men in the chairs. Both wore white shirts and dark jackets, their faces shadowy in the gloom. The one nearest the table held a sheaf of papers on his crossed thigh, and a pencil. He asked the people in front, "Did you know Joaquín?" They shook their heads. He waved them on. Maria stepped before him, trying not to see the floating hair.

He asked, "Did you know Joaquín Murieta?"

"Yes."

"Where you from?"

"Río Cosumnes." He scribbled on the paper.

"Your name?" He looked at her.

She stood thinking, as gray light briefly washed across his cheek and nose, the last of the viewers leaving. She had hoped to cloister her strength. Still, she had come to ask this man a question, and couldn't afford to upset him. Looking over his head at the framed likeness of a white-haired man hanging on the wall, she murmured, "Mary." Life was balance.

He scratched on the paper and nodded at the jar. "Say if it's him."

Not intending to look, she asked, "Captain Love, he kill other men too?"

"Nope. Just Joaquín Murieta and Three-Fingered Jack there." He rose from his chair and accidentally bumped the table. At that instant Father Sun blazed brightly through the wall of windows, brilliant light sparking off the glass jars, clearly illuminating the reddish brown hair moving like moss at the bottom of a river. It drew her unwilling eyes.

Pedro stared blindly at her through the brandy, his mouth a silent scream. The tails of his mustache waved in gentle synchrony with his hair and the shreds of pale flesh on his neck. Below that flared the flat shoulders of the table. Stiff. Dry. Dusty.

Giant wings whumped into the room. Concussive, pulling her inside out. The air shrieked. She barely heard: "Holy Jesus, we ain't got all night. Say and git on outa here, squaw."

Power suffocated and blinded her. Her legs collapsed and she slumped to the floor. Men's voices howled in the maelstrom. Rough hands yanked her. The room whirled in chaos. Through the crackling wind she heard Isabella cry, a voice demand: "It's him, ain't it. It's him!"

"Yes." She managed, struggling to her feet to face Condor. Yes. She had known it would be Pedro.

The fractured air aligned itself as the bird settled on the jar and gripped the wide lid with its talons. Molok thrust his naked pinkish head at her, scowling, red eyes unblinking. His wings stretched from one side of the room to the other —

wings slashed with white, the tip feathers wide apart as if grasping the air. Below him, Pedro's gray eyes stared. Next to Pedro, Quapata's claw of a hand curled, the scar on the stub of the finger exactly where she had applied the herbs. The men in suits stood motionless as rocks.

Molok asked the courteous question, "Where are you going?"

A yipping howl came from behind her. She turned to see Coyote, tongue draped limply over the humps of his incisors. "Give her a peck," he said. "She wants to die."

But the power of Condor flowed into her and filled all the hollow spaces. She expanded until she was tall as the building and broad as the bird's wingspan. Her voice came quiet and steady within the wooden walls:

"I go to the home place. In time of rain I will wear the mist rising from the river. In the long dry I will wear the dust of the earth. I will sing and dance to celebrate the spirit in all things — life rising from the ashes, the living feeding upon the dead, the eternal cycle. I will help the plant and animal people repopulate the shores and teach the new people to know them. I am old, Molok, in decay. I am food for the new ones to root in, and someday they will talk to birds. They too will hear spirits in the boulders and the river and the trees. Someday they will listen."

Endnotes

MARY. Local old timers remember stories of an Indian woman named Mary, who lived to old age in the vicinity of Bridge House. She is said to have had a child with reddish hair, but no husband. She worked for the local ranch women, treated the sick with herbal remedies, and for many years delivered most of the babies. John Sutter's diary records a "Mary," Indian wife of Perry McCoon and mother of baby William "Billy" McCoon. Heinrich Lienhard's diary tells of "McCoon's mistress," a beautiful Indian named Mary, who tricked drunken Sutter out of thousands of dollars when he was camped with his Indian miners.

JOHN AUGUSTUS SUTTER (originally Suter) was a complex figure — part vainglorious pretender to rank, part chronic debtor counting on miraculous upturns of fortune, part visionary, entrepreneur and self-publicist, part generous host and booster of California's interior. He spoke better Spanish than was credited in this book. Much has been written about him. His portrayal here is consistent with Richard Dillon's *Fool's Gold* (1967) and Kenneth Owens (ed), *John Sutter & a Wider West* (1994). Escaping a mountain of debt and a warrant for his arrest in Switzerland, he abandoned his wife and five children and sailed to the new world. He later dodged creditors in Missouri and arrived in California in 1839, soon afterward being joined by mountain men encountered on the trail, including Pablo Gutiérrez and Sebastian Keyser (Kaiser). Sutter went to Hawaii on the last lap of the journey, acquiring sailors and native Hawaiians (Kanakas). His land grant and fort on the confluence of the American and Sacramento rivers was well located for the fur trade, indeed for an empire. Lienhard and others documented Sutter's use of Manu-iki and many young Indian girls — as the joke went, he was indeed the "Father of California." The Micheltorena War has been variously interpreted. Dillon describes an outfoxed and incompetent Sutter hoping to acquit himself gloriously on the field of battle. The present book simplifies the movements of that war. Exactly why the battle produced no more injuries than a decapitated mule remains uncertain. Sutter's treatment of the Indians at the fort was arguably better than they received in the missions — he paid for labor, if sparingly. After his wife and family arrived, his lifestyle changed and his son paid off his father's debts (not the one to the Russians) by selling his father's land to the men who developed the City of Sacramento. Buried in Lititz, Pennsylvania beside his wife, Sutter died an embittered old man, having spent his last years in a futile attempt to lobby the U.S. government into compensating him for his fort, livestock, and supplies. His life demonstrates the opportunities afforded by the old West to a man of modest origin and extravagant ambition. Sober and possessed of better judgment, he might indeed have become the King of California, as he is described on a plaque on the house of his birth in Kandern, Germany.

PEDRO VALDEZ is a fictionalized, fleshed-out representative of the handful of Mexican pioneer soldiers who went to the Sacramento Valley with Sutter to develop an Indian militia and "pacify" the frontier. The Sheldon family has forgotten the name of the "Spanish friend" to whom Jared Sheldon is said to have handed his son during the shootout with miners, so Pedro became that man. For personal background he became the son of old Pepe. Dmitry Zavalishin, a Russian scientist, linguist and diplomat who in the early 1820s was attempting to lay the groundwork for a Russian takeover of California, wrote later from Siberia (where he was exiled) that he had met a man called Pepe near San José who constantly talked about rich sites of gold in the foothills. Pepe was considered mad. Zavalishin writes, ". . . he was a tall, lean old man with wild, roving eyes . . . almost naked and barefoot, in a threadbare cloak . . . but he gave very definite answers to my questions and displayed no insanity at all." During the gold rush "native Californians" like Pedro were in fact discriminated against, flogged and even summarily hanged in the mining regions. Retaliation and racial violence were common and well documented.

THE MIWOK PEOPLE were named by anthropologists a generation after Maria, based largely upon language — *mí-wa* being their word for man. The meaning of *sacayak* has been lost. Remarkably autonomous, villagers identified themselves only as the people of that particular headman. Thus, when Padre Duran of Mission San José enticed or abducted Valley people to the mission and asked them their tribal name, they said Kosum-umne — the people of *Kosum*, Salmon. Duran marked that on his map. John Sutter established the present spelling when he identified the Rio de los Cosumnes. Today, mortar holes in the boulders and a grassy depression for the dancehouse mark the site of Maria's village. On the mound behind the vanished roundhouse grows an enormous oak. The top and all but one major branch was recently removed, but the tree is putting out more growth. Many of the original plants and animals have returned to the riverbottom; the salmon-run is history, though lone individuals have been spotted. Hydraulic mining, which was just beginning at book's end and may not have existed in the area until 1858, deposited at least 16 feet of silt in the riverbed, covering all but the top of Sheldon's damaged dam, the top of which is still visible to divers.

ELITHA CUMI DONNER, her family, and the events of the Donner Party rescue are close to history. To reduce confusion with Elitha's name, the youngest sister was called "Ellie," though her real name was Eliza. The stories of the baby nailed to the wall, the $10,000 stitched in the quilt, the Brunner's failure to answer Elitha's letters, and the happy day in which the Indian women gathered marsh-grass nuts and feasted on hornet grubs are from Eliza's published memoirs 65 years later, assisted by Elitha — the first break in the Donners' long silence. By

Eliza's account, Frances remained at the Brunners with her sisters until recovered by Elitha, while other accounts place her with the James Reeds in San Jose. Not long after Ben and Elitha took the girls to Sacramento, Mr. Brunner was convicted of murdering his nephew and was incarcerated in San Quentin. Most people today would be surprised at the extent to which the survivors were blamed and, especially the females, made sport of on account of the cannibalism. During the Donner Party rescue, George McKinstry penned a lewd, unprintable note to Lt. Kern about "man eating women," which is preserved in the California State Library. Except for her cooking, little is documented about Elitha's life before she married Wilder. She is not known to have spoken on behalf of Indians or to have worked for John Rhoads, and there is no evidence of a romance. Regarding the San Francisco property, the earthquake and fire of 1906 destroyed records, but a *San Francisco Chronicle* story in 1928 told of the town "doing itself proud" by giving lots to the "Donner orphans" (names omitted) in 1847. The timing fits with the Houghton account of Elitha accompanying McCoon to San Francisco and not returning for a couple of months. In an undocumented endnote to his revised edition of *Winter of Entrapment*, the late Joseph King says that James Reed orchestrated the property gift for Elitha's cousins Mary and George, whom he adopted, and that they subsequently lost it in court battles with squatters. McGlashan's history is the apparent source for this interpretation.

BEN WILDER is represented as faithfully as historical records allow, including his role in the miners' shoot-out with Jared Sheldon. The *Sacramento Union* quotes are verbatim. Wilder's words and actions after the shooting were orally reported by Mrs. Marguerite Gordon of the Eating House, who later worked for the Sheldon family. Shortly after they were married in 1853, Ben and Elitha took the Donner girls from the Brunner's yard in Sonoma and cared for them in their Sacramento cottage on 18th and K streets. Via paddlewheeler, the little girls journeyed to school in the Dominican nunnery in Benicia. Wilder and his brothers acquired Rancho de los Cazadores, but lost it when the U.S. Lands Commission ruled the title invalid. After a brief return to mining, he bought a farm a few miles away from Sacramento in the Franklin area, where he and Elitha lived for 50 years and had six children. Wilder became a conservative pillar of Sacramento County. Their eldest son, George Donner Wilder, hung himself after his wife and three children burned to death in their house on the Wilder ranch. Another adult son was thrown from a horse and died of a fractured skull. Elitha's grandchildren remembered her as a dignified old woman sitting quietly on the porch overlooking the fields. In 1923, at nearly 91, she died and was buried in Elk Grove Masonic Cemetery next to her husband. As recently as the 1960s her great-grandchildren hesitated in school to identify themselves as descendants, because of jokes about cannibalism.

PERRY MCCOON, an English sailor, was hired by John Sutter to help with the cattle and pilot the riverboat. Sutter records that he caught McCoon stealing calves, that McCoon deserted during the march to war, and that he "rec'd his title" to the pig farm on the Cosumnes River (no title was granted). On February 5, 1846 Sutter mentions McCoon's marriage to widow Lewis and, 4 months later, her burial at the fort. The memoirs of a visiting doctor suggest to some that McCoon beat her to death. Badly injured, she had miscarried. Dr. Duval describes her youth and beauty and expresses sorrow, but oddly omits the cause of her wounds. On June 1, 1847 Sutter records Perry's marriage to "Mis Donner." The Houghton memoir describes the wedding feast. The cattle drive of Sheldon, Daylor, McCoon, Charles Weber and others to Coloma in 1848, which led to their discovery of gold in Weber Creek (Placerville), is documented. "Dry Diggings" yielded up to $17,000 per week, mined by Indian workers until they were massacred as described. In 1943 the author of *Early Day Romances* writes that McCoon wasted his wealth drinking and gambling, losing self-respect and pride in his appearance. His sale of mining claims is speculative, but County records say he sold G. McKinstry all or part of his ranch for $25,000. McCoon died at Bridge House in a riding demonstration, the number of witnesses suggesting a contest. His grave site is unknown, but could lie beneath the white quartz rectangle emerging from the old asphalt near the author's lawn. A hand-hewn block of white marble is cemented in the adjacent rock wall, the faces covered.

GRIZZLY HAIR is patterned after an impressive Miwok leader who organized his people into a gold-panning cooperative and whose funeral drew hundreds of Indians from miles around — mentioned by Steven Powers in *Tribes of California* (1877). In the present book Grizzly Hair is given the role of the unknown Indian leader(s) who organized the valley peoples and coordinated with Estanislao, who led the mission exodus and is credited with the 1829 "rebellion" against the Mexican presidios — a war that had the effect of retarding further Mexican incursions into California's interior.

JARED DIXON SHELDON, an educated and skilled millwright from Vermont, arrived in California in the 1830s and became California's first contract engineer. He built water-powered mills in Los Angeles, Marin, Bodega Bay, Contra Costa (for José Amador) and Mission San José (on Mill Creek) before building one on his rancho. His life in California and that of his partner Bill Daylor, was well documented in Sheldon's letters, papers, and outside sources. Sheldon and Daylor are buried side by side in the Slough House Pioneer Cemetery, formerly the Omuchumne burial ground. The fight Manu-iki caused at the fort was described by Heinrich Lienhard, who said Sutter was afraid of Daylor afterward. The hanging at Rancho Omuchumne occurred at a later date. The events of Sheldon's death in the first of California's water wars are taken from written and oral histories — the news article and Sheldon's proposal to the miners verbatim. Daylor loaned Sutter only $7000 for the passage of his family, another man loaning a similar amount. Daylor's motive was suggested by Lienhard's colorful description of Frau Sutter. In the declining gold rush community of Bridge House, Jared Sheldon's cabin stood until the boards rotted, the large bloodstain visible on the floor. Remnants of his mill and dam can be seen at the river's edge today, when not silted over. The remarkable oak-trunk mill spindles still exist, but need a permanent home. The spiked cannon was removed by the Grimshaws, repaired and fired by the men every Fourth of July until one year, when overloaded with powder, it exploded. Sheldon's widow Catherine, who became a noted midwife, made a success of the Slough House Inn, which still serves spirits and meals and is the scene of boot-stomping dances on summer weekends. She left John Mahone, who imbibed too liberally as he worked there, and visited Utah relatives. Returning to California, she married Dennis Dalton, and died in 1905 at the age of 73. She is buried in the Slough House Pioneer Cemetery, the key to which can be requested at the Inn. A descendant lives in the Greek-revival house Mahone built for Catherine in 1852, a short walk from the Inn. Son William Chauncey Sheldon (little Will) prospered, fathered a family and maintained his father's papers.

SARAH RHOADS DAYLOR and her second husband, William Robinson Grimshaw, founded a large clan, as did the Gaffneys with whom they are intermarried. The old Cosumne Store, rebuilt across the road after the floods of 1862, still faces Daylor Road, now State Highway 16. Across the road where the washed-out original adobe stood are three houses owned by Grimshaws, who still work the land and, with other farmers, sell produce at the roadside stand. Sarah, whose hair was dark, lies beside William Grimshaw in the Slough House Pioneer Cemetery. Grimshaw penned one of the most engrossing personal memoirs of the period covered in this book.

JOHN PIERCE RHOADS, the giant of the Donner Party rescue, was truly a man to match the mountains. He and his family are represented faithfully, including their rich gold diggings near the present town of Folsom. Their removal of gold from Dry Creek nine months prior to the usual gold-discovery date is Rhoads family history, as is Father Thomas Rhoads' scouting of California for Brigham Young and his return to nascent Salt Lake City with a barrel of gold — which legend says gilds the Angel Moroni atop the Mormon Temple. Thomas married again (plural wives) and founded the Utah branch of the family, which spells the name Rhoades or Rhodes. John Rhoads married Mary Murray in 1854, a year after Elitha married Ben Wilder, and later served in the California Legislature. In 1866 at age 48, he died of pneumonia and was buried in the Slough House

Pioneer Cemetery. His raft ride on belted logs down the raging rivers to alert Sutter's Fort of the stranded immigrants is family legacy — the Bear River portion noted by other sources. Most historians credit him with three trips to the summit and a fourth attempt being turned back by snowmelt floodwaters. His descendants meet annually to clear the weeds and paint the iron fence around his grave

SALVADOR and LUIS are historical Indians who worked for John Sutter. In his fort diary Sutter calls them "good boys" from the "tribe of Cosumne." They were in fact killed by their white companions, and eaten. Joseph King probes their origins (*The Californians*, April 1996, published the month of King's death).

THE OMUCHUMNE were massacred as described, and Daylor's letter was published as quoted. The episode is also described by killer-participant M. Case in the *Oregon Historical Quarterly* (1900). The editor's preface says the " . . . conflict was between a system of peon and contract labor and free labor" and the Oregonians, representing free labor, employed the only method available — "brute force." In other words, disliking the labor system, they exterminated the labor force. Pedro's retaliation was fiction. Quapata was a child at the time, one of two Omuchumne orphans provided for in Daylor's will, and was not a bandit. It is not known what happened to Maria's people at Rancho Sacayak; they might well have been massacred, as were other whole villages.

LEWIS KESEBERG, his cannibalism, his trial at the fort, the morbid jokes and the contention that he developed a taste for human flesh, are the subject of ongoing speculation. Although his reputation has recently undergone some sanitization, what was unknowable then remains unknowable today. The Donner money — estimated at over $14,000 — was never found. An educated and intelligent man, Keseberg bought a hotel, restaurant and brewery in Sacramento, but was plagued by business failure and the care of two epileptic, uncontrollable daughters, one mentally retarded. Phillipine Keseberg, said to have been a buxom woman with an eye for other men, bore him seven other daughters, most of whom died young. A friend wrote that Keseberg was loathe to talk about his Donner Party ordeals, which had become something of a fixation bordering on "derangement of mind." Poverty-ridden in his last years, he died in 1877 and is buried in the Old Sacramento City Cemetery, or, more likely, in the pauper's cemetery near the old County hospital.

MARY MURPHY and her abuse by William Johnson are from Mary's letters. She is buried in the town her rancher-developer husband, Charles Covillaud, named for her. William Johnson left California and went to Hawaii.

RANCHO SACAYAK is noted in early Sacramento County histories, though being unsurveyed (a requirement of a Mexican land grant), it had no boundaries. About the time Elitha left her adobe, an Irish miner named John Driscoll built a rock house nearby. Over the next 53 years Driscoll expanded his holdings for stock-raising, purchasing adjacent land from departing miners, as did his descendants for another 50 years. Unknowingly they were piecing the old rancho back together. In the 1930s grandson Art Granlees acquired the property of Vyries Brown, an ancient prospector living alone in his dilapidated frame cabin, and built a new house a few yards away (the author lives in it). By 1970 the Granlees family had sold their combined 2,600 acres — except for the 12 acres around the house — to a developer who renamed the subdivision Rancho Murieta; the logo depicts the legendary bandit.

GOLD RUSH TOWNS. Marysville is a thriving city. Katesville and Cook's Bar vanished with the 49ers. Michigan Bar lasted longer, then withered after 1920. Sutter Creek, Amador City (smallest incorporated California city) and Drytown are quaint Amador County towns on Highway 49. Ione (formerly Bedbug) is a rural town. The little that remains of Fiddletown's commercial center is virtually unchanged since 1852, including the Erauw's brick mercantile that may well be the site of Murieta's interrupted card game, and a Chinese apothecary (Dr. Yee's) locked since the Gold Rush with herbs and cures still on the shelves, recently reopened as a museum. At Sloughhouse (modern spelling) a couple of businesses besides the Inn remain, but Cosumne is entirely agricultural, though the store, rebuilt in 1862, still stands. The surviving structures of Bridgc House were torn down by the developers of Rancho Murieta in the early 1970s.

JOAQUIN MURIETA is and always was a blend of historical fact and gold rush mythology. The legislative debate about the reward occurred. A maimed hand was displayed along with the head, but historians believe the villainous "Three-fingered Jack" was a fiction of the bounty hunters — a sort of bonus offering (See Remi Nadeau, 1974). Many old-timers who claim their forebears were acquainted with the real Murieta say his hair was blondish. Aided by the head and hand, which he exhibited in Stockton and San Francisco, Captain Love succeeded in getting the State reward. The grisly display later made the rounds of gold rush towns. In the 1890s the head came to rest in a San Francisco museum of medical curiosities. Some historians believe the earthquake of 1906 threw it off the shelf where it lay in broken glass and alcohol and was quickly consumed by fire, while others believe it was rescued and is the same head that sits today on a TV in Santa Rosa, property of a Mr. Johnson, who inherited the relic from his grandfather (colorfully described by Richard Rodriguez, 1992). Many descendants of pioneers tell family stories of Murieta's long and peaceful life after his purported death.

THE CONDOR-SKIN COSTUME was stolen after the Indians refused to sell it to John Sutter. He "acquired it" and gave it to Russian collector I.G. Voznesensky, who recorded that the natives ran in fear of it "as if they had seen the Devil." It was in the tsar's private collection until the Revolution. Modern Russian anthropologists have concluded the robe's origin was the Cosumnes River. The identity of the thief is unknown, so McCoon became that man. He had opportunity and motive — to get back into Sutter's good graces after marking his cattle as his own. The robe can be seen today in Russia in a collection of Miwok artifacts in the St. Petersburg Museum of Archeology and Ethnography. The Miwok people would like it back, as it was rare even in the 1840s and is imbued with spiritual significance. The bad luck which has fallen upon recipients and viewers of this artifact is indeed remarkable.

OLIVER WOZENCRAFT wrote the reservation treaty with the Indians, the goods listed quoted verbatim. Unfortunately for the native people, Wozencraft resigned from government service and is remembered as a persuasive advocate for federal dams and subsidies for railroads to the West. The story of Indian reservations in California is one of the sorriest episodes in U.S. history.

All minor characters with European names are historical — including William Tecumseh Sherman, who surveyed Jared Sheldon's land grant, acquired land in the Slough House area during the Gold Rush and a decade later played a key role in the Civil War; General Mariano Vallejo, Edward Ord, John Frémont; William Leidesdorff, from whose rancho the town of Folsom sprang; and Leland Stanford, who sold dry goods in Sacramento and Stockton when Wilder was hauling. Stanford is remembered for the university he founded for his son and for being one of the Big Four who built the first transcontinental railway. George Donner's acquantance with Abraham Lincoln was as described.

About the author:

Naida West attended schools in Idaho, a one-room schoolhouse in Montana, and high school in Carmel, California. She holds a PhD in sociology from the University of California, Davis. Her career includes interpreting German to English in Germany; serving on a school board and other tribunals while mothering three children in Sacramento; teaching college in Sacramento and Davis, and consulting in California government with an emphasis on environment. Now she stays near her small ranch, writing and enjoying the natural world along the Cosumnes River. West is also a sought-after speaker. An anthology of her collected historical articles, as well as the prequel of *River of Red Gold* will soon be published. She is working on a sequel set in 1870-1890.